part one

The Sea Maid's Music

"*Uncivil Seasons* made me lose a whole working day. It held me, held me too long. It has Malone's richness of detail, his dialogue, and his gift for presenting characters, his inventiveness and his admirable style. There's a feeling of solidity to the town, to its people, the countryside, and the whole North state."
—Malcolm Cowley

"He's created two of the most memorable police detectives ever to appear in mystery fiction. Together they make a formidable pair—fresh and unforgettable. Equally engaging are the colorful characters the detectives encounter. Mr. Malone has written a rattling good mystery; he has also written an excellent novel…Vivid imagination…beautifully rendered…A rich diversity of cast, a compelling plot, prose of often poetically haunting beauty—impressive language in any kind of novel."
—Evan Hunter, *New York Times Book Review*

"Excellent…Engrossing as a detective story, it is also a 'mystery play' in the old sense of the word. The mystery it attempts to penetrate is not the obvious one but the eternal mystery of mysteries: What is life's purpose?…To get to the bottom of one of Malone's books is always a searing experience, like plumbing a well and finding oneself looking at the faces of the stars."
—*Chicago Sun-Times*

"A mystery of class and conscience, and it's a beauty. Malone sets his plot spinning on the first page and delivers enough twists and turns to keep readers of the genre more than satisfied. What elevates the book way above the mystery's customary standards is the author's intelligent handling of character and setting. He wants to entertain, but never at the expense of your brain…Among other virtues, Malone's ability to create believable characters from every social class is impressive. He makes us see Hillston whole. The dialogue rings true throughout…First class…an entertaining, intelligent book."
—*Newsday*

"Much has been made of the highbrow mysteries of Umberto Eco and Gabriel Garcia Marquez, [but] here in America we have also managed to produce an unusually funny and knowing use of the genre in Michael Malone's *Uncivil Seasons*."
—*The Nation*

"It bears Malone's imprint—the vividly drawn ambience…a stylish gift for language…characters come alive…a tender and believable romance."
—*Washington Post Book World*

"A purely perfect book. It's filled with action, suspense, intelligence and a sense of humor so droll it makes you happy just to know someone still thinks like that…The deft and deadly way Michael Malone dissects the town's maneuverings and mores is alone worth the price of the book. The only problem with *Uncivil Seasons* is that it's too short. I want Malone to write more, and quickly. When you read him, you will too. A joy."
—*The Atlanta Journal-Constitution*

"I really loved it. His grasp of people and place is wonderful. Most writers who are this good at plotting tend to neglect character; this is certainly not the case with Michael Malone. Cuddy Mangum, in particular, will remain in my mind forever."
—Lee Smith

"Intimate and believable, *Uncivil Seasons* is an examination of the human condition, in the form of a murder mystery. Malone's antic muse enlivens his evocation of a small Southern town. He is a wonderful writer, a master of both the sad and the funny. His humor runs comfortably from the jauntily ironic to the downright hilarious. And the dialogue! This is lovely, crisp dialogue, often promised on flap copy but seldom delivered on the page. The mystery, which is as twisted and murky as one could hope for, doesn't detract from the characters or the ambience; rather it adds a rich dimension of passion and rue."
—*The San Francisco Chronicle*

"Malone's novel has been compared to Faulkner's *Intruder in the Dust* and Harper Lee's *To Kill a Mockingbird*, but on the whole it's superior to both. It lacks the heavyhanded racial dogma of *Intruder* and the sentimentality of *Mockingbird*. A meticulously plotted detective novel with strong characters and a solid sense of place, *Uncivil Seasons* is a real find…Splendid as the mystery is, it's Mr. Malone's creation of a fictive world—the sense of real people living complex lives in a real place—that makes the novel so rich…*Uncivil Seasons* is that rarity, a mystery novel that invites rereading. Highly literate, sophisticated, evocative, it's grand entertainment."
—*The Kansas City Star*

"A pure delight. It's funny, it's sad, it's chilling, it's tender. It is also—hurrah, at long last!—a genuine whodunit that has you suspecting everyone by turns."
—*Book of the Month Club*

"Malone is one of those few writers working today who truly has a sense of what he is about as a writer. To read his work is to partake in a genuine meditation on what it means for people to live with and among each other. As with Dickens, the spirit to whom Malone most clearly gravitates, we come to know of the pains and joys of living the human comedy in a deeper way…"
—*The New Haven Register*

"Filled with fascinating characters…The town and its people come alive for readers. Malone is a fluent, creative writer, and his characters are brilliantly delineated. This is a book that shouldn't be missed."
—*The Minneapolis Tribune*

"The grace of this intricately drawn novel lies not only in its gripping plot, but also in the rich array of characters [and] lively dialogue…*Uncivil Seasons* is a must for those who enjoy a well-crafted detective tale. Malone's prose is vigorous and exciting, his characters glow…"
—*The Detroit Free Press*

Uncivil Seasons

a novel
by Michael Malone

SOURCEBOOKS LANDMARK™
AN IMPRINT OF SOURCEBOOKS, INC.®
NAPERVILLE, ILLINOIS

Published by Sourcebooks, Inc.
P.O. Box 4410, Naperville, Illinois 60567-4410
(630) 961-3900
FAX: (630) 961-2168

ISBN 0-7394-1985-4

Printed and bound in the United States of America

For Barry Hoffman
"Round up the usual suspects."

The eye of man hath not heard, the ear of than hath not seen, man's hand is not able to taste, his tongue to conceive, nor his heart to report, what my dream was. I will get Peter Quince to write a ballad of this dream. It shall be called Bottom's Dream, because it hath no bottom; and I will sing it in the latter end of a play, before the duke; peradventure, to make it the more gracious, I shall sing it at her death.

—Nick Bottom, a Weaver
A Midsummer Night's Dream

chapter 1
Monday, January 17

Two things don't happen very often in Hillston, North Carolina. We don't get much snow and we hardly ever murder one another. Suicide is more our style; we're a polite, college town, and our lives are sheltered by old trees. Maybe once a year a blizzard slips around a corner of the Smoky Mountains and blusters its way east, or a gale swells up from Cape Hatteras and runs across the Piedmont to break up our agreeable liaison with nature; but usually storms lose interest along the way. Whenever one does barge through town, merchants stockpile sleds as recklessly as Carolina blockade-runners once stowed tobacco and cotton. Schools close. Cars spin off the road. People have accidents.

They commit murders, too, but much more often in thought and word than deed. There is some impertinence in being a homicide detective in a town that wants to go on believing it is still too small and too temperate to require such expertise. That I should be the detective obliged to remind them of their susceptibility seems a further affront to Hillston, for I'm one of them. My mother is a Hillston Dollard. Her family has sheltered the town since its founding; they founded it. They sheltered it with pride; defensive, unchallengeable pride in the town, and the Piedmont that circled it, and the state that circled the Piedmont, and the country that circled the state. That's what Dollards did. It was the family business. For me to be searching for killers among us would have struck Hillston as an improper lack of family feeling, except that, of course, as everyone said, we rarely murdered one another.

The trouble was that now Cloris Dollard was dead, had been found dead last Sunday, her skull crushed. She was my uncle's wife.

• • •

"The sky looks like snow," I told Mrs. Lawry Whetstone.

"Never happen, sugar," Susan said.

"Probably not."

I was standing naked beneath my overcoat beside the bedroom window of the Whetstone summer cottage, glumly looking across the January gray lake toward Pine Hills Inn. The Inn was Hillston's oldest restaurant; old enough to boast it had been reduced to the degradation of serving as the stables for invading Federal troops during the War of the Confederacy. My circle ate at the Inn. Snug in a booth there an hour ago, Susan Whetstone had repeated that she just couldn't see the sense in her divorcing Lawry and ruining everything. She'd poked at the shrimp sunk inside her avocado, and brushed her blond hair up from the nape of her tan neck and said, "No, sugar, it's better this way." Susan and I had been having an affair for eighteen months; a year ago, I hadn't thought it was better this way. Now I no longer asked her to leave Lawry, but she hadn't seemed to notice I'd stopped, and she went on refusing to come away with me. It seemed impolite to point out she needn't worry about my feelings, especially after it had become so clear that Susan was not a worrier.

Susan's husband, Lawry, was a vice-president of C&W Textiles, Hillston's biggest industry, a century-old complex of mills and manufacturing that Lawry was determined to haul, against the will of its elderly patriarch, into the hightech gloss of what the newspapers were in the habit of calling the New South. Lawry flew around to places like Japan and Houston and neglected to take Susan with him. He'd been away in Atlanta for two weeks now, either buying or selling. "Who knows, who cares," said Susan, no backseat careerist.

I was standing by the window. She was stuffing designer sheets and towels apparently stolen from Hyatt hotels into the hamper and pulling the beige-checked coverlet over the bed. She found my shorts and tossed them at me. She'd already showered and dressed again; she had a postcoital efficiency I found depressing.

"Justin, it's 1:30. I better run. Laurel Fanshaw told me somebody, she wouldn't say who, was going to bring a motion to impeach me off the effing Charity Ball committee if I wasn't at this meeting today. I bet it was Patty. I can't believe you were so gaga over her; she's such a bitch."

"I was sixteen." I lit a cigarette. "You better run."

"Aren't you supposed to be back at work by two?"

"I'm supposed to check Cloris's 'socialite connections.' Aren't you one of them?" I brought Susan her suede boots. "That's what Captain Fulcher told me today." I mimicked my chief's fidgety face. "'Nobody can beat Senator Dollard's wife to death and rob her blind in her own house while I'm at the helm. Check out everybody, Savile, but don't step on any toes. You can be sure nobody in her circle carted off a crate of Mrs. Dollard's silverware, right? You know, my wife has the same pattern! Grand Baroque." I did a set of his mouth clicks.

Susan said, "Funny man. I love it when you do Fulcher. He is so tacky."

"He'd be crushed to know you think so; he wants to be 'in,' like you."

"Not as 'in' as you, sweetie." She shoved her foot into the magenta boot by pushing against my bare leg. "I like that scar on your leg." She opened my overcoat and ran her hand down my calf. "I think it's the fact that it's a bullet wound that turns me on." She walked to the dresser mirror to watch herself slide into her mink coat. "On TV, they said a robber killed Cloris. Meanwhile, it has got to be the creepiest thing I ever heard." Her hand stopped, lipstick poised.

I asked, "Did you ever hear of anybody really disliking Cloris?"

"Come on! You think somebody killed her on purpose? Get real, Justin." The lipstick plummeted into the suede purse. "Bye bye. I loved it today. I'll call you."

Shivering, I walked barefoot into the kitchen; like the rest of the cottage, closed for winter, the room smelled thickly of stale air. The table and counters were piled with summer's leftovers: white sail bags, OFF! cans, black flippers, badminton birdies. In their empty refrigerator I'd put my bottle of Jack Daniel's. I poured my fourth drink of the day, carried it out on the screened porch, and stared across Pine Hills Lake, a dark, flat oval ringed by the coves where, in summer, Hillston resorted in old-fashioned vacation homes. Somewhere on the other side, behind banked evergreens, was the Rowell Dollard cottage. When I was a child, I'd been brought there often, balking, to play with the daughters of the woman whose murder I was now assigned to investigate.

When I was a child, we called the place the Ames cottage, because back then Cloris had been married to a man named Bainton Ames. It was only after his death that she'd married Rowell Dollard, and so become a relative of mine, because Rowell was my mother's younger half-brother; and so become, because Rowell was a Dollard and a state senator, just the kind of person no one in Hillston wanted to believe could ever be beaten unconscious and then smothered with her own pillow in her home on Catawba Drive, which was (as Captain Fulcher reminded me) the best street in town.

I'd grown up on Catawba Drive, but had not driven for a long time along its shaded, twisting road until last Monday, when I was called to come look at Cloris Dollard. I was called by authority higher than Captain Fulcher's, because the circle closed ranks.

Because my father had played music on weekends with Cloris's first husband.

Because I'd been a (reluctant) usher at Cloris's second wedding. (Reluctant because I didn't like Rowell Dollard, who persisted in trying to give direction—his own—to my life.)

I was called in because Mother's cousin was the state attorney general. He'd gone over Fulcher's head to relieve me of all other cases, so that I could devote my time to discovering who'd killed Cloris, and then telling him about it the day he returned from his golf resort.

Because my mother's oldest brother (Uncle Kip) was a U.S. senator. Because one of my mother's grandfathers had been governor, like his father before him.

There was no need for me to worry about getting back late from lunch. In Hillston, family talked louder than money. Usually, although not always in our case, they spoke the same language. Captain Fulcher did not care for me, but he was afraid to make it obvious. He assumed that sooner or later I would tell Mother's people to find me a job as a judge or a senator, and then it would be better for him if I had never become aware of how covetously he despised me. His pink, frantic jowls flinched whenever I referred to Mrs. Dollard as Cloris.

After my childhood I had come to call her Cloris, but I'd rarely seen her. She was only a large, handsome shape passing me on the golf course or on the dance floor of the Hillston Club. Last Monday, I'd stood on the vast yellow carpeting of the vast colonial bedroom, and followed the smear of dried blood and the track of scattered pearls that led to the queen-size bed where Cloris Dollard had lain dead all night on a daisy coverlet, her suit ripped loose at the shoulder, a shoe absurdly dangling from her foot, the pillow now taken away from her face so that Richard Cohen, our medical examiner, could say what was immediately clear: someone had broken her skull, someone had pushed hard enough on her face to crush her nose. I'd stood, looking down on her body, and remembered her voice when I was a child, a full, warm, smoker-deep voice that made all her words sound like laughs.

And I recalled one moment from the summer I was six. Cloris and my mother, both in their bathing suits, stood on the dock at the Ames lake cottage, watching Uncle Rowell swim out to pull upright the little sailboat Bainton Ames had just capsized. Cloris was tugging up her suit straps and saying to my mother, "Honey, you're crazy, don't envy me! Thank your stars you're so petite and don't have to lug these damn things around with you everywhere you go!" She put her hands beneath her breasts and pushed them up. I recall my sudden wonder at all that amplitude of flesh, so different from my slender mother's body. I recall my squirming flush as I realized they were talking about their breasts.

When I called to tell my mother that Cloris was dead, she had sobbed, "Oh, my God, where's Rowell? Is he there? Oh, poor Cloris. I'll come over. Poor Rowell, poor Rowell. And his primary!"

Like her half-brother, Mother had been bred a Dollard. She knew that primaries were the family business.

Out on Susan's porch now, hairs rose from the goose bumps on my bare legs. A colder, quicker wind swirled up inside my coat, and my muscles tightened to shrink away from the gusts. Gray swells on Pine Hills Lake slapped up at a gray swollen mass of clouds that had hurriedly spurned over the sky and blotted the day out. It looked very much like snow. As my head tilted up to finish my whiskey, I noticed a different shade of gray steam skyward from the crest of the piney hill that sloped up from the side of the Whetstone lot. At first I thought of a fire, then saw that it was chimney smoke, then seemed to remember that hidden in that evergreen foliage was the vacation compound belonging to old Briggs Cadmean, president of C&W Textiles.

Hillston was a quiet college town, but it took the clattering noise of Cadmean's mills to pay for so much quietness. For the past fifty years Cadmean had owned the mills; he was the hub of the wheel. Eighty now, he was seldom seen socially. His pleasures had presumably been pecuniary and domestic: he'd made millions, he'd married often. Two wives had left his ugly downtown mansion on the arms of their lawyers; two had left in expensive coffins. Now he lived alone. I'd heard that his children, some of them old themselves, had all fled from him—several by dying. Why should his summer house be open in January? Surely, at his age, he too was not forced out here by a clandestine affair? Did the compound even still belong to Cadmean? I couldn't remember if Susan had said he'd sold it. She'd said something about it today at lunch, but I'd been drinking at lunch, and I forgot things when I drank. What I forgot first was how frightened my Dollard relatives were that I would start drinking again. "Some men can't handle it," Rowell had often informed me. "You seem to be one of them." Rowell had plans for me that meant he had to keep the skeleton gagged in the closet; to him the noise of ice in a glass in my hand sounded like the rattle of bones breaking loose and shaking the doorknob. I threw what was left of my drink toward the lake and went inside to get dressed.

• • •

At 2:30 I was walking unsteadily up the wide stone steps of the municipal building when I was stopped by Sister Resurrection, a tiny, old black woman who'd been trying to save Hillston for half a century. She always stopped me when I'd been drinking, somehow she sensed that's when I was most likely to agree with her. Now she shook her makeshift cross at me and said, "God's ready to put a stop to all this trash! He got no time to mess with mercy now! Praise Him!"

I said, "Why shouldn't He have time? He had time to start the whole mess."

She had no answer, or didn't care to share it, and marched in her fluttering rags away, insistent that we all rejoice in the imminent Armageddon. I followed her and stuffed five dollars down in her sweater pocket.

Inside on the fifth floor, Cuddy Mangum, Hillston's other homicide detective, stood in the hall, fiddling with his scores on a college basketball pool that was tacked up above the coffee machine. Captain Fulcher couldn't fire me because of my family; he couldn't fire Cuddy Mangum because Mangum was discreetly running the department for him. He wanted to fire us both.

At Cuddy's feet sat the dirty, white, unclipped little poodle (more or less) that he brought with him nearly everywhere he went, despite Fulcher's demands that he stop. The dog's name was Mrs. Mitchell, or Martha. He'd named her for the wife of Nixon's crony John Mitchell, and with her light frizzy bangs and sharp nose she did somewhat resemble that lady. Cuddy said he'd found Mrs. Mitchell abandoned on Airport Road the day he'd returned to Hillston from Vietnam, when he was feeling that the government had done to him about what it had done to Mrs. Mitchell, when they both had just been trying to help out.

As I came down the hall, Cuddy waggled his eyebrows. "How was your lunch break?" And he gave his crotch a few quick pumps.

I said, "Cuddy, that's the kind of gross, white-trash social style that gets you assigned to investigate ax fights in the By-Ways Massage Emporium parking lot, while I'm off interrogating Daughters of the Confederacy with our toes dangling in their private pools."

He winked his caustic, blue-jay eye down at me. "Is that where you were? I told your visitor you were off doing something hushed up and high-class, but *my*, I didn't know it was toe-dangling! Sort of shrivels you up though, in January, doesn't it, all this dangling? Now, was this pool water? You sure it wasn't *lake* water?"

I pointed at my cubicle and felt in my jacket pocket for a cigarette. "Who's in there?"

"I don't know, but I'm in love with her." He blocked me with his tall beanpole body; his white acrylic "ski" sweater smelled like pizza. He sighed loudly. "Now, tell me, Justin Bartholomew Savile the Five, why'd I have to grow up gross and country, and you so classical ivy and antebellum with your mama's folks that used to be the governor and all just running the state so big, why when their wives get whopped on the head, the attorney general has you put right on their case without a kiss-my to our fathead captain, not to mention *me* and my four years' seniority."

"You've got pizza on your sweater. Is that what you got for lunch again? Pizza, a Coke, and a Twinkie?"

"Hey, well, I can't afford to eat in those upper-crust tumbledown spots like where you and Lunchbreak Whetstone just got back from. Ye Olde Pine Hills Inn."

"I guess you want me to ask you how you knew that?"

"Dee-tection." He stuck his big bony hand in my jacket pocket and pulled out the Inn's inscribed matchbook. "It's never going to work with you and Lunchbreak, you know? What with you thinking *est* is Latin for *is*, and her thinking it's those lessons she took where they teach you how to tell people 'I hear what you're saying,' when you don't plan to pay any attention to what they've said."

"You just don't like Susan."

"Um. There's no putting anything past you today, Mr. Esse Quam Videri." (Once I'd made the mistake of translating for Cuddy the North Carolina state motto.)

I said, "You know, I'm very tolerant of your hillbilly affectations. Mine are just as native as yours. My great-granddaddy studied the classics and went to law school, too."

"Well, you've got me there," he grinned. "In fact, except that I'd have to get so pretty and preppie and go act in amateur Shakespeare theatricals, wearing jackass ears and tights, I almost wouldn't mind being Justin the Five, so I could go out gobbling ye olde nouvelle cuisine with a blond adultress in a beat-up barn, and come staggering back to work smelling like bourbon and—"

"Good Christ, don't you ever shut up?"

"Only when I...." And he began his graphic pumping again as he wandered back to erase his basketball game scores. Cuddy changed his projections continually on the basis of sudden, powerful hunches; he had never even come close to winning the pool. "Ask her if she'll marry me," he called over his shoulder.

I opened my office door and realized what Cuddy had been talking about. She sat in my father's old Yale chair staring with oddly yellow eyes at the papier-mâché ass's head I'd stuck up on the hat rack.

"It was part of a costume," I said.

"Mr. Savile? I was told you'd definitely be back by two

o'clock." She turned around the clock on my desk and pointed. It said 2:25. "My name is Briggs Cadmean."

I said, "Pardon me" and "I'm sorry," and went around her to hang up my overcoat. I hit into the side of my desk and lurched against her chair. "I was detained. Briggs Cadmean?" She wore a lavender down jacket with jeans and scuffed riding boots. She had a lovely face and an annoyed look. She was clearly not the town's oldest business magnate. I returned stiffly to my seat. "Is *the* C&W Briggs Cadmean your grandfather?"

With an even more annoyed look, she stuffed the book in her lap into a new briefcase. "Father."

"You're kidding."

"No."

"Are you the youngest?"

"Yes. Number nine. Out of wife number four. Now that you have my lineage." She was looking me over strangely. She looked familiar to me, too, but then, Hillston's circle was not large. I was thinking: hunt club (boots), charity tennis, political cocktails, dance. "Excuse me. Haven't we met?"

"Probably." She was not terrifically forthcoming.

"Miss?" I asked. "Mrs.? Ms.?"

"If you prefer to be formal, how about Doctor? Or Professor?"

"Are you an M.D.?"

"No. I teach astronomy at the university."

"My dad taught surgery at the medical school here," I said. "He didn't think Ph.D.'s should call themselves doctors. But I will if you want me to."

"What you call me doesn't matter much, since I'd like to keep this as brief as possible."

We were not hitting it off. In fact, she slid her chair back a significant inch away from me. "I'm here," she said, "because my sister-in-law asked me to drop in. Joanna Cadmean. She'd like to know if you could come talk with her. About Cloris Dollard, I understand."

"Pardon? Joanna Cadmean?" I was looking for a cigarette; I hid them from myself.

"She's the widow of one of my half-brothers. And she's staying out at my house for a few weeks. She came here from St. Simons Island for Cloris Dollard's funeral. She's staying because she was thrown riding; she's on crutches now, with a bad ankle. At any rate, she's worried about something, and she'd like to talk with you."

"What's she worried about?"

"That somebody's trying to kill her, too."

I found a cigarette. "Any particular reason why she thinks so?"

"A premonition."

I leaned my chair back and dismissed this Joanna Cadmean. We'd already had four other wealthy women call in, frightened that they, too, would be murdered soon, for their sterling or their diamonds or their too many years of capital and status. I said, "I'm sure it's just that the news of Cloris Dollard's death has upset Mrs. Cadmean." I picked up the silver letter opener Susan had given me and balanced it on my fingers as I quoted: "'Such tricks hath strong imagination.' *A Midsummer Night's Dream*."

Her response was to raise an eyebrow. "I saw your performance last week." Obviously, not a theater enthusiast either.

"Mrs. Cadmean," I shrugged, "has spooked herself."

"Yes, she has a strong imagination. In fact, she's a psychic."

"There, you see," I said, and smiled.

"A real psychic."

I smiled some more. "Visions and auras and foresee the future?"

"That's right."

"Tea leaves or Ouija board?"

The yellow eyes were flat as metal. "Please don't be cute."

I let my chair come back down on all fours. My neck flushed. "I'm sorry. Exactly how do you mean, 'a real psychic'?"

She stood up. "If you keep records here, go look up her maiden name. Joanna Griffin. When she was in college, she got to be pretty famous for her work with your department."

I stood up. "*That's* who your aunt was? Joanna Griffin? The Hillston psychic?"

"Yes."

"The one who found the two coeds' bodies?" I looked across at Mr. Cadmean's namesake. "Well then! Who's going to kill her?"

Now she looked bemused. "She didn't say. Ask her."

"Why me? Why does she want to see *me*?"

"I have no idea. As I understand it, she doesn't want to talk officially to the police, and I believe she knew your mother. We're out at Pine Hills Lake."

"Ah. You're staying at your father's summer house?"

"The lodge belongs to me." She walked to the door.

"I'll come out. Should we have dinner first?"

She zipped up the lavender jacket. "No, thank you."

I wasn't surprised. "Well, then, I'll drive out to the lodge after I eat alone. Around eight?"

"Fine. Joanna said to be careful about the road; she said it's going to snow."

I opened the door for her. "Is that a psychic prediction?"

Her hair shook out behind her shoulders. "No, that's probably the weather report. Do you know where the lodge is, Mr. Savile? It's the compound next to Lawry Whetstone's cottage."

I followed her out into the hall, wondering if she and Susan could possibly be friends, and if Susan had told her about us. She so ostentatiously disliked me, I was reluctant to think it had taken only our brief conversation to make her feel that way.

As we passed Cuddy's office, he lunged through his open door and said to Briggs, "Ma'am, would you like to marry me?"

She surprised me by leaning down to pet the poodle, Mrs. Mitchell, and then laughing. "I might," she said, "but not today."

"Well, how about going out for a pizza and a Twinkie?"

I was pulling on my overcoat. "Cuddy Mangum, this is Professor Briggs Cadmean. This is Detective Lieutenant Mangum, a great believer in marriage."

He cocked his head at her. "Not *the* Briggs Cadmean that owns Hillston! Honey, you don't look at all like your pictures in the paper. Listen, in fact you ought to talk to them. They don't do you justice. They make you look great big and bald and sneaky and about eighty years old!"

Briggs's surprising rumbling laugh suggested to me she didn't care much for her father.

"Excuse me, Cuddy. I'm going to walk Dr. Cadmean to her car."

"I don't blame you." He nodded toward the double doors at the end of the hall. "But what about V.D.?" He wheeled around to Briggs. "That's just our captain's name. Van Dorn. We call him V.D. to watch him chew up the insides of his cheeks."

I interrupted their laughter. "I'll be back."

"I'll mention you dropped by. Miss Cadmean, if you change your mind, I could be at the license bureau in the morning." Cuddy ducked back into his office.

I opened the door to what I incorrectly assumed was her father's new Lincoln, then watched as her big black car surged into Hillston's afternoon traffic. Something wet caught on my eyelashes. I looked up, and saw snow floating out of the dark sky.

• • •

"Um!" Mangum unlocked the door to the records room. "Joanna Griffin! Amazing. And asking for you like a sphinx out of a story, when the only people that call me out of the blue are trying to sell me light bulbs."

"Joanna Cadmean. She married a Cadmean."

"Isn't there anybody in Hillston besides me that's not part Cadmean or a damn Dollard like you?"

"My name's not Dollard. My name's Savile. I'm the only Savile in Hillston. There must be two hundred Mangums."

"At least. And I'm hoping to add more."

"Even if they're part Cadmean?"

"Well, hey, nobody's perfect." Pencil tight in his teeth, Cuddy rummaged through the file cabinets. "Okay, here it is. Griffin, Joanna. Looks like a couple dozen cases here. Also looks like she was what you might want to call a volunteer worker. I don't see where they ever paid her a damn penny."

"How do you charge for visions?" I took the file from him.

"What's her name, Jeane Dixon does all right. Course, she's on a big scale. Like, will Elvis come back from the dead? Lord, I hope so. Well, don't hog it. Read."

The file began decades ago, when one day a Hillston girl of good family had walked into the police department and shyly announced to the desk sergeant that she knew where the bodies of two missing local coeds were buried. They'd been missing for over a month. She was taken to the office of the young assistant solicitor, Rowell Dollard.

The girl explained to him and to the incredulous police that whenever she saw photographs of the missing coeds, she saw them being forced down wood basement steps into a black space. She went on to describe, in precise detail, what turned out to be a half-burnt, long-abandoned country church thirteen miles south of Hillston. Even as the squad cars followed her lead, bouncing over the clay-clotted road into overgrown woods; no one really believed the girl. They didn't believe her until the two corpses were dug from their shallow graves in the church basement, behind the wood steps.

After the department agreed that she couldn't have killed the coeds herself, after a student confessed that he had, they asked Joanna to tell them what her secret was. She said she didn't know. Images like these had been coming into her head since she was little. Naturally, she didn't like it. Not only was she a freak to her schoolmates, the visions themselves brought on violent headaches, and were followed by a terrible depression. She was horrified by the discovery of the bodies. So were her parents. Embarrassed, they had her put under observation at the university, where she was a freshman. There, parapsychologists asked her to look at the backs of cards and read what was on the other side. She did so. The university concluded that if there were such a phenomenon as mental telepathy (and about this they disagreed), then Joanna Griffin was telepathic.

The Hillston police became less skeptical. When a local

three-year old disappeared, his mother begged the police to call in Joanna. Joanna told them where to find the well shaft he'd fallen down, and still lay in, alive. She picked a suspected arsonist out of a lineup and recounted each moment of his crime to him so vividly that, terrified by her sorcery, he confessed both to that, and to two other unsolved arsons.

Of course, sometimes her sibylline visions were too vague to follow, and sometimes she had nothing at all to tell the department that had sheepishly gotten into the habit of calling her in whenever they had no leads and the news was publicly wondering why. The papers called Joanna everything from a mystic to a charlatan, and one literary journalist dubbed her "the Carolina Cassandra."

Then suddenly, after two years, Joanna stopped working for the police and left the university for a term. When she came back to town, strangers continued to pester her with demands that she locate misplaced trinkets and wandering spouses, that she tell them where to find good jobs, that she bring back their dead. She asked them please to stop asking.

"Can you imagine," Cuddy said, "having no choice but to really see what's going on in the rotten world? You know? Not being able to blink your eyes? Seeing all the old smut in the heart, and the tumor on the bone, and somebody's future that's never going to happen? God damn! Can you imagine being her?"

There was a rumor that she'd attempted suicide in college, but that her family had hushed it up. Then she'd eloped with one of the Cadmean sons, and the visions, as far as anyone knew, had ended. "Marriage'll do that," Cuddy remarked. Perhaps after she had become a member of his family, old Briggs Cadmean forbade her to hallucinate, thinking it unseemly for a daughter-in-law of his to be even mentally trekking through creek bed and alley, feeling her way to the deserted, or raped, or stabbed. Dreaming her way to death.

Cuddy closed the file of yellowing papers. "I thought I heard she died."

"Christ, I'm almost scared to go meet her."

"Well, if you get a chance, ask her if she can help me win the basketball pool."

"All right. So long, I'm going out."

"You just got here. Why don't you come up to my office and do some police work, just to keep your hand in. Take your pick. Who keeps stealing Mr. Zeb Armel's Pontiac every night and driving it 'til the tank's empty? And my bet's Zeb Jr. Who is exposing his private parts to Mrs. Ernestine Staley when she walks down Smith Road to collect her mail? And, my question, why in the world did he pick her? Who held up the Dot 'n' Dash? And, of course, why is there blood and fingertips all over the By-Ways Massage Emporium parking lot?"

"Sorry. I'm on special assignment. I'm going to East Hillston about the Dollard jewelry."

"Across the Divide? Over to where us poorfolk were herded together and told, 'Let them eat Twinkies.' That East Hillston?"

"Right."

"Well, don't ask any tattooed greasers to step outside, General Lee."

I left him at the elevator door and crossed the marble lobby back out into the snow.

Never ask a greaser with tattoos on his knuckles to step outside, especially if he's smiling, and combing his hair with a switchblade. Those were among the first words Cuddy Mangum ever said to me. And although we'd been born in the same year, in the same town, we were never in one another's homes until after I joined the police department ten years later, and we met again in the hall where I'd seen him today. He'd made the remark our senior year (mine in a New England prep school, his in Hillston High). I was back home to escort a debutante to a dance, and we'd come in our formal clothes at dawn to an all-night diner. As soon as we sat down, three hoods leaned into our booth and began making vulgar cracks. I asked them to step outside. Somebody tall and thin, seated by himself at the counter, all of a sudden spun his stool around and faced them. He said, "Wally, don't talk dirty in front of a lady. I think you left your brains out in your Chevy;

why don't you and your pals go look for them, how about?"

And after a volley of muttered obscenities, Wally clanked off and his friends followed.

It was when I came over to the counter to thank Cuddy Mangum that I got the advice never to ask tattooed greasers to step outside. He added, "They never read your rule book, General Lee."

"Mind if I ask—is Wally a friend of yours?"

"He's my cousin." And my rescuer spun his stool back away from me and picked up his textbook and his doughnut.

Ten years after that, when he and I were introduced by Captain Fulcher, I said, "Oh, we've already met."

Cuddy took a doughnut out of his mouth and nodded. He said, "Especially now you're in the police business, don't ask a tattooed greaser to step outside."

It was his parting shot whenever I told him I was going to East Hillston, far from Catawba Drive and my family's circle. Cuddy leaned out into the hall while I was waiting for the elevator.

Chapter 2

I inched my old Austin timidly into East Hillston. I hadn't been drinking long enough not to be still afraid of the snow. With me was a list of Cloris Dollard's stolen property that probably wasn't very accurate. She had been a woman of property, but not a careful or a frugal one. She'd spent her life as cheerfully as all the money she'd given to Hillston charities, and all the money she'd spent to buy the random wealthy clutter of belongings she'd given away or left behind. What had proved less fragile than their owner—and had not been stolen by her murderer—Cloris's daughters had come from other cities and taken home with them, or stored in the basement. Rowell, who liked to keep things, would not let them touch his wife's room.

I had searched in the house through the clutter, looking for a clue among boxes of clothes, photographs of golf trophies, her first husband's sheet music, and her daughters' camp crafts; among drawers of old theater programs, packets of seeds, keys and buttons whose uses had been lost for years. I was looking through a past of good looks, marriages, travel, civic duties, through the loose ends of an easy life, for a clue to tell me that Cloris's death had not happened, as Fulcher believed, by the unlucky accident of indiscriminate violence, but for a cause particular and personal, and so discoverable. I'd found nothing.

Now I was doing instead what Cuddy had long ago warned

me detectives actually do for a living. I was walking, with a list of stolen property, into every pawnshop, secondhand business, and disreputable jewelry store in town. I was waiting for someone to give me a clue. Most of the stores are in East Hillston. None of the owners had seen any of Cloris Dollard's property. Not unless they'd seen on their customers some of the used clothes she was always donating to Goodwill.

The good will performed locally by Cloris Dollard and her friends, and by Susan Whetstone and her friends, was for the benefit of this section of town called East Hillston, which meant poor Hillston, which meant the area bordering the side of downtown Hillston that had gone out of business when Cloris and her friends had stopped shopping there twenty years ago and had driven off to the new malls and had never come back except for charity's sake.

Sister Resurrection walked fast along the streets of East Hillston, dawn to dark, the smell of her rotted sweaters as familiar as her stick with its wood cross taped to the top and her unsparing eyes that kept waiting for God to burn up the world. Men and women who worked the lowest-paid assembly line jobs at C&W Textiles lived here; so did most of Hillston's blacks; so did the few Greek and Italian families, after three generations still known to their neighbors as "the foreigners," who owned corner groceries and submarine sandwich shops. They lived here in all that were left of the massive Victorian frame houses built after the Civil War, when East Hillston had been the center of town. Boarded up or doled out as shoddy apartments, the old homes were rotting beneath layers of bad paint and cheap linoleum. Beside them, even shabbier little oblong boxes had been thrown up on what had once been big lawns where summer parties played croquet. These little 1940s duplexes, faced with stucco or aluminum siding, now hid behind all the pickup trucks and rusty Chevrolets scattered over the yards. The worst place to be from in Hillston was East Hillston. It was where Cuddy Mangum had grown up.

The Mangums had lived three blocks from the old, shambling, two-story Gothic house that somebody named Pope had owned as far back as the town records went. Somebody named Pope had been on the police books as far back as those records went, too. At present, various assortments of Pope brothers and their wives lived in the house and were periodically arrested for stealing cars, hijacking cigarette trucks, and brawling in public. Long ago, their mother Edna had just picked up her raincoat and walked out of the house. She'd left when her youngest boy was twelve. She'd never come back. The boys' father, T. J. Pope, had died while waiting trial for murder: he'd killed a mechanic who overcharged him.

Cuddy said the Pope brothers were hereditarily unreformable, but their marauding was checked by a congenital stupidity (evidenced by their having hidden three thousand dollars belonging to Cherokee Savings and Loan under a junked bus in an old cardboard suitcase that had "Edna Pope, 1002 Maple Street, Hillston, N.C." tagged to the handle), and so, at any given time, a few of them were likely to be sidelined by prison.

Cuddy Mangum kept up with the Popes. He called me with the latest news shortly after I'd gotten home from East Hillston and was changing into a suit to go meet the psychic Joanna Cadmean out at Pine Hills Lake. His call came when I'd just hung up the phone and poured a drink after listening to my uncle Rowell Dollard tell me, again, to go arrest someone for killing Cloris. I thought the ring now was Rowell calling back. My uncle was persistent. He hated to lose. At fifty-eight he played squash twice a week, and he played and played until he won. If I beat him two out of three games, he'd pant, "Let's make it three out of five." Captain Fulcher was scared that if we didn't find Cloris's murderer fast, Rowell would do it himself, and then have all of us fired, as, long ago, he'd gotten V.D. Fulcher's predecessor fired. Rowell liked to do things himself; he'd insisted on acting as a father to me even during the time when I already had one.

The call, however, was from Cuddy, using a British accent, "Lawry Whetstone here, old boy. Understand you've been banging my memsahib. I say, bad show."

"What do you want, Cuddy? A part in our next play?"

"What are you doing right now?"

"Changing my clothes."

"You know, I wonder if you're not some kind of pervert. There's something un-American about the way you're always playing the piano and changing your clothes. Want to get in on a real arrest; score with V.D.? Meet me at the Popes' house on Maple fast as you can."

"Christ, what have the Popes done now?"

"Charlene called up the station . . ."

"Graham's wife?"

"Preston's. Charlene is Baby Preston's wife. Can't you keep up? Old Graham's wife gave him the heave while he was in the tank for trying to collect insurance on a semi he poured kerosene all over and lit a match to about the time everybody was getting out of church and strolling by his house to watch him do it. Whooee, I love those Popes! Graham's wife's the daytime bartender at the Rib House now, but she put on a lot of weight snacking on the job and lost her looks. Charlene called...."

I kept straightening my bow tie. "Jesus Christ, Cuddy, how do you know all this?"

"These are my people, white boy. My grandma's sister married a second cousin of the Popes'. That's why I don't have the heart to go over there alone and arrest Preston for whinging off two of Luster Hudson's fingers with an ax outside the By-Ways Massage Emporium, which is what hot-to-trot Charlene—who was whinging Luster, as was well known to everybody in East Hillston *but* Preston—just got through telling Sergeant Davies took place. Now, Officer Davies says we ought to close the By-Ways, says they're showing obscene motion pictures in the back. I says, 'Ummmm, are they ever! But doesn't it make you so mad, Hiram, how they blip off every eighteen seconds, and you got to plunk in a few more quarters to get to the good stuff?'"

Sergeant Hiram Davies was past retirement age and a rigid Baptist deacon. "Okay, Cuddy, force yourself to hang up, and I'll be right over."

"I knew you couldn't stay away. You love this low-life blood-and-lust detective work, doncha?"

"That and the long lunch hours."

• • •

When I skidded scared in the slush around the corner of East Hillston's Maple Street, I could hear gunshots, and then I saw Cuddy hiding down beside his patrol car. I braked next to him and yelled, "Get out of here!"

"They're not shooting at me!" he yelled back.

"Jesus Christ! Who are they shooting at?"

He was twisting his arm around inside his neon-blue parka. "How the hell should I know? I just got here! Where the hell is my gun!" He didn't always wear his revolver, and often couldn't even find it.

Up and down the snowy street, lights popped on in the duplexes. People cracked their doors and stuck their heads through. Cuddy hollered at them, "Will you folks please get on back!"

I rolled out of my Austin, slid into the patrol car, and flipped its siren on. Mrs. Mitchell was hiding under the dash. In about five seconds, the shots quit. As soon as they did, a young woman ran out the door of the Pope place and jumped down the cinder blocks that they used for porch steps. She slipped face first in the wet snow and started to scream as loudly as the siren. Cuddy and I scurried to her. It was Charlene. She hissed at him when Cuddy asked her if she'd been shot, and then she went back to screaming. I'd pulled my gun from the shoulder holster I always wore, because once when I hadn't, a drunk at a KKK rally had shot me in the calf and splintered a bone. I crouched, ran toward the porch, and yelled into the door. "Police! Come out of there!"

I heard things banging around inside. From next door I heard a man call out, "It's the police for the Popes."

A door at the back slapped shut and Preston Pope came running across the driveway, headed for a van that had white horses in blue moonlight painted on it in iridescent color. Shoving past the metal junk piled on the porch, I leapt down and got to him in time to grab Preston's leg. He kicked like crazy, and we whipped back and forth in the snow until Cuddy ran up and shook him off me, yelling, "Preston! Cut this shit! I'm gonna hurt you!"

The youngest Pope went limp then, so quickly Cuddy almost dropped him, and mumbled "Mangum, don't listen to that bitch! I swear . . ." But he gave up the effort and just stood still. We were all three panting, and puffs of smoke from our breath blew all over the place.

Charlene Pope was still out in the middle of the yard hugging herself. Charlene looked like somebody on the cover of one of the magazines you could buy in the By-Ways Massage Emporium. She had bleached white hair and black eyes and breasts hard as apples, and she was somewhere between fifteen and twenty-five. A black acetate bathrobe was slipping down off her shoulder; the only other thing she had on was one pink, fuzzy bedroom slipper.

Cuddy scooped her other slipper out of the snow. "Come on, Charlene. Let's all go on back in the house and see what the problem is."

She had a high, twanging voice that got away from her when she raised it. "Y'all got to be crazy out of your minds! I want you to arrest his ass and get him out of here!" She shook both fists at her husband. "Goddamn fuckhead!"

Cuddy said, "Now, don't talk dirty out in the front yard in your nightgown, Charlene." He, Preston, and I went inside, and finally she followed us, already with a cigarette in her glossy purple mouth.

Local news was loud on the color TV, and Kenny Rogers was simultaneously singing a love song loud out of stereo speakers on the mantel above a fireplace that was used as a trash can. The Pope living room looked like a K-mart warehouse, like a cheap motel that didn't care who came there or what they did there, and didn't bother cleaning up afterward. Thin, green carpeting was oil-slick with grime and puddled with stains, and cluttered with bent Coke and beer cans, ashtrays, country-and-western tapes, electric drills, balled-up bags of junk like corn puffs and barbecued potato chips, and God knows what else. Foam stuffing poked out of the black vinyl couch, where a skinny orange dog lay on a beach towel. One shade was ripped in half and there were chunks gouged out of the plaster. On two walls were textured, color photograph portraits of various Pope boys and their brides, the boys in rented baby-blue tuxedoes with black piping. On another wall was an auto parts shop poster of a hefty blonde, naked and knee-deep in surf. On the floors along the walls were stacks of car stereos, CB systems, about seventy cartons of cigarettes, and five televisions—one with the screen smashed. I said, "So these are your Popes."

Cuddy said, "My, my, this is *messy*." Two windows were broken and gunsmoke lay thick in the air. He poked open another door and peeked in; he looked down the halls and tilted over to see up the stairs.

Preston picked a revolver up off the floor and handed it to me. "There ain't nothing in it," he said defensively.

Charlene shrieked, "That's right, you'd still be shooting if there was!"

Wiry and sullen, Preston came at her, snow still white in his beard and on his jean jacket. She backed away, making faces. He said, "I wasn't shooting at her, I was just shooting."

"Cleaning your gun?" I asked.

"Blowing off. You know."

I said, "Not exactly."

Charlene said, "He is so *stupid*, I can't stand it another second."

"Well, let me tell you this, this bitch here is a cunt."

"You dumb prickhead!"

They started toward each other again, and Cuddy slid between and elbowed them both. He asked Preston, "Where's everybody else, where's Graham and Dickey?"

"Greensboro. That's where she thought I was too."

Charlene hissed back at him. "I came over here to pack up

my own personal belongings that don't belong to you."

I said, "In your robe?"

"I was getting ready to take a bath. I can use the tub if I want to, I guess!"

Preston was yelling again. "The hell you can, you can't use nothing in this whole goddamn house, 'cause none of it's yours, 'cause the goddamn water belongs to *me* and the goddamn TV belongs to me too!" He spun around and jerked out the TV cord, which just left the Kenny Rogers tape going at high volume.

"I'm leaving," she said.

"You're not leaving," he said.

"Yes, I am too!"

"Go ahead and try!"

"Well," Cuddy said, "why don't you at least go throw on a few clothes, Charlene." He turned her toward the stairs in the hall. "What with all the windows broken, it's kind of drafty." Actually, they had the oil heat up to about ninety degrees; even with the ventilation, the place was so hot I decided to take off my overcoat and brush out some of the slush.

Cuddy put his hand on Preston's shoulder. "Preston, you need to calm down. You don't seem to be paying attention to the fact that you're getting arrested."

Preston said, "What for?" but he was watching Charlene try to go up the stairs while looking back down at us.

I said, "Are you kidding? Assault with a deadly weapon?"

"Charlene's never gonna say that."

"Is he kidding? What do you think your wife's *been* saying?"

"Forget her. Y'all got eyes. She's out of her fucking gourd!"

Charlene yelled from the top of the stairs. "In case you hadn't noticed, you stupid asshole, you're *screwed*, Preston! What are you gonna do now, huh? What are your big brothers gonna do for you now, huh? Huh, baby shithead?"

He jumped. "Just let me go kill her, okay?"

Cuddy said, "Whoa. Let's not do that right this minute. Let's have a talk, you and me, and this gentleman is Lieutenant Savile and that was his camel-hair coat you tore the pocket off of."

Preston said, "I'm sorry."

I said, "It's all right."

Cuddy said, "Now, listen, Preston, you wouldn't like to be moving in with brother Furbus for, oh, about a year, would you?"

Furbus Pope, the eldest brother, and probably twenty years older than Preston, was in the state penitentiary on a larceny charge.

"Okay, what's the deal?" he mumbled.

"Well, first of all, why did you shoot at your wife?"

"Let me tell you something about Charlene...."

"In a minute. Second of all, I'd hate to think for your health's sake, you were going through—" Cuddy glanced over at the floor, "oh, six or seven hundred packs of cigarettes a day while you were sitting around watching all those TV sets."

Preston said, "You want one?"

"And third of all."

Preston now slumped down onto the couch and pulled at his hair. The orange dog finally sat up. I'd decided it was dead.

Cuddy wiggled his fingers. "Third is the matter of a couple of Luster Hudson's fingers, which I hear rumors you took off him with an ax."

"Says who?"

"Guess."

"Luster."

"Guess again."

"That bitch." Preston dug his fingernails into the side of his face and started it bleeding.

"*Now* you can tell me about Charlene." Cuddy sat down. I stood by the door, where I could watch the stairs. The dog came over, sniffed at Cuddy's leg, and then wandered back to the kitchen.

Young Pope had gotten himself so depressed by now, he had to keep taking long breaths while he talked. "Couple of weeks ago I found out Charlene and Luster Hudson had something on."

"Couple of weeks ago you found out," Cuddy said, and looked at the ceiling.

"Well, it was Graham found them out, and he told me. So, Charlene, she says it's a lie, but I don't believe her because she's on nights at C&W along with Luster and she's not showing up home. And then Graham saw her and him dancing at the Tucson Lounge. So I said, 'One of these times, Charlene, you're gonna open that door and there'll be a gun in your belly.'"

"That's telling her," Cuddy said.

"So she said, 'Don't think I haven't hidden your damn gun where no way you're gonna find it.' So I said, 'I don't need a gun to—'"

I said, "Let's skip to the part where you chop off Hudson's fingers."

"It was Luster came at me with the ax."

"Any particular reason?"

"He had it in his pickup."

Cuddy said, "I think what Lieutenant Savile means is, what did you *do* to Luster before he looked in his truck to see if he had an ax handy?"

Preston mumbled something.

Cuddy took out a package of cheese crackers. "Come again? Seemed like you said, 'Torched his bike.'"

"Yeah."

"Torched his bike."

"I said, *yeah*. I'm looking for Charlene, and I seen his Harley outside the Tucson Lounge and so I look in and I see him and her out on the floor and so I take a rag and stuff it in his tank. And so I torch it."

"All right." Cuddy nibbled tiny bites of the cracker.

"So he comes for me at the By-Ways but Graham's with me, so Graham ducks and comes up under Luster's knees and I get hold of the ax and that's when it got his fingers."

I said, "You just left Hudson lying there bleeding?"

"He's the one left, and he knew why, too. I chased his goddamn truck a block but I gave out and threw the ax at it."

"Good Christ," I said. "What about the man's fingers?"

"Aww, shit, it was just the tips. Graham picked them up and

looked and it was nothing but the tips."

"I don't suppose you're keeping them in a jar on your bureau?"

Preston was shaking beer cans that sat on the floor; finally he found one with something to drink in it. Mournfully he told us, "Y'all got eyes. Charlene brought this all on herself."

Cuddy said, "I don't see where *Charlene's* the one in trouble."

Preston flared up. "Well, that's where you're wrong because I've about had it with that little girl and she's gonna wind up in a divorce, I swear she is!"

Cuddy said, "That's harsh," and gave me his blue-jay wink.

I hadn't heard noises from upstairs in a while. I said, "Excuse me, I think I'll just go see if Charlene's taking another bath."

"Oh, hell!" Cuddy untangled his long body from the plastic swivel chair. "I forgot! Back stairs!" By the time I got to the top, we all heard the motor rev outside and the tires whir in the snow.

Cuddy yelled, "Too late!" and I yelled, "Is she in *my* car?" and the three of us ran onto the porch, but it was the iridescent van whose engine Charlene was racing out in the street, while she shouted through the open window, "*I'm taking it*, it was *my* money paid for it!"

Preston hopped up and down, but couldn't shake Cuddy's grip. "*You get back here!*"

"Get fucked, shithead!" Charlene popped the clutch, tore up a gear, and was gone.

"Sweet lips," Cuddy said.

Preston's mouth was working hard but words had failed him. Then he bolted back inside up to the second floor.

The upstairs of the Pope house convinced me that they'd put all of their housekeeping efforts into the downstairs living room. In a bedroom that could only have been Charlene's, Preston yanked the top drawer right out of a dresser and was shaking his socks and several dozen "Arouse" condom packets onto the floor. Then he slammed to his knees and pawed through everything.

Cuddy said, "What'd she take?"

Preston said, "Nothing," and began tossing undershirts around.

I wandered out to the bathroom. Nobody's been taking a bath, because the tub was full of small gray velvet sacks. I opened one of them.

"Hey, Cuddy, you want to hang on to Preston? We have a problem here."

"What you got?"

I brought the sack back into the bedroom and pulled out an ornate dinner fork. "Cloris Dollard's silverware."

Cuddy said to Preston, "I don't guess you got it with Green Stamps, did you?"

Chapter 3

Downtown, we booked an even more morose Preston Pope. I left Cuddy with him and went to visit Joanna Cadmean.

It was snowing so hard by the time I'd driven to the lake, I had trouble finding the turnoff to the Cadmean compound. Although I'd often looked at it from the bedroom of the Whetstone lake cabin, I'd never really seen it, because when you're as wealthy as the Cadmeans, you can afford a lot of trees. Even when my mother's people had had money, they hadn't had that kind of money.

In the black water, a covered sailboat, a motorboat, and a canoe were shadows, moored for winter beside two long docks. A beach (for which somebody had trucked in a great deal of white sand at considerable cost) led up a slope of pines, and at the top, lights looming, sat the huge lodge with its big windows that looked, over the heads of the pines, down on the lake below and the smaller houses that ringed the water.

Inside, the lodge turned out to be the handsome, rustic sort the rich liked to build in the Appalachians and out West in the 1920s, with the cavernous stone fireplace, bare log beams girdering high ceilings, and a few bluish American Indian rugs thrown here and there. A porch stretched halfway around the first floor, and an open balcony across the second. In the middle of the roof was an odd octagonal turret with an outside walkway, like a watchtower. The furnishings were spartan.

I'd recognized my mother's car among the others clustered along a driveway lit by the porch lights and already glazed with snow. Mother's old sable coat hung on the coatrack in the hall, and my mother, a small, still-pretty woman of a buoyant disposition, sat uncomfortably swallowed by a bent-willow chair near the fire. She was chattering away at someone on the couch when the young woman, Briggs, led me in.

"Justin! Whatever in the world are you doing out here tonight? Oh, Briggs, you invited him. I didn't know you knew Briggs, honey. My God, your coat's all torn up. Joanna, this is my son, Justin. He's a policeman. I wanted him to play the piano or use his imagination or something, and Rowell wanted him to be governor, but he's a policeman. I don't know why he ever went into such a morbid profession in the first place, though I suppose you could say his father did cut open people's brains for a living."

"Lt. Savile, hello. It was nice of you to come."

I came around the couch to meet the famous mystic. Expecting....I don't know what I expected. Madame Blavatsky? Carmen, in Mexican clothes with gold earrings and big clay beads she'd made herself, ruffling a deck of tarot cards? Saint Theresa?

What I saw was an unexpectedly beautiful middle-aged woman dressed in a pastel sweater and tweed skirt very much like those all my mother's friends wore on winter days at home. But despite her ordinary clothes, the chignon in which she wore her waved light hair and the sculpted cast of her features made me think at once of some Archaic Athena, some goddess quietly standing to support a temple. And always afterward, from that first look until the end, I thought of Joanna Cadmean as such a statue, Delphian, cool, and impenetrable as stone.

Her right foot, thickly wrapped in Ace bandages, the toes covered by a white sock, was propped up on the redwood coffee table. In her lap was a spiral-bound artist's sketchbook; with a pencil she was drawing faces rapidly, swirling from face to face without lifting the point and, strangely enough, without even looking at what she was drawing. If there was anything else "odd" about her (other than her beauty), it was her stillness. Her large, wide-set eyes—not at all the sharp Svengalian jabs of light I associated with psychic powers from old movies—were a deep, still gray. Her voice was peaceful, quiet, and slow, nothing like the intense, animated cheer habitual with Southern women like my mother, to whom she now said, "Your son came out to see me, Peggy. I invited him out."

As I bent to take Mrs. Cadmean's hand, she quickly turned the page of the sketchbook over to a blank sheet.

"You asked him? Whatever for?" My mother tilted her head for me to kiss as she spoke. "I ought to be grateful. I haven't seen him in ages, except on the stage. He's in the Hillston Players. Weren't you in that a long time ago? They just did *A Midsummer Night's Dream*. He played the one that gets turned into a donkey. I saw him there, and then at Cloris's funeral, and now I run into him all the way out here. You didn't go to Cloris's services, Joanna."

"No. I went to the grave."

"Well, and now you're stuck in Hillston. Joanna fell off a damn horse and broke her leg."

Mrs. Cadmean smiled. "Sprained my ankle. Your mother brought me a care package." Beside the couch was one of the wicker baskets my mother called her "Shut-in Surprises." This one included more historical romances than I could imagine a woman like Joanna Cadmean wanting to read.

"It was my fault," Briggs was saying to my mother. "I shouldn't have put her on Manassas."

Mrs. Cadmean pulled a plaid blanket down over her legs. "No, it's not the horse's fault. I started thinking something upsetting, and I frightened him. He wanted to get away from me, that's all. So he threw me."

"Well, that's a weird way to put it," my mother said. "But that's the way Joanna was even when she was little." Mother turned to us. "She used to tell us that we were *colors*. Really! She'd look at us, like this, *hard*, and she'd see these different colors around us like a neon sign. If she didn't like a boy's color, well! She wouldn't have a thing to do with him. Oh, God, Joanna, remember when you told Mrs. Mott at church she had a round lump like a grapefruit in her stomach, and she was dead of cancer a month later?"

I asked Briggs if she had any whiskey.

Mother sang her nervous laugh. "Why, yes, it is so bitterly cold, why don't you just bring me and Justin a teeny, tiny sip of something, Briggs?" She held up thumb and forefinger to measure a quarter inch.

Briggs left the room, and Mother went on. "I was a sort of robin's egg blue, wasn't I?"

"You still are." Mrs. Cadmean smiled and began to draw again.

"Good! I was afraid maybe you'd say I'd turned all smudgy black inside." Mother touched her finger to the lace wrinkles at the edge of her eyes. She started to remember what colors other childhood friends had looked like to Joanna, while I waited for my drink. My father and I had grown so accustomed to Mother's Ferris wheel of language, that on the rare occasions he and I had been alone together, we'd been astonished by the silence and could never think how to get past it. We'd play eighteen holes of golf with fewer words than Mother would use to describe a wait at the bus stop. She'd been by my father's hospital bed talking of orioles that had come that morning to her birdfeeder, when he'd died, silently, his hand on hers. "...And Joanna, what was so spooky was up in Judy Fanshaw's room, you were *eight*, when you said Cloris was stark white with a red rim, like a blood-red moon! And it gave us all the creeps, and *now*, all these years later, here Cloris is, murdered! And the newspaper came over here, Justin, to interview Joanna, but she wouldn't talk to them."

I sat down near the fire. "Briggs said you live on St. Simons Island now, Mrs. Cadmean. It's beautiful there. How long since you've lived in Hillston?"

"Fifteen years. I left after my husband, Charles, died." Her handsome head was still as marble. "But I come back from time to time. I was here last summer."

Mother scrambled out of her deep chair to help Briggs with the drinks. "I was just thinking last week, Joanna, how Cloris broke down in the middle of your Charles's funeral, because that summer she'd lost poor Bainton in that freak accident on the lake, and now here you'd lost your husband too. Can you believe that was fifteen years ago? Now, here we are at Cloris's..." Mother sipped away a fourth of my already minuscule drink before handing it to me.

The shadows of the flames from the cave-like hearth darkened the pallor of Mrs. Cadmean's face as she turned toward me, wincing as she jostled her ankle. "It was to inquire about Cloris Dollard's death that I asked you here."

Mother said, "The attorney general has assigned him exclusively to Cloris's investigation." The attorney general was Mother's cousin.

Mrs. Cadmean said, "Really, Mr. Savile?"

"Oh, Joanna, call him Justin." Mother saw me look inquiringly at my empty glass; she put her arm through mine and led me across the shadowy vaulted room to the huge window at the far end, trilling back, "Ladies, excuse us. Let me just go take a look at this snow. I'm a little worried about driving. But I do have my chains. Do you have yours, Justin?" When we reached the window, she spoke sotto voce. "Will you please be careful?" She nodded at my glass.

"I'm fine."

"Jay, please remember the strings Rowell had to pull to get your license back." Jay was my childhood name, now used in emotional emergencies.

"I'm fine."

Mother pulled away, her nostrils tightened, and she called out, "Look! It really is snowing hard. The ground's completely white."

Briggs came over to watch the swirl of heavy flakes fall into the arc of floodlights. White streaked invisibly into the white sand and vanished into the lake. Briggs said, "I can't remember the last time Hillston had snow like this."

Mother's eyes blinked. "Six years ago," she said. She ran for her coat. "Joanna, I'm going to leave here before it gets too deep. Justin, please don't stay long. Rowell's coming to go over some family papers, and I think you should be there." She saw I was tempted to say something, and hurried away to the couch. "Stay off that foot, Joanna. And if that newspaperman pesters you again, why don't I ask Rowell to call up *The Star* and have him stopped? Briggs, would you like one of Mirabell's puppies? She had eleven! Isn't that a very Irish thing for an English setter to do?"

After Mother left, Briggs excused herself to go prepare a lecture.

I said, "Are you old enough to be an astronomy professor?"

She put another log on the fire. "I'm twenty-nine. How old do I have to be?"

"You don't look it. You're only five years younger than I am."

She said, "You're thirty-four? You don't act it. Good night."

I poked at the fire with the iron prongs. "I don't think the professor likes me, Mrs. Cadmean."

She smiled at me, the gray eyes steady. "She certainly gave that impression. Go ahead and smoke if you like." She said this just as I was telling my hand to move to my pocket for my cigarette case, and wondering if I should.

I sat down in the big bent-willow armchair beside her. "What would you like to know, Mrs. Cadmean?"

"Please call me Joanna. We've met before. Not exactly met. You won't remember. It was a very painful time for you. I was at the cemetery the day of your father's burial. I liked your father. He was perceptive." The eyes smiled. "Not a word I use lightly."

"Thank you." I lit the cigarette. "Yes, it was a painful time." If she had seen me at the cemetery, she had seen me hit Rowell Dollard hard enough to make him stumble back into a wreath of lilies, hit him when he told me that if it weren't for my drinking, my father wouldn't be dead, my mother's life wouldn't be ruined.

Joanna nodded, as if she were following along with my

memories. There must be that advantage in having a reputation as a psychic; you simply sit there and nod, and people believe you are seeing straight through to their innermost hearts, either because they want you to, or because they desperately do not. "You look much better now," she said, "than that day."

"Thank you. Let's hope so. I was a raving maniac back then."

"That's not true." She spoke softly and with a compelling self-assurance; all her remarks had this odd quiet authority. On her lap her long white fingers moved over the coarse wool of the blanket, like the fingers of a blind woman touching a face. "Tell me about Cloris's death," she said. And picking back up the sketchbook, she began to draw again.

"Well, I'm not sure what you want to know. Do you mean police details? She was killed between ten and midnight, a week ago Sunday, at her home. In fact, she'd left early from the last performance of *A Midsummer Night's Dream*, the one my mother was telling you we did here in town."

"You played Bottom. I've always liked Bottom for feeling so comfortable in fairyland. I'm sorry to interrupt you. She left early?"

"Sometime after the second intermission. She told someone then that she had an upset stomach."

Mrs. Cadmean looked over at the tap of snow gusts hitting against the window. "Is the theory that she surprised a burglar?"

"Yes. This evening we recovered the silverware and have arrested a suspect."

She didn't seem much interested in this fact. "Some coins were taken? I think I read in the paper."

"A collection that had belonged to her first husband, Bainton Ames."

"Yes. Bainton had showed me his coins often."

"They were kept in a safe in her bedroom. It was flimsy, easy to jimmy open."

"She was beaten over the head, is that right?"

"With a trophy from her desk. The blow killed her. But the killer also smothered her. With a pillow."

"Another play," Mrs. Cadmean said.

I assumed she meant *Othello*, but the plot of a jealous husband's suffocating an unfaithful wife seemed to have little bearing on the Dollards.

I watched the beautiful profile stare silently into the fire, her eyes darkening, unfathomable as the black lake outside. "Did you find a diary, Justin?"

"Pardon? A diary? No." I stood up. "Why are you asking me all this about Cloris's death? Miss Cadmean said you think someone is trying to kill *you*. Do you think they're the same person?"

The pencil scratched firmly over the page, blotting the drawing. She closed the book, and shut her eyes. Just as I began to worry that she was preparing to go into some kind of trance, she said calmly, "You know a little about my...past."

"I know you're the psychic, Joanna Griffin. My partner Cuddy is a great admirer of yours. The truth is, from the way he's talked about you, I thought you'd be a whole lot older. His file on you stops about fifteen years ago. He thought you were dead."

She tugged down the cuffs of her sweater sleeves; it was a curiously nervous gesture in someone so otherwise composed, and one she repeated a number of times during our talk. "Your friend is right. Joanna Griffin did pass away a long while back. I guess you could say I went out of business. So, now I want to be very careful in what I say to you... I asked you about a diary because I think Cloris wants someone to find it."

"Rowell would know if she kept one, wouldn't he? Her husband. Do you know Rowell Dollard?"

Her voice dropped, and she looked down at her sketch. "Oh, yes, I know Rowell."

"That's right; he was assistant solicitor when you worked with the department. Were you friendly with him and Cloris?"

"I was friendlier with Cloris earlier, when she was married to Bainton Ames. My husband and I used to play bridge with her and Bainton." Joanna smiled, pulled over the sketchbook, and started a new drawing. "Cloris and I were different in personality."

"Yes." As earth and air.

"But we played bridge very well together. People occasionally accused us of cheating, but it was just…"

"Mental telepathy."

"I suppose so."

"Could you use it to help my partner win the basketball pool?" I was joking but she gave me a serious answer.

"Unfortunately, Justin, it doesn't work when I want it to. Just when it wants to." Now she began speaking with the slow precision of a translator, her pencil pressing harder into the paper. "Thoughts…pictures…come to me *very* vividly. At times they are so strong, I have to act. When I went that first time to the Hillston police, about where the two girls were buried? That picture of the graves in that basement felt like the kind of headache where you can't bear the slightest sliver of light in the room."

"I've had that kind of headache too, without any accompanying epiphany."

She turned and looked so deeply and for so long without blinking straight into my eyes that I grew embarrassed by the intimacy. Finally she whispered, "You have very beautiful eyes. They're quite open."

Neither of us spoke until a whistle of wind blew down the chimney, flurrying sparks in the fire. Then she said, "I have to be careful. I get a strong feeling, inescapable; but who's to know what it means, if it's even true. Sometimes it's nothing."

"Sometimes the bodies are buried there in the cellar." I felt very uncomfortable. "Will you say who you think wants to kill you?"

"One reason I have to be so hesitant is that these pictures are most intense when I'm ill, or upset. Even a fever from a cold. They came strongest when I was younger. They weren't pleasant, most of them. I'll tell you one I never told the police. When Charles was dying, I was at the hospital with him one night when I suddenly saw an image of Bainton Ames out in a boat on Pine Hills Lake." She stopped to erase part of her drawing.

I pulled my chair to the fire. The room was too large, the log beams too high over my head, the corners too shadowy. I began to want another drink. "Was that the same night that Bainton actually drowned?"

She nodded. "Yes. But in my...vision, his death was not an accident. There was somebody hidden in the boat behind Bainton, somebody who leapt up and struck him on the head, somebody he knew." She moved her leg slightly with her hands and smoothed the blanket.

A twitch behind my scalp pulled at my hair, even while I was thinking, easy enough to say all this so long after the fact. "Who was the somebody?"

Again she didn't respond to my questions, but said, "Finally, my uneasy feeling about Bainton's death grew so acute, I told Cloris. She was, naturally, reluctant to believe me. She didn't believe me. In fact, she was angry. There was a painful scene. She asked me not to mention my, as she called them, *fantasies* to her again." The even voice dropped. "Well, that was many years ago."

Snow had stuck in an oval around the corners of the huge window, making an old-fashioned frame. Through it, black lake and black sky were slipping into each other. With my shoe I pushed a log deeper into the fire's cave.

She kept drawing. "You see, Justin, a week ago Sunday, out on St. Simons, I dreamt that Cloris Dollard came to me and told me to find her diary."

"You mean you just *dreamt* she had this diary?"

The gray eyes frowned, disappointed in me. "Dreams are often wiser than the people who have them. They are, in many cases, certainly more honest."

I held up my hands. "God knows."

"In my dream, Cloris was dead. Her hair was bloody, and her face blank white. She held out her hand, unclenched her fist, and pearls spilled from it."

"You had this dream the night she died?" I came over to her couch and sat down.

"Yes. She said she'd been killed because Bainton had been killed."

"Before you'd heard about her murder?"

"Yes."

"You could have read about the head wound, or someone could have told you about it after you got down here, and you fed the details back into the dream without knowing it."

"I could have."

"But you didn't?"

"No." She lifted her long white hand from the opened sketchbook and turned it toward me.

I whispered, "Good Christ." Covering the page was a drawing of Cloris Dollard *exactly* as I had looked down on her that Monday morning. She lay on the flowered quilt, one arm turned back, one foot dangled off the bed's edge. Joanna had drawn the pillow pressed over the head, drawn the pearls on the rug below, drawn even the ripped right sleeve of the suit. Nothing about that sleeve or about the pearls had been in any public report I'd read. She took the sketchbook back from me, and said quietly, "I told you the images I see are very vivid, Justin."

I stood up to walk. "What do you mean she said she was killed because Bainton was killed? Bainton Ames died years ago. We have a man now in custody, a petty thief from East Hillston, on this Cloris case. You don't think he killed her?"

"Do you?"

I turned and stared at her. "I don't know. Who do you think killed Cloris? If he'd pressed you, what would you have told the reporter?"

She held her hand over her eyes; it was a large hand, milky white, naked without a wedding ring. "Nothing. I don't feel I should say anything, not until there is some other... some *external* evidence."

"Why not? We're not going to arrest someone just because of a dream you had."

She shook her head no. I leaned closer and touched her hand

and was startled by its heat. "Will you tell me why you believe someone is trying to kill *you?*"

Her eyes went dark for an instant, then she blinked and they were calm again. "Nobody is trying to kill me now."

"But Briggs said…"

"I have the premonition that somebody will…decide to try to kill me. But hasn't yet. That must sound odd." Her hand came up to her neck, and I thought I saw a white scar, very faint, on her wrist at the edge of the sweater's cuff.

"Mrs. Cadmean, it all sounds odd to me. I hope my saying so doesn't bother you."

She took my hand and examined it, turning it over, pressing her fingertips into my flesh. "No, it doesn't bother me. I stopped believing some time ago that it was my fault I wasn't as…" She let my hand fall and looked up at me. "Wasn't as *numb* as most people. I used to think everyone felt as much as I did; they simply didn't let it show. I was," she looked away, "deceived. They don't."

"If you thought ordinary people had your gifts, yes, you must have been disappointed." The phone rang, and I jumped. "Shall I get it?"

"I'm sure it's for Briggs. There's an extension up in the tower."

"She's up there on the roof?"

"It's her study. Her telescope's up there."

The phone stopped. The snow had muffled all sound.

"I should go," I said. "If there's ever anything I can do, if you want to talk, will you call?"

She nodded, and I found myself leaning down again to take her hand. She raised mine to her cheek and held it there for a moment. Then she said, "Here, take this." She tore a page out of her sketch pad. On it was a drawing of me, done with a skilled and strong line.

I asked, "Am I this sad?"

"Yes."

I rolled the paper and put it in my coat pocket. "Do you have a feeling when—if somebody is going to try to kill you—*when?*"

Then Joanna Cadmean made the most bizarre statement of our conversation. She said serenely, "I expect I'll be home long before Easter."

"Back on St. Simons?"

"I mean I will have died. And gone, I assume, somewhere. I don't expect this little world is all, do you? It's certainly never felt like home to me."

"Died! Christ, what makes you think such a thing?"

The beautiful head turned slowly toward me, the eyes still as a statue's. "Cloris told me. I heard her voice. Three days ago, while Briggs and I were in the riding ring. That's why Manassas shied and threw me. It was death. Animals don't like it."

• • •

Outside, I wiped snow from my windshield with a pine branch. While the car was warming up, I took out the drawing. It was amazing; it was no more than a few lines, but it was like looking a long time into a mirror. I turned the sheet of paper over. On the back were faint sketches of tiny heads, hideous gargoyles, their eyes tormented, their mouths gaped open with rage.

At the bottom of the drive I looked back up at the lodge. High above me the light from the tower turned the snow to a white mist, as if I were far off, lost at sea, and on top of the Cadmean roof an arctic lighthouse warned me away from frozen reefs.

Chapter 4

Even though he'd had to leave his wife watching television alone back in Crest Hollows, shove himself back into all three polyester pieces of his wine-colored suit, and drive his new white Mercury back into town where slush could splash on its chrome, Captain V.D. Fulcher was happy, because he'd heard that Preston Pope had seven placesettings of the Grand Baroque sterling belonging to the Rowell Dollards, and that told him that Preston Pope had murdered Mrs. Dollard, and that told him the case was closed and that the important people in Hillston would think well of him for letting them forget in a hurry that homicides ever happened in Hillston to important people.

"Except Preston didn't do it," Cuddy said again.

"I don't care which one," Fulcher told him. "Graham. Furbus."

I said, "Not Furbus. Furbus doesn't get out for two more years."

Cuddy tipped a box of Raisinettes to his mouth and tapped it. "Furbus is the only Pope that *would* kill somebody. Took after his daddy."

Preston had certainly been saying he didn't do it, and his brothers didn't do it; he'd been saying so for three hours. He was less certain of what he *had* been doing eight nights back. Finally he decided he'd been out in his van looking for Charlene; that was what he usually did between 10:30 and 1:00 in the morning. When I got back to the municipal building from the lake, and called my mother to tell her I'd gotten back, Preston was still saying that he'd never seen the silverware until I held up the fork, which was what he'd said to begin with.

I said, "Maybe Charlene brought the silverware over to bathe in."

Cuddy said, "Did Dickey or Graham do it?"

Preston shook his head violently.

"Did you do it?"

"You already asked me that a million times! I swear to God, I didn't choke that lady!"

"We know you didn't choke her," I said. "Did you smother her with a pillow?"

"Aww, shit!"

Cuddy bent his head and looked closely into Preston's eyes. "This is real serious, Preston. *Real* serious. This isn't what you're used to, you got to understand that in a hurry."

Preston's pupils blurred with tears that he swiped at with his fists. "I got eyes, I can see shit when I step in it, don't you think I can? Y'all got to help me! Get Graham, he'll tell you I didn't do nothing."

I said, "We have a call in for him right now, believe me. How about this, Preston, did you and maybe Graham and Dickey go over there to North Hillston and rob the place, and you *didn't* kill Mrs. Dollard? Maybe she was already dead?"

"No way!"

"How about, maybe after you *finished* stealing everything, somebody else came in and killed her? Any idea who?"

Preston was sunk down in his chair, rubbing his wrist raw with his chain bracelet. "I don't even know where the lady lives. I just want y'all to believe me, that's all I want."

At 9:30, Fulcher, splashed with another pint of his rampant aftershave, trotted in smiling, and we all went back to the beginning. Preston begged us to believe he would never rob a house with a woman in it, much less kill her. Then he asked Cuddy if

he should confess to the burglary (even though he was innocent), so that then he wouldn't have to stand trial for the murder (of which he was also innocent, but for which he might
nevertheless go to the gas chamber). Then he said he was so
hungry he couldn't think anymore. "Anymore?" Cuddy said, and
got him some cheese crackers and a Coke.

Upstairs, just before eleven, Graham and Dickey Pope, dragging two policemen along with them, rammed into the front
room like bears after a cub, and yelled at us to give them back
Preston. They swore their baby brother had been at home drinking beer and watching the basketball game on television with
them every minute of the night of the murder. Told what Preston's alibi was, they swore that, come to think a little harder,
they'd been out in the van looking for Charlene with him every
minute of the night of the murder. The two of them, dribbling
wet snow, crowded in on Cuddy. The younger, Dickey, with his
black, curly hair and long-lidded blue eyes, was the best-looking
of the Popes; as always, he wore a shiny cowboy shirt. Graham
was ugly and over six and a half feet tall with a beer belly and the
short, tangled beard after which Preston had modeled his own.
Graham shouted, "God damn it, Cuddy Mangum, you know that
boy ain't killed the goddamn woman."

"You watch your mouth," said Captain Fulcher.

"How come all her silverware was in his goddamn bathtub?"
Cuddy shouted back at Graham.

The Popes stared at us without a word and then stared at
each other. Finally, Dickey said to Graham, "That little son of a
bitch; if he did it, I'm going to kick his ass!"

Graham said to us, "Y'all put the fix in, is that what's going
on here? Well, God damn it!"

Captain Fulcher had them both locked up as accessories.

We'd already sent Preston to bed; he'd gone back to trying to
tell us what Charlene was like.

"He did it," Fulcher said, doing the clicking noise with his
mouth that made him sound as well as look like an agitated hamster.

"Nope," said Cuddy.

"Listen to me, Lieutenant."

"All right."

"Somebody killed the Senator's wife. Somebody robbed her first. Preston Pope robbed her and Preston Pope killed her."

"Your logic's real persuasive, but I'm gonna have to disagree."

We were in Fulcher's office, crowded in with his civic awards and bowling trophies. Photos of his children—now teenagers who wouldn't give him the time of day—grinned gap-toothed in plastic cubes on his metal desk.

"That house is way out of Preston's league," Cuddy said. "Besides, if he had been there, he'd have left behind his fingerprints, his car keys, and his dog."

I took out a cigarette, but Fulcher tapped the NO SMOKING Lucite bar on the edge of his desk, and I put it back. He added an apologetic smile. I asked Cuddy, "What makes you so sure?"

"Charlene. Listen, Justin, there wasn't a mark on that girl. Here he was ranting and raving how he was going to kill her for whoring around, and he hadn't even *slapped* her."

Fulcher punched his finger on our report. "Six shots fired!"

"Not at *her*. That's first. Number two is, Preston's got a snapshot of himself and his mama in his wallet. He didn't smother any fifty-year-old woman."

Fulcher looked smug. "His mother deserted him, don't forget that."

With a pencil, Cuddy drew a quick series of overlapping triangles on his pad. "V.D., I'm *real* sorry you took that psychology extension course last summer."

"Don't get smart, mister."

"All right."

"And don't *ever* call me…that." Fulcher couldn't bring himself to repeat his initials and spluttered to a stop.

"So where's the rest, where's all her jewelry and the coins?" I said. "We looked at the Popes'. They're not there."

"They're somewhere," Fulcher announced. "You find them. I want Preston Pope pinned to the wall. I want this case closed fast." He worked into his overcoat. "I'm going home. It's sleeting out there." He called his wife on the phone and told her so.

As soon as the door shut, Cuddy snapped his pencil in two.

"Christ." I lit my cigarette. "Can you believe Fulcher's parents had the gall to name him after General Earl Van Dorn?"

"Yeah." Cuddy threw the pencil pieces at the wastebasket. "Just because they wore silk sashes doesn't mean those damn Confederate generals of yours weren't idiots too."

"What'd you call him V.D. for? You're going to get yourself fired."

"*You* can support me. That suck-butt'll never fire you."

If Fulcher had known Rowell Dollard was going to arrive ten minutes later, no doubt he would have stayed to be congratulated. We saw my uncle as we were on our way down to the lab. Cuddy'd had a patrolman bring over every pair of shoes, boots, and gloves Preston had in the house, for forensics to check them out.

• • •

Senator Dollard was in the foyer, standing by himself in the middle of the black and white marble parquet floor. He looked like a part of the design, with his perfect white hair and perfect black wool overcoat, and his furled black umbrella with its silver head. His face, ruddier from the cold, was tilted up at the full-length portrait of Briggs Monmouth Cadmean that was hanging lavishly framed above the double doors to the courtroom, with a plaque below it saying he'd given Hillston the entire building. Our hollow footsteps on the marble startled Dollard. He turned, swinging the umbrella like a racquet and reminding me of the last time we'd played squash, when he'd slammed into the wall hard enough to slit open his cheek.

As soon as he saw us, he said, "Has he confessed? Pope?"

I shook my head and introduced Cuddy, who immediately said that in his opinion Preston Pope wasn't responsible for the crime.

Rowell looked at me the whole time Cuddy was talking, but

he turned to Cuddy when he stopped and said, "Then I hope you'll find out who is."

"I'm going to try, sir," Cuddy answered. "I'll be down in the lab, Justin."

Dollard gave a small nod as Cuddy walked away. "Is he in on the case?"

I said, "Now."

From his days as solicitor, Dollard knew this building and our procedures well; he'd followed our investigation the way he played squash, and Fulcher was terrified of his daily phone calls. Mother said Rowell's involvement was his way of coping with what had happened to Cloris, that he would never forgive himself for losing her because he hadn't been there to protect her, because he had never been able to convince her not to leave the house unlocked, not to trust strangers, not to realize that the world was dangerous. He insisted that only a stranger could have killed his wife, because no one who knew her could possibly want to hurt her. "Who in *God's name* would kill Cloris? She had more friends than anyone I ever knew!"

About Cloris, Dollard was right: I had interviewed many of those friends, and by their testimony, Cloris Dollard had been the most amicable woman in Hillston. The friends were all certain, like her husband, that she had suffered by hideous chance at the hands of a transient madness. Not only had *they* not killed her, they couldn't think of a single soul who might have, "unless he'd gone crazy." And none of them knew anyone who might have gone even temporarily insane.

Everyone had liked Cloris. She'd liked everyone. I'd talked to a dozen members of First Presbyterian Church who'd spoken with her after services that Sunday morning, when she'd been "maybe a little quiet, but her same sunny self underneath." I'd talked to her daughters, whom she'd called that afternoon in Phoenix and Baltimore; they said their conversations had been largely about grandchildren, and unremarkable. I'd talked to Mr. and Mrs. Dyer Fanshaw of the Fanshaw Paper Company, on whom she'd paid an ordinary afternoon call at their estate in

North Hillston, two wooded meadows away from the Dollards' own brick colonial. I'd seen her myself in the audience at the Hillston Playhouse during the second intermission of A *Midsummer Night's Dream*, for she'd been chatting in the aisle with Susan Whetstone. Susan had said she couldn't remember what they'd talked about, but it certainly wasn't that Cloris expected to be murdered, although she had mentioned that her stomach was upset. I had in fact interviewed most of Hillston's inner circle, and it had very politely informed me that no one in it was a burglar and a killer.

Although I hadn't let Captain Fulcher know it, I had even checked out that Rowell Dollard had actually gone, as he'd said, to the suite he kept over in Raleigh for nights when he worked late during sessions of the state legislature. If Cloris had died no earlier than twelve, Rowell could conceivably have rushed back in the hour and a half it took to travel the unbanked, unlighted, two-lane road between Hillston and the state capital. He could have smothered Cloris, and then sped back to Raleigh.

But, so far, I could think of no motive. If Rowell Dollard secretly kept a mistress, no one had ever heard of her; if he secretly owed millions, so far I hadn't found out to whom, and at this point he had as much money as Cloris did anyhow. Even if they'd used the estate she'd inherited from Bainton Ames to help build Rowell's career, the perks and payoffs of that career were now worth considerably more than his wife's private possessions. If he secretly hated her, Hillston hadn't noticed. Rumor was, among Cloris's many friends, that as a bachelor Dollard had "worshiped" her even when she'd been married to Bainton Ames. They told me now, "He loved her just the same 'til the day she died." They thought it was the most tragic thing they'd ever heard, for death to part the Dollards after all Cloris had suffered, and when Rowell was destined for even greater office.

Standing there in the foyer under the donated gilt chandeliers, I noticed how Rowell's eyes, which were somewhat protuberant— pressing forward, like his voice and his manner—tonight looked sunk back in his skull, their color dead in his florid face. I said,

"Rowell, do you want to see the report on the arrest?"

He hesitated, also unlike him, then answered, "No, just tell me." I gave a summary of Preston Pope's statement while he stared past me down the empty corridor of closed doors and at the courtroom doors behind us, the doors—he had told me so often—to Washington.

We stood alone in the middle of the big marble floor. When I finished talking, he asked, "But you don't share this Mangum's opinion, do you? About Pope?"

"I'm not sure yet."

"I see. Walk me to my car, Justin, all right? By the way, your mother mentioned something odd tonight. She said you were out to see Joanna Cadmean earlier. Something about her wanting to talk to you about Cloris." He paused for my response, but I made none, because I wasn't certain what I wanted to say, and he added, "I can't think why. As far as I know, Cloris and Joanna Cadmean hadn't met in years." He waited again. "I did notice she visited," he stumbled, "the grave. It surprised me at the time."

"Isn't that why Mrs. Cadmean came to Hillston, for the services?"

"No! I'm sure she's just here to see her in-laws. She's staying out at the compound with the youngest Cadmean girl, isn't she? The one that teaches at the university?" Dollard walked toward old Cadmean's portrait, then hurried back, as if he couldn't think standing still.

"Briggs," I said.

"Typical of old Briggs to name a daughter after himself. I don't think he liked any of his sons."

"I don't think his daughter likes him. Mother told me tonight on the phone that Briggs moved out to the lake because she couldn't stand to live in that brick mausoleum with her father."

We crossed to the tall, brass-trimmed front doors. Outside, rain had already started washing the slush over the steps and into the sidewalk gutters; by morning there'd be no trace of the aberrant snowstorm.

Rowell was tapping the umbrella's silver knob against his lips. "Did Joanna Cadmean say what she wanted to know?"

"She wanted to know if Cloris kept a diary. Did she?"

"A diary?" He was surprised. "Why? No, Cloris didn't keep a diary."

"Are you sure?"

"Of course, I'm sure! Cloris was a totally…open person. She always left everything out where anybody could see it. I would have known. She would have *read* it to me." He kept shaking his head. "What did she mean, a diary?"

I decided to tell him. "Mrs. Cadmean says your wife told her in a dream to look at a diary."

Thoughts were shifting through his eyes as he stared at me. The eyes looked angry; but then, they often did.

"She said she dreamt Cloris came to her and said she'd been murdered, and told her to read the diary."

Rowell began pacing again, tapping the umbrella tip loudly on the marble.

I added, "She described details I just don't see how she could have known."

The ruddiness of his complexion deepened in his neck and ears, and his voice dropped. "Did she say who?"

"Who what?"

He snapped, "Who killed Cloris."

His tone startled me. "She gave the impression that she had somebody in mind, but she won't say who. It's just a dream. I don't know why she chose to tell me about it. Even odder, she talked more about Bainton Ames than anything else. Another dream she'd had years ago, at the time of *his* accident; she dreamt that it was no accident. That it was murder. And she really almost had me convinced."

Rowell kept rubbing his lips back and forth over the umbrella's silver handle. He said, "Do you know who she was?"

I nodded. "A psychic. A mystic. She worked with you back when you were a solicitor."

"She did not 'work' with me. She was somebody who came to the police and volunteered certain premonitions."

"She knew where the bodies were buried."

The umbrella twitched in his hand, and the knob scraped against his teeth. "You understand," he said softly, "this woman is preternatural. You have no idea." He turned around to me. "She's also insane, Justin."

"Insane? She acted perfectly normal. You know, I would have thought you'd be the last person to place any credence in…"

His face flushed. "She is *not* normal. How can you say she's normal?"

"I mean, coherent, pleasant; you know what I mean. Obviously she's not *normal*. Listen, Rowell, if somebody tells you they're Jesus Christ, they're crazy. But if somebody tells you on Monday that X is going to be killed on Tuesday and X is killed on Tuesday, it doesn't make them crazy. It makes them pretty damn clairvoyant."

Rowell nodded. "Or a murderer."

"Good Christ. You're not suggesting *she* killed Cloris? She wasn't even in Hillston. For what possible reason?"

"For God's sake, of course I don't think that! Don't be absurd! I'm suggesting you stay away from that woman."

His command irritated me. "How much do you know about Mrs. Cadmean personally?"

His voice was curt. "I doubt I've seen her more than five times in the last fifteen years."

"She never remarried. Was her marriage to, what's his name, to Charles Cadmean, happy?"

"I have no idea. I assume so."

"Is there any possibility she might have been involved with Bainton Ames? I'm sorry if this is awkward for you."

He was glaring at me. "Why awkward?"

"I suppose because Bainton was Cloris's first husband. And, quite honestly, people have said you were already involved with Cloris back when they were married."

His mouth twisted to a sneer. "People?"

"They don't say it critically."

"They shouldn't say it at all." He put his hand on the door's brass bar. "How I felt about her isn't any of their business. And it isn't any of yours." His voice got loud enough to echo off the marble walls of the large empty space. "And I suggest you spend a little less time listening to Joanna Cadmean's hocus-pocus, and a little more convicting the thug who killed Cloris!" The senator banged open the door, and his umbrella caught in it as it swung shut. When I tried to help, he jerked it free and started down the steps. At the curb, rain was streaming past the tires of the silver Mercedes he'd left parked there.

I was turning away, when, from behind the small, antique cannon fixed to the side of the stone steps, someone darted suddenly at Dollard with a long stick. I yelled "Rowell!" and sprang down after him, but I saw before I reached her that it was Sister Resurrection, even this late, haunting the streets, assaulting people with the promise of apocalypse. She was dressed as she always was. Rain beads hung from her knots of hair and ran down her shapeless sweaters, soaking into her split and laceless tennis shoes. Rain, like the world and the flesh, had meant nothing to her for many years.

She had her cross pointed at Rowell and was chanting as he shoved past her to pull his car door open, "It won't be long! The dragon coming! I heard the voice say, 'It won't be long.' That old serpent, he got the chain in his teeth, and he snap it! He *snap* it, and crawling out of the lake of fire and brimstone. He shall be *loosed* out of his prison!"

"Get back!" Rowell, his face white, was in his car now, tugging on the door. "Will you get her away!" Sister Resurrection touched her hand, shriveled as a claw, to his. She had a hissing whisper. "God getting ready. We shall arise anew! Say yes! Say yes!" He shook the skinny arm off his sleeve, slammed the door, and left her, fallen to the curb.

I tented my coat over my head and leaned down. "Sister, you all right? You shouldn't be out in this cold rain. Come on. It's late." I pulled her to her feet. She was weightless and tense as wire, and the smell of her clothes in the rain was even fouler than usual. "You go on home. It's late." I pointed down the sidewalk toward the Methodist church two blocks east, where the minister had made her a place in the basement near the furnace. "You'll catch cold."

I doubt she had heard me, but, still chanting her garbled revelations, she turned, and with her quick stiff stride, hurried away, her makeshift cross in one hand, and Rowell Dollard's black umbrella in the other, jutted out before her like a sword.

Chapter 5

The Hillston police are stationed in an annex connected through the basement to our new municipal building, although most HPD offices (like the detective division) have been moved into the main building itself. The lab people never come upstairs if they can help it, and Etham Foster, who runs the lab, would just as soon nobody ever came down to the basement, either. He's a wary, saturnine black man of about forty, who looks like the basketball player he was; he had gotten himself through college playing that game, and said he had never picked up a basketball again after the day they handed him his diploma. When I walked into his lab, his long fingers were picking with tweezers at the bottom of Preston's boot. And Cuddy, chewing on a glazed doughnut, was standing like a stork against the wall, watching him.

Cuddy looked up. "Look who's here, come down to pay a call. You and the Senator wrap it all up?"

I said, "Sister Resurrection just scared him to death."

Foster glanced at us, then went back to placing bits of fuzz in a plastic bag as if he were alone in the place.

"Good," Cuddy said.

"She was out front under that overhang, just about frozen."

"You know why she stays around this spot so much? She's got a grudge against the powers that be, and this is where they be."

Foster turned his back on us and switched on the light under his microscope. Cuddy went on. "You know Sister Resurrection used to have a kid, a long, long time ago? Yeah, ain't that downright amazing to think of? But he went bad, raised hell, and got himself shot."

"I hadn't heard that."

"Well, this is a little bit of local East Hillston lore that wouldn't necessarily have come to your attention over on Catawba Drive."

"Who shot him?"

He licked glaze off his fingers. "Cop."

"You're kidding."

"Sure. I'm a great kidder." He walked around to Foster. "Okay, Doctor Dunk-It, what you got?"

Foster slid in another slide without looking up. "No yellow fibers anywhere on your man's shoes."

"Good. And no prints of his on the silver, either."

Foster said, "Doesn't mean a thing."

His drawer was filled with fragments of Cloris Dollard's life: fuzz from her yellow carpet, gravel from her driveway, hairs from her cat, blood from the top of a trophy that said she was the best woman golfer in Hillston. Etham Foster knew Mrs. Dollard as precisely as my father had known where against the skull to place the drill. I said, "Tell me about who did it, Etham."

"I told you. Man was careful."

We had little more than that to go on. Since Cloris Dollard had never bothered locking her house, we didn't even know whether her murderer had entered before or after she had come home. Her house was so sheltered by its grounds that no neighbor had seen or heard a thing, even if she'd struggled. And we'd lost nine hours before the Dollard maid's arrival the next morning. We knew the upstairs phone had been yanked from its cord and that Cloris's purse had been thrown in the grass by the stone gate, and we had a list of all Senator Dollard thought but wasn't sure had been taken by whomever had pulled open all the drawers and cabinets in the handsome house and had left in its bedroom a dead woman.

I said, "Pros don't kill people."

Foster finished looking at a piece of glass taken out of Preston's boot tread. "Didn't say pro. Said careful."

"Come on, can't you give us *something?*"

"Give you a Marlboro butt off the driveway that wasn't there more than a day, and nobody in the house smoked."

"It's too bad the neighbors and two ambulances and a half-dozen of V.D.'s new patrol cars drove all over the place before they called you."

Foster said, "Right," and would I mind not smoking in his lab, and Cuddy said, "He can't be a detective without smoke coming out of his nose." His eyes looked dull blue and angry. "Was Mrs. Dollard taking this guy on a guided tour or what? 'Well, now you've loaded up the silver, and don't forget that little TV, come on up in the bedroom 'cause I've got some jewelry and rare coins I think you'll like, locked up in a little safe you probably wouldn't even have noticed all on your own.'"

"Maybe she thought if she offered him things, he wouldn't hurt her," I said. "Maybe he only hit her because she went for the phone or maybe it started ringing and panicked him into hitting her." I rubbed my hand against the back of my own skull. "Or, let's try this possibility. He already knew the house, and knew her, and he meant to kill her." *But who in the world would want to kill Cloris? She had more friends...*

Cuddy said, "How tall was she?"

"Five nine and a quarter, plus heels."

"Preston's too short."

Etham Foster looked back up. "You don't know she was standing."

"And Preston's not strong enough, either. To pull her up on that bed—and what the crap for?—and shove down a pillow so hard he breaks her nose? I don't believe Preston could do it, much less, he's just not that goddamn mean!"

I was thinking of how Rowell had flicked Sister Resurrection from his sleeve as if she were a gnat, knocking her down on the curb. I said, "Maybe anybody can be that mean."

Cuddy slapped his hand loud on the counter. "Oh, don't start that dorkshit 'everybody's rotten under the thin ice' moralizing again! The only thin ice you ever knew anything about, somebody served you in a whiskey glass!"

Unhurriedly, Foster walked away from us to open the refrigerator and take out a tube of somebody's blood. My blush had brought sweat out over my lip. "Get off my back, Mangum, you've been picking at me since I got down here. Why are you so pissy?" We stared at each other, until he reached up and pulled on both his ears with his knuckly hands. "I'm scared," he said, "the powers that be're gonna railroad Preston because it's easy. Nothing personal."

"Except you think those powers're all my kinsfolk. You're a snob."

He blew out a sigh, and then he laughed. "Whooee, Doctor D, listen to the white folk spat!" Foster ignored him and smeared the blood on his slide, and Cuddy tossed my overcoat at me and said, "Okay, Preppie, let's get out of the man's lab. Don't you ever go home, Foster?"

Foster didn't look up, but said, "Your man had big hands," and he held up his own, fingers spread the way they would have stretched over a basketball. He added, "Shut the door."

Upstairs, while Cuddy fed Mrs. Mitchell a cold hamburger, I told him more about my visit with Joanna Cadmean.

"She couldn't be *that* good looking."

"That's not the point, Cuddy. The point is, she knows who killed Cloris. The same person who killed Cloris's first husband."

"How about Cloris's second husband Uncle Rowell?"

"Maybe."

He said, "I'm kidding."

"I'm not."

Chapter 6
Tuesday, January 18

I am an insomniac like my father, who wandered around his house at night like a ghost and now, from time to time, visits mine. I have always had to drug myself unconscious with detective fiction: reading on about pure nastiness and someone else's guilt until I can fall backward into nothing, like in snow. When I awaken in the night, I need to get the light on quickly and find my page before the real mysteries slip in, before I hear voices, before I see ghosts. When I was little, my father would come at my request with what he claimed was a magic stethoscope, and would check for signs of monsters lurking. I did not doubt his power to keep them away.

This morning I had a nightmare that woke me up. It was pitch-black night in this dream, and I was in our old sailboat out on the lake. Pine Hills Lake is fairly large—seven miles by almost two—but in my dream the lake was boundless, an unshored, black, flat expanse. Out of the silent dark, Bainton Ames's powerboat suddenly came flying at me, his white bowlight shooting up and down across the water. Then the dream went up to that octagonal turret on top of Cadmean compound. Joanna Cadmean was standing there at its window, wearing the gray suit Cloris Dollard was found dead in. And now Mrs. Cadmean's eyes did look like a mystic's, unblinking, crazed. She had her arms out as if she were waiting to embrace someone. I knew it was her eyes making Ames's boat head toward me. Someone was kicking away from his boat, churning foam. And I jumped too, just as the boat ripped through my bow, and exploded, and flames spumed along the water, rimming me in.

So, I was awake at five, and rather than fight for sleep until Cuddy came to pick me up, I put on a monogrammed robe Susan Whetstone had given me that I didn't much like, and, my bare feet tiptoeing on the frigid wood steps, I felt my way down the three flights from my bedroom to my kitchen.

Most of my salary goes into the mortgage and upkeep and furnishing of a narrow Queen Anne brick house in the south part of Hillston that overlooks the lawn of a women's junior college, named Frances Bush after its nineteenth-century founder: my house had once boarded her students. Five years ago, after I'd finished law school in Charlottesville, and confused everybody and annoyed Rowell by going to work for the Hillston police, I'd bought the house with money my father left me. No one wanted to live downtown then, and old houses there were cheaper than trailers. Obviously, as had been pointed out to me, it was too much house for a single man. It was also too much house to heat: the rooms were large and had high ceilings, and on each floor a big Victorian bow window sucked in the cold air robustly with a laissez-faire disdain for my modern fuel costs.

At five, then, in the kitchen, I wrapped myself in a blanket and ate leftover spaghetti while I finished reading the department's copy of the old coroner's report on Bainton Ames's drowning accident that I had started studying before I went to bed, having found it in the vault of old files last night. There was little in it to suggest that Cloris's first husband hadn't died exactly as the coroner had concluded: accidental drowning while under the influence of alcohol. His dinner companions that night had confessed that the five of them had drunk five bottles of wine, and everyone knew that Bainton did not normally drink.

An unlucky accident, people had said, and added, "but not surprising." Bainton Ames, a preoccupied, farsighted man—for decades chief industrial engineer of Cadmean Textiles—had his eyes focused on future machines, or ancient coins, or seventeenth-century music; the present had been a blur. When Ames drowned, people said preoccupation had killed him.

One midnight in mid-August fifteen years ago, he had left the Pine Hills Inn, where he'd dined with four men big in the Atlanta textiles business. Against their advice he'd set out across the lake in the twenty-two-foot inboard powerboat Cloris had given him as a lure into the world. Headed back to the Ames cottage on the opposite shore from the Inn, he had presumably slipped, knocked himself out, and fallen overboard. The boat had sped on pilotless into a marina, where it had blown up a gas tank. The explosion had terrified all the residents, and that summer, boating after dark was banned.

A few weeks later, they discovered that Ames had not been in the boat when it exploded, because a teenage boy, swimming around under old Briggs Cadmean's long pier, had bumped into a swollen body bent around a piling, and had unhooked Ames's jacket from the bolt it was caught on.

After her husband drowned, Cloris had their lake house closed. Two years later, she married the still-bachelor Rowell Dollard, and he and her daughters persuaded her to reopen it. Rowell bought a new boat.

My father, who every weekend for years had played violin in Ames's amateur string quartet, was furious with his dead friend for ever having tried to pilot the Chris-Craft, even in the daytime. When Cloris later married Rowell, my father said, "Well, good Christ, Peggy, Cloris certainly runs the gamut. First Euclid. Now Mark Antony. Don't you think your brother Rowell is a little too *relentlessly* athletic?"

But the Ames girls liked their sporty stepfather, who taught them how to water-ski and dance. And by all accounts, Cloris loved him. In old photographs of them together, I could see that she shared with Rowell something florid and heated, something that made you think she enjoyed her marriage bed, in the same way she enjoyed her golf and the club dances at which she and Dollard won prizes as the most polished couple on the floor. They traveled. They were well-to-do; especially after Cloris sold Ames's sizable shares of Cadmean stock to a Mr. Paul Whetstone, who turned Cadmean Textiles into C&W Textiles, and turned Lawry Whetstone into a vice president.

And Cloris had the easy, warm sociability necessary in the wife of a politically ambitious man. So Rowell swam, with the same seriously energetic strokes with which he did his laps on the lake each summer morning, into the state senate. Cloris was proud of him. So were Mother's people. He was proud of himself, as he said when he advised me to do something I could be proud of.

Time had worn away her past with Bainton Ames. She was Cloris Dollard. And Ames was to most current lake residents, "Oh, that accident that blew up the marina. Man fell out of his boat."

All I had to suggest that the man had been pushed rather than fallen was the distant dream of a woman my uncle thought mad. After fifteen years it was going to be close to impossible to prove Joanna right; the boat was gone, the marina was gone, the body was rags over bones. I didn't even know why I wanted to prove her right; it wasn't Bainton Ames's death I was being paid to investigate.

When I woke up in my kitchen, my head flopped over on the Ames file, my hand still around a fork wrapped in spaghetti, Mother was rapping on the back pane. "Jay! Jay! Wake up!" She had her hand to her mouth. "Lying there like that! You scared the life out of me!" We both knew she'd found my father like that, the day of his first stroke, his arm flung out across his desk; on it, accounts of other people's medical problems.

"Justin, please don't tell me you've been drinking all night." She took my face in her hands. "You haven't suffered a relapse?"

"What time is it? No, I haven't been drinking." All my bones felt bruised.

"Quarter to ten." She let out her breath in a little laugh, relieved by her decision to believe me. "It's freezing in this house.

My God, son, just throw open the windows; it's warmer outside!"

"To ten?"

She rubbed at the arms of her old sable coat, the gesture, like her face, girlish. "Aren't you supposed to go to work? I let your phone ring its head off."

"I unplugged it. Stop staring at me—I said I haven't been drinking."

"I didn't know you could unplug phones. I'm sorry, but your feet are *blue*, Justin! I'm going to turn up your thermostat. I can't understand why you want to live in a house that you can't live in."

"I like the woodwork on the doors. I don't like flat doors."

I made coffee while mother hurried through the house to see what my life was like. Its reality always seemed to surprise her. I said I wanted to ask her something.

"Ask me what? Rowell said you've arrested poor Cloris's murderer. I'm glad it's over."

"It's not over." I handed her a cup. "That last Saturday, when you and Cloris went shopping, the day before she died, tell me again, what sort of mood was she in?"

"Fine, she was fine. We had lunch, and I bought a scarf, and she got some papers copied. I told you. That's all. What do you mean, not over?"

"What papers? You didn't tell me about any papers."

"Well, it's nothing to do with her dying."

"I said, tell me anything, it didn't matter what."

"I probably did mention it. You never listen to half the words I say, anyhow." Mother sighed. "Your father always said, 'Half's plenty.' Well, if it matters, we went to CopiQuik. She said, 'As long as we're right here.' She had a big folder of papers she said had been Bainton's. It surprised me because why, after all this time, be copying anything of Bainton's, and I remember I said, 'Cloris, whatever for?' Well, she'd found them in a box in the basement, she was a terrible pack rat, like you, because there were these textiles people wanting them now. They wanted to know if Bainton had ever figured out how to make this—now, it was a funny word, inert, inertial?—some kind of loom. Seems like Cloris said something about making copies of the papers to show to old Briggs Cadmean. That's all I remember, so don't ask me anything else. I was trying to get to the off-ramp of that idiotic new beltway before a mile-long truck going ninety hit me."

Further questions led her only, by looping cloverleaf turns of language, to news of her departure. She had, in fact, come to see if I had suffered a relapse; she *claimed* she had come to tell me she was driving to Alexandria, Virginia, to baby-sit her only grandchildren—the two belonging to my younger brother, Vaughan, a gynecologist, and his wife, Jennifer, who were off to Antigua on the Club Med plan. Vaughan was the mirror in whose clean image Mother had always asked me to scrub off my flaws. As a child, he had never given her a moment's trouble. As an adult, all he asked of her was baby-sitting. Vaughan was still annoyed with God for postponing him. He resented the position of second son; in his view, I had long ago abrogated the privileges and responsibilities of primogeniture. ("I hate to have to say it, Jay, but it's really pretty crummy the way you've let the folks down; you've really loused up pretty bad.") He never hated to have to say it at all; he couldn't even keep from smiling.

I said, "Tell Vaughan 'bon voyage.'"

Mother poked her forefinger into each of my geranium plants on the window ledge, and watered one of them. She asked with sly nonchalance, "How do you like Briggs?"

"Which Briggs?"

"The girl, of course, Justin."

I said, "I don't. Too cold."

"Baloney. Susan Whetstone's the one that's cold. Of course, she must love it over here." Mother patted my hand. "That was pretty catty."

"I'll say." I poured another cup of coffee.

"Look." From her purse Mother took a small newsclipping. "It was in this morning's paper." Beneath an old photograph of Joanna Cadmean that made her look a little like Grace Kelly was a headline: FAMOUS PSYCHIC COMES HOME AFTER GIRLHOOD FRIEND MURDERED.

I scanned the two paragraphs. "That damn Bubba Percy! He even blabbed that she's staying out at the compound."

"He says maybe the police ought to ask Joanna who killed Cloris."

"Mother, I am the police, and I did ask Joanna."

"You did? Who did she say?"

"She didn't say anything."

I took a pack of cigarettes out of the back of the cabinet where I hid them from myself.

"Oh, Justin, I wish you'd stop smoking. If I could quit after… I started when I had you, I was eighteen, and I stopped when your father died, in March that'll be six years, so that's… If I could quit after all those years…"

"Then I will too. I'm sorry. I didn't get much sleep."

"Well, you'll quit when you start feeling bad enough about it. You never have been as feckless as you like to imagine. You probably feel bad about sleeping with Lawry Whetstone's wife."

The match burned my thumb. "Who told you that?"

"Nobody. Whatever else would you be doing with her?" Mother sat down with her coffee. "Justin, I had no idea you were so naive as to let me convince you I was. I'm not opposed to adultery; but I am old-fashioned enough to think it ought to be serious."

"Mother, please don't tell me you and Dad were having affairs. I couldn't take it this morning."

She looked fondly at the gold ring that was to me as much part of her hand as the bent little finger she said she'd deformed by playing Chopin's "Revolutionary" étude before her bones were mature. "Your father and I were…oddly in love, though he was occasionally a little less aware of it than I was. But of course, I realize not all marriages are lucky. Why, my God, I liked Bainton Ames perfectly well, but it didn't stop me from being really happy for Rowell and Cloris."

"Wait a minute. You *knew* for a fact Rowell and Cloris were having an affair, at the time of her first marriage?"

"Well, nobody said it. Rowell was already in politics. But of course I knew. He'd been in love with her for years. And people in our circle more or less knew. I thought you knew."

"It doesn't surprise me. I remember I *was* surprised when she married him. She always seemed very nice. I liked her."

Mother frowned. "I don't understand why you dislike Rowell so. He went out of his way to advise you all through. And after your father died…"

I went around the table and pulled my little space heater closer to her. "Dad didn't like Rowell, either. You know that. You know what he said to me once? He said Rowell was the kind of man who would have made it to California over Donner Pass."

"Well, I don't know what in the world your father meant by that—which is nothing new."

"He meant Rowell would shoot the Indian. Cut loose the dying ox and pull the wagon himself. Drink the horse urine. Eat the dead. He meant Rowell would *get there*."

My father had added that he himself would have probably been the one in a Western movie who didn't fire his gun in time and was therefore tomahawked by the Apache, who didn't lash his horse hard enough to leap the chasm, and couldn't hold fast enough by his fingers to the scrabbling rock of the edge, and so never made it to the final reel.

"Dad said that once Rowell and he were out on the dock looking at some ducks on the lake that Cloris was feeding bread to, and Rowell said, 'Damn, if I had a rifle right now, I could blast them all right out of the water!'"

Mother said, "I thought you enjoyed those hunting trips with Rowell."

Looking down at the Ames folder on the table, I said, "I did. Let me ask you something. What if Cloris found out Bainton had actually been pushed—not fallen—but been pushed out of that boat when he drowned? What if someone had told her that?"

"Who! That's a horrible thing to say! Cloris never thought such a thing."

"What if she'd just recently found it out, just before she died. Would she have told anyone?"

"She would have been *devastated*. When Bainton drowned,

Cloris felt horrible! I've always thought that's why she and Rowell waited those two years. That, and his career." She washed out her cup. "Jay, are you going off on one of your tangents?"

"Mother, just a minute, what was Bainton Ames doing while Rowell and Cloris were having an affair? Was he having one? Is it possible he and Joanna were lovers?

"God, that is the funniest thought imaginable. I don't say this meanly, but Bainton and Joanna both always struck me as a little on the cold side. Bainton never looked up from his designs long enough to even notice Cloris, and I think Joanna married poor Charles Cadmean because he kept asking her and she didn't have anything else to do. Joanna never seemed to care much what happened to her life. Why, it never seemed to cross her mind that she was beautiful." Mother stood up and pulled on her gloves. "Of course, she was four or five years younger than I was—I was already up in Virginia when she was in high school and college—and we weren't close when I got back, so I probably shouldn't even talk about her."

"If she didn't love Charles, more reason to turn to someone else."

"Well, it wasn't Bainton. I really have to run, honey. Don't bother to kiss me. I'm sure your lips are frozen. And calm down." And out she fluttered.

I opened the coroner's report again. I knew Ames's death was tied by knots, years tightened, to the death of Cloris Dollard. Except I didn't know it; I had only heard dreams. I needed what Joanna Cadmean had called the "external evidence." I started making phone calls.

• • •

To let Cuddy in, I had to get out of the shower and back into my robe. He blinked his eyes at my wet hair and bare feet. "Excuse me! I've been ringing your bell for ten minutes. Guess I caught you on your lunch break."

I ignored this and started back up the steps to my bedroom.

"Your photos are out in the car. My, it is freezing in here!" He followed me up the three flights, with a loud charade of gasping. "Why don't you move into someplace nice, and level, and warm?"

"This is nice. Anybody who has a photo wall mural of Cape Hatteras beach in his living room shouldn't talk about what's nice."

"Everybody in River Rise has got one, they're built in."

"I don't doubt it."

"What's the matter with it? The only time your place is nice is springtime, when you can spy out the top story on the Busher girls—all catching the rays on the grass and reaching behind their pretty backs and unfastening their suit tops."

"You're in a better mood. Where were you?"

"At the office. Doing V.D.'s paperwork."

"Where was I supposed to be?" I threw the coverlet over my bed, a four-poster I'd bought at a used furniture store that had subsequently changed its name to Antiques Ltd.

"Following a lead on those coins, is what I told V.D. He's not happy. He had to let Graham and Dickey go. Looks like they *were* drinking beer the night of the murder, and looks like they were doing it at the Rib House, and in comes Joe Lieberman and says he's got about twenty folks to swear to it."

Joe Lieberman was the Popes' lawyer; they gave him a lot of business. I'm sure he had three stereos in his car, if he wanted them, and four TVs in his house, and all the cigarettes people would leave him alone to smoke.

Cuddy took off a ski cap that said GO TARHEELS!, stuffed it in his parka pocket, and sprawled out on the bed. "But V.D.'s got it jimmied so he can hold Preston, the mad-dog killer, and they moved him across town. Preston asked me would I go get Charlene for him. Aww, lordy, humankind, don't it break your heart? So I went over and tried, but she wasn't much up for it."

"Back at the Maple Street place?"

"Nope. Luster Hudson's. He rents a little house off the 28 bypass, raises hunting dogs. They tried to chew their way out of their pen when I drove up. Ole Charlene finally came to the door in her black number and told me I was lucky Luster was out of town. I said, 'I wantcha, but this is business,' and I told her what had happened to her husband since she saw him last."

"What'd she say?"

"I only knew one lady with a messier mouth, and she had three or four big scars down her face and rolled drunks in Saigon."

"Charlene wasn't sympathetic."

"That about says it all. She told me she had a real man now, a big man she could lean on instead of carry, and she went on with that awhile like a Loretta Lynn song. So the idea is baby peckerhead can insert his privates up his own privy for all she cares. I said, 'Where is Prince Luster so bright and early in the morning when he works the night shift?' She said he quit C&W and was on to a better life in the dog market. I said, 'Well, even if it does seem the thrill is gone between you and peckerhead Preston, seems like a good proletariat union volunteer like yourself wouldn't want to see a working man railroaded by police and capitalists.' She said Preston'd never worked a day in his life. She had me there. Her new love's off somewhere unknown in the Great Smokies with his dawgs."

"Did she know those silver sacks were in there?"

"I asked her that very thing. Says I, 'Charlene, sweetheart, one more question, and I'll let you go on back and feed those dogs before they eat each other and put Luster out of his new business. When you were taking that bath yesterday, did you notice anything in the tub besides yourself—clanky stuff belonging to a rich murdered lady?' That's when the doorknob slammed into my dick and I lost interest."

"Why didn't you bring her in? Christ!"

"Let's hold off a little bit, see what Graham can find out. What's that scratchy singing?"

"It's Ma Rainey."

"Come again?"

"An old blues singer. One of my blues records."

"Where do you get all these folks from?"

"I bet Willie Nelson likes her."

"Sounds like she's singing up from the bottom of the reservoir through a tin can."

"It's a very old recording."

"Hey, well, I *knew* that. You wouldn't have it unlest it was old." His jay eyes peered ostentatiously around my bedroom. "It's all old. My mama had a chest in her kitchen looked like that one." He meant the pine hutch with a white metal countertop where I kept my sweaters and shoes: "Yessir, she was ashamed to death of it, it was so country. I'd been wondering where it got to. All right, let me just lie here and take a nap while you plow through your wardrobe awhile looking for something to put on. Will this old thing hold me?"

On our way out, Cuddy snooped into my front room and took the cloth off an oil painting. I'd started a self-portrait. In the family attic I'd found the easel that had belonged to my father, who did landscape watercolors and who had, to his deep pleasure, a picture—a clump of spruces at the golf course—hanging in the university museum.

Cuddy said, "The bow tie's good. You got the polka dots just right"

"You don't think it looks like me."

"Looks like a cross between Bobby Kennedy and Susan Whetstone."

"Maybe that's what I look like."

"Well, that's true. But you mostly look like Senator Rowell Dollard. Sorry. You think maybe I look a little like Jimmy Carter before he wore out. When he was leaning back in the porch rocker with his fluffy hair. What was the name of that old girlfriend of yours, the one that was so crazy about Jimmy Carter? Why can't I come across somebody like her?"

"Well, you keep telling me you're too ugly."

"I know I'm ugly, but it's the kind of ugly that's getting real popular."

He was still talking when we walked outside to the patrol car.

"Savile, the thing you need to do, you want to be a detective like in your books, you got to do more than mope and fuck and puff your lungs to soot. *Dentists* can oil paint. You want a hobby more on the lines of bloating up big and fat and raising orchids. You want to take up something even kinkier than Shakespeare playacting."

"Well, I play the piano in the middle of the night. Not too different from playing the violin on cocaine."

"Shit, you can't count that. All you know how to play is 'Malaguefnia' and 'The Sting.'"

"That's not true, and I don't think any of your hobbies—like your wall display of a bunch of different kinds of beer cans—puts you up there with Hercule Poirot, frankly."

"Who?"

"Christ, open the door to the car! It's freezing out here!"

"I don't know how you could tell. Hop in the backseat, Martha."

The frizzy little dog scrambled over the headrest. Cuddy, driving with a doughnut clamped in his teeth, now informed me, "Here's the truth. Your trouble is, you're too domestic. You got too many towels. Sideboards. Relatives. You ever hear of Philip Marlowe's mother coming to visit him at the office? Listen, the thing you have to do is to get out in the rain and let your trench coat get all soggy. You got to get lonesome, Lieutenant Savile. You're not lonesome enough, that's your real trouble. That and a nutty imagination. And don't remind me how you solved who poisoned Mrs. Ormond last year, 'cause that was pure *luck*. Doughnut?"

"No. How can I get lonesome with everybody traipsing in on me all the time?" I shook four vitamin C capsules from the bottle I kept in my briefcase. "I didn't get any sleep, and I don't want to get run down—and don't say a word." I also had a hangover I didn't mention.

Cuddy pawed through the bag and found the doughnut he was looking for, a vile jelly one. He said, "Anybody else ever tell you you were a hypochondriac?"

"Yeah. She's probably a judge in Atlanta by now."

"Where to, General Lee?"

"Pine Hills Lake. I want you to meet your mystic. Then I'm going to Cape Hatteras, you know, like on your wall."

"Kind of cold for the beach, and I don't know if V.D.'s gonna love your taking another vacation so soon after the last one, when you and Susan Whetstone slipped off to—"

"I'm going to see Walter Stanhope, you know who he is? Well, he used to have V.D.'s job, fifteen years back, before Rowell had him fired, and I found out on the phone this morning from Hiram Davies that Stanhope retired to Cape Hatteras. So I want to ask him something. You want to come? It's four hours."

"No, thanks, I'll just look at my wall. But you got to listen to me, Stanhope's not how to find out who killed Mrs. Dollard."

"Trust me."

"That's what my ex-wife said."

Chapter 7

Cloris Dollard kept the past, whether she'd kept a diary or not. She didn't sort it, or label it, and from all reports of her habitual sanguinity, she didn't dwell on it. She just kept it in cardboard boxes. Tossed into a fur company's box were hundreds of photographs—her unedited biography from scalloped black and white rectangles of herself as a habitually sanguine child, to color Polaroids of her and Rowell posing last summer at 10 Downing Street in London. Over the past week I had studied these pictures. I felt close to this big, tan, blond woman with the loud, warm voice I could remember yelling at me, "Pull that canoe on in, hey you, Jay Savile! Get your body over here and eat some lunch with my girls!"

To Captain Fulcher, the fact that the Senator's wife had been murdered was the tragic but ancillary aftermath of the fact that she had been robbed. I didn't believe that anymore. I believed she had been robbed because she'd been murdered. I believed she was dead because Bainton Ames was dead. I believed Joanna Cadmean. And I wanted to hear more of her dream.

At the Cadmean lake house, young professorial Briggs came down from her tower with a green ribbon through her hair, like a vine in strawberries, and engaged in a quick spate of stichomythic wisecracking with Cuddy Mangum about professional women and the merit of the solar system. All she said to me was,

"Is Mr. Mangum always so…"

"Juvenile?"

"Jocular."

I said, "He doesn't know what jocular means," and Cuddy said, "I do too: well-endowed," and she excused herself to go find her sister-in-law.

Cuddy sighed. "I believe I drove her off with my lewdness. And just when she was about getting ready to want to marry me."

"You've already been married. Why do you want to do it again?"

"Improve," he said. "Besides, Briggs was married before too. Married a hippie when she was a child. It didn't last long. He turned capitalist on her after all he'd said. She woke up one morning and he'd shaved off his beard. Imagine! After that, it all went in a downward spiral."

Another surprise. "Are you making this up, Cuddy?"

"Nope. She told me on the phone last night."

"Why'd you call her up?"

"My my, don't be tetchy. You can't keep 'em *all* on the bench."

Joanna Cadmean came in and sat down on the couch where she'd sat before, the same pillow cushioning her foot on the coffee table. In winter light, the great vaulted space of the lodge living room was sharp, even harder than it had felt last night shadowed by snow. She wore the same skirt and the same long-sleeved sweater. On the floor beside her was the morning paper open to Bubba Percy's article on her. Her sketchbook lay next to her on the couch; she picked it up and began to draw in that odd, unlooking, resolute way, while Cuddy and she talked about her past work with the police. Drawing, she sat in the bright, cold light and told of old nightmare visions, of seeing the lost she'd been asked to find, already dead in secret graves, hair growing wild.

I asked her, "Did you ever, do you mind if I say this? Did you ever think you were crazy?"

Mrs. Cadmean smiled at me. "Oh, I expect I *am* crazy."

"I mean, well, did you ever want to get away from being you? Want to change? Did you suffer from what people said about you?"

With quick sideways strokes, she crossed out the face she was sketching and turned the page. "When there was that external evidence, Justin, to prove me right, people said I had a great gift. When there wasn't, they said I was a charlatan or a lunatic. Neither the praise nor the censure of other people came to mean much to me."

Cuddy said, "I don't expect there's anybody who doubts you've got an amazing gift." I could tell he was as impressed with her as I had been—with her beauty and her strange incandescent self-possession.

The calm gray eyes turned to Cuddy, crooked toward her in the bent-willow chair. She said, "The trouble with the kind of gifts the gods give, Mr. Mangum, is they cannot be declined, or exchanged, or even," she looked down at her drawing, "set aside for a while. You cannot say 'No, thank you' to the gods." One hand closed over the wrist of the other, covering what I felt must be scars. Then she looked up at me. "Now, Justin, you wanted me to look at some photographs of some men? Men who may be connected to Cloris's death? Are they in that folder? Mr. Mangum, we seem to have made a convert of your friend overnight."

Cuddy said, "Hey, he's got ESP! I mean, not like you, but he's always saying things that you're thinking, or singing songs that are in your head, you know. One night, a couple of years ago, he called me up and said, 'Are you okay?' and I had in fact just had the puerile notion of sticking a dirty revolver in my mouth—tasted terrible—over some real sad news about my ex-wife getting married that morning. If I'd had ESP, I wouldn't have ever introduced her to her new love, much less hauled that same man across a rice paddy on my back."

"I'm sorry." Her eyes went black in the sudden way I'd noticed before, a bruised look coming into them and then vanishing.

In the manila folder were blowups of a dozen random mugshots I'd asked Cuddy to bring me—mixed among them pictures of the three Pope brothers. One by one as I handed them to her, she touched her hand over the surface, shook her head and placed them facedown beside her on the couch. She paused no more over Preston Pope's face than any other, although when she came to Graham Pope's, she did go back and hold the two pictures up and comment on the resemblance. The only time she even hesitated was at a photo of a bull-necked, blond ex-Marine with dulled eyes and a long arrest record, a local hood, Cuddy said, who had died ten years ago in a car crash.

"No, I'm sorry," she said. "Nothing. Of course, that means nothing too, you understand."

Then I gave her the photograph I had brought in my briefcase. She dropped it, and as I leaned down to pick it up, I noticed the long fingers of her oddly translucent hand trembling in the folds of her skirt. "Why are you showing me this?" she whispered. Cuddy twisted over to see the picture I'd taken from among the jumbled stack in Cloris Dollard's cardboard box. On the back, in her broad script, was scribbled *Pine Hills Lake house*, and on the front Bainton Ames sat slumped in a beach chair, papers on his lap; near him his step-daughter lay on a towel, my mother in her bathing suit stood in the sand, holding a cigarette, and in the shallow water, Cloris Ames and Rowell Dollard—both tan and well muscled—stood laughing together, their handsome faces close enough to touch.

I said, "They look like lovers, don't they?"

Mrs. Cadmean turned her eyes to the huge window, where light sparked like static over the pine tops and down across the flat gray lake. I spoke quietly. "Is there anyone in *this* picture you associate with Bainton Ames's death?"

Her response was to struggle up awkwardly onto her crutches and limp across the long room to the window. Cuddy had to jerk in his legs as she went past.

"Did the two of them arrange Bainton's accident?" I asked her.

Her back was to me, her hands tight on the crutches. She shook her head no.

"Did the same person kill Bainton who killed Cloris? Mrs.

Cadmean? You said, she died *because* of Bainton. Did the same…"

"I know no *fact* to suggest so." Her voice was soft but distinct in the hard angles of the room. "Do you?"

"Not yet. Do you *believe* so?"

She kept staring out to the empty lake as if she were waiting for someone.

Cuddy looked up, his face uncharacteristically hushed, as I walked around him to go stand beside her. It was then that I realized that from the Cadmean window you could see across the northern tip of Pine Hills Lake to the dock and the small half-moon beach of Cloris Dollard's summer cottage, now boarded up; with some effort I could distinguish part of the back deck, where whoever had taken my old photograph might have stood to snap it—perhaps the other daughter, not seeing what the camera saw. From the tower with the telescope, Briggs could probably see right into the house itself.

Standing by Joanna Cadmean's side, and without turning to look at her, I asked her, "Is it Rowell?"

Her eyes closed, then opened, peaceful gray. They looked a long while at the lake.

I followed Mrs. Cadmean as she moved along the window. "That's what Cloris told you in the dream, and when you heard her voice at the riding stables, she was warning you against him?"

Cuddy looked at me, startled. "Why not?" I told him. "Maybe Rowell just grabbed up the coins and things at random to make it look like a robbery, and dumped them, and Pope somehow stumbled on the silverware."

She said in so low a voice I barely heard her, "Bainton's coins were very rare; some collected by his grandfather were especially rare. I know Rowell liked them. He liked to keep what was rare."

I said, "Like Cloris?"

"Was she rare?"

I said, "But why kill Bainton? What's wrong with divorce? The estate? He built his career on Bainton Ames's money."

Joanna Cadmean swung her crutches toward me. Her voice

was like the light coming off the ice outside. She said, "He built his career on what I told him."

Cuddy asked, "What do you mean, Mrs. Cadmean? The publicity from your discoveries when he was assistant solicitor?"

"At first." Her voice melted into its soft stillness. "My…insights remained helpful even after it seemed best not to make them public."

Cuddy said, "You mean, you were working with Dollard on his courtroom presentations?" She nodded, and he turned to me. "Well, according to Fulcher, your uncle never lost a case."

Yes. Dollard had campaigned on that record and gone to the state senate on it and with it won the worshipful envy of men like Fulcher.

Mrs. Cadmean reached her hand out to me. "In the past I've found my perceptions grow stronger the closer I get to the place where the death occurred." She took my hand in hers, its heat and tension were startling. "They are stronger here in Hillston than they were on St. Simons."

We were all quiet for a moment. Then I said, "I'll take you over to the Dollards' house."

Cuddy unwound himself and stood. "I suppose we could. Couldn't hurt."

"Let's go now," I said. I wanted to go back there too.

She excused herself to change her clothes, and I was surprised again by her attractiveness when she returned in a stylish red wool dress and wool cape. Outside, she walked awkwardly on the unfamiliar crutches, dodging the puddled ice that was alarming all Hillston, a city unaccustomed to the cold.

• • •

Mrs. Cadmean said nothing as we drove in past the Dollard gate and along the crackling driveway up to the imperturbable expanse of red brick and white wood. An orange Pinto was parked in front of high rhododendron bushes whose stiff brown winter leaves seemed to have given up all hope of spring. Inside, a Mrs. Teknik was vacuuming; she had replaced the former cleaning woman who'd quit. She said that this woman had refused to come back inside the unlucky house. "Colored people," she said, "believe in ghosts."

I said, "So do I."

The house had been restored to order, Etham Foster's men having long since abandoned the search for proof of an intruder's identity anywhere on the premises. Upstairs, my uncle had had the bloodstained yellow carpeting torn off the bedroom floor, and the blond oak queen-size bed was stripped to its mattress. But his wife's clothes still hung in their closets, her toiletries still lined the white wicker shelves in her bathroom. Dust lingered in the light over the vanity table where Cloris Dollard's perfumes, combs, and jewelry boxes sat in geometric patterns utterly unlike the untroubling disarray in which we'd found them that first Monday morning we'd been summoned there. In fact, it was not that the house had been returned to order, it had been put in order: premises that had once looked like an unresolved quarrel between two incompatible decorators now had swung in favor of Rowell Dollard's opulent fastidiousness. Downstairs the stiff, silk, pearl-hued chairs and settee made a precise square with the gray mantel, and no longer gawked askance at the painted wood secretary I'd seen so piled with magazines and gloves and so stuffed with scraps of paper, pointless pencils, and unmailed letters that it would not close. Everywhere in this house, now, the disorder of life was missing.

By holding to the rail and to my shoulder, Mrs. Cadmean was able to climb the curved stairs to the bedroom. Her body heat against my side shocked me; her arm burned across the back of my jacket. Her other arm clutched a shoulder bag. In our slow ascent I said, "I don't like the idea of your being out at the lake by yourself."

"Briggs is usually with me, and before she leaves to teach, she fixes everything so I'm quite comfortable."

"Still, couldn't you go to your father-in-law's in town?" She shook her head. "Way out there," I said. "What do you do?"

She smiled the strange cold smile that had scared me at the end of our first conversation. She said, "Oh, I prophesy."

"If you get…worried, you'll let me know?"

"I'll let you know," she said. "Is that the bedroom through there?"

"Yes."

"And, Justin, should something…happen to me, ask Briggs for a letter. I don't mean to be coy, I want you to understand. So, tonight, I'm going to write everything down for you."

"All right." My shoulder felt abruptly cold when her hand moved away to take the crutches. I left her, as she had asked, alone in Cloris Dollard's bedroom. The sound of the crutches moved slowly across the bare wood above me.

Downstairs I searched through the wood secretary, the study desk, and the bookshelves for anything Cloris might have used as a diary. Then I went down to the basement, where I found no boxes of anything resembling technical papers that might have belonged to Bainton Ames.

"Savile, you are tangling with the big boys now. Why'd you let me go on believing *you* were rich?" Cuddy was in the study, looking at Rowell's framed diplomas.

"I tried to disabuse you, but obviously the idea meant too much to you to give it up."

"Now I see Uncle Rowell's place, and Cadmean's play-house—not even his real house!—I wonder why I bothered being jealous of you all these years."

"Me too."

"Yassir, things have clearly slumped for you since all the slaves done run off your place and jest left the corn rotting in the fields, like some old, tall, dead, yellow-sashed soldiers." He started on the other wall of bookshelves, reading the spines.

"Christ, you love to talk," I said.

"I can't rely on my features, Lieutenant."

From the other wing the vacuuming buzz stopped loudly. I heard Mrs. Teknik mumble, then I heard a sharp "Where are they?" As we hurried back out into the entryway, Rowell Dollard, his scarf very white between his black velvet collar and his flushed ear, was starting up the stairs.

"Rowell," I called. "Sorry to intrude again. I assumed you'd be in Raleigh."

His face was swollen with suppressed irritation. "I understood from Fulcher that you people were finished here, Justin. I don't mean to be uncooperative, but…" Then his eyes were pulled away from us and turned up toward the landing at the top of the stairs where, soundless, Joanna Cadmean stood braced by the angle of her crutches. When he finally spoke, his voice was hoarse. "What are you doing here?"

She answered mildly, "Hello, Rowell."

Florid, he backed down the steps toward me. "Why is she here? Why have you brought her in this house? What in hell kind of hocus-pocus are you pulling, Justin?"

Cuddy loped up the stairs to help Mrs. Cadmean down. I said, "I'm trying to find out who killed Cloris."

"How so?" Dollard snapped.

"Any way I can."

His black overcoat still buttoned, the senator strode across the entryway to the study door, his head quivering from the effort to control his voice. "I'm sorry, but this is not tolerable. I'll have to ask you all to leave." The door shut sharply behind him. I suspected he was telephoning Captain Fulcher.

My apologies to Joanna Cadmean for having subjected her to so painful an encounter were acknowledged, if heard, by a nod from some far-distant and chilling place. In the car, Cuddy's little dog whimpered on the floor of the backseat where Mrs. Cadmean sat silently until we were back out on the bypass. Then she asked, "Is there no phone in Cloris's bedroom?"

"There was," I told her. "After the jack was torn out, I suppose they must have had it removed."

"Because standing in there, I kept hearing her phone ring. Very loud. There was no image really of what might have…taken place. I simply kept hearing the phone ringing over and over. Except I did see coins. Coins falling in the air. Bainton's, I suppose. I recall from the papers back at the time, one of the men Bainton had been with that night was talking about the coins. Odd. Falling like a storm." In the rearview mirror I watched Mrs. Cadmean's steady, peaceful eyes gazing out as the unleafed trees went blurring past. I noticed that the eyes never blinked.

• • •

All the way back to town Cuddy said, "I don't know. I don't know. It's nutty."

I reminded him that he was the one who had first told me just how accustomed the Hillston police were to exactly Joanna Cadmean's kind of detection.

"That's true, but mind if I say something personal?"

"Yes." Mrs. Mitchell nosed herself under my elbow.

"Hate is blind and so are the hots."

"Meaning?"

"You ought to take yourself off this case and go back to your regular assignments."

"Sure!" I leaned over and punched in his cigarette lighter. "And leave you to run the only case the town council and the newspapers care anything about! Get your name on this one, Mangum, and maybe you can squeeze out Fulcher."

"Get fucked, Justin."

"You sound like Charlene. Okay, okay. I apologize. You're just trying to help. Like always. How are hate and 'the hots,' as you so eloquently put it, blinding me?"

We were both angry. I was smoking; he rolled down the window and let in the freezing wind. He said, "You know what I'm talking about. You *want* to believe Senator Dollard killed his wife, because you hate him. You hate the way your momma thought you ought to let her little brother be your great white father. You hate the way she loves him so much and admires him so much, and, and, and. You're jealous."

"Oh Jesus Christ! Now you sound like Fulcher's psychology course. And who am I jealous *for*? Cloris Dollard, or my mother?"

Is it for them I have 'the hots'?"

"You said it, not me. I had in mind Joanna Cadmean."

"I'm not even going to respond to that, it's so absurd."

"I watched you, General Lee. You gloop around her like some soulful teenager with sore nuts, mooning over the high school art teacher." The anger loosened and left Cuddy's face; he grinned. "In fact, now I remember, you *were* in love with your seventh-grade Latin teacher, weren't you! What was her name?"

"Mrs. Berry."

"That's right. It was because of her you majored in classics. You know what's amazing that I bet you never thought of? We're older now than Mrs. Berry was *then*! What could she have been—twenty-seven at the most? Here she was, an Older Woman—up in a tower of knowledge and power there was no way you could climb—and the damn truth is, she was a *baby*!"

"I'm not going to drop the Dollard case."

"I didn't think you would," he said, and rolled the window back up. "You can lead a horse to water but a jackass likes to mix his own drinks."

Chapter 8

Graham Pope's former wife, Paula, tended bar at the Rib House, out on the bypass, on the other side of Hillston from Pine Hills Lake. Almost as big as its parking lot, the Rib House stretched between a Toyota dealership and a pitch-and-putt course that was closed for the winter. Its long-tentacled machine, there to feel through the weeds for balls, had been left waiting like a giant mantis in the grass. The Rib House, in a regrettable effort to resemble a Victorian train depot, had stuffed itself with semi-antiques, beginning with a mechanical gypsy fortune-teller in a glass case by the door. In trolley cars, plywood gazebos, and papier-mâché caves, large families ate at long tables without talking—except to yell at their children to stop running back to the salad bar. Even if the parents hadn't apparently worn out conversation years back, they couldn't have heard each other. The Rib House was a clangorous blare of herded suburban flight from life at home together. Hand to my ear, I made phone calls while Cuddy walked Mrs. Mitchell outside.

By half past five, on every level surface, vast dripping ribs of pig and cow were being devoured. A lengthy line of more hungry families craned out necks to meter their progress, while they stood discussing whether they should order "The Hombre" or "Big Mama" or "Little Dude," as poster-size menus labeled these platters.

Paula Pope was a creamy, fat woman somewhere near forty, with hair so black and skin and eyes so lovely she looked as though some cartoonist had drawn Snow White's face inside a moon. She was working fast, puffing at a loose curl, and frowning fretfully as she plopped cherries and pineapple chunks into huge frozen pink and lime drinks that she topped with paper Confederate flags. "I'm divorced," she said to Cuddy for openers. "We're friendly, I guess, but we're divorced; so don't come asking me about Graham Pope, because I don't know."

Cuddy said, "How you doing, Paula? This is Lieutenant Savile. Paula Pope."

"Paula Burgwin." She wiped her small hands on a towel when I offered mine, and we shook. "I got back my own name. Do you know what it cost me? Fifty-five dollars."

I asked her if she'd heard about what happened to Preston and she nodded the way you nod when the highway patrol asks you if you know what the speed limit is. "What can you tell us about it, Paula?"

"Not a thing, except it's probably not true. You two want a drink?" Cuddy had a beer and I had a whiskey, and for a few minutes we both tried to pick up the check.

"You keep up with Charlene, don't you?" Cuddy asked, licking at his beer head. "Preston wants to see her, real bad. Is it all over between them? Because she gave me that feeling."

Paula was mixing two more fishbowls of icy pink foam. "You wouldn't get her to believe it in a million years, but Charlene's acting real dumb." She added, "That don't mean, compared to Preston, Charlene oughtn't to be teaching over at the university." She giggled like a child. "Charlene says there's this brainy girl at C&W that's big in the union that told her she was naturally smart and oughta do something with herself."

Cuddy said, "I'll have to go along with that. Preston, now, is slow, no getting around it. So what makes Charlene so unnaturally dumb these days, and can I have two bags of those beer nuts over there? And bring Justin something to eat too."

"I'm not hungry," I told her. "I'd like another whiskey. Weak."

"Because she's young, is all," Paula said. "Everybody young's dumb. Weren't y'all dumb? One weak Jack Daniel's." She had a pretty hand, set apart from the creamy arm by a crowded charm bracelet. Her arm looked as if its skin were so tight it would pop if something pricked it.

"Oh, lord," Cuddy said with a sigh. "I've been waiting and waiting for a chance to get young. I was always old, working to get myself to where I could have a ball being young, and now Paula, you come telling me, 'Remember when.' I'm so sad, I got to have a pizza, can I order a pizza here at the bar? Justin, I want you to try some of this pizza."

Promptly at 5:30 a rail-thin black man complaining about the cold weather came to replace Paula at the bar, and the three of us found a little cable-spool table free in a corner, and I bought her a strawberry daiquiri and had a third drink, and Cuddy ate an entire pizza the menu named "The Kitchen Sink."

Paula said, "Charlene traded a moron for a goon, is all."

"I bet you mean Luster Hudson," Cuddy mumbled, cheese stuck to his fingers.

"Thinking there's men like Luster makes me worry I gave up on Graham." Her high, small voice struggled against the dinner clatter around us. "Well, I'll tell you one thing, last night Charlene asked me over there for supper, where she's moved out with Luster, called me up and said we had a lot in common now, and invited me."

"Ex-Popes Club, huh?" said Cuddy. "Y'all could get a lodge and play bingo."

"That'd be funny if it wasn't sad. So, anyhow, I went, and you know what that man is doing with a bunch of dogs?"

"Not feeding them," Cuddy said. "And speaking of Luster's dogs, business must be better'n it looked, for him to quit C&W, did you have that feeling? Didn't he make pretty good money on the forklift at C&W? He say anything about that?"

"He didn't say anything about anything. So, do you want to know what he does with those dogs? Well, I happened to go to the bathroom, and I heard this little kitten crying its eyes out in a box with holes punched in it, so I brought it out, and I said to him—Charlene was outside getting the bottle of wine she'd stuck in the snow to cool off." Paula paused to offer me nachos and eat half a dozen herself. "I said, 'Whose cute little kitten is this?' Just trying to be polite, even though I don't much like Luster and vice versa in a big way—you could tell he was mad at her for even inviting me over, and he was about as nice as a snake. You know what he told me? Says, 'I get them from ads. I use them to hunt my dogs with, if it's any of your business.' He sat right there with the TV on, and told me that, like he thought I'd say, 'Oh, that's nice!' He was obtaining those kittens under false pretenses and then siccing his dogs on them, I couldn't even believe it! Then he says, 'Put that damn cat back where you got it,' but I set it down on the floor, and it ran right over and climbed up the leg of Luster's jeans, like I'd told it to go scratch out his eyes. And so he yanked it off and threw it against the wall, hard. And so Charlene opened the door, and the kitten tears out and runs up a tree and can't get down. So you know what he did?"

"Shot it," I said.

Cuddy said, "I see you're getting a feel for Luster's personality. I had to bring Luster in one time, me and five guys that used to play pro football, and we ran the patrol car back and forth on top of him for a while so we could get in close enough to put the cuffs on."

Paula sucked away half her daiquiri through a straw. "He wouldn't even let me use his ladder to get that kitten. And he wouldn't let Charlene do it either. And so he says, 'I don't have to put up with somebody coming in my house and telling me what to do.'"

I said I could imagine Charlene's response to that.

"She didn't say a word. And you want to know something else, Charlene's scared of Luster. I really think that's why she wanted me to come over, so she wouldn't have to be by herself with him. She was glad he was going off to the mountains. She thinks she's all excited about Luster, but what she is, is scared, if you know what I mean."

I said, "I think that's an interesting observation," and she smiled with a shy hesitation that was taking a while to decide she'd been complimented.

Cuddy licked his fingers. "She told me she had a *real* man now."

"That's right,' that's what she thinks she thinks." In one long sip, Paula finished whatever liquid there was in her drink. "I don't know any real men."

"Well, hey, what about us?" said Cuddy.

She looked at me, her spoon poised to scoop up the pink slush. She said, "What about you?"

I said, "I wish I could, ma'am," which she knew wasn't really true, but a way of saying I liked her, and she gave me a nod and closed her mouth over the Snow White pretty teeth and scooped up more daiquiri. I asked her what had happened to the kitten.

"Luster said he didn't want me in his house, is what he said, and I said, 'Thanks for supper, Charlene,' and went and got my car and parked it under the tree and climbed up on the car top and just about killed myself and got the dumb kitten." She held out her right hand so we could see the red scratch streaks. "It's at home. You two want a kitten? I don't even like cats all that much. You think your little dog would like a kitten, Cuddy?"

I said, "If you ask me, you sound like a real woman."

She dropped the spoon in the empty glass. "Too much of one." She giggled, then sighed. "Well, how bad trouble's Graham in? Did he steal that new Mustang of his?"

"Not that anybody's mentioned," Cuddy said.

I asked her, "Have you ever seen him or his brothers in the company of Senator Rowell Dollard, the man whose wife's been killed?"

She laughed. "I doubt it."

"Ever heard them talk about him?"

"They didn't talk much politics—except 'Shoot them all.'"

Cuddy said, "How about, hear them talk about some old coins, jewelry, a sapphire and diamond bracelet?" Paula turned the charms on her own bracelet; she shook her head. Cuddy went on, "I got two notions. One is, Preston stole that stuff from whoever stole it. The other one is, Preston never saw so much silverware in his life 'til Mr. Savile here showed it to him. And number two means Graham and/or Dickey dropped those little bags off at the house on their way to Greensboro. *Or*, number three, old Albert Einstein Charlene needs a real lawyer a lot more'n a real man." Cuddy wrapped his pizza crusts in a napkin to take out to Mrs. Mitchell.

Paula said, "Well, if Charlene put that stuff there, and I'm not saying she did because I never knew her to steal a thing, she sure didn't know it belonged to that dead lady, because Luster was watching about the investigation on the news and told Charlene to shut up so he could hear because she wasn't listening. And I tell you the truth, Cuddy, I wouldn't put a lot past my in-laws, but they're not killers. Graham tore in here this morning and said you folks had planted that silverware on Preston because y'all had to get somebody fast, this lady being a Hillston big shot and all. How can you eat all that pizza and stay so skinny? If I *look* at a pizza, all my buttons pop off."

Cuddy held the last cheesy triangle about an inch from her nose. "Honey, don't blink," he said.

She giggled again. "Well, this was real nice, but I've got to go feed two kids and a cat. I shouldn't even say this, and this is all I'm going to say, but if I was the two of you, I'd talk to a man called Ratcher Phelps, you know him? He's the one Graham and Dickey would go to if they had something special."

"Who?" asked Cuddy. "I never heard of him."

"Oh, he's tight. Old guy. Only reason I know is I've heard Graham on the phone telling people if they used Ratcher Phelps they had to be careful, because Phelps wouldn't put up with sloppiness." Paula then explained that the only way to open negotiations with this Mr. Phelps was by asking at his East Hillston business, the Melody Store, if he had banjo sheet music for "Moonlight Bay." "You have to say it was your mother's favorite, and you want to play it for her birthday."

I said, "Mr. Phelps is a sentimental receiver of stolen goods, I take it?"

"Don't Savile here talk old-fashioned?" Cuddy asked Paula. "He likes everything old. He even rides around on horses, pretending to be a Confederate general."

"He's talking about a pageant at the Hunt Club, that's all, Paula. I like your bracelet," I said. "Could I ask you where you got that particular charm there, do you mind?"

She raised her dimpled wrist. "This one? Oh, it's some kind of an old stone bead I dug up myself in the backyard when I was little. I think it belonged to an Indian." The charms jingled as she shook her hand. "This is my whole life, right here."

"Pardon?"

"Well, like here's a Bible-camp medal, third prize for backstroke, if you can believe water could ever hold me up once upon a time, and this is for high school choir."

Her voice came out in slight pushes of air, as if it were trying to escape the weight of her body, as if it were something delicate caught inside, still singing, like the cat in *Peter and the Wolf*. She said, "And this one is one of those Purple Hearts, have you seen one? It was my first boyfriend's that he got in vietnam. I was real young. We were going to get married but it didn't work out that way. And here's my wedding ring." She spun it on its chain. "Do you know what I found out? Graham stole it out of a jewelry store in High Point, if you can believe that."

"It has the sad smack of truth," Cuddy said.

"And this little pin here, my mama got this for twenty-five years' service on the loom at C&W. Mr. Cadmean presented it to her himself. They had a whole ceremony. Now they just lay people off and don't even wave good-bye to them. Here's my boy Giffins first tooth. And well, so on and so on. My whole life, right here on my arm." She let it fall onto the table.

Cuddy sighed. "Paula, I sure wish you'd stop talking like the end is near."

A curl shiny as a blackbird spilled over onto her forehead; pushing it back, she touched her broad face, puzzled, as if she'd never felt the flesh before. She said, "Oh, I don't mean my life's over. I just mean I can see what it is now. It'll just be that some more." Her giggle was like a small bell, unreverberant; swallowed by the racket of food. "I mean, I used to wonder, is all, and now I know."

Chapter 9

"The Popes are out," I said an hour later, flipping my cigarette into one of the big cuspidor ashtrays sitting under Mr. Cadmean's portrait in the municipal building's lobby. "From the way Paula talked, I'd say Graham really thinks we're trying to frame his baby brother. You don't suppose V.D. could have actually dumped that silverware in their bathtub, do you? He'd do anything for Rowell."

The instant the elevator door opened on the fifth floor, Captain V.D. Fulcher was standing there. He yapped at Cuddy. "Where have you been? Is that that dog?!" Mrs. Mitchell jumped behind me, and I hid her in my coat.

"Going up, sir," Cuddy said, and pushed the button, but Fulcher shoved his fake-madras shoulder against the door.

I asked, "You been waiting in the hall for us long, Captain?"

Fulcher had his mouth click going at a quick tempo. "Do you two ever bother listening to the radio dispatch in your car?"

Cuddy said, "I like Loretta Lynn better. He likes Mama Rainey."

"Ma," I said.

"Where've you been all day?" Fulcher wasn't spluttering; that meant Rowell hadn't called him, which surprised me. I said, "We got a lead a couple of hours ago about a possible fence for the jewelry and coins, and we followed it up."

"I don't suppose you found out much of anything?" Fulcher's face was so smug, I started to wonder if, despite our advice, Preston had decided to confess. "Come to my office." Our leader marched ahead.

•   •   •

In fact, we hadn't found out much of anything from our lead at the Melody Store. Ratcher Phelps's response to my wanting to play "Moonlight Bay" on the banjo for my mother was to regret that he was unable to help me, especially considering that he was always happy to assist the police.

"It must have been your overcoat, Savile," Cuddy said. "I should have asked. You just don't look like a banjo player."

Ratcher Phelps smiled. He was a small black man of sixty-some, wearing a black pinstripe suit with an American-flag tiepin and square, yellow-topaz cuff links. He had the rhetorical lugubrious look of a well-to-do funeral director, and smiled with aggrieved disappointment at our suspicions that he might be trafficking with petty thieves. On the way from the Rib House to East Hillston, we'd called in a check on him, and the last charge against Phelps was twenty-five years old, when someone who hadn't liked him much had phoned the station to say there were four-dozen Lady Bulova watches in his car trunk. Since then, not so much as a parking ticket had brought him to the department's attention, although he had a nephew either less virtuous or less careful.

Mr. Phelps's ostensible business was musical instruments. It was in his Melody Store, while mentally adding up the spinets and electric organs all around him, that he told us sadly it was always the same old story. "And the years don't change it, and the government won't change it, and nothing I see's going to turn it around, and, gentlemen, I guess that if I let it bother my tranquillity of mind, I doubt I'd sleep peaceful, which I do." He counted the burnished trombones and glossy clarinets that hung glittering out of reach on the walls and were purchased through high-interest installment payments by the parents of East Hill-ston's state-famous high school band.

"That's good. You get your rest," Cuddy said. "Poor Lieutenant Savile here's an insomniac, and my upstairs neighbors are too much in love. Now about these emerald earbobs I was mentioning."

"It is dispiriting and grievous to me," Phelps said, rolling his tongue around the words as if he were readying his lips to play what he had to say on one of his saxophones, "the same old way when white people rob and steal what belongs to some more white people, the first thing to transpire is the black people get paid the call by you people."

"That about takes care of all the people," said Cuddy. "Let's drop all of them for now except the ones called Pope, and talk about a diamond and sapphire bracelet."

"If you young men want a clarinet, a harmonica, if you are inclined to a piano in your home, we can talk 'til you buy or I close. But, gentlemen, I don't sell jewelry."

I said, "Do you buy it?" and he showed me his cuff links and smiled his sad, insincere smile. I tried again. "Do you buy rare American coins, and might you be interested in a reciprocal exchange? For instance, an upcoming appearance of your nephew William Phelps currently involving petty larceny, but susceptible to abatement."

His lips repeated *reciprocal*, either because he liked the idea or liked the word and intended to add it to his already palaver-ous style.

I said it again for him: "Reciprocal." My lips were a little numb after three drinks, and I thought maybe I'd mispronounced it.

His morose filmy eye lamented the Fall awhile before he said, "Such as, to what?"

"Shoplifting," I said.

"And suspended," Cuddy added.

"I know a Mister Dickey Pope," he said. "Who used to buy strings and picks from me for his guitar. But I haven't seen him since summertime. Maybe he gave up on his playing." Phelps's gloom suggested this would have been a wise decision. "No, not since summertime."

I said, "Anybody besides Popes come to mind?"

"No, sir, they don't. What would these jewels and these American coins happen to look like if I was to happen to glance down at one on the sidewalk in the midst of my constitutional?"

I described them. Only the rarest of Bainton Ames's coins had been kept in the bedroom safe and only they had been stolen; the rest, the less valuable type sets still sat in their small vinyl boxes in the Dollard study. Among the missing, according to the detailed records Ames had kept in his neat, spidery hand, were a 1907 Saint-Gaudens double eagle, an 1841 "Little Princess," a Bechtler's five-dollar gold piece, and an 1880 Stella Liberty head with coiled hair; the last alone was worth at least sixty-five thousand dollars.

Phelps shook his head sorrowfully. "Isn't that something? A couple of old dirty coins are worth more than all my horns put together."

Cuddy said, "I know what you mean," and rapped a beat on a snare drum so wretched-sounding that Phelps's eyes moistened even more. I bought a collection of simplified Gershwin songs, and he came close to selling me a new piano.

"Nice to meet you," I told him.

He moistened his lip. "The feeling is reciprocal."

• • •

In his office now, V.D. Fulcher was turning the plastic cube that contained photos of his offspring from child to child. Cuddy and I were listening to him ask us again, "Who is this unidentified black source you say doesn't know anything? There's getting to be too many nigrahs in this case."

I said, "You mean like the head of forensics?"

He bounded across to the file cabinet and jerked open the drawer, flashing the plastic digital watch he wore with the face on the inside of his wrist.

"I mean," he gloated, "I have one of Mrs. Dollard's earrings." There was an unavoidable twitch of surprise from us both that Fulcher must have treasured. "You know who had them? Reverend Hayward."

Cuddy said, "I didn't realize Reverend Hayward was a nigrah! My, my, he looks as white as you do."

Fulcher said, "You're treading, Mangum. That crazy old colored woman Hayward takes care of came into the vestry today and dropped this in the collection plate by his elbow." He unclenched his fist, and green flashed out. "He couldn't get her to tell him where she got it. You know who I mean. The Bible nut. Sister What's-Her-Face. She had a pretty expensive umbrella, too. Might be connected."

"It's Senator Dollard's," I said.

Cuddy said, "Damn, you *are* psychic."

In the interrogation room, Sister Resurrection, indifferent to a destiny less than universal, paced out a square along the walls, so that Fulcher and I had to keep rotating on our chairs to see her. Harriet Dale, the only woman on the force with whom Fulcher felt comfortable, stood by, boxy and tight-curled. Cuddy had gone back in disgust to the lab.

"We ought to have her sedated," Fulcher said, exasperated.

"Good Christ," I told him. "We ought to let her go home. What the hell good is holding her supposed to do?"

"What's with you, Savile? Ogilvey'll be down in a second. Then we'll make some progress." Ogilvey was our consulting psychiatrist.

"I doubt it."

In the gray cotton dress that Harriet Dale had somehow gotten on her, Sister Resurrection looked a third her usual size, but her sermon was the same, and in no evident way had she responded to Fulcher's demands that she tell him where she'd found or stolen Mrs. Dollard's earring. By the time Dr. Ogilvey arrived, she was in stride with the measure of the room she walked: "God is sick and tired of all this trash! The day coming He got to lay down His head. God fixing to move the mountains, pull over the sky, and lay down His weary head. No more shall He walk in the garden in the morning. No more shall He fret on the sinner's hard heart. Matthew and Mark can't hold Him back, amen. Mary weeping can't hold Him back, Amen. His little baby Jesus can't hold Him back. Hear the voice, hallelujah, say yes. God fixing to loose the Devil's chains."

"This woman is schizophrenic" was Dr. Ogilvey's prompt diagnosis. He threw in "hebephrenic" and "a hundred percent delusional system," and advised us our duty was to take her to the state institution. As for extracting from her the original whereabouts of the jewelry, his offhand estimate was that it would take him five years of daily work to bring her to acknowledge her own name, and in fact he doubted he'd ever succeed. Some years back I'd been forced to talk to several psychiatrists; this was the first time I'd believed one.

"What about if we sedate her?" pleaded Fulcher, but Ogilvey just pulled back on his car coat and left. The captain followed the doctor out, arguing the point. "I'm going home," V.D. let me know over his shoulder. "We're having company, and I'm already late."

"Well, Sister," I said. "Would you like a cigarette? No? Mind if I smoke?" Mrs. Dale began giving me a worried look. "Sister, you know that silver-haired man who knocked you down last night? That earring belonged to his wife. My mother was a friend of hers. And now somebody's killed her. What's your opinion, ma'am?" Mrs. Dale's head jerked up; she thought I was talking to her. "Share your thoughts. You think that silver-haired man might have killed his own wife? Did that earring fall out of his car?"

Sister Resurrection was edging along the wall and shaking her head. She began again. "Shadrach, Meshach, and Abed-nego they were walking in the middle of the fire. But the flame of the fiery furnace never teched a hair of their head. The dragon he spits up fire in the night. High up. Down it rain."

"Umbrella won't help?"

She shook her head, back and forth. "Down it rain."

I stood up, and scared Mrs. Dale. Clearly she was torn between her assumption that I had interrogation techniques beyond her training, and her instinctive feeling that I was deranged. I said, "I'm going to call Reverend Hayward now, and he'll come to take you on home."

This alarmed Mrs. Dale enough to make her step forward. "She hasn't been released, Lieutenant Savile."

"Has she been charged?"

"No, sir. But I don't have the authority…"

"I have the authority."

With relief, she gave up her struggle. "Yes, sir." Such is the comfort of rank.

•　•　•

Back upstairs, where I hadn't been all day, Officer Hiram Davies peered at me over his bifocals with eyes earnestly innocent at sixty-four. Behind the front desk he still sat at attention in the uncomfortable wood chair where he sat all day, fearful of sloth and forced retirement.

"Here," he called. He handed me a neat stack of his memo sheets and added a reproach. "I hope I got them all right."

"Hiram, let me ask you a favor? Don't mention my having called you about where Walter Stanhope lived."

"How come? Is something wrong?"

"No, but…"

"Nobody told me he wanted his whereabouts kept secret. Lots of people know he moved to Cape Hatteras."

"I know, that's not—never mind, just please don't volunteer the information that I was asking."

His nostrils pinched tight. "Are you saying I'm some kind of blabbermouth, because—"

One of his lines rang, and he transferred a call downstairs with elaborate precision.

I said, "One more thing, and I'll stop pestering you."

"You're not pestering me."

"Burch Iredell, that guy that was coroner here back ten, fifteen years ago?"

Davies pushed in on his bifocals as if that would help him see
what I wanted.

"Is he still alive?"

"What do you want to know about all these old people for?"

"Maybe I'm planning a reunion."

"That's not true. Is it?"

I apologized. "It's just a joke. Is Iredell dead?"

"He's in the V.A. hospital over in Raleigh." Davies sat up
straighter, his shirt stiff with starch to hold off the future. "But
his wife's passed away. She attended my church for many years."

"Hiram, tell me, do you remember when Mrs. Dollard's first
husband died? Bainton Ames?"

"Well, yes. Bainton Ames. He drowned."

"Back then, do you remember, did anybody ever suggest he
might have been murdered?"

He pushed on his glasses some more, uncertain whether I was
checking to see if his memory was failing, or actually coming to
him for help. "They thought he'd been blown up with the boat,
then along comes his body miles away. Then they thought he'd
fallen out."

"That's right. You have a good memory. Anybody think he'd
been pushed out?"

Davies's eyes went away to the past and came back puzzled.

He said, "Now, isn't that funny, because Captain Stanhope
did ask that same question, now I think back. Is that why you
want to see him? There wasn't anything to it. He was fired, you
know." He said this as if getting fired were a profound moral fail-
ure. Then with careful fairness he added, "He got another job,
some kind of security work. But he was pretty bitter. Then I
heard he just retired. I heard all he does now is fish off in the
middle of nowhere."

"That sounds pretty good to me, Hiram."

Davies shook his head in a nervous tic, scraping his collar on
his thin neck. "No, it's not," he said. "It's not."

Alone in my office I felt myself dropping back into the weighted depression that had always tugged me down when I didn't keep drinking once I had started. The rush of impulse just to walk out and find a bar scared me. Instead, I started smoking. The memos in Davies's small, precise hand all looked accusatory. One said, "Call Candace," which was Susan Whetstone's code name, and the name she wished she'd been given at birth. Another said, "Call Mr. Briggs Cadmean." He was doubtless returning the call I'd made earlier about the papers my mother had said Cloris Dollard was planning to show him. The man who answered the Cadmean phone now didn't say whether he was a secretary or a butler or a son, but he came back on the line finally and told me Mr. Cadmean would be happy to see me; right away would be fine.

Then I called Susan, though I felt guilty phoning her home, and she told me she was coming over to my place tonight after going to a bridal shower because we couldn't meet tomorrow. Tomorrow, two days early, Lawry was coming home. I said again I really thought she and I should take some time to think things over, and she said she was coming anyhow. I said I was tired, and she said, "Good. You can be passive," and laughed.

I tried the former police captain, Walter Stanhope, long distance again. I'd been trying during the day first to find out his phone number on Ocracoke Island, then to reach him. This time, just as I was hanging up, he answered. He answered like a man who didn't expect to get phone calls unless somebody had died. His voice had an unused, rusted sound, and he said very little except to repeat an inflectionless, indifferent "okay." On the spur of the moment, I decided not to explain until we met why I wanted to talk to him. Instead, I said I was coming out to the Outer Banks to fish and just wanted to pass along Hiram Davies's regards, and maybe pick up some tips about what fish were running.

Stanhope said, "It's January."

"I like surf casting in winter. Truth is, I'm trying to get away from things in Hillston."

"Okay. Up to you."

I told him I'd call tomorrow after the ferry ride.

"Up to you," he said again, and hung up.

My stomach had knotted and was rumbling from hunger. I ate three Tums tablets and tried to call Susan back to say I had to leave town, but now no one answered. I picked up the silver letter opener she'd given me and absentmindedly pricked blood from the palm of my hand.

Across the room, the insignia on the back of my father's old chair said LUX ET VERITAS. He had believed in both. Cuddy Mangum believed in luck. Sister Resurrection and Joanna Cadmean believed in voices. Perhaps because for a short time I'd heard voices, too, they made as much sense to me as truth, light, and luck: I had an impulse to call Joanna Cadmean.

Professor Briggs Cadmean answered the phone at the lake house.

"How's Mrs. Cadmean feeling?"

"Fine. She's up here with me now; would you like to talk with her?"

"In that tower? How'd she get up there?"

"I helped her. She thought it'd be interesting to look through the telescope."

"I have to go out of town tomorrow," I explained. "If anybody asks to see her that you don't know, or even if you do know them, stick around, all right? And would you let me know who it was?"

"Is something wrong?"

"Probably not. If Senator Dollard gets in touch with her—"

"He called this evening."

"What did he want?"

"I don't know. He talked to Joanna."

"Put her on."

"What's the matter?"

"Probably nothing. I'm sorry. Let me speak to your aunt, please."

"Joanna isn't my aunt. You forget my father's patriarchal persistence. She's my sister-in-law. I have brothers in their fifties."

Joanna Cadmean came on the phone, her voice as peaceful as a hypnotist's. Rowell Dollard, she said, had called and spoken to her abusively, had charged her with insanity ("Not the first time I've heard that, of course."), and had told her never to come to me again with her delusions.

"Did he threaten you?"

"He said, 'I won't let you do this to me.' Is that what you mean?"

When she again refused to move into town, I suggested she invite some friend over during the hours Briggs had to be away, and she promised she would. For one thing, two strangers, who'd read Bubba Percy's newspaper article, had already come out to the lodge to ask her to tell them where their runaway teenage son was living and why he had left them. "I'm going out to Hatteras to see Walter Stanhope, Mrs. Cadmean. About Bainton Ames. Do you remember him?"

There was a long pause.

Finally she said, "I don't think that will serve much purpose, do you? After all these years, surely there's not going to be anything he can tell you."

"Well, the old story is that Dollard pushed Stanhope into resigning over a series of bungled investigations. I'm wondering if it was really because he had gotten onto something about Ames's death. Obviously he's got no stake in protecting the senator."

Another pause, then she spoke slowly. "Perhaps. But digging up the past? I don't think it's necessary."

"I don't understand. I thought that's what we were trying to do."

"I confess, I used to be rather frightened of Captain Stanhope when I was young. I don't think he liked having me around much. Even then he seemed to me a very dissatisfied man."

I said, "So am I." I meant about the case, but she said, "Yes, I think so. You have your mother's eyes, but in yours there's a dark rim around the iris."

"Pardon?"

"Midnight blue. Very dark. May I say something, Justin? Let

go. You aren't to blame."

"Pardon? Blame for what? What did my mother say to you?"

"She didn't say anything." There was a mild small laugh. "Don't forget, I'm the crazy psychic. I always say weird things. Thank you for worrying about me." She said good-bye.

•   •   •

Down in the garage, Lieutenant Etham Foster was stooped over unlocking his car parked in the space next to mine. I said, "It's only 8:30. What's your family going to say seeing you so early?" Then I realized I didn't know whether Etham had a family or not. He had never spoken of anything but the problem under the lens.

His sheepskin coat hung on his nearly seven-foot frame, like beach moss on a tall winter tree. He said, "What they always tell me, 'It's in the oven, heat it up.'"

This was more of a response than I'd expected, and it led me to say, "Give me a second, Etham. Let me ask you something. Wouldn't you figure if you got hit on the head in a powerboat with side rails, you'd fall down *in* the boat, not over the side?"

"No idea. Never been in a powerboat."

I pulled myself up on the hood of my Austin so I wouldn't break my neck trying to talk to him. "So, what's your guess, did a robber kill Mrs. Rowell Dollard?"

"Not paid to guess, that's your department."

"He knows he can't hock those coins. They're too rare."

"Like you said before, he could already have the buyer set. Could be something else he wanted; something you don't even know about. Nobody knew she had it but her."

I tossed up my car keys and caught them. "That's good. Nobody but her, and *him*. Like a diary."

"She jots the killer's name down?"

"Maybe it was already in there."

This time when I tossed the keys, his big hand flicked out, and they disappeared inside it. He said, "Your mind's racing," and threw them back. Bending himself into his car seat, he added, "I heard you just sprang Jessie Webster on your own hook. You got something on Captain Fulcher you can lean against when he finds out?"

"Yeah. A big family. Is that Sister Resurrection's name, Jessie Webster?"

"Oh, yeah, most of us have real names too. Did you think it was my momma named me Doctor Dunk-it?"

"She might have. My momma named me Justin Bartholomew Savile the Fifth and called me Little Jay until my father died."

"You're still pretty short," he said, and I'm fairly certain he came close to almost smiling.

While I was watching Foster drive off, Cuddy came out carrying Martha Mitchell and digging in the pockets of his bright blue parka for the keys to the new white Oldsmobile he kept parked as far from everybody else's cars as he could manage. He told me that Davies had found out for us that of the four textiles executives who'd eaten dinner with Bainton Ames the night he died, two were themselves now dead, one was on vacation, and the last (a Mr. Bogue, now president of the synthetics division of Bette Gray Corporation in Atlanta), could be reached at his office tomorrow.

"I need my own theory," Cuddy said. "You got yours, and now it looks like V.D.'s getting the idea you and Sister Resurrection pulled the murder off together."

Finally he tugged out of his jeans the big key chain that had long been a department joke, for on it were a rabbit's foot, a miniature horseshoe, and a Saint Christopher's medal. ("Don't laugh. Chairman Ho had nothing to match it," he'd say.) The dirty snow of the rabbit fur had a Junior Mint stuck to it. "Well, time for Cudberth R. Mangum, M.A.—as my momma once had my name listed in the Hillston phone book—to go slosh around on that water bed you think's so trashy, and flip on the tube. Martha and I got twenty-two channels of big tits and loud guns waiting. I just love it." He cocked his head at me. "You ought to get home too. You don't look so good. You're starting to look like that painting of yours."

"I didn't get any sleep. Or food."

"You coulda had a pizza instead of those whiskeys. Go set a couple of your sideboards on fire, warm up your house, and crawl in bed. Go home, hear me?"

"I'm going to see Briggs Cadmean."

"Which?"

"The fat, bald one."

"Good."

"Then I'm going to Hatteras."

"You're going off the deep end is where you're going."

I opened my car door. "That's all right, I know the way back."

Cuddy shook his head as he walked away.

Chapter 10

I couldn't see the Cadmean mansion until I was waiting, freezing, at its door, and what I saw then was about a block's worth of bricks the color of old blood. Between the house and the street spread a high fence of iron spears; the long front lawn was an arboretum crowded with immense trees, each labeled with a metal plate and all indigenous to North Carolina—balsam fir, longleaf pine, palmetto, spruce; the largest were two magnolias and a red maple with the frayed ropes of an old swing hanging from it. The side of the house was sheltered by a tall latticework walkway, twisted with thick, leafless grapevines. It made sense that a little girl growing up here would have started looking out at the stars; she certainly couldn't have seen much sun down below. The big rooms inside were as crowded and dark with wood as the yard. Wood inlaid floors and wood paneling were crammed with wood chests, paintings, Spanish chairs, and marquetry tables. Clearly the strangely empty spaces of the lake lodge had been the girl Briggs's reaction to this press of pudding-thick furniture.

To come upon old Mr. Cadmean's own beaming manner in the midst of this gloom was disconcerting. The elderly black housekeeper who'd finally come to the door led me up a dark, boxed stairway into a pink children's room wallpapered with Victorian Mother Goose characters. There, like a mammoth stuffed walrus in a toy shop, Cadmean lay on the floor in a disheveled gray suit, his huge arthritic hand working delicately to place a mirror into the bedroom of an extravagant dollhouse. Crouched beside him, a beautifully dressed little girl, five or six years old, watched with her lips pursed critically.

"There!" he rumbled. "Now Miss Mandy can look and see how pretty she is." He stood a miniature doll in front of the little mirror.

"Grandpa. I told you already. Her name's Two Eight."

"Honey, Two Eight's no kind of name for a sweet pretty lady. Let's call her Mandy, isn't that a nice name?"

"I don't like it," she said. "Now put this rug down right by the bed." With a peremptory point, the child handed him a doily.

"Mr. Cadmean. Sorry to intrude."

His enormous head swung around as he lumbered up onto all fours. "Oh, Justin, there you are. Good. Come on in here and meet one of my grandchildren. This is Rebecca Kay Cadmean. Isn't she just as pretty as a little doll?" He beamed.

"Grandpa. Be quiet." The child smacked her palm over his mouth.

I'd seen Cadmean rarely since going away to school, but as a boy, I'd sat in the pew behind him in church and watched the back of his big, already bald head bounce in time to the hymns, his big hand swipe at a fly or float an envelope into the collection plate. Now, at eighty, he looked almost exactly the same— the fat still solid, the shrewd yellow eyes lidded as a bear's, the small lips curling (like his daughter Briggs's, like the granddaughter's, too), the same habit of patting his stiff bent fingers up against the shave of his cheek, making a rhythmic sound of the scrape.

Rebecca was there for a visit; her mother, who'd brought her, was off somewhere tonight, probably at the same bridal shower as Susan Whetstone. The inner circle wasn't large. We left Rebecca rearranging the doll's furniture as the old housekeeper complained querulously that she couldn't get the child to mind her.

Rebecca agreed. "I'm not going to bed, no way, José."

"Regina Tyrannosaura," Cadmean chuckled at me, and

brought me back down the stairs, one hand clenched on the rail, one arm tucked through mine, like a barge hooking itself to a tugboat. "Let's us go down to the office. Can you believe this weather! Had to get two fellows from C&W to come over to unfreeze my kitchen pipes. In Hillston!"

A fire blazed under a walnut-paneled mantel, gleamed on brown leather armchairs and on a spaniel sleeping by the hearth. The office, as he called it, looked more like a small museum honoring the history of C&W Textile Industries. On its walls were engravings of the earlier factories, framed citations and advertisements for hosiery, underwear, and work clothes ("The Men Who Built America Were Wearing Cadmean Jeans"), and photographs, and maps of Hillston. On tables sat scale models of textile machines.

Mr. Cadmean banged at the fire with another log from his woodstack, then opened a liquor cabinet in the wall next to the mantel. Over the mantel was an oil painting of an unhappily beautiful woman in a formal summer gown with a little copper-haired girl leaning against her side, their hands clasped on the woman's billowing lap.

"You don't drink, do you, son?" he asked, holding up a bottle.

"Yes, sir, I'll have a whiskey, if you don't mind."

His mouth, fleshy and pretty as Henry the Eighth's, made a kissing noise. "Allrighty. I had the notion I heard you weren't a drinker."

"I don't drink as much."

His laugh rumbled. "I don't do anything as much." The glass he handed me was cut with a Gothic C. "And I hate it." He clicked his glass to mine. "I certainly do hate it. You know who that is?" I was looking up at the portrait.

"Your daughter, Briggs, isn't it?"

His breath rumbled slowly through his huge body. "That's right. Her and her mother. A sweet, sweet lady." He shuffled closer to the painting, the fire reddening his scalp. "Just that pretty, too. She was my favorite of all I married. Last and favorite. I hated like hell to lose that woman. I'll tell you this, I

just about killed your daddy when he told me she was dead. Yep."
He shook his ice hard. "I took him by the coat, I didn't even
know I was doing it, and just about killed him."

"He was her surgeon?"

"That's right. Brain tumor." Cadmean squatted, his stiff joints
popping like the fire, and dropped in another log. "Well, hell, poor
fellow, his eyes got big as milk saucers. I apologized later on. But I
couldn't believe she'd left me, like *that*." He snapped his fingers one
sharp crack, then turned around and chuckled. "Your poor old
daddy said, 'I'm having you thrown right out of this hospital!' Said,
'You can't hold on to her by *shouting* at her all night long!' I said,
'Try   it,
Savile, go ahead. I paid for this goddamn hospital!' Yep, I was in a
state. Have a seat, son."

"How old was Briggs?"

"Baby was ten years old." An ice cube cracked in his teeth.
"Hardheaded as a mule." He sank himself down in the big leather
armchair across from mine. "I hear Baby and Joanna drug you out
there to the lake on some foolishness."

"Rowell told you?"

"That's right." Ice bulged one cheek, then the other. "What
do you think of my daughter? Mighty pretty, isn't she? And
sharper than a serpent's tooth and always was."

"She doesn't appear to like me."

Ice glistened between his small, even teeth when he grinned.
"Me either, son. You find me a man she does like that's not some
Communist hothead or a damn pansy covered with ivy, and I'll
kiss his fanny. Baby's done everything she could to spite me.
Everything in the world she could think of. Because I didn't have
the heart to come down hard. She was like a little doll left me of
her mother."

His fire was so hot I had to shove my chair back; beads of
sweat were running down the line of my chin. I said, "She seems
to be doing all right. A college teacher."

"Oh, shit, college teacher. That's right. Had to go up North to
school, just had to go. Like a fool I let her, and the next thing I get's

a telegram, a *telegram*, telling me she's married some scrawny little New York anarchist Jew she met at some rally to stop folks like me from making money. Eighteen years old, and she sends me a god-damn telegram. I couldn't believe it!" He pawed at his vest pocket and pulled out a cigar, the tip of which he poked into the fire.

"I heard they divorced."

A long, low growl bubbled past his lips.

"She's lived out at the lake since she came home?"

After Cadmean puffed his cigar tip bright red; he stared at it in disgust. "It's hers," he grumbled. "Like a fool I gave it to her mother and like a fool her mother left it to her. Baby hasn't set foot in her own home for five years and seven months. My own flesh!" His fat palm thudded on his chest like a priest's mea culpa, except Mr. Cadmean had given no indication that he believed the cause of their estrangement lay in him. Then, with an abrupt jerk, his body shook off the subject as he pushed out of his chair and refilled our drinks. "Hell. Women! I truly love women. Truly love them all, big, little, white, and black. I love textiles," his twisted forefinger waved around at the room's evidence, "and I love women, certainly do. Any kind of woman except a loose one. That sort I've got no use for. None. I had two divorces with women that turned out to have the morals of a cat, and both times I was as shocked as a baby with his finger in a light socket. How come you aren't married? I had half a dozen kids when I was your age."

"I lived with a woman in law school I thought about marrying; she decided she'd rather be a judge."

"You don't *think* about marrying. You *do* it. Judge, hunh? Shit. Isn't that good whiskey? Here, hold this." He handed me his drink while he prodded the fire into a roar. "Justin, let me tell you this. Women are going wrong. Men, shit, men are nothing but rooting pigs and hogs grabbing in slime, always will be. But women, now. Women are the dream, son. The grail. They're what the war's about, what you're beating your brains to get your snoot out of the swill and look up at something better for. Come to America and what do you see? That's right, you see the Statue of Liberty. Hunh? A woman. A dream. A whore's worse than the worst man ever lived on this earth, because a whore's fallen down from the *sky*, son." He raised his huge arm and let it plummet to his side; then he reached over and took back his glass. "From the sky. Am I right?"

"I like women too."

His yellow eyes squinted at me. "You just have to remember one thing. One thing. They're all crazy."

"Is your daughter-in-law, Joanna?"

"As a loon!" His head nestled back and forth in the tufted leather. "Now, tell me, is that what you wanted to see me about? If Joanna was nuts? You could have saved yourself some gas." He leaned across and patted the air as he would have patted my knee if he could have reached it. "But I'm appreciative you came out in all this ice, because I am truly enjoying our talk. Folks think I'm some kind of misanthrope or senile fool or whatever they think because I've got so I can't abide standing around someplace with no chairs listening to a bunch of phony society goats suck up to me and nose their hands in my pockets. I'll do what I do. And one thing I'll do is take care of my own. Because I love my own." He grinned. "And I enjoy talking to my own on a winter's evening. What did Joanna want?"

"She has a feeling about who killed Cloris Dollard. She thinks it's connected to Bainton Ames's death."

"That so? Crazy as a loon" He threw his cigar into the fire. "Who does she think did it?"

"I'd rather not say."

He nodded. "Never any sense repeating geese gabble. I thought you already caught your man. Some East Hillston jailbird."

"No, sir. Actually, Mr. Cadmean, what I wanted to ask you about was some technical papers of Bainton Ames's that Mrs. Dollard brought over here to you shortly before her death. Do you have them?"

The old man pushed his forefinger in at the bubble of his lips. "What papers?"

"As I understand it, designs for something called an inertial loom."

Cadmean looked at his drink, then put it down. "No, I haven't had a talk with that woman in years, except in a goddamn reception line. What are you getting at, son?"

I told him what my mother had said about Cloris making the copies, and he went to straighten a picture frame on the wall. "Well, hell, I don't know what Peggy thought she heard about these papers, but either she didn't hear right or Cloris changed her fool mind. Cloris wouldn't know a technical paper if she blew her nose on it, besides. And Bainton Ames worked for me 'til he died, you know. Whatever he designed, I'd already have anyhow." He crooked his fingers now. "You know what this is? Come over here."

Behind glass on a mat was a collection of faded checks with an etching of the original Cadmean brick mill printed at the top. He tapped the glass. "This is real currency. See what they say? Three dollars. Twenty dollars. The Cadmean Company. Back before the War between the States, we paid with our own money! Printed it and paid with it. Just as good as a bank's. Better! Who the hell knows you at a bank? What do you want some old papers of Bainton's for?"

"I just wonder if there's some connection between them and Cloris's death."

His palm played its scraping rhythm on his wide cheek. "Oh, shit, son. That doesn't make a lick of sense. Bainton's been dead for almost twenty years."

"Well, almost fifteen. Are you sure you can't recall any such conversation with Cloris Dollard? Do you know what textiles people might be interested in papers like that? Mother said some men asked Cloris about them."

"I can recall plenty of conversations with Cloris. That woman ran her mouth like an automatic bobbin loader. But none worth listening to and none anytime lately." He tapped an old photograph. "Now, look at that factory there. Isn't that the prettiest thing you ever saw? It broke my heart to have to pull that building down. And you know what? We found some old gold-shafts under the foundations! Isn't that something? Going back to colonial times. You heard how people say they were sitting on a gold mine!" His chortle stopped as suddenly as it began. "Now my board's trying to stick up something so ugly it wears down my soul to have to look at it every day."

His arm crooked in mine, he led me around the room as if it were an art gallery. I stopped at a photograph of Cadmean shaking hands with Franklin Roosevelt. "Parachutes," he told me. "Yep. Overnight, we switched from ladies' hose to parachutes, working our fannies off, and here's Mister Frank thanking me personally. All his boys were jumping out into thin air hanging on to my parachute. Wearing my B.V.D.s." His laugh rumbled down along the arm pressed against mine.

"You go in everyday, then?"

"Damn right I do. Day I don't, send the hearse and start digging a big hole. I love work. Work is love, son. Am I right? I love every shuttle, every bolt, every man and woman that works at that place. Hell, some of them have been with me longer than you've breathed the air. Loyalty. That's what work is. I'll tell you one thing. I've got a bunch of young snots pushing at me now, who, you unscrew their heads and you're looking at a goddamn computer inside. Shit, telling me we got to cut back and lay off and get out of cotton. Conglomerating this and importing that and union diddling and tax diddling. That's not C&W. *This* is C&W," he tapped first at an old magazine advertisement claiming that a boy who'd walked barefoot to school had built a factory that now put socks on America's feet, and then at a photograph of a dozen women, half of them black, on an assembly line, each face turned obediently to the camera. "Whites and Negroes, sitting side by side! So listen here, don't say I'm against progress, because that's a lie." He steered me to a complicated model on a table by the wall. "You're wondering about Bainton Ames? Bainton Ames was progress. And I grabbed him like *that*." His fingers snapped. "I didn't like the icy son of a bitch, but I grabbed him. I bet you don't anymore know what this is here than those young deal makers like Lawry Whetstone who wouldn't know a shuttle if they got their balls caught in one."

"It's a loom."

"That's right. What kind?"

I shrugged. "Did Bainton Ames design it?"

"He did. Yep. He did indeed, right before he got himself drowned. This pretty thing was our first high-speed shuttleless loom. A rapier loom." He shoved the miniature steel rods in and out on the model. "You know what a shuttle loom does? Shakes. Breaks down. Uses a lot of power. Makes a lot of noise. People go deaf. I went stone-deaf myself once for six goddamn months. Shuttleless loom purrs like a little kitty, compared. No, I don't hate progress, long as it's real. But I'll tell you this. Most of it's a pile of acetate." With a grinning nod, he rubbed my wool jacket cuff between his fingers. "I'm back on my goddamn coal, now the Arabs are squatting on our faces, and if I'd had my way, I'd never gone off it. Nice jacket. I bet you understand me, Justin."

"Well, I don't like acetate." I sat back down with the drink I'd left on the table by my chair.

"You don't look like you do. See this?" He tapped a piece of the model. "Bobbin loader. Used to be, back in the sixteenth, seventeenth century, when they wound the yarn around a skein, they called it a bottom. I saw you in that Shakespeare play. Just had to go, with so many of my acquaintances in the cast. Bottom the Weaver. I noticed that, an old weaver like myself. You did a good job; I laughed out loud. That Bottom, he got himself into quite a fix, didn't he? Hunh?"

"Yes, sir, he had a most rare vision. I thought I saw you in the audience. Maybe Cloris mentioned something to you there?"

"Never saw her. That place was jam-packed, wasn't it! Hillston sticks by its own."

"Why'd you hate Bainton Ames, Mr. Cadmean?"

"I didn't hate him."

"I'm sorry. I understood you to say you did just now."

"I didn't like him. There was nothing in his head but ideas." Bent over behind the display table, Cadmean kept working the moving parts of the loom model. "Ideas are fine, truly fine, on paper, but they don't warm the bed. A man who lives by ideas will betray his brother. 'But a faithful man who can find?' Proverbs."

The tiny machine clicked and rattled. Squinting over it, he looked at me awhile. "Leave all this old mess alone, son. Bainton's dead and gone. And Cloris left her fool house open to trash and trash got in and killed her. It's happening more now. Even down here. I hate it. But she's buried now. You let Rowell get through his troubles in peace. He's got a primary coming up before long. You're his people."

The fire was hot on the side of my face; I loosened my tie. "I work for the same state as he does, sir. I realize he has a primary. But I have a murder."

Cadmean stopped the loom suddenly with his palm and came slowly back toward the fire, his small lips puffing in and out. "Let me say something. Everybody's got a little shit on their shoes, son. Everybody. People like us don't track it into the parlor and wipe it on the rugs. That's all. You know what I mean?" His stiffened fingers reached across me, picked up my glass, and held it in front of me.

I knew what he meant.

"Now, you excuse me. I've got to go see about that little princess I'm baby-sitting. What do you want to bet she's no more sleeping than a hoot owl? Selma'll bring you your coat. Truly nice seeing you again. You look like your daddy. Take care driving on that ice, now."

Shuffling past, his fingers squeezed an instant into my shoulder, then ruffled the back of my hair. I couldn't imagine how his hand could be so cold in that room. The fire spat back when I flung my ice at it.

Chapter 11

Oh, I knew what he meant. He meant all the things that our kind of people were too polite to say in Hillston—just as they had been too polite to say Cloris was not faithful to Bainton Ames.

He meant me to translate his parting remark out of the code. "You look like your daddy. Take care driving on that ice, now." He meant me to think about my car accident on Catawba Drive in the snow six years ago, the accident that had brought on my father's second stroke.

"I thought I heard you didn't drink" was code too.

He meant me to remember I was a Hillston Dollard, blood kin to men of high degree, and I was bound in a circle of courtesy, and I was closely guarded there.

Just as my mother's family, when they arranged to have rescinded my expulsion from a New England prep school, never let it be said in Hillston that I'd been expelled for getting a girl intoxicated and keeping her out all night.

And when I dreamt and drank away my college years, Dollards arranged to degrade an arrest for drunken driving to a speeding ticket, and they never told Hillston I had a drinking problem; they said the late sixties were demented.

And when drinking got to be the only dream I cared about—being a dream of magnificent swaggering prerogative, coarse and bountiful, unshackling me from my future and pillaging my days like a corsair—my people never told Hillston my problem had gotten worse.

And when I dreamt to hear voices uncivil as the times, when ghosts dashed against my windows and whispered to me, when ghosts could fly faster than I could floor the car, my people told Hillston I was too ill to accept my ROTC commission. They did not say that the pleasant Blue Ridge Mountains hospital to which they'd taken me boarded only those addicted like myself to the heedless seductions of drink.

A year later when they came to take me home, we all kept on keeping silence. Only my younger brother, Vaughan, said openly that grief over my commitment had caused my father's first stroke, and Vaughan, everyone knew, cared nothing for Hillston, or even the state. Whenever I'd complained to Rowell, "Pick on Vaughan. Let *him* go into politics," Rowell had impatiently frowned. "He's not a Piedmont man. It's got to be you, Jay. All Kip has is daughters. And I don't have anyone. There's just you." Whenever I said to my preoccupied father, "Please get Uncle Rowell off my back," he told me, "Shrug your shoulders. He'll fall off."

I went to the law school where Rowell arranged to have me admitted.

And two years after that, certainly no one let it be said that drink had made me crash the car while driving my father home from a Christmas party. They blamed it on the snow. And when, in the spring, my father died, Rowell brought me down from the Blue Ridge Mountains hospital to which I'd been sent, so I could stand with my people at my father's grave.

And Rowell stood with me. Even when I struck him for whispering there by the grave what I knew was true. Even when I insisted on living in Hillston as something no Dollard had ever been. For they had been college men and lawyers, and even some of them drinkers, and some more or less mad, and most had held public office. But none had ever been public officers, in so individual a sense.

Like my psychiatrists, my people had among themselves their theories about why I wanted to spend my time with criminals. My mother's cousin the attorney general wondered if alcohol had given me a taste for gaudy violence. My mother's older brother U.S. Senator Kip thought I'd read too many books. Her younger brother State Senator Rowell said I needed time 'til ambition took root.

But no one said anything to Hillston. People not in the circle had no idea I'd had a "really serious problem," much less that all my pastimes—playing the piano, painting pictures, refinishing furniture, putting on plays—were hobbies I'd developed in a sanitorium, were habits to replace habits.

Because I said nothing either, not even to Cuddy Mangum, who probably thought my mother's people had pulled the requisite strings to keep me from going off to jail or war, whereas I'd simply on my own gone off a different deep end. Which is what I meant when I told Cuddy there in the parking lot that I knew the way back.

To Mangum, in the beginning, my joining the police was only another of my social pastimes. My arrival at my first homicide in white tie and tails (I'd come to the victim's house directly from the town's Charity Ball) led him to conclude I'd cast myself as the inspector in a drawing room romance, a mystery novel.

But I had chosen detection carefully. In college I had studied classics, electing to learn about the distant past because I had known so long so much of a closer past, had been told since childhood so much of what my future would be: it would be the family business, public office. When Rowell decided his ambitions for me would have to be postponed ("After the mountains, you're too vulnerable for courtroom law, and you can forget running for office anytime soon. We're going to have to wait a good ten years to fade this mess."), when Rowell decided to wait, he told me that in the interim I had two choices—I could go into business law, or I could accept a position on his staff.

But I chose public office. I chose the police.

Ironically, it was a remark of Rowell's at my father's grave that confirmed my desire. He said, "What you've done grieves me, but I can't say it surprises me. I was a solicitor too long for anything to surprise me. In that building, there're no mysteries in the end."

After my training, I was rushed through promotions because that's what Captain Fulcher thought the Dollards wanted him to do. And I knew they wouldn't tell Fulcher anything different. They had to hold me up out of the mud, because I was wrapped in the flag of their name.

I had never wanted to be a lawyer. I didn't want to prosecute crime, or to defend it. I simply wanted to solve the mystery. I wanted to pull down my visor and on a common field ride to where mystery contracted to an instant, like the *crack*! of splintering wood, where no one knows from what castles the jousters have come, and justice is a blind queen on a dais who cannot see the coats of arms on their shields.

Detection was to me a knight, whereas law was only a squire to my people. A loyal, discreet British butler. And I had read enough mysteries to know how often the butler turns out in the end to be the villain.

What Mr. Briggs Cadmean meant me to remember was that I was indebted to that butler's discretion, nevertheless. I had been sheltered by his family service. When Cadmean reached over my chair and held up before my face my empty whiskey glass and didn't say a thing, he meant that when I had come home from what my family referred to only as "the mountains," the circle had stood by me, in a ring. And they expected that courtesy returned.

Rowell liked to make speeches to me. "You have a duty to this family. You have inherited a sacred trust, and that is the honor of serving your state. Don't you feel that, Jay?"

Well, now I did.

Chapter 12

"Listen here, Lieutenant. Whatever your name is, y'all got no right to come in here and harass me! They could fire my ass, called off the line by the police like that in front of everybody and his goddamn brother. Y'all think just because I'm nobody and a woman, it's open season on Charlene Pope. First Mangum, now you. And you really want to do something for me, you get that baby Preston's big brothers off my back. I don't belong to the goddamn Popes!"

"Savile."

"What?"

"My name is Lieutenant Savile."

"Listen, right this minute, far as I care your name's Lieutenant Shithead, and I don't care if you think I think so either."

Charlene and I were having our talk inside a Plexiglas cubicle from which her elderly shift manager observed the floor; he'd politely offered to go away to buy himself a Coca-Cola.

It was almost ten o'clock at night by the time I'd left my empty glass beside Mr. Cadmean's models and driven across Hillston to stand here looking at the originals. Beyond the window the great hall of machines kept whirring and clattering, even at this hour, blending, carding, combing. Fed by their workers, the huge looms tirelessly kept weaving Cadmean's cloth.

Charlene (her bleached white-yellow hair pulled back in a

ponytail, and wearing a smock over jeans and an orange mohair sweater) was in the same mood I'd seen her in on Maple Street. Now she also had purplish pouches under her eyes and a large scab in the corner of her lip.

Suggesting she sit down, which she wouldn't, and offering her a cigarette, I said, "I'm not trying to harass you."

"Sure, what do you call this? I smoke my own." She proved it by pulling a pack of Marlboros from her pocket and flicking her plastic lighter on in front of the match I was holding out.

"I'm trying to find out why you'd called us yesterday and said your husband was responsible for the fight at By-Ways Massage."

"You tell me," she mumbled.

"Does that mean you wish you hadn't?"

She shot a fast stream of smoke out of the side of her mouth; she was watching the men and women moving about in the plant beyond the glass, as if she thought one of them might suddenly turn on us with a machine gun.

I said, "One thing I can assume is, you wanted us to come over there and see that silverware. There're easier ways to leave your husband, aren't there, than getting him arrested for murder?"

"Don't you start saying I did things when I didn't do them."

"What things didn't you do?" I noticed a man with prematurely white hair and a black moustache staring in at us as he went by. Turning her back, Charlene hurried to stand on the other side of a tall file cabinet where she wouldn't be as easily seen.

I said, "Well, we don't much think Preston committed the Dollard murder."

"Fine." She was smoking faster than anyone I'd ever seen, holding in her other hand the little tin ashtray she'd snatched off the desk quick as a shoplifter. "I could care less, but fine."

"Or the robbery. We don't think his big brothers did it either."

"How come? Don't put it past them, mister. I could tell you stuff about the Pope boys." She went back to her cigarette.

"No doubt. Incidentally, what was it you took out of your

husband's bureau drawer when you left on the spur of the moment in the van yesterday?"

Veins bulged in her neck "Did that prick tell you I stole that money?! Goddamn him! That was $675 *I won* in Atlantic City on our vacation, and we were saving to go to the beach this summer and it belonged to me and I took it. And just let me see Preston tell me to my face I stole that money!"

"Preston didn't say you stole it."

Confused, she stopped her cigarette midway to her mouth, and I pointed at it. "Did you know, somebody who didn't live at the Dollards' left a Marlboro butt in their driveway the night of the murder?"

She blustered, "So?"

"Mrs. Pope, was that silverware there in the bathroom when you got to the house, or did you put it there? And, if you put it there—for whatever marital cause—where did you find it?"

She stabbed out her cigarette hard enough to shred it. "I'm not talking to you. I never killed a fucking fly. Y'all are off the wall."

Outside, the throbbing noise was endlessly the same. I came around to lean on the metal desk across from her. "Nobody said you killed anyone. Your, I guess, former sister-in-law Paula told us—"

"Paula!" With a jerk she knocked two cigarettes out of her pack; they fell to the floor and I picked them up.

"Paula told us she doesn't think you knew that silver belonged to the victim."

Charlene let me light her cigarette this time; her eyes, black as pea coal, had gotten glittery with fear.

I said, "I wonder if you came across the silver and figured it was stolen and thought you'd get back at Preston for causes I can certainly imagine. If you don't want to come talk to him, all right. All I want from you, Charlene, is where you got the sacks."

She was whispering now. "I never saw it."

"That's not true, is it? I should and will pull you in, Charlene, but I don't want to have to."

"Please. Listen to me, Mr. Savile. Y'all got to leave me alone! Please! I never saw it."

"Do you remember where you were the night Mrs. Dollard was killed? A week ago Sunday?"

Her teeth scraping across her lower lip pulled the scab off so a line of blood the color of her lipstick started down her chin. "I was with a guy called Luster Hudson the whole night, out at his place. Preston and I are separated. Luster can tell you I was there. He's in the mountains now, delivering some dogs."

"You remember that far back? I don't think I would."

"Listen, you sure would if the fucking cops—" She stopped and wiped at the blood with her fingers. I handed her the hand-kerchief in my jacket pocket; she just stared at it. I said, "Here," and took it and pressed it against her mouth.

Behind us the door swung open, and a small young woman with short red curls and hostile blue eyes charged in yelling, "What's going on here?" Above her jeans she wore a too-large sweatshirt with a badge identifying her as a union representative named Alice "Red" MacLeod. She couldn't have been more than five one or two in her work boots, but she seemed to be under the impression that she was a great deal larger as she elbowed me away from Charlene and repeated, "Okay, what are you doing to her?"

I said, "Pardon me, I'm Detective Lieutenant Savile. I'm speaking here with Mrs. Pope."

"What about?" In her huge sweatshirt she looked like a high school student on a stage crew, but there was none of that swollen adolescent blankness in her attractive face.

"It doesn't concern," I looked down at her badge, "the union."

She spun around. "What happened to your mouth, Charlene?"

Dabbing with the handkerchief, Charlene shook her head, her eyes miserable. "Nothing. I bit my lip. He's just asking me about Preston, the guy I'm married to, but, like I told you, I moved out. It's nothing, honest. Okay?" She looked at me. "Can I go now? Give me a break, how 'bout. Okay?"

Alice MacLeod said, "You don't have to talk to him, do you

understand?" Then she wheeled on me, leading with her tilted chin. "What do you want with her?"

"I don't see how it's your business, Miss…MacLeod."

"Anything on my floor on my shift is my business." Her voice was North Carolina, but farther west, mountain sharp.

I said, "Mrs. Pope, the best thing you can do for yourself, listen to me, is cooperate with us voluntarily."

Miss MacLeod pulled Charlene away by the arm. "Do you want a lawyer?" Charlene shook her head no.

Going to the door, I told Charlene, "We're finished for now. If you don't think I'm trying to help, wait 'til you meet my chief."

She nodded, without meaning it, and I left.

I'd gotten all the way outside and was tugging the collar of my overcoat up over my ears to start the walk past all the railcars and trucks bringing Cadmean raw fibers to weave and taking what he wove away to sell, and past all the hundreds of cars his workers had bought with the money he paid them for making him so much more; I was still standing there staring up at the disinterested stars his daughter studied when I was jabbed in the back by the fingers of Alice "Red" MacLeod, who still wanted to know what was going on.

Her breath clouded around her face, one of those British schoolchild faces, freckled milk, one of those faces brought over from Scotland's Highlands by vanquished followers of Bonnie Prince Charlie, a stubborn fighter's face. "Is Charlene in trouble?"

"She has information involving a murder."

"What murder?"

"Mrs. Rowell Dollard's."

She sucked in the cold air.

"Yes. The best advice you can give her is to tell us what she knows."

"She's scared out of her wits."

"Of what?"

"What do you think?! Of you. What's your name again?" It was not a friendly question.

"Savile. Justin Savile." I took off my glove, found my wallet,

and showed her my identification, which she examined stu-
diously. I said, "You're going to freeze out here. Would you like to
step back inside and I'll explain, if you're really interested in
helping Mrs. Pope."

"Tell me here."

I told her that Preston was being held for possession of stolen
property thought to be connected with the homicide. She listened, frowning up at me, her fists balled under her crossed arms.
"Okay," she nodded when I finished, "I'm going to talk to her."
She spun away, then back around. "Sorry I jumped down your
throat. I don't like cops."

"Why not? We're workers too."

"Depends on what you're working for."

"Mind if I ask, is Red a political nickname, or does it refer to
your hair?"

She studied my face.

I smiled. "Or your temper?"

A puff of air blew from her mouth. "All three," she said.
"Bye." And was gone.

Behind me the lights of C&W spread across the night like a
small town. Old buildings, saw-toothed at their roofs with
skylights, hooked on to the new, flat buildings Cadmean didn't
like. Other buildings were under construction, their scaffolding
bare. Huge spider-tanks were painted pretty colors and inscribed
with their owners' initials. High smokestacks spit out the waste
of power.

Spits up fire, I thought. Sister Resurrection's fiery furnace.
The dragon spits up fire, and down it rain.

Chapter 13

It was only when I opened the door to my house and realized that all the lights were on and the heat had been turned up to at least eighty and the shower was running hard up on the top floor, that I remembered that Susan Whetstone had told me she was coming over. My rapping on the tub's glass stall, as she had apparently not been able to hear me until then, in no way appeared to startle her. The impenetrability of Susan's composure continued to impress me. Both hands still lathering her hair, she said, "Where have you been?"

I said, "You sound like we're married, which only you are."

She said, "I can't hear you," and slid the door closed.

I walked back down to the first floor and ate two jars of yogurt and a muffin while reading the day's junk mail and bills. I swallowed four aspirin with some tomato juice, turned down the thermostat, picked up Susan's mink coat, which was spread open on my couch, and her suede boots, which were toppled over in the middle of the rug; I shut off the lights, climbed the stairs, took off my clothes, and went back into the bathroom. The shower didn't stop until I was brushing my teeth, staring at the red streaks in my eyes.

"Where have you been?" Susan said again.

"Working on the Dollard case. Tell me again, Susan. You can't think of *anything* else Cloris said to you that night at the play except she had a stomachache?"

"Oh, for God's sake, her stomach hurt, and wasn't the play good, and when was Lawry coming back."

"Why'd she ask that?"

"Well, she didn't know about us, if that's what you mean. She said something like, 'I think he's annoyed with me.'"

"Annoyed with you?"

"No, with her."

"Why?"

"Who knows, sugar."

"Was she upset, was she joking, was—"

"Not back to this again! I told you, she just yapped at me a few seconds at intermission." Susan dropped the balled-up washcloth to the floor of the tub. "Who cares."

"Seems to me the conversation would stick in your mind a little better considering the woman was murdered an hour later."

"Considering I'm not a psychic, how was I supposed to know that at the time!" Susan stood in the tub, appraising with thumb and forefinger the girth of her waist, the hang of her upper arm, the firmness of her inner thigh. Her thighs were brown and slender. All of a sudden, they reminded me, distressingly reminded me of one hot August afternoon—it must have been the summer of my seventh birthday—when my father was driving us up to Virginia to visit his parents. I had yielded the front seat to my younger brother, Vaughan, and had fallen asleep in the back; my head on my mother's lap, at the cuff of her red-and-white-dotted shorts. I woke up, my cheek sticky hot and stuck to the skin of her thighs. My eyes opened on a magnified world of gold-haired skin, whose tanning over the summer months had been an assiduous undertaking, discussed at length. ("Oh, Rowell, here you are already black as a berry, and I still look like an absolute fish!") I pulled away from her thigh and saw the red imprint I'd left, and the stain of saliva that darkened her shorts. Then I lay my head down again in a new place, shivering with the pleasure of the cool, sinking soft flesh. I kept still there, pretending sleep, until finally she carefully slid away from me, and picked up her book.

In the bathroom mirror, now, my adult face flushed with blood. I couldn't stand here naked, looking at a naked woman, and thinking about my mother's thighs. I turned away to wrap a towel around me. Susan was saying, "All right? I talked to Lawry right after I got home from the play. There was a message on the service to call him back and I did. All right? I said, 'Why does Cloris Dollard think you're mad at her?' and he said he had no idea why. All right?"

"I'm trying to find out what her *mood* was, Susan."

"Her mood! What's her mood got to do with a robber hitting her over the head? Justin, come on. Anyhow, why are *we* talking about it? I know, it's your *job*. You better watch out, sugar. You're beginning to remind me of my husband."

I rinsed out my mouth and spat. "I thought you loved Lawry."

"I do...So, I thought you had this case all solved. People were saying at Patty's tonight that they heard on the news you all had arrested some creep. Meanwhile, that has got to be the most boring party I've gone to in a month." She tilted her head, twisting water from her hair.

Susan had tan blond hair and sharp, beautiful bones and a perfected body kept the same tan blond color throughout the year by regular exposure to various beaches. Naked, she looked as if she were wearing a white bikini. I handed her one towel that she wrapped around her hair, and one that she tucked in over her breasts.

She said, "Laurel Fanshaw got blotto and puked all over the kitchen."

"Charming."

"She said she'd felt like throwing up ever since she got pregnant. She gave Patty a gorgeous Marimekko wall hanging. I don't see why they wanted to give Patty another bridal shower anyhow; she's already been divorced twice."

"If Patty has a tag sale, let me know, would you? I could use some more pillows and sheets."

"Funny man. And how's your funny partner, Mr. Mangum, the good ole boy? Were you two out together, I bet?"

"Cuddy's fine. Why are you so hostile, you think maybe we've gone gay?"

"Funny, funny. That man is so fake."

"Are you kidding?"

"Oh, forget it." She stepped out of the tub.

I said, "I'm sorry I'm so late. Pardon, pardon, pardon. How come you're washing your hair?"

"I always wash my hair when I'm bored. If you're going to stay out all night playing cops and robbers, why don't you get a TV?"

"I don't like the way they look."

She shoved me away from the sink, leaned into the mirror, and said with the mildest pretense of sincerity, "I'll tell you what I don't like, sugar. I don't like the way I look."

"Oh, yes, you do."

"Joel gave Patty a face-lift for an engagement present."

I stepped behind her. "We aren't engaged."

She pressed her fingers against both cheekbones and pulled the tan blond skin tightly outward. Next to the thin platinum wedding band, the big square diamond flashed in the mirror. We both watched my hands come around and loosen the tuck in the towel until it fell away, and move over her breasts, and then downward until they dropped below the mirror's view. In a while she rubbed back against me, her hands still on her face.

She said, "I thought you were going to be passive."

"I am."

"Oh? Something didn't get the message." She looked at me looking at her.

I took her hands and pulled them down around my back and held with mine. We watched her nipples harden.

"I can't stay too long," she said. "I've got to go out to the airport early. Lawry's in a vile mood about some stupid business deal of his falling through, or something."

"I'm going to have to call him about this Cloris thing."

"Is it midnight?" Susan asked.

"No."

"Do you know if it is or not?"

"No."

"I want to leave by midnight," Susan said.

"All right."

"You should have come back sooner."

"Do you want me to hurry?" I pulled the towel from her hair.

•   •   •

When I woke up it was nearly four and she was gone and all the downstairs lights were on. I woke up because of another nightmare. I was playing Bottom again, that final Sunday performance of A *Midsummer Night's Dream* at the Hillston Playhouse, a small downtown movie theater we'd bought when it went out of business like most of the stores around it. We were doing the scene in the woods in which my cronies run off terrified after Puck transforms me, changes my head into that of a donkey, and Titania, the fairy queen, takes me off to her bower to make love. Titania, to my disturbed surprise, was Joanna Cadmean. Old Mr. Cadmean sat in the front row, his bent fingers patting the knee of his daughter Briggs, whose hair had been cut to short curls, like those of the C&W union representative, Alice MacLeod. Then it was intermission, and I saw Susan in her mink, standing in the aisle—as I'd actually noticed her that Sunday—talking to Cloris Dollard. Now Cloris was braced on Mrs. Cadmean's crutches, and her nose was crushed in. Everyone pretended not to notice. Then I was in a car with Rowell Dollard, driving through the snowstorm back to the theater—I don't know why I'd left—and trying frantically to get back there before intermission ended and I had to be onstage. I had on Bottom's homespun costume, and the huge papier-mâché ass's head lay on the car seat between us.

In the dream, I knew I had to keep out of my mind my certainty that Rowell had killed both Bainton Ames and, fifteen years later, his own wife. I knew that if I couldn't void my brain of my suspicion, Rowell would be able to read it there and he would try to kill me, too. But the more I fought to erase the images, the more vividly detailed they grew, like an iris opening in a film. Beside me in his black overcoat, his face from the snow-light as silver as his hair, Rowell kept staring, harder and harder, into the side of my head, until I could feel he was seeing through my skull to what was in there. I sped up, pushing the accelerator to the floor, but nothing changed. The tires floated on in snow so deep all boundaries of the road had disappeared, and the front beams shone out at a white, endless lake, billowing around us. Then we were sliding down the long hill and into the curve at the bottom of Catawba Drive, near my parents' home, the hill that had been in my dreams before. And down there, in the middle of the intersection, black rags in the snow, stood Sister Resurrection. Rowell snatched up the papier-mâché mask and jammed it over my head, and, blinded, I still saw the tree like the ghost of a giant looming. Then I heard the siren coming, as years ago I had heard it, waiting in the crashed car, holding my father.

I woke up uncovered and shivering. In the bathroom two white towels lay strewn on the floor. I showered to warm myself enough to stop shaking; then I put on some jeans and a heavy sweater and an old leather jacket. My tackle box, and rod and reel, were out on the back porch, icy to the touch.

When I pulled into a truck stop for breakfast an hour later, the world was still dark, and the woodpeckers and mockingbirds were just beginning to complain about the weather.

Chapter 14
Wednesday, January 19

A poor pink started to wash through that blue-black opulence the sky has just before dawn, and I had come out of the little hills of the Piedmont and passed in the night with the trucks the scruffy little egg and hog farms, ramshackle in leached fields, the red clay and cornstubble and piney gum woods, lifelong familiar and so invisible. East on 64, I was sloping down into coastal lowlands, into flat earth fallow for the bright-leaf tobacco, and for cotton, the old king—throneless since Appomattox—like Bonnie Prince Charlie after Culloden Moor.

Wind was cold off the bright water of Albemarle Sound. Far away the wakes of menhaden and shrimp boats already ruffled, luring the white gulls down. As I met the ocean, the sun blew up over the horizon line, and I turned south off the causeway into the wilderness preserve of the Outer Banks. I was alone on the road for an hour. Shafts of sea oats bowed shaking to a sandy highway that warned of the dangers of leaving it.

Waiting for the ferry to Ocracoke, I fell asleep, and fell back asleep, crossing. And missed again the wild horses, descended from the mounts of buccaneers, that summer after summer I had never seen, though straining beside my father against the boat rail, binoculars at my eyes, gulls screeching in and out of view.

Ocracoke Island, to which former Hillston police captain Walter Stanhope had retreated, hides across rough water at the farthermost tip of Cape Hatteras. These are the barrier isles, spars of sand dunes, some heaped high as a hundred feet, all forever shifting, the longest stretch of wild shore on the eastern coast. Between the Banks and North Carolina are tangled inlets, too shallow and too dangerous for successful commerce, haunts of pirates and blockade-runners. Between the Banks and England swells the gray sea. They call Cape Hatteras the Graveyard of the Atlantic and boast of over two thousand ships buried there, lost beneath the foaming spume.

When I was a boy vacationing on the Banks, my father walked me out along the bleached plank fence on Diamond Shoals to see the black-and-white-striped lighthouse, the tallest in the country, the placard bragged. And yet, still defeated by the flat sea below, where rusted smokestacks and iron masts speared out of the waves like the arms of monsters drowning. From the Indies with Verrazano, conquistadors came here, and fled, conquered by swamp and the secret spars. It was in through the Outer Banks, past Kitty Hawk, that Sir Walter Raleigh—who wore clothes of silver and in one ear a pearl, and who dared more gorgeous madness than other men could dream—sent his colonists, saying, "Bring me gold to win back the favor of my queen." At Manteo the earthworks of their fort are tended grass now.

The Outer Banks are a place to risk a dare, like courting queens, like flying; or a place for men, like Blackbeard, who need to be lost. Walter Stanhope, namesake of Elizabeth's captain, had come back here to retire, among people still holding, in their faint Devonshire accents, a distant memory of Raleigh's extravagant dream. Stanhope had come to lose himself here at the edge of the sea.

After some inquiries and some wandering among the narrow, sand-dusted streets, I finally found him, around eleven, out on the island's oceanside, surf casting on the empty beach, a tin bucket wedged in the sand beside him.

"Mr. Stanhope?"

"Right."

"Sorry to startle you. You're not an easy man to find."

"Savile?" He was a thin, reedy man in his late sixties, with a gaunt wrinkled face brown as my gloves. He wore a beat-up winter police jacket and frayed green rubber waders, a crumpled hat and sunglasses, and he clamped in his teeth an empty cob pipe.

"Yes, sir. Justin Savile. Thanks for seeing me. Regards from Hiram Davies. He's well."

"Okay." Pulling down his sunglasses, he looked at me as if people were something foreign and their purposes dubious.

According to Davies, Walter Stanhope had lived alone since his wife had died; he had no other family. He was a native Banker, who actually had worked in Hillston only a decade. It was said that old Briggs Cadmean had been instrumental in maneuvering the city council into first appointing Stanhope Hillston's police chief. What had impressed Cadmean was the man's management of a flare of civil rights disorders in the small coastal town where he was then chief. Stanhope's Hillston predecessor had a brutish reputation that, in Cadmean's view, might give our city a bad name. It had been under that earlier man's regime that Sister Resurrection's son had been killed.

"Drive okay?" Stanhope finally asked and pushed his sunglasses back up over his eyes.

"Fine. Catch anything?"

"Some." In the bucket two croakers floated.

"Kind of windy out here, isn't it?" I wiped at the tears already chapping my cheeks.

"I guess. Not so bad. Where're you staying?"

"I don't know yet."

The glasses came down again. His eyes were the color of the sea, an impenetrable grayish green. "Lotta places are closed up."

"I noticed. Looks like you lost some houses, too. I haven't been out on the Banks in a while."

Stanhope reeled in, unhooked some kelp from his lure, and cast. The whir of his bright brass spinning reel sent the line on and on over the ruffled waves. "Lost some in '73. Whole place'll be gone before long. The Army Corps of Engineers finally quit messing with those dune walls. Guess they figured they'd poured enough millions into the water. Hurricane tides sucked the groins right out." He stopped with a brusque rasp of his throat, as if surprised to hear his voice go on so long.

I said, "Amazing the sanguinity of the human race, rebuilding on sand that already slid out from under you."

"Amazing the stupidity."

By now I was close to a jog trying to stamp the sting from my numb toes. "Can I buy you a cup of coffee, Mr. Stanhope? Maybe some lunch?"

"I've got coffee at home…You really come here to fish?"

"Well, sir, to tell you the truth, I hoped you wouldn't mind if I asked you a few questions about the old days in Hillston, and maybe get some advice. Had you heard that Rowell Dollard's wife was murdered January the ninth?"

His teeth, tannic colored, shifted back and forth on the pipe's cracked stem. "During a robbery, I heard on the news."

"I'm not so sure I think so."

"I'm retired, fifteen years." He reeled in a few turns on his line. "I don't much like looking back. What did Hiram say to you about me?"

"He said your dismissal was totally unjustified." It was totally untrue that Davies had said so, but nevertheless accurate. I added, "A lot of people in Hillston say you were a good chief, Mr. Stanhope. I think maybe too good."

"I don't much like Hillston," he said, and added a few minutes later, "You work under Van Fulcher?"

"Out from under him, as much as I can. We're not friendly."

The sunglasses were pulled back down the hawked nose. "I used to work under some of your Dollard kin. We weren't friendly."

"Fulcher's better at going along with them than you and I are."

I interpreted his tug on his line as a nod. He reeled in,

hooked the lure to the guide, and said, "I live over there." Then he picked up the bucket and started toward the weedy dunes behind us, his feet sliding easily as he climbed through the soft sand. Silently we went past a collapsing plank walkway now jutting out into the air, the shore beneath it shifted away; its house's windows were boarded, and old beer cans, left doubtless by partying trespassers, cluttered the porch. "That your car?"

I nodded. "Can I leave it there?"

"Up to you. Austin 100-4?"

"Yes, sir. Used to be a nice green."

"Parts must cost a penny."

"About what I earn."

Far down the beach, scouted by furtive sandpipers, a solitary man moved with a metal detector, as though he had been condemned by Herculean gods to sweep clean the coast. "Stupid," said Stanhope when I pointed at the treasure hunter.

I said, "Well, they used to claim Blackbeard's gold's still buried out here somewhere in the dunes near where he was killed."

"There's no gold." It seemed to be a flat statement about life. Stanhope motioned me across the deserted highway and down a narrow cul-de-sac, dark with moss-hung oaks and yaupon.

"There might be," I called ahead. "Things get buried."

His head jerked back at the sea. "Lot of gold out *there*." He said "out" as my father—a Tidewater Virginian, had—"oot." Clearing his throat through a voice that sounded, as it had on the phone, rusty from lack of use, he added, "At Nags Head, men used to tie lanterns to their horses' necks, drive them along the coast dunes. To trick the ships into smashing on the reefs. They'd loot the wrecks after the drowned washed off." He stopped at the door of a tiny bleached-wood cottage and added, "I don't much like people," and took his tackle and bucket inside.

Like its owner, Stanhope's living room was brown and worn and sparse: no pictures, few books. There were, however, long shelves of records, and as soon as he came in, he put on a stack of LPs. The first was string music, perhaps Mozart, very quiet. He also had an old television, with rabbit ears covered by foil, that sat beneath a cabinet neatly lined with conch shells whose shiny peach inner curls were the brightest color in the room.

He asked hoarsely, "Are you hungry?"

I admitted that I was, and at a small Formica table in the small kitchen, we ate the fish chowder he had left to warm on the stove top.

Telling Stanhope about the Cloris Dollard case was not easy, as he did not so much as nod, but I faltered on through his silence until I'd explained everything I'd come to suspect. Then we sat there without a word. Finally he said, "You want that coffee?"

"Thank you, yes. You see, if Cloris found out Rowell had killed to get her—and maybe he also had done something under the table about selling Bainton Ames's textile shares to Whetstone, I don't know—but if she was going to *leave* him, or *expose* him... Rowell wants to go to Washington, Mr. Stanhope. One more term in the state senate's all, and then he wants to run for a congressional seat. If he had to choose between Cloris and his ambition..."

Stanhope combed the pipestem through thin, brown hair paler than his scalp. "Killed the woman he killed for?" he asked in the inflectionless tone his voice kept.

"Well, this is fifteen years later. Maybe they were fighting and he did it accidentally. Panicked and tried to make it look like a robbery."

"Why'd he come home from the capital in the middle of the night to accidentally kill her?"

"Maybe she called him in Raleigh; she said she was leaving the play because of a stomachache, but maybe she was actually upset about Rowell. The last time he can confirm his whereabouts in Raleigh is 9:50. That's plenty of time for him to drive to Hillston. We've got 'til midnight for time of death."

Stanhope brushed his eyebrows. "Joanna Cadmean put this notion in your head?"

"No, not really."

"Okay."

"Look, you know yourself Mrs. Cadmean's not just some kind of nut. I've been back to the newspaper files on her. The bodies in the basement like that! She's listed as instrumental in the solving of at least thirty crimes."

He poured coffee from a tin pot. "I don't deny it," he said. "Dollard got a lot of use out of that girl."

"She thinks you didn't like her."

"Didn't."

"Why?"

Staring into his empty pipe bowl, he shook his head. "No reason. Superstition. Gut."

"Did Rowell dislike her? I mean, then? He hates her now."

Stanhope looked at me for a while. Finally, he cleared his throat with a cough. "I'll say it this way. How that girl Joanna felt about her…what she called visions, was how she felt about Rowell Dollard. She'd do anything he'd have wanted her to."

I stopped looking for a match and took the cigarette out of my mouth. "She was infatuated with him?" I didn't want to believe this.

As he handed me his box of kitchen matches, Stanhope nodded. "He was taking her to bed. Not that it's anybody's business."

"Are you sure? It's hard to believe. What happened?"

"Hard to believe of him?"

"Of her. Well, she was, what, only eighteen?" I saw Mrs. Cadmean at the top of his stairs. *Hello, Rowell*. "What happened?"

"Guess it ended. Dollard got promoted, moved to Raleigh."

"How do you know they were lovers?"

"People talk. People are sloppy. People are spiteful. And I'm a good cop. Was." He slid his pipe along his teeth.

Leaning over toward him, I said, "Tell me. You *did* think Dollard might have killed Bainton Ames. Didn't you?"

Instead of answering, he dumped the two fish from his pail into the sink and started scraping their scales off.

I went on. "You think what I think, don't you? Rowell was in that boat, he pushed Ames out, and then swam to shore. He's an impatient, violent man. He wanted Cloris, and Ames wouldn't divorce her."

His palm on the fish, Stanhope carefully slit open its belly. "I considered it," he said.

"But couldn't prove it?"

His head shook no.

"Why consider it?"

"It's a long time ago, Mr. Savile."

"It's not since Cloris was murdered."

Stanhope wrapped his fish in foil and put them in the small refrigerator before he said, "Okay. Hiram told you I thought it. I did think it. That he *might* have. That he had motive and means. That's all. Okay, it puzzled me that Ames hadn't been in the boat when it hit. The skull contusion," he ran his long fingers through the back of his hair, "surprised me. Too deep and sharp to have happened in the water. Far back here on his head. He hit falling, should have hit landing on the boat floor."

"Yes! So how'd he get over the rail?"

"Lots of ways besides Dollard's pushing him. Accept that first off. But I knew about Dollard and Cloris Ames. And I knew Dollard was at the same restaurant as Ames the same night eating dinner."

"He was?"

Stanhope took his pipe off the window counter and sat back down. "He left his car in the lot overnight. I asked him why. He said there was a short in the ignition. There was."

"How'd he get home? He didn't live anywhere near the lake."

"I asked him. He said, a friend."

"Who?"

"I asked him. He said it didn't concern me."

"You couldn't find out?"

"I tried. But then," he stood up and took the cups, "I lost my job."

I lit a cigarette. "The coroner's report said one of the textiles men Ames had been talking to, the men from Georgia, thought he saw Ames walking with somebody toward the docks; I think the somebody was Rowell. But the man said he couldn't give any description."

"I had a talk later on with one of those Georgia guys. Hogue? Bogue?"

"Bogue. Impressive. How can you remember that?"

His eyes crinkled the deep crow's-feet around them. "It's a case sticks in my mind. Bogue was, all four were, close-mouthed about whatever business had been going on at this dinner. It was around the time there was a lot of tangle with pro-union activity in some of the textile mills. I figured they might have been up to Hillston about that, planning strategy. We had our hands full for a while. Back then old Cadmean was dead set against the union. Bainton Ames was dead set for it. On principle. Don't think he had much of a grasp of the politics one way or another. So I figured they were up talking strategy to Cadmean, and then Ames was just supposed to take them out and they'd smooth him over with a polite meal. Pine Hills Inn had rooms back then, they were staying the night." His throat rasped into a cough, and he stopped for a few minutes to rest his voice.

"Anyhow," he went on. "What I remember is this Bogue was itchy to know if we had some coin, some kind of rare gold piece he said Ames had brought over to the inn for him to look at. They both collected. This was a new acquisition Ames was excited about. Bogue said he'd looked at it again right before they split up outside, and Ames had put it back in a little envelope in his pants pocket. Bogue wanted to know, if we had it, could he buy it? His friend's just dead a day now. He wants to go see the widow about a coin."

I said, "So, you don't much like people?"

"Not many… Now, the coin wasn't on the body. I didn't see how it could have fallen out, unless Bainton dropped it outside on the dock or in the boat while he was fishing for his keys, and didn't notice. Not like him, though."

From the back of the house the phone rang. It surprised Stanhope, and frowning, he left the kitchen. What surprised me was that he had called Bainton Ames by his first name, and I was going to ask him how well they'd known each other, when he walked back into the room, his thin mouth working hard on the gnawed pipestem. He stared at me so seriously I thought perhaps he had been given news of someone's death. He said, "That was Mr. Briggs Cadmean on the phone. Wanting to know if you were here."

"What?"

"I figured, some kind of family emergency, so I said yes. But that wasn't it."

"How the hell did he know I was here? Hiram Davies! What did he want? Is he on the phone?"

"No." Stanhope went back into his living room and turned off his record player. I followed him. "He hung up. He wanted me to know—"

"I don't believe this!"

"He said you were set on stirring up some nonsense from the past that had nothing to do with the investigation."

Stanhope watched me pacing the little room.

"Said, fact that you'd come down here showed you'd gone haywire, he put it. Said he hated to say it, but you had a history of mental trouble."

"God damn it."

"Said I should calm you down. And just as well not mention he'd taken the trouble to call, for your family's sake. Just concerned about you."

We were facing each other across the kerosene heating stove that stood out from his wall. Finally I asked him, "Why'd you tell me, then? And why the hell did he think he could ask you to calm me down?"

"I owed him favors, he put it." Having said this in his flat tone, Stanhope returned to the bedroom. He came back clearing his throat repeatedly and carrying a scuffed black violin case. For a bizarre moment I thought he was bringing me the one that had belonged to my father, which I knew my mother still kept at home. Then he said, "You called up, I thought about it. I said, okay, come on. So. You came. I don't much like looking back."

He set the case down on the worn-smooth corduroy covers of his couch, and snapped open the clasps. "Long time ago, some of us used to play. Not much. Just a little on weekends. Bainton Ames and me."

I understood what he meant. "And my dad."

"Some. It was no big thing."

"I don't know if you knew. My dad died, some years back."

"Yes, I know." He closed the lid on the bright ruddy wood of the violin.

I sat down beside his coffee table; under its glass top, shells were carefully arranged on sand. I said, "I hope you aren't just agreeing that I'm on to something because you knew my father. And otherwise you'd think I was unbalanced too."

"No. But I wouldn't have let you come out. I think it's possible you're on to something. I don't think Mr. Cadmean would bother making a call if you weren't on to something. I just don't know what the something is. When somebody tells me, they hate to mention it, but they're disinterestedly eager to keep somebody else quiet, I wonder why. Where's the string tied? Motiveless benevolence?" He shook his head. "But you probably notice I'm not much on the species. Forty years, arresting them for hating each other and trying to grab whatever the other one's got—it's enough."

We sat listening to the kerosene bubble in the stove, and to the wind, and the tireless surf.

I said, "They can surprise you."

"Not enough. I stick to fish now."

I pointed at his shelf of records.

He nodded. "Yes. And to music. Music's just itself. No motives."

"People wrote it. People play it."

"It doesn't care who. Not a bit." As he stood up, he scratched his brown long hands through his hair. "You even bother to bring along any tackle?"

"It's out in the car." I smiled.

"If you want to, go get it," he said, and coughed. "There's a cove on Silver Lake I'll show you, down some; you might get a bass. Crankbait'll sometimes stir one up in winter. Up to you. They call you Justin now?"

"Pardon?"

"Used to call you Jay, didn't they? Seems like they called you Jay last time I saw you." He held the tan thin hand out at the height of his waist. "You ought to quit smoking," he added, and held out my coat.

Chapter 15

Before I left, my two-pound bass wrapped in foil, Walter Stanhope let me use his telephone to make some calls, which I charged to the department. Mr. Bogue of Bette Gray Corporation in Atlanta told me busily he couldn't possibly remember a conversation with Bainton Ames fifteen years ago, and thought it could hardly be relevant now, but he'd have his secretary send me a memorandum should anything come to mind. He said briskly that he still very much regretted the loss of Bainton Ames, and now, of Mrs. Dollard. And, yes, he had spoken to a police chief about the coin. He was sorry to hear others were missing now. If we recovered them, he would be interested in purchasing a few from the owner. The coin Ames had shown him fifteen years ago was, he recalled, an 1839 classic-head Liberty quarter eagle minted in Charlotte, North Carolina. It was a poor sister of the star of the Ames collection, an 1841 quarter eagle known as the "Little Princess" among numismatists, but still quite something to possess. He added that he'd lost another chance at just such a piece only two years ago at an auction in Washington, D.C., and concluded in a hurry, "Was that all?" I took down the name of the auction gallery.

Then I called Hillston to tell Cuddy I was going to stay overnight on the Banks. He told me to come back now. He said, "You know that wall in that Shakespeare play you were just in?

That wall you peeked through and the lion ate your girlfriend? That wall's about to fall on your head, old Mister Bottom. And it is the only thing between you and V.D.'s snapping teeth. I am in reference to that wall being your fancy kin and friends. They are falling off. Old Cadmean called up here."

"And Hiram told him where I was! God damn it."

"I jumped on Deacon Davies, but he didn't mean no harm. He got real peevish: yes, you told him not to mention it, but how was he to know that meant including not to Mr. *Briggs Cadmean* who had donated the very floor he was standing on! He thought maybe you meant don't mention it to *me*."

"God damn it."

"You already said that. What's with that fat old bald man? What'd you say to him last night? He must have hopped up and down on V.D. bad about your trying to string up Senator Dollard."

"I didn't say a word to Cadmean about Rowell."

"Well, something rubbed him wrong. You better come home. Old V.D.'s saying you may need some quick R and R, by which I mean Restraint and Roughing Up. Says you're bonkers and he's gonna have Dr. Ogilvey come see you."

"Oh, great."

"Um hum. There's more. Says Harriet Dale, our lady flatfoot flathead, told him she was 'scared' of you, the way you and Sister Resurrection were shooting the breeze on the same frequency downstairs yesterday. Listen here, General, when it gets so the only friends you got at headquarters are white trash and nigrahs, it's time to pucker and pick up the bugle, and I don't mean 'Charge!' As my daddy said after forty-two years on the line at C&W, 'Enough's enough.' And the truly bad news is Preston's told Fulcher he *did* pick up that silverware. Off the side of the road on Wade Boulevard around two in the morning the night of the murder. While out cruising for Charlene. He claims it caught his eye when he stopped for a red light and emptied out his brains into the ashtray. 'Those sacks must have fallen out of the killer's car,' he tells us. I'm real disappointed in Joe Lieberman. He's already talking plea bargaining for Preston. Fulcher's got

Ken Moize and the other justice boys hot to trot. Murder one. They're going for it."

"Where's Charlene?"

"Can't find her. We're looking."

"She might have gone after Hudson."

"The Great Smokies are great big."

"Well, who knows Hudson? Did he have any friends?"

"Let's not take time out for humor. Speaking of which, I'm going out now to eat supper at Ye Olde Pine Hills Inn. I'm trying to go suave, see, and I said to myself now where would old suave Savile take a girl? So what's good there? How's their pizza? I'm taking Briggs. I wanted you to be the first to know, in case you found out."

"Briggs?"

"Junior. The professor. I took six Valiums and called her up, and I think I heard her say yes."

"So why are you telling me?"

"On accounta your tone right now."

"She was supposed to stay with Joanna Cadmean."

"I'll talk to Mrs. Cadmean. Not to worry. I'll make her promise to lock up. Listen to this, I'm going to take over my basketball pool, and let her take a whing at it. She never saw a game in her life. But well, hell, why not? So get on back. Not that there's all that much we can do anyhow. If you see some fellows in white coats with a net on the front steps here, don't stop to chat."

"Could you start a check on the late-night gas stations on Raleigh Road? If Rowell drove back and forth twice that Sunday, maybe he got some gas, God willing."

"Savile, you are *stubborn*. Anybody else ever tell you that?"

"Rowell Dollard, for one. Constantly."

"Well, I hate to spit on your birthday candle, but you got about as much chance of pinning either one of those killings on him—I don't care if he's Jack the Ripper—as you got of getting Lunchbreak Whetstone to cook you three squares behind a picket fence. Adiós and happy holiday."

"What holiday?"

"Lawdy, Ashley, you don't know it's a state holiday? Today's General Lee's birthday! Yaahoooo! Shall we rise? We shall rise!"

I said, "Your jocularity is getting me down," and hung up. I felt too tired to drive for four hours. As it turned out, it took me closer to five. And it was 8:30 when I reached Hillston and changed clothes, and headed across town to C&W Textiles.

I was stubborn.

That I was stubborn had moved into familial myth long ago when, at age six, I'd trekked one night in cold rain to the home of a fellow first grader three miles away, whom I rightly believed had stolen my harmonica. That was, as it proved, my first case of detection, and one involving the police as well, for a patrol car had found me on North Hillston's winding roads, trudging, sodden, home to Catawba Drive with my harmonica.

That I was stubborn had kept me bloodied and facedown in mud through the autumns of junior high school, attempting to play the game of football, for which I had little talent and less bulk.

"No, you have your father's talents, and my character," my mother would say. "That's a Dollard will. We're all stubborn."

"Everybody in the state of North Carolina is stubborn!" was always my father's reply.

On vacations, to the beach or the mountains, the only times I remember his being so garrulous, my father would say (as furious drivers passed him on the shoulder, or waitresses refused to let him order what he wanted), "North Carolina is such an ornery state. Virginia may be stuck up. But North Carolina is stiff-necked. You won't give in, you won't give up, and you won't move out. Did you know, Jay, until recently, ninety-nine and a half percent of the people living in this state were *born* here, and the precious few of us that weren't are looked on with considerable suspicion?"

In proof, he would always point out that we claimed to be the first colony, even though we were a lost one; that our state was named after the only British monarch misguided enough to get his head chopped off (Charles I) and was half-settled by the crazed Highlanders who thought they could win that kingdom back for Charles III; that our president, Andrew Johnson, had been the only chief executive to get himself impeached; and that, in the seventeenth century, we had even been mad enough to declare war on Virginia!

My father would say, "The hornet's nest, that's what General Cornwallis called Carolina. Now, Virginia yields to no one in considered revolution, but, good Christ, you Tarheels rebel against polio vaccinations!"

"And proud of it," I would call from the car's backseat.

And Mother would add, "Our Edenton ladies had their tea party long before the bragging Bostonians, and what about our Culpepper rebels, and your great god Thomas Jefferson, sweetheart, did nothing but plagiarize our Mecklenburg Declaration of Independence!"

And beside me Vaughan would turn the pages of his horror comic book as Carolina cars swept in a rage around us, "First In Freedom" on their plates.

And in school I was taught that we were indeed a stubborn state: the first colony to vote to leave old England, the last to ratify the new constitution. In the Civil War, first we wouldn't secede, and then—though we lost more men than any other Southern state (and my mother, a Daughter of the Confederacy, could tell me the names of all those dead from whom I descended) and lost more men than this whole country lost in Vietnam—we wouldn't surrender, not until seventeen days after Appomattox. And for ten years after that, while Federal troops guarded farmland matted with weeds, we rankled, stiff-necked. And now on the front-bumper plate of Preston Pope's van rides a cartoon Johnny Reb, sword high, screaming, "Hell no! I won't surrender!"

And when, at fourteen, I broke my heart refusing to stop trying to date Patty Raiford, who was ostentatiously in love with a senior (the first of her many husbands), Mother would say to my father, "Little Jay comes by his stubbornness honestly. Honey, he's a Tarheel. My God, if I hadn't been a Tarheel, I would have let you just slip away back to that awful girl from Alexandria. Remember her? She had the biggest bosom you would ever want to see. I never did believe those breasts were real, were they?"

And my father would say with his soft smile, "Good Christ, Peggy, I haven't the faintest idea."

And Mother would lean around from the car's front seat and say to me, "Now, that's a Virginia gentleman, I want you to know. That's a Savile."

At my father's grave, Rowell Dollard had hugged his arm across my back. "You're a Dollard, Justin. I won't forget it. Don't you."

Chapter 16

Under the lights, coming around the curve onto the Hillston beltway, I noticed the tan Camaro behind me, and the image stirred that when I'd driven home, a tan Camaro had been parked across the street near the entrance to Frances Bush College. The car was still behind me after I took the C&W Textiles exit, and when I pulled into the Dot 'n' Dash, it went by at a crawl. I waited; in a few minutes the tan nose edged, bouncing, out from the side street behind the store.

My escort kept behind me as I passed through the chain link gates that hem in the town of Cadmean's mills. For five minutes I leisurely cruised up and down the long parking aisles, until finally the Camaro simply stopped in an open space behind me, and shut off its lights.

I reversed fast, slowed as I passed by, took down his plate numbers, and then continued on backward until I found a parking space.

Inside at the big board by the time clock, the driver of the Camaro walked by me without a look. Waiting for the elevator, he pulled off his orange John Deere cap and stuffed it in his mackintosh pocket. I remembered that combed-back white hair and the black moustache; last night out on the plant floor, he'd stared in at Charlene Pope long enough to make me remember.

The elderly division manager could tell me nothing about

Charlene Pope's present whereabouts; her future at C&W—if we were indeed thinking of arresting her—appeared to be in doubt. On the other hand, he was pleased to tell me about the floor's instructional supervisor and elected union representative, Alice "Red" MacLeod, once I had assured him that far from being under suspicion, Miss MacLeod had proved a model citizen of cooperation with the authorities. Flat in the face of his own disapproval, the man obviously liked her, and, fears allayed that her politics had brought her to grief, that she might have incited a workers' riot or kidnapped the governor, he let me know that "in spite of how it looks," Red was "a crackerjack," "a little steamroller," "smart as a whip," "sound as a dollar," and, in general, as industrious, reliable, and judicious as a socialistic union troublemaker, only twenty-nine and female, could conceivably be.

This time, instead of talking in an icy parking lot, she and I drank horrible coffee in an institutional lounge walled with vending machines. This time, instead of a sweatshirt, she wore an apple-green turtleneck, and instead of opening with "What's going on?" Red MacLeod whisked in and said, "Have you found Charlene? Hi."

"Hello. No. We have a car cruising the house where she's supposed to be staying. She didn't call in sick?"

"Nobody's seen her since last night. And look, last night after you left, she shut me out *fast*. She wouldn't talk and she sure wouldn't listen. All she would say was how people had to leave her alone."

Unspiraling a glutinous pastry, Red shook her head; the curls bounced like the ribbons my mother liked to coil with the edge of her scissors into bows on packages. "Look, I'm sorry I couldn't help out. If I get a chance, I'll try again. Okay? How long have you smoked so much?"

I threw onto the tray the empty matchbook inscribed PINE HILLS INN. I said, "Not long enough."

"It's hard to quit." Her eyes were earnest blue.

"But you managed, no doubt. Please don't brag about it."

"No brag. I can't smoke in class, so I had to quit. I miss it."

"Class?"

"Frances Bush. I go in the mornings. This is my last term. That's why I work the two-to-ten. A little old, but better late..." Having unwound her sugary concoction, she broke it into six even strands, pushed three toward me, and began eating the others.

"Somehow you don't look like your typical Busher," I said. "There's no brand name sewn to the rear of your jeans."

She took a count of four, staring at me, and then she smiled. "I get tuition," she explained. "The woman that founded the school, Miss Bush, worked this scholarship deal out with Cadmean Company, sometime back in the nineteenth century, for a woman working in the mills. They give one a year. Next fall I'm hoping to go to the university. To law school."

I cracked the edges of my styrofoam cup, bending them down like petals. "And then what? Do you know?"

"Sure!" Freckles of confectioners' sugar stuck on her Highlander chin. "I've always known. I want to be governor of North Carolina."

"Oh, my God."

"What's so funny!" Her freckled fists crossed under her arms.

"Nothing. That's what *I* was supposed to be. But you go on ahead."

"I will."

"Brush off your chin first."

Her hand flew up to her face and then back under her arm. I saw she bit her fingernails. I said, "Mind if I ask you where you live? Not on campus, do you?"

"Why?"

I ate one of the sticky strands. "Because I live across the street from Frances Bush. In the narrow brick house with the blue shutters?"

She didn't appear to know it. After thinking it over, she decided to say, "I just moved to Tuscarora, an apartment."

I smiled. "That's only two blocks away from me. You know, your old academic ancestors used to live in my house; it was sort of a Frances Bush dormitory annex. Sometimes I think I can hear them in the house giggling, and climbing the stairs in their high-button shoes." And sometimes I thought I could hear their ghosts in tears alone in iron narrow beds. I said, "Two blocks away. I'm glad to think I'm bound to have met you anyhow, even without Charlene."

She didn't speak, and we studied each other's eyes. Hers were serious and azure and very tired. Then I told her, "You're twenty-nine, you come from near Boone up in the mountains, you never call in sick, you work too hard, and you've never been married."

She snapped, "Not a crime, is it? Who told you?"

"An old gentleman admirer of yours. Your division manager. I'm thirty-four, I come from Hillston, I've got a law degree, and I'll trade it to you right now for the name of that man with the black moustache over there to your left—don't turn your head—by the wall phone, and I've never been married either."

"Do you call in sick a lot?" She bent down and retied her bootlace. "It's Ron Willis, why? Just a loader here at the plant. And a company stool. He's a creep. He's also a junkie."

"Any connection to Charlene? Relative? Friend of any of the Popes? Old boyfriend?"

"I don't know. Do you want me to find out?"

"Would you do that, Governor? And would you tell me, too, if you could join me for dinner tomorrow night?"

Her leather laces twice-tied, she straightened slowly back up in her chair. "I work nights, you notice?"

"Lunch?"

"I eat between classes. It's ten minutes."

"Are you planning on wending your way to the governor's mansion all alone? Or are you living with someone, or engaged or anything discouraging like that?"

"I'm just busy. Why do I have to be engaged?"

"Why do you always answer a question with a question?"

"Why do you ask so many?"

"I'm a detective."

"Why aren't you a lawyer if you've got a law degree?"

"How about breakfast, and I'll answer your first five

questions. I'll even throw in a few pointers about how to get to be governor."

"I'd appreciate it if you'd stop kidding me. Obviously, the idea is to work up in local politics."

"Who's kidding? I can be of assistance. I know an old family recipe for working up in local politics. My great-great-grandfather was a governor of this state. Eustache Dollard. And my great-grandfather."

She sat back. "For real?"

"As far as anyone could tell."

"Dollard. Like Senator Kip Dollard?"

With a paper napkin I rubbed the pastry crumbs from my fingers. "Don't forget the attorney general."

Her fist went to her mouth. "Oh! And Rowell Dollard. His wife; you must have known her. Look, I'm sorry."

"Thank you." I stacked our cups on the tray, and she pulled it from my hands and dumped the contents in the wastebin. She said, "Thanks for the coffee. I ought to get back on the floor. Let me know about Charlene, will you?" With the sudden celerity that was gradually startling me less, she turned back toward me. "Are you still holding her husband?"

I explained that in all probability Preston Pope would be indicted by the grand jury tomorrow.

"But Charlene says she doesn't care about that. What's *she* so scared of? Being charged as an accessory? Is she afraid of her husband, or his family, or what? Because she sure is scared."

I already knew what Charlene was afraid of. I knew because at the Rib House, Paula Burgwin had told me. Charlene was afraid of Luster Hudson.

Her fingers were waving in front of my face. "Hey!"

"Pardon?"

"I said, I eat breakfast at the Bush Street Diner. At seven thirty. That's probably too early for you. Bye." She waved the small freckled hand and spun away.

I caught up and walked her back down the twisting turns of concrete steps, each landing painted a different pastel color, and hurried with her along the hall toward the rattling whir of the indefatigable looms. Then, quite suddenly, she turned, startled, her lips parted. She asked, "Why are you whistling that?"

"Pardon?" In fact, I hadn't noticed that I was whistling anything although apparently I often did. "I don't know. Just popped into my head. I don't even know the name of it." It had been some slow, lamenting tune of which I could do only the first phrases, reiterative and dolorous.

"It's an old mountain ballad; it's 'Lass from the Low Country.' I can't tell you how weird this is. That was my grandfather's favorite song. He used to always whistle it like that." She looked at me solemnly. "I mean, I was thinking so much about him today. Today's the day he died, January nineteenth." Her Scottish face, pink and white and stubborn-chinned, went on staring up at me luminous in the neon light. "Do you do that a lot?" she asked.

"Apparently."

Slowly, she nodded at me, and vanished behind the steel doors.

I didn't move. I felt as if I were being nudged off a cliff, falling into a new self, impatiently telling the old, "Why do you keep saying you love Susan, when you don't?" I said aloud, "I don't love Susan." A man coming out the double doors beside me said, "If you say so, buddy." I grinned at him. "She doesn't love me, either." He called over his shoulder. "Join the club."

Chapter 17

It was 10:20 when Fulcher's call came. I'd gone home and decided against trying to warm the house, and had washed out the lipstick-smeared glass Susan had left on the kitchen table, and then had filled it with bourbon, and then had poured half back into the bottle.

Today I'd driven nine hours on little sleep; my skin was dry, flushed hot, and my bad leg with its chipped bone was hurting. I'd already called old Cadmean's house twice, even though Walter Stanhope's last words, delivered with his bluff hoarseness, had been a warning: "I were you, I'd be leery of the man with the strings. But up to you." Now I was told that Mr. Cadmean was in bed. I had a feeling it wasn't true. I also had a strong urge to call Joanna Cadmean, but decided that I was foolish to worry about her. Cuddy and Briggs were probably back there at the lodge now. My earlier jealousy of them seemed now a kind of gluttonous evasion; evidence that having invested so much time in wanting Susan, I had to feed any dissatisfaction with amorphous claims to other women. What a loss of my past to admit I didn't want to marry her at all, didn't even like her.

Back in the living room, and without turning on the lights, I sat at the piano and tried by touch in the dark to pick out the melody of "Lass from the Low Country," pick out the sad sweet Celtic grief that had come across the ocean with defeated dreamers.

Above the piano was framed my favorite of my father's land-scapes, a pencil-and-watercolors sketch of the Rappahannock River, banked with the tight-leaved, lime-green trees of early Virginia spring. I looked up at the picture and saw, reflected in its moon-silvered glass, Joanna Cadmean's face. Slowly she smiled. Then her face contracted, as if she were stepping backward, away from me. My heart loud, I spun around on the piano stool, but there was, of course, no one standing in the dark soundless room.

Outside, a car motor started. So vivid had been Joanna's image on the glass, that I leapt up, jarring my throbbing leg, and ran to the front door to see if she had somehow gotten in the house and were now leaving. The car had reached the corner, and was just turning into the intersection. It was the tan Camaro from C&W, Ron Willis's car; obviously he had been watching my house again. Spying for whom? Himself, the Popes, Cad-mean, Rowell? And why? To find out what I was finding out? Blackmail? It was even possible Fulcher had someone undercover trailing me, gathering violations of the rules manual to back him up when he told my family I was fired.

Dizzy, I closed the front door and leaned against it in the unlit foyer. Something white fluttered at the top of the stairs. Probably what I saw was a sliver of a neighbor's light, shining in through the white window curtain. What I thought I saw was Joanna Cadmean. This time she was standing at the edge of the second-story landing, one hand on the banister. Her hurt foot, unwrapped and bare, was held out in front of her as if she were about to step off into air. A veil of white gauze fell, like netting around a bed, from her head to her feet, enclosing her.

With her free hand she raised the gauze. And beneath it she was utterly naked. Pulling the cloth over her head, she flung it away, and it floated timelessly down the stairs toward me.

I shut my eyes quickly, but when I reopened them she was still there, still naked, moon-pale and gleaming. Then suddenly she raised both arms to me, as she had in my dream the night before, drawing me up to her embrace. But when her hand let go of the rail, she lost her balance and pitched forward and fell, soundlessly. I cried out loud, "Christ!" and plunged for the light switch. Illuminated, the hall shrank, the steps shortened to a finite number, and there was no one on them. I walked back to the piano and my drink.

And then at 10:20, I felt my way to the insistent phone by moonlight.

"This is Van Fulcher."

Too worn down to be much interested in the tirade I expected, I said only, "Yes."

"I just this second got the call from the station. I want you to get out to Pine Hills Lake right away. Mrs. Charles Cadmean just committed suicide."

The glass fell from my hand. "Joanna Cadmean?"

"I guess so. Yes, right. Mr. Cadmean's daughter-in-law. We've got to handle this right, Savile. I'm going to call Cadmean up right now. I'm at home. It's going to take me a while to get over there. Ambulance and squad car are on the way. I want you to—"

"She's dead?"

"Yes. I—"

"How?"

"Jumped from some kind of tower at the Cadmean lodge out there. You know where this place is?" Fulcher's voice was quick and high with excitement. He always found death exhilarating.

I asked, "Jumped? Who said jumped? Who called it in?"

"Well, it's tragic. Rowell Dollard. He's out there. After what he's already been through! Sergeant Davies took the call. The Senator's badly shaken, I guess. This is ticklish, Savile, it being the Senator who found her. You follow me? So, considering, we'll postpone getting into these stunts I know you've been pulling. And you get out there. Do you know where it is? Savile? Savile, are you listening to me?"

"Yes, I'm going. Good-bye." I picked up the pieces of broken glass as I waited for Etham Foster to answer the phone at the lab.

●　　●　　●

The moon kept ahead of me, a hard ball of light rising through the black smoke of the clouds, climbing over the black trees, heading for the back glassy lake. I could see up the hill, through all Cadmean's thicket of pines, the harsh blue and red patrol lights spinning. Their colors flickered on the silver Mercedes that was parked in the driveway, right in front of the porch steps. On the gravel beside the car, covered in white cloth, lay the shape that had brought all the lights, and brought the men who now knelt around it, like Magi at a moonlit creche.

"She's dead?" I asked.

"Oh, yeah." Dr. Richard Cohen, our medical examiner, looked up, bald, unshaven, exhausted. He was my age, with the pouched, weary eyes of a man much older. "Oh, yeah. Dead on impact. Her neck's broken." He pushed himself to his feet, and tapped the edge of the Mercedes' hood. There was a dent in it. And blood on it. Cohen's hand, pale and black-haired, vaulted in an arc from the car roof to the ground. "Like this. She hit here, see. Bounced off."

I pulled my collar up around my ears and closed the lapels over my neck. He nodded, blowing on his hands. "Cheesh, it's colder than a witch's pudendum. I might as well have stayed up in Brooklyn. And they told me this was the Sun Belt."

"Where's Dollard?"

"Lying down inside. I tried to give him a sedative, but he wouldn't take it."

"How did it happen?"

"According to him, she insisted he go up there to that tower with her." Cohen pointed over his head at the octagonal study on the roof of the high lodge. A shaft of light came out of the open door, silhouetting the rails of the balcony. "She doesn't say a word, *bam*, she opens that door. And over she goes. He couldn't get to her in time." Cohen's words floated on the cold air, like mist.

"She was on crutches."

"Right, they're up there, by the rail." He rubbed his eyes. "You knew her? So what was her problem?"

"What was he doing here?"

"Ask him. He told us she called him up, said she was upset and had to talk to him. I wish I'd brought a hat."

I gave him my tweed cap; it fell low on his narrow head. "How long's she been dead, Richard?"

"Less than an hour. You want to take a look? Then I'm headed home, okay? I've got a baby to walk."

Together we knelt down, and he tugged away the sheet and shook his head. "Good-looking for—what? Forty-two, three?"

"Forty-eight, I think."

"Looks younger. Well, okay, she hit here." He turned the head. "This tibula's broken." The arm was unnaturally twisted back. It was the hardest part of her to look at.

"Five ribs broken. Cheek's crushed. But what killed her was the neck. Instantaneous. It's a long drop."

I touched her hand; it still felt warmer than mine. "What's this?'" Her wrist was smeared with a small streak of fresh blood.

Cohen shrugged. "Scrape; it's nothing. This is interesting: see these faint vertical white streaks? Old scars. Too old really to tell much, but I wouldn't be surprised if she hadn't made a serious attempt way back when."

"What would you say, could anyone have survived that fall?"

He looked back up at the tower. "Improbable. But people have jumped out of planes and survived it. People do amazing things."

The moon loomed between the vaporing clouds and shone on the motionless face, cool and still, white except where blood gritted the skin. The gray steady eyes were open, unblinking, focused far beyond this moment. The handsome head was twisted to the side, and the line of its profile, Delphian, serene, was as untroubled and disinterested as stone. She wore a dress of thin white wool, too thin for such weather, and around her neck were milk-white pearls, and tight in the hand of her broken arm, a white silk scarf.

"Say, come on; can I go now, Savile?"

"Just a second, do you mind?"

Officer Pendergraph had gone back to the squad car; he was young, raw-faced, and energetically working against letting me see he was bothered by mortality. I said, "You all right, Wes?"

"Yes, sir, I'm fine."

"Was there a note?"

"No, sir. We didn't find one anyhow. We looked."

"Get a statement from Senator Dollard?"

"Dr. Cohen said leave him alone 'til you people came."

I told Pendergraph to call the station and try to hurry Foster's forensics crew and the photographer. The task relieved him. "They're on the way," he came back to tell me.

The murky vaulted space of the lodge's huge living room was reddened by the embers of a fire gleaming beneath the smooth embedded stones of the mammoth chimney. Beside the antler coatrack, the telephone was off its hook. I replaced it and called the Pine Hills Inn, too late to page Cuddy Mangum there. I reached him at his apartment in the River Rise complex where he'd taken Briggs. I told him not to bring her home, and told him why. Then I walked slowly through all the spare, chilly rooms, checking their windows. Nothing was out of order. Finally I sat down on the couch across from Cohen, who'd pulled one of the bent-willow chairs over to the fire embers and was resting his head in his hands, elbows to his knees. "Your hat's on the table in the front," he said.

"Richard, I want you to tell me two things. What's there to indicate a struggle? What's there to indicate she was pushed?"

His hands opened and his head came up, pale and thin above the wiry black border of hair. "Pushed? Who by? By Senator Dollard? Cheesh!" He nodded slowly. "Well, okay, sure. Somebody could have shoved her; that or jumped, fall would be about the same. Struggle? I didn't see any claw marks on his face, if that's the kind you mean. But who knows." He thought, yawned, and thought some more. "I'd say, pushed her from the back, *bam*, no warning, if he did it. Seems like I saw a snag kind of thing, down the dress front. Rail splinters probably. Headfirst, see." He pantomimed the motion and the fall. "Yeah, headfirst. Gutsy woman, if it was her idea. I'm going, all right with you? Fading fast here."

"You writing probable suicide, or what?"

"I'm writing broken neck for now. You can decide how it got started." He yawned through his words. "Goo'night "

The door to the first-floor bedroom was closed. I opened it. It had been her room. By moonlight I saw the basket of gifts from my mother, still untouched, on the dressing table. Over a rocking chair back were folded the sweater and plaid skirt I'd first seen Joanna Cadmean wearing.

"Justin?"

His voice came from a chair in the dark corner. Then Dollard stood and his silver hair moved into the light. "Justin? Did they take her away yet?" His face was ashy; his pupils black, distended to the rims of his eyes.

"No"

"Justin, *God*, this is dreadful! Dreadful!"

"Yes."

"I should have suspected…"

"Yes? Suspected what?"

"She was just standing there by the door, up there. Then she opened it. And went out on the balcony. And just *leaned*…and…then she was gone. Just gone! I *heard* it, Justin. My God! She was mad…mad. Completely insane!" His mouth opened, gulping air like a swimmer.

"Yes. You already told me she was insane." I stooped to the lamp and twisted the knob. At the click, Dollard stepped backward and covered his eyes. He wore all gray, gray sweater and gray slacks. He looked old. I said, "I'd like you to take me up to the study now and show me how it happened." I turned toward the door and let him pass through first. One of his hands kept rubbing up and down against his arm.

The door to the balcony was open, the tower was cold as outdoors. Its huge gray telescope shadowed a wall. The instrument pointed straight out across the black lake, pointed at the summer house that had once belonged to Bainton Ames. Silent in the room, we listened to a siren coming nearer.

As Dollard told me where she had stood and how she had moved, I stepped out onto the pine-plank balcony. Yellow crutches lay on its floor. Caught in the rough log rail were tiny threads of white wool. I leaned over. Far down, directly beneath me, gleamed the silver car, beside it the white motionless shape. Beyond the pines, from the foot of the hill, came headlights bouncing. Foster's men and the photographer. It was still too soon for Captain Fulcher. I walked back inside, pulling the door closed with the edge of my sweater.

"Have a seat, Rowell."

"We'll talk downstairs. It's too cold up here."

"In a minute, please. It *is* cold. Why were you and she up here?"

"She asked me. She insisted I look at something. Something to do with Cloris."

"What?"

"She never said." Rowell sank down in a chrome and black leather chair beside a desk heaped with papers and maps of the stars. He said, "I don't think there was anything to show me. She began talking wildly. And then, she jumped! For God's sake, can't we do this in the morning? I'm upset, Justin, God!"

Watching him, I lit a cigarette. I found a paper cup with some water in it to use as an ashtray. "Why were you over here at all?"

"She called me. I've already explained all this. She begged me to come."

"Why?"

He didn't answer.

"Why did you come?" I was speaking as softly as he was. "An insane woman you clearly dislike calls you up at night, and you drive all the way over here from North Hillston? Why?"

He still didn't answer, and I turned and leaned down to the telescope sight, and looked through it, into blackness. Pushing it upward, I saw, very clearly, cold and unblinking stars. "Why, Rowell?"

When I turned back to him, Dollard thrust his head forward, the shadows behind him moving. "It's a private matter."

"Not anymore."

His hand pressed hard against his arm. "Justin. She was hysterical. She was raving."

"So you tell me. I'm asking you, about what? What was she raving about before she just turned around on those crutches and pulled herself up and over the rail? In her raving, did she happen to say why she suddenly decided to commit suicide? While you stood and watched? Why did you happen to be here when the impulse just struck?"

He stood. "What's the matter with you, Justin? For God's sake!"

"Tell me why you came here."

"You're the one who let her into my house! Into Cloris's bedroom! You listened to her insane mutterings!"

"So did you, some years back. They weren't so insane then, if I recall your comments to the press."

For a long time, Rowell stared at me, his eyes protuberant, his face tight. Then he stepped quickly forward and touched his hand to my shoulder. "Justin, what I'm going to say is in absolute confidence. I want that understood."

I didn't speak, or move. Finally he stepped back and turned his eyes to the wall of books. His voice was broken by struggles with silence. "When I first knew Joanna Griffin, she was quite young. I was young. We were thrown together by her...involvement with, well, apparently, you have read all about that. She...fell in love with me, I guess you'd have to say. And, well, we had a brief, a *brief* relationship. I broke it off. She was not a stable person, even then. As she proved. Now, that was thirty decades ago! And now!" He stopped suddenly, walked back, and sat in the chair. "Now she comes back to Hillston and begins making incredible accusations. By involving you, she involves the police. And then she does this!" He stabbed his finger toward the balcony. "I don't know why!"

I said, "I don't believe you, Rowell."

When he raised his eyes, they were as glazy as marbles. "What?"

"I don't believe she committed suicide." I dropped the cigarette into the paper cup and listened while it hissed in the water. "I think you killed her."

"What did you say?"

"I said, you killed her."

He whispered at me, "You're as mad as she was. In God's name, why should you think such a thing?"

"Why?" I leaned against the books and watched him. "Because I know what her accusations were. Because she made them to me. And to Lieutenant Mangum. Because I know she believed, absolutely believed, that you are guilty of murder. You killed Bainton Ames in order to marry Cloris."

A dusty red mottled his cheeks, spreading up his face to where the vein in his temple jumped.

"I think she believed you killed Cloris too."

"Oh, my God!" All the color disappeared from his face.

"Because Mrs. Cadmean would never have 'asked' you to come over here, would never have 'asked' you to come up in this tower with her, because she was deathly afraid of you. Afraid you were going to kill *her*, too! That's right. So strong was her conviction that her sister-in-law came to my office Monday to tell me about it." As I went on, Dollard's face froze, like the face of a man put under a spell, "*Because*, Rowell, Lieutenant Mangum just told me he was over here this evening, and he spoke to Joanna Cadmean and she was not at all in a suicidal state. She was getting ready to go to bed. She had no intentions of inviting you over. And I think a check of the toll calls out of this house tonight is going to prove it."

Outside, light jumped up from the flash of the photographer's camera. I could feel Dollard's eyes frozen on me as I moved out of the room onto the balcony. Down on the driveway, I saw Foster crawl around the front of the Mercedes. I called, "Etham," and the willowy black man leapt to his feet and rammed his hands into the pockets of the sheepskin coat. "Yeah, what?"

I called down, "Thanks, okay? As soon as you're through, they can take her."

"Can I get up there?"

"Come on when you're ready."

Rowell sat rigid in the black chair, breathing with his mouth open.

He said, "Justin, why are you doing this to me? I don't understand."

"Why not? You had already called here yesterday and threatened the woman. You came here tonight, and forced, or cajoled, your way in. You ordered her to keep quiet about her premonitions, just as you just now ordered me to keep quiet about your having seduced her. And when she told you she *knew* you were guilty, you shoved her over the balcony. That's all. She probably climbed up here to try to escape you. I expect if she hadn't struck your car, you might have simply driven off and left her, assuming we'd call it an accident. Just as people thought Bainton Ames's drowning was an accident."

A noise came from Dollard's throat and his hands squeezed on the chrome armrests.

I said, "I'll try hard, but maybe I won't be able to prove you killed Ames. Just as Walter Stanhope wasn't able to prove it."

Startled, his head jerked up.

"But, Rowell, I *can* convict you of killing Joanna Cadmean. And I will."

"I really believe you mean this," he whispered. "You're serious! I'm your *family*." He came fast out of the chair, his voice louder. "After all, *all*, you've already done to hurt your mother, you can't mean to do this! This will kill her!"

"It will hurt her to hear what you've done, yes."

Suddenly he made a sound like a laugh, derisive and sharp. "This is insane! Justin, think! Even the accusation could do irreparable harm. And not only to me!" His indignant expression darkened abruptly and his face was purple. "I'm not listening to any more of this. This is intolerable! Nobody in his right mind would put up with it."

I stayed by the door as he strode toward me. I said, "If you'd wanted us to think it was an accident, you shouldn't have broken this chain."

His head swiveled to the brass door chain I held up, its catch twisted where it had been snapped from the bent lock. "And you shouldn't have wrenched her wrist," I said, "so hard you tore off her watch." I stepped over to the corner, bent down, and gathered the two pieces of the watch I'd seen on Joanna Cadmean's wrist both times I'd been with her. The band of gold links was broken. Near the watch lay a brass letter opener. I pointed down to it. "Did she try to protect herself with this? Is that how her arm got broken? Did you take the phone downstairs off the hook so if Briggs called, she'd think Joanna was talking with someone? And your scarf, Rowell? Did Joanna grab at your scarf as you shoved her toward the rail? Is that why it's down there in her hand now?"

Slowly, horror closed Dollard's eyes: I listened to footsteps start to climb the stairs far below us. When they reached the first landing, he shook himself, then walked to the door without seeing me as he went by. I spoke to his back, to the lush gray sweater that looked no less rich and assured now than it had before. I said, "Just don't leave the house. Thank you."

Without turning back, he mumbled thickly, "You're going to regret this."

I picked up the extension phone on the desk and called the River Rise apartment and asked Cuddy how Briggs was doing.

"Cruddy. Same as me," he said. "She's okay, don't worry. It's feeling responsible, you know, that's the worst. I mean, my sense is she and Mrs. Cadmean hadn't met more than a couple of times before now. Listen, she wants to come over, and I'm gonna bring her. We both feel awful, tell you the damn truth. But that lady acted *fine*, Justin. She didn't seem down, she seemed almost, hell, jolly. I swear I can't understand it!"

"It's not suicide, Cuddy."

I heard his long whistle, like a wind. "Dollard?"

"I think so. It looks that way."

"Shit a brick. Well, you were right. And I was wrong. Damn.

How'd he get in there? She told me she was going to lock up. I *told* her to."

"I don't know yet. I guess she let him in. Okay, would you go ask Briggs if Joanna told her about any kind of letter or note or something she'd written to me and put somewhere."

While Cuddy was gone, I listened to the ambulance doors snap open and shut, and its motor spit in the cold, and the keen of its siren leaving. Foster opened the study door. I waved him in.

Cuddy came back on and told me Briggs hadn't been left any message about a letter for me. He said, "Be there soon as we can. Justin, I'm sorry."

Foster and the photographer crowded me out of the study. Downstairs, I went to the door and watched Rowell, motionless in his black overcoat, standing outside by his car, boxed in by my car and Foster's and the squad car whose noiseless light kept spinning, throwing fire over the lake.

In Joanna Cadmean's room I began my search for the letter I felt certain she had written me, but had not yet made known to Briggs, because she hadn't thought she needed to yet. There were very few belongings through which to search: one suitcase on the floor of the closet. One drawer indifferently arranged in the bureau. She had required little. I emptied Mother's wicker basket, and ruffled the pages of the pile of thick romances, heroines in white by ruined towers, pierced by moonlight.

I found what I was looking for in a book under the bed; one of those small-print, yellowing collections of Shakespeare's complete works, pages separated from the cracked spine, the kind of book that summer houses have on musty shelves. Mrs. Cadmean had written the letter on the notepaper given her by my mother. She had placed the dozen sheets, whether by design or accident, midway through the play *Hamlet*. Her handwriting was scrolled and ornate, but perfectly clear, perfectly linear on the page. At the top of each sheet the red cardinals sat on a dogwood branch, symbols of the state.

January 18

Dear Justin,

You said just now on the phone you planned to go speak with Mr. Stanhope. If you did, he may have told you something about an incident in my life, when I was a young girl, and involving Rowell Dollard. It is true. I was hurt by it. Perhaps I should have told you myself, but it has no bearing on this matter.

It is also true that when I first told Cloris of my terrible instinct that Rowell was responsible for Bainton's drowning, she said I had fabricated the story because of my dislike of Rowell. Our friendship came to an end because she didn't believe me.

It is not true that I fabricated the story. But I have to confess, when I that Cloris had spoken to me in my dream about a diary, in fact, she had telephoned me, last month, in the ordinary way. Let me explain. I have had an interest, since my childhood, in old coins. I suppose I liked feeling on their faces the many hands that had touched them through so much history. Bainton had often shown me his collection. I knew it well. And so I noticed in the testimony surrounding his death the mention of a coin he'd brought to the inn to show someone the night he died. It was a coin he'd recently acquired.

Justin, I saw that coin *this summer*, back in the collection. I know I am not mistaken. I could only conclude that Rowell had taken it from Bainton that night, and all these years later put it back with the others.

This summer I visited Hillston (at my father-in-law's request—he wants even relatives I suspect he doesn't much like to keep in touch). And this time, I paid a call on Cloris (Rowell was, I believe she said, in Washington that weekend), and asked her if we might not reconcile after our quarrel. She agreed. We had a good talk. Afterward, I asked if I might see Bainton's coins again. I was stunned to see the presumably missing gold piece there. But I didn't mention it. Bainton had died so long ago, and I suppose I felt the cruelty of asking her to accept a truth about Rowell that would shadow the life they had, by all accounts, so happily lived for so many years.

But I did take the coin out of its case, and studied it, and I commented on the fact that it was the only one with no label on its paper envelope.

Shortly before her death, Cloris phoned me to thank me for making the overture to renew our friendship. And she said, laughing, that she had wanted me to have that coin of Bainton's as a gift, since I'd taken such an interest in it, and after I'd left, she'd set it aside to mail to me, along, she said, with a pretty leather diary she was sending to her daughter. But she'd packed them up somewhere, and could-n't put her hands on them—as she said—but they were somewhere in "this madhouse" and one of these days she'd send it along. It was very typical of her.

But I never received the coin. And then, a few weeks later, I had my dream, and the next morning I was told that she'd been murdered. Justin, I don't *know* if Rowell killed Bainton. I, perhaps foolishly, decided only to intimate my feelings to you by talking about dreams without directly producing evidence that would involve me in testimony about the past. My encounter with Rowell at his house and his truly cruel attack on me over the phone make even clearer, if I need further proof, just how vicious I can expect him to be.

The coin is a two-and-a-half-dollar, Liberty-head gold piece, Charlotte-minted in 1839. Bainton kept very careful records. He had only one. I feel strongly that the coin is still in that house. I think Rowell could not bring himself to dis-card it as easily as he has discarded the living.

That was the end of her original letter. In a different pen, another sheet followed, dated tonight.

Dear Justin,

Briggs and your friend, Lt. Mangum, have just left for their restaurant, and I'm going to take my poor ankle to an early bed, with another friend of yours, Shakespeare. (I regret I missed the chance to see you in A *Midsummer Night's Dream*, a favorite of mine, as you might expect.)

I have the strong feeling you're thinking of me now. I thought of calling, but hate to intrude any more than I already have on your sympathetic ear. I will mail all this tomorrow. You can decide what's best to do with it, if anything. I'm going home.

You have been very much in my thoughts. Upsetting thoughts, of your falling a long way. But perhaps only into something new. Everything around you is white. I can't tell if it's something good or bad. (Always the Sibyl's way out, isn't it?) But please take care. You know, I trusted your eyes from the first moment I saw them. They see the possibility that there are more things in heaven and earth than are ever dreamt of in all the Horatios' philosophy. For believing so, dear Justin, I thank you. We are only mad north-by-northwest.

Joanna Cadmean

I folded the small, scented sheets back in order. This was no deathbed letter, and not even the Polonian fool Captain Fulcher would believe it was. On the table by the bed was the sketchbook, some of its drawings torn out. I turned over the pages. A gray shadow of Rowell's enraged face looked out at me, uncannily like the look he had just now given me as he strode out of the study. Across the sheet, Joanna had drawn a series of vertical lines, like the rails of a balcony, like the bars of a cell.

I walked back out into the bitter cold night, and charged Rowell Dollard with murder.

part two

Bottom's Dream

Chapter 18
Thursday, January 20

The snow began to fall again early in the morning after Joanna Cadmean died; thick, sticky flakes this time, large as new buds of white azaleas. By dawn they covered Hillston, snowslip heavy on the trees, the downtown stores wheyfaced, staring out at one another across the white, silent roads. I walked onto the steps of the municipal building and saw the whole slumberous city, lulled and hushed by snow.

Rowell Dollard was not in custody; he was not even booked. He was in a private room at University Hospital under the care of a personal physician who said his patient was the victim of hypertension and acute prostration brought on by the shock of the violent deaths of his wife and Mrs. Cadmean. The pull of medical rank pleased almost everyone who had been sitting all night in Van Dorn Fulcher's office. Dollard's near nervous collapse was, said the state attorney general, "just the sort of holding pattern we need right now."

The A.G.'s name was Julian Dollard. He was my cousin. He had driven very quickly over from Raleigh for this informal hearing, which was also attended by Judge Henry Tiggs, a man I'd known since childhood. Everyone listened sleepily to Rowell Dollard record his statement for the stenographer until Rowell simply mumbled to a stop and said someone should call his doctor right away. His statement was the same one he had given me: Mrs. Cadmean had jumped for no cause she made known.

By dawn, V.D. Fulcher looked as if he were ready to check into a ward near the senator's. The captain's pink, whiskery jowls were twitching. His splutter had stammered into incoherence as he tortured himself with calculations: where should he truckle, and how? Word that Rowell Dollard could legitimately seek sanctuary in a hospital bed was the happiest news the captain had had since he heard the Jaycees were giving him a plaque and Mr. Briggs Cadmean was going to attend. Fulcher's problem was not that I thought there was sufficient evidence to charge Dollard. And certainly not that Cuddy Mangum and Etham Foster agreed with me. It was not even that Fulcher himself—after clicking his mouth hard up in the tower study for fifteen minutes and twice rereading Joanna Cadmean's long letter to me—did not believe with much comfort that she had committed suicide.

Fulcher's problem was that Hillston's current solicitor had said flatly that there were unignorable grounds for reasonable suspicion against Rowell Dollard, even if he was a state senator. This solicitor, Ken Moize, not only was not a Dollard, he was not a Hillstonian, not even a Carolinian, having only lived in the state since the age of fourteen. Moreover, this outlander Moize didn't even like the A.G., Julian Dollard, whose job (Fulcher whispered) he probably coveted. Fulcher's problem was that he needed to decide whether Julian Dollard would override Moize to protect his kinsman; or, whether Julian would feed Moize a little tidbit of Rowell (an indictment), to avoid the public howl Solicitor Moize might let loose if he could prove Julian party to a cover-up, oust him, and snatch up and wolf down the attorney generalship for himself.

So buzzed poor Fulcher's mind. He couldn't even be sure but that *Julian* disliked his cousin Rowell Dollard, jealous of the backing the state moneymen (like Cadmean) had always shown the Senator, their man in Raleigh for many years, and one they'd expect to see go on being their man for years to come. Fulcher's quandary was that if the ship was sinking and he ought to desert, where was the shore? And what if, as he paddled off, whiskers frantic above the waves, he should look back and see the big vessel majestically right itself and sail, with all its power churning, away from him? What then?

So, for most of the night, he sat fretful and let us fill his office with smoke—he couldn't tap his Lucite-bar warning at me because the attorney general, copper as old money from his recent vacation at a golf resort, was pilfering my pack—and let us litter his floor with the yellow crumbs of Cuddy's crackers and the foil of the solicitor's gum. Until finally it was decided that nothing had been decided, except that Joanna Cadmean was a corpse now, in a waiting room at Pauley and Keene Funeral Home, dead either by her own hand or by misadventure at the hands of person or persons unknown. And both the city prosecutors and the state prosecutors would study the evidence, and one another, until they could decide, in due time, where the ship should dock.

Only one decision was made: Fulcher decided after everyone but Cuddy and I had left that I had overstepped my authority, and was therefore to take two weeks' leave of absence. Inspired by the convenient collapse of Senator Dollard, he phrased my suspension in a medical way: the leave I was on was sick leave; my sickness was overwork. Clearly, wherever Fulcher thought the big boat of power was headed, he didn't much believe anymore that I ranked among the officers, and although still a first-class passenger, I was now one who could, with impunity, be kept for two weeks from eating at the captain's table.

I left Cuddy in there arguing with him about me. Passing under the wry, yellow, lidded eyes of Briggs Monmouth Cadmean varnished in oil, and clattering across the black and white floor of the rotunda, I walked out. I stood at six in the morning at the top of the steps looking over the still, blanched facade of downtown Hillston, where I had lived all my life, and, shaking, I pulled on my gloves and wrapped my scarf tighter. Across the street, my car was as white as a cairn of heaped stones.

Up the sidewalk through the slant of thick, blossomy snow came a black umbrella. Beneath it a man's ratty overcoat fluttered out as if there were no one in it; the bottom dragged stiff and wet in the drifts. Sister Resurrection was marching from her home in the church to her post by the hall of government. I walked down to meet her, my legs unsteady enough to keep me close to the balustrade.

"Good morning, Mrs. Webster," I told her, and touched my cap. My voice startled me by coming out a hoarse whisper. "Like a fairyland out here, isn't it? Mighty cold for a walk, though."

Although she didn't speak, she did stop, and I bent down to look at her under the umbrella. She wore a child's red toboggan cap and red mittens with white stars over the knuckles. The wizened folds of her neck were open to the gusty snowfall.

I said, "Well, things are bad. That silver-haired man we were talking about; I believe he's killed somebody else now. She was actually, now I come to think of it, a little in your forecasting line of work."

Sister Resurrection walked around me, and began a march as precise as a sentinel's, up and down, at the base of the steps. A hum rose out of her throat, and then a chant. "The King of Babylon," she said, "he wox angry. He got the iron walls. He got the fire burning. He throwing God's childrens into the fiery furnace. But God Almighty don't mess with Babylon. He makes His people for to walk through the valley of the shadow. God Almighty He taken that fire and He wet it with the tears from His eyes. He snatch that fire and He *squeeze* it." Umbrella high, she balled tight the red mitten of her free hand. "And squeeze it. And making a chain to hold the Devil just a little while longer. Just a little while longer. Just a little, my Lord, just a little. And then we laying down our heads and sleep."

I said quietly, "Amen."

And "Amen," she replied, and looked into my eyes and through them and beyond.

I said, "Here, if you're going to stay out, here, Mrs. Webster, do you mind?" and undid my long wool scarf and wound it high around her thin neck and tucked it in. Unmoving, she stared beyond me, then turned back to the march of her weariless warning.

But as I was brushing snow from my car, I felt all of a sudden her scratchy hand pluck at my arm, and when I looked around, she began to tug at my sleeve, her grasp oddly strong. Pointing the black umbrella ahead, she pulled me with her into the street. She let go, hurried a few steps ahead, whirled back, motioning with her fluttery arm for me to come; rushed on, turned back, called me with her arm again. Down the empty streets I followed the small dark figure, no one but the two of us in the white ghost town. The unplowed road billowed around us soft as sheets. On we floated, like sleepers silent, until abruptly she darted off to the left.

Lurching after her into the side street, I saw her stop and rattle her umbrella at the painted glass front of the Tucson Lounge. Gaudy at night with noise and rows of red electric bulbs topped by a red neon cactus, it was in daylight just a dull, raw wall. In its gutter, snow was falling on black plastic bags and soggy boxes of drinkers' debris, bottles and cans and stench. Sister Resurrection wheeled around and pressed against me, her eyes rheumy clouds that suddenly sharpened to jet. Her hand flew up and grabbed at my coat arm and, the fingers wriggling inside the mitten, she pulled me down with her to a crouch at the curb. The hand flew out again and pinched hard at my earlobe. "Trash," she said, and pointed down, twisting her head and pointing back at the window of the bar behind us.

I nodded. "Yes, you're right."

"The harlot sitting on the dragon's back, she wearing the crimson and purple robes, she wearing gold and wearing jewels." Her red-mittened fist jerked away from my face, yanked up her hat, and squeezed the ear beneath. She breathed out slowly, "Wearing *jewels*." And for a wink of a moment only, I saw a self come into her eyes, saw her be there seeing me. Then she was gone again; murk clouded the pupils and they lifted skyward.

I touched my ear, burning still where she had grabbed it. "Ear jewels?" I whispered. "Is this where you found that earring? Here in the trash?"

But unhearing she sprang to her feet and scurried through the snow back the way we'd come.

Back in front of the municipal building, I heard her as I

climbed into my car. "She hold the cup of fornication and drinking the blood of my Jesus outta that cup. She Babylon. God throw her down from the iron wall and dogs shall lick her blood."

• • •

At the Bush Street Diner near Tuscarora Road, I was asleep with my face pressed into the side of the booth when Alice "Red" MacLeod tapped my shoulder and scared me. "I told you 7:30 was too early for you."

I bolted upright, shaking my head, and she added, "Are you all right?" Tugging on her book bag, she slid into the booth.

I said, "I'm fine, it just doesn't show."

She unbuttoned a plaid parka; beneath it she wore a pink fuzzy sweater the color of her cheeks. "Sorry I'm late; I had some union phone business. More rumors about shutting down my division. This creep named Whetsone had us 'analyzed' and says we're not 'competitive.'"

"We've met," I said. "Sounds like him."

While we ate eggs and coffee, I explained what it was that had kept me awake all night, that Joanna Cadmean was dead, that the suspected murderer was my uncle. She said, "Justin, I'm really sorry." She thrust forward the stubborn chin. "And it's just disgusting what they're doing about it. They fired you!"

"They suspended me, while they decide if they can afford to fire me."

"What are you going to do now?"

I made an effort at a laugh. "Well, first I'm going to take it lying down for about eight hours."

"How in hell do people like them always end up running the world?"

"God, I hope that's not a serious question."

"Oh, yes, it is. It sure is. It's *the* serious question, Justin."

I looked across the plastic tabletop at the solemn blue eyes. "You called me Justin two times," I said. "Would you mind doing it again?"

Her blush moved up from the neck of her sweater into the freckles, and she frowned. "Isn't that your name?" And she went back to piling scrambled eggs on her toast like pâté, eating quickly and pleasurably. "Aren't you hungry?" she asked, cup to mouth.

"Not really." The food at the diner did not look as if it had improved since my last visit, the night Cuddy rescued me from his cousin Wally's switchblade; the old picture of eggs and bacon on the menu had an unappetizing anemic pallor. My head was logy, and my hand shook so that finally my cup of coffee just slipped through my fingers and crashed onto the tabletop, sloshing me and the table with scalding liquid. I jumped out of the booth, shaking my pants, and she jerked a wad of paper napkins from the container and started to sop up the dark stain.

"I'm sorry," I said.

"Look, I do things like this all, I mean all the time. Don't be stupid. There. You better go home and go to bed."

I took the sticky napkins from her, both of us holding on to them until finally she let go. And smiling I said, "All right. I will. I wonder if you'd like to come too?"

Her face crinkled, the eyes stayed grave. "No." And she sat back down. Then she smiled. "You better go home and go to *sleep*. I'm going to European History: World War I to the Present."

"That'll depress you."

"No, it won't. It'll make me mad. It always does."

"Yes, you're a warrior, Alice 'Red' MacLeod."

She nodded, pulled over my plate, and ate everything on it. While doing so, she told me she had two pieces of news for me. Last night, Graham and Dickey Pope had stormed into the plant when the shift ended, looking for Charlene. They told Alice they didn't know Ron Willis, the white-haired man with the black moustache. And no one else she'd spoken to had heard of any connection between Willis and Charlene; except that one woman had told her she'd heard Charlene had taken up with a man called Luster Hudson, and Ron Willis had once palled around with Hudson when the latter had worked at C&W as a forklift operator. I thanked her, and she said she'd love to help me put Willis away; he was a stoolie paid to keep watch on union activists like herself. She said Willis had once told her floor manager the lie that she had a long affair back in Boone with a black Communist social worker.

"What was the lie?" I asked.

"That he was a Communist."

"Oh."

She looked across at me, her chin up. "It's over. He had to choose between me and somebody else, and he didn't think he ought to have to. But I thought it would be better for everybody if he did."

"You're…"

She cocked her head. "Archaic. High-minded. Unliberated. And a hillbilly."

"What I'm trying to say is, you're very pretty in the morning. Christ, I sound like a teenager. I think I'm falling in love."

This time she didn't blush; she just looked, and then she said, "Go home. I'm late. Here." And hauling a coin purse out of her book bag, she took out three folded dollars.

I said, "No."

"I asked you, remember? Plus, I ate your breakfast."

"If you're so unliberated, why won't you let me pay?"

She said, "God, I hope that's not a serious question," and hurried into her parka and slid fast out of the booth. "Look, are you going to bed?"

"The prospect seems to fascinate you. Are you sure you couldn't give World War I the slip?"

"Your eyes aren't even in focus. I think you're already asleep."

I pulled myself out of the booth and touched my toes five slow times. "Wide awake. In fact, I'm about to embark on a new career. Breaking and entering."

"For a good cause?"

"Yes, ma'am, Governor."

"Okay." She slung the bag over her small straight shoulder. "Bye."

"See you tomorrow, 7:30, Alice."

• • •

When I reached the North Hillston colonial I planned to break into, there was a car already parked out in front. A white Oldsmobile, like a big ice floe in the white snow. The house was Rowell Dollard's, and the car was Cuddy Mangum's. In the front seat sat Mrs. Mitchell. I tapped the glass against her skittering paws. Cuddy was already inside, and he started yelling as soon as I opened the door. "Where'd you go, you damn jackass?!" He stood at the top of the curved stairs, hand inside his coat, probably looking for his gun.

"What are you doing in this house, Mangum?"

"Guess. Now, Justin, why in holy shit did you run off that way? I come out and you're gone wandering off in the snow like old Doctor Zhivago. And so I ask your pal Sister Resurrection out there— wearing, I do believe, your scarf like she ate the rest of you—I ask her, 'Sister, did you see a good-looking crazy man go by?' But we don't speak the same lingo the way you and her do, and all I got for an answer was that God's in a *real* bad mood and lost His patience with trash, which I hope was not in reference to me."

By now I had crossed the Dollard foyer and had climbed the stairs to the landing.

Cuddy shook his head. "You know, maybe you do need a sick leave. You look bad. You haven't even changed your clothes, and that scares me. And excuse me being lewd, but did you maybe come or pee in your pants?"

I said, "What are you doing here? It's coffee."

A sleepless night had reddened the blue-jay eyes and shadowed the old acne scars. He still wore the three-piece herringbone suit he'd put on (or bought—I'd never seen it before) to take Briggs out last night to dinner. I'd been telling Cuddy for years that if he really wanted to take over the department; he had to stop wearing things like Elvis sweatshirts. Maybe love would be his tailor. I said, "Nice suit."

He tilted his head at me. "I know you, General. I may not know you, but I know you. I suspicioned there might be an attempted break-in at this residence coming up, and I figured the police ought to be on the scene. And since you ain't the police, being as V.D., that old spitlicking toadeater has fired, excuse me, *suspended*, your ass, I figured I would save you from the temptation of committing an illegality. Call me Tonto, for you are sure enough the lonesome ranger now."

"You're the one waltzing around his house without a warrant," I said.

He rippled his bony hand in his jacket pocket, tugged out a loud tie, and then the paper. "Oh, I gots de warrant."

"How?"

"Mister Ken Moize. And I got something else for you, you just going to love." He crooked his long skinny arm and darted it at the open door of Cloris Dollard's bedroom.

Inside, boxes were piled on the bare mattress of the queen-size bed. Cuddy loped around the bed and patted them. "I was just tidying up the lady's closet a bit waiting on you, because it didn't look to me like anybody'd paid it much mind, and this box here," he tapped a cardboard crate labeled Mumms' Champagne, "well, sir, it was full of little children's clothes still with the price tags on them. I guess she was planning on sending them off to her little grandchildren. So I wonder, maybe this was where she kept stuff she hadn't gotten around to mailing off to folks, like Mrs. Cadmean said she was going to. And so, what you're gonna love, Kemo Sabby, is what was down at the bottom." He reached in and his hand came back out holding a red Moroccan leather book, gold-stamped and gold-leafed. The blank pages of the diary fell open to a small clear envelope. Inside the waxy paper glittered the golden coin. Cuddy held it up so I could see the classic smooth brow of the profile of Liberty, and the date, 1839.

Chapter 19

Still dressed, I fell asleep and didn't dream and didn't wake until a thudding jarred one eye open to see by the carriage clock beside my bed that it was 5:30. I staggered to the back window and looked down in the gray light at my yard where Cuddy Mangum stood pitching up snowballs at the side of my house. When I jimmied open the window, he yelled, "We got to go to the hospital. Luster Hudson's beat up Charlene Pope. Open your damn door, I've been kicking it for ten minutes, haven't you got any ears?"

"Bad?" I called.

"Nothing permanent, but it doesn't sound pretty. Contusions, abrasions, hematoma, as per usual. Mankind! My car's out front."

I couldn't tell if the sky was 5:30 dusk or dawn; the snowdrifts looked higher now, and the tree branches sagged with white weight. I yelled at his back, "Is it tonight or tomorrow?"

Cuddy swiveled back around. Wearing his neon-shiny parka in all that white, he looked like an astronaut on the moon. He said, "General, don't talk crazy when I'm working so hard to persuade people you're sane."

"Is it 5:30 P.M.?"

"More or less. Come on! I've got four more cases besides this one, you know. This crime-doesn't-pay notion has never really gotten across to the populace. I'll wait in the car. Martha wouldn't come. She can't take the weather. Probably home biting the professor. She's jealous."

As his heavy Oldsmobile crunched out through the snow, he said, "Don't you ever change your clothes? Want a Big Mac?" His hand rummaged in the bag beside him and brought out the dripping hamburger.

I said, "What happened to Charlene?"

"Okay, okay. Desk clerk, real pisspot at the Interstate Budget Motel, heard her screaming. 'Course, he hated to intrude, he hears so many folks screaming out there, so he turns up his TV. Then this pickup zooms off, cutting right through his boxwood shrubs, so now he goes to check, because screams is one thing, and shrubs is another. So, when he notices the room door's open and the heat's escaping, he strolls on in and sees Charlene on the floor between the beds, and so he calls us in case she's dead, and we ask him why he didn't bother to let us know. He's mostly torn up about who's going to pay for all this breakage and who's going to clean up all this blood. And I say, 'You are,' and then I sort of accidentally drive over some more of his boxwoods backing out in a hurry."

"How do you know it was Hudson?"

"Description matches: big, blond, ox-headed, and pig-eyed. Plus the plates match. He checked in there last night as 'L. Smith.' Catchy. Sounds like he was flashing a wallet as fat as Woodrow Clenny's on Saturday night." Woodrow Clenny was a legendary Hillston pimp, whose throat had been cut years back by one of his employees. Cuddy said, "So he shows at the Budget and then Charlene shows later in her van. Ask me why she went. I'll say this, when our pal Paula told us Charlene wasn't as dumb as Preston, she gave her too much credit."

"Hudson. Did you get him?"

"Nope. Three cars out looking. We leaned on the guy that's been feeding his dogs, but he swears all he knows is Luster says he's going to Asheville, and he pays him to feed them. We got a man on this guy anyhow. Well, too bad Little Preston didn't torch Luster's bike when Luster was sitting on it. Isn't that B.M. good, referring to the Big Mac, naturally?"

It was at least making me feel better than I had in a while.

Cuddy said, "I passed our coin to Ken Moize. It fits the description in Mrs. Cadmean's letter."

"And the one on Bainton Ames's list?"

"Yep. Worth more now, lot more, than Ames paid for it. Mr. Ratcher Phelps would weep to know the appreciation." Cheeks sucked in, he slurped at the semisolid milkshake through the straw. "And I wired a photo of the coin down to that Mr. Bogue in Atlanta to confirm. And let's see, what else. Mrs. Cadmean had no liquor, no drugs in her system. She made no toll call to North Hillston inviting your uncle over. Don't throw up your racquet yet, but I do believe Solicitor Moize is coming your way on the senator. Dick Cohen wouldn't go for suicide; filed his report 'open, pending investigation.' So, really all we need now is for Dollard to make a full confession, and we've got him."

"How is Rowell?"

"Resting. No visitors. Fulcher tried hard to keep the newsboys out of the cookie bowl about Dollard's even being out there at the Cadmean lodge, but somebody (it wasn't you, was it?) leaked it to Bubba Percy at *The Star*." Steering with one skinny hand down the blank, unrutted road, he dumped a fistful of french fries into his mouth.

"How's Briggs doing, Cuddy?"

"Oh, okay. Like I say, still at my place. After she got back to the lodge, she didn't feel up to staying out there alone. And I don't want to crowd her right now, so mind if I pass the night on that rickety couch with the catpaw feet of yours? If Lunchbreak's coming over for a snack, I'll step out in the yard."

"Fine."

"Junior Briggs's daddy called out there to the lodge after you left, huffing and puffing and tried to make her come stay with him at his house." Cuddy shook his head and sighed.

I said, "He wants her back."

"Well, hey, he ain't gonna get her."

"Who is, you?"

Frowning, he looked over at me. "That bother you? Let's get straight, General." His eyes stayed on me, asking me.

"No," I said. "Damn it, will you watch the road! It doesn't bother me a bit."

He grinned. "Why the hell not? You got a nerve not being dismal. I'll tell you this, when God got around to making that woman, He'd finally figured out how to do it. He was *inspired* that morning. Then He fell into a slump and came up with Lunchbreak."

"Talk about sounding like a Loretta Lynn song! Do you *want* me to fight you for her?"

"Hell, no. You're too good-looking and rich. Well, I thought you were rich. 'Course, now you're out of a job and gone crazy and let your clothes get all messy, I guess maybe I could take you on. Holy shit!" Suddenly he twisted the steering wheel. "Look at that Buick! That joker's lost it! Jackknifing, look at that, with the brake pedal to the floor!" Cuddy slowed, pumping gingerly, until the wide car ahead of us managed to spin out of its circle without leaving the road. "No chains, no brains," Cuddy snapped. "So hey, Mister Preppie, we gonna duel or what?"

"If Briggs is gettable, go get her, Cyrano."

"Say who?"

"Don't kid me, Cudberth, you already slipped up and told me you had an M.A."

"Well, that's true, but I didn't get it in French drammer of the *fan de sickle*. And anyhow, you want to know what a big nose really means?"

"It means jocular. Take the turn, take the turn, you're passing the hospital!"

Charlene's room was crowded. There were two other patients in it, both elderly, one watching *The Merv Griffin Show* and the other telling her to turn it off. Around Charlene's bed were Paula Burgwin, Graham Pope, and Dickey Pope. No doubt Preston Pope would have been there too if Cuddy had been able to talk Fulcher into releasing the suspect into his custody for the visit. But the law had Preston now. The grand jury had gone ahead with their indictment of the youngest Pope for the murder of Cloris Dollard; bail was set at two hundred and fifty thousand dollars, which was a lot more CBs and cigarettes than Graham and Dickey had in stock to offer a bondsman as collateral. Joe Lieberman hadn't even tried to negotiate.

By the bed, Graham, hairy and bear-big, was shouting. "Now, God damn it, Charlene, you tell me who did this to you and I'm gonna kill the son of a bitch!"

"I'm gonna kill him too," said Dickey from the other side of the tilted bed. He had a comb and a pair of pliers sticking out of the pocket of a black satin cowboy shirt with roses sewn across the yoke. Any inconsistency between their vaunts to avenge Charlene now, and the fact that, only days ago, both these Popes had described her to us as the whoring bitch whose head they planned to bash in—for breaking Preston's heart, and then squealing on him to the cops for pure spite—was obviously not troublesome to either.

In the chair beside the bed, Paula Burgwin, plump and teary, sat holding Charlene's hand. Charlene's face on the snowy pillow was red with cuts and bruises except for where a white bandage swaddled her nose. Hard red lines were painfully distinct across her throat. The worst was her eyes—they were gorged with blood so red that no white showed, and black circles puffed around their sockets. Her right hand was in a cast. Paula kept patting her left one.

I had to swallow a few times before I said, "Christ, Cuddy," and they all looked at us coming into the room.

Graham puffed up in his huge down vest. "Y'all get out of here!"

"Get out of here!" echoed Dickey.

Tears ran over the sides of Paula's round cheeks. She said, "They want to help, is all."

"Shit!" Graham was wheezing like a bellows. "Help send my little brother to the chair. Mangum, they get my brother, I'm gonna kill you, I'm telling you now."

"Kill 'em both," Dickey said. "Let's bash 'em, come on!"

"Call the police!" shrieked the old woman in the next bed, her stick-thin arm waving her IV tube so jerkily I had to grab at the swaying stand. I stepped over and told her, "It's all right, ma'am. We *are* the police. Excuse us, please." And I pulled closed the white ring-curtain that partitioned the room.

Cuddy said, "Graham, cut this shit. The sad fact is, Preston has signed a statement that he picked up that silverware on Wade."

"It ain't true. He never saw it. He knows better'n lie to me."

Cuddy nodded fast. "I wish he'd known better'n tell so many different stories to Captain Fulcher downtown, 'cause it does have a way of giving the impression of a lie."

Graham weaved toward Charlene. "He did it for this goddamn bitch here. Trying to save her ungrateful whoring ass. Excuse me, Paula."

Cuddy whistled. "For Charlene? That's noble. That's not brainy, but that's noble. You hear that, Charlene?" He moved to the bedhead now and spoke softly. "Lord, lord, Charlene. I'm real sorry. Now, I want to hear you tell me who did this to you."

Graham yelled, "She won't tell us. I swear she's in on the goddamn fix."

Charlene's lips moved stiffly until she could whisper, "Get fucked, Graham."

Cuddy smiled. "That's my girl! You haven't lost your sweet-talking ways. Now, how did this bad mess happen?"

She stared at the ceiling. Finally she managed to mumble, "I went to bed and I woke up this way."

Cuddy said, "Come on, tell me, because the fact is, I already know."

Her head moved slowly, painfully, away from us, and the hand in the plaster cast hid her face.

Cuddy said again, "Come on, sweetheart; after Luster finished showing you what a real man he was, where did he go?"

Now Graham swelled almost to the ceiling. "Luster! God damn it, I knew it!"

"Let's go get him," hollered Dickey.

I blocked the door while Cuddy called, "Whoaa, boys. Back up."

"Are you sure you're the police?" came the reedy voice from behind the curtain. "I think I ought to call the nurse."

"Go ahead," Paula snapped. "I sure can't get her to come for me."

I asked Graham, "Do you know where Luster Hudson is? Because we don't."

"He's no place where I can't find him!"

"Graham!" Paula stood up, tugging down on her sweater, then raising her small pretty hands so the charms jingled high as her voice, "Graham! You listen to me for once. What good's getting killed gonna do?"

Dickey said, "Paula, cram it, who asked you?"

Graham knocked him on the back of the head. "Shut your mouth, Dickey!" Then he tried to hug Paula, rumbling, "Little lady, don't you worry about me."

She said, "I'm not, you damn goon."

"She's just all upset," Graham explained to us. "Paula has a heart just as soft as a little baby bird."

Paula replied, "It's not as soft as your head."

Finally we succeeded in pushing the Pope men out into the hall, and I said to Graham, "All right, if you find Hudson, you'll call Mangum, deal?"

Dickey sneered. "Y'all bring a bag to put the pieces in, and bring one that don't leak."

Graham said, "Dickey, will you shut your mouth? Now, listen here to me, Mangum. Charlene planted that crap on Preston. I know it. I talked to him serious today, and he never saw it. The way I see it now is Luster made her do it."

I said, "I'm getting the same feeling."

Graham swayed back and forth above our heads, his hair and beard brown, shiny tangles. "So, here it is. I'm gonna find Luster Hudson for you, and I'm gonna leave that son of a bitch just about enough teeth to talk through to tell you he made her do it. And then you send me Preston home! Come on, Dickey!" Down the green hall they stomped, twice the size of the old women in robes who clutched the arms of bored nurses and shuffled, inch-by-inch along, trying by constant motion to keep away from death. I watched them, lit a cigarette, and slumped against the wall. Finally, I said, "Hell. It fits. The beating, the money. I think Graham's telling the truth about Preston; Preston's covering for Charlene."

"Yep, Preston's the Duke of Windsor, okay. Well, getting your Harley incinerated and even the *tips* of your fingers shaved off could make a fellow less churlish than Prince Luster want to get even. Okay, if Luster and Charlene planted it, did they know who it belonged to? And you see that No Smoking sign?"

I told Cuddy about the encounter with Sister Resurrection and her intimation that she'd found the earring at the Tucson Lounge, "According to Preston, remember, that's where Luster and Charlene hung out every night."

Cuddy said, "Them and every other honky-tonk freak in Hillston. You better put that cigarette out before a nurse asks me to arrest you."

"Well, I don't think Charlene knew about the murder until she heard it on TV, just like Paula said. Question is, what about Luster? Where'd he get all that cash the motel clerk saw?"

"Selling dogs?"

I felt sick. "It was just robbery all along."

"Hold on." He yanked at his hair for a minute. "Dollard might still have unloaded the stuff. Or, Luster could have been working for Dollard. Or for somebody."

"Or Luster could have killed Cloris all on his own. You just saw his hands dented into Charlene's throat in there!"

Cuddy nodded. "He's mean enough. And dumb enough."

I thumped back hard against the wall.

"Calm down," Cuddy muttered. "Now, another thing is, this could all be separate from what happened to Joanna Cadmean, or what happened to Bainton Ames, too, okay? And maybe it's not separate. We don't know." He went back into the room, and, crushing out my cigarette on the sole of my shoe, I followed him.

The two elderly patients had reconciled their differences and were both quietly watching a game show in which couples clawed their way to the stage for the chance to guess behind which curtain waited the price-tagged paraphernalia of a better life.

Paula was leaning over Charlene, still stroking her hand. Bending down beside them, Cuddy said, "Charlene, listen. Wanting to protect that pig Hudson would be real stupid. Wanting to protect yourself from that pig by freezing us out would be real stupid too. And you're not stupid. We're the only ones can help you."

The red, horrific eyes moved from his face to mine. "Sure," she hissed, flinching, her lips held still. "Like Shirley."

Paula explained. "She means a friend of ours seven or eight years ago, and the thing is, Shirley asked the police to help her because her ex wouldn't leave her alone and said he had a knife and all, and the police told her they couldn't get into it until Jack *did* something. He had to do it first, is what they said."

Charlene turned her eyes, acerbic and dry, back to us as Paula added, "Well, what happened was, Jack killed her. She bled to death right there on her floor."

Cuddy nodded, "Okay, I remember when that happened, Charlene, and if Shirley'd come to me instead of whoever she went to, it *wouldn't* have happened. But this is different. Understand that. Okay? Now, we can go two ways. One is, you tell us where Luster went, and we lock him up on felonious assault. Two is, you don't, and we lock you up as a material witness. Both ways, Luster's not going to be able to get to you."

She just looked away.

I stepped in front of Cuddy. "Charlene, would you like a cigarette?" She didn't say no, so I lit one and held it to her lips and moved it away and then back again. Then I said quietly, "You know, we're not the only ones who want to protect you. It sounds like Preston does too. He's risking a murder charge for you. I don't know how much you might have to forgive him for—quite a bit, probably—but it does look as if he's forgiven you beyond where maybe most men would go. Is that fair? I don't mean just that you left him. I mean, he must know Luster forced you—I think he did force you—to plant that silverware in the Pope house and then call the station so we'd come out and pick Preston up. But I don't think you knew what that silverware would mean to us. Because Luster lied to you. You didn't know the silver was connected with a murder. If he's told you you're an accessory, he's lying. I don't think you are."

She kept staring at me as I put the cigarette back to her swollen lips.

I went on, quietly, "And so, maybe it's not Luster Hudson that's the better man. You think?"

As I smiled down at her, tears welled over the bruised eyes.

"Charlene." My voice dropped quieter. "Luster just wasn't what you thought he'd be. That's all. Listen. I've made the same mistake. God, we all have. But I'm very sorry it had to cost you so much." I held the cigarette down to her again. "Now, everything's going to be all right. That's a promise. And so would you mind if I just ask you this? Will you tell me, do you know where Luster is now?"

I waited, and finally her head shook no, almost too slightly to see.

"Or where he *might* have gone?"

Another no.

I leaned closer. "He called you to come to the motel. And you went because you were afraid not to?"

After a longer wait, her head moved slowly up and down.

"Yes. And you were right to be afraid. Here. Look, would you like a sip of your juice here?" I put out the cigarette and placed my hand behind her head and carefully raised it and held the paper cup to her lips. Her eyes, still filled with the unfallen tears, stayed on mine. "You brought him some clothes to the motel? And what else? The rest of the stolen property?"

Her head moved no in my hand, her eyes frightened.

"You didn't know what you were bringing?"

Then, after a moment, she struggled to whisper, "A gym bag kind of. Locked. Had to pick it up from somebody."

"All right," I told her, nodding. "Thank you. Good. Will you say who?...No? All right. That's all right." I let her head back down on the pillow, but kept my hand on her hair. "We'll put that aside. Charlene, why did Luster beat you? Did you tell him that you'd been talking to us, and that we were looking for him?"

She nodded yes, and I kept on smoothing her hair back from her forehead.

"And did you tell him you were scared maybe he had killed Mrs. Dollard, and that's why he had the silverware?"

She stared at me, her mouth quivering.

I said, "Were you really with him the night Mrs. Dollard died? It's all right that you said you were before. Just tell me the truth now, just go on."

Charlene's unhurt hand was kneading the starched white sheet. She looked at Paula and Paula murmured, "Tell him," and then Charlene's head turned back to me, and she shook it softly no.

I nodded. "You weren't with him. All right. Charlene, did Luster Hudson kill Cloris Dollard?"

The tears now spilled over her eyelids and slid down into the bandage. She winced as the salt of the tears touched her broken skin. Finally, her chest moved and she whispered, "He said he didn't, but I swear he did. The guy gave me the gym bag. Ron Willis."

Paula squeezed Charlene's hand. I stepped back and said, "You did the right thing, Charlene. I want to thank you. All right? You rest now, and Paula'll be here with you." Paula nodded vigorously. I bent back down to the bed. "And we'll have an officer right outside this door. Hudson's never going to hurt you again. I'm giving you my word. Now you go back to sleep. Good night. We'll leave you alone now."

Back out in the hall, Cuddy caught up with me near the nurses' station and said as we went down in the elevator, "My my my. That was fine, Justin." He gave his low, windy whistle. "Now, why can't I get a bedside manner like that? You get that from your doctor dad? I almost fell into a trance myself, just looking on. A brain of steel is just not doing the trick for me; what you need in this world is a silver tongue."

When he returned from calling headquarters, I was slumped down in a sofa in the main lobby lounge. I said, "If I hadn't been so damn sure, so *blind*, maybe Charlene wouldn't be up there like that."

"Well, hey, what about me? Don't hog all the guilt. You told me to pull her in, remember? And what about *Charlene*? She could have told us about Luster any time she wanted to. Okay, so we find Hudson and see what's in that bag. And we find Willis. And we don't know Dollard is out. He sure isn't out of the running on the Mrs. Cadmean case."

I said, "I think I can give you the plate numbers for Ron Willis." I found the piece of paper in my wallet. "WY-2252."

"You sure you're not psychic?"

"He tailed me out to C&W and was very interested in my talk with Charlene out there. He knows Hudson. But he may not have any more to do with it than the gym bag transfer."

"My, you keep busy. Okay, I'll put in a call."

"Let's go over to C&W. He works there."

"You work too many hours for a man's already been fired."

"I haven't been fired."

"Well, General, let's just say, you're in the cannon and the match's mighty close to your balls. You took me a little too literally when I advised you to get lonesome. Actually, what you need is some friends in high places. You need to…"

Then I saw the plaid parka spinning in through the main doors. I introduced Cuddy to Alice MacLeod at the information desk. She said the hospital had called the plant to check on Charlene's insurance. We waited for her while she went up to visit, and then followed her back to the mills. Ron Willis had not shown up for work. Nor did he ever return to his apartment, across the street from which Cuddy and I sat waiting for him in the cold Oldsmobile.

Late that night, while I threw blankets and sheets on my couch, Cuddy started winking his eyes and making Vs with his long skinny fingers, as he said, "Well, you are smooth. You want some advice?"

"No."

"Here it is. Marry her."

"Who?"

"Red MacLeod."

"I told you. I just met her. Good Christ, you're always trying to get everybody married. You and my mother. You go ahead without me, all right? What do you want, a double wedding out in my backyard?"

"Well, hey, wouldn't that be a sweet thing?" He snapped off his galoshes and slid his feet out of his Hush Puppies loafers. Both his big toes stuck out of holes in his socks. "But let's hold off 'til the snow's not so deep. Because I want Briggs to wear some high-heeled sandals. I just love that kind."

"What in the world makes you think she's going to marry you?"

Shaking blankets out on the couch, he said, with no smile, "Faith, hope, and that poor lady, Mrs. Cadmean. I asked her. While Briggs was getting on her coat. And she said, yes, as a matter of fact, she had that feeling. Oh, well, okay, I believe her, why not?"

"No reason."

That night I dreamt again of Joanna. She was going to marry Rowell in the white dress she had died in.

Chapter 20
Friday, January 21

At noon the next day I hurried past Sergeant Hiram Davies at the switchboard while he was looking down at his bologna sandwich; he never went out for lunch, fearful he'd be forced to retire if he left his desk. At the end of the hall I waved in at Cuddy Mangum (eating a loaf-long grinder while talking on the phone), then slipped inside my office and shut the door. Everything was the same there; somehow I'd imagined the room would be redecorated or mossy with cobwebs.

Everything was the same with the case, too. Neither Luster Hudson nor Ron Willis had yet been found. Preston Pope was still in custody. Rowell Dollard still was not. But when the grand jury met again on Monday, they seemed likely now to decide Rowell should be charged. There was simply too much evidence. Foremost was the letter to me. It was indisputably in Joanna Cadmean's handwriting. The Liberty coin found in Cloris Dollard's diary was indisputably the same model that Bogue had been shown by Bainton Ames that long-ago summer night. Ken Moize, who had asked me this morning to come to his office, also told me the coroner had ruled out accidental death for Mrs. Cadmean—judging that the balcony rail was too high for her to have fallen over unintentionally, especially on crutches, moving slowly. Between the other two possibilities—homicide or suicide—the coroner had elected not to choose. I said that one thing troubled me: why had she, so indifferent to her beauty, been so beautifully dressed that night if she weren't expecting anyone?

"So what? Maybe she gussied up for Mangum." Ken Moize, an eagerly earnest native Midwesterner, had his helmet on, and an exalted look; he was prancing to joust just as soon as someone handed him a long enough lance and a wide enough shield. Moize had wanted me in his office by ten to give him a full briefing on my investigation of Bainton Ames's death, as well as any theories I had about Cloris Dollard's and Joanna Cadmean's. With his tape recorder spinning, it felt a little less lonesome off the deep end.

I'd had a number of other phone calls this morning after I'd come back from the diner and my third breakfast with Alice. Ratcher Phelps had called. Rowell Dollard had called. Both wanted to see me. The third call was from Lawry Whetstone, whose secretary I'd asked to tell him to get in touch. He said, small world, that I wanted to see him, because he wanted to see me. Lawry didn't say what he wanted to see me about, but I assumed I knew—he wanted to accuse me of having an affair with his wife. And so we agreed to meet at my office at 1:30; my office was more convenient for him since he was eating downtown, and more comfortable for me since I didn't want this talk to happen in my house. I didn't want it to happen at all. I'd been expecting his accusation for months, and worrying about it, and feeling guilty about it, and imagining how I was going to respond to it. But the call had never come.

And now, just when it was clear to me that Susan and I were no more real together than mannequins embracing in a store window, just when I had begun worrying and feeling guilty and imagining how I was going to get *Susan* to admit we didn't care enough about each other to risk the waste and hurt—now here came Lawry's call. Now the secret was out, shame wriggling me up on the scaffold even as the scars of the A were fading from my breast. As Lawry hung up, I found myself in a twitch of resentment—like the thief arrested on his way to return the stolen goods. For more than a year Susan had refused to leave her husband for me; now what was I going to do if, instead of demanding that I leave her alone, he announced that he was getting a divorce, and Susan was mine?

So, not much liking myself, I defiantly walked into my office and waited. I had no idea what style of confrontation to expect. Lawry and I had, of course, met; we'd even played tennis. But I avoided him: if I saw him in the club locker room, I'd go home without changing my clothes; if I saw him at a cocktail party, I'd keep to the other side of the crowd. This was to be our first and probably our last private conversation.

Lawry Whetstone surprised me. Sleek and Florida-blond and cruise-tan as his wife, he breezed in and sat down on my black wood chair and comfortably rubbed the pastel checks of his wool jacket against the LUX EX VERITAS insignia on its back. He had a great deal of rich hair, close-trimmed in back, and a deep dimple in the middle of his chin. His weak feature was a bobbed nose too short for his face, and he had a habit of pulling on it as if he could make it longer. He crossed his legs, looked briefly at his suede boot, and then briefly at me, and said, "How about this snow? Wouldn't you love to go cross-country skiing? Ever tried that? Sorry you couldn't make lunch. This new Italian place in the Monmouth Building, I've got to say, it was great. Some smart people are starting to do some smart things downtown. About time, right?"

I nodded. I was trying not to smoke. I was just waiting.

Lawry glanced appreciatively at his cashmere coat, which hung from my coatrack. "So maybe they'll turn old Hillston around," he said. "Look at what's happened in Richmond and Baltimore. Why not Hillston, right? Tear out all this old junk."

"I like the old stuff."

"Who doesn't?"

I could hear the pulse in my ears as I kept waiting.

"Okay," he grinned. "You're busy, I'm busy." Lawry stroked his close-trimmed sideburn with affection. "Anyhow, Susan says she told you Cloris Dollard mentioned me at that play, the night she died, about how she was feeling 'bad' or something about me?"

"Pardon?"

"Dollard's wife, right? Should have gotten in touch earlier, I guess, but who thinks these little things are going to matter. To be honest, I didn't connect the times right off. Because the damn thing is, I think I was trying to call her from Atlanta just about the time she died."

"What?" My pulse and the muscles of my face hurried to adjust to the news that Whetstone was apparently here not to talk to me about Susan, but to talk to me about Cloris Dollard. "You called Cloris Dollard Sunday, January ninth?"

"Right. Called her twice. The first time she said she was just leaving to go to the Hillston Playhouse—weren't you in that Shakespeare thing they did?—and so would I mind calling her back. So I did, around eleven, eleven fifteen, that night. No later. I crashed pretty early." He finished stroking his sideburn and went back to pulling on his nose. "Thing is, she didn't answer. Phone all of a sudden clicked off. Around eleven. You can check the time with the hotel; don't they keep telephone records? I was returning her call. How this all got started was, she asked me to do her a favor. I guess that's what she was telling Susan she felt guilty about. I mean, I hardly knew her. Still, it's sort of a bummer hearing she got killed."

The Dollard phone transcripts for that Sunday had, I thought I recalled, included among Cloris's many long-distance calls, one to Atlanta, but given the department's premise that robbery was the motive for the crime, morning calls had not been followed up. I asked, "What favor?"

"Right. Well, I was down in Atlanta on business, and C&W, I guess, told Mrs. Dollard I'm staying at the Hyatt Regency, so she catches me in on Sunday morning. I was half-asleep, to be honest. It was damn funny. Out of the blue." Then Whetstone sat back with a silky rimple of his pastel suit, and waited expectantly for me to invite him to continue. He had an effective rhetorical trick of luring you on by pausing. When I said, "And?" he recrossed his legs and told me that Cloris Dollard had called him for advice: an Atlanta textiles firm had approached her recently about purchasing any drawings there might still be in her possession executed by her first husband, Bainton Ames, shortly before his death; designs for an innovative type of loom that was supposed to cut costs and labor.

"Why should they want a design at least fifteen years old?" I asked.

"Oh, back then they couldn't be bothered with energy efficiency, you know; they all thought Ames was some kind of half-baked, genius-type nut." Whetstone opened his eyes wide to symbolize madness. "But now it's the thing; everybody's into saving power, et cetera. So, okay, Mrs. Dollard digs out these old Ames folders, but naturally she doesn't have the foggiest what she's looking for, so she zips over to old Cadmean here in town, and he tells her anything Bainton Ames designed belongs to *him*. And he grabs the papers away from her. So, that was that. Mind if I smoke? Ever try these Ultra Lights? Pretty damn good."

I pushed over an ashtray (one I'd made up in the mountains), and Lawry slid from his pocket a leather-and-gold cigarette case that was exactly like the one Susan had given me and I could feel now in my breast pocket being beaten on by my heart. Why had old Briggs Cadmean lied to me by saying Cloris had never brought him any designs? Why lie? I asked Lawry, "What does this have to do with her calling you?"

"Oh, I'm C&W, too." He gave me a collegial shrug. "She liked to ask men's advice; you know the type. So, okay, she says she's started getting p.o.'d at old Briggs; he's such a senile old bullshitter, I'm not surprised. So, he tore her head off about the designs, and she's p.o.'d, et cetera, you know: 'Who is he to tell *me*?' She's the inventor's widow, right? And what she wants to know is, does Cadmean really have the right to stop her from selling them?"

"Well, she had the copies she'd made," I said. "Did he grab the copies?"

"Copies? Oh, I guess, well, I didn't know about that."

Staring down at my note pad, I kept doodling the word *Cadmean*, making stairs of it. "My mother was with Cloris when she had some copies made. She mentioned it."

"Nice tie," Whetstone said suddenly. I looked up and saw him studying my chest. "Dior?"

I flipped the cloth over and read the label. "Valentino. What exactly did Cloris want your advice about?"

"Nice tie. She wanted me to get in touch with the textiles guy who'd approached her. I said I would, and I'd call her back. Just to be a nice guy, right?"

"Was this a Cary Bogue at Bette Gray Corporation?"

He grinned as if I'd just told a clever joke. "How'd you know Bogue?"

"He was with Bainton Ames the night of his death; way back. I've been looking back at the reports."

"Right." Whetstone nodded. "I actually gave Bogue a call on this Mrs. Dollard thing, and he mentioned that drowning episode. Did you know this? Pretty interesting. Ames was so pissed then at old Briggs Cadmean, he was planning on walking out. That's why Bogue was up there, negotiating about getting him to come down to Atlanta. Ames had come up with some new rapier-type loom, I guess."

I had to get out of my chair and start walking. Why hadn't Bogue mentioned this to Stanhope at the time? Had Cadmean known Ames was leaving him? Walter Stanhope's rasping whisper came back. *If I were you, I'd be leery of the man with the strings.*

Whetstone gave me the ingratiating smile that he followed with the pause.

"Leaving why?" I asked. "Did Cadmean know?"

"Couldn't say who knew. Way before my time. The story I heard was that Ames had a burr in his butt about old Briggs's roughing up the union types that were agitating back then. Ames—now, this is all according to Bogue—Ames was trying to pressure the old man into going union by holding the designs out on him, and when Mr. C. called his bluff, Ames said he was taking his ball and was going to go play elsewhere. You know how it was in the old days. A little sandbox and everybody kicking sand. A more personal-type lifestyle, know what I mean?" Whetstone leaned smoothly forward and twisted his cigarette out half smoked. His eyes were as blue and as empty as the sky, and they were the precise color of his pocket handkerchief. I had been dreading the possibility that I would *like* Lawry Whetstone. But I didn't like him.

Now he smiled broadly, his teeth slightly bucked and intensely white in his tan face. "The thing is," he said, "it's all so rinky-dink. I mean, about the dumb designs. You know? Bogue told me it was no big deal; sure, he was curious to see the drawings, but what he really wanted was an intro to talk about buying some kind of coin collection. He's a coin-type nut. But old Briggs, that's just the sort of small beer he has a hernia over, the loom thing. How the designs belonged to him. That man is so out of it. And too full of himself to step down."

I sat back. "What do you mean, out of it?"

Whetstone pulled on his nose and then glanced at his nicely buffed nails. "Ever met our Mr. Cadmean?"

"Yes."

"Well, then you know what I mean. How he loves every square inch of C&W. How *FDR* shook his hand for beating the 'Krauts and Japs' with his parachutes. Et cetera. Right? Whereas, news flash. We *are* Germany and Japan. Old Briggs hasn't got even a rudimentary grasp of what's going on at C&W these days. But you'd have to kill the old shit to get him out."

I leaned back on the rear legs of my chair. "That's not what I hear from him. He says he's down there all day every day."

Whetstone laughed; his tan fingers laced around one knee; on his right hand, a gold college ring. "Right! And the peacock spreads its tail on NBC every day too. But it doesn't negotiate the deals, now does it? I like to say, 'Corporations aren't made out of whole cloth': obviously, if we'd counted on the cotton mills for capital, Chink imports would have closed C&W down years ago, the way they have most of the old man's buddies. Nobody wants to tell him, but his beloved mill is just a dinosaur we have to work around until we can cart off the bones." His grin invited me to share in this corporate fun, but instead I tore the scribbled note off the pad, and asked him to repeat the times and contents of his calls to Cloris Dollard on the day of her death. He did so affably.

Then he surprised me by leaning over my desk and picking up

the silver letter opener Susan had given me. It was the most recent of her gifts and the one that had prompted my asking her again to stop buying me things, and her telling me again that one of the advantages of having an affair was it gave her someone else to shop for. Shopping was her occupation. Now Lawry tapped his forefinger on the silver blade's tip. "Are you in a real hurry?" he asked. "Susan give you this?"

I kept my eyes on his, their blue blankness impossible to interpret. "Yes," I answered. "She did."

"Nice." He placed it back at a pleasant angle to the rock crystal desk garniture. "I've got one too," he added. "Listen, have you got a minute, Justin? To be honest, this Dollard thing was a kind of excuse to come in."

Here, then, it came. And what I couldn't understand was why he was smiling the energetic salesman's grin that was too kinetic to be so close to the eyes' blue blandness.

"Justin," he said, and I felt his body as well as his voice hone toward me. "Justin, Susan really enjoys herself with you. She really does. The thing with you's been a good deal for her. You and I have never laid it out, but let's take it as programmed in—and filed. And go from there. Right?"

My throat felt dry as sand, dry as mornings in the mountains when I would awaken to the faint jiggle of the nurse's tray and wonder why she, a stranger, should come with such efficient comfort into my estranged delirious room. It took me a minute to wet my throat enough to reply. "I don't know what to say, Lawry. I hadn't realized you knew about my relationship with Susan. I can only—"

He broke in cheerfully. "Come on! Let's be real! This is today. You knew Susan and I have always been open about all our affairs."

I reached into my jacket for my cigarettes. "No, I assure you. I didn't know you *had* 'affairs.'"

He grinned. "Well, you knew of at least one affair that one of us was having." And he pointed at the gold-trimmed case in my hand. "Come on, Justin, everything's fine, not to worry, okay? Long as nobody's got herpes." He guffawed, then looked at me. "You know, Susan told me you weren't going to make this too easy."

"Make what easy?" The sweat was starting across my upper lip, and heat pulsing into my hands. "Make *what* easy?"

Looking at his coat, he said, "Well, to be honest, what would you say to the possibility of a foursome? How does that strike you?"

"A foursome?"

"You know." He gave his nose a few short pulls, and turned to me and smiled.

"No, I don't." But I was beginning to suspect that I did, and the skin of my scalp warmed.

Whetstone's voice became confidential. "Look. I'd really enjoy getting something together, and so maybe you would too. I've got this gal I've been seeing, works in Personnel. She's pretty damn great, believe me. And we've tried it with another couple." He nodded at me encouragingly, as if he were selling me insurance. "It worked out fantastically, just great. So, okay, what I'm proposing is, how about getting her together with Susan and you and me, and see what happens? Susan says fine with her—you know her, she's adventuresome, right?—but she didn't think you'd go for it. But me, I like to say, nothing ventured, nothing et cetera. I promise," he laughed, "we won't do any coke around you. She tells me you really don't like getting into that. Okay?"

I stood up fast. "The answer's no."

Undismayed by my face, Whetstone rose from my father's old chair and advised me, "Remember the old cliché, don't knock it 'til. Think it over. Maybe you've already got somebody else you're into things with now. I don't know what your lifestyle is, but somebody new'd be okay with me, if it's okay with Susan. Does she know her? I mean, no real reason it has to be this gal I was mentioning before. Slash is slash, right?"

I hit him. I didn't know I was hitting him, I didn't know I'd come around the side of my desk to do it, until I was watching my fist fly into his jaw and seeing his tan complacent face shoot backward, the mouth open in suprise. His head clattered loudly down the front of my file cabinet to the floor. From down there he rubbed his blue handkerchief over his jaw and then stared at it eagerly. There was no blood. After that, he looked up at me; his unclouded eyes giving no signal at all of what he might say. Then he bounced agilely to his feet, wiggled his jaw, and said, "What's with you? You some kind of S&M macho cop type or something? I'm beginning to wonder about Susan's taste."

"Me too," I said.

The doorknob turned, and Cuddy Mangum's head poked through. "Excuse me," he drawled. "I thought I heard the sound of violence. Y'all playing squash, or what?"

I said, "This is Mr. Whetstone. He just brought us some information."

"Sounds like it wasn't very good news," Cuddy said.

Whetstone pulled his cashmere coat off the rack and wiggled his finger at Cuddy. "You ought to do something about this guy." He shook the finger at me. "He's a nut."

"Well, we'll give him some more shock treatments," Cuddy replied. "Let me walk you out, Mr. Whetstone. Our chief's in the hall, and he's not very stable either." He turned to me sternly. "Savile, go to my office."

I said to Lawry, "If you want to continue, I'm at your service."

"God Almighty," Cuddy muttered. "He wants to fight a duel."

Chapter 21

Cuddy Mangum's cubicle was stacked with crates of paperback books, for which he had the same ravenous appetite that was set loose upon the candy bars and crackers whose boxes and cellophane wrappers littered the area near the wastebasket, giving his floor the look of a movie theater after a Saturday matinee. On one of his walls was a poster of Elvis Presley, and on the other a blackboard, and on the blackboard were scribbled notations of the sort always there, for Cuddy thought aloud with chalk in what he called an academic way, although I'd often suggested that it was actually from detective films that he'd acquired his diagramming habit. This he admitted: "Well, hey, of course. How do you think the Indians learned how to sneak up on the buffaloes except from watching the dance? The whole twentieth century comes out of the movies— luvvv, everything, don't you know that? You're the smoking detective and I'm the chalking detective. I've got six channels, movies is all they show. Some of them are real old black and white ones; you'd like those."

Cuddy apparently had eliminated Rowell as a suspect in Cloris's killing on principles of schematic parallel structure. Despite his continual reminders to me that it is only in books that the same character commits all the murders, he was, in his investigations, strongly drawn to any congruity in modus operandi.

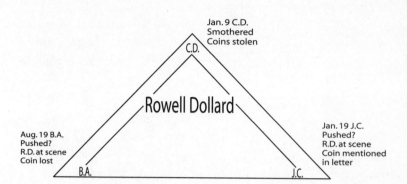

Here not only the obvious significance of Rowell's presence at the scene on the nights of both Bainton Aimes's and Joanna Cadmean's deaths, and the significance of their both falling (or getting pushed) were figured in; he also had inscribed in his geometric angles the fact that there had been discussion on both nights (Ames at the restaurant to Cary Bogue, Mrs. Cadmean to me by letter) of the 1839 Liberty quarter-eagle coin that was subsequently found in Cloris Dollard's closet. He also seemed to think relevant the coincidence that both falls to death—separated by fifteen years—had taken place on the nineteenth of the month; the only fact in the cases that seemed to me to *be* just a coincidence.

I was studying his triangle when he loped back into his office and poked me pedagogically on the collarbone. "General Lee," he said, "you are on the hill at Gettysburg, and if you will look around you, most of the coats you see are blue."

I said, "Yours is gray." He had on again his new three-piece herringbone suit.

"You are not supposed to be here. You are particularly not supposed to be here whopping your girlfriend's husband in the jaw, who, by the way, just probably established Mrs. Dollard's time of death for us at about 11:07, which is the time he said her phone clicked off, and which is jest a leetle too quick for the senator to have zipped in from Raleigh to kill her. However, I must say, I didn't like old Lawry either. He had too many teeth, and every one of them was perfect. On the other hand, why wasn't *he* hitting *you*? You're the adulterer. 'Course, I'm not too up on the customs of the porticos-and-polo set."

"Let's drop it," I said. "I've got to go. Rowell asked to see me this evening. I don't know what for. And Ratcher Phelps wants to see me too, so I'm going there first. Want to come? I'll explain in the car."

Pulling straight up on one of his many cowlicks, he looked like a lanky puppet dangling from his own hand. "Sorry," he sighed. "I've got an armed robbery, and an exhibitionist. And I have just returned from another little drive that was your idea, and that may be enough for me. But I had to testify in Raleigh anyhow, so…"

"You saw Burch Iredell? You got out to the vets' hospital?"

"Yep, I slid on over through the slurp and saw your old coroner for you about the Ames drowning. Hiram Davies neglected to give you an update on Mr. Iredell, because time has bullied him around in the meanwhile, bad. I asked him if he could remember back fifteen years, he said he could remember back to the Flood. I said this was more like a lake. I asked him, 'Mr. Iredell, you have any thoughts about whether back fifteen years ago Mr. Bainton Ames (since you were coroner back then and you signed the official papers) might have been, unofficially, murdered, and if so, sir, by whom?' Well, Mr. Iredell said he certainly did have a notion Ames was murdered. Said the man sitting across from us had done it. Said this man shot Ames with the same rifle he'd used on JFK."

"Come on," I said. "Are you making this up?"

Cuddy flopped down in his chair and threw his long legs over the edge of the metal desk. He sighed, "I wouldn't have the heart. You eat lunch? You tore out of the house so early to eat breakfast with Alice the future governor, I bet you're hungry. You want that extra grinder? It's meatball. I'm losing my appetite from falling in love."

I ate the gooey sandwich, leaning my head over the wastebasket, while I told him why he'd better get back in touch with Cary Bogue. Then he told me more about his visit to the former Hillston coroner.

"Now, where the nurse wheeled Mr. Iredell out for us to have our little talk was the so-called recreation room of this veterans' hospital, which speaking as a vet, all I can tell you is, it's a funny way for a country to say, 'We appreciate it, boys,' because this particular snotgreen-painted place was truly ugly and had gotten all tumbledown—and was el-cheapo for openers. And I sure wouldn't want to get recreated there—the reason being almost everybody I saw was about as scrawny and lost-looking as a plucked fowl escaped from Colonel Sanders. All this recreation room had was a little old black and white TV with furry channels, and some worn-out jigsaw puzzle boxes of the Grand Canyon, and these plastic checkers that the fellow that had allegedly murdered Mr. Ames was playing a game of solitaire with. Now, this alleged murdering fellow didn't have any legs, had his pajamas folded over with safety pins, and he looked to me more the meditating type than your Mr. Iredell seemed to think he was, what with accusing him of killing Ames, JFK, the little children in Atlanta, plus being a North Korean spy who's been slipping into Iredell's room every night and stealing his desserts and planting electrodes in his head. Which the latter may be true, because your Mr. Burch Iredell, by the way, had a sort of sit-down disco movement to him, including his eyeballs, that didn't seem to wear him out at all." Still seated, Cuddy suddenly flailed himself about in palsied gyrations, his eyes spinning like Ping-Pong balls in a bingo hopper.

I said, "Will you quit kidding?" I had spent in the mountains many unending mornings in such a recreation room, among the checkers and the spasms, where each minute stretched like an orange pulling loose from the bough, too slowly to see it let go. I said, "Look, it's nothing to kid about."

Cuddy shook his head. "It ain't my joke, General. It's the Lord's. If you think that's kidding, you should have seen some of the fellows out there couldn't make it down the hall to get to this recreation room. Let's just leave it that your Mr. Iredell's opinion is not going to be much use to Ken Moize in a court of law. Because law's got no imagination." Cuddy blew out another long sad sigh. "Humankind," he said, "is breaking my heart." Then he shuddered off the subject, and scooted his chair over to a paper package lying on one of his book crates. "Now, tell me, which one of these do you think? Which goes better with my suit?" He pulled out two ties. "I'm trying to improve my image so I can get Briggs junior to marry me. Women are always after you, and all I can figure is, it must be your clothes."

"They don't marry me."

"Oh, they will when you mean it. Come on, which one?"

The first of the ties looked like a summer lightning storm, and the other one had orange squares on it. I said, "Are you seriously asking me?" He nodded morosely. I took off my own tie and handed it to him. "This one," I said. "Trust me."

"That's what my ex—"

"I know, I know."

So I went by myself and tieless through snow now crunchy as brown sugar to see Ratcher Phelps in East Hillston at the Melody Store. Up front a young woman was clerking, and back among his pianos, Mr. Phelps sat in his black suit and black patent leather shoes and sheer black nylon socks. He was playing a banjo and talking a song to himself, as solemn as a family lawyer at the reading of a will. He kept on with it as I walked toward him: "If you need a good man, Why not try me?…" His long spoon-curved nails plinked a last sharp chord as I finished the verse for him in a soft whistle, my ears going pink as I heard myself doing it. He said, "Hmmmm," his moist doleful eyes quickly blearing over a look of wry interest. "You know that tune, Lieutenant?" he asked.

"Yes, sir. 'Big Feeling Blues,' isn't it? I have it on a Ma Rainey record, with Papa Charlie Jackson playing banjo."

"Hmmmm." He placed the glittering instrument carefully on top of the spinet behind him and gave a slide of his hand to his hair. The hair was a flat black color that looked dyed and straightened; he combed it with a deep side-part. "You like the blues?" he asked me. I nodded. He nodded back. He said, "I have it in my remembrance that a piano," he skipped his hand, a diamond ring twinkling, over the spinet's keyboard, "that a piano is your particular favorite. Who do you like on blues piano?"

I told him, "I like Fletcher Henderson. Lovie Austin. Professor Longhair. I like this lady Billie Pierce a lot. I like mostly old blues."

He nodded in a stately way and repeated his oleaginous "Hmmmm," and then we rested with that.

"Well, Mr. Phelps," I began, "on the phone this morning you mentioned wishing to discuss this matter of reciprocity with me. Here I am." I sat down on a piano bench across from his.

Wetting his lips and pursing them a few times for practice, he said, "Young man, I have deliberated in my mind, and I have gone to my heart and asked it. And I believe that your," he paused, searching among the spinets for a word, "your misimpression about my business, which is the business you see here before you, and not the jewelry business, *was* a misimpression."

I smiled, nodding. "Mr. Phelps, I am here as a music lover. And I am here alone. And anything you may kindly choose to say will be held in the uttermost confidentiality. I give you my word."

He accepted it with five slow nods. "Let us then," he said, the voice warming, "let us then take a supposing. Suppose on that constitutional walk I believe I told you I have the habit of taking?"

"Yes?"

"Suppose those particular articles I believe you told me you were looking for, suppose they came to my notice, and the individual which they did not belong to also came to my notice? Now, in such a supposing as that, what would be interesting to know is if you people have any remuneration in mind for the recovery of those lost articles…throwing in that unnamed individual for no charge?"

I gave him a very serious frown. "Mr. Phelps, Mr. Phelps. I thought we had already settled on your remuneration—when we came to our agreement on the matter of your nephew Billy, and his upcoming trial. Here you are raising the rent."

Like a minister of an old Ming dynasty, he stood up, small, portly, and sedate. "Billy," he said, "is my sister's baby. That poor widow grieves over her boy, and I in my heart at night in bed, I grieve over her, and a little extra re…muneration would go far to help ease her trials, and rent. That lost property is valuable property. According to you white people that lost it, now. I wouldn't know. Worth more than all you see before you."

I stood up too, and we studied each other. Meanwhile, at the front of the store, a fattish child with idolatrous eyes spluttered notes out of the brassy, bright trumpet the clerk had taken down for him; his mother watched, pleasure and distress both in her face.

Finally, I asked Ratcher Phelps if he had the stolen jewelry and coins with him. He said this was a music store. I asked him if he knew where the goods were, and who had them. He asked me to find out what the reward would be if he answered that question, and then ask it again. He offered me another of his suppositions: it would be astute of me to hypothesize that the more quickly I returned with an agreeable figure, the more likely I was to be present at an upcoming rendezvous between Mr. Phelps and the unnamed seller of the Dollard property. I was to suppose that Unnamed had contacted Phelps out of an urgent need for immediate cash.

I asked, "Are we talking about a Mr. Luster Hudson?"

Phelps rubbed his topaz cuff link, big as a cat's eye, on the black sleeve of his other arm.

"Ron Willis?" I asked.

"Young man," said Ratcher Phelps, "we are talking about Ma Rainey and Billie Pierce." He picked up his banjo, cradling it across his dapper pouch. "And," he added, leading me to the front of the store, "up here let me call to your attention a book of Fats Waller's melodies that I am partial to, and I believe you would find them interesting to undertake."

With a hand on his shoulder, I stopped him. "Mr. Phelps, now, let's spell this out, all right? I get this money for you, and you've got to promise me I'm going to be there looking on when those coins are turned over to you."

His perfectly specious smile rippled over the deep black jowls. "Oh, young friend," he said. "Let's just play the tune. Let's not sing out all the words."

Chapter 22

I don't like hospitals. My father liked the clarity of urgency there. I don't like the sterile smell, the sealed windows, the sharp quality of light and life insisted on. When I was a child, University Hospital meant to me the big square building that wanted my father to be in it most of his time, and that would call him away loudly out of his sleep, insisting that he return. As this building was also the ogre-haunted, inexplicable maze into which, from time to time, elderly relatives of mine would walk, never to come out again, simply to vanish from my life, I was always terrified that my father, too, would be snapped up by whatever monster crouched hungry behind some turn of the endless halls. He, a surgeon, always joked that no doctor and no nurse of his acquaintance would be caught dead staying in University Hospital as a patient; they knew too much to risk it. "Good Christ, Peggy," he'd say, "whatever happens, just keep me at home in bed and let me sniff chicken soup." But, of course, the ambulance that sludged through snow to the foot of Catawba Drive where I sat in the smashed car, holding my father, blood from my mouth sliding onto his unconscious face, that ambulance rushed him straight to University Hospital, where they are supposed to know how to make the bad things stop happening. And after six months more, he was caught dying there; while west in the mountains, in a hospital of recreation rooms, I was caught alive.

Rowell Dollard had once come to visit me in the mountains to tell me I was killing my father and was killing myself. Today I was coming to University Hospital to visit him, and hear him try to convince me he was not a murderer too.

Outside Rowell's door, Officer Wes Pendergraph sat reading *Sports Illustrated*. Inside, on the angled pillows, the silver hair gleamed as if it really were indestructible metal not subject to the dissolution of color and flesh that had in two days withered my uncle's face. The face, gazing out the flat window, did not turn until I said, "Rowell."

"Justin. Well." His eyes moved toward me; in them, anger too weak for his customary passion. "Your mother telephoned me from Alexandria."

"Yes, I spoke with her too."

"What did she say to you?" Rowell asked.

I didn't say she'd called crying and bewildered; how could Joanna be dead, Rowell be her murderer, me be his accuser? And crying, asked, had my suspension from work been brought on by a relapse into an alcoholic craziness? I told her only that it had not, and that other than so saying, I would not discuss with her the investigation of Rowell Dollard. "He's *family*, Jay," Mother had kept repeating. I said to Rowell now, "She is naturally distressed. She wants to come back to Hillston, but she has to stay with the children until Vaughn and Jennifer return from Antigua. She asked me to send flowers to Joanna's services." Actually, by Joanna Cadmean's will, there were to be no services, merely private cremation. Old Briggs was apparently making the arrangements.

"Will you sit down, please? I can't see you." Rowell's voice, once so heartily senatorial, was now faltering.

"All right." I pulled over the vinyl chair. "How are you feeling?"

"They've brought my blood pressure down. But there's an embolism lodged in my lung."

"Yes, I was told. I'm sorry."

"I'm not supposed to laugh too hard and send it to my brain. That is, under the circumstances, hardly likely... You've been taken off the investigation."

"Yes."

"I would still like to talk with you about it"

"As you say, the matter is out of my hands. If your lawyers think you should talk to anyone, talk to Ken Moize."

Dollard inched up farther on the pillows. "I said I want to talk to *you*."

"All right."

"I did not kill Cloris! I cannot believe that you could have thought I did."

I looked at him a long time, then I said, "I owe you an apology for having believed otherwise."

Dollard let his breath out abruptly, as if startled to realize his lungs were filled.

I added, "But it is Mrs. Cadmean's murder the prosecutors are taking before the grand jury Monday."

"I am not guilty of that, either. She died exactly as I told you."

"Would you believe it if *you* were still solicitor! Does it look like suicide to you?"

"No." His protuberant eyes fixed on mine. "No. It looks like murder. It *was* murder. Her own."

"Her own?"

His head raised from the pillow, his neck veinous. "Yes! Listen to me. Joanna murdered herself…so that I would be convicted."

"Jesus, Rowell! That's preposterous."

"Is it? I've lain here thinking about everything, and I know it's so." His voice quickened, and he stopped himself, then began again slowly. "She must have been planning it for years. She planned it perfectly."

His eyes closed shut but moved restlessly beneath the lids as he went on in the strange thin voice. "You, Justin, were the perfect one to use. The perfect one to go to first."

"What do you mean by that?"

His head lay motionless on the pillow, the eyes shut. "You are a sympathetic person. And an imaginative one. You are too young to know many of the circumstances of the past, but close enough to care. You are a relative of mine. And you don't like me."

Neither of us spoke. Outside, the clouds filled with a rusted rose color, and day's light slipped lower in the room. From the hall filtered to us the rumbling screak of tray carts.

Then Dollard spoke again, his voice still as the time. "Joanna hated me. She never forgave me for breaking off with her. It was…unacceptable to her. After I ended it, while she was still at the university, she called me…continually, at all hours, pleading, threatening. She was *obsessed*. One time, she demanded I come to her dormitory room or she would cut her wrists. I refused, I didn't believe her. I was wrong. I found out she had nearly died—*would* have died, if her roommate had not returned unexpectedly from home. She has done this before, Justin. Don't you see?" He stopped, pacing his breaths with concentrated effort, while outside the red darkened.

I stood by the sealed window to watch night come on. I said, "You are telling me Mrs. Cadmean plotted her suicide to make it look as if you had murdered her?"

"Yes."

"*She* took the phone from the hook, she broke the door chain in the study, she tore off her own watch?"

"Yes."

"And your scarf, in her hand?"

"She must have picked it up in the hall. I didn't notice. I was terribly upset, Justin! God! She led me up to the study. Do you think if she had been trying to get away from me—on crutches!— I couldn't have caught her?"

"She could have been already upstairs. You could have forced her upstairs."

His eyes stared at me but were seeing back to that night. "She stood there, and *smiled*. And said, 'This time I am leaving *you*. And this time you will suffer.' And then…she jumped."

"Again, Rowell, we're back to, why were you there? She did not call your house on the nineteenth. That's a fact."

His forefinger knuckle rubbed against his lips. "No, she didn't. I had phoned her earlier myself; I admit that. I was furious that she had been in my home. That she'd manipulated you into bringing her there. It was then she told me if I didn't come over that night…She threatened me."

I looked around at him. "With what? That's the point, isn't it?" He pushed the knuckle hard into his upper lip.

I said, "Rowell, you read the letter Mrs. Cadmean wrote me."

"*Lies*! Incredible lies. That's when I knew how long she had planned this…monstrous…" His voice faded.

"You know we have checked, and she did come to Hillston last summer, and there is a record of a call from your number to hers on St., Simons Island at the time she said Cloris called."

"For God's sake, can't you understand?! I called her, to demand that she stop her vile accusations to Cloris. *She would never let me go.*" Rowell's voice itself sounded penned by a furious frustration. "When she married Charles Cadmean, I thought that would be the end of it, but, no, the letters…*demented* letters, Justin…kept coming. Years later, after Cloris and I married, they still kept coming. This has gone on half my life! I don't mean all the time. But she besieged us. It was maddening. We never knew when. Years even could go by. We would forget. Then late at night, the phone would ring and it would be her again. That voice! You have no idea… Upsetting Cloris dreadfully. Telling Cloris how she'd been made to suffer. Telling her I had—," he pressed his hand against his forehead.

I said quietly, "Had killed Bainton Ames?" He said nothing. "We know you were at the inn the night Bainton died. Why did you take his coin? Good Christ, Rowell, why did you *keep* it?!"

Straining, Dollard pulled himself upright on the bed. "Justin, Joanna *put* that coin there in Cloris's closet two days ago. She must have. That's why she made you bring her to my house. She was upstairs alone, wasn't she?"

I sat back down. "And where is she supposed to have gotten it?"

"It's a duplicate."

"No, it's genuine."

"For God's sake, Bainton's was not the only one of that series, was it?! There must be dozens of them. You have to find out where she bought it. Can't you see how *long* this woman has been plotting to ruin me? She wants to kill me!"

I said, "She's the one who's dead, Rowell. That's a rather extreme form of revenge."

"I tell you, she was psychotic!"

I shook my head. "Everything you tell me, especially if true, especially if she did hate you this bitterly, all the more reason for you to get rid of her."

"*She killed herself.* Justin, Justin, please. She actually believed that I would come back to her! When she spoke to me at Cloris's grave, she actually believed that now I would come back to her. She had *waited.* I told her she was out of her mind. *She killed herself.*"

Behind us the door whooshed silently open and a young doctor, an East Indian with deep, placid eyes, entered the room. "Sir," he said in a purr, "I must say to go. Senator Dollard must be staying undisturbed." With long, attenuated fingers he lifted Rowell's wrist to take his pulse. I told the doctor I was just leaving. "Good, then," he murmured.

Passive and quiet in the hands of the hospital, Rowell looked up at me. He said, "Will you help me, Jay? She plotted against you, too."

I said, "Do you have any of these demented letters she's supposed to have written you?"

He shook his head angrily. "Of course not. I tore them up. Why should I keep them!" He saw that I did not believe him, and closed his eyes.

At the door, I asked, "One thing, Rowell. Excuse me, Doctor. Would you be willing to give any monetary reward for the recovery of Cloris's jewelry, and the coin collection?"

"Do you know where they are?"

"I'm in contact with someone who thinks he can buy them."

"Is this coming from you on your own? Or from the department?" Rowell's voice was rising again, and the doctor held up an admonishing hand at me.

I said the department had no knowledge at this point of my informant.

"Send him here to me."

"I can't do that," I said.

He brushed his hand irritably at the doctor, who was trying to wrap a blood pressure band around his arm. Then he muttered, "Five thousand dollars. If he'll bring those things directly back here to *me*. They're mine."

"Just one thing more. Did Cloris ever mention being approached in the last year by a man named Cary Bogue, who wanted to see some technical designs Bainton left behind?"

Rowell shook his head. "What do you mean?"

"Had she kept any of Bainton's Cadmean Textiles files?"

"There might have been some in the basement. I don't know; what if there were? Justin, what are you talking about? For God's sake!"

But the doctor took me firmly by the arm. "No more. Good evening." He pushed the door shut behind me.

In the hall, Wes Pendergraph dutifully stood up and dropped his magazine on the chair seat behind him. Obviously he hadn't been told of my suspension. "How's it going, lieutenant?"

"Fine," I said. "Anybody else been in there?"

"You better believe it." He showed me his pad with the names on it. In addition to his private physician, Dollard had been visited by several lawyers, by his senatorial aide, by his secretary, by the lieutenant governor, by the A.G., by Judge Tiggs, and by Briggs Cadmean. Pendergraph shrugged. "The doctors are going nuts, but, gosh, I can't keep men like Briggs Cadmean and them out, can I? And the news guys! This Mr. Percy from *The Star* won't quit!"

"You're doing fine. Take it easy, Wes."

Down in the lobby, I telephoned Etham Foster and asked him to check the coin Cuddy had found in Mrs. Dollard's diary again against Ames's records: Was it the *same* coin? I telephoned Miss Briggs Cadmean at River Rise, where she was still staying, and asked her if she had heard what Joanna was saying on the phone to Rowell that time he had called when they were both up in the tower study. She said no, she had left the room so as not to overhear their conversation. I telephoned the Melody Store and said to its proprietor, "That song we're singing without words, Mr. Phelps? I have an offer of five thousand dollars."

Ratcher Phelps hummed. "Well, well now, indeed I believe you and I are going to get along, Mr. Savile. I appreciate this, I want you to know. I'll be in touch."

Hanging up, I noticed through the glass booth Paula Burgwin hurrying toward the elevators; she glided by so smoothly wearing her fake fur hooded jacket, I thought of a lady bear on skates in an ice show. Paula was carrying a vinyl flowery suitcase. In it, she told me, were clothes for Charlene Pope, who was being released from the hospital and was going to move in with her. She explained, "Cuddy Mangum's promised us some—whatdoyoucallit?—surveillance, but I'm taking a week off from the Rib House to stay home with Charlene anyhow. I just hope they don't fire me, you know?" Paula asked me to excuse her breathlessness. "I've been racing. I just got off work, and I wanted to get here quick as I could. Who wants to stay in a hospital longer'n they have to, do you know what I mean?"

"Yes. Tell Charlene to do what Mangum tells her. You're a good friend." I held the doors as she tugged the bag into the elevator.

"She's family, is all," Paula replied. "Bye bye, thank you."

So I left the hospital, where they can't always stop the bad things, and never the worst. I went out through those wide doors that I had watched so intently as a child from the backseat of Mother's car. Watching for my father to appear again, absently patting the pockets of his long white coat, searching for his cigarettes. I would count every person released by those doors, saying to myself, he will come before I count twenty of them, before I count forty of them leaving. I would sit waiting, watching for him to escape again from the terrible vast building that I imagined as the lair of some invisible dragon who snatched away family, the dragon from whose imperishable thirst I had fled, on coming of age, to warm meadhalls where, of course, I found out the dragon comes too, leering jealous through the windows, watching, waiting.

Chapter 23

The wall of iron spears around the Cadmean mansion was gated and locked across the driveway. Snow shiny in the starlight was frozen, on the turreted bays and conical roofs, and frozen on the winter vines of the latticed arbor, and frozen on the branch tips of all the high, thicketed trees through which, flickering, I could see lights, here and there, in the dark red house. It was close to ten. No one answered the buzzer I pushed at the gatepost, or even came, inquisitive, to a window at the sound of my horn. I gave up finally and drove on through Hillston to C&W Textiles Industries.

Back in the 1840s, John Cadmean, the first of the Hillston industrialists, had not only built on the property where the mills still stood new homes and a school and a church for his workers, but he had erected his own mansion, a huge, awkward attempt at Greek Revival, right next door to the factory. All he had to do was walk across the plank path thrown over the mud street, and there he was among his clattering looms. He wanted to be close. He did everything personally. He had even persuaded the people of Hillston to help him personally lay tracks in the middle of the night for his own railroad, tracks to run right up the street to the warehouse doors, tracks to run precisely through the right-of-way of the Virginia line that held the monopoly for freight service through the Piedmont—that Virginia monopoly being the reason why he had to start his own railroad in the middle of the night. And when the workmen from the Virginia line came in wagons and tore up a hundred feet of the illegal tracks, this first of the Cadmeans had talked a state judge of his personal acquaintance into issuing warrants for the outsiders' arrest. The Cadmean line remained.

Hillston then was a roughshod, graceless town where rowdies, some of them named Pope, spilled out from cheap-fronted frame saloons and fought down among the lame vagrants, the whores, and the scrawny farmers crowding with mules in the dirt-swirled streets. Hillston stayed through the century's turn as graceless as it had begun. And although by 1900 the shrewdest brigands to survive the Confederacy had bullied enough bulk of wealth to buy colleges and build conservatories and pave streets and ride upon them in open carriages with their wives, Hillston stayed still what my father, the Virginian, once said it had never stopped being: a mill town founded by a coarse breed with the trite, threadbare vision that the grabbing and holding of money was in itself a pursuit worthy of the word *civilization*; a town of a heart's-core rapacious greed plastered over with a thin smear of bromidic morality and a vulgar aesthetic. He said this at a dinner party to which—as I recall—my mother had invited both Mr. Briggs Cadmean and Rowell Dollard, neither of whom agreed with him. It was probably the only time I saw my father anywhere near as drunk as he all too often came to see me.

Old Briggs, hidden tonight behind his iron wall, was a direct descendant of that man who had allowed no right-of-way to impede his trespass. Thinking so led me to consider another congruity unmentioned in Cuddy's triangle of deaths: Bainton Ames and Luster Hudson and Ron Willis had all worked for Cadmean. Of course, half the people in Hillston did. Hillston was his; he had inherited it. If there were secrets about these murders the old man protected behind the iron gate, how was I to force a lock more than a roughshod century strong, even if I found the secret out?

The new C&W business offices (whose procedures, according to Lawry Whetstone, old Briggs failed to grasp) sat precisely where that first Cadmean had built his house. The new C&W gate was open, steel mesh rather than wood planks, and I drove through it to wait for Alice MacLeod to come rushing out from among the moil of bundled workers.

I'd seen her once today already. This morning, like the morning before, I had arrived early at the diner and was waiting for her with breakfast and with flowers—silk ones I'd taken out of a vase in my living room. This morning we had talked more about her and more about me; and listening and talking made me more and more want to listen and talk to Alice MacLeod. In fact, the thought—not the thought, the sensation—came, that I wanted to be near Alice MacLeod as profoundly as I had wanted, seven years ago, to be near whiskey.

"Hi," she said under the C&W lights, and I said, "Hi," and we stood there jostled by the ravel of men and women headed shivering toward their cars and homes.

We moved through our talk slowly in the general direction of the old Volkswagen she'd parked at the far end of the first lot. Then, over her shoulder, I saw someone I thought I knew. Edging the area of new C&W construction at the border of the lot were three work-trailers up on blocks. Behind them were rust-brown girders, the low skeleton of what, according to signs, would be eventually C&W ELECTRONICS DIVISION. The person I thought I saw peering out one of the trailer doors was Ron Willis, and when the moon slid over the spider tank atop the main factory, so that I could see his oddly white hair before he pulled on the orange John Deere cap, I knew that it was Willis.

"Go home, I'll come there!" I abruptly told Alice. And I started running hard toward the trailer, cutting across aisles of moving cars. I was not close enough to catch him when Willis saw me and saw that I was coming for him. He sprinted off around the side of the trailer. I heard a car rev, and then the tan Camaro came out fast. I was right in his path. A gun came out of the driver's window and shot wildly. Screeching, cars all around us bucked to a stop as I flung myself off the Camaro fender, got to my gun, fired, missed, and started running again back through the lot, cursing out loud because my Austin was parked all the way at the other end of the plant, and Willis, horn blaring, was in a fast weave through the astonished traffic.

Then I heard the VW's horn, and Alice was backing at high speed toward me. I tumbled by hops into the seat beside her as she reversed gears.

"Go!" I yelled. "He's at the gates!"

"Was that Ron Willis?"

"Yes." I reached over her hand and jerked the wheel. "Left! Through there. Okay, just get me close enough to try to shoot out the tire! Watch out! *Jesus Christ!*"

She had sheered in a thudding tilt up on the curb and was passing around the right side of the line of cars exiting at the factory gates. I could hear the metal on my door shriek against the steel post.

"Take a right!" I leaned out the window. "See him?"

"Yes. Damn this damn car!"

By now we'd fallen half a block behind. We were going to lose him. The Camaro bounced over the top of the rise ahead on Wade Boulevard.

"*Now watch it,*" I said. "Watch the snow! You're skidding!"

As we came over the crest of the hill, I saw that halfway down the other side, the rear of Willis's car was starting to slip sideways. He brought it back in line, sped up, slid again, and then his brake lights came on and stayed on, and he began to pinwheel in the icy crust, spiraling down the street. A station wagon coming from the opposite direction cut away from him, went off the road, and hit a mailbox on the corner. The Camaro slid sideways up onto the sidewalk in front of us.

"God, I'm going to hit him, I can't stop!" Alice yelled. But she did stop. With two feet to spare.

Gun in hand, shaking, I was out of the VW and at the Camaro door when Willis suddenly accelerated, blinding me with splattering slush. His car lurched forward, and jerked me loose from the door handle I'd grabbed. I fell away, rolled out into the street, fired two shots into the rear tire, and one into the back window. This time the Camaro smacked into a parked van on the other side of the street, and stopped. The woman driving the station wagon screamed. A teenage couple hopped out of the parked van. As I pulled Willis from his front seat, he kicked at me. I hit him in the stomach, and he dropped to his knees in the brown, oily snow.

"What the fuck are you doing?" he gasped, his white hair flopped over the dazed eyes.

I said, "I want to ask you a couple of questions." I told him his rights, which he assured me he already knew. Then I cuffed his hands behind him to the streetlight.

No one was hurt. The teenagers were confusedly shaking glass slivers out of their hair. The woman in the station wagon had bitten her lip and was deeply upset because she'd only driven out to buy some coffee. She kept repeating this fact as a great injustice: "All I went out for was a can of coffee." Beneath a scarf, her hair was in plastic rollers.

When I reached Cuddy Mangum on the phone, I told him to send along a squad car, and to radio for a wrecker.

"Justin," he groaned. "Will you please just stay home, so I can?"

I said, "I am at home, on sick leave. This is a big collar for you, Mangum. If you want to score with V.D., better get over here quick."

My weak leg buckled as I walked back from the Dot 'n' Dash to the intersection. The teenagers were staring at Ron Willis. The woman with hair rollers was staring at the gash now bent into her car's front end. Alice MacLeod was staring at me. "Are you limping?" she asked, her hands tucked under her arms, her eyes filled with a caring so wonderful to me that smiling wasn't enough and I laughed aloud. "I'm fine. How are *you?*"

She was laughing too. "You mentioned us going out somewhere tonight. Was this it?"

"Well, wasn't it pretty exciting for a first date?"

She looked past me at Willis, who scowled and yanked around to turn his back on her. She said, "I was happy to help, believe me. Did he kill Mrs. Dollard?"

"I think he knows who did, if he didn't. Good Christ, Alice MacLeod, where in the world did you learn to drive like that?"

"In the mountains. We drive like that all the time."

"*Thunder Road!*"

"That's right. All that bootleg whiskey weighing down the trunk keeps us from fishtailing in the snow. You ever driven in the North Carolina mountains?"

"I've been driven in the North Carolina mountains. I'm going to tell you all about it as soon as we get out of our clothes." We were slopped with mud and slush from head to foot.

Far off I could hear the siren coming as she took my hand and looked at my watch. "It's only 10:25," she said. "Where next?"

Chapter 24

It was nearly midnight before I opened the door to my house, stepped inside behind Alice, and saw that there was going to be a scene.

Before that, Cuddy Mangum had booked Ron Willis, a surly man in his late twenties whose demeanor vacillated between whining indignation and a drug-sustained loud bravado. Willis denied he had given a gym bag to Charlene Pope to give to Luster Hudson, claimed he had no idea where Hudson was, and snarled that he refused to say anything else. He also said did I know my girlfriend had been "a nigger's whore?" Cuddy pulled me out of the room and locked Willis up for the night.

Down in the foyer, Cuddy told me that my tie had gone over so well with Briggs Junior, as he called her, that he would never forgive me for having telephoned his house when I did. Then he winked down at Alice, standing there with us, and said, "Governor, I'm trying to get this lady to marry me. That's her daddy up there on the wall giving me a nasty look." He pointed at the portrait of old Mr. Cadmean above the courtroom doors.

"Good luck," Alice said.

I told her, "Mangum's a little nuts on the subject of marriage."

"Well hey, why not?" Cuddy grinned. "Now if y'all two would come get married with us, and stop this tearing around the streets shooting off guns like *The French Connection*, we could all play bridge together and then go home. Be a foursome. Y'all play bridge? I love it."

"Good night, Cuddy," I said.

He took Alice's hand in his huge gloves. "Now listen, Red, I know old Sherlock here looks pretty pitiful now, but take my word for it, he used to be a pretty snappy dresser."

I said again, "Good night, Cuddy," and he waved his keychain of talismans at us and rubbed the rabbit's foot lavishly against the side of his nose. Then Alice drove me back to pick up the Austin, and then she followed me home.

The scene I saw coming, I saw as soon as I realized that my furnace was clanking heat up through the radiators and that Susan's mink coat was draped over the banister. She had never before come over to my house when Lawry was back in Hillston, so I was shocked. But then I had never before hit Lawry in the face, either.

"Well, sugar, it's about time. Where the crap have you been?!" Susan spoke just as Alice walked through the open door into the living room, and it was too late for me to do anything but walk in after her.

Susan was draped full-length on the white canvas couch. There was a bottle of Campari on the floor beside her, and a wineglass. She was wearing black velvet slacks and a black cashmere sweater and she was reading a hardcover book she'd brought with her, entitled *Mommie Dearest*. She did not move when she saw Alice, except to toss her head so that the mane of blond hair shook.

I stepped toward her so annoyed it amazed me that she blandly smiled when I asked, "What are you doing here, Susan?" Then I turned sideways and gestured an introduction. "Alice MacLeod, this is Susan Whetstone. Mrs. Whetstone is an old friend. What did you want to see me about, Susan?" I had told her again on the phone yesterday I wanted time to think; again she hadn't listened.

Now Susan sat up. "God, what happened to you?! Have you been rolling around in the slop out there?"

I said, "Yes."

Susan was still ignoring Alice, who stood next to me, still buttoned up in the plaid parka, her jeans and boots as soiled and soggy as mine. I kept talking without much hope for the conversation. "Alice has just helped me capture a suspect over on Wade Boulevard."

"What fun," said Susan, with a grin, and now she looked at Alice as if the latter were modeling a bizarre outfit she didn't plan to buy. She asked, "Are you a police...person too?"

"No," Alice said,

"No? Just another old friend?" And now Susan looked at me. "Or a new friend? Mighty sweet of you to play cops and robbers with Justin when it's so cold out, and at midnight, too. I thought you'd been fired, Justin. Are you a private eye now?"

Alice said to me, "Thank you for the offer of a drink, but I think I'll go home now." I could feel from the heat on my ears that they had blushed as red as Alice's hair.

"No, wait." I caught at her arm but it tensed, and I let my hand fall away. "Let me walk you to your car," I said.

"It's not necessary," Alice said.

"Oh, don't leave on my account," called Susan, stroking her hair up from the nape of her tan neck.

"I'm not," Alice said.

"You just got here. And you both look like you could use a drink. Meanwhile, have we met before, Alice? Did you say her name was Alice, sugar?"

I said, "Susan, please."

Her eyes grave and a darkening blue, Alice looked back at Susan. "Yes, my name is Alice. No, we haven't met. But I have met your husband. I work at C&W."

"You do?" Susan smiled. "What do you do there? Let me guess. You work on the line, just like in that movie *Norma Rae* with that short girlfriend of Burt Reynolds's playing a redneck with all those children by different fathers. Isn't it boring how little bitty the world is?"

Alice said, "No, I don't find the world little or boring."

"Lucky you."

"Yes. Good night." Alice walked out of the room, and I followed her.

Outside by the Volkswagen I said, "I'm sorry. I had no idea she would be here. I should have told you. I'd hoped to end—"

"Please." Alice's hand waved away my words. "There's nothing to apologize about. And I'd rather you didn't try." Her voice was as brisk as the air clouding her words. She was in her car now, but I was holding the door open. She tugged at it. "Would you please let me shut this?"

"Alice, let me talk to her and then come over to your apartment? Will you? Please? I'm so sorry for putting you in an awkward—"

She said, "I didn't feel awkward." And she pulled the door closed, and drove away.

Back inside, Susan stood at the unlit fireplace, watching herself brush her hair in the mirror above the mantel.

I said, "You were a bitch. What are you doing over here?"

She looked around and widened her eyes and then turned back to the mirror.

"Susan, let's…"

"Let's what, sugar?" She kept brushing.

"Talk."

"Talk away. Don't you want to change first? And bathe? Look at yourself."

"Lawry told you what happened?"

"He thinks you're crazy." She kept her eyes on her image.

"Because I didn't care to join his four-way fuck!"

"I told him you weren't into group things. He never listens to me. He said you knocked him down." Now she curved sideways, and looked at me, her head tilted into her hair. "That kind of turns me on."

I walked away and sat down in the rocker next to the couch. I asked her, "Will you answer a question? Have you been having other affairs? Since we've been involved?"

"Affairs?"

"Sex." I watched the big diamond move with her hand, dead in the muted light.

She glanced at her brush, pulled the loose hairs from it and balled them between her fingertips. "Do you want to know?"

"That means you have. Why didn't you tell me?"

"You're so old-fashioned, honey, I didn't think you'd want to know. It wasn't serious."

I glared at her until she shrugged and turned back to the mirror. Then she asked, "Who's that girl?"

I was quiet, listening to the rattle of the water in the radiator. Then I said, "I'm in love with her."

Susan spun around. "What? You're reading me the riot act, and you're balling that dirty little redneck hippie?"

"That's enough! And I'm not sleeping with her. I just met her."

Susan came across the room and stood over my chair. "You *are* nuts, you know that?"

I stood up, knocking over the wineglass as I squeezed past her to move away. "Listen, Susan. I've been trying to say this a long time, and now I'll just say it right out. I don't think we should see each other anymore. You never had any intention of divorcing Lawry. I don't know why I wanted you to. Let's just stop it right here and now."

"No," she said, as if I'd asked her if she wanted another drink. "I don't want to stop it."

"I *do*. I'm sorry. I don't want to see you anymore. I'm very sorry if this is hurting you."

"Oh, crap, Justin. Not again. We've played this scene before. Don't pull this on me tonight about leaving Lawry." She picked up her purse from the floor, put her brush in it, and started looking through its depths for something else.

"I don't want you to leave Lawry," I snapped. "I think you two suit each other just fine."

"Now, don't be sarcastic." She found a gold tube of lipstick.

"I mean it." I raised my voice. "Will you look at me!"

Her head swung up. "What in hell is the matter with you?"

"I said I mean it! I want us to say good-bye. I'll walk you to your car. Is it out back?"

"Are you pissed because I told you I screwed somebody else? Grow up."

"I'll get your coat."

After examining the lipstick tube carefully, she closed it and dropped it back in her purse. "Is this a joke? It's not funny."

"I'm serious."

"Oh, fuck. This is ridiculous." She laughed with a short, harsh sound. "A month from now, when you want back…"

I stunned myself by yelling, "I'm going to marry Alice MacLeod!"

Now she stared at me, her mouth in a grimace. Then she hissed, "You shit!" and bounded off the couch and slapped me across the face. I let her do it. The edge of the platinum setting of the big square diamond cut into my lip. I let her slap me twice more, and then I grabbed her wrist and pulled it down.

I said, "I'm sorry, Susan. I haven't behaved well. I wish this didn't have to be painful. You act as if it sounds like its coming out of nowhere, but…"

She yanked her arm away. "You are so full of it. I don't know why they ever let you out of that nuthouse." Swooping up her purse, she stalked into the hall and stabbed her arms into the mink coat.

I went after her. "Be honest, God damn it. You don't love *me*. You never have. I was somebody to slip off and eat lunch with. That's it."

She shook the perfect blond hair free of the fur collar. She said, "Sugar, all you ever were to me was a dick. And that doesn't mean cop."

The door slammed behind her, and the hall shuddered.

Chapter 25
Saturday, January 22

The next morning I opened one eye to squint at my brass clock, and instead I saw an old, loud-ticking tin alarm clock with two bells on top. Beyond it on a papered wall I saw a photograph of Martin Luther King, and beside that a poster of an Appalachian bluegrass festival. I turned over and I saw the red tangle of Alice MacLeod's hair. I was only an instant surprised; after that, I felt that I was looking at my life, familiar and sure as when, after traveling home from New England schools, mile by mile beside the highway, granite turned to red clay and each bend of the road was felt before seen.

I was awake and had been visited by no ghosts in white dresses—or in white hospital coats. I was freshly awake and had scarcely slept.

Last night at one when I'd rapped on the door of her basement apartment and, squatting down, had tapped on a window, Alice had pulled back the blue cotton curtains and told me through the glass to "Go away." Had not her upstairs neighbor, a brawny man I immediately detested, come down in his T-shirt to the landing of the old, partitioned house, and asked her if she wanted me "gotten rid of," she probably would never have let me in. Mud-clotted as I was, I didn't look very reputable, and I think that helped her decide in my favor.

Embarrassed, she opened the door, and embarrassed, I followed her in. I stepped down into what must have once been the kitchen of the house, down into a room that was like seeing Alice MacLeod herself, fully, for the first time. The pine furniture looked mountain-made. On the unvarnished floor was a dark-blue oval rag rug, and thrown over the couch a wedding-ring-patterned quilt of pale bleached blue. Filling a corner was a wooden handloom, its shuttle resting among green hues of thread. A typewriter was crowded by textbooks on a card table, and plants in rubber pots leaned toward the light.

"What are you doing here?" she asked.

"This is a wonderful room."

"Thank you."

"I came to ask if you would marry me," I added, shivering in my sodden clothes.

"No, I won't. Good night." In the green wool robe that fell over her bare feet, she stood stiffly upright, like a small red marigold.

"I wonder if you would give it some thought," I said.

"I don't even know you."

"Oh, yes, you do. Don't you believe: 'Whoever loved that loved not at first sight?'"

"No."

"I do," I assured her. "I want to be around you every minute you'll let me." I sneezed.

"You ought to get out of those clothes."

"All right." I pulled off my coat and jacket together, and grabbed at my sweater.

She almost smiled. "You ought to go *home* and get out of those clothes."

"Listen, *please*," I said. "I'm sorry about tonight. Susan is some-one I was involved with because I didn't care what I was doing, and neither did she. I just told her I have fallen in love with you. Could I please stay and talk to you awhile? I know it's late, but tomorrow's Saturday. No World War I to the Present." I grinned, holding my breath for her answer.

Alice frowned at me, and then she frowned at a faded photo-

graph on the mantel of the wide, low cooking fireplace. In the photograph a young, thin, serious-faced couple looked uncertainly at
the camera; he in an army uniform, with Alice's eyes; she in a cotton dress, with Alice's hair. After studying their picture, Alice
walked out of the room. She came back with a large pair of folded
denim overalls, their soft blue as pale as the quilt on her couch.
"Okay. You can wear these," she said. "Bathtub's back there."

I took them from her, saying, "I hope they belonged to your
father or your brother or your grandfather and not to that fellow
who wanted me 'gotten rid of.'"

"No brothers," she said, but she called as I walked off. "And the
guy upstairs is gay."

And so afterward I went out in her backyard and scrounged for
fallen branches to crack over my knee, and together we built a fire
with them, and we talked about the mountains. We talked about
our pasts, as though we could see them in the bright leaping fire.
And hour by hour, our eyes, spellbound, interwove all difference.
So that, when long into the night our voices sank lower, like the
fire gleaming quiet and warm, and I took her hand, our palms,
wordless, spoke on together in conference too tenuous and sensible
for speech.

When we went near morning to her bed, I had learned that her
grandfather had beveled the corners and plaited the ropes beneath
the yielding feathery mattress on which, in the dark blue dawn, we
slept.

Early Saturday as I left Alice's home, I was singing. I was thirty-
four and had long ago stopped listening to love songs as though
they had anything to say to me. Indeed, I was faintly surprised to
realize that people kept on writing the songs, and that new lovers
would be forever stepping into the dance I thought I had left for
good. And now, walking along the cold crystalline sidewalk in
those overalls, I had a feeling of such glad buoyancy, such big-
hearted, lighthearted amplitude, that I expected my feet not only
to dance but, like Paul Bunyan's, to bound over the houses, and my
eyes to wink at breakfasting families of birds in the top branches of
trees.

Chapter 26

In my living room, I sat thinking about Alice, thinking that Alice was the source of Joanna Cadmean's vision of my falling into something new, whether good or bad, she couldn't say. I was also waiting for someone to pick up Cadmean's phone. Then, after I was told for the fourth time that old Briggs was unavailable, I decided to use a family connection. I called Cuddy's River Rise condominium and spoke with Cadmean's daughter, and with some difficulty persuaded her to find out for me her father's whereabouts. When my phone rang shortly afterward, I assumed she was calling back, but instead I heard a voice whose rusty cough I recognized before he finished asking, "Could I talk to Mr. Justin Savile? This is Walter Stanhope. From the Banks."

"Hello, Mr. Stanhope. This is Justin. How are you?"

"Don't mean to intrude. Wondered how it was going."

This morning, in my own expansive state, his calling felt to me a gesture of enormous outreaching. I told him, "Sir, I'm following in your footsteps. I've been suspended." Then I told him of Joanna Cadmean's death and of the evidence that linked Rowell Dollard to it, and linked Rowell, by the coin, to Bainton Ames's death as well. I told him of Luster Hudson and Ron Willis and Charlene Pope, and of Lawry Whetstone's information. I told him that far from being further harassed by old Briggs Cadmean, I couldn't even get past the old man's iron gates to speak to him about why he had lied to me when he claimed he'd never seen the Ames designs that

Cloris had wanted to sell to Bogue.

"Ah," replied Stanhope. "Cadmean lied? Find out why. And why Bogue lied."

I told him everything Rowell had said to me in the hospital: that Joanna had plotted to kill herself in order to take revenge on him.

"Know she tried suicide before?" asked Stanhope. "Back in college."

"Yes, sir, I was told, but…"

He cleared his throat slowly. "Something didn't go into the report on that attempt. I guess, her dead, no harm saying it now. Doctor told me at the time he released her back then. She'd just had an abortion."

"Abortion?" I think this fact shocked me as much as her death.

"Not a very good one."

"My God. Dollard's?" And neither she nor Rowell had ever had another child. *Think of me as your father*, I could hear Rowell saying.

"I'd expect so." Stanhope stopped to cough. "I were you, I wouldn't shut out any possibility 'til you're sure."

"Pardon?"

"Sure that Dollard's not telling the truth about her. People can hate a long time, even ordinary ones, and she wasn't ordinary." In the background I could hear the recording of the baroque violin music stop, then in a moment another record begin.

"But to plan out her own murder like that? It'd be diabolical."

"People can be diabolical, if you want to use that word."

"But she was psychic, Mr. Stanhope. She told me she felt like there was a phone ringing while Cloris was being assaulted, and now we've found out Whetstone actually was trying to call, right then!"

"Not saying she wasn't clairvoyant. Know for a fact she was. Saw her prove it." I could hear him try to swallow. "But both can be true. The way she used to look at Dollard; it was past what most people would call love."

"Mr. Stanhope, I'm convinced she's right about Rowell killing

Bainton Ames. And I thought you agreed."

"Maybe he did. Could be she thought she could get him back by blackmailing him. Could still be true he didn't kill her. You said out here how she told you she was going to die soon. Could be she'd already planned it."

"No, what she said was somebody was going to *kill* her."

"So why didn't she protect herself? Why wouldn't she leave the lodge? Another thing; you just said it struck you funny how she was all dressed up that night, not like her regular style. That sticks out to me too. Excuse me." I could hear his muffled coughing and the wheeze for breath.

I said, "Are you all right, Mr. Stanhope?"

He said, "Okay."

"Do you mind if I ask, have you seen a doctor?"

"Yep, I've seen a lot," he replied, and changed the subject. "Well, think about that white dress. I'll tell you what I thought when you told me: dressed up for a wedding."

I had thought of that too, while Rowell was talking there in the hospital. And I had dreamt it. But I didn't want to think it; I didn't want to believe she'd made me a part of her plot.

Stanhope was asking, "Could she have planted the coin in that closet?"

And I could remember how she'd suggested she go see Cloris's bedroom, remember her going back into her own room before we left the lodge, remember the shoulder bag pressed tightly to her side as we climbed the Dollard steps together. "'Yes," I said. "And I guess she could have had the letter to me already written. And I guess if Mangum hadn't come to take Briggs out to dinner that night, she could have already figured some other way to get rid of her, once she knew Rowell was coming." I was fighting hard against what I had already started to believe yesterday as I looked into Rowell's eyes in that white room. "But the broken chain and..."

"Just saying," Stanhope whispered in his graveled voice, "keep it in mind. Up to you, but I'd try tracing that coin, and same, if you can, for the leather diary. Where were they bought, who by? And what's the C&W connection? That's what police can do. It's just no fun."

Before hanging up, Stanhope made a dry noise that could have been a laugh. "Never knew why people figured justice *ought* to be stoneblind, but I always knew she *was*. Looks like here you've got plenty of evidence to get Dollard for killing Mrs. Cadmean, which maybe, maybe now, he didn't do. And no way at all to convict him of killing Bainton Ames, which maybe he did do."

"I've got the coin."

"Well. You know juries. And after fifteen years, well."

"Maybe, Mr. Stanhope, if Joanna Cadmean did commit suicide, she realized exactly what you're saying now; she knew we couldn't get Rowell for Ames, but could get him for her."

"Could be. Kinda doubt that was her motive." His cough started again.

As we said our good-byes, I told him I had hopes of getting married by summer. He wished me well. "Hope is all I have to go on now," I said, and thought that I was beginning to sound like Cuddy Mangum. I added that the woman I wanted to marry me was from the mountains and had never seen the Banks, and that I'd like to bring her out there. "And I'd like to have her meet you then, if that's all right. Maybe in June?"

There was such a long pause, I wondered if he had put down the phone, but then he said, "Okay. I'll try to be around."

I didn't ask him what he meant, because I knew. And I stood still by the phone, with the sense that I was suddenly pinioned by this unspoken sentence of death, as if my happiness with Alice were some great bird shut into a cage so small that its wings crushed, bent against the bars. But soon enough I would forget to think there was a cage; everyone does, even the dying.

I hadn't moved when the phone rang again, scaring me. This time it was Briggs Junior, who told me that her father could be found for the next hour at the Hillston Hunt Club, and could be found later this afternoon at Joanna Cadmean's cremation, which she herself did not plan to attend. "Such rites seem beside the point," she explained.

I asked her to have Cuddy meet me at my house at five, and added, "Let me just say, Briggs, I think Cuddy Mangum is one of the finest men I ever knew."

"Are you saying that because you don't expect me to realize it?"

"No, not at all." Somehow, whenever she and I spoke, we were quick to assume the other's hostility. I mentioned this observation to her now, and said, "You know, you and I so instantly got off on the wrong foot, I thought we were destined to end up in love."

She said, "That's only true in books."

"I thought most of the true things were in books. I just wanted to say I shared your view of Cuddy, that's all." She didn't answer, and I went on, "Sorry, I'll keep quiet. But if we're going to play bridge together for the rest of our lives, we're going to have to learn how to talk to each other."

"Bridge? I don't play bridge."

Poor Cuddy's suburban dream of a table for four. Alice had told me she didn't play any games at all. And I had already played too many hands in a pacified recreation room, feeling beneath my fingertips the ruffled corners of the worn cards; looking out at winter mountains leaf into spring, swell into thick summer, then fall. Cuddy believed if he waited until he could get everything ready at once, make all arrangements, forget no detail, then life would begin for him like a birthday party at last, and keep on noisy and warm always. But in Briggs's voice I kept hearing a disengagement cool as her stars, and it worried me for him.

• • •

At the Hillston Hunt Club I found old Mr. Cadmean. In a mammoth, black hunt coat and a fur cap, he stood smoking his cigar in the middle of the club's indoor riding ring. At his feet in the loose sawdust earth lay a fat, elderly cocker spaniel. Cadmean held in his arthritic hand a lunge line; at the other end, on an enormous black horse, trotted his little granddaughter Rebecca Kay, plump and glossy as an apple in her red snowsuit. She was so tiny, the stirrup leathers had been tightened right up into the saddle skirts, but she was posting with a determined scowl and in good rhythm and thudding with her boots on the huge horse's withers whenever he forgot her slight weight was up there and slowed to a walk around the circle Cadmean was turning. A woman stood by, watching, her teeth tight on her lower lip; I assumed she was the child's mother.

"One two! One two! One two!" called Cadmean from the hub of the moving wheel. "Manassas, move your fanny! Kick him, honey! Good girl!" It surprised me to hear that this dutifully trotting horse was Manassas, the stallion who had thrown Joanna Cadmean weeks back.

"Can I jump, Grandpa?" yelled Rebecca, pointing at a low set of crossed bars behind Cadmean. She raised herself up and forward into a half seat.

"No!" cried the mother, and Cadmean growled, "No, ma'am," at the same time.

The little girl said, "I'm not a baby, I'm almost six!"

"Manassas is a baby," Cadmean was saying as he turned and saw me walking toward him, my shoes digging deep into the soft dirt.

"Hello, Mr. Cadmean." I stood outside the circumference of the stallion's trot and watched his white eye roll at me each time he snorted past. In a few minutes I said, "I've been trying to reach you for days, Mr. Cadmean."

"Have you?" He didn't look at me. "Well, looks like you found me, too. I thought I heard tell you were excused from work due to illness. Might be dangerous traipsing around sick like this." He switched hands on the line, and his bent fingers came up to shift the cigar along his small, fleshy lips.

"No, sir. That's not why I was suspended. It was for tracking dirt onto the parlor rug."

The lidded yellow eyes stayed with the horse and rider. "I believe I warned you about that very thing," he said.

"You did."

"That's right. I thought I did."

"Let me offer my condolences about Joanna." My offer was met with a nod. I added, "I'd like to attend the services this afternoon, if you have no objection."

"She put down she didn't want services, but I'm certainly not going to let her go without Reverend Campbell saying a few words over her. She was a Cadmean by name, and no nuttier than some of the others, God knows." Then abruptly he flung out his arm and introduced me to Rebecca's mother, wife of another of his sons, a gentle-faced, timorous woman whom he obviously terrified. As we exchanged hellos, the old man pulled in on the lunge line, halted Manassas, took Rebecca off over her protests, hugged her over her protests, handed her to her mother, and told them to go across the street to the Fox and Hound Restaurant and order their lunch. Rebecca parted unhappily while issuing her own command. "You better come soon, Grandpa."

"Isn't she something?" he beamed as they left the ring. "Reminds me of Baby. Did you come here to ride, Justin?"

I stroked Manassas down the white blaze of his head, while his mouth nibbled wetly at my hand. "No, I came here to see you," I said. "But I used to ride."

"I know you did. Now, who told you where I was?"

I smiled. "Why did you refuse to talk to me?"

"Where's my daughter?" He moved his cigar over to the other side of his mouth.

"Why did you call Walter Stanhope and tell him I was crazy?"

Cadmean laughed out loud. "Well, son, we got the kitty full. Somebody's got to call."

"Go ahead."

He laughed again, and we stood there until Manassas shook himself and backed away tugging at the lunge line.

Cadmean handed me the line. "Here. Ride him."

"No, thanks."

"Oh, come on, let him get the kinks out. I'll tell you this. I wish I could still get up on an animal that pretty without every joint and bone in my body screaming its goddamn head off. These are the good times, son. Don't throw them away saying, 'No, thanks.' Things just get worse and worse. They truly do. You'll wake up one morning, and it'll hurt just to move. Go on. I've got to go take a leak. I just took one, half an hour ago. That all goes to hell too. Come on, Duchess."

His old cocker spaniel lurched to her feet and paddled after him as he left me standing there with the horse and walked with his stiff carefulness to the stable office door.

I thought about it, and finally unhooked the lunge line, climbed up, and rode Manassas. At first I was tense enough to let the horse fight me with a skittish backward dance; I was nervous that I would not be able to stop thinking about Joanna Cadmean and that Manassas would feel this and would try to throw me as he had her. But finally his rhythm took me over, and I met him there and we had worked up to a canter when Mr. Cadmean came back, scraping his fingers up against the shave of his fat cheek as he watched us. When a young boy in chaps entered the ring, Cadmean called me over. The boy took Man-assas to walk him, and Cadmean, the spaniel, and I went outside and crossed the snow-curbed street. I said, "Maybe Hillston ought to invest in snowplows."

"Look over your head." Cadmean pointed at the glassy sun in a cloudless sky. "Let God plow. He's the only one doesn't come begging me for donations to buy His equipment." He paused. "I take it back. Every time I turn around, His preachers are sliding their buttered hands in my pockets."

We entered the paneled bar of the Fox and Hound Restau-rant. It was busy with boasting businessmen and Hillston women rich enough to ride. Between us we knew most of them. The bar was ostentatiously sporting: hunting horns, crops, ribbons, and etchings of red-coated riders hung on all available wall space. The bar had been modeled on the proprietor's notion of a British country pub; all the wood was varnished almost black and gouged with scratches, all the fabric was faded cabbage roses, and even the Cokes were served in pewter tankards. Above the rows of liquor was a stuffed fox who appeared to be running fast without caring where he was going, for one of his eyes glanced at the mir-ror behind him and the other one stared out at us. In the middle of the floor was a large Franklin stove; beneath it, Cadmean's spaniel, which he'd brought right inside with him, flopped over exhausted from her walk across the street. Cadmean took us to a far corner away from everyone else. He sat down in a chintz armchair under an engraving of two fox hunters taking a fence while a third fell from his horse on the way.

Sitting down across from the old man, I said, "All right. I rode your horse. Now, will you answer my questions?"

"Good horse. Am I right?"

"Very."

"Fine, fine horse, Mr. Manassas. Whiskey?" The bartender had come over with a deferential stoop.

I said, "Bloody Mary, very weak."

"No whiskey?" asked Cadmean. "Well, I'll have my whiskey, Mr. Gilbert. A double, how about?" Then he settled into the uphol-stered chair and gave one long slow stroke to his bald scalp. He said, "I called home. It was Baby found out for you where I was. Selma was glad to hear her voice after all this while."

I said, "You don't waste much time."

He nodded. "I don't have much time to waste. Where is she? She hasn't been at the lodge since the accident. Is she coming to the services today?"

"No, she said she was not."

His mouth twitched. "I don't understand her, I just don't. Where is she?"

I shook my head. "I'm sorry. I don't think it's for me to say. If Briggs wanted you to know, she'd tell you."

"Justin, you just told me you're not going to play the only card you've got in your hand." His puffy lips pushed in and out like those of an old sea bass. "That sort of stymies our game, doesn't it, hunh?"

"Maybe it's not the only card I have," I said. "But before I turn over any others, I'd like to know why you called Walter Stanhope." We sat waiting while the bartender placed down our drinks tenta-tively, readjusted them, lifted them, rubbed his cloth over the wood beneath, put them back, and finally left.

Cadmean said, "I told Stanhope—good man, Walter—the same thing I told you: no sense in muddying old stagnant water, making a mess." As if in demonstration, he swirled his drink until the amber liquid slopped over the sides.

I said, "That water was already stirred, Mr. Cadmean. And now, not only are Bainton Ames and Cloris dead, so is your daughter-in-law."

His big head swayed sadly. "I know. I know. It's just pitiful. I couldn't even believe it at first. But I told you," he sighed, "Joanna was a crazy woman. She's proved me right. I certainly hate to think of something that bad having happened out at my lodge. I built it, and I had some happy times in it."

I took the plastic stick with its fox on top out of my glass and sipped at the Bloody Mary. "You understand," I told him, "Monday, Rowell will be charged with her murder."

"Why don't we wait 'til Monday to see what happens on Monday, how's that?" Sucking in a piece of ice, he bared his teeth and crunched it in two. "Tell you what I know today. Know Rowell's in a hospital bed, and it's a goddamn shame. Shame about his health, and his primary, and shame about the shit that geese are going to gabble."

"Yes," I nodded, "I expect whatever happens Monday, you'll have to fund another friend to run in your primary this spring, Mr. Cadmean."

Swallowing the ice chips, he smiled agreeably. "Oh, well, I have lots of friends."

"Perhaps you should have made Lawry Whetstone one of them."

"Why's that?" Cadmean's lidded eyes squinted at me. "Fact is, I don't like Lawry. I don't believe there's a natural fiber in him. I believe he'd as soon put his pecker in a plastic balloon as a living moaning woman, and I got no use for a man not more particular."

I said, "I don't like him either. But I appreciated his coming in to say Cloris told him herself—the day she died—that she'd brought you those designs of Bainton Ames's. And that you had confiscated them from her. It made me wonder why you bothered lying to me about that." He watched me sip at my drink. I went on, "It made me wonder so much, I started wondering if maybe you decided you better get hold of copies she told you she'd made on those papers. Copies she probably kept in her safe. Maybe in her purse. Like the purse we found thrown into the grass beside her driveway."

Turning the whiskey glass in circles on the dark table, Cadmean shook his big bald head as if I'd given the wrong answer to an easy question. "Shit, son, that's pretty farfetched, isn't it? You know I was watching a Shakespeare play while poor Cloris was getting robbed. A play where a fellow has himself turned into an ass, am I right?"

"Oh, I didn't wonder if you did it personally. I don't believe you'd personally crack open the head of even a loose woman."

His eyebrow went up at this and stayed there, sardonic. "I appreciate your good opinion," he said.

I took out a cigarette; I kept them now just in the pack—the case I'd put in a box with the other gifts I was returning to Susan. I said, "No, sir, I didn't think you were over there personally rummaging around in the Dollard house. What I've been wondering was if maybe you arranged to have someone else do that errand for you. Or arranged to have someone else arrange it. Someone from C&W. You know, the same way C&W men come over and unfreeze your pipes when you ask them to. Maybe two somebodies. Maybe Luster Hudson and Ron Willis."

He took a cigar out of the hunt coat, rolled it between the stiff, twisted fingers. "Luster Hudson. And Ron Willis. I don't recall those particular names." Now he began to lick at the cigar with a tongue pink as a cat's.

"No? They're C&W. I was wondering if you'd asked Ron Willis to follow me around town the last few days. Which he did."

Cadmean looked at me, his lips puffing in and out.

I smiled back. "I know you've taken a real interest in my where-abouts, from your long distance calls. Problem is, Mr. Willis got a little nervous from being wanted for questioning in a murder case, and he got a little more nervous, it turns out, from being pretty full of cocaine, and the result was he took several shots at me."

"Mighty happy to see he must have missed," said Cadmean,

pulling out a box of wood matches and waving the flame of one beneath his cigar. "Where is he now, this drug-addict fellow?"

"He's in jail now."

"That so? You think he killed Cloris?"

"No. He has a very good alibi for that night. Not a Shakespeare-play alibi, but just as good for his purposes. I'm interested in whether he got those papers from this friend of his, Hudson, who maybe did kill Cloris."

"I read it was gold and jewelry that robber took, not papers. What would some old robber want with those?"

I finished my drink and patted my mouth with a paper napkin that also had the fleeing fox on it. "Mr. Cadmean," I said, "the bad thing about using violence is, by its nature you can't keep it on a lunge line. You can harness a waterfall to your mill, but what if there's a flood, and the dam breaks? You can hire a thug to take some papers from a lady's house while you and she sit watching a play, but what if the lady gets a stomachache and leaves early and catches that thug helping himself to her silverware and anything else he sees? And what if that thug got scared, or just thuggish, and killed her? You see what I mean? Once you let violence loose, it's out of control."

He nodded. "A lot like alcohol-drinking. Am I right? All depends on the drinker." With a noisy gulp he finished off his whiskey. "A lot like car-driving in the snow. All depends on the car. And the driver." The ice snapped between his teeth. "No, I don't believe I know these two fellows of yours. 'Course, if they did kill poor Cloris, I'm going to have to let them go from C&W." He watched his ash as he slowly rolled it loose on the edge of the ashtray. "Now, let's go back to Rowell a minute. Huh?" His eyes seemed impervious to the smoke coiling past them as they peered at me. "What you got against your uncle, son, except he helped your mama put you in a loony bin to dry out."

I leaned forward into the smoke behind which Cadmean's moonwide face bobbed. "What I have against him," I said, working to keep my voice as tranquil as his, "is I believe that he's a murderer."

"Who of? Joanna?"

"That's certainly what the prosecutors think. But the person I *know* he killed is Bainton Ames. One reason I know it is that Rowell has never said to me that he didn't."

"No hope in hell you'll get proof, son."

"That may be true."

"And why want to?"

"You say you wouldn't want to have murderers in your factory. I don't care to have any more of them than I can help in my state's senate."

"Oh shit, Justin." With a cracking snap of his fingers he called over the bartender from the other side of the room. "You can't clean the dung off the world. It just keeps flying. You can't dig out the road back to Eden, don't you know that yet? Another drink?"

"No, thank you."

"Sure?"

"Yes."

"Alrighty."

"I do know you can't," I said. "So let's just say I want to find out for sure, for my own satisfaction. How's that?"

Cadmean gave his skull another stroke. "That's different. Check, Mr. Gilbert, if you will, sir." He slid an ancient curved wallet from his back pocket and paid with cash. There was nothing in the wallet but a great deal of cash; credit cards were not to his taste, he said. Pawing up a handful of jelly beans from the bowl on the table, he pushed himself with a grumble out of the chair. With a snort, the old cocker spaniel shook herself instantly awake and followed her master on his progress through the room, stopping when he stopped to squeeze a shoulder, rub a head, or kiss a hand. At the door he suggested that we go for a walk.

I buttoned my coat. "Aren't you supposed to be joining Mrs. Cadmean and Rebecca in there for lunch?"

"The girls'll be fine. That woman's so scared of me—now, isn't that amazing?—she can't even eat when I'm around. Just diddles with her fork."

So I crossed back over the street with him, slowing my steps to his as we trudged into the snow-splotched wet field of the jumping arena bordering the stables. There we wandered about among the scattered red and white gates, and the hogback rails, and the plasterboard walls painted to look like either bricks or stone. We could hear the snow melting, and the earth sucking it in.

"Sun's working," Cadmean grumbled. "I told you it would. Now. Let's play some poker." He put his gnarled hand through my arm as we stepped around a gully of icy mud. "You see my Baby, am I right?" I nodded. "You interested in her?"

"She's interesting, yes."

"She's damn pretty."

"Indeed she is."

"Smart."

He bobbed his head, and then slid his hands into the deep pockets of the old hunt coat. After a few more yards, he growled, "Well, I want her to come over and see me." I nodded again. "I want her to do something else." He looked at me. "I want her settled down before they dig my hole. I want her with a man that can make her happy. Right sort of man."

"What kind is that, Mr. Cadmean? Surely not the sort with a history of mental trouble. I believe I'm quoting correctly your remark to Mr. Stanhope about me." Leaning against the fake brick wall, I thought with some pleasure about the inevitable clash between the old man and Cuddy Mangum, whose name the industrialist had doubtless never heard, unless he'd heard it from Cuddy's father, who'd worked on the line at C&W all his adult life.

Cadmean navigated the puddles, came up to me wheezing, and stood to scrape the bottom of his old black-laced boot against the wall edge. "Oh, shit," he grinned. "Forget what I said to Walter. I'm the one all for burying the past. You're the gravedigger won't let it be." His small eyes smiled with a sleepy malevolence. "All right, son. Let me hear your answer. Can you bring my Baby over to her own home, to sit down and talk with her own daddy for one evening's time—and doesn't it crush your soul to hear me have to ask it? Can you bring her?" The only sign of his feelings was a rapid twitch that began at the side of his mouth.

I looked at the bearish eyes; in the sun they were yellow as sulfur. I asked, "And if I do?"

"Well, then," he started to walk again, Duchess tilting toward his heel, dottering along beside him, as fat and old as he. "Well, then, I guess in trade I'd lend you a shovel to help close up that grave of yours. I guess I'd tell you a story. Now, understand me, this would be just a story, and it's not one I'll ever tell again, and it's not one if you wanted to tell it to somebody else and give me the credit for it, I'd ever say that I'd told you. Hunh? If you were to go blabbering, I'd be obliged…" (And he grinned, his discolored teeth oddly old behind the baby-pink lips.) "…I'd certainly be obliged to tell whoever you'd talk to, that, well, you had a history of mental trouble. This here is a private story for your own satisfaction. Not for Ken Moize. I'd like your word on that."

I looked across the road to the stubbled farm fields where a chicken hawk swooped tirelessly on the watch for a snake or a careless mouse. I said, "All right. You have my word. Tell me the story."

He grinned. "Why don't I tell it after you bring over my little girl?"

But I shook my head and kept walking, too quickly for him to keep up.

He called, "Hell, hold up, son." So I waited for him to slush stiffly through the sinking snow. "Hell, I hate being old," he was muttering. "Truly, truly hate it. But I like your gumption. You're stubborn as me." He took my arm again, and we ambled on around the maze of jumps. His other hand scraped its monotonous song against his cheek as he began to tell me his story: "A while back, one summer, there was this man who designed my machinery—and this is a man I treated so well, giving him so much stock, he came to hold the chits for a goddamn 10 percent of my business—this particular man decided on the sly to peddle his fanny to the highest bidder. And, same time, to peddle those designs he'd been doodling behind my back, besides."

I interrupted, "As I understand it, Ames opposed you for trying to keep the union out of C&W."

Cadmean stopped short. "Now, wait. Wait. Don't 'understand,' just listen. This is a made-up story, wasn't that clear? And I'm the one making it up. There's no names to this story. Huh? You just listen, all right?"

I said all right, and he clumped forward again through the mud. "Well, now, I happen to hear that some business acquaintances who'd come up to see *me* were sneaking around on this visit and setting up a private-type meeting with this particular two-timer. I happen to hear because I make it my business to hear. Everything." He gave me a sideways glance. "Now, pretend the place they were meeting was mighty close to where I have a summer home, and say I also keep a nice boat. Still have it. I enjoyed a spin in that boat. Pretend that night I spun it over to the marina next to Pine Hills Inn, just to keep a personal eye out, see if my sad information of this two-timing was accurate."

I whispered, "Go on."

He nodded, "Good story, am I right?"

At the end of the field, out of the stable trotted two young matrons, one on a gray, the other on a dun mare. They'd been in the Fox and Hound earlier, and I knew them both from those social and civic affairs that, like medieval feast days, ordered the calendar of Hillston's inner circle. In their black and red riding outfits, the two waved merrily and Cadmean swept off his fur cap with a bow as they whisked by us. "Ah, women, lovely women!" he groaned. "I truly could have married another half a dozen if the Lord hadn't shut off my tap." He guffawed loudly and the women turned their heads and waved gaily again. Watching them trot away off among the trees, Cadmean squeezed my arm. "Why in hell don't you get married? You and Baby, now. You two are certainly good looking, both of you. Good blood. Good families. I believe I could get a fine litter of grandchildren out of the two of you. 'Course, they'd be goddamn stubborn."

I stepped away, folding my arms, but I said nothing to disabuse him of his suddenly evident plans to breed me to his daughter. Instead, I told him that yes, his story was fascinating.

"I figured you'd think so," he chuckled. "Well, I'll finish it. Say I took a glance into that inn window that night, and I see all my old pals are sure enough having a little gab with the two-timer. I also see, looking miserable over by himself at the bar, a certain good looking fellow, maybe about what your age is now, who I happen to know is cross-eyed in love with a foolish woman that's already married to this betraying man I've been talking about. You follow me?"

I said I did, and he smiled.

"So, I go back to my boat, diddle around there—pretty damn put out and trying to ease my soul." Cadmean stopped again and hoisted himself up on a hay bale we'd come upon; he gazed complacently around him, as if that too were a way to ease his soul. He looked on one side at the dark feathery trees fronting the blank sky, then turned around and looked across the street to where small white swamps of snow seeped into the brown and yellow grass of the meadow. The hawk still circled.

Cadmean beamed. "Isn't that the prettiest thing in the world? Winter fields. I got no use for people putting down the Piedmont like it was some scruffy patch between the mountains and the beach."

"The mountains and the coast are beautiful," I said.

"It's all beautiful. God on the land never went wrong. People now, I think He gave up and turned people over to Lucifer." Cadmean pulled out another cigar while I found a last cigarette and we each lit our own, and I waited.

Finally he mumbled, "So," his lips a circle of smoke. "Here's the part of my story for your special satisfaction. Say, when I'm sitting down there in my boat, I see my false friends out on the inn's porch arguing with that design man, and he looks a mite weavy on his feet from not being the kind to hold his liquor. After the others walk on back inside, he stands there looking down at something he's pulled out of his pocket."

The coin. So far, each thing Cadmean had said fit precisely with what Cary Bogue had long ago reported: the arguing would have been their trying to convince Ames not to take his boat across the lake after having so much to drink. It was what happened next that I wanted to know. I asked, "And?"

"And? Well, *and* this in-love fellow pops out of the inn and catches up with the other one, right about where his boat's moored. And they talk a bit. And they yell a bit. And maybe it's talk about this also two-timing woman they both want to hold on to. The way I said before, men are rutting hogs, and, son, that's a fact of nature no sense denying. And this in-love fellow gets carried away with his feelings and slugs my design man right in the face a good one, and down he goes, clunk, on that hard concrete walkway by the dock. And off the other one goes not even looking back."

My heart had quickened fast enough to sweat my hands inside their gloves. Had Rowell simply left Ames lying there on the marina walk?

"He went off to his car in the lot?" I asked.

Cadmean shrugged, puffing up smoke at the cloudless sky, watching it rise. "So, there I sit and there the other one lies flat out. I'll tell you this. I didn't feel like going helping that man up after he'd stabbed me in the back. But he didn't move and didn't move, and I'm starting to think, maybe he's accidentally dead from that fall under the influence.

But pretend, here comes the in-love fellow back and he about jumps out of his skin when he sees the other one still laying where he'd socked him. So he picks him up. Now, son, let me rest my old voice. You use your imagination." Cadmean's sleepy yellow eyes moved back toward me.

I stared at him. "He put the body in the boat and took off."

"All right. That sounds like a good ending to this story."

I said, "And he motors out into the middle of Pine Hills Lake, throws the body overboard, jumps off himself, and swims ashore."

Cadmean's cigar slid around in his pink puffy lips. He shook his head. "My story ends at the dock. My eyes are good, they truly are, but not good enough to see across a big old lake in the middle of a summer night."

"You heard the explosion when the boat hit the pump?"

"My ears are good as my eyes."

I tried to keep my voice even. "And you never said *anything*? Why didn't you tell Stanhope?"

Cadmean's little, eyes widened innocently. "Tell him what?"

"Christ! That Rowell murdered Bainton Ames!"

"Now, son, now." He leaned over and squeezed at my shoulder. "I don't know what you're talking about."

I walked off, wheeled and stared back at him. At the stable end of the muddy arena I could see the teenage boy leading out Manassas, now unsaddled and looking like some Tartar chieftain's steed, the winter hair of his pasterns like high shaggy black fur boots. I said to Cadmean, "Fifteen years! And you know what! You *told* Rowell what you saw, didn't you? Christ, you've had him by the balls for *fifteen years?*"

Pulling off his fur cap, Cadmean scratched his bald skull. "Well, that's a mighty uncomfortable figure of speech… I'll tell you two things about Rowell. He was a good husband to Cloris. He's been a good state senator to this area. He's a Piedmont man. He does what he can for us."

"He's *your* man."

Cadmean squished the cap back on. "I'm a Piedmont man. So are you. I love where I live. Don't you, son?"

I told him, "Ken Moize can subpoena you. You've withheld evidence in a felony."

"Have I?" He pulled out the cigar and studied it curiously. "Have I? I thought I was just telling you a story. In exchange for you arranging a visit. And seems like you gave me your word you'd get Baby to come see me. So why don't you go do it, son?"

"You're amazing! You stand there and tell me you'd commit *perjury*, and then you expect me to 'keep my word'!"

He looked at me with an astonishing benign affection. "Justin. I don't believe you think a gentleman's word has anything to do with what other people do or don't do, or say or don't say. Keeping his word just has to do with his having given his word. Am I right? That's the kind of gentleman I want to see my girl bed down with."

By now I was pacing back and forth about twenty feet off from him. I yelled, "Just what are you going to do if Hudson and Willis won't keep their mouths shut! If you sent them over to Cloris's, and we can tie you to it, you better believe that's a subpoena you'll *have* to answer. Christ!"

Cadmean spit out his cigar and ground it into the mud. "Oh, now we're back to your story. Well, I don't believe I'll worry about that. I'm an old man, and worrying's bad for the little bit left of my health. Like I said, son, this philosophizing of yours about brute violence and all getting on the loose, and how it can't be controlled...It all depends." And then with a jerky quickness I wouldn't have thought possible, he jumped down from the hay bale, threw up both arms, clapped his hands sharply, and in a booming shout called, "Manassas! *Huh! Huh! Huh!*"

Off at the field's end, the black stallion broke loose from the startled stableboy, reared with a shivering whinny, then bolted toward us. Duchess bounded to her feet and started barking.

Mud flew up with a smacking pop as Manassas' hooves slapped at the ground, flying closer. He was galloping straight toward me, his neck stretched, mane shaking, nostrils huffing out white smoky air. His eyes wild on mine, he kept coming almost as if old Cadmean, like a wizard, had communicated to him some silent command that he come trample me to death. At the last instant, when I could feel his breath in the air, I leapt sideways to the barrier of the hay bale.

Cadmean stood right where he was, as serenely as if he watched a child skip toward him bringing flowers. Only inches away from crashing into the fat old man, the horse sheered off at an angle, legs prancing mud up on Cadmean's pant legs, then whirled around and stopped himself in front of his master, who reached calmly in the deep pocket, pulled out the jelly beans, and held them up. Manassas mouthed them out of the big, twisted fingers while Cadmean, cooing, rubbed the sweated neck. "Good boy," said the old man with a chuckle, and peered over at me. "Controlling brutes, now, son. It all depends," he said quietly, "on who's in control. Huh?" He thrust his fingers through the bridle strap and tugged the nuzzling animal into a walk beside him back across the thawing field.

•　•　•

Two hours later, when I came quietly into the crematorium of

Pauley and Keene Funeral Home, Mr. Cadmean, in a dark suit, his bald head bowed, stood alone among the empty chairs as the Reverend Thomas Campbell, who had baptized generations of the inner circle, including mine, prayed that in heaven Joanna Cadmean's soul would find the peace that life should not promise and cannot give; while Mr. Pauley with a discreet forefinger pushed the button that slid her rich, black coffin smoothly and slowly into the fiery furnace.

Afterward, I walked Mr. Cadmean out to his limousine and said I'd like to ask him one question. "Did you ever tell Joanna the story you told me?"

"What story was that, son?"

"The one about the designing man and the in-love fellow."

His driver opened the back door to the C&W company limousine. Cadmean carefully lowered himself into the plush seat, then shook his head. "I don't recall that particular story," he said. "But I never told Joanna any love stories. I truly never had the feeling she was the kind of woman would want to hear them. Would you excuse me now? I need to get back to my mills. I've got a young snot been giving me a hard time. He's in for a surprise. I'm an old man. But I'm not as old as they think. Huh? I appreciate you paying Joanna your respects. I like a man with good manners. Principles, I've got no use for. Ever notice how most of the slime of the world gets flung there by men with principles? Take care, now." The big car turned slowly toward home. Home was Hillston. All of it.

Chapter 27

"General, I had made plans to fling my skinny body over what you might call the chasm between Junior Briggs and her old man Fatso the Bald because I hate to see a family frost each other when it's a family I want to put my name to, and I'm the one liable to end up catching the icy breeze. But I don't know about talking Briggs into going over there. All this terrible stuff you tell me that old rascal's said, not to mention *done*, lordy! I don't know. Why did you say we can't go to Moize? My future pa-in-law ought to be in jail!"

I said, "Cadmean does love her, Cuddy. It's been five years since Briggs's even gone to his house."

"Well, now, love. Nero loved Rome. To hear him tell it, he only burnt it down so he could redo it prettier. I saw that on TV."

"Don't worry. I didn't think you'd been sneaking around reading Suetonius."

"Who?"

Cuddy Mangum roamed my kitchen drinking my beer and complaining to Mrs. Mitchell about the contents of my refrigerator and shelves. "Honey, just eat it. I know it looks all crumbly and rotted, but he doesn't have any *American* cheese. What kind of soups are these tall skinny cans supposed to be? Bisque? Vissysuave? Don't you have any meatball vegetable?"

We were there waiting for a visitor. Mr. Ratcher Phelps had telephoned shortly after my return from the funeral services to say he was ready to pay his call. I confessed I wasn't going to be able to hand him a check for $5,000 today. In his sonorous dirge of a voice, he replied, "Patience is a woman I've kept company with all my life, and I've got the trusting heart that gives a man tranquillity of mind."

We were waiting and Mr. Phelps was an hour late.

"Maybe," said Cuddy, gnawing at an old stale loaf of French bread, "maybe Parson Phelps and his girlfriend Patience took time off to go at it back behind the pianos." And he gave his crotch-pumping gesture.

I shook my head. "Mangum, I thought love was going to refine you."

"You never know what love's gonna do. Look what it's done for you: losing your job, punching husbands out, you and Red running wild and slobby in the streets. Is this bread bread, or is it bricks?" Teeth clenched on one end of the loaf, he was yanking wildly at the other with both hands.

"It's old."

"Of course it's old. It's yours, isn't it? I think it's got two of my teeth in it, too." He gave up and let the loaf clatter to the table. "Anyhow, what you don't know is, one reason Professor Briggs Junior is so crazy about me is because I'm so, let's call it, loose. How's that? *Loose*." He jiggled all his lanky limbs in an attempt to convey a languid, easygoingness. "And she's uptight. I mean, not really uptight from the inside out, but a little bit from the outside in. Due to her losing her ma and hating her pa—wonder why?— and due to that phony-leftist ghoul she slipped up and married up North. That creep actually *beat* her, on his way to a Hooray Hanoi march, and if I ever come across him I'm gonna be tempted to do to him what a guy from Hanoi did to a friend of mine. Oh, lord, you know: we all plum lost our innocence to the sixties. I oughta be ten years younger. Know what I mean? 1965 to '75, Uncle Sam was an old acidhead. Good politics, though."

I sat down across from him with my yogurt and said, without planning to, what I never had said in five years of almost daily conversation. "Cuddy. I want to tell you something, all right?"

"Shoot."

"You say you lost a decade. Well, so did I. I was in a sanitarium. Twice. A hospital up in the Blue Ridge." His jay eyes looked into mine, warm in the sun coming across my shoulder onto the table's clutter of food. "They called it 'acute alcoholism.' But it wasn't just drink. I was, well, okay, I was pretty crazy." Blushing, I rubbed hard at my ear. "It's not the sort of thing I want people to know. But I've told Alice and I've always felt bad not being open with you about it. So…well, that's it."

The sun moved in among the bony shadows of his face. "Aww, General," he said quietly. "I'm glad you said so." Then he smiled. "But I've known it for years."

"Known what?"

He rolled his blue eyes extravagantly. "That you'd gone to the bin, as my grandma used to say when they took her spinster sister there for being too much of a friend of Jesus—even though the hymn says you're supposed to be. But she fell into the habit of too-long nightly phone talks to Him, and they were on a party line."

I was rattled. "Don't kid me. You knew?"

"'Course I knew. So what? I told you, everybody went crazy back then. You should have seen me out in those rice paddies." He grimaced. "No. I take it back. You shouldn't have seen me."

"That's different."

"Not much."

"You didn't bring it on yourself."

"I brought my first wife on myself trying to get out of going."

I found him another beer in the back of the refrigerator. "Who told you?"

"Guess." He snapped off the can top. "Right. Old V.D. Fulcher wanted me to keep an eye out, let him know if you slipped up."

"Why didn't you tell me?!"

His Adam's apple bobbled as he drank. "Never saw you slip up." I pushed the yogurt away. "Rowell must have told Fulcher."

"Probably." Cuddy squatted down by the cabinets. "So, I wasn't open with you either. And another thing I never told, I'll tell you now it's true confessions. Your old love Lunchbreak made a play for me about a year ago. That time I came to that cast party y'all had when you did, what was it? *The Philadelphia Story.* She was high and wanted to know if I wanted to step into a back room and get that way too." He had his head in the cabinet, looking among the cans there.

"Did you?" I asked.

"Nope." His head poked around the corner of the cabinet door. "Don't you have any junk food in this house? Nothing in here but a million jars of vitamins. I crave junk food. Some of us never had the willpower to kick our bad lunch habits the way you did."

Then the doorbell rang and Ratcher Phelps came in, sanctimonious in his black suit, as if he'd arrived to show us a catalogue of caskets. Instead, what he carried was a cardboard box. Holding it on his knees, he sat on the edge of the couch cushion and accepted a snifter of brandy to war against his lumbago. "Young gentlemen," he said, "my party was not punctual, and consequently I apologize for keeping you waiting, but I needed to ascertain for certain that my party was not hiding and watching where I went."

"Let me see the coins," I said.

Phelps smiled sadly and snuffed at the brandy. "Suppose." And now he began another of his hypothetical propositions. "Suppose when I leave, you were to find a box on your stoop, and maybe it has coins in it, and maybe it doesn't."

On his feet quickly, Cuddy snapped, "Look here, Parson, why don't you—"

But I waved him down and asked him to show Phelps the mug shot of Luster Hudson he'd brought with him. "Mr. Phelps," I said, "I have a photograph here I wonder if you'd glance at, and give me a nod if it reminds you of your unpunctual party."

After the briefest look, he gave me the nod, adding, "Ummm. I guess that's what you white people would have to admit was a ugly face."

Cuddy said, "Yep. Luster's the bad kind of ugly. I'm the good kind. Now, let's move on. You told Lieutenant Savile on the phone that you'd explained to Mr. Ugly you had to check out this merchandise, and locate your capital. You have such a fine reputation in the business—"

"The music business," interrupted Phelps.

"That Ugly actually trusted you to cart off this stuff! And you're going to meet him with the money. Right?"

"Well, this isn't all the merchandise, and there was a down payment." Phelps moistened his lips, and then he chugged the entire brandy as if it were water.

Cuddy asked, "Meet him where for the rest? And when?"

Phelps's moist, bereaved eyes were peering into the empty snifter.

"Would you care for another?" I asked him.

"Why, just a morsel," he replied, and stared politely at the ceiling while I poured the snifter half full. "Thank you. As to the 'when,'" he said, "one o'clock this morning." Phelps peeked up through the bottom of his glass. "As to the 'where,' where might you say my remuneration may be at?" Now he spun the snifter and scrutinized me through it, his eye like an owl's, shrewd and inquisitive.

I assured him arrangements were being made, but repeated that I'd already explained I didn't have the money with me.

He nodded. "The thing is, I'm accustomed in my business, the music business, to deal on the down-payment plan, and being as I've just put down a thousand dollars on this particular transaction, I am short, and I am troubled by that fact."

I said, "I could give you a check of my own for eight hundred, but anything more would bounce."

Cuddy whispered, "Are you crazy?" but I wrote out the check anyhow, while Phelps tossed down his second brandy with long liquid swallows.

Neatly folding my entire checking account and tucking it into his vest pocket, he said, "The 'where' is a little alleyway next door to a white people's dance place named the Tucson Lounge, if that name's familiar to you."

"Yes, all right," I said. "We'll be there at one A.M. You stay away."

He shook his head mournfully. "It would be agreeable to me,

Mr. Savile, to stay to home, being that I am not partial to the music they play at the Tucson Lounge, but this party is going to be waiting and watching for my car to drive up. And then I get out and walk and then I put down the money and then he picks it up and then he puts down something for me. The fact is, you need me there."

He was right, and we worked out a plan together. When we finished, Phelps stood up and handed me his empty glass. "You people be just as careful as I'm going to be," he told us. "This particular man is a running man and a scared man and this man already showed me a gun and rubbed it a little too hard into my neck." Phelps pointed out the small bruise just under the drooping lobe of his ear. "That gun was by way of impressing on me not to do just exactly what I'm doing." He studied each of us in turn. "And I ask myself, why *am* I doing it?"

"Well, sir, you're a good citizen," suggested Cuddy.

The short portly body bowed its Mandarin bow. "Exactly what I decided must be so," said Ratcher Phelps.

Cuddy added, "Plus, you love your nephew Billy. Plus, five thousand dollars' reward is better'n messing with stolen goods nobody smart would try to fence for the next ten years. Plus, I've heard Luster Hudson's views on the race to which you have the honor of belonging, and I imagine he hasn't been too shy about sharing those views with you."

Phelps bowed again.

Cuddy asked, "Just how much more does Mr. Ugly think you're going to pay him for this stuff? And where does he think he's going with the money?"

The box under his arm, Phelps sauntered over to my old upright piano, where he played a run of scales with his left hand. "He didn't specify his travel plans, but he knows he needs to go somewhere new, fast. And the sum he mentioned was twenty-five thousand, and the sum I mentioned back was fifteen thousand. Of course, you gentlemen tell me those articles are worth twenty times that."

Cuddy whistled. "Whooee. He thinks you've got fifteen thousand in cash! That's a lot of pianos, Parson."

Phelps changed keys, modulated through a series of chords, while his whole face sagged into a mask of despair. "Mr. Savile," he sighed. "Talking of pianos, you need a new one."

I told him, "Well, it needs to be tuned."

"It needs to be..." He rolled his tongue thoughtfully, and then smiled. "Ostracized. That's what it needs to be. Ostracized." He set the box down beside him, and, standing there in his overcoat and fedora, romped through "Maple Street Rag," wincing at the sticking keys and flat notes.

"Well, *hey*!" Cuddy clapped. "That was fine!"

Phelps told me sadly, "I hate to see a man that says he likes Fletcher Henderson having to play his tunes on a piano this bad." He flashed his aggrieved, specious smile and wished us a good evening. We were to meet again at midnight.

When Cuddy came back inside with the cardboard box, he rolled his eyes. "My, my! Look what I out of the blue found on your front doorstoop."

"You know," I said, holding up the Photostat, "this picture of Hudson? Remember that mug shot of the punk we showed Joanna Cadmean? The big blond guy you said had gotten killed in Vietnam. That guy and Hudson look a lot alike. Remember how she kept staring at that photo out at the lodge?"

Cuddy had opened the box. "Stare at this," he whistled. Out of the satin jewelry bag, he poured bracelets, a necklace, and a single emerald earring. Unsnapping a leather case, he held it up for me to see the ten clear-plastic, labeled envelopes, within each of which was a single coin.

"Damn it," Cuddy yelled. "Don't put your fingers on them."

But I had already seen an envelope that I was astounded, and sickened, to find among the others in that case. It wasn't supposed to be there. It made no sense there. On the other hand, it was the only way that everything did make sense. This envelope was labeled, like all the others, in Bainton Ames's methodical spidery handwriting; the words identified the coin inside this envelope as his "1839 Liberty-head quarter eagle, Charlotte mint." With my handkerchief, I held up the packet by its corner. The profile of Liberty gazed with the same exquisite disinterest I'd seen on the coin—now at headquarters—that Cuddy had found in the diary that was supposed to have belonged to Cloris Dollard. The same coin, and Ames had only owned one.

Twenty minutes later, we were in Etham Foster's lab, and his saturnine face, brown and dry as toast, was glowering at us. "I ought to report you two."

Cuddy winked. "Why, Doctor D, we're the ones got the goods for you."

"Yeah. And jumbled them all up, too. If you Dick Tracys have smeared my prints!" Away he stalked on the stilts of his legs.

And so in another hour we knew that the two coins were exactly the same model; that according to Ames's records he had at no time ever had two of the same model; and that the envelope in the stolen case was definitely in Ames's handwriting. There had not been anything at all written on the envelope found in the diary.

I slumped against the wall. "Well, that's why Joanna Cadmean told us the envelope was blank when she supposedly saw the coin in the case last summer. She couldn't risk trying to forge Ames's handwriting."

Foster had dusted the leather case and was working with his microscope on the prints. Now he looked up. "Come here." Elation inched into his voice. "It's Hudson, okay. A big, fat, juicy thumbprint, right *there*. On the corner of the case. Look." He pressed his own huge thumb over the Photostat of Hudson's print. "The size of mine. Look." Glee, pushed out of Foster's voice, escaped by making him rub his hand rapidly up and down his long thigh. "I *got* him," he said. "He stopped being careful. They always do. And that's all I need. Now it fits. Didn't fit before. No prints at all on that diary. Except y'all's, of course. Why not Mrs. Dollard's, see? That lady flimflammed us, Justin, that psychic of yours. She was good. I'll say that. Flimflammed us, see?"

Yes. I saw. Finally. Joanna had done just what Rowell had claimed.

And Rowell had done just what Joanna had dreamt.

And neither of them had been careful enough.

Foster stood, one gigantic foot on his metal stool, his hand out-spread as if he were dribbling an invisible basketball. "Another thing," he said. "We got in touch with that auction gallery of yours in D.C., Savile. One of these quarter eagles did come on the mar-ket there a few years back, like that guy Bogue said. Agent that bought it wouldn't reveal over the phone who he was bidding for. But we can subpoena him if we need to."

Cuddy sighed loudly. "I think we know who he was bidding for. Joanna Cadmean. Fuck the ducks." He tilted his head at me sadly. "We've been had, General. You know, that night at the lodge she was hustling me and Junior out the door so fast and saying how we should make a night of it, and I thought the whole time she was just matchmaking."

"Theories," snorted Etham Foster, stooping over his micro-scope. "Real evidence is where it is at, my men." His mood broke through again, giving his voice almost an effusive sound. "I knew there had to be more for me than a dumb Marlboro butt. And here it is!" His hand rubbed happily along his lean flank. "Don't slam the door."

"I think Doctor Dunk-it is bidding us adieu," said Cuddy. "Come on, General, let's sneak out of here before somebody gets the idea you're trying to do your job."

On the way back to my house, Cuddy said, "So we grab old Lus-ter, good old all-American solo, and bring him to V.D., and get us some medals, and unlock poor little Preston Pope so he can try to win back Charlene's affection."

"Fine. Will you please be sure you have your gun?"

"Listen, Sherlock, I've got to go to Moize with all this crap. The coroner's got to be filled in too. Remember that thin ice you used to spout about? We're dancing on it."

"I don't know whether I wish we could suppress the two coins and let Moize go ahead and prosecute Rowell for Joanna. Or let Rowell just fade in peace."

"Whoaa." He turned to stare at me. "Don't go closing family

ranks on Lady Justice, General. I'll bust right through your ivy vines and come after you. I mean it."

"Watch the road. I know, I know, hell. Well, he didn't kill *her*."

Cuddy leaned back, pushing his thin arms straight out on the steering wheel. "Yep. That Mrs. Cadmean took us in, rolled us good, and left us in the street in our shorts. Lord, imagine that kind of hate dripping drop by drop down on your brains for thirty years. Humankind! Maybe I oughta go into a monastery and just pray. It's gotten so sitting on the benches in the damn River Rise Shopping Mall is enough to break my heart just watching the sadness and meanness go by."

"He didn't kill her. But he did kill her baby. She'd had an abortion just before she slashed her wrists."

"Don't tell me any more."

"And he did kill Bainton Ames. Let me out at my car. I'm going back to the hospital."

Now Cuddy grinned, his sharp features splintering into new angles. "What hospital? No need to check into your old room at the booby hatch. How about a Trappist retreat for us both? We'll find one with cable TV, where they'll let us bring Junior and Red, and we'll live happy ever after, planting zucchini."

"I suppose you haven't read *Candide* either."

"*Candy*? Sure, I read it. I read everything with a blow job in it."

I said, "Cuddy, I hope just because I told you about being in that sanitarium, I'm not going to have to listen to you joke about it from now on."

He pulled to a stop behind my Austin and waved out the window at two Frances Bush students, one of whom casually gave him the finger and went on talking with her friend, as they walked through the gate. "My my, such rudeness," he sighed. "Aww, listen, if people can't joke about the ones they love, next thing you know they want to burn queers and bomb Iran. Love's a joke, General. Why, it's just the best joke on life there is in the world, if you wanta know the capital T Truth. How about a Baby Ruth?" He tugged a candy bar out of his pocket. "You know, now, our generation *worked* on being rude. But these youngsters don't give the appearance of knowing the difference. Imagine that." He tossed the candy bar into my lap.

I asked, "What's in this thing?"

"You never had a Baby Ruth? No wonder you went totally psycho and had to be locked up. These are sorry times. I can't believe that young woman flipped me the bird! It must be enough to drive a gentleman like you crazy again. Here everybody is, lonesome bags of shit in satellite orbit around a big black hole, meaning so-called civilization, and not only does this generation not even bother pretending to ape any ethics at *all*, they're rude! Speaking of apes, you just gonna love Luster Hudson. Adiós."

Chapter 28

"How are you, Rowell? Rowell?"

"Yes. I suppose you came for your informant's money, Justin. It's there by the bed."

Rowell Dollard had made out the check to me, his signature less thick and sure than it had always been when scrawled across the bottom of the homiletic letters I used to angrily crumple in the waste can at law school.

Seated in the wheelchair beside the flat hospital window, he looked shrunken within the gray wool robe, black monogrammed with his initials but now too large for him. The unlighted room was nearly dark, and empty anyhow of belongings that he would want to see as part of his life. On a tray, food lay untouched in glutinous positions. On a table, ribbons drooped from flowers in cardboard vases.

I stood across the room from him to say that the man to whom I would be giving the check was risking his safety, if not his life, to lead us to Cloris's killer.

Dollard might have been blind, his eyes looked with such fixed opaque blankness at the window glass. "Who killed her?" he asked quietly.

I sat down in the vinyl chair. "A man named Luster Hudson. He worked at C&W."

"Robbery?"

"Yes. But it may be more complicated than that; he may have

been working for someone."

Nothing in his face changed. He wasn't interested.

I said, "I have the jewelry. And the coins."

"You didn't bring them."

"No."

The perfectly combed silver hair was motionless; the outline of his head as still as a medallion, and lined by moonlight slatted through the half-raised venetian blinds. "I didn't think you would," he said finally.

I was watching his reflection in the dark window. "I expect you know what I found in the case," I said. "And what finding that second coin in the case means."

"What is that, Jay?" He asked the question politely, but as if he were not involved in the answer.

"It means that Joanna put a coin in the diary. To convict you of murder."

I leaned sideways in my chair so that I could see his face now. "And the same coin in the case means that the night you killed Bainton Ames, you did pick up his coin from the marina walkway, and you did keep it. Odd how the same coin both absolves and convicts you."

He didn't speak, but his body seemed to become even slighter inside the handsome robe, as if the aging of years had been collapsed into minutes and his flesh wasted as I looked on.

I asked him, "Why did you strike Bainton Ames that night?"

Dollard's head turned carefully toward me. His face, all ruddiness clarified, was frail now and nearly delicate, the eyes and mouth expressing nothing. "I assume you've talked with Briggs Cadmean. He surprises me, telling you. But he always did surprise me."

I asked again, "Why did you knock Ames down?"

Rowell was looking past me out the window. After time went by long enough for me to hear the calm noises and the blurring, hummed voices that are the sound of hospital evenings, he answered, "Bainton said something about Cloris I couldn't allow him to say."

"All right, but *then*, when you came back, Rowell! And found him still lying there!"

He said nothing.

"Was it," I asked, "because your car wouldn't start that you came back?"

Preoccupied, he slowly nodded.

"When you saw Bainton was still unconscious." I bent farther forward, into his line of vision, "Why in *hell* didn't you go for help?! So you knocked him out, so what? Why come back and kill him?!"

Rowell's eyes blinked, and he pressed his hand over them. "I thought he was already dead."

"But he *wasn't*, Rowell. There was water in his lungs. He drowned. If you hadn't panicked about protecting your precious political career. If you hadn't taken him out in that boat and thrown him over and killed him, Rowell, he wouldn't have died."

Earlier today, imagining confronting Rowell, I had assumed he would deny that he'd taken Ames into the boat; I thought he would claim he had picked up the coin where Bainton had dropped it and then left, and that the dazed man had eventually gotten up, motored off alone, and toppled overboard. But instead my uncle gazed at me, curiously. He asked, "Political career?"

"Come on! Christ! That's why you covered it up. And you got your reward, too. Old Cadmean's blackmail took the curious form of financing your ambition. Your goddamn ambition."

He turned his head calmly away from me. "My ambition?... Considering my name, I don't think I had much of that. Certainly not enough." The robe slipped, and he pulled it back over his legs. "I had a little. But I had to flog it. My brother Kip had to flog it in me." Rowell's voice was so hushed, I kept myself perfectly still in order to hear him. "Even then," he went on, as though in private meditation, "even then, I knew Dollards were supposed to play in a different league."

"You're a state senator."

"State senate isn't much, Jay. Not much to end with; maybe to start." His hand, bruised bluish from the IV needle, moved gently down the gray wool over his legs, which rested on the props of the wheelchair. "I think I was a good solicitor. Probably I should have stopped there."

"Yes!" I burst out. "My God, how could you bear being under Cadmean's thumb all these years?! Him and Joanna Cadmean! Both! Jesus. I pity you."

His face flinched and some of the color came back and some of the old anger deepened his voice. "Your pity is not something I want or need." He pulled himself straighter in the wheelchair, tightening the gray robe around him.

And so we sat together in silence in the dark, impersonal room, until he asked mildly, "What have you said to Fulcher and Moize?"

"Nothing yet. Cadmean won't say anything. Ever. Doubtless you know that."

"Moize, I expect, will try to indict me only on Joanna, whatever you say." His tone was bizarrely detached, as if he were discussing some court case in which his interest was merely professional. "The other...is so long ago."

I said, "There's no statute of limitations on murder."

Moving his forefinger softly along the rubber wheel of the chair, Rowell said, "Jay, this will disappoint you, no doubt. But if you'll think back to your criminal law classes...Perhaps you never attended many...Though I had hoped when you enrolled at Virginia...Well, if you'll think back, you'll recall casebook examples I expect Mr. Moize also recalls."

"What are you talking about?"

Dollard waited for the energy to speak. "If I struck a man in anger, that was assault. If I then returned and discovered that man—as I thought, dead—and I removed his body, that was disposing of evidence. Neither striking him in anger nor removing him is murder. Nor, by precedent, is the combination premeditated murder." Rowell said all this seriously but dispassionately, as though he actually were in a law school classroom.

"There is no statute of limitations on manslaughter either, Rowell."

"True." His hand began to move again on the wheel, barely touching the rubber tread with his fingertips. "But I rather think...I have been through...a lot. And I have already paid this state—as the play says, doesn't it?—some service. And I rather think a jury will be inclined to mercy." His head kept staring straight out the window when he added, "I'm just sorry you can't feel the same inclination."

Upset, I stood and started walking. "Why, Rowell? Why didn't you call an ambulance?!"

"I told you, I thought he was dead. I couldn't hear his heart at all. And…and…" Now the voice faltered for the first time, and the silver hair began to tremble slightly. "And then, I didn't think. You don't know what you'll do until you do it. Yes, I must have picked up the coin. I must have carried him into the boat." He spoke softly, pausing often, seeing what he said. "I didn't think until I was swimming and I heard it blow up and the light was in the water, and then I had already chosen…what I couldn't even regret." He fought through a slow, struggling breath. "Do you want the truth? I was too weak to bear the shame of having killed him…I was afraid it would cost me Cloris. I would lose Cloris. I…She…" Rowell's head fell suddenly to his chest, then came quickly back up, and his throat tightened with a strange constricted noise. "Ambition?… She was my ambition. She was my ambition." His bruised hand squeezed hard around the wheel. "And her, I won."

High in the window, moonlight shuttered through the blinds and shadowed his face. And when the moon moved on, I saw that he was crying, tears following one another down into the tremulous mouth. He made no gesture to brush them away, and they hurried from his eyes and nose onto his neck and soaked into the collar of the gray robe. Grief shook through him, breaking up his words as he said, "She's gone, Jay. I didn't believe it until these last few days here. I put off believing it. I put it off and off, and it wouldn't stop being true. I've lost her. She's gone." And he bent over in the chair as if an unbearable pain had twisted through his body.

"Rowell." I came around the back of the wheelchair so that I stood close beside him. "Please don't…You're not supposed to get—"

He grabbed up at my hand and crushed it in his. "I don't care. You see? I *have* lost her. When you've lost, you're not scared you'll lose." Letting go, he breathed in a last long shudder until his body was still again. I waited there beside him. Finally he pulled a hand-kerchief from his pocket and blew his nose. He said, "I'm all right. Go sit down."

"I'm sorry," I told him quietly. "I'm sorry for your pain. To have kept this inside, too, for so long. I can't say I wish I had left it all alone. But I hope you will forgive me for the poor way I handled it. I...I judged you unfairly. I ask your pardon. I wanted to think you guilty. Even of killing Cloris to protect yourself."

He twisted his head to see me. "Why? Why? Was it because I pushed at you so hard?"

My eyes closed, weighted shut. "Why flog in me an ambition it seems neither of us really had?"

"I just wanted you to be better than me."

"It always felt like you wanted to prove me worse."

Rowell shook his head, the silvery hair whitened by the moon. "I'm sorry. No... I loved you."

"It didn't feel like it," I said.

"All I hated was your weakness." He looked away, back to the window.

"I hate it too, but I'm forgiving myself. So should you, Rowell." Reaching across the bed, I picked up the coat I'd left there.

His arms stretched out along the rests of the chair, his hands hanging motionless above the wheels. He said, "I think I'll leave that to a higher judge than I'm going to get in Hillston. Are you leaving now?"

"Yes, I have to." I buttoned my coat. "You should rest. I'll go talk to Moize, now. I'll come again tomorrow. I'll do what I can."

At the door, I looked back at him, still and gray by the black, empty window. "Good night, Rowell. I'm sorry."

He whispered without moving, "Jay? This isn't the life I meant to have."

Chapter 29

The Tucson Lounge on Saturday night was a place for Hillstonians to go in fumbling, sentimental quest of a feeling they had heard in the sound of songs and seen in the size of films, and thought would be theirs, and would be better than their insensible weeks, if only they clotted together in a place like the Tucson Lounge. This feeling was some amorphous heightening of impulses, nationally inherited and both fed and sedated by a week of television, which was too small and flat for the size of the impulses. This feeling was some mixture of anarchy and of nostalgia for undefined hurts, and of lust enhanced by the romance of love, and of xenophobia boiled over by sports and news into a fine and otherwise failed (not even attempted) sense of all-American spirits joined, and so each enlarged to the size of film and the sound of song.

And all this was made possible for these Hillstonians by the alchemic solution at the Tucson Lounge of beer and music and bodies and flaring lights. All this found expression in bloodied knuckles, in throats sweetly choked-up close to the band's booming speakers, in couples rubbing hot-eyed against one another on the dance floor. All this found its correlative with the national heritage in the Tucson Lounge's western decor. Outside blinked the red neon cactus. Inside over the long bar ran a mural of a cattle stampede in a dust storm: steers plunging off the wall away from the endless, open background; a train rushing westward into space; a solitary cowboy sitting on his horse in bittersweet, patriotic, lonesome sufficiency and self-regard.

Across from the painted cowboy, I leaned on the bar, gun heavy beneath my arm, and watched the hand of the big round Budweiser clock fall from the twelve. Behind me up on a rough wood platform, the Boot Hill Boys, a country-and-western group (mountain-country taught on fiddle and piano and guitars; western-dressed in fringe and boots) wailed of invisible tears and trembling lips and the solace of barroom buddies.

Cuddy Mangum and I had arranged with Ratcher Phelps that I should be the one to wait inside the bar, since, of us three, I was the only one Luster Hudson had never seen. "Not that I think even Luster's dumb enough to show up in public," Cuddy had said, "but if he does, you'll spot him."

I'd stared again at the photograph of the cropped-haired, ox-sullen head whose thickness narrowed nothing at all as the neck bulged into the shoulders. "I think so."

"Yep, you'll spot Prince Luster right away. He'll be the one snapping folks' backs in his biceps, and chomping the tops off the beer bottles and spitting the glass chunks at the band."

An hour ago Cuddy and I had left our hurried meeting with the stunned and fretful Ken Moize, who had until Monday to decide what to tell the grand jury he wanted them to do with Rowell Dollard. I told him why Joanna should want us to think Rowell had killed her. I didn't tell him Cadmean's story about that summer night at the Pine Hills Inn.

As Cuddy dropped me off in front of the Tucson Lounge, he said, "The cavalry is coming. Wait for it, you hear me? If Parson Phelps chickens out on us, I'll just take his car and stick Sister Resurrection up front wearing his fedora. The black people all look alike to Luster anyhow."

It was now 12:30. I'd drunk one whiskey and four Coca Colas. I'd seen a Dodge mechanic bloody the nose of a collegiate fellow who kept insisting (out of a code the mechanic didn't honor) that a tap on the shoulder gave him the inalienable right to slow dance with the mechanic's date, who giggled each time her escort was tapped, and giggled higher when the collegian was knocked backward into the passion-glazed couple behind him. I had heard from the Boot Hill Boys a dozen variations on the sad imperfectability of human love. I had gone three times to the bathroom (posted COWBOYS), and the third time had sidestepped somebody's vomit on the floor.

The restrooms were off a rear hall across from a fire exit, and it was from the small glass pane in that door that I was to watch the alley for Hudson. The Tucson Lounge fronted Crowell Avenue, where Sister Resurrection had brought me in the snow to see the trash. Beside the bar was an open-ended pedestrian alley, and there, blocking the entrance, Ratcher Phelps was to drive his black Buick, with Cuddy Mangum hiding in the backseat. Exactly at one A.M. Phelps was to walk to the middle of the alley, set down the brown bag containing the money (actually, wrapped packages of Cuddy's memo pads), then instead of waiting in his car for Hudson to replace this bag with the rest of the jewelry, Phelps was to leave. As soon as Hudson touched the bag, which Phelps was to position just across from the fire door, I would move to arrest him, Cuddy being, by then, out of the Buick and covering me.

This short alley backed onto Jupiter Street, which ran one-way and was not much used: most of the buildings in the block were empty victims of the suburban River Rise Shopping Mall. I had been worried about not having anyone in position to block off the Jupiter Street end, from which we expected Hudson to approach, but Cuddy was certain that if Hudson (who was slow) ran, we could outrun him.

On the Jupiter Street corner leaned a decayed hotel, its shaded siderooms hiding from the alley's view. Except for the perverse residence there of a famous old lawyer who was a friend of Cuddy's, this hotel, the Piedmont, had decades ago lost whatever respectability it may have once claimed. For years the same drunks grew old in the lobby, watching the same parade of hookers, runaways, illicit lovers, and drifters whom Fulcher delighted in sending patrolmen to hound out of Hillston. I had taken the photograph of Luster Hudson to the desk clerk and had passed it among the limbo of derelicts in the musty foyer, and no one had seen Luster Hudson tonight inside the Piedmont. The clerk was hostile and averted his eyes; the drunks asked me for money.

Queasy with the thick sour stink of urine and beer, I kept waiting by the Tucson's fire door. At 12:35 I called Alice on the wall pay phone. I said I wanted to tell her that last night with her I had felt, finally, what I had in the past asked, unanswered, of drink: that there was nothing else to ask for, because there was nothing missing. She said only, "I know." And I said that I already knew that she knew.

"I know," she said.

From then on, I just stood waiting, pretending—when men lurched past me headed for the COWBOYS door, and women lurched past me, some with wide smiles, headed for COWGIRLS—that I was using the phone again, or waiting to use it, or waiting to be sick, or looking for love.

Then, at twenty 'til one, I saw Dickey Pope, bright-faced with sweat and high blood and drink, staggering up to me on his heeled boots. He had a deep cut over his cheek, and his black satin shirt with its yoke of roses was ripped open to his navel. Dickey was unzipping his jeans, his other arm thrust out to shove open the men's room door, when I registered on him.

"Fucking Lieutenant," he belched. "What's happening?"

I said, "What happened to you?"

"Nothing. I'm just having me a *good* old time!" He took his hand from his open fly and waved it back at the blare of noise down the hall. "Hey. Joe Lieberman says you're gonna turn Preston loose."

"Maybe."

He swayed toward me with unfocused belligerence. "You better. You savvy? I'd love to kill you." Dickey threw in this last remark casually, not even looking at me.

"Really? Is Graham here with you?" I was thinking that if Graham were around, I should either get rid of him before Luster arrived, or tell him what we were doing and ask for his help.

Dickey chortled, throwing his arm around me. "Graham's on a goddamn hunting trip. He don't even sleep. He's *tracking* something." Dickey was so delighted with this conceit that he hugged my shoulder.

I said, "If you mean what I think you mean, Luster Hudson's still in Hillston."

Dickey pulled away, crafty-eyed. "My brother Graham raised Preston from a baby," he said, and backed through the door to the men's room, with a slurred, "Fucking Lieutenant!"

When Dickey came back out, I followed him into the bar to see if he'd lied about not being with his brother. But I didn't see Graham—the size of a buffalo and hard to overlook—anywhere in the crush. Dickey fell into a booth beside an underage, overripe girl wearing a sequined jersey, inside which he immediately plunged his hand. She poured a stream of beer over his head, and he rubbed his hands in his black curls and then stuck his fingers in his mouth.

I walked back to the hall and waited some more. At five 'til one, a drunk couple went behind a recessed partition at the end of the passageway and made love. I could hear their grunts between the band's twanging chords and could feel the thumps along the wallboard.

At 12:59, craning my neck to peer down the dark alley, I saw the nose of Ratcher Phelps's black Buick. I checked the push bar on the door again, my palm so moist it slid along the steel cylinder. Slipping my gun from its holster, I held it inside my coat. There was no one anywhere in the alley.

I felt Phelps coming an instant before I saw him, small and straight in a checked overcoat, his feathered fedora at a conservative angle. He carried a brown paper bag rolled at the top.

Phelps had come only a few yards toward me when, from Jupiter Street, two of the old scavenger drunks I'd seen in the Piedmont lobby wobbled into sight.

Mr. Phelps hesitated, reluctant to put the bag down until they were gone. But one of them, scratching at the stubble on his chalky face, came wheedling over. "Hey you. Got any change?"

His companion slapped at him feebly. "You asking a nigger for money?"

I was straining to see around them as they crowded against

Phelps, and then suddenly Hudson was coming up fast behind the two old drunks. He was not as tall, but he was as big as Graham Pope. He had about a two weeks' growth of dirty-blond beard and wore a muddy fleece-lined jean jacket.

Hudson knocked through the tiny derelicts, grabbed Phelps, half his size, with one beefy fist, snatched the bag away with the other, and then, almost lifting him, slammed the small black man without a word into the brick wall. "God's sake," moaned Phelps, his hat tumbling away. Hudson grunted, "Shaddup, coon, and lissen." I was terrified to wait, fearing that if he opened the bag, he'd kill Mr. Phelps. I was terrified not to wait. Phelps said, "Just a—" and Hudson shoved his hand over Phelps's face and banged his head harder against the bricks. I jumped out around the door yelling, "*Hudson! Police!*" He reeled about, Phelps slumping to the pavement behind him, and fired the big automatic suddenly in his hand. The bullet burned past my ear, wood chips splintering back from the door into my neck. From the left I heard another shot, Cuddy's, that missed, and I was shooting too, as Hudson spun, already running. Cuddy was already flying past me after him, as I stumbled over the crouching drunks in my way.

Swinging off-balance around the corner onto Jupiter Street, I saw everything with the most intense swelling of sensation. The Piedmont. By the snow-heaped curb, Hudson's pickup with three basset hounds howling in back, lunging on their chains. Cuddy in a crouch, gun out, shouting "Halt!" Hudson turning. The Mustang behind Hudson across the street. The huge shaggy shape of a man jumping to the Mustang's hood, lifting something shiny to its shoulder.

Hudson was firing and Cuddy's revolver flew spinning away over the sidewalk.

And then I had stepped in front of Cuddy, pushing him down behind me, my arm shoving him back, and in my other hand I felt my gun keep shooting, and I heard Hudson keep shooting, and I heard a cracking echo.

And the whitest light exploded inside me, blowing up too fast and too big, distending the light through me so there was no room for me inside my body. And still so expanded were my sensations that I even had time to think how strange I had time to think I was dying, time to think how strange it should be Rowell's words I was hearing—*Jay, this isn't the life I meant to have.* And time to think of Alice. And time to feel beneath my head the sliding sheen of Cuddy's parka before the black sky widened.

part three

The Seasons Alter

Chapter 30

Of the first long timeless night, I have no memories at all. How long it was, I was not to learn until much—until months—later. Of how far I had traveled into that darkness, how nearly I had touched the faint sinking banks I floated toward, I had no sense at all, until slowly and from a dim, clouded immensity of height, pain reached down for me and in a blast hooked through me to snatch me up. The dark water felt so restful, felt languorous warm, and the huge squalling shape that grappled to lift me was so cold and screeched at me so loudly, that I kicked out at it to let me fall back, drop deeper and deeper into the muffled lake, to let me slip listless down deep into the quiet quaggy muculent dark. And so falling I would escape again into the timeless night.

But more and more persistent, this intolerable creature would come back for me with its grapple to gouge me up into the sharp cold. More and more precipitant, more and more intrusive, until, unable to fight free, I was snatched through the eclipse.

I was jolting with convulsions I couldn't stop, and thinking, "I have to get back. This is too far to ask me to go, and too fast. If I'm not held back, I'll die, sucked up into that mire of light."

Then there was an *I* there, hearing voices that were not me.

I heard voices, calm and medical. "Dad?" I was saying, but there was no voice to take the word outside me, and no one answered.

Time came back voluminous.

My mouth moved. With the strangest labor it brought out the sound, "What's wrong?"

A cry I knew came saying, "Oh, my God." Then I heard my mother's weeping and felt her hand. "Jay? Jay? Jay?"

"Can you," I sank away and, flailing, swam back, "make them stop this pain?"

But she couldn't stop it. Nights and days labored on and were the same to me. The same black, as profound as the slime at the lake's unfathomed deep. My eyes were pressed shut, closed with tight weight.

Time wove on, and finally my hand came up and felt, and my head and eyes were wrapped with thick tape and gauze. I heard someone moving gently around me. I asked, stuttering and frantic, "Am I blind?"

"No. No. We don't think so. Just sleep. You're all right."

"Alice?"

"Yes."

"Alice?"

"Yes, it's me."

"Where…"

"Yes, you're in the hospital. Don't try to talk."

"Where…"

"You were shot. But you're all right, you're all right now."

Memory blasted everywhere through my body. My fingers grabbed up at the mask of bandages over my head and at the tubes tangled in my nose and the tube needled into my hand.

"Justin! Stop it, stop moving!"

"*Cuddy?* Where's Cuddy!"

"He's fine. He wasn't hurt. Lie back!"

But by now I was heaving in spasms, and then there were doctors back, hands and voices looming around me.

Day by night, like the old delirium, my self drowned and surfaced, plunged and swam back to air. Ghosts already drowned clutched at me, or groped sightless past me. Joanna. Cloris. Bainton. My father. Day by night the pain funneled toward the places where two bullets from Luster Hudson's gun had entered my body. The first had passed through my bent leg into my stomach. The second had taken away a tiny back corner of my skull.

Voices came and went. Cool medical voices that advised in whispers, they couldn't promise anything. "I'm afraid he isn't out of the woods yet, Lieutenant Mangum, but don't say that to Mrs. Savile at this stage in the game."

Voices of my relations. Alice's voice, reading to me from her textbooks, hurrying history by me, and with it, time.

Day by night, rambling quietly in a stream of words, Cuddy's voice: "Hello, General. *O Bottom, thou art changed!* I saw that in a play. Once again, you took them too literally when they told you to go on sick leave. You came close to showing us Stonewall Jackson had nothing on you, jumping in front of me like that, you're so dramatic. Being in reference to the fact that General Stonewall got himself shot and went west to the Great Chancellorsville Above, and being in reference to the fact he was what you might want to call a hero, which don't ever do again, you hear me? Welcome back."

• • •

"You still here, Sherlock? What? 'Come again?' as my grandma was always saying to her pappy after he got the palsy and lost the free use of his lips. Can't you talk any plainer than that? 'What happened?' You mean nobody bothered to mention that Luster shot you? Well, Luster shot you. Next time you save my life, would you try to do it so you can keep a little closer grip on your own? I can't keep taking all this time off to troop over here to University Hospital to see if you've checked out. I'm a busy man. I'm trying to get engaged to Junior, plus V.D.'s flying all over the place to the Southwest Moneybelt, licking toadies, trying to get a big-city job out there and leaving behind a mess on his desk that's a revelation of his so-called mind.

"Come again? I think Justin's asking us about Luster. I know it's hard to believe, Alice, but this man used to be a real smooth talker. Well, now, Luster. Luster is a corpus delicti. Nawsir, you didn't kill him. You did just what it says do in the manual, Wild Bill. You shot him bull's-eye as anything, right in the leg.

"Nope, it was Graham Pope gave Luster the *coup de grass*. I don't know if you had a chance, you were so busy knocking me down and trying to squish me, chance to notice somebody great big standing on the hood of a Mustang with a Western Field 550 pump gun, twenty gauge, firing three-inch magnum shells? Well, that was my deputy, Graham.

"No, you're right. It's a shame. I was looking forward to asking Luster a couple of hundred questions about him and C&W myself, but Graham hadn't read the manual."

• • •

"Good evening, General Lee. Now, you scared us bad last night, slipping away again. Pull yourself together. Bubba Percy down at *The Star* got halfway through your obituary, had you joining all your fancy ancestors up in Preppie Heaven. But I told him, 'Bubba, you rot-eating hyena, that man's not about to die. He's got a closet full of clothes he's never even worn. Plus he owes me $69.50 for jumping on top of me and bleeding all over my JC Penney parka.

"Speaking of owing money, we got a *bill* here from Mr. Ratcher Phelps. He wants the city to reimburse him for the $233 in cash he claims he was carrying in the wallet he claims was removed from his person by those two old drunks in the alley. Says I, 'My, my, you mean right there in the middle of the guns of Navarone, which you might have thought would scare off such jittery tiny little rummies as those two, you mean those two eensy-weensy winos whipped around from where I saw them scrabbling away, and coolly relieved you of that much untraceable money?' Says Phelps back, 'Young sir, Greed knows not Fear, and an inebrious man has no ears, and it is devastatabalistical to me that when the white people get robbed, you people come running, but when the black people get robbed—yea, in the very midst of laying down their lives for the white people—that's when you people turn your backs, and perambulate the other way.'

"Well, he had me there. Says I, 'Parson Phelps, think of nephew Billy, out of jail and back on the streets up to his childish pastimes. And doesn't a citation of gratitude from the mayor of Hillston himself mean more to you than filthy lucre?' Know what he said? He said, 'No.' Now, who'd suspect he could talk so short? So, I get him the money, don't ask where from, but Hiram Davies would go rabid and chew up his desk. So now Phelps says, 'Here's the rest of it' The 'rest' meaning a bill for, one, dry-cleaning his coat; two, replacing his fedora; and three, outpatient services to paint Mercurochrome on his noggin. Meanwhile, Savile, *you* owe Phelps seventy-five dollars a month for the rest of your life, which needs to be a *real* long one.

"What for? Why, the new piano installed in your living room you gave him that eight-hundred-dollar down payment on. He threw in the stool 'cause he took a fancy to you."

●　●　●

"Well, my my! They took those coils out of your nostrils. Tell you the truth, they didn't do a thing for your looks. 'Course, you still look a little too much like the creature from the black lagoon, what with all your hair gone under that wrapping, and I'm really not all that crazy about your scruffy beard. But on the other hand—now don't rile up, Peggy Savile—ma'am, you do have yourself a handsome son somewhere underneath it all. Now if he'll just go back to sleep and stop pestering us with all this begging for sips of water, maybe we can play us some more bridge before they throw us out. Is that Ms. Woods, R.N., on again? Umm ummm, she was so short-tempered to my little poodle last night. Where'd Junior and Alice go? I swear, sometimes I get the feeling those girls aren't really trying all that hard to learn how to play this game, Peggy. Do you get that feeling? Lordy, they already owe us four hundred and fifty thousand dollars, and they're still trumping their own aces. Can I offer you a glazed doughnut, ma'am? I see you're watching the basketball game. A blue-through Tarheel, you sweet lady!"

• • •

And days of nights passed by. And not until then was I told how long the timeless while had lasted. Not until then was I told that outside the sealed window of my hospital room, everywhere on the trees along the branches swollen buds had burst to petals, unleafing snow and rose.

Chapter 31

They said it was the third week of March. It might as easily have been in my dreaming one night or one year since I'd felt myself fall back into the sheen of that blue parka, but by the moon's time, a few days more than two months had circled round, passing by. Two months that would have no past. I thought how less than a twinkling of an eye must time be to the dead.

They told me I had been unconscious for three weeks, and only semiconscious for three more. They told me that two doctors had given me up, and a third had flown into Hillston from Baltimore, and contradicted them, and snapping off his surgical gloves had flown back away. They told me that I was lucky, and that I would be living from now on with a shorter intestine, a stiffer right leg, and a head made harder by a small plate of steel. They waited no longer to tell me that Earth had turned tumbling on without my knowing, slanting the Piedmont to spring, because doctors were going to cut away my bandages to see if I could see, and everyone was concerned that for me to see the world so changed since last I saw it would bring about a relapse.

But what I saw after the chilling blade snipped, and weight lifted gauze by gauze, was light brightening until it hurt, and then the white and rose Highlander face of Alice MacLeod. And that hadn't changed at all.

"Hi," she whispered. "I was saying when you hung up: I love you."

After a few minutes, another face leaned down and winked a blue jay eye. "Let's move on out of the mush, you two," said Cuddy. "I've got an official ceremony to perform. This is business." He waited until the warm, limpid eyes of the doctor from India finished searching in mine, finished touching my face with the same long, thin, careful fingers I had seen months ago feel for Rowell Dollard's pulse. Then Cuddy said, "Here goes. Now watch me mess up. *Dulce et decorum est pro frate* just about *mori*."

In his hands was yellow shine that unfolded into a long, fringed, yellow sash. With studious pats he draped it across my hospital shirt. "I memorized that," he said. "You want me to tell you what it means? 'How sweet it is to throw your body down for your soul brother.' More or less. Doctor Dunk-it was my consultant. Don't you just love it? It's old. That sash is old, too. That sash is a genuine Confederate sash I bought in Washington, D.C. This auction agent that found the coin for poor old Joanna Cadmean helped me locate this sash. I told him you were dying and I wanted you to be buried in it."

"I don't know why in the world," said my mother to Alice MacLeod, "men think *women* are so sentimental."

"But, General, even though you fooled me, you can keep it anyhow if you want to."

"Why, my God, Alice, I remember how Justin and his father both cried all the way through *Bambi*."

"Oh, didn't that movie just break your heart?" sniffed Cuddy. "But now, *Dumbo* was even sadder than that. Did y'all see *Dumbo*? Remember when they chained up his momma? Oh, my!" Cuddy blew his nose, yanking a Kleenex out of the box beside Mother's Shut-in Surprise.

The next week I was put in a wheelchair by the window so that I could watch the Lenten sky blossoming, and the cardinals swaying on the thin branches of the dogwood trees. Seated there, by the window, my thoughts were often with Rowell.

The state had made its decision. At a new inquest, Hillston's coroner had ruled Joanna Cadmean's death an apparent suicide. Probably no one would ever know if she had really spotted the original Liberty-head coin in the case. Perhaps she had seen it, but I preferred to believe that Joanna had never seen the coin Rowell confessed he had picked up from the marina pavement and, years later, returned to the case. And returned there as a token of what? Possession? Guilt? Cancellation of the killing itself, itself tangible evidence that Bainton Ames had never removed the coin from the case that night, and so had never left his house that night, and so had never drowned?

If Joanna Cadmean had *not* seen the Liberty-head coin, but had only dreamt it, then her final case for the Hillston police department transcended all the other mysteries the department had brought, in earlier years, before the oracle of her extraordinary gift. If she had only dreamt it, she was (as Rowell told me) preternatural; and I think she was.

And, ironically, if Joanna had only trusted her gift, had she not assumed she would need "real" threads to weave her spell, had she not found—as we now knew—a duplicate coin in Washington, and bought a diary in a St. Simons shop, and used the brass letter opener to break off the door chain inside Briggs's tower study (leaving on the brass blade some fragments of the chain's metallic paint for Etham Foster's microscope to find), had she not erred in the other infinitesimal, inevitable ways people in the tangle of the real world must err, no doubt we would have all gone on believers. No doubt Ken Moize would have persuaded a jury to condemn Rowell Dollard for killing her, killing her, though, in only thirty seconds and not for the thirty years she believed he had actually taken to murder her heart.

But as it was, Ken Moize accepted the coroner's new verdict that a mentally unbalanced woman had killed herself. Moize still did go to the grand jury about Rowell Dollard. And he did obtain an indictment. Because Rowell voluntarily confessed. After long discourse with our attorney general and with the other men who live at the capitol of the state, Moize agreed to accept the plea of nolo contendere then entered by Dollard's lawyers. The charge agreed upon was involuntary manslaughter, resulting in the death of one Bainton William Ames. The judge, who was not

Judge Henry Tiggs, found Rowell guilty, sentenced him to two years in prison, reduced the sentence to one year, then made him eligible for parole in six months, and then allowed whatever time the Senator needed to recover from what proved to be a paralysis of his right arm caused by his embolism to be counted toward his serving out his sentence.

Rowell would be paroled before he ever entered a cell. And if this did not seem just (as it did not to some local journalists), the judge announced in his summation that, in view of Rowell Dollard's personal suffering and his public service ("And," said Cuddy, "let's face it, his family name."), the court was inclined to be merciful. Naturally, Dollard had resigned his state senate seat and his candidacy in the upcoming primary, and our state, said the judge, could be assured that this man was thus punished well enough to satisfy justice.

They told me that before his transfer to the new state medical facilities in Raleigh, Rowell Dollard and I had lived for two weeks on the same hospital floor along the same corridor, and that often in the long nights after visitors from the world outside were required to leave my room, he had came in his wheelchair to wait beside me, never speaking, just waiting there, beside the sealed window, watching out.

● ● ●

One bright day when haze motes spun up in my room like seafoam, Cuddy Mangum stuck his head in the door. "You decent?" Then he ushered in a thick cluster of Popes, all noisily hushed and stiffly dancing so as not to take up too much space.

Dickey had his comb and his pliers in a new aquamarine cowboy shirt yoked with lariats. Graham had taken off his down vest and put on ten pounds. Somewhere lost behind Graham, Preston moved furtively. And on either side of Cuddy stood Paula Burgwin, in a muumuu, and Charlene, whom I'd last seen as a platinum blonde and who was now staggeringly black-haired and appeared to be wearing a Puerto Rican costume from *West*

Side Story. Of Charlene's own recent stay in this hospital, there was only a thin white scar over the bridge of her nose.

The Popes jostled for position until Cuddy, like the nervous director of a school play, prodded Paula forward, and she—obviously elected speaker for the group—said, "Mr. Savile, how're you doing?"

"Call me Justin. And much better, thank you, Paula, and how about you?"

"Well, I am trying to lose weight, is all, if you can believe that, and I'm on this Scarsdale Diet thing, you know the one where that lady shot him, and," she giggled, "it's a real good diet for me because I can't even afford half the things he expects you to—"

Graham bellowed, "God damn it, Paula, will you get on with it?"

"Yeah, Paula," said Dickey from the mirror over the sink where he was combing his hair. "Will you stop running your mouth?"

"Shut up, Dickey." Graham cuffed his brother in the side of the head.

"Listen, y'all goons," Paula said, "Justin *asked* me how I was doing. I'm doing fine." She turned to me with the Snow White smile that showed her small, perfect teeth. "Well, I lost my position at the Rib House, but I'm seeking other employment at this time."

"I don't know why," growled Graham.

"Anyhow," Paula told me, "if they'd let me get a chance to say so, we all just wanted to come see how you were doing and tell you we're sorry about your getting hurt and we appreciate what you did to help Preston out. And Charlene got a suspended sentence, for giving evidence against that goon Luster. We appreciate that. And, well, that's all."

Preston sidled out from behind Graham and nodded and ducked back.

I said, "Listen, I appreciate what *you* did, Graham. I probably wouldn't be here if it weren't for you."

"Hell with it," Graham grumbled. "I'm just sorry Hudson's dead. I wanted to mess that son of a bitch up in person, and I wanted him to remember who was doing it."

Charlene had stuck a cigarette between her magenta lips, but Cuddy pulled it out before she could light it. She stepped forward now, orange skirt flouncing, and frowned at the ceiling. "This is all my fault, I guess. I hope you ain't going to hold it against me." She stepped back as if she'd finished a recitation.

I told her, "Don't be silly, Charlene."

Cuddy sighed. "Let's say there's nobody here without some M&M's melted on their hands; by which I mean Messing Up and Mixed Motives."

"Not Paula." Graham tried to hug her, but the muumuu slid away from him. "This little angel of a mother here never bad-mouthed a soul in her life."

Paula giggled. "I guess you never heard some of the things I've said about you, Graham."

"She was teasing," he explained. "Okay, lieutenant, you ever want to go hunting something with *four* legs, you look me up. We got to hit the road, I guess."

"We got to split," echoed Dickey, and they all left but Preston, who passed quickly by my bed, his hand inside his leather jacket, and dropped out of it a car's AM/FM tuner onto my sheet, then hurried away after his family.

"I didn't see that," said Cuddy.

I asked him, grinning again, "Did you round them up and make them come here?"

"Well, it is April Fool's today. But I believe this was Paula's idea."

"Good Christ, did she give in and go back to Graham?"

She and their two kids went back to the Maple Street house. Because Charlene came to our conclusion that Little Preston did a noble deed trying to keep her out of the state pen where her sweet-talking ways might have gotten her face torn off and her hair (umm! you notice that?) ripped out by some of the inmates there, whom I have seen at the lady convicts' wrestling finals, and I don't believe even Graham would take them on without a sledgehammer. So Charlene the Hot Tamale has kissed and made up with Preston, and love's gonna live there again. Paula went on back because she didn't want Charlene to have to live in that house again with the Pope boys unchaperoned, which she believes no woman should have to do, and I can see her point. But Paula is not living there, as she put it, as man and wife. She is holding herself in reserve, like those Greek ladies in *La Strada*."

"*Lysistrata.*"

"That's right. One of those foreign films. And speaking of man and wife, look here." He loped around to the bedside, tugging out a small jeweler's box; in it was a diamond ring in a circle of tiny sapphires the color of his eyes. "You think Junior'll like it? I put it on my Visa card. I just have the feeling she's going to say yes. Don't you?" Head tilted, he grimaced.

"I hope so, Cuddy. She ought to."

He flopped down into the wheelchair and spun it in a circle. "Oh, lordy, if she doesn't, I'm gonna, I'm gonna…." He stopped and sighed loudly, for the first time in our acquaintance robbed of his rich mint of words.

I said, "Did you buy those clothes to propose in?" For he was wearing a Harris tweed jacket with a gray wool knit tie.

"First, I tried on a bunch in your closet, but the pants were knickerbockers on me. Tell you the truth, I came into a little extra money. This is going to spook you, Justin. I almost didn't want to tell you. You remember those basketball scores Mrs. Cadmean gave me the night she died, off the top of her head? I won the pool. I won the damn NCAA basketball pool! First time in my life! Can you believe that?"

I could see Joanna's face, see the perfect smooth profile, feel the calm gray eyes on mine, hear her voice soft and absolute as a dream saying to me, Let go—saying to me what she could not tell herself. I said, "Oh, yes, I believe it." The face moved close to mine, translucent now.

Cuddy was saying, "No, I already wore these clothes when I took Junior over to see her old man."

The gray eyes closed and the face faded away.

I said, "Sorry? You got Briggs to go see Cadmean?"

"Ummm."

"How'd it go?"

He spun the chair in a slow circle. "I'll say this. If you stood between her and her dad in your shorts, your pecker wouldn't be too much use to you afterward, due to falling off from frostbite." Cuddy yanked up his hair. "I hate to confess this because I am a strictly moral man, but I *liked* the fat old bastard."

I laughed, and winced. "I also hate to confess it, as he is not a strictly moral man...any chance Ron Willis will tie Cadmean in for us about those Ames papers?"

"I deeply doubt it."

"It's not over, Cuddy. Luster was working for somebody. I just know it."

"Doctor D's happy. He found some of that yellow carpet's fibers on Luster's sneakers. Plus a speck of Mrs. Dollard's type blood, plus a sliver of some kind of expensive grass the Dollards had planted out there, plus dog hairs, plus Lord knows what all else; so he's happy, and Ken Moize is happy. Luster did it. And the state rests. We've got nothing on Ron Willis except his whinging a few shots at you, which appears to be a popular Hillston pastime. He can prove where he was the night of the robbery. Just because he knew Hudson and just because he handed Charlene a bag, doesn't make him a murderer. Or even an accessory. Meanwhile, Hophead Ron has come up with some real fancy lawyers that wouldn't use Joe Lieberman to lick their stamps, and they are arguing he wasn't even shooting at you. Just disturbing the peace, under the influence, and driving so as to endanger."

"I think old Briggs hired Willis to find somebody to steal those copies of the Ames papers. Cloris *had* them. Somebody took them."

"Oh, lordy. You are stubborn. Well, it wasn't Cary Bogue; he said he never saw them, and for us to stop pestering him. Anyhow, Fatso the Bald and I didn't get into that aspect of our relationship when I was over there. It was personal."

"What did you say to him?"

"Not much. I've been told that I'm a talker, but between your mama and my future pa-in-law, I believe I've been overrated."

"So, what did he say?"

Now Cuddy jumped out of the chair and blew up his cheeks and poked his finger at his pursed lips. "Says, 'Who the shit are you, son? Huh? Huh? Huh?' Says, 'I truly, truly believe I know you from somewhere, your particular ugly face strikes a chord of memory in my old ossified vicious self-adulating mind. Didn't your daddy used to work on my line? Huh? Huh? Now, shit, you're not diddling with my Baby, are you? Even if that child did sew a stone up in my heart. Because if I hear—and my ears are big as the sky— if I hear you are not doing right by my Princess, I'm going to have to send some boys from C&W over to pull off your arms and club you to death with them. Son.'"

I said, "Let me quote a friend: 'You are messing with the big boys now, Mangum.'"

He winked, "Oh, I expect that man is going to just love me if he lives long enough. I'm not going to let him see his grand-children unlest he improves his character."

"Forget it, Cuddy. He's too old for improvement. And I'm not sure what's coming along behind him is any better."

"Are you in reference to Lawry Whetstone?"

"For one."

"The Whetstones are on a cruise to the Caribbean. What with you whopping him and throwing her over, they needed to rest up. Fatso gave me the news when I was over at his castle that he personally sent old Lawry off on this vacation and told him don't rush back. They don't appear to be too friendly." Cuddy ate two chocolate turtles out of the box on my bedside table, then leaned over and shook my foot. "All right, now, when are you going to unhook your catheter and come on back to work? Not that it's as much fun around there now that old fathead V.D.'s left us to go tame the West."

"Have I still got a job?"

"Yep. Fact is, the new captain's a friend of your family's, you know how family connections always help. He even got you a raise so you could make your piano payments." Cuddy draped his (apparently new) London Fog raincoat over his lanky shoulder.

I pulled myself carefully up on the pillows. "New captain? Have we got a new captain? Who?"

At the door, sun twinkled the blue-jay eyes. "Oh, a real brainy guy."

"*Who?*"

"Me." He waved a salute and closed the door.

Chapter 32

I was home by Easter, sleeping on the couch downstairs across from my new ebony spinet. Above the piano, beside my father's watercolor, now hung the pencil sketch Joanna Cadmean had drawn the first day we met; Alice said it didn't look like me.

Propped on my cane, I watched Alice, day by day, move through the house, and leave it rich with her presence, with a vase pulled forward on a table, with apple juice shining in the refrigerator, with her small earth-dark gardening gloves placed one upon another in the windowsill.

While she was gone, I followed her days, saw her walking along the aisles of looms at C&W. Lying on my couch, I was taking tests with her across the street, worrying if this morning's exam had indeed, as we had predicted, begun with this question or that. I was going back, sober, to college.

Seated at my new piano, I was always listening for the click at the door and the quick steps coming closer. At every car's brake squeaking outside the house, my heart expected her, hours before I knew she could possibly return.

My own first public outing was to take place shortly before I resumed work at the department, under my new chief, Captain Mangum. I was asked to Easter services at the large stone church I had attended as a child, as a restless captive peering at the back of old Briggs Cadmean's glossy skull, but that I had not entered since my father's funeral. It was Alice who (to my mother's delight) asked me to go to church with her.

Across from her at the kitchen table, I said, "Red MacLeod, Lenin is writhing."

"Why?" she asked, and poured more syrup on her pancakes.

"I thought you were a Communist."

"Wasn't Christ? I'm a communist with a little *c*." She smoothed the syrup in swirls with her knife. "Most Communists with a big C are just Fascists without the nice clothes."

"Are you speaking as a weaver, or as a politician, or as a churchgoer?"

"All three," she said, and began eating.

I watched her. "Alice, why don't you marry me now and then run in this district primary? It might be nice to have a Christian communist state senator named Savile."

She laughed, leaned over and kissed me, tilting the small, stubborn chin. "First of all, Mister Savile the Fifth, even if you do con me into marrying you next month, which is not practical, and not reasonable…"

"How about if I say, all right, *take* the damn sideboard out of the dining room, will that do it?"

"This sideboard is hideous. And second, if somebody out of this house goes to the senate, the name's going to be MacLeod the First. Unless, of course, you want to run against me."

"Ah *tempora*. You and Briggs." I poured her a third cup of coffee. "You ought to get old Cadmean to finance your campaign. You're one of his. He'd love to buy you…. Can you be bought?"

"Bought to do what? And for how much? I'm practical. So's Cadmean. Just last week the union and he bought each other off. What he wanted to buy was 'cooperation,' and we sold it to him."

"Meaning what?"

"Are you really interested?"

I was very interested.

"Well, Mr. Cadmean invited all the shop stewards to this special board meeting, where he got us to testify so the board would vote through his plans to put this new loom system in the cottons division. That's my section. To update, instead of cut back. Now, that means shutting down for the time it takes to install the system, and then, after it goes in, laying off some workers."

I put down my fork. "New loom system?"

"Okay, so why does the union agree to 'cooperate'? Because, Mr. Cadmean makes a big tearjerker speech about how it's better to lay off a few people now than to let the division get shut down completely because we keep running at a loss. Because if we have to shut down, everybody loses." Alice cut some more squares of pancakes with quick sharp slices.

I asked, "Why should the union believe him?"

"Because there is a faction on the board fighting Cadmean to phase out the textiles completely; they want C&W to move more into their electronics; they want the plant space. And frankly, if they're willing to give me assurances they'd pay to train the people now assembling their clothes so they could assemble their computers instead, that would be fine with me. But Mr. Cadmean comes out sounding like the great American philanthropist and making the board sound like heartless capitalist capital P pigs, and everybody gets choked up about loyalty to 'the old mill,' and fighting the Asain labor peril, and they vote him everything he wants. Why aren't you eating your pancakes? Are you in pain again?" She looked at me seriously over her coffee cup.

I said, "Are you talking about a direct projection inertial-loom system?"

Alice stared at me, her cup dark blue as her eyes. "Well, you're always a surprise." So was her boss.

• • •

Sunday night, rain thudded at the bedroom's bay windows, and the big oak scratched at the glass, but to me wind and rain sounded peaceful as mist.

Unfastening her green robe, Alice said, "So, you think old

Cadmean's really going to show up tomorrow to see you? What do you think he wants?"

"He's the one who made the appointment and what I think is, he's too conceited to miss a chance to grandstand. But who knows what he wants, except he wants his daughter. And who knows what she wants, except to spite him. Good Christ, I can't believe she turned Cuddy down."

Alice slipped beneath the covers. "Justin, how many times do I have to tell you, Briggs didn't say *no*. She told Cuddy, 'Ask me again in a year.'"

I pulled myself up, careful of my leg. "Why? You don't have to wait a year to *decide* if you love somebody. If you do, you do. Like us."

She hugged against me, her cold nose on my chest, and wove her fingers through mine. "You're not fair to Briggs. She has a lot of bad junk to sort through about her dad. I mean, to be sure that she's not marrying somebody either because Cadmean doesn't approve, or because he *does*. Plus, is it really *her* Cuddy wants, or is it marriage? And, Jesus Christ." Her hair, scratchy silk, made goose bumps along my shoulder. "Who in our generation wouldn't be at least a little ambivalent about marrying the local chief of police?"

"How about a local detective lieutenant?"

"That's bad enough."

But her mouth and her hands as she now slipped up over me was evidence beyond doubt that she and I were stubbornly, perfectly right.

She whispered, "Now, don't hurt yourself again."

"About that sideboard. We'll haul it to the backyard. We'll sprinkle it with the leftover cigarettes, and the leftover Jack Daniel's, and set it on fire. Say yes."

"Yes."

She moved above me like a flower swayed, like white peonies and red poppies and rose mountain laurel swayed; and I was the new shafts of spring earth, and so joined with her that there was no way to tell what was earth growing up, and what was flower.

Chapter 33

Easter Monday two letters came in the mail. Both were endings; one was also an inheritance. The first was a postcard from Susan Whetstone of a hotel swimming pool in St. Thomas. It bore neither salutation nor signature and was brief: "Why did you send those things back? You are so full of it." Unless she'd already found someone else to give the gifts to, Lawry now had two of a number of expensive things, including a gold chain I had never worn, with the initials JBS.

At the heading of the other letter was the name of a legal firm in Cape Hatteras. It advised me formally of instructions received last month from a client, Walter Charles Stanhope, regarding a bequest. Mr. Stanhope's desire was that in the event he should predecease me, I should come into possession of property of his, consisting of a three-room house and a lot fifty by a hundred feet at Shore Walk on Ocracoke Island, North Carolina. This letter ended: "I regret to have to inform you that Mr. Stanhope passed away at his home during the night of April 10. The house has been closed. Please advise us at your earliest convenience as to your wishes in this matter."

In my living room, holding the lawyer's letter, I saw myself creak open the bleached-gray door of the small house, shadowy under mossbearded oaks. I saw the fishing rods inside the door, saw the phonograph records still on the turntable, saw the conch shells dusty pink in their cabinet. Standing by my car in Hillston, I walked into Mr. Stanhope's bedroom, which I had never entered, and took down the black, frayed, dusty case of his violin from atop a mahogany wardrobe, and sat down on the bed where he had died, and held it. Standing in the noise of downtown Hillston, I traveled back along the coast of the silent Outer Banks, back along the thin, flurried wild oats rustling together as they bent away from the sea, back where spume of the gray waves rolling in from an old world was salt in my eyes.

At the municipal building, Cuddy Mangum stood in the corridor outside my office, pinning to the bulletin board more of the notices with which, Etham Foster told me, our new captain was rapidly reorganizing his unnerved department.

"You're early," Cuddy said, spitting thumbtacks out of his mouth into his hand. "B.M., referring, of course, to old Briggs Monmouth, isn't showing up 'til four, if then. Plus, he says we're going to meet downstairs in the courtroom. Says he's too old to climb all these stairs and too fat to ride in the elevator. Fact is, the old bastard just wants to refresh our memories about who paid for that courtroom and who thinks he still owns it." Cuddy rubbed his eyes; there were dark circles under them now.

Leaning on my cane, I followed him into the big corner office where the Elvis Presley poster had replaced Fulcher's bowling trophies, and where there was finally room enough for all of Cuddy's books. He tapped his pencil on the large metal desk. "Now, listen here, Justin. The hardheaded truth is we just haven't shown Mister Moize enough to tie Willis in on the Dollard case. He's not going to take it to the grand jury. So I don't want you to limp off brokenhearted." His head at its old waggish tilt, he added, "You must have come in here six hours early to traipse around showing off your cane, which does have that Ashley-gimping-home-to-Tara look to it, I'll give you that." He stood, looking out his window over the little skyline of Hillston, now flat-edged in the bright spring sky. "Maybe I should get a cane," he said. "Maybe that would help."

I told him, "Alice thinks Briggs may change her mind one of these days."

"Well, I hope Alice is going on inside information." His head shook away thoughts, and he turned back. "Seeing as you have shown up a week before the doctor said to..."

Then there was a knock at his door, and Hiram Davies, frozen-faced as a palace guard, stepped in. "Captain, Mr. Moize needs to see you right away. I'm sorry if I interrupted. Excuse me." With a starched nod, he backed out.

"What now?" Cuddy said. "Okay. How about start going through these reports, General." He tapped a stack of papers on his desk. "Crime marches on, you know." He sighed and yanked up on his cowlick and left.

So for an hour I read laconic tales told by patrolmen of my fellow Hillstonians; most of them mysteries only in God's plot, which has always escaped detection. A car dealer on the bypass borrowed a friend's shotgun and blew off his own head because his business was failing; his body was discovered by his eight-year-old daughter. A fight took place outside the college bierhaus between two high school students and two Pakistani university undergraduates whom the locals mistook for Iranians; one, an epileptic, was hospitalized. A battered wife blinded her husband by throwing liquid Drano in his face. An East Hillston senior citizen's lung was punctured by a knife wound inflicted by a four-teen-year-old mugger. A North Hillston boy on speed killed his mother's miniature chow. Last, there was a report with the heading, "Refer to Savile—homicide." The body of a coed had been found Friday night; someone had raped and strangled her as she walked back to her dormitory from the library through University Arboretum. I was supposed to find out who.

I heard Walter Stanhope's hoarse whisper. *Forty years, it's enough. I stick to fish now.* Forty years, before he'd retreated to the outermost edge of the land, retired to the place where prophetic Indians had stopped the first Lost Colony, and then with all their people had fled west and west and west away from the endless waves of pale dreamers from an old world, themselves fleeing west. Forty years; that left me thirty-five more to go.

I went to the morgue to see the body of the young murdered

woman, and then I drove across town with Etham Foster to walk the path through University Arboretum to the place, strewn with rain-blown pink and white petals, hidden in a canopy of leaves, where she had died, and where no one had found her until Saturday morning in the rain. "Just my luck," grumbled Foster. "Rain."

At 4:15 I was sitting at the table where, when court was in session, the prosecuting attorneys sat. I sat and blinked at the afternoon sun angling through the tall sets of dusty windows, and thought about my new case. On the dais in front of me rose the high empty judge's bench, flanked by the furled flag of the state of North Carolina, with its motto, *Esse Quam Videri*, "To Be Rather Than Seem." Beside me the empty pews of the jury box sloped up to meet the oak wainscoting.

The murdered girl's name, said the report I held, was Virginia. Virginia. That name of the first girl born to the first colonists, the name of the first Protestant born in the new world, born on the Outer Banks to a governor grandfather named White and a father named Dare, christened in honor of a Virgin Queen for whose favor Sir Walter Raleigh had dared the dream of gold. The Lost Colony had vanished, including this firstborn of my people, this Virginia White Dare, had vanished and left only a mystery carved in a tree, a single world of warning or prophecy, the word *Croatoan*. But no one had been able to interpret the mystery, and no one had been warned away, and whites dared to keep digging the gold beneath the forests of tall pines. Raleigh had died on the block, and his dream was now a land of Hillstons.

• • •

Briggs Cadmean, wearing a rumpled poplin suit and holding an unlit cigar, came into the courtroom. He squinted at the hard light for a moment before he moved. Then down the tiered aisle he shambled with leisured interest, running his stiff fingers along the backs of the empty oak chairs, stooping with a groan to pick up a littered newspaper off a brown-cushioned seat.

"Good afternoon." He smiled, reached for and shook my hand. "Justin. Mighty happy to see you in church yesterday and on the road to recovery. You had my prayers, son. I know a parent's heart. I've lost five of my flesh and bone. None left to me but my Baby, and two foolish sons so scared of me they moved out of the goddamn state." He waved his cigar at the windows. "Isn't this the prettiest day you ever saw? All that rain just washed the world young. Between the apple trees and the cherry trees and the azaleas, I just want to fill up my lungs with Hillston! You know what they say, 'If God is not a Tarheel, then why is the sky Carolina blue?' Am I right? What can I do for you today?" By now Cadmean had settled himself carefully into the large spoke-backed chair where, during sessions, the court recorder sat.

I said, "You're the one who made the appointment."

He nodded. "Where's Captain Mangum?"

"He had a meeting. He sends his regrets."

"Huh. You like Mangum? Smart man, am I right? New breed."

"Yes."

"His people were tenant farmers, you know that? Country people. His daddy came into town applying for a job at the mills, came in his bare feet."

"What did you do, have his genealogy traced?"

"Captain Mangum like his new job?"

"Yes."

Cadmean grinned. "I talked to a lot of friends of mine. I heard they were getting ready to appoint a new chief. I'm all for progress, always have been."

I said, "No reason why if you're asked your honest opinion, you shouldn't be happy to give it."

Old Cadmean rolled the cigar between his palms while he told me, yes, he was always happy to be of service to the city he loved. His huge bald head swiveled slowly as he spoke; doubtless to indicate that the perimeters of this courtroom were a ready example of his affection for Hillston. He said, "Shame you never got to see the old courthouse, Justin. Man with your fine taste would have liked it. I was a teenager when it burnt down. I remember getting shown the ruts in the steps where the colored people had rolled up the whiskey barrels back when they were running the town for the Yankees in the days of Reconstruction. Couldn't even read, and they were running the town drunk as baboons. Well now, progress."

I said, "While you're throwing your unprejudiced voice behind the new breed, Mr. Cadmean, I've got a name for you. Somebody who believes in progress and wants to get into state politics one of these days."

"Who is he?"

"It's a she. Alice MacLeod. Your great-grandfather sent her to college."

He grunted. "Oh, her. Bush Scholarship. Yep, Alice is something. She's not a scared woman. Scared women give me the fidgets. Wants to get into politics, hunh?" The fingers scraped up the fat cheek. "Hunh. Well, maybe I ought to sit down one of these days and have a talk with her."

I said, "You'll run into the same problem you're going to run into with Captain Mangum. She's not for sale."

"That so? Wouldn't it depend on what I wanted to buy?"

"What can I do for you, Mr. Cadmean? I'm afraid I need to get back to work pretty soon."

"That thing over in the Arboretum Friday night?" He shook his head. "Didn't that make you sick? What kind of girl was she?"

"Not the kind that wanted to get raped and strangled."

Turning his chair so his back was to the shaft of sun, he squinted at me. "I saw Rowell last week."

"Yes, he said you'd come. I went to Raleigh yesterday afternoon to visit him."

"Must weigh down your soul."

"Mine, yes. But I think his own actually feels a little lighter. Confession has a way of doing that. Is that why you're here?"

"Joanna was a crazy woman. I believe I told you that. Pitiful. It just makes me want to cry."

"Does it?"

"Doesn't it you, son? Killing herself for spite."

"Yes, it makes me want to cry. I'm sorry she died. I'm sorry she couldn't let go."

"What of?"

"Believing she could force someone to love her. As you know, Mr. Cadmean, it can't be done."

The eyelids lifted to show more yellow.

I pulled my leg off the cane I was resting it on, stood up, and, sun in my eyes, walked toward Cadmean's brooding face. I said, "I hear the board at C&W met this past week and decided to install a new inertial-loom system in the textiles division."

He pursed the sea-bass lips. "Well now, Justin. Who told you that? Yes, I won that vote. I had some opposition."

"I heard you had to scramble pretty hard."

He nodded. "I truly hate it when I have to. It reminds me I'm getting old, and that's something I hate even more."

"Mr. Cadmean, tell me something about this new system of yours. Are your engineers making use of Bainton Ames's designs?"

"Could be."

"Where'd you get them?"

He surprised me. He said, "Cloris gave them to me day before she died. Brought over a whole box of Bainton's other old stuff besides."

"Why'd you tell me she didn't?"

The old man patted his hand at the air near me. "Something the Preacher Solomon says, I believe, is a prudent man concealeth knowledge. But a fool's mouth is his destruction. I make it a practice not to answer folks, 'til I know *why* they're asking a particular question. Hunh? You told me those particular designs were tied up with poor Cloris's getting herself killed. Well, I didn't believe they were. I thought you'd gone haywire, tell you the truth. But, naturally, every now and then I'm mistaken."

I asked him, "Did she give them to you of her own free will?"

Cadmean bared his small even yellow teeth. "It's not my way

to use force against a member of the fair sex. I love women."

I said, "Not loose ones. Not Cloris Dollard."

"That's true, son. And I told her so to her face. Told her something else. She had no business holding those designs back from me all these years, a whole carton of stuff mildewing down in her basement, not letting me know Bainton had advanced his ideas as far as he had way back then. 'Course, she didn't anymore know what was in those files than a cat can read."

"So why'd she bring them to you when she did?"

"Well now," he rumbled. "That's a long story."

"Is that why you came here? You enjoy telling these long stories, don't you? I'm not sure I have time for another one. But I'll listen to a short version."

I walked back to my chair and sat down. Cadmean pointed at my cane. "How long you going to have to be on that cane, son? Is that leg busted for good?"

"Probably not. Do you know Ron Willis?"

"Mighty happy to hear it. Well now, Mr. Willis used to drive a forklift on the night shift; in cottons."

I smiled. "That's another thing you were too prudent to reveal last time we talked?"

"No. I didn't know it then. You obliged me to find it out after that pleasant walk we took. I like to know as much as I can about anybody working for me."

"Did you arrange for Ron Willis to rob Cloris Dollard of the Xerox copies she'd made of those designs?"

"Oh, I already answered that question for Mr. Moize and the answer was no."

"You would so testify?"

Cadmean pushed the fat pads of his fingertips together. "I recall Solomon also saying there were six things the Lord hates, and one was a false witness who breathes out lies." The big gnarled fingers interwove, flew apart, interwove. "And another one was a heart that devises wicked plans. You want to hear this short story?"

My shadow, looking strange to me with its wavery cane, nodded.

He pulled out a thick brass lighter and held it up into the sun. "Why don't we wait for Captain Mangum?"

"No, sir. I'm afraid you're going to have to put up with a small audience."

"All right, then." The fat old man scratched his song against the shave of his cheek with the lighter, his little, lidded eyes on me. "Say there was a man from Atlanta named Cary Bogue, a sort of rival of mine, a ferret and a hog. Maybe you already heard how he came up into our state and tried to work a shady deal that fell through when Bainton died. Say this ferret had gone right then and there to Cloris; says, 'Let's *you* and me dicker, and while we're at it, I would truly love to get my hands on all those old coins of your departed one.' Well now, maybe Cloris was not the sort of woman I'm particular to. But she was a feeling woman, and this Bogue showing up the day after her husband died, came across to her a little too much like a carrion crow, so she told him she was making a vow: 'Not you, not now, not ever.'"

I said, "Skip on ahead some, Mr. Cadmean."

Slanted light made a play of our shadows against the wall while Mr. Cadmean gazed around the sun-smoky courtroom. "Fine," he said. "Let's skip to a few months back when Mr. Bogue fell into conversation with somebody from Hillston who knew Cloris. And Bogue mentioned how he'd, all those years ago, wanted those pretty coins *and* those designs, and how maybe he still did, because maybe Ames was so smart he could see the god-damn future far enough ahead nobody could be sure they'd still quite caught up to him. You follow me?"

"Yes."

"That's good, Justin. I appreciate a good listener."

"Who is this somebody from Hillston?"

Cadmean flicked open the lighter; flame shot up and he blew it out with his pink, puffed lips. "You know him, son. I believe I heard you did to him what he tried to do to me."

I knew he meant Lawry Whetstone and saw in the sleepily watchful eyes that he was aware I knew.

I said, "I don't appreciate the comparison. Another thing,

Lawry knew what I was 'doing to him,' and he didn't care. And that, I'll confess, makes me feel even shabbier about it."

He nodded. "You're old-fashioned. Like me."

"Not exactly."

"Well, *I* didn't know I was getting two-timed. But I found out." The lighter flicked again. "And I did care."

"And?"

"And I'm afraid my vice president's liable to be disappointed when he gets back from—what do you call it again? Cruising? I'm afraid Lawry was hoping my board wouldn't want to tie up so much capital in any new looms just now, when he's so pressed for cash to finish that electronics plant of his." Cadmean shifted his huge bulk in the chair. "My vice president spends a lot of time conglomerating and socializing in big-money places, like Atlanta. I'm truly a simple old man. I've found out it's easier to keep your house in order if you stay home and live in it. Sort of like keeping your wife to yourself, am I right? Another thing I'm old-fashioned about is credit. It appears my vice president had arranged to lease on credit a bunch of machinery for his new plant from a place in New England that, pitifully enough, had to go out of business. But this credit was on a mighty short leash. That's why not getting my capital is going to be a disappointment to him."

"But I bet you're going to enjoy telling him."

"Oh, I am." Cadmean probed at the bones padded beneath the bald scalp. "I don't believe he's going to be all that surprised. Lawry and I already had a little talk about his last trip to Atlanta, when he ran into Mr. Bogue and Mr. Bogue was in a position to offer him a little capital in a hurry to hold off those creditors."

"And in exchange, what was Lawry offering Bogue?"

"Using my imagination, I'd say he promised he'd talk a foolish woman into selling Mr. Bogue some coins, plus some designs she had no right to sell." Cadmean's puffy lips pushed in and out as he got up from his chair now and came across the room. "Problem is, Lawry forgot to remember one thing about women. They change their minds. Like *that*!" The fingers snapped in a loud crack, and then he continued his walk, going all the way over to the other side of the large room from me, to the jury box, where he eased himself down into the front pew. He put his cigar back into his breast pocket and set the lighter down on the rail in front of him, turning it to the sharp slant of sun.

"She decided to give those papers to you," I said. "But then you were so obnoxious to her, she decided she'd sell Bogue the copies she'd made."

Cadmean leaned his crossed arms over the jury rail. "I truly wouldn't be surprised. I didn't know about those copies. Didn't know 'til you told me. Cloris was too sly for me. Women have fooled me all my life."

I ran my pencil through my fingers, tapping it on the report in front of me, point to top, top to point, while Cadmean stuffed his hand into the pocket of his jacket, took out and slowly unfolded a piece of paper. "This thing here is another copy. The original came to my attention a few weeks ago, and I had this made up because I thought you'd be interested." He pulled out some bifocals and slowly put them on. "This was in an envelope addressed to my vice president Mr. Whetstone at his Atlanta hotel, but Cloris didn't get a chance to locate a stamp to put on it before she passed away." The old man rubbed at his mouth and then began to read slowly. "'Dear Lawry. You were so upset on the phone this morning....'" Cadmean looked up, over the glasses. "By the way, this letter's dated. Dated January 9. Day she died. You all right over there, son? You look puke green."

I pushed my cane out to rest my leg on again; it had been a long time since I'd been up this many hours. "I'm fine. Go ahead."

"Well, Cloris goes on a little about being sorry to let Lawry down; then she says, 'When you first asked me if Bainton had left any papers, I thought, well, my stars, why hold a grudge against Bogue after all these years. And the girls could have the money. Still, it just didn't seem fair to C&W. That's why I took them to Briggs. But after that old SOB—'"he paused and waved the sheet at me. "Can you believe that woman called me an SOB?" "'—said what he did to me, I thanked my stars I'd gotten those Xerox copies made, and I called you back. But, like I told you this morning, now I can't bring myself to sell them,'" Cadmean's thin copperish eyebrow lifted, "'without talking to Rowell about it first. I know we agreed I wouldn't mention anything about this to him, because of his loyalty to Briggs. But he and I have never kept any secrets and I don't want to start. So, like I said, I'll put the copies in the safe, and we'll wait until you get back to Hillston and Rowell's home, and if he says okay to give you the copies, and not tell Briggs about them, fine. And there's no reason why Mr. Bogue ought to get mad at *you*, but I just want to say I'm sorry if I put you in an awkward spot. Apologies, Cloris.' Interesting letter, am I right?"

Sun reflected back from Cadmean's glasses as he refolded the sheet. Then with that surprising suppleness I'd seen once before out in the muddy field by the stables, he picked up the lighter off the rail in front of him and set fire to the paper, holding it by its edge in the big stiff fingers until I would have thought they'd be burnt. I jumped, then sat back. With my cane, I couldn't have reached him in time to stop him, even if I'd been willing to give him the satisfaction of trying.

I said, "These are handsome oak floors. Seems a shame to burn holes in them. It's also against the law to deface public property."

"Justin, you're a wry man."

"Not as wry as you, sir."

He grinned. "That's true too."

"What was the point of that little bit of drama?"

"Son, you suspected me of hiring some bumblers to rob a woman that ended up getting killed." He groaned, bending over to pick up the ashes and to dust the floor with his hand. "Well, that's insulting."

I said, "I assume Luster Hudson got this letter out of Cloris's purse when he went over there to get those papers for Whetstone. Willis got it from Hudson. And kept it, as insurance. And what do you want to bet, you got it from Willis. Now, how did that happen?"

"I've learned a lot of sad things in a lot of sad years on this pitiful earth, Justin. One of them is, if a man can be bought once, he can be bought twice. Hunh? You just have to offer him a little bit more than he was getting the first time. A sad tale of betrayal came with that letter."

I looked up. "What'd you give Willis? The mills?"

Cadmean swayed his big head. "Now, you know that's something I'd never sell." The teeth flashed. "And not about to let anybody else sell it. Or shut it. Not 'til they dig my hole."

I clipped my pencil to the report. "Willis has somehow acquired some very expensive lawyers. I can use my imagination too. As far as imagination goes, you're a lot of things, Mr. Cadmean, but I'm not sure being a psychic is one of them. How do you know Whetstone was negotiating with Bogue for fast capital?"

Cadmean smiled. "You're right. I don't have visions like poor Joanna. What I have is friends. All over the South. When you've been in a business for, let's see, almost seventy years, because I was ten when I started on my daddy's line, when you've been at it that long, and you're not a complete son of a bitch, and I'm truly not, son, you're liable to end up with a few friends. And my vice president was not a discreet man."

If Cadmean was right—and the fact that Lawry Whetstone was cruising the Caribbean while the board canceled his plans to cut back the textiles division suggested that Cadmean was right—then Lawry had taken a considerable risk when he came to me with a story so close to the real one in order to find out what I knew; when he even insinuated that Cadmean was behind the theft. As, indeed, I had concluded. I saw Whetstone, blandly tan, turning the gold college ring, waiting for me to ask him another question. *This Dollard thing was really just an excuse to come in.* Had he planned deliberately to end our conversation with his proposed foursome to outrage me and obscure his motive in making the only personal contact with me we'd ever had? *Sugar, I told Lawry you wouldn't be interested, but he never listens.*

Yes, there was little reason to doubt Cadmean was right, and that Ron Willis, for who knows what price, had sold him the letter that told him he was right. Whetstone must have decided Sunday after Cloris called him that he'd rather not wait to hear what Rowell would say, because he knew what Rowell would say, because Rowell was Cadmean's man. Cloris must have not only told him in that Sunday-morning call (*She was a totally open person, Jay; she never kept anything back.*) where she was putting those copies of the designs, but told him she was going to be out at the play all evening. Easy enough to call that evening to be sure she was leaving. Easy enough to call Ron Willis from Atlanta and tell him to go take the papers and make the theft look like an ordinary robbery. Whetstone knew what Willis would do for money, because he was already paying Willis to spy on people like Alice. He already knew Susan would be at *A Midsummer Night's Dream* that night, and so he phoned her and left her a message to call him back as soon as she got home. Easy enough, too, to call the Dollard house to warn Willis to get out because Cloris was also on her way home.

Easy enough to think nothing could be easier than getting those copies for Bogue (for whatever reasons of rivalry with Cadmean or revenge against him or curiosity about the designs themselves, Bogue had wanted them), in exchange for whatever financial help Bogue was going to give Lawry to help him rival or revenge himself against Cadmean's power at C&W.

It must have been a shock to find out Willis had subcontracted the job to a man as stupid and vicious as Luster Hudson, and that Cloris had come home too soon from the play. To find out Hudson had tried to take revenge on Preston Pope and had returned to Hillston from wherever he'd been sent. To find out Susan had been talking to me about what Cloris had said. That Willis wouldn't stay put and was terrified of Hudson and paranoid about me and in the habit of taking more cocaine than was fashionable, and then shooting off guns. The last shock must have been when old Cadmean showed him Cloris's letter.

I stood up in the sunlit oval and pushed in my chair. "Of course, Mr. Cadmean, I don't believe you want Lawry's felonies to come to light. You like things the way they are. As I recall from your other little story, this is just the way you like to have people in your employ. I'm not sure Lawry's going to be as much use to you as Rowell was; I very much doubt you're going to run Lawry for office."

He rubbed his hand roughly over his face. "Thank God his daddy's dead and gone."

"I don't know why you even bother mouthing the words." I picked up my report. "The thing is, I'm not interested in playing cat and mouse with you. I'm on a cane and don't enjoy the scampering. So I won't. What I am going to do is tell Ken Moize everything you've said. It's his job to decide whether he wants to spend the taxpayers' money to listen to Willis perjure himself, or whether he's just going to put him away for assault against me."

"There certainly doesn't seem to be any *proof* that Mr. Willis sent Hudson to poor Cloris's house. Or that Lawry hired Willis."

"Like I said, it's not my job to make that decision. And chasing you for my own satisfaction has gotten to be a waste of my time. What accommodations Lawry and you and Moize make don't interest me as much as finding out who just killed a girl named Virginia Caponigri."

There was a noise and the doors behind us opened. Cuddy Mangum, shielding his eyes, stepped inside, a clipboard under his arms. "You two still here? Hello there, Mr. Cadmean. Sorry I got held up, but Justin here can fill me in."

I said, "One thing we were talking about was how Mr. Cadmean had given you his vote of confidence over at the city council."

"Was I saying that?" Cadmean threw up his old hands in innocent openness.

"I appreciate everybody's vote," Cuddy said.

Cadmean grinned. "Some votes count more than others, that's a sad fact of democracy."

"Umm," said Cuddy.

Mr. Cadmean puffed up his lips. "Well now, you think you deserve this job?"

Cuddy said, "I know I do."

"I'm as smart as you are, son." Cuddy had started back up the sloped aisle toward the double doors when Cadmean added, "I want you to bring my Baby over to see me again."

Cuddy turned. "I don't know if I would even if I could; but I can't. Briggs's not going to be around for a while, soon as her term's over. Seems like she said she was going off west somewhere to look at a telescope."

"Well, shit, son!" Cadmean roared. "Shit! Don't let her get away! Women are truly the wonder of the world, they're Eldorado and the mouth of the Nile. But you got to remember. Not a one of them has got a lick of sense. I married four of them, and two of those got a pack of coyote lawyers to gouge through my pockets. And there were some others I woke up in time *not* to marry. Women are going wrong. I swear, they're getting to be just about as hoggish as men, plus all of them are just as crazy as loons on top of it."

Cuddy blinked and sun flashed through the blue. "You old bastard, if you hadn't believed all that bullshit, maybe you wouldn't have had so much trouble with your women." He waved the clipboard at me. "Meet you back upstairs, General Lee. We got a lady thinks she saw somebody suspicious hanging around the Arboretum." The oak doors closed behind him.

As Mr. Cadmean shambled over to my chair, he held out his gnarled hand. "Good man, Mangum. Come on. Between my arthritis and your leg, we ought to be able to keep up with each other."

"I think we can manage," I said.

And so we walked back through the courtroom and out onto the black and white marble floor of the rotunda. Cadmean turned at the doors to look up at his varnished portrait. "Shit," he whispered. "I was old then. If there's one thing I can't stand the thought of, it's the world going on its merry way without me in it."

"You want it to come to a halt when you do?"

He grinned. "That's exactly right."

"Well, that's something else you can't do anything about."

"What was the first something?"

"Acquiring your daughter's affection."

From the middle of the patterned floor, he circled back to me.

"Justin, you don't want to waste your time. Don't waste it trying to hurt my feelings. Don't get yourself believing I care whether you want to listen to my stories or not. There's always somebody who does. Always will be."

"'Til they dig your hole. Or are you planning to keep talking from the grave?"

He chuckled. "Could be. Keep your ears peeled. Hunh! You sure were something in that donkey head, son."

I pushed against the brass filigree of the door bar. I said, "What if Rowell hadn't made that nolo contendere plea? What if there'd been a trial and we'd subpoenaed you? Would you have perjured yourself?"

The pink lips pursed against his forefinger. "There wasn't a trial," he said.

"But if there had been?"

The old stiff fingers squeezed my shoulder. "Son...son. 'Sufficient unto the day is the evil thereof.' Hunh?"

Outside, the afternoon sun glowed red on all the buildings. I stood with the old industrialist at the top of the broad stone steps that were guarded by empty antique cannon, fired last in 1865 for a lost dream and a cause undefendable. Beside me a long sigh rumbled from Cadmean before he spoke. "I'll tell you this, Justin. Sometimes I think when I think about my Baby looking up at those tired old stars of hers, what if it was my privilege to be up there, looking down? What do you think I'd see? Hunh?" His sulfurous, low-lidded eyes gazed down over Hillston. "Well, I'd see a little tiny ball of slime, wouldn't I? And nations of bugs crawling crazy all over it. And I bet up there I'd be able to hear something I've always suspected. God laughing His damn head off like a scorching wind. Am I right? Take care of yourself, son."

I stood there, watching him carefully descend the gray stone steps one by one, watching him stiffly pull himself into the backseat of the waiting limousine and with a wince of pain tug shut the door.

All he couldn't do was make his child want to spend a night under his roof. All he couldn't will, with the powers of influence, was love. Just as Joanna couldn't will it, not even with sorcery, or revenge its loss with death.

I stood there until from behind the stone balustrade, I heard the voice of Sister Resurrection, as always, faithful at her station by the house of law. She began to speak suddenly, as if she'd been listening to the old man whose bones, like hers, were brittle, and whose eyes were as ancient and as hard. I heard her before I saw her, so her sharp, impatient chant came up to me in the warm sun like the keen of a ghost too haunted to wait for the dark.

"The time is come. How long, O Lord? God fixing to melt the mountains. Make a path. God fixing to overthrow Pharaoh. Joseph's neck in a collar of iron. Cut it loose. The blind shall see the mountains tremble. Make a path for the anger of the Lord. Praise Him!"

Around the corner of the cannon the small figure of rags came marching, her hair snow wool and matted with bits of earth. The filthy sweaters hung fluttering to her knees, and she had again her wood, handmade cross in both small black hands. Leaning on my cane, I made my way down the steps to where she stood, still speaking. "God Almighty's sick and tired. He gonna loose the Devil's chains."

I touched her arm, and she spun to face me. I said, "Mrs. Webster, God knows I don't have any right to ask you this, but don't you believe there's any chance for love at all?"

The clouded black eyes blazed out at me like a sudden flame. "*I carrying it!*" She spit the three words up at my face, and then thrust forward her crossed sticks of wood. "You want it? Take it."

Startled, I stepped back and said, "No, ma'am."

Clouds passed over the eyes like smoke, and she turned away and began again to prophesy.

Please enjoy the following preview of
Time's Witness, Michael Malone's second
Justin and Cuddy novel, available from
Sourcebooks Landmark.

Prologue

Of charity, what kin are you to me?
—*Twelfth Night*

I don't know about Will Rogers, but I grew up deciding the world was nothing but a sad, dangerous junk pile heaped with shabby geegaws, the bullies who peddled them, and the broken-up human beings who worked the line. Some good people came along, and they softened my opinion. So I'm open to any evidence they can show me that God's not asleep at the wheel, barreling blind down the highway with all us dumb scared creatures screaming in the back seat.

My name's Cuddy Mangum. I don't much like it. Short for Cudberth, by which I suspect my mother meant Cuthbert, though I never called it to her attention. Everybody's always known me as Cuddy. Cudberth would have been worse. Or Cud.

A few years back, at the start of the eighties, I was made police chief here in Hillston, North Carolina. If you ever read a story by Justin Savile, you know that, but chances are you've got too cute a notion of who I am. Justin's loved me for years without a clue to my meaning. He sees things personally. Me, I look at the package, and the program. According to Justin, I'm somewhere between young Abe Lincoln in cracker country and the mop-up man on Hee Haw. A kind of Carolina Will Rogers without the rope tricks. And Justin's always adding to his portrait. He never read a book without looking for everybody he knows in it, and it didn't take him long to find me chasing after a dream like Gatsby, wearing some buckskin moral outfit Natty Bumpo left behind. I'm not saying his views aren't flattering. But if my arms had had the stretch of Justin's imagination, I could have bounced through the state university free, playing basketball, instead of slapping concrete on the new sports arena for four years to pay my way.

Justin and I are natives of the same tobacco and textiles city in the North Carolina Piedmont. But his folks shipped him out of Hillston early, off to some woodsy New England prep school, then to Harvard, where his imagination got away from him for a while, and they had to lock him up in a sanatorium near Asheville. I saw it once; it looked like Monte Carlo. Afterwards, they smuggled him into law school in Virginia, but he ran home to Hillston and threw them into a hissie by joining the police. I've heard his reasons. They're all personal.

I didn't have near enough the imagination for the first place I was shipped after college, and after too long a while slithering through rice paddies in the Mekong Delta, I crawled back to Hillston as fast as my psychic state allowed. I wanted a master's degree from Haver University, and I wanted to get to know my wife, Cheryl. It turned out she'd made other plans with a fellow I used to like. She was my last living family, if you want to call her that. My folks are dead. A long time ago, my sister Vivian's boyfriend, going drunk into a curve at eighty miles an hour, smashed them both through a steel rail on Route 28. He survived, and died in a motorcycle accident three months after he got out of traction. His parents still owed University Hospital over twelve thousand dollars. For his personal motto in the Hillston High yearbook, this boy had them write, "I want to live fast, love hard, die young, and leave a beautiful memory." That year, six different East Hillston guys had this same motto. Vivian's boyfriend was the second to get his wish.

In 1931 my daddy walked into Hillston barefooted. The first big building he saw was Cadmean Textile Mills, so he took a job there sweeping floors. His folks worked a farm fifteen miles outside the town. They didn't own it, and they couldn't feed him. After forty-two years on the Cadmean line, he didn't own the house he died in. He did own a long series of large cheap cars loaded with chrome that he buffed with a shammy rag on Sunday afternoons. I don't know if there was anything else he loved. Any dreams he kept, he kept private. Mama never learned to drive the cars. She had bad teeth and a purplish birthmark across her right cheek that she covered with the palm of her hand, and she was shy about going anyplace except the East Hillston A&P and the Baptist Church of the Kingdom of Christ. By third grade, I'd stopped asking her for help with my homework. Her tongue would stutter struggling to decipher the big printed letters, and a thin line of sweat would rise just above her lips, and her birthmark would blush purple.

I didn't have the best thing, which is class. Here in the South that means an old family tree, with all its early rough graspy roots buried deep down in the past where nobody has to look at them. And I didn't have the second-best thing, which is looks—because the hard fact is, resembling young Abe Lincoln is no asset at a high school sock hop. But I had the third thing, which is brains. So I was lucky enough to learn how to see where the light was, and where to look around for the switch. I don't mean moving out of East Hillston, but I mean that too. I've got a job that makes some use of my brain, and is some use to other people. I've got eight walls of books. I've got a new white Oldsmobile my daddy would have just admired. I own a condominium in River Rise, west of town, so big I haven't had time to furnish half of it. It's big enough for love to have some space, because let me tell you, love likes a lot of room; it's hate that does fine when it's cramped. I've got so many former neighbors to prove that fact, it comes close to breaking my heart.

Justin Bartholomew Savile V is a Liberal Democrat, a group just about abandoned by everybody except the upper classes. Justin's father (J.B.S. IV) was the kind of Virginian who'd name his son J.B.S. V; his hobby was running Haver University Medical School. Justin's mother is a Dollard. Well now, Dollards. For a couple of centuries they've sat slicing up the pie of the Carolina Piedmont and passing the pieces around to each other with polite little nods. "Why I don't mind if I do, thank you so much." Justin's great-great-grandfather Eustache Dollard was one of the state's best-remembered governors (mostly because his daddy had led a charge into the Wilderness against the Yankees without bothering to see if anybody was behind him), but also because Eustache had chiseled his name into a hundred large-sized public buildings, including the state penitentiary. From what I've read about the governor, Dollard State Prison's a fitting memorial.

Like I say, Justin loves me. Once he even came real close to getting himself killed, leaping between me and a bullet. He didn't think, his genes just jumped forward like they thought they were back in the Wilderness. So I keep that in mind, his body stretched over me, soaking my hair with blood, when I think about another time, the day I came to see him in the hospital. It was the look in his eyes when I told him the Hillston city council had just made me chief of police, and consequently his superior. That look was there for just a blink before pleasure took it over. Oh, it wasn't envy or jealousy or distaste. It was a look of pure unvarnished surprise. See, it hadn't—it couldn't occur to Justin that some East Hillston wisecracking white trash, with a mama so ignorant she'd named him Cudberth by mistake, could walk so far off the line as to embody the Law. Lord knows what innocent notions Justin has of Abe Lincoln's political savvy. Now, personally, he was happy for me, and proud of me. He loved it when I taped my poster of Elvis up behind my desk. If I'd called him on that blink of surprise, he wouldn't have had a clue to my meaning. And the God's truth is, Justin Savile's the kindest man I ever met.

My friend Justin's blink is sad proof of the power of the package and the program, the same ones that are walking a black man named George Hall into the gas chamber at Dollard State Prison on Saturday unless the governor changes his mind. So me, I'm for a new program, not to mention a new governor. Like George Hall, I can't rely on kindness.

Chapter 1

I was over in Vietnam trying hard not to get killed when the death penalty went out of fashion back home. That was 1967. At the time some kind folks thought we had us a moral revolution going that couldn't slip back; it was racing along the road to glory, chucking war and racism and sexism out the windows like roadside trash. These sweet Americans could no more imagine a backward slide than Romans could imagine their Forum was going to end up a cow pasture in something called the Dark Ages, much less a big litter box for stray cats tiptoeing through the condoms and cigarette butts.

So when I joined the Hillston police, everybody figured the death penalty was gone for good, like racks and thumbscrews. Turned out it was only gone for nine years, seven months, and fourteen days. Then a death row huckster told the state of Utah he wanted them to shoot him, and Utah had to fight off the volunteers eager to oblige, and the United States was back in the habit of killing people to stop people from killing people.

Nobody'd heard a word from the governor, so my state was still planning to kill George Hall at nine o'clock Saturday night. It used to be, before the moratorium, executions at Dollard State Prison were scheduled early in the morning. Then, after the Supreme Court changed its mind and told the state that capital punishment wasn't cruel and unusual after all, somebody over in the Raleigh legislature decided that on the other hand, it was cruel to make condemned prisoners sit up all night waiting to die at dawn, since studies showed that not too many of them could sleep. So they changed the time of death to midnight. But given the fact that our Haver County D.A., Mitchell Bazemore, held the national record for death penalty convictions (forty-four, so far, and still counting), before long the staff at Dollard starting protesting about the late hours—the doctor on call at the gas chamber had a daytime job in a clinic at Haver Power and

Light—and eventually they scheduled executions for nine P.M., or as close to it as they could manage.

George Hall was the first man I ever arrested in a homicide case. He was young, black, unemployed, and he shot an off-duty cop outside a bar in East Hillston. With the officer's own pistol. George was sitting on the sidewalk beside the gun when I happened to drive by. "I'm not running, just don't shoot!" was the first thing he said to me. His nose was still bleeding from where this particular off-duty cop had stuck his pistol in it. At the time, a fidgety toady named Van Fulcher was chief of police; he showed up fast, and relieved me of the case even faster—not because he was wild about either justice or Bobby Pym, the dead cop, but because whenever a case looked likely to interest anybody with a camera (and a black man shooting a white policeman was about as likely as you could get in the Piedmont Carolinas), Captain Fulcher suddenly felt the urge to take a personal interest: "Go hands on" was how he put it. So Fulcher went "hands on" in the Hall investigation, which was a short one. So was the trial. George had a court-appointed lawyer, who tried to persuade him against pleading not guilty, since he didn't think the jury would go for self-defense. This public defender wasn't a very bright guy, but he was right about that jury. While half-a-dozen witnesses said it certainly looked like self-defense to them, there having been a reasonable appearance of the necessity for deadly force on George's part to prevent his own immediate death or serious injury, not a one of these witnesses was white. The jury didn't even stay away long enough to order dinner. This was 1976, and, at the time, like I said, I thought capital punishment was out of fashion for good, except in places like Iran and South Africa. But after three appeals and seven years on death row, George Hall was about to become Mitchell Bazemore's next victory on his way to the national record. Friday morning, I told George's brother I never thought it could go this way, and George's brother told me to go fuck myself. Friday evening, I went to a dance.

For ninety-six years running, on the Saturday before Christmas, the Hillston Club had held its annual Confederacy Ball. Every year the town's inner circle, which liked to refer to itself as "our number" or just "us," let a committee at the Club tabulate this "number" and send them creamy gilt-bordered invitations. The elected drove through North Hillston, where they all lived on windy roads, over to the Club, and there they two-stepped around a mildewed ballroom for a couple of hours, pretending it was 1861 and still possible they were going to win the War. The men grew mustaches and strapped on swords they claimed were inherited. The women ballooned out of BMWs in hoop skirts, with gardenias pinned to their hair. My information comes from Justin, who loved any excuse to dress up in a costume, and had a handmade gray brassy outfit looped with gold tassels that he frisked about in there every year.

Except this year. This year the entertainment committee had not only dropped the word Confederacy from their invitations, they'd changed the date from Saturday to Friday. A black man was scheduled to be executed at Dollard Prison on Saturday, and there'd been considerable publicity regarding the case, because in the years George had waited on death row, his younger brother, Cooper Hall, had become a pretty well-known political activist with an instinct for what his enemies (and that was most of Hillston) called media manipulation. I'm not saying the Hillside Club acted out of worry over what Coop Hall could do with their planning to dance the Virginia reel while his brother was being gassed to death. The number'd been raised on good manners, and they were feeling genuinely queasy. Peggy Savile, Justin's mother, and my source, made a motion to cancel the ball entirely, but after some "frosty" discussion, the motion was defeated five to four in secret ballots that fooled no one. Still, even Judge Henry Tiggs, Retired, who'd once called an attorney with a sardonic black colleague up to his bench and drawled at him, "Get that nigrah out of my courtroom," even Judge Tiggs probably wasn't comfortable with the thought of stumbling through a waltz under the mistletoe at the exact same moment somebody he'd sentenced to death was paying his debt to society by inhaling for three or four minutes (up to six, if, like Caryl Chessman, he was determined not to breathe too deeply) the vapors from a sack of sodium cyanide eggs dropped into a little sulfuric acid.

So it was decided to move the dance to Friday, and unanimous to substitute black tie and formal gowns for the antebellum costumes, which undeniably had the smack of nostalgia for the Age of Slavery, or at least might give that tacky impression to people not of the number. That last included me, but the doorman didn't notice when I tugged Justin's invitation out of my rented tuxedo, laid it out on his open white glove, and strolled into the foyer, ducking a chandelier that burned real white candles.

Earlier, back at my bureau mirror in River Rise, I'd tried putting different hands in different pockets, looking for the nonchalant effect. Martha Mitchell was disgusted; Martha's this little more-or-less poodle I found dumped out, just a puppy, on Airport Road the day I got home from Vietnam; she had Mrs. Mitchell's nose and bangs, and she appeared to have been treated about the same by her relations. Since I knew the feeling, what with the Nixon gang dicking us both around in the worse way, I gave her a ride to Hillston, and we've been splitting Big Macs for nine years. So Martha, lying on my king-sized waterbed, lets go with this sigh while I'm practicing nonchalance at the bureau. She's a proud lady. Well, hey, here I am, youngest chief of a city its size in the whole South, modernized my department with some drastic innovations like computers, women, and blacks; dropped the crime rate 11.75 percent my first year, not to mention the crime rate inside the force—bribery, bigotry, and occasional mild brutality being the oldest favorites; with a half-column and my picture in *Newsweek* magazine stuck to my refrigerator door by a magnetized tiny pineapple. SCHOLAR COP is the headline on this piece: I'm going for a history Ph.D. at a slow pace.

So Martha squirmed on the waterbed, embarrassed for me, while I tried out one hand versus two in the slippery pockets of those rented trousers. I told her, "Honey, don't give me that

Marxist wheeze. There's things about my life story you don't even know, so get your toenails out of my waterbed before I find you floating around in the closet." Martha's listened to my conversation a lot longer than my ex-wife Cheryl did; she's not much on repartee, but she hangs in there.

I decided on one hand, so that's how I walked into the Hillston Club ballroom, heading for the waltzy music and hum of voices, past a ceiling-high Christmas tree burning some more real white candles, past a blond beautiful drunk girl in a strapless red satin gown lying on a couch against the wall, her arm over her eyes, past Mr. Dyer Fanshaw trying to unhook his wife's stole from the catch on her necklace.

"Well, why, Chief Mangum, surprised to see you here." A. R. Randolph, short, stout, shrewd, and ignorant as a hog, was shoving towards me, one hand in his back vent, tugging his pants loose from the crease of his buttocks. These folks were so used to their Rhett and Scarlett rentals, they were having trouble with their own clothes. "Dammit." He jerked his head at the girl in red satin. "That's my damn granddaughter passed out on the damn couch, and it's not even ten o'clock."

"Looks like she might be a real pretty girl when she's feeling better." We shook hands when he'd finished playing with his underwear. "Surprised to see me? Why's that, Atwater?" I let Randolph's Lions Club set up their October carnival in my municipal building parking lot, so I called him Atwater and joked some circles around him. He got a kick out of it. He was more than twice my age and a thousand times my income, inherited the construction company that had built Haver University and just about everything else in Hillston, including the River Rise complex and the state-funded four-lane bridge over the Shocco River that you could play a full game of softball on without worrying about interference from traffic.

He stepped closer for confidentiality. "Figured they'd need you over at the state prison. What I hear is, the Klan's going there tonight and bust up that vigil. All those 'Save George Hall' nuts. That's what I hear."

"Well, now, rumors. A rumor's kind of like the flu bug. You don't know where it came from and you don't want to spread it around." I gave him my country grin. "Those Klan boys aren't as young as they used to be. They'll all be home watching HBO. It's too cold and messy out there for politics."

"I heard you had a tip they were going to hassle those pro-lifers tonight."

Luckily I was already grinning, so my laugh sounded friendly. "You got to keep up with the lingo, Atwater. Pro-lifers are the ones that are against killing fetuses, and for killing grown-ups. Whereas Coop Hall's group is anti-pro-capital punishment, and most of them anti-pro-lifers too. You with me?"

"Well, they're wasting their time, whatever they call themselves."

"Probably."

"Cuddy, the historical fact is, mankind has a right to protect ourselves against scum. And that's always the type that gets themselves executed."

"Um hum. Historical-wise, three popped right into my head. Socrates, Joan of Arc, and Jesus Christ. Talk about scumbags, whoowee!"

His plump face wrinkled. "Now hold up, Chief, if Christ hadn't been killed, we'd none of us be redeemed today."

"Well, you got me there, Atwater."

Neither one of us was looking at the other one during this chitchat. He was watching his friend Dyer Fanshaw still trying to detach his wife from her stole while she ignored him and hugged everyone who walked close enough. I was looking over Randolph's head into the ballroom to try to spot either the man I'd told myself I was coming to see, or the lady I'd told myself I didn't care if I saw or not. The man was Julian Lewis, once attorney general, now lieutenant governor, hoping to move up another step. The lady was Mrs. Andrew Brookside, wife of the man Lewis was running against. Except when I knew her best she wasn't married; she was sixteen and her name was Lee Haver.

One wall of this ballroom was glass doors; each one had its

own wreath. In front of them, tables floating with white linen stretched along, crowded with crystal punch bowls, beds of oysters in their shells, and platters of tiny ham biscuits. Every four feet, a waiter stood waiting to tilt a glass ladle of champagne punch into any receptacle held up in his vicinity. (Some members had obviously lost patience with their little crystal cups, and had moved on to water glasses.) The waiters were the only black people I saw in the room, except for the mayor, the mayor's wife, the president of Southeast Life Insurance Company, and half the band, which sat on a little dais, behind shiny red shields draped with holly garlands and labeled The Jimmy Douglas Orchestra. The band was pumping through "The Anniversary Waltz" (maybe celebrating a near-century of these affairs), but only about fifty couples were dancing (or forty-nine; I don't know what old Judge Tiggs and his wife were doing, maybe the tango, or maybe one of them was trying to leave the floor and the other one didn't want to). The rest of the guests looked like they were scared to lose their places in the punch line.

"You know Dyer Fanshaw?" Randolph tugged me towards the couple.

"Let me take a wild guess. Does he own Fanshaw Paper Company?"

"Chief, you kill me. Dyer, will you leave that woman alone and say hello to our chief of police? You see him in *Newsweek* last month?"

"Cuddy Mangum," I said, just as Mrs. Fanshaw broke loose, tossed me a fast hello, and rushed into the party.

"Everything under control?" Fanshaw asked while we shook hands.

"Personally or criminally?"

"Mangum kills me," Randolph explained. "He means the George Hall business, Chief. Don't you, Dyer?"

Dyer did, so we talked awhile about whether the governor would stay Hall's death sentence (they didn't think he would), and whether there'd be a riot at Dollard Prison between the vigilants protesting execution and the enthusiasts demanding it.

I explained why I had my doubts. "First of all, it's freezing rain out there, which discourages philosophical debate, and second"—I shared a little of the inside track—"I talked to Warden Carpenter an hour ago, and the place is quiet as an opium den. I talked to the FBI, which pays about two-thirds of the dues at our local Knights of the KKK, and they don't have a plan rattling around in their heads. And I talked to somebody working with the George Hall vigil, and she says they can't get *Action News* to come, which they surely could if there was a hundred-to-one shot of even a poke in the eye, much less blood in the dirt."

My business leaders were relieved and disappointed, and tickled to be in the know. Then they talked for a while about how Governor Wollston could follow his heart since he wasn't up for reelection, and about whether Andy Brookside had made a mistake resigning the presidency of Haver University to run on the Democratic ticket, since—even if he was a war hero married to a millionairess—having an assistant campaign manager like that Jack Molina mouthing off against capital punishment was going to kill him in the polls; not that they cared—they were Republicans and loved to see Democrats beat in their own heads with their own baseball bats. I asked if Brookside was here tonight, and they said, sure, he went every place there were more than a dozen voters penned up in a room with only one exit.

Then some more stocky financial spokes of the inner circle herded around us. A lot of this group I knew by name, but we weren't exactly what you'd want to call golf partners. I recognized a bank, a towel company, a "Hot Hat" barbecue franchise (all the roofs had red neon pigs tipping top hats), and a lot of real estate. Most of these men looked like their bow ties were choking them. The bank (still growing the mustache he'd started for the reclassified Confederacy Ball) jumped right into the George Hall business with the interesting theory that the problem with capital punishment these days was that it wasn't cruel enough. "Listen here, it's painless! They put you the hell to sleep, come on! In the old days, they'd flay you alive, burn you—you'd think twice."

"Dead is dead," said the towel company, shifting his cummerbund to the right.

"You wouldn't say that, Terry, if it were your feet in the fire."

I had to agree with the bank; between gas and disembowelment, or getting stuffed with gunpowder and blown all over China, or having my head crushed by an Indian elephant, I'll take American technology any day. I told them, "Folks don't have any imagination anymore. You know what happened if you killed your daddy in ancient Rome? They sewed you in a cloth with a monkey, a poisonous snake, a fighting rooster, and a wild dog, and they tossed you in the Tiber."

The notion stopped them cold for a minute, then the bank nodded. "That's what I'm talking about. Punishment. And I'll tell you something else, it ought to be in public, like they used to. Put them on TV. It's supposed to be deterrence, right? Make people watch."

I said, "Speaking as a keeper of the peace, gentlemen, crowds make me nervous. Last time we hanged somebody in public was in the 'thirties, over in Owensboro, Kentucky. What I read is, twenty thousand folks piled in for the show, and a third of them set up refreshment stands. 'Make them watch' isn't exactly the problem. It's the fights over good seats."

My figures led the real estate man to mention how he'd managed to buy six seats for the Super Bowl, which led to complaints about Cadmean Stadium at the university, which led to speculation about the illness of "poor old Briggs," meaning old Briggs Cadmean (of Cadmean & Whetstone Textiles Industries), a big bald sly S.O.B. of about eighty-five, and, to hear him tell it, the private owner of Hillston. I had to walk by Cadmean's picture on the way to my office every day; he'd paid for the municipal building and wanted everybody to know it. In this eight-foot oil painting in the lobby, he's got the rolled-up blueprints in one hand; the other hand's pointing down the hall towards the men's room. Once the old bastard had claimed to my face that he was personally responsible for my promotion to chief. I was dating his youngest daughter at the time. The rest of his offspring were male, long dead, or looked it, and this girl (he'd named her Briggs after himself and called her "Baby") was his favorite. She hated the sight of him, and turns out he thought I'd bring them together as a thank-you note for my new job. I had to disappoint him. Deep down, Briggs Junior wasn't any fonder of me than she was of her dad, though she just about convinced me otherwise. She was an astronomy professor, and I think what she really loved the most was stars. Justin always said she was about that cold, too. Last I heard, she'd taken a position out West, where there wouldn't be so much population between her and the sky. She sent me back my ring before I finished the Visa payments, and about a month after she left, Cadmean flagged me over to his limousine on Main Street, and accused me of reneging on a deal he'd never bothered to call to my attention. He had the morals of a grizzly bear. Justin liked him.

"Poor old Briggs," Fanshaw was saying as he looked over at the passed-out girl on the couch who was about to deep-breathe herself out of the top of that red satin strapless. "Well, God knows, Cadmean had a good long life, and he's dying the way he wants to."

"How's that?" I said. "Just temporarily?"

"See what I mean?" Pointing at me, Randolph nudged Fanshaw. Then the quartet of business leaders said they were headed to the bathroom before their wives cornered them, and did we want anything. I was the only one who appeared to find this question peculiar.

Randolph told them he'd be down later, and turned back to me. "Nahw, Dyer means Briggs won't go to the hospital. What I heard was, he said, 'I paid for the damn hospital, but that doesn't oblige me to let those suckbutts get their hands on me, so I go meet my Maker with my fanny in a pan and a tube up my dick.'"

Fanshaw tightened his nostrils. I gave him a wink. "A sweet-talking man. He's got a lot more to explain to his Maker than a bare backside."

They both chuckled their agreement. And that's when I saw Lee Haver Brookside. Actually it was Justin I saw first, as they

swung past the crowd onto the dance floor. Justin stood out, due
to being the only man at the party in white tie and tails. He was
the kind who'd wear an English hunting outfit to a barbecue picnic. Now he and Mrs. Brookside were waltzing in big slow loops,
so I saw her back where his hand rested just above the black
folded silk, then the white of her neck and shoulders as her head
turned. A diamond flared like a match in the braided coil of dark
gold hair.

I said I thought I'd go get some punch. "Nice to meet you,
Mr. Fanshaw."

"Same here." He nodded at Randolph, like I'd passed a test,
and told me, "Call me Dyer. The real bar's downstairs in the
men's lounge. That punch won't do a thing for you."

"Mr. Fanshaw, what I paid for this outfit, I don't want to
waste it on a john. I see enough line-ups of men during the day."

Fanshaw chuckled, and Randolph said, "Huh?," and I gave
one shoe a quick rub on the back of my trousers, put my left hand
in my left pocket, and walked into the party.

For the most part, the club style seemed to be to mix the
sexes for dancing, and split them up for conversation. Seated at
little tables, women, their long dresses glittering, smoked themselves almost invisible while telling each other what must have
been mighty funny stories. Men stood in black glossy huddles,
nodding at everything everybody else said. The Reverend
Thomas Campbell (an old tall Presbyterian, in a tuxedo) and
Father Paul Madison (a young short Episcopalian, in a collar)
had crossed the line and were chatting with our new black
mayor's wife, whose fixed smile must have been hurting her jaws.

"Chief Mangum," called the rector, grinning dimples in his
cheeks. He didn't look any older than he had in college, and in
college he'd looked about seven. "Come buy a ticket to Trinity's
Christmas lottery. And talk Mrs. Yarborough here into it too."

"Well, Paul," I said, squeezing in, "maybe I should remind
you, soliciting in public's against the law. Plus, our first lady's a
Baptist, right, Dina? How you doing?"

In her fifties, pleasant-looking but not pretty, Dina Yarborough was a thin light-skinned black woman with stiffly waved hair and a careful voice. "Fine, thank you. Nice to see you, Cuddy. Isn't this a lovely party?" I'm sure she'd almost rather have gone to the dentist for a root canal, but you couldn't tell it from her eyes.

"It's my first time," I said.

"Mine too," she nodded. "It's an annual affair?" I didn't hear any sarcasm, so maybe she didn't even know about those ninety-six years of hoop skirts and yellow sashes under the Stars 'n' Bars.

Both ministers leapt in fast, Campbell by nodding in a coughing fit, and Madison by waving a thick card in my face. "Worthy cause," he wheedled. "Add sleeping quarters to our soup kitchen."

I said, okay, I'd take five. He said I could send a check; I said I had money in my wallet, and he said, "Five hundred dollars?"

Old Campbell (his was the richest church in town) laughed while I was gasping, "A hundred dollars each?! What are y'all raffling?!"

"A Porsche. Only two thousand tickets to be sold." Paul Madison put his hand over his heart. "You've got a great chance, Cuddy."

"You're raffling a Porsche for a soup kitchen?"

Madison grinned like a pink conscienceless baby. "Jim Scott donated it. Here's the thing, you raffle small-change stuff like, oh, a cord of wood, nobody wants it. A Porsche, that's a big temptation."

I winked at Dina Yarborough. "Paul, I thought you guys were in the business of fighting temptation."

"Frankly," coughed Campbell, a sad craggy man, "we at First Presbyterian have stayed away from this sort of thing."

Madison already had his pen out and was writing my name on the damn ticket. "If Trinity had y'all's endowment, we'd stay away from it too. How many did you say you wanted, Cuddy?" My glare hit his dimples and bounced off.

"One," I whispered.

"One?"

I snatched the ticket away from him. "Thank you, Father

Madison. Mrs. Mayor, would you care to dance?"

"Hey, There" thumped to a close about thirty seconds after we got going, so we stood waiting while I asked her, "Where's Carl? Off hiding one of those vile cigars of his from the public? I keep telling your husband, tobacco made Hillston. A smoking mayor'd be patriotic here."

"Not if they're Cuban cigars." Her face loosened into what so suspiciously looked like wryness that I decided her question about this ball's being an annual affair was about as innocent as the Trojan horse.

I laughed. "Lord, Dina, tell the mayor to give me a raise or I'm going to leak it to the Star how he's trading with Fidel. Come on, let's go get a drink." But before we could squeeze out of the crunch of dancers, Dina's brother, the president of Southeast Life Insurance, tapped her for the next number. Tapped me, that is; his fingers boring into my shoulder like he was looking for a major nerve to paralyze. He said, "My sister promised me this next dance," in a tone that suggested I'd dragged her onto the floor at gunpoint. And I dropped her hand as if I'd gotten caught doing it. Lord, the South. None of us can shake off all the old sad foolishness.

On my way to the food alone, I smiled at anyone who smiled at me. Then out of nowhere, a wide elderly lady in a lacy bed jacket stopped me with two steel forefingers on my lapels, and dared me to contradict her. "You were in that magazine. *People*."

"Excuse me?"

"I saw you. I forget what it said."

I told her, "Ma'am, I missed that one. *Newsweek* said I was tall, gangly, innovative, and indefatigable."

"That's the one I saw." She eyed me suspiciously. "What did it say your name was?"

"*Newsweek*? Seems like it said my name was Chief Mangum."

"That's right." Reassured, she patted my elbow. Thousands of dollars of diamonds were slipping dangerously around on her fingers. "I'm Mrs. Marion Sunderland."

"Not the Mrs. Marion Sunderland that owns the Hillston

Star and Channel Seven? Listen, what happened to those reruns of *Ironsides*? You know where Raymond Burr's in a wheelchair and has to catch the crooks secondhand? I wish you'd put those back on the air."

Mrs. Sunderland took a beat before she surprised me. "I believe that article also described you as whimsical. They misused the word. You're a little odd, but you don't strike me as capricious."

"Well, I think debonair's really the word they were after." I leaned over and patted her arm in return. "Mrs. Sunderland, I want you to take some professional advice. Next time you go honky-tonking, you ought to leave those rings home in a vault."

"Mr....Mangum, I only go out in public among friends."

"I bet that's what Julius Caesar said." She surprised me again with a laugh that would have been loud on a woman twice her size. Then she invited me to "call on" her, then she introduced me to two friends hovering nearby, a fresh-scrubbed octogenarian widow of a department store, who said she couldn't hear and just ignore her, and a Sunderland grandnephew who appeared to ski for a living. I spotted Paul Madison hunting through the dancers like Cupid through a cloud bank, so I slipped away without out a word of warning to his next victims. No one else stopped me before I reached the buffet, where Judge Tiggs was trying to load his plate with deviled eggs, and his wife was trying to block his hand.

"Hey." Somebody pulled me down by the elbow and kissed my cheek. "I'm surprised you came." It was Alice, Justin's wife. She's a small beautiful copper-haired lady from the North Carolina mountains. Justin met her three years ago while we were investigating some folks that worked on her floor at Cadmean Mills, and the best move he ever made was to marry her as soon as he could talk her into it. Bluest eyes you ever saw, clean as the sky, and clear as we all used to figure truth was. Alice believes in truth, and loves politics, and claims she can keep the two in shouting distance. We argue a lot. Justin says that's why he invites me to dinner twice a week, so he won't have to "box around about ideas" with her himself. "Can you believe this man?" Alice would say. "Smart, educated, and he sits here and says he's not interested in ideas, whatever that means."

Justin would check his wine sauce. "It means, for Christ's sake, I don't care why Prohibition got voted in when it did. I thought we were trying to figure out if Billy Gilchrist's too bad a drunk to be a reliable stool pigeon." Justin would talk your head off about the people in the case at hand, but analyzing history bored him.

I put down my buffet plate and kissed Alice back. "Well, look at you." I turned her around. "An old commie union organizer like you, used to go out to dinner in a sweatshirt with Emma Goldman on it, used to love a good brainy fight and a Hostess cupcake and don't try to deny it 'cause I've seen the wrappers." The waiter offered me a cup of punch, which was hard to drink because of the baby strawberries floating in it. "Now, Lord, Lord, Alice. Justin the Five's got you all pregnant and dolled up in this swanky thing, looks like you borrowed it from Jackie Onassis last time y'all got together."

"How do I look?"

"Like Christmas." Her gown was a dark green velvet and her red curls were like ribbons. "You look like the prettiest Christmas present anybody ever got, by which I'm sorry to say I don't mean me." I kissed her. "Congratulations, Red. But please don't name that child Cudberth, 'specially if it's a girl. Is that Scotch? Where'd you get it, the men's room?"

"Ladies' lounge. You know, I don't like the way liquor tastes anymore. I guess that's lucky." She gave me the drink. "I'm going to kill Justin."

"You're talking to the police chief. But I didn't catch what you said."

"I told him I wanted to tell you I was pregnant."

"You know he can't keep a secret. Good detective though, I'll give you that. He tells folks his secrets, then folks tell him theirs, then we put the cuffs on them and haul them off." I reached for a ham biscuit, but the waiter waved me away and tweezered one onto a plate stamped "Hillston Club." I held up four fingers; he held up one eyebrow, then humored me and piled them on. "Alice, tell me about Mrs. Sunderland. How much say does she have at the paper?"

"Does have? Probably none. Could have? Probably lots."

"You know her? Didn't the *Hillston Star* endorse you?"

"She's one of Justin's godmothers."

"Can't hurt."

She laughed with her chin raised. "Cuddy, I never denied it." Alice is in the state legislature now, which she wouldn't be if it hadn't been for Justin's name, and for old Briggs Cadmean's tossing a big chunk of money into her little campaign—out of some peculiar impulse that had nothing to do with late-blooming feminism. Now I'd heard she was also working to get Andy Brookside into the governor's mansion, but I'd avoided discussing it with her.

We watched Justin waltz Mrs. Brookside in and out of duller dancers. The Jimmy Douglas string section was giving "Lara's Theme" all they had, fighting back against the buzz of talk. "Isn't my husband beautiful?" Alice smiled, happy as a cat.

"Motherhood hormones are eating up your brain, Red."

"Well, he is. He looks like Paul Newman used to."

"When was that?" We watched some more—his black coat-tails, Lee's black gown lifting as they turned; her shoulders, his shirt front a bright white blur. "Married him for his looks, huh? I always thought it was his cooking."

"Go break in on them, so I can dance with him. You know Andy's wife?"

"I did a long time ago." Alice gave me too straight a look, so I turned towards the buffet to scoop up some cashews, and I had a handful near my mouth when Lee saw me staring at her, and smiled. It was just a polite smile, then it went away as she recognized me; her body tightened, pulling Justin out of step for an instant.

Alice was talking. "Well, I feel like I ought to be at the vigil anyhow, but Jack Molina agreed if I could put some pressure on Andy's position, or get to Lewis tonight, that might do more than holding up another placard at the prison. And now he's not even here."

"Who's not here? Brookside?"

Alice was either looking at me funny or I was getting too sensitive. She said, "No, Julian Lewis, Julian D-for-Dollard Lewis, Justin's whatever he is, cousin, the lieutenant governor."

"He's not here? Damn it." I had promised George Hall's new lawyer, an old friend, that I'd come to this dance, corner Julian Lewis, and give him some reasons why he should persuade the governor to stay tomorrow's execution. Not that a lot of people hadn't been giving the governor a lot of reasons for a lot of years, but last-minute reprieves appeal to some politicians. They're catchy; the press likes them too. But as for Lewis caring what Alice thought, I didn't see why she thought the lieutenant governor would listen to anybody who was trying to stop him from taking over his boss's office, even if Alice's mother-in-law was Lewis's aunt. Plus, Lewis wasn't going to think a damn thing the governor didn't tell him to think. As for her influencing Brookside—in public, he too had stayed away from the Hall case, soothing his liberal constituency by keeping Professor Jack Molina (one of the Hall Committee coordinators) on his campaign staff. I looked around the ballroom. "Where is Brookside?"

"Go ask his wife." Alice took my plate away from me.

"I don't dance."

"Oh bullshit, you're a great dancer."

"Honey, now that you're a mama, you got to watch your language."

She mouthed something that was pretty easy to lip-read, as I let her nudge me onto the floor. I eased my way through a cluster of younger dancers calling coded jokes from couple to couple while they circled. One pair just stood with their eyes closed, rocking softly back and forth.

Justin stopped the instant I touched his shoulder, and smiled like I'd brought him a million dollars, his long-lost dog, and news that the lab was wrong about his having cancer. I tell him, with that smile I don't know why he isn't in politics, except a year in the loony bin makes nervous voters nervous. I said, "Excuse me, may I?" And he said, "Hey, Cuddy, wonderful, you came!"

"Why is everybody so surprised?"

"Have you two met? Lee Brookside. Cuddy Mangum, my commanding officer." Justin did a little bow—I suppose straight from childhood dance class—and said, "Thank you," to her, "Pardon me," to us, and walked backwards smooth as a skater through the crowd. When I turned around to Lee, she had her hand up ready to rest on my shoulder. "Hi," I said. Her hair was pulled back in its loose knot, away from her face, a smoky ash-blond, and her eyes, which I'd remembered as blue, were actually gray like an owl's feather, flecked and warm. I hadn't looked this close in her eyes in a long, long time; the last time I'd looked, on a Saturday morning in June, we'd both been crying. It's easier to cry at seventeen. We were standing on a little wooden Japanese bridge in her backyard—except with that much land and trees and gardens, you don't call it a yard—and she was telling me her mother wouldn't let her see me again, not through the summer, not after she returned to private school in the fall, not, in fact, ever. I kept saying, "Why?" but we both knew why, and I don't blame her now for not letting me force her to say it. After that, I'd next seen her a year or so later when she came to my house in East Hillston, called me a coward, and slapped me across the face. After that, only in passing.

I took my hand from my pocket now. "You still mad?"

She said, "My God, how long has it been?"

"Don't start counting. How'd you like that French college?"

And she laughed years away for a minute. "Oh my, was I ever young enough to go to college?"

"Hey! I'm still going."

"You are? You're the police chief."

"That's true, too."

She still had her hand held near my shoulder, but lifted it back so I moved forward and circled her waist, and we started dancing. I couldn't really remember what it had felt like all that while ago, pressed together in the gym under the sagging streamers and balloons, or in some school friend's hot dim living room, not moving when the records changed. Now she felt cool and sure, accustomed to dance with strangers. There was something sad about her eyes, but it was hard to imagine her crying easily anymore. We danced at first without speaking, at one point passing close to Justin and Alice; Justin was humming, Alice smiled at me, and wiggled the fingers woven with his.

Finally Lee moved her head and asked me, "So you stayed in Hillston. You always wanted to travel."

"I've traveled some." I summed up two years in Southeast Asia, then six months in Europe (on the G.I. savings I'd planned to use to buy Cheryl and me a house), seventeen months teaching school in Costa Rica, a summer in New York City, when I decided I wanted to be a police detective. I said I still like traveling; I take a special package charter some place new every vacation I get. Last year it was Nova Scotia; the year before, Haiti. I said, "But mostly Hillston, since I've been with the police department here."

"Why the police? I mean I guess I always expected to read how you'd...I don't know, written the history of the United States." She was squeezed against me by a wild-spinning couple.

I backstepped us away. "Well, probably the more history I read, the more I figured, crooked as the law is, it's straighter than lynch mobs and posses on the loose, right? I'm a great believer in capital-L Law. And Hillston's home. So here I am, enforcing the law in Hillston."

"Hillston's gotten so big." Her hand lifted out of mine to gesture at the room. "I used to think I'd find myself seated beside you at a dinner, but I never did."

"I used to think that too." I didn't tell her that when I'd first gone to Paris, I'd get the dumb notion to rush off to a certain park or museum because I was sure that's where I was going to see her stroll by.

She'd stayed abroad after college. Her first husband was a French mountain climber; I'd read in a paper that he'd died in a hotel fire, only twenty-seven years old. I remember thinking: the

French mess up in Vietnam, the U.S. sends me over there, I'm lucky and escape, Lee's husband makes it up Mount Everest but can't get out of a suite on the Riviera. Six years after his death, she'd married Brookside. She had no children.

"Andy was there the same time you were," she said, her neck arching back to look up at me. "In Vietnam. Have you two met?"

"Over there? Nope, we never did run into each other." It was interesting—"Andy"—the matter-of-fact assumption that everyone knew who her second husband was, which of course everyone did. The "Have you met?" probably meant local politics, since I doubt she figured young Major Brookside had ever swooped down in his jet to shoot the breeze with the boys in the mangrove swamp. Well, maybe she'd lived so long in a world where everybody knew each other, that's all the world she thought there was. I mean world, too. Randolphs and Fanshaws, now, they counted in Hillston, and Cadmeans and Dollards might own the Piedmont and have a long lease on the state, but Havers had been so rich for so long, they were on the big map. When Chinese and Kenyans and Danes smoke your cigarettes, you can build universities with your loose change, and you can expect even your collateral daughters to marry heroes; you don't need them to marry money. That message her family had sent to the little Japanese bridge—well, you could see their point. I've got my All-State Guard plaque and my dinky combat medals in my bureau, I've got my three-inch *Newsweek* clipping on the refrigerator door. Andy Brookside's got a cabinet full of football trophies, a Congressional Medal of Honor and a presidential committee appointment to study that sad war, a Pulitzer Prize for the book he wrote after he studied it, a *Time* magazine cover, and Lee Haver. There's no catching heroes. They've got the gods running interference for them, you know what I mean? The gods keep them wrapped in a glow, you can see the shimmer when they come in a room.

I said, "Well now, this is a pretty place. Never been in here before, myself. You come to these Christmas parties with your family back then?"

She didn't answer. A tiny blue vein in her neck tensed against the diamond necklace around it. Then, after a silence, she said, not smiling, "You know, I hated you for a long time."

The rush of old intimacy shocked me. I tilted my head to look at her; it felt like that sudden fall that jerks you awake when you nod off in a chair.

Her eyes searched in mine until finally she said, "You remember that day I came to your house with the box of letters? Right before I left for France? You wouldn't even talk to me. You wouldn't look at me. Your mother left us standing there in your living room, and shut the door to the kitchen. I think she was crying too. She asked me if I wanted a glass of tea, and you snapped at her, 'No, she doesn't.'"

I said, "I remember it very well. You threw the letters at me and slapped me in the face."

Her palm moved inside mine as she pulled her hand away. We stopped there in the middle of the dance floor.

"You're the only man I ever hit," she said.

She put her hand back in mine. Other couples seemed to be moving around us, but far away, small and shadowy, as if the room had suddenly doubled in size. We moved together. Then I heard, coming from a distance, the rustle of applause, and I realized the music had already stopped.

I was going to ask her if she'd like that glass of tea now, when through the knots of applauding couples I saw Andy Brookside walking towards us, tall, bright-haired, full of energy, his handsome head nodding right and left; maybe he thought folks were clapping for him instead of the band. He touched Lee's arm, and claimed her. "I'm sorry, darling, I got caught up in a conversation." (It was the first I'd seen him all night, and I wondered if he'd been down in the men's lounge where the "real drinks" were.)

She said quietly, "There you are."

He put his arm through hers, saying, "Shall we?" before turning to me with a friendly, expectant face; I didn't see a twitch of phoniness in it, and I was looking hard.

Lee stepped away from him to introduce us. "Have you met my husband, Andy? Cuddy—" And then the beeper in my breast pocket went off, which meant that Sergeant Davies at headquarters had decided I needed to make a decision, which to him could mean anything from Mrs. Thompson had called again because Clark Gable was back in her attic crawlspace, to Officer Purley Newsome had put another dead cat in Officer Nancy White's locker, to a gang of terrorists with Uzi machine guns were holding the entire downtown population of Hillston hostage.

I turned the beeper off. "Excuse me, I better go phone in."

"You're a doctor?" Brookside smiled, then showed me how he'd won the nomination. "No, wait...Cuddy, Cuddy.... Of course, Mangum! Our police chief. Last spring at the Jaycee's breakfast panel, 'Improving Town and Gown Relations.' Right?" His handshake was professional but not stingy. "Good to see you. Tell me, what's your sense of the George Hall situation?"

"Lousy for George Hall," I said.

"Naturally, yes. Of course, I meant the governor. Clemency."

I said, "I don't think so. But then I'm not in tight with the powers that be."

Lee had been standing there, her fingers touching a jewel on the necklace. Into our silence, she suddenly said, "Andy phoned the governor yesterday, asking him to extend mercy," then she looked up at Brookside as if to make sure it was all right to have told me. There was something uncomfortable between them, which was odd in such a poised couple. I mean, I knew why I felt uneasy—I was half back to eighteen years old—but I certainly didn't suppose I was what was troubling the Brooksides.

"Um hum...." I looked from her to him. "Well, there's mercy, and then there's justice."

"True." There was nothing in his eyes but earnestness.

"Hall's supporters wanted not just clemency, but a pardon. At this point, they're just trying to get the stay of execution. And if you're planning on making any statement about 'mercy' of a little more of a public nature, seems like waiting much longer might make it pretty moot."

He gave me a stare. "I know."

Mr. and Mrs. Dyer Fanshaw shuffled in a bored fox-trot near us. Mrs. Fanshaw smiled brilliantly at Lee, then patted the clumps of diamonds strung on her own neck. Every city employee in Hillston (including teachers, including tax clerks and garbage collectors, including me) who filled out a form or washed his hands or signed a check, did it on Fanshaw Paper. It adds up to diamonds fast. She cooed as they swerved close, "That is just a beautiful, beautiful dress, Lee."

Lee smiled brilliantly back. "Oh thank you, Betty. Yours too. Merry Christmas."

I excused myself again to go telephone, but Lee touched my arm. "Cuddy, before you go? Is it true there've been threats against the group George Hall's brother organized? Jack Molina, on Andy's staff, says so. He's been working with—is it 'Cooper' Hall?"

I nodded. "There're threats against just about anybody who steps in front of the public and moves enough to catch their eye."

She stared at her husband. "But you're protecting them?"

"Coop Hall? I can't. Not unless I locked him up, and maybe not then. Oh, I could catch whoever did it, but if they don't mind going to the trouble, and they don't care about getting caught, anybody in this country can kill anybody they want to."

"Lee?" Brookside reached for her arm again.

I backed away. "Thanks for the dance, Mrs. Brookside." She offered her hand again, so I took it. Her fingers were cold, colder than they'd been when I'd held them before.

Out in the lobby, I saw Father Paul Madison, small and eager, selling Mrs. Sunderland's grandnephew a chance to own a Porsche. I waved good-bye, but he held up a palm to stop me, so I waited.

"Cuddy," he said, brushing blond hair out of his eyes, "don't take this wrong, please, but would you know anybody I could lean on to make a contribution to the George Hall Fund? We're seven thousand in the hole."

"You mean, like me? And why should I take it wrong?"

He blushed. "Well, you're the one who arrested George in the first place, but then I know you're a friend of Isaac Rosethorn's."

"Isaac's charging you guys seven thousand to represent Hall?"

"Oh, no, nothing like that much. It's the paperwork, and phone calls, and now we need to hire an investigator to go back over—"

My back was still tightened with memories of Lee. Paul stopped in midsentence, peered at my face, then he lowered his head. "You don't think we'll get the stay?"

I said, "No. Do you?"

"I'm praying we will."

"You are? Looks to me like you're selling Porsches."

His blush spread over his ears and neck. "Cuddy, I'm sorry I upset you," he said. When I didn't answer, he gave my arm a rub. "You still mad about what happened at Trinity?"

I said, "Only when I think about it." He was referring to a protest rally that the Save George Hall Committee had staged in October on the steps of his church, Trinity Episcopal, to which they'd invited a very left-wing movie star who happened to be on location in North Carolina; they'd sent a lot of news people advance word, but neglected to do the same for the police— meaning me. I also suspected they'd taunted the Klan into coming; at any rate, ten showed up in robes, with a few Aryans in combat fatigues, plus a hundred hoods with nothing else to do. I didn't have enough men there to handle it. Mud clots got thrown; we made four arrests, and the evening news shot a lot of footage. I was so angry at Paul and Cooper Hall, I came close to arresting them too. It was right after that that Isaac Rosethorn offered to take on the Hall case. It was also right after that that *Newsweek* called me up.

Paul was saying, "And look, drop by the soup kitchen someday. We've got a new stove. Eight burners and a built-in grill. Mr. Carippini bought a range for his restaurant, so he gave us his old one."

"Isn't he Catholic?"

"Sure. Listen, this stove's been blessed by a bishop."

"Father Madison," I grinned back at him, "please don't turn to crime; you'd run me ragged. About your Hall Fund, why don't you ask Mrs. Andrew Brookside?"

"You think?"

"I think she's sympathetic. But you may have to say you won't use her name."

Madison looked puzzled, then nodded. "Oh, right, Andy Brookside. Politics." He acknowledged that little world with upraised palms, then with a soft whistle blew it away.

As I waited for the cloakroom attendant—an old black man with a completely specious grin, and "Hillston Club" embroidered on his jacket—I glanced at the couch by the tree, but the girl in red satin was gone. Inside the ballroom, Justin and Alice were talking to Mayor and Mrs. Yarborough. They all turned when the Jimmy Douglas Orchestra struck up "God Rest Ye Merry Gentlemen," while behind them brass-buttoned waiters trooped out of an open door carrying gleaming platters of shiny roasted turkeys with red ribbons on their legs and circled by white candles burning in bright little apples. Everybody clapped.

ABOUT THE AUTHOR

Michael Malone is the author of nine novels and two works of non-fiction. Educated at Carolina and at Harvard, he has taught at Yale, at the University of Pennsylvania, and at Swarthmore. Among his prizes are the Edgar, the O.Henry, the Writers Guild Award, and the Emmy. He lives in Hillsborough, North Carolina, with his wife, Maureen Quilligan, chair of the English department at Duke University.

For Jack, Patrick, and Daniel,
who gave me a name worth keeping.

For Ceili, who loved well.

And for all those who find ways to go on:
Better days are coming for our little hearts.

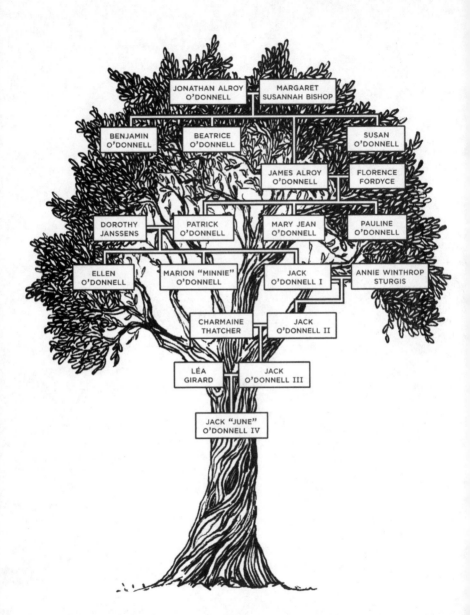

The O'DONNELL FAMILY

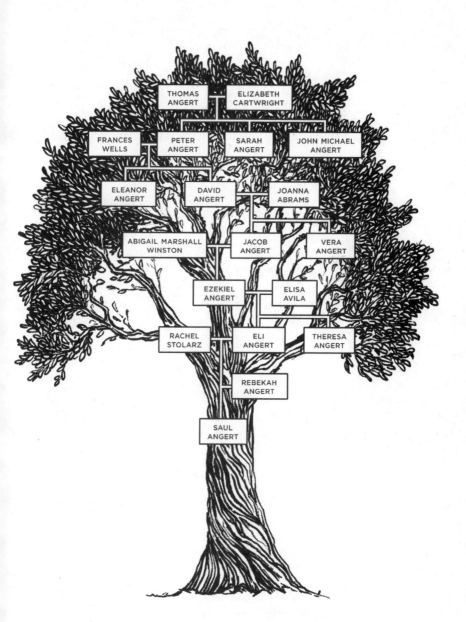

The ANGERT FAMILY

One

FROM my bedroom window, I watch the ghost flutter. She shifts and warbles in the dark yard, her pink sheen caught in moonlight. I wonder if she's looking up at the spread of stars or if she's facing the farmhouse, watching us. Maybe things like her don't have eyes. Maybe they wander, unseeing, through the world.

At the edge of the clearing, the sudden shuffle and bob of branches draw my eyes from the ghost. A couple of giggly sophomores I recognize break through the brush and hesitate, half-shadowed, as they scour the hilltop our house sits on.

They look right past the shimmering pink spirit and focus instead on the cherry tree that sprawls out in front of our porch. The tree's as old as the town itself, planted by my great-great-great-great-grandfather, Jonathan "Jack" Alroy O'Donnell, when he first settled here. He, like Dad, could talk roots into spreading anywhere, but part of the reason Jonathan stayed in Five Fingers was

1

the taste of the cherries that grew on this hill. *Like heaven on earth,* Dad used to say, *like the silent world before anything had gone wrong.*

Within months of his arrival, Jonathan had started a farm a couple of miles from here, closer to the water, where the earth mixed with sand. For two generations, the O'Donnells built a legacy of roots and branches. It's been four more since the Angerts, my family's mortal enemies, foreclosed on the farm. But the cherries from that land are still sold in grocery stores and farmers' markets, at festivals and fairs, beneath hand-painted signs and vinyl banners reading JACK'S TART.

The sophomores, Molly Malone and Quincy Northbrook, run toward the tree now, folded in half like they're trying not to block a movie-theater screen. Neither of them sees the ghost, but they both shiver as they pass through her, and Molly stops and glances back. Quincy's halfway up the tree, trying to shake down the empty branches. He hisses at Molly, and she runs to stand below him, folding her shirt up like a grocery bag as a few shriveled cherries drop.

Gravel crunches then, and headlights swing up the curve of our long driveway. In the tree, Quincy freezes like a raccoon caught robbing a trash can, but Molly's already running, halfway back to the woods with her spoils. At the breathy honk of the car horn, Quincy drops from the branches and takes off full tilt after her.

Hannah rolls the Subaru's window down and shouts, "Yeah, that's right! You'd better run, punks!" She shakes her head in mock disapproval then looks up at me, affecting surprise. "But soft!" she calls. "What light through yonder window breaks?"

"It's me," I yell back.

"Wait. June? You're positively glowing. I thought that was the east and you were the sun."

"Yeah, I'm ovulating. Common mistake."

"Well, get those incandescent ovaries down here. We've got death traps and deep-fried John Doe waiting for us."

I pull on my canvas tennis shoes, swing my leather backpack over my shoulder, and flick the lights off. But something makes me take one last look at my room from the hallway, at the wild constellations of green star stickers Dad and I tacked on my ceiling when I was six years old. I'd been sure back then they'd glow forever—that nothing Dad touched could dim.

Mom even used to say, "June, your daddy's the sun."

And he was. He could make anything grow. He warmed every room he stepped into. When he touched an animal, it would lie down and nap. He even went away in the winter, like the sun so often did, and without him the house became cold, lethargic.

It's been almost ten years since he died, and not a single star sticker still glows. But some people are too alive to fully die, their stories too big to disappear, and he was one of them. I see traces of him all over our magic house. I hear him in the creak and groan of the floorboards as the summer nights stretch them, can visualize him sitting at the foot of my bed, saying, *Other houses have support beams and foundations. Ours has bones and a heartbeat.*

I close my eyes and listen to the house hum and yawn, stretch and curl. Outside, Hannah honks, and I close the door and jog downstairs.

In the soft light of the kitchen, Mom and Toddy, my stepdad, are laughing and tickling each other like freshmen on a first date while they choose a bottle of white wine from the fridge. Shadow and Grayson are in the living room, standing on the couch, playing a gladiator video game with motion sensors.

"Han's here," I announce, and Grayson screams something like *katchaaaaaaw* over my words and kicks the air.

Mom yelps with laughter and squirms in Toddy's arms, turning her sparkly Torch Lake eyes on me. Dad always said they were the first part of her he fell for. They met far away from here, but she was a little piece of home to him, so he swept her up and brought her back with him, because he wanted all the home he could have in one place.

Mom smooths her T-shirt down over her improbably toned stomach. "Tell Hannah hi!"

Toddy wraps her waist in his arms and rests his chin on her head. "Go anywhere else after the carnival and you need to let us know, Junie," he adds. "Don't you girls get in any trouble."

"Never." I feign indignation and turn down the narrow hall for the door.

"Love you, baby," they both call.

Outside, the throng of moths surrounding the porch light disperses around me. The hens, as usual, are asleep in the grass beyond the decrepit chicken coop, no cares in the world. As I slide into Hannah's passenger seat, everything feels particularly *right* in a way I can't explain. Like the whole world's in harmony.

The house, the woods, the hens. Hannah in her floral minidress and me in my ratty summer tank top and shorts. The spirit.

I scan the yard for any hint of the wobbly pink thing. "Saw the ghost," I tell Hannah.

Hannah pops a piece of gum into her mouth then holds the pack out for me. "Which one?"

The cozy pink presence isn't the only one that has drifted across our yard since before I was born. "Feathers," I answer.

Hannah chews on her lip. "Good."

The other ghost—the shadowy one we haven't named, that plume of darkness that makes you feel nauseated and cold if you brush against it—only ever appears before something bad happens. Even when we hadn't actually seen the blackish thing, we'd know it had been there because all the animals on our land would freak. The always serene hens would flap, peck, break their wings, sometimes even kill one another. The normally merciful coywolves would mutilate rabbits and sparrows and leave their uneaten bodies on our hillside, scatterings of grisly omens. The last time it came was three years ago, the night before our porch collapsed and I broke my foot, but I haven't actually seen the dark ghost in ten years.

Not since before the worst Bad Thing.

Hannah starts to reverse down the hill and into the woods. "Ugh, your house always makes me feel the feelings. I swear, there's no place more nostalgia inducing than that leaning stack of lumber."

I nod and look out the window.

"Is she here now?" Hannah asks as she reverses slowly down the driveway. "Feathers?"

I point out toward a curve in the edge of the forest where I can barely make out a pink tendril caught in moonlight. "There," I tell Hannah. She gazes out toward that point with a dreamy, contented smile, then returns to easing down the driveway. "I wish you could see her."

Hannah lifts one shoulder in a shrug. "I just like knowing she's there. You know, not everyone gets to be best friends with someone who has a guardian . . . ghost."

"Han, if she were my guardian ghost, don't you think she would've intervened when I got bangs?"

"Who says guardian ghosts don't have a sense of humor?"

When we were little, I saw the pink ghost all the time. Hannah couldn't, but she could *feel* it. Sometimes we'd chase the shimmer across the yard and run through it, as if it were the spray of the sprinkler. It felt soft and lush, like running through a million falling feathers, thus our nickname for it. Dad always called it the Sprite, and when Mom shot him dubious looks— *you shouldn't toy with the kids like that*—he'd wink and say, "You know, Léa, to enter the kingdom of heaven, you must become like a child."

Then she'd smile as she turned back to hanging laundry, or rolling dough over the floured counter, or trailing her fingers along the gauzy wind-rippled drapes, and say, "Five Fingers loves its stories."

Like most transplants to this place, Mom had a hard time accepting the strange things that happened on our land as anything other than the shared imaginings of wild, summer-dazed minds and a town-wide tendency to exaggerate.

Five Fingers *did* love its stories, but Dad's were true. Our house *is* magic, in some small way. The skinny halls and wallpapered rooms, the gnarled forest that encircled our hill—together they do all kinds of impossible things. My whole life kids have crept onto our property at night to make wishes and look for spirits, or to steal cherries from the first Jack's Tart tree with hopes of shrinking their dogs' tumors, healing their grandparents' melanoma, even clearing up their acne.

As we pull onto the wooded road beyond my driveway, something flutters in my peripheral vision: the shift of a shadow, the undulation of something inky in front of the gatehouse.

My blood chills. My stomach clenches, a knot tightens my throat, and there's a jarring halt in my heart. But when I glance in the rearview mirror, there's nothing there. No shadowy thing, no darkness.

It's gone, I tell myself. *It's been gone three years. It's not coming back.*

Hannah flicks the frayed edge of my jean cut-offs. "June?"

"Huh?"

"You okay? You look sort of . . . not."

I shake my head. "Sorry, just distracted."

It's gone.

Still, tonight's feeling of rightness has been disturbed. Something *off* buzzes in the air, like a single hornet circling my head, always out of sight.

Two

WE leave Hannah's car parked by Meijer and join the crowd rollicking across the highway toward the high school. The organ music playing on loop in the Tunnel O' Love overlaps chaotically with the *whoop* and *dingdingding* of carnival games, and sweet, fatty smells mingle with the pine in the air.

We follow the curling path to the red-and-white ticket booth at the entrance to the school's parking lot, and I try to leave behind any thoughts of the dark presence I imagined back at the house. *It's gone; it's not coming back. It was never there.*

Hannah squeezes my arm and squeals in excitement as we step into the ticket line. She may be painfully shy, but she loves crowds.

Our friendship couldn't be any more of a teen-TV-drama cliché if we tried: Hannah Kuiper is a shy yet extroverted, violin-playing salutatorian. I'm a socially comfortable yet severely introverted underachiever who, if given the option for a weekend excursion, would choose Desert Island over Theme Park. She's a waify, blue-eyed blonde, and I'm a dark-eyed, even darker-waved brunette who wore Hannah's current pant size back in the seventh grade. Mom attributes my relative brawn to the fact that I, like Dad, never stop moving.

As we near the front of the line, Han rises up on her tiptoes, searching the crowd beyond the booth. "I think I see Nate Baars," Hannah says.

"How," I say, "in this writhing mass of Vineyard Vines shorts and North Face fleeces, did you pick out one little Vineyard Tendril–North Freckle?"

"Why are people crowded around him like that?" she asks, completely ignoring me. I squint and follow her gaze to the base of the Ferris wheel. Nate's standing with a dozen kids from our school, most of whom have already graduated.

"Weird," I say. "I've never seen people line up to hear someone make a fart noise with their armpit before. Is that Stephen Niequist with him?" I gesture to the rail-thin blond boy in the grandpa cardigan, Hannah's academic rival.

She shrugs. "Weirdly enough, they're friends. *No* idea what those two have to talk about, but I see Stephen's car at Nate's house all the time."

Nate and Hannah live on the same street. We used to ride bikes with him when we were kids, before the natural current of high school took him and us in two very different directions. One direction being distinctly *toward* flatulence-based humor.

"Maybe the world's ending and Nate just found out he's allowed to choose one person to save," I suggest. Truthfully, Nate is *exactly* the kind of boy who might draw a crowd—he's all suntanned muscle and shiny, chocolaty hair—if he weren't so ridiculous. But he is, and so this visual makes no sense.

"Maybe he won the lottery," Hannah says, "and now he has fifty new best friends who want a piece of the pie."

The gaunt woman in the admission booth calls us forward, and we trade twenties for highlighter-pink wristbands. We wander partway down the aisle on the right and stop before the House of Mirrors, staring up at the pink archway over the entrance. "Hey," Hannah says gently, taking my hand. She juts her chin toward it. "Maybe this year?"

The House of Mirrors was always Dad's favorite, and it's mine too. There's something so thrilling about wandering around only to get yourself un-lost—especially when the thing you're lost in blurs the line between dream and reality, possible and impossible. Like our house and our land. Like Dad himself.

Hannah and I come to this carnival every year, but I haven't been into the House of Mirrors since Dad died.

"What do you think?" Hannah says, studying me.

I shake my head. Hannah squeezes my hand then lets go. "Maybe next year."

We stand in silence for a few more seconds, like we're at an altar or a grave and not five feet from a game where you shoot plastic clowns with mounted water guns.

"Huh," Hannah says, breaking the reverie. I glance sidelong at her. Her eyes are back on the group at the bottom of the Ferris wheel. Now that we're closer, it's apparent that Nate is not, in fact, the center of their attention. He and Stephen are standing off-center, a little bit behind the others, and as a gaggle of middle schoolers jostles past, a gap in the group shifts to reveal the person they all seem uniformly focused on. At first, I can only see his back. He's on the tallish side of average and the thinnish side too, but he somehow takes up more space than someone his size should, as if his presence bends everything around itself.

He turns a bit, and I get a partial view of his profile, but I still don't recognize him. Clean-cut dark hair, uniform five-o'clock shadow. A T-shirt whiter than I've managed to keep one in the time it takes to get from the cash register to the door. The kind of dark, slim-fit jeans you can get away with wearing to a Five Fingers wedding.

I realize then that the reason he stands out so starkly against the backdrop of our lakeside town is because he looks unnaturally *clean*. Even the tattoos covering his pale arms manage to look cleaner than plain Five Fingers skin.

Hannah takes a step past me, trying to get a better look. "Is that..."

A couple of people laugh, and Nate Baars smacks the stranger on the back. He turns then, so I can see his full profile, and he forces a fraction of a smile before discreetly maneuvering away. The curvature of the group shifts to accommodate his movement.

"Is that ... a moderately attractive stranger?" I finish Hannah's thought. "The most elusive legend in all of Five Fingers?" Hannah doesn't seem to hear me. "Han? Do you know him?"

Mandy Rodriguez, who graduated two years ago, grabs the boy's arm and pulls him into a hug. Something along the lines of *good to see you* passes between them, and Hannah releases one crack of laughter before red splotches rush into her cheeks. "Not exactly."

The boy turns to wave as Mandy and her friends move off toward a cart selling fried-dough elephant ears. In that moment, his face becomes fully visible.

Unmistakable.

"Oh my god," Hannah gasps. "It *is*. It's him."

"Saul Angert."

The buzzing I felt back at the gatehouse swells within me now. It's not a hornet or a bit of darkness circling me. It's everywhere, everything. It's Saul Angert. Saul Angert, and the fact that he shouldn't be here.

And that I definitely shouldn't be here with him.

Three

"HOW long has it been since anyone's seen him?" Hannah asks.

"Three years," I answer automatically.

"Right," Hannah says. "Of course."

Three years ago everything changed for the Angerts, like ten years ago it changed for my family.

I was about to start high school, and for the first time since second grade, he and I were going to be in the same building. We'd spent the fourteen years prior avoiding each other, and, barring a few brushes, we'd done a good job.

I was nervous to see him on a regular basis, but a little excited too. My parents had never been the rule-setting type, so the more they drilled into my head that I *must, at all costs, stay away from the Angerts*, the more I obsessed over keeping tabs on them. I wanted to know everything about the people I wasn't allowed to know.

Saul and his twin sister, Bekah, were my personal forbidden fruit, the one thing in Five Fingers I could never touch.

"God, why do you think he's back?" Hannah says.

I shake my head. The snag in my throat returns. At this point, it's more like a double knot.

"Maybe Santa got my letter," Hannah pans, then shoots me an apologetic smile. She's had a crush on Saul for nearly as long as I've been under strict orders to avoid him.

One of my earliest memories is of Dad perching me on a stool in our summer-warm kitchen and telling me about the Angerts— what they did to the O'Donnells way back before I was born, how they still treated us. And, most importantly, what happens when we cross paths with them. I have dozens more memories like that one, snippets of panic and curiosity whenever I spotted one of them at the grocery store or in our elementary school's bus lane, fear and embarrassment when we met at the neighborhood pool and I watched Dad's face storm over.

Hissed insults in parking lots.

Ignorant backwoods dick, from Saul's father, Eli.

Elitist asshole, from Dad.

Yanked arms and hasty retreats.

Slammed doors and peeled tires.

Even years after Dad was gone, Mom dragged Shadow and Grayson away from the Cone's walk-up window, milkshake-less, when she saw Bekah Angert working the register.

So I spent much of the summer before freshman year mentally preparing myself to get regular, prolonged, and up-close looks at the supposed face of evil. But when my first day came, Saul wasn't there.

"We should go say hi," Hannah says timidly, like not even *she* believes that. She knows the sordid saga of the O'Donnell/Angert feud, but as with most things that cause her displeasure—spiders and peplum tops and that Richard Harris song about the melting cake—she tries to ignore it.

"Hannah, *no.*"

When the bus dropped me off after my first day of high school, I wandered toward the Angerts' summer cabin. I watched from the woods as Saul trekked in and out of the front door, carrying taped-up cardboard boxes and milk crates full of records. He looked less solid then than he does now; he looked wilty and tired.

"I was seriously starting to resign myself to never seeing him again," Hannah forges on.

That was what I'd thought three years ago: that the packed car meant the Angerts were leaving town. But the next day a group of upperclassmen—Mandy Rodriquez among them—marched up to my locker and asked if I was the reason Saul had transferred last minute. It turned out he was going to spend his senior year at boarding school, the pretentious arts academy two hours south of town.

The news traveled fast, and by lunch everyone was speculating that Mandy was right. People paid attention to what our families did. They knew about the bad blood, and the pains we took to avoid each other, because, for all intents and purposes, Dad and Eli Angert were local celebrities: Dad for the cherries and general magic surrounding our house, Eli for a series of boring-ass man-vs.-nature novels the *New York Times* had lauded, and the both of them for the roles their ancestors played in the founding of Five Fingers.

I understood why Saul's friends would think Eli had yanked Saul out to keep space between us, but it was impossible to be sure. After all, the Angerts had had their own Very Bad Thing happen a few months before, and even from a distance, I could see the family slowly falling apart. A few weeks before Saul left, Rachel, his mom, had ditched her job as the school nurse and moved to Chicago without his father, who—much to Mom and Toddy's displeasure—moved full-time into the summer cabin that bordered our property.

Weeds had quickly overrun the once magnificent garden, beer bottles and cans had piled up on the front porch for weeks, newspapers had lain at the lip of their driveway getting soggy, and when someone knocked the mailbox off the post, Saul's father hadn't bothered to fix it.

I expected things to settle down and Saul to come home, at least for the summer. But he didn't, and, after art school, he left for Vanderbilt without so much as a weekend home first. Then I resorted to tracking his movements through covert Google searches, history cleared on the off chance that Mom or Toddy ever used my computer. A year ago, Saul turned up in a "10 Under 30" feature *New York* magazine ran. Six months ago, I watched Toddy angrily stuff the local newspaper into the kitchen trash can, and when I fished it out, one of Saul's terrible junior high yearbook photos stared back at me alongside a piece alerting Five Fingers that its very own Saul Angert had sold an untitled book of essays to

Simon & Schuster. I'd been watching for it to pop up online or in bookstores but never heard another peep about it.

Three years, and in all that time, he'd never come home. And yet now here he is. Standing a few yards away near a pile of puked-up popcorn, as if he never left.

"It's a miracle," Hannah says hazily. "A back-to-school miracle."

Or a tragedy I've brought on with the sheer force of my curiosity. My mind flashes to the darkness I saw undulating across the gatehouse earlier.

The nameless thing is gone, was never there. You imagined it.

"How long do you think he's here for?" I say. "I mean, he can't be staying, right?"

"I have no *idea*, Junie." Hannah's voice strains under nerves and excitement. "That's why it's *essential* we hang out with him tonight."

A thrill of curiosity and panic shoots through my stomach. "Hello? Hannah? It's me, June, your best friend who's forbidden from interacting with him."

"I know, I know!" she cries, glancing between me and the group below the Ferris wheel. They've rearranged again so that Saul's facing our direction, and I jerk my gaze away before he can catch me looking at him. "But," Hannah begins, "this is quite possibly a once-in-a-lifetime opportunity. Don't act like you're not curious."

"You know what curiosity did to the cat."

"Convinced it to help its shy cat-friend woo her childhood crush?"

I laugh despite myself. I can't blame Hannah for trivializing my family's feud with the Angerts. Even Mom used to roll her eyes at Dad when he did things like steer us away from the shore and back to the car when we turned up for a beach day only to find the Angerts there. Backing out of the parking lot, Mom used to sigh in exasperation as Dad mumbled under his breath: *Think they're better than everyone, just 'cause they paid thousands for a piece of Ivy League paper and some froufrou shoes.* Before he died, we stayed away from the Angerts only because *Dad* did. But after, I think we all started to wonder if he'd been right: if the Angerts' hate for us really *did* somehow cause our bad luck.

It wasn't just us who said it. The whole town did—maybe just for fun, but they said it. Once, when I was in middle school, I even overheard a teacher explaining it to a substitute in the lounge: *The families hate each other so much that when tragedy strikes one, fate lashes out at the other. And when they cross paths? Well, they don't. And for good reason.*

But Hannah would never hear of it. *Bad things happen, June,* she'd say. *They just do. To everyone.*

"Pleeeeeeease." she says now, bouncing on the balls of her feet. "Let's just say hi."

"Hannah, my mom and Toddy have literally *two* rules: no swimming at Five Fingers Falls and no Angerts. You know this."

She squeezes my arm and says, "Sorry. I get it. I do. I'll just have to be happy knowing that, in another universe, the one where your family doesn't hate Saul's, we're having a lot of fun tonight. You, me, Saul, and"—she pauses, tipping her head toward the Ferris wheel—"*Nate.*"

I look over, and as if on cue, Nate spots us. He waves with the unfettered ferocity of someone stranded on a desert island trying to catch the eye of a chopper flying past.

"Are you kidding, Hannah? You just dreamed up another universe and you made *Nate Baars* my unofficial date! You could've chosen anyone!"

She laughs and waves back. "He's not that bad," she says. "Besides, he's Saul's cousin. He's the whole reason I know Saul."

"*Know* is a pretty strong word for someone you've never spoken to. Aloud, I mean."

Hannah waves off my comment. "You used to think Nate was super cute."

"In the fifth grade!" I say. "He didn't have that walk yet."

"Oh please, since when aren't you into boys who walk like they just dismounted a horse after fifteen hours of riding bareback?"

"He probably has chronic hemorrhoids."

"Junior," Hannah says reproachfully, and I know she's serious because she never uses my full name. Or, at least, my full*er* name. Despite my being a girl, my full name is Jack O'Donnell IV, after my father and his father and his father's father, who apparently got *his* name because he was the spitting image of *his* father's father's father, Jonathan "Jack" Alroy O'Donnell, pioneer settler of Five Fingers and purveyor of magic cherries.

Mom used to call me Jackie, but Dad always called me Junior or June. After he died, everyone else started to too. "Oh my God!" Hannah grabs my arm again. Her face is reddening rapidly. "They're coming over here. I'm so sorry—I think I just willed that to happen. Oh my God, am I a witch?"

19

The tension in my throat snarling again, I glance over my shoulder. The Ferris wheel group is disbanding, but Nate and Saul are distinctly headed in our direction.

"Shoot," Hannah says, as if she weren't just begging the universe for this exact scenario to unfold. "He's actually coming over here! What do we do?"

I search for somewhere to hide. Hannah, realizing how actually terrified she is to talk to her forever-crush, also searches for somewhere to hide. I book it toward the House of Mirrors, and she chases after me. I spin back to her, my heart jarring at the realization of what I'm about to do. "Wait."

Hannah stops short, wide-eyed, and I glance toward the entrance, the spurt of adrenaline from seeing Saul spurring me on. "I want to go in alone," I say, and Hannah's face twists with worry. "You want to talk to Saul; now's your chance."

She and I lock into a staring contest. I can practically see the debate happening in her mind. "Hannah. You can do this. You can talk to him."

She shoots another glance over her shoulder and takes a deep breath. "Okay. Okay, go."

I kiss my pointer and middle fingers and hold them out to her. Hannah does the same, our two fingers meeting in the middle like a tiny high five. "When I get back, be ready to tell me which song you chose for your wedding processional."

Hannah's eye roll evolves into a grin, and I turn and step into the dark, where everything becomes me.

Four

THE room glows neon. Blues, purples, pinks cross-fade along the edges of mirrors, and so do the versions of me they reflect. The whirring of the fans dulls the screeches and giggles of the other people hustling through the maze as I take my first steps.

I come up against an unexpected pane of glass, then veer right. As I move, I allow myself to forget where I'm going, like Dad used to do—he loved to lose himself first. Then, only when he was sure we were in the epicenter of whatever maze he'd led us into, he'd make a plan and swiftly guide me out.

"When you've been as lost as I have," he once said, "you get good at finding your way home, June-bug."

I feel him in the whip of the fan-stirred wind. Like he's rustling my hair, egging me on. *By the time Jack the First was your age*, he'd tell me, *he'd flown across the Atlantic with Amelia Earhart, gone over Niagara Falls in a rubber ball, and climbed Backbone Mountain to catch a falling star. By now, Jack II had saved dozens from drownin' in an Alaskan mega tsunami, using only a sliver of glacier for a row-boat, a broken pine for an oar, and a box of cherries for medicine. By your age, Junior, I'd stopped a tornado with a matchbook and a glass factory.*

I turn into a new room, all semblance of laughter and chatter fading. Blue-green arches frame the mirrors here, and swipes of glow-paint on the floor create the illusion of ornate tiles. This, I decide, must be the epicenter.

Channeling Dad, I become more purposeful with my turns, but when I change directions I come up against cool glass, and my breath catches in my chest. I laugh off my surprise the first few times it happens, but eventually my lostness, my aloneness, starts to unnerve me. It's been too long since I've seen anyone else.

And I keep remembering that outside these walls there's an Angert, and Bad Things happen when an O'Donnnell crosses paths with an Angert.

Bad Things happen, and I'm locked in a glass labyrinth with no escape.

I stumble forward and collide with another mirror. My pulse quickens. I try to calm myself, try to keep moving.

Another collision.

Keep moving. I turn and jolt to the left.

A pane of glass stops me. I spin right.

Keep—

I slam hard into someone as I turn the corner, barely managing to stifle a scream.

"*Shit,*" someone—a boy—gasps. In the strand of neon green

light, I see his hand clutching his collarbone. Either my skull or my teeth just slammed into it, but apparently I'm too high on adrenaline to feel any pain.

"I'm so sorry!" I stammer, moving forward with my hands held out apologetically. "God, I'm sorry. I thought you were—"

He looks up, the light slanting across his face.

Saul Angert.

That's who I'm looking at. Who I just bit. Saul "If You See Him Dying on the Side of the Road, Keep Going" Angert.

He raises one hand and massages his clavicle with the other. "It's fine. You were right. I *was*."

"—the ghost of Jack the Ripper." The words escape like air from a tire.

"Oh," he says. "I thought you were going to say, *having a complete meltdown about being trapped in this god-forsaken nightmare.*"

My heart hammers against my ribs. "No. The vibe I got was definitely Jack the Ripper."

His laugh is gravelly and warm, so at odds with his coolly rigid appearance. His dark hair is cropped close on the sides and a little longer on top, pushed back in a smooth swoop away from his forehead, and now that I'm closer I can see the minor imperfections that keep his face from being perfectly symmetrical: the slight turn of his right canine tooth and the lone dimple on his left cheek. He takes a half step back. "Well, I'm sorry I scared you."

"Oh please. I scared myself. *I'm* sorry I bit your collarbone," I reply. "If it helps, it's super unlikely I have rabies." *Despite what you might have heard.*

Although if he knew who I was, would he be standing here?

He gives me that scratchy laugh again. "Oh yeah. Right. I'm not sorry—*you* are. That's what I meant to say."

"I was just being polite," I say. "I feel no remorse."

"Wow," he says with mock disbelief. "Stone cold."

I tip my head down the mirrored aisle. "Most of me *is* made of glass, so."

"Most of you *are* made of glass."

"I feel like if you're not in uniform, you're not allowed to police someone's grammar."

When he smiles, his mostly straight white teeth glow blue along with his white T-shirt and pale arms, except for where his tattoos cut inky shadows through the light. He *is* handsome, in a way. Just not *my* way, which is usually either (1) brawny pseudo-lumberjack types whose personal hygiene regimen amounts to a lone spray bottle of Febreeze or (2) NOT SAUL ANGERT.

It would be best for me to walk away now. I know that. But I'm standing face-to-face with someone I've heard about my entire life, Googled regularly for at least three years, and never, before now, spoken to.

And I haven't burst into flames. The ceiling hasn't collapsed, the earth hasn't opened to swallow us, and he's acting pretty . . . normal.

Which, I assume, can only mean that he doesn't recognize me. Did *not* Google *me*.

I'm a little offended. And guilty. Also curious, and shaky with adrenaline. Like I'm about to jump off a diving board or crest the peak of a roller coaster.

"Well," I say, not so much *returning* to my senses as chasing them down with a hatchet. "Good luck."

Saul nods, and I turn a corner toward the outer ring of pink and blue mirrors. I watch him in the reflections in front of me as I go. He's trailing me a couple of yards back, the faint trace of a smile curving one corner of his mouth. I stop and face him. "What are you doing?" I say. "You can't follow me. That's cheating."

"Who says you're going the right way?"

"If I'm not, then why are you following me?"

"I'm not," he says. "This happens to be the right way. I'm just trying to get out of here. It's purely coincidence."

"Fine. Then you can go in front of me."

He shakes his head. "Are you kidding? I'm not going to let you cheat off of me. You bit me and didn't apologize."

"That was self-defense," I say. "At that point, there was still a *ninety-nine* percent chance you were the ghost of an English serial killer."

A slow smile spreads across his face, and for a second we're silent. Another thrill bubbles up in my chest. My midsection feels like a shaken-up champagne bottle, fizzy and light.

"Fair enough," Saul says.

I start moving again.

He gives me a few yards' head start before he follows, and again my eyes keep rebounding toward his reflection. Whenever he catches me peeking, a microscopic river of embarrassment jolts through my atoms, and the corner of his mouth twists up in a quiet way, like we're sharing an unspoken joke whose punch line is *our families hate each other, ha-ha!*

Or at least that's what the punch line is for the few moments before I take a distracted yet forceful step and slam my face into a mirror. Saul lets out one rough laugh, then jogs over to where I'm clutching my nose and groaning. He ducks his head to get a better look. "You okay?"

"Could be worse," I say, still covering my nose. "A cartoon anvil didn't fall on my head."

"Lemme see." He pulls my hand away from my face, and his dark eyes zigzag over my nose, which hurts way less than my dignity. Now we're *really* close, and I can smell his wintergreen toothpaste and his laundry detergent, and something else that's warm and a little earthy.

He brushes his fingertips over my nose. "That hurt?"

If his voice had a taste it would be like one of those artisanal chili-pepper dark chocolate bars. If it were a color it would match the eyes that are currently boring into mine.

A memory resurfaces: his name at the top of the MARRY column in the KISS/MARRY/KILL chart Hannah wrote on her closet wall in seventh grade. The image doesn't quite exterminate the butterflies in my stomach, but it *does* remind me that if Greg Schwartz turns up dead, Hannah will need a very good alibi.

"Doesn't look broken or anything," Saul says, narrowing his gaze to peer at me through the neon light.

It's probably my turn to talk, but his hand is warm on my shoulder and we're standing, like, six inches apart, and the vast majority of my brain has already rejected the memory of face-planting into a smudgy fun house mirror so that it can fully devote itself to screaming, I WONDER IF SAUL ANGERT'S MOUTH TASTES MORE LIKE COOL MINT OR SPICY CHOCOLATE.

Finally, Saul releases my shoulder, and it's then that I notice the fullness of the noise in here, the eerie music and wash of voices pulsating from everywhere. I spot the barely visible gap where one mirror flares right and another just left to hide the opening between them. I lean to the right until the two separate in my vision. "Hey, guess what," I say.

Saul stares at me for a long moment. "What?"

"I win." I slip between the panes and out into the buzzing night. As soon as I set foot on the asphalt, my eyes land on Hannah and the bowlegged boy beside her.

"June *freakin'* O'Donnell," Nate Baars calls to me.

Saul's shoulder bumps mine as he emerges behind me, and all the fizz in my chest turns to lead and sinks. He lowers his mouth beside my ear and murmurs, "O'Donnell, huh?"

But he doesn't say it like it's an accusation. He says it like a joke.

He brushes past me to meet Hannah and Nate, then looks back with a faint, mocking smile.

He said it like he was waiting to, like he knew who I was the whole time.

Five

"HOW is it I went in after you and I've been out for, like, fifteen minutes?" Nate half-shouts at me, because he half-shouts everything. "Whooped your *ass*, girl."

"So you guys met," Hannah stammers and gestures toward Saul and me as we awkwardly join them.

"No," I say at the same time Saul says, "Yes."

I think I was wrong; it was hornets in my stomach, not butterflies, and now they're migrating toward my face. Saul's gaze meets mine, and his coal-black brows pinch together, wrinkling his forehead. We both mumble some variation of *sort of*.

Nate guffaws. "You guys don't know each other?"

"We haven't *formally* met," Saul replies. He holds out his hand to me. "I'm Saul."

"Oooh, that's right," Nate says. "Your families hate each other. Dude, this is *Junior*." Then, as if worried Saul might mistake me for

28

one of the *other* Juniors whose family the Angerts hate, Nate adds, "You know, like Jack O'Donnell IV." And then one final clarification: "She lives in the haunted house."

Dryly, Saul feigns shock. "Oh, *that* O'Donnell."

I can't tell if he's mocking Nate or me. His pupils stretch and shrink as they take me in: tiny telescopes honing in on a predator, or maybe prey. Fine—*good*. If he hates me, that will make it easier for me to hate him too. Like I'm supposed to.

He's still reaching out to me, and Hannah nervously titters, so finally I take his hand. I'm hoping for a floppy palm, preferably slick or sticky. Instead, his hand is a lot like his voice: both leaner and rougher than you'd expect from his almost sterile appearance.

Not my type, I think.

Your best friend's childhood crush.

The son of your dad's mortal enemy.

"Nice to meet you," Saul says.

A voice like late-summer corn husks.

Laugh like brewing coffee.

Hands like sun-warmed sand.

"You too."

Hannah laughs nervously again, then Nate claps his hands together and barks, "Well, that was weird." Saul barely acknowledges him, and I study my shoes and wonder how Nate managed to get him here when the two of them seem to be the sort of cousins who've never met. "Anyway, what do you kids want to do next? Ferris wheel? Scrambler? Carnival-food binge session?"

I look to Hannah for some assurance that she didn't promise our night to Nate Baars while I was in the House of Mirrors. She sways on her feet, one hand on her hip, as she scans the carnival, studying everything but Saul and me.

Dear god, she promised our night to Nate Baars.

"Actually," I start, "I'm, um . . ." *Not allowed to hang out with you.*

"Scrambler?" Hannah says abruptly, voice high and wobbly. She looks faintly green and less faintly miserable.

"Scramblaaaaah," Nate wails and then—no exaggeration— whoops and gallops toward the line. Saul strides past us with his hands in his pockets, leveling a glance over his shoulder. I grab Hannah's arm and hold her back from the group, infusing my glare with the heat of a thousand Junes.

"The moon, Junie!" she hisses. "I'll owe you the *moon* if you go along with this."

Glancing between her and where the boys are walking ahead of us, I feel my resolve crumbling under my curiosity. "Fine," I say. "The moon, a million dollars, and one solid kick to Nate's crotch."

Hannah drags me after them into the queue just as Nate's launching into an unnecessarily long story about his weekend that roughly amounts to: *I climbed a rock; I jumped into a lake.* Saul just sort of nods along, his expression lacking any sign of interest. Even the way he moves seems contained, cautious, thoughtful compared to how Nate bounds and gambols.

I try and fail to picture clean-cut Saul Angert among the mucky bike racks and beat-up kayaks attached to the cars in the Five Fingers High parking lot.

Though they're both lean and dark-eyed with weirdly elegant posture, it's equally hard to reconcile Saul as the son of Eli Angert, several of whose books I read for a Michigan literature unit last year. Mom and Toddy had offered to write me a note to get out of it ("As you know, our daughter's allergic to Angerts . . ."), but I was too embarrassed.

So I read (and appropriately loathed) Eli's books about Men Learning to Be Men: full pages describing brown liquor in crystal glasses, paragraphs devoted to the silence of the woods, diatribes about mercy-killing injured does, and more than one passage juxtaposing a masturbation scene with a sermon on the brutality of nature.

You could take the average Five Fingers boy, age him up forty years, and get an approximation of Eli Angert. But I can't understand how a boy like Saul could be born in a place like this, or what would bring him back once he escaped.

At the front of the Scrambler's line, a man with pitted cheeks and a straggly ponytail checks our admission bracelets, and a stroke of benevolent genius hits me.

"Hey, Saul," I say, pulling my backpack off my shoulders as the four of us cross the metal platform to some open cars. "Ride with Hannah? I wanna get a picture of her on the ride, and it'll be easier from another car."

He shrugs and pulls his hands out of his pockets, only to stick them right back in when he realizes he has nothing to do with them. "Sure."

Hannah shoots me a mortified look. It was a sort of mom-y thing for me to do, I know, but I wasn't the first person to make this night uncomfortable.

"I'll ride with you, Han," Nate offers.

Hannah's eyes widen, and she opens her mouth like she's about to excuse herself from the ride entirely.

"Saul already said he would," I say and grab Nate's leathery elbow to steer him into the car across from Hannah and Saul's. I rest my backpack on my thighs, and once we get the lap bar down, I rifle through my bag for my phone to maintain the pretense of taking a picture.

"Smile!" When I glance up, I find Saul's eyes already on me. A spurt of heat blooms in my chest.

Oh no. I definitely think he's hot. And worse, I want him to look at me.

Meanwhile Hannah's grimacing with anticipation of the picture I'm about to take, so I force my eyes to my screen and snap a few. Saul's not smiling in any. He's just staring intensely at the camera.

"Good?" Han calls to me.

"Good." I will my voice steady. "You guys look like you just found out bacon doesn't exist anymore, so good."

"Don't eat bacon," Saul says. "Vegetarian."

"There is no such thing as a vegetarian in Five Fingers," I say.

He lifts one shoulder in the barest of shrugs. "I know. That's why I was exiled."

Hannah laughs, a bright sound that makes Saul crack a partial smile. When his eyes flick toward me, they burn my skin, and I'm horrified and embarrassed and guiltily thrilled.

I swivel in my seat toward Nate and wait for my blush to fade, my heartbeat to slow. "Smile," I say, and Nate flips off my phone.

The metal arms of the Scrambler screech to life, the ghoulish music resumes mid-note, and we start to spin. I catch the tail end of a gravelly laugh hidden in the noise.

I feel it in my stomach as neon colors whip around us.

Because I have an insta-crush on Saul Angert. Because I am a horrible friend and a traitor to my father. Because when Angerts and O'Donnells get together, Bad Things happen.

Six

BY the time we've disembarked the Scrambler, I'm still not sure Hannah has looked Saul in the eye, and her misery has become more blatantly visible. I grab her elbow and say, "Would you run to the bathroom with me?"

"God, yes."

As soon as we duck between the port-o-potties into the shadows of the parking lot, Hannah blurts, "This reminds me of when I had that hot dentist."

"The one whose hand you accidentally licked?"

"Saul keeps *trying* to make conversation, but, like, there's a giant invisible hand in my mouth, and I'm suddenly deeply convinced I still have braces."

"Open," I say. Hannah sticks her tongue out. "Oh shit, Hannah, they're back! Your braces are back! You have haunted teeth!"

She sighs. "This is terrible. I've set off a chain reaction that culminates in my dying alone, in a doily-covered apartment, beneath a pile of coupons."

I kneel on the asphalt and dig through my backpack for Dad's old flask. Hannah glances anxiously between it and the crowd beyond the port-o-potties, then rubs the spot between her brows. "Will that make me puke?"

I wave a hand toward a sign that reads, DEEP! FRIED! CANDY! "*Everything* here will make you puke."

She sighs, swipes the flask, and takes a quick swig. "Okay, now put that away before we get arrested."

I laugh, though I'm pretty sure she's not kidding, and take a long sip myself before tucking it back in my bag.

"What was I thinking?" Hannah says. "I can't even *talk* in front of him. I couldn't when we were kids either."

"To be fair, when we were kids, he was, like, thirty-eight."

"Juuuuune," she groan-laughs. "He's twenty-one! I'll be eighteen soon—it's not a big deal."

"Whatever. Let's get back to your sugar daddy and make sure he gets you into his will before it's too late."

"I hate you."

"Love you back." I kiss my fingers and hold them out to her. Still shaking her head, she does the same. "By the way," I say as we head back toward where the boys are waiting for the bumper cars, "if you guys get married, should I call Saul Dad?"

"Jack O'Donnell IV," Hannah says, "you're so grounded."

Maybe it's the shot of whisky I took, or the meteor shower glittering across the sky; maybe it's the group of fifth graders clustered on curbs watching trails of light streak across the black with sleepy awe in their eyes, or how the night air cools and thins, but from this moment on, the carnival becomes something gentler.

The music mellows, voices simmer. The trees sway as if rocking to a lullaby. And as the four of us meander from ride to ride, Hannah loosens up and acts like herself. She talks about school and tells Saul about how she got into violin. She asks him questions about Tennessee, Vanderbilt, the summer writing residency he just finished at York St. John. She even laughs good-naturedly when Nate makes jokes or just generally does something to suggest he'd like some applause, like jumping over a trash can for literally no reason.

Each time Nate out-Nates himself, I catch myself meeting Saul's gaze, like we're sharing another private joke. It happens so many times I resolve to hang back and walk behind the others just to stop myself from eye-flirting.

I keep forcing Hannah and Saul to ride with each other "so I can get pictures," but after the Kamikaze—a pendulum ride with a metal arm that swings you in a loop—I don't have to force them anymore. It's evident this pairing is becoming permanent all on its own, which makes my head feel cloudy and my spine burn with an unprecedented and sickening breed of jealousy.

Fifteen minutes from close, we join the line for the last ride, the Ferris wheel.

"Okay, not that I don't love me some Junior," Nate says, "but I demand a ride with Hannah."

She blushes and glances sideways at Saul, who shrugs and says, "Sure."

I hate it. I hate that Hannah just asked Saul's permission to ride with Nate, and worse still I hate that I hate it. I shouldn't care.

I shouldn't *be* here. I should've left as soon as I saw him.

We reach the head of the line, and Nate and Hannah file in first. Their bench rises, and another lowers to the metal ramp. Saul holds out an arm, gesturing for me to go first. I do. Silently. Awkwardly. Miserably.

He slides in beside me and waits for me to get my backpack into my lap before pulling the scuffed bar down. We're mute as our bench lifts to lower the next for loading. Both of us look around for a while, studying anything but each other. The possibility of our car detaching and plummeting to the concrete doesn't gnaw at me like the immediate distress of being alone with him, of feeling Saul Angert's hip against mine.

"Did she blackmail you?" he says.

I finally look at him, and his face is serious. "What?"

"You clearly don't want to be here with me. So how's Hannah keeping you here?"

"Oh. She asked."

"Do you want to know how Nate got me here?"

"Guns?" I hazard.

"Yeah." Saul nods. "Guns."

I fight a smile. "Wait, really, how?"

"He likes your friend," he says coolly. "He needed a wingman. Shit, sorry—that sounds a lot creepier than the last time I said it to a seventeen-year-old girl, four years ago."

"God, this is rapidly becoming a bad teenage retelling of a Shakespearean comedy."

"How so?"

"Hannah's not into Nate," I say. "I don't think they would be a good match."

Saul shrugs lazily. "I don't know. He's a little goofy, but he's a good guy."

Neither of us says anything. Moments pass, and the silence accumulates, thick and heavy between us. To break it, I say, "Eighteen."

"What?"

"You can rest easy. You said the word *wingman* to an eighteen-year-old girl. Far less humiliating."

One corner of his mouth curls up. "Agreed. Far less humiliating."

"The bigger concern is that you used the word *wingman* and it's not 1986."

Saul's eyes narrow, but his grin widens. "Wow, you *do* hate me, don't you, Jack O'Donnell IV?"

My stomach turns inside out at the sound of my name in his voice. This isn't how he's supposed to be, and it's definitely not how *I'm* supposed to be *with* him.

Saul swears and grips the lap bar as we jolt up another notch to let more people board below. Nate's and Hannah's feet dangle over us, swaying in the lake wind, but Saul's just staring at the ground. "Not a big fan of heights?" I say.

"What gave it away? The fine sheen of cold sweat that just sprang up all over my body?"

"Actually it was your white-knuckling." I flick his hand with mine.

His fingers latch on to my hand and hold it there. "Hey, sorry about your hand," he says, tightening his grip. "Turns out I need it now, so you're going to have to find a new one."

I laugh. I warm. I burn. Guilt springs up in me. "I have something more effective than a hand in my purse, if you'll let me go," I say. When he does, I fish out the flask.

His smile now looks like how his laugh sounds: inviting, warm, uneven. I pass him the whiskey and watch his throat move as he chugs a little. He wipes his chin with the side of his hand and passes back the flask. "Thanks. Aren't you a little young to have that?"

"No, haven't you heard? They've changed the drinking age since your childhood here thirty-five years ago."

"Hilarious. So funny."

"I can tell you think so by your raucous laughter, Saul."

"I have to admit," he says, "I'm a little surprised it's true."

"What's true?"

"You O'Donnells hate us."

Heat rushes into my face. After making it this far without broaching the feud, I'd expected to finish the night without acknowledging it. "Oh, deeply," I answer, unsure whether I'm kidding or serious. Right now I don't hate Saul Angert. Nor do I want him to know I ever thought I did. "And you guys hate us too, right?"

He nods solemnly. "I'd wish you dead, but we don't need another ghost in that house."

I don't laugh. I can't. His gaze has me frozen. Like he's a Gorgon and I'm the sap who wandered into his temple. I'm worried I've lost track of the silence, that maybe we've been sitting here like this much longer than appropriate. "My house isn't haunted," I say.

"Glad to hear it," Saul answers.

"It's magic, but not haunted."

His face remains neutral. "Magic."

"I'm serious."

"Okay, Junior." He braces himself against the bar as we rise higher. "What's magic about your house?"

"You don't have to call me that," I tell him.

"What would I call you?"

"June, Jack, Jackie, whatever you want."

"I want to call you Junior."

"Fine."

"But I like Jack too."

"Whichever."

"And June's cute."

"Adorable," I agree. "Makes me sound like a tiny golden retriever puppy."

We surge upward one last time, straight to the top of the Ferris wheel, and again Saul locks my hand against the bar with his, and again I like it more than I should.

"So, June." His voice is taut as he pries his gaze from the asphalt below. "What's magic about your house?"

I shift my hand in an attempt to free it, but instead Saul slides his fingers through mine and grips them for dear life.

"Well, what have you heard?" I ask.

"The coywolves." He closes his eyes. "That if you leave shoes in the yard, the coywolves take them."

"One hundred percent. Every time."

His dark eyes open to find mine. "You're messing with me."

"I'm not. You really never left flip-flops in our yard when you were a kid? I thought everyone did that."

"Everyone did," he says. "I didn't. What else?"

"The coywolves never—or *almost* never—kill our chickens. Dad said it's always been that way, since Jonathan Alroy O'Donnell first came here."

Saul fixes me with another serious stare. "That can't be true."

"Dad called our woods a thin place, where the world and heaven overlap. He said that's what made our house magic—why that first cherry tree Jonathan planted grew overnight and the animals would lie down together."

Again all true, except, of course, when the dark ghost appeared. But that seems like a tally in the *yes, definitely haunted* column, so I don't mention it. A chill rolls through me at the thought of the writhing darkness I imagined tonight.

"And do you have proof of this, Jack?"

"We've never kept our chickens in their coop. We just let them roam the hill."

"Wild." Saul stares vaguely at our hands as the Ferris wheel begins to twirl in earnest. Cool wind ripples over us, carrying the contented noise of carnival-goers upward, and he relaxes a little. "What about the ghosts?" he says. "I remember kids used to go to your house at midnight, try to see ghosts in the yard."

"There are two of them, and anyone can feel them, but my dad said only Jacks could see them. He called them sprites. We don't really know what they are."

"And the Window Whites?"

He's talking about the little white puffballs that float in our windows and doors, like sentient, unblown dandelions. No one knows what they are or why they sometimes drift listlessly in our doorframes and other times disappear for weeks.

"They land on the glass and move around for a while, then float back into the woods," I tell Saul now. "My mom thinks they're just blossoms or pollen."

"And the rearranging hallways and rearranging woods?"

I shrug and look down at Saul's hand and mine. My stomach dips. "You think it's all just made up?"

"I think Five Fingers likes its stories."

I laugh. "You don't sound like someone who was born here." He says nothing, and I continue: "I have some hazy memories of opening a door and finding myself back in the room I thought I'd just left, and a dozen memories of walking straight out from my house through the woods toward the setting sun, only to end up back at the hill. And there's this massive tree Dad called O'Dang! We'd go looking for it all the time and only find it, like, ten percent of the time. We always knew, though, that if we stepped into the forest and the sky was misty but sunlit, we could find it."

As the words spill out, all my blood feels like it's freezing and breaking through my veins. I try not to think about the tree. I try not to think about the woods, because the next thought I have is always of the Worst Day.

All the minuscule details stored in perfect vividness by my eight-year-old brain: the dryness of the air and dirt that week, the blue petals that fell in a perfect circle from Mom's hydrangea, the weeks when she fed me only Froot Loops and macaroni, either because she was too sad to cook or because I was too sad to eat anything real.

If our house *were* haunted, there'd be more than two ghosts fluttering on our hill. If it were haunted, Dad wouldn't be gone.

"I'd like to see it." Saul's husky voice brings me back to the humming night.

"The tree?"

"The house," he says. "All of it."

I study him for a long stretch during which neither of us blinks. "You really never sneaked over? Not once?"

"Once I got as far as the woods." He shakes his head. "I remember when you did, though. When you got stung by the bees?"

I stare down at the purple stripes of a psychic's tent. "Yeah?"

That was the day I started to believe that being *close* to the Angerts was dangerous. It was also the day Hannah's crush on Saul reached legendary heights. Hannah and I were seven, so Saul must have been about ten. She and I had snaked through the woods out toward the Angerts' summer home. We found Saul and Bekah building a tree house—or, rather, *she'd* been nailing boards to a trunk, hanging on them to check their strength before climbing up to nail the next one, and Saul had been taking pictures with a clunky film camera that looked like a prop from a movie set.

Hannah and I crept close to get a look at the kids I wasn't allowed to play with—she knew them a bit through her neighbor Nate. Saul had his back to us as he crouched in the mud, snapping photographs of something we couldn't see.

I study him in the Ferris wheel's light, comparing him to the boy I saw on that day. "Your ears were bigger back then."

Saul's head tilts back, and the corners of his eyes crinkle in laughter. "Actually, I think they were the exact same size they are now, but the rest of me was considerably smaller."

His hair was longer then too, but just as neat. Bekah was the opposite, hair wild and limbs muddy and thorn-scratched. As I watched the mysterious Angert twins that day, a fallen branch cracked under my foot, and when Saul spun toward the noise, I stepped onto a collapsed log. It made a hollow sound beneath my sneaker, because it *was* hollow, or mostly hollow, give or take a hornets' nest.

The wasps swarmed at once. Hannah started screaming and ran toward the Angerts' cabin. Bekah and Saul both came toward me, like they were going to fight the things off with their hands, but even in my earth-splitting panic I knew: The wasps hadn't just attacked me for stepping on their house; they'd attacked me for getting too close to the Angerts.

Going toward the twins for help would only make things worse, not to mention the trouble I'd be in when Dad found out.

I turned and ran. Through the woods all the way back to my house, the hornets trailing me the whole way. Mom saw me hurtling toward her from where she was sitting out front, reading on a papaya-yellow blanket beneath the cherry tree. She stood and came running full speed. She swept me off the ground and over her hip, barreling for the front door. Inside, she dumped me into the tin tub downstairs and cranked the faucet to full blast. As the icy water spit from the showerhead, I watched the hornets die in the pool forming around me, the beating of their wings slowing to a fizzle and then nothing, no movement at all.

I spent the rest of the day in a Benadryl haze, covered in calamine lotion, and Dad had had to pick up Hannah from the Angerts' cabin, which had him more furious with *them* than me.

When he got back, I heard him and Mom talking in the hallway outside my room. *Angert girl got hurt too*, he said, and I could tell from his voice that he thought this was only fair. *Completely covered in poison ivy. I mean, eyes swollen shut, everything.* Mom's heavy sigh disapproved of his obvious glee, but she didn't say anything. That was how it was. He couldn't be talked out of anything, and he could talk other people *into* anything.

"That was the first time I saw you up close," Saul says beside me. The breeze lifts my hair from my shoulders, and goose bumps wriggle up where Saul's gaze just glanced off my neck.

"No it wasn't."

He lifts his eyes to mine. "What do you mean?"

"The hornets were the second time. The first time was at the YMCA pool. I couldn't have been more than five years old. We showed up after you, and your dad made you leave. On your way out, you dislocated your shoulder. Like an hour later, I nearly drowned. That was the day my dad first told me about your family."

Saul tilts his face skyward and shakes his head as if addressing the stars directly.

"What?" I press.

"Nothing. It's just . . ." He slumps into the bench again. "What a convenient concept. That every bad thing that happens to you was caused by the person you hate."

"So you don't think bad things happen when our families cross paths?"

"June," he says. "Every single outdated, low-budget, under-repaired ride we've taken tonight not only *could have* but *should have* killed us, O'Donnell and Angert or not, and yet here we are. Together."

"I'm honestly kind of surprised the guy who's currently drawing blood from my hand with his fingernails as we dangle three stories above an asphalt parking lot would be willing to jinx us like that, but okay."

He faintly grins. "You already bit my collarbone *and* got your just reward when you plowed into a mirror that's probably never, in its forty years of life, been cleaned. Even if we *were* to be disciplined by the universe for speaking to each other, I think we've gotten enough punishment for the night."

"How did you know the mirror was the same age as you?" I ask somberly. "Were you born in the same hospital? Hey, what was the world like before the Internet?"

"How old, exactly, do you think I am?"

"I don't know—what's the last year a person could've been born and still know what a *fortnight* is?"

"It was one thing when you took *wingman* from me. I won't let you disparage *fortnight* too."

"Seriously, though," I say. "What about the thing at the YMCA? I mean, you left in an ambulance, and an hour later a pimply lifeguard was hunched over me, forcing water out of my lungs."

Saul lifts one dark eyebrow. "That shoulder's been on the fritz my entire life—all forty? Fifty years of it? Loose ligaments. Ended my baseball career before it ever began. I'd call that a blessing, not a curse. No, Jack O'Donnell IV, I don't believe your mere presence dislocated my shoulder. I believe our great-grandfathers pissed each other off and this town turned it into something big and impossible and legendary because this is Five Fingers, and everything has to be big and impossible and legendary. It's a coping mechanism for our ungodly winters."

I stare at him, trying to decide whether or not I agree. Five Fingers might be a town of tall tales, but that's because enough of us have seen enough of *it*—the stuff that's worth repeating until it becomes a tall tale—to believe in it. Dad said we lived in a magic house, and we do. He said the Angerts were dangerous to us—do I really draw the line there?

And then there's the thing too big to ask about: If *our* bad things don't turn into *their* bad things and vice versa, then what about what happened to Dad and Bekah? Ten years ago, he was totally healthy, then weeks after *she* was diagnosed, *he* was gone.

And three years ago, when she . . . on the day they lost her . . . my foot plunged through the porch and I broke a bone for the first time in my life.

We're silent for the rest of the ride, and when the car touches down, Saul disentangles his hand from mine, and we step off to meet Nate and Hannah. Talking about all this has stirred up memories I do my best to leave settled on the floor of my mind, and it's impossible to pack them away so quickly.

As the four of us make our way toward the Meijer parking lot, I feel empty, like a wrung-out sponge. I don't have the energy to care when Saul and Hannah walk ahead of us, though I *do* notice Nate's disappointment now. And I don't care that the only goodbye Han and I exchange with them is a walking wave, like, *Probably see you never!*

I don't care when I see Saul loiter against Nate's passenger door, watching us climb into Hannah's Subaru, or when he calls scratchily, "Have a good fortnight!"

Because I'm Jack O'Donnell IV, and for at least three reasons, I have no business having a crush on Saul Angert.

Seven

"WELL, I hate to say it," Hannah sighs, as we cruise into the blue-green forest that hides my house, "but a night with Saul Angert was hardly worth the moon."

I will myself not to blush, to stamp out the traitorous hope in my chest. "What about the tracker I'll have to wear on my ankle if my parents find out about it? Was it worth that?"

"He used to seem . . . *sparklier*, didn't he?"

My insides twist and snag. "Yeah, super sparkly. Like a tiara for a Barbie doll. I thought you were having fun."

"With no help from him. What a wet blanket. Almost makes you appreciate the Nates of the world."

I think my face is on fire, or maybe just crawling with fire ants.

"But still." Hannah bumps the volume up a couple hundred decibels and cranks the windows down so the heat can beat and roar against our ears. "He is *fine*, isn't he?"

"Just not Barbie-tiara fine," I shout.

The moon shines through the foliage cupped around the raw-boned road, turning everything silver and sublime. "There, June!" Hannah cries pointing up at the sky. "Your gift in all her glory. Please accept this as payment for causing your perfectly good night to be Angerted."

"Do I still get to kick Nate in the crotch?"

Hannah's laughter gets lost between the layers of sound, and I laugh too, because that's the way the lake air works: It carries the feelings you exhale into someone else's inhalations, it syncs your heartbeats, connects you to everyone else who loves it like you do.

That's what Dad used to say, anyway: *Lake people are sponges; we all absorb the same mix of life and minerals. We recognize it in each other and share it when one of us gets dried out. You're a sponge, Junior, like me. When you're dry, you have to go back to the water to survive.*

Hannah sings along, her right arm flinging out to gesticulate wildly and her wispy hair flaring around her face. She's most beautiful when she's this relentless kind of happy. Maybe that's when everyone is their most beautiful, especially to those who love them.

I thrust my right arm out the window and catch Hannah's hand with my left. We sing until our throats fray, and for a while, everything is how it should be.

By the time we rumble past the shabby gatehouse to the grassy hill my home sits on, I'm starting to feel full again. Hannah parks beside the green-trimmed garage Dad built, and the motion sensors catch the car's hood, triggering the porch lights. A flutter of moth wings stipples the ghostly glow of the bulbs, and my eyes skim the windows, the Whites bobbing in their corners.

Hannah kisses the index and middle fingers on her right hand, and I do the same. "Love you, baby girl."

"Love you more." I climb from the car and jog to the porch, listening to the crunch of gravel as Hannah reverses into the ring of woods.

I pull my keys out but freeze, a sudden prickling on my neck. When I turn back toward the yard, Hannah's headlights have vanished beyond the hill. Everything is dark and still, apart from the twin glints of eyes a few yards beyond the porch.

A lone coywolf stands with its reddish tail high and front leg bent, its narrow face caught in the edge of the porch light and its fox-like ears trained toward me.

I don't know quite what makes me do it, but I lean down, slowly, to untie my sandals, my gaze still locked with the coywolf's eyeshade.

Tapetum lucidum, Dad explained to me as a kid. *Eyeshade. A special reflective surface behind the retina that lets some animals see better at night. It gives the image another surface to bounce off of toward the brain, if the first one fails in the dark.*

The coywolf watches me step out of my salmon-colored espadrilles and lift them by their leather ties. I take a few cautious steps, set the shoes on the walkway, then retreat.

The coywolf sets her foot down and picks her way toward my shoes, haunches rolling as she moves. In one swift motion, she drops her snout, snatches the shoes, and darts into the trees.

I stare after her, a laugh building in my chest, followed by an ache. I can picture it so clearly: Dad's back and mine silhouetted by the moonlight as we sat in the yard listening to the cicadas and crickets. So many calm nights when we just *listened* to our thin place for hours. "Can you hear it, June-bug?" he would whisper. "The heartbeat of the world?"

Eventually we'd hear the door creak on its hinges and Mom's bare feet patter across the porch. "Bedtime," she'd hum, and Dad would look back at her and smile, say nothing. Then she would float down to the grass and sit on my other side, pulling my head against her chest to run her hands through my hair.

"Magic," I whisper, aching for those lost nights. I turn to go inside and find one lone Window White bobbing in the doorframe. I cup it in my hand, its softness barely palpable as I lift it toward my face. Something strange happens then: One moment it's floating along my lifeline, the next it seems to disperse into my skin, as if it were never there. I wait for it to reappear, but when it doesn't, I stifle a shiver and let myself inside.

The house is dark and silent as I creep through, nearly tripping over an amorphous pile of shoes in the foyer. Mom and Toddy aren't great at laying down the law, and while I'm not a particularly tidy person, the hands-off approach works even worse with Grayson and Shadow. They're always leaving their stuff all over the house, and I'm always tripping over it.

I steady myself on the credenza against the wall, and my stomach twists and jerks low at the sight of the vase full of blue hydrangeas resting there. I wonder where Mom got them. After Dad died, she let the bush out front wither to nothing, and when the winter snow finally thawed, she yanked it up by the roots and left it down on the curb with the trash.

The sight of it, for some reason, had started to make me sick to my stomach; sometimes when I saw it, I forgot how to breathe. For ten years Mom made sure there were never hydrangeas in the house.

I push the vase behind the only framed picture that sits there: one of Mom and me—I'm just a toddler—both of us perched in Dad's lap in the yard, wearing crowns of weeds we made together.

An ache begins behind my heart and spreads through my chest like roots.

People used to ask if it bugged me how quickly Mom and Toddy got together. I'd tell them it bugged me more when people didn't mind their own business. Those who didn't *really* know Dad would balk; those who did would laugh.

The general consensus in Five Fingers seemed to be that Mom married Toddy because she was helpless without Dad, because he didn't have life insurance and she didn't want to work or know how to fix the toilet when the tank wouldn't stop running. Because she was too pretty to be alone. All these arguments I now understand to be Midwestern ways of shrugging and saying, *She's French.*

For as long as I can remember, my friends' parents have regarded Mom with a mix of intrigue and wariness. But if they assume she doesn't know how to work hard, it's only because she makes work look easy. Earthy and romantic.

She won't wash a dish unless the lather of the soap will please her hands at that moment. She doesn't bake a pie unless she can delight in rolling the dough, in using flour-covered hands to brush the sweat off her forehead, in pressing the crust's lip with perfect dessert-fork indents. She can turn something as strenuous as toiling in the garden into an almost euphoric ritual.

But she also regularly gets massages, visits gourmet shops to buy tiny blocks of herbed cheeses that cost the same as oversized bags of shredded cheddar, and has her favorite perfume shipped to her from Europe.

In Five Fingers, shoe-stealing coywolves are less of a mystery than she is. But she always says that what she loved best about Dad was that, to him, she wasn't a mystery at all.

I sometimes think that's also what drew her to Toddy. He's stable and predictable. Kind. Plus he and Dad knew each other all their lives.

I think Mom married Todd Kemper because they understood one another and what they had lost. They fell in love while they held each other in the wake of that loss, and, together, in the bitter work of staying upright while their hearts broke, they found something sweet.

He'll never be Dad. And, *yes*, sometimes that bothers me. But with Toddy, there's no pressure to strip, bleach, or scrape Dad from the walls. He's in the floral wallpaper that lines the kitchen and the deep grooves in the mudroom's hardwood floor, where we stomped around in ice skates. With Toddy, it's okay to keep all the old pictures on the walls, to leave the albums set out in the wicker basket by the massive television he brought when he moved in. It wasn't even a question that Mom would keep wearing that first, jewel-less wedding band on her ring finger, beneath the one with the large princess-cut diamond that Toddy added.

He gave me a ring at the ceremony too. It was beautiful— peridot and two side diamonds—but I couldn't bring myself to love it like the fifty-cent spider necklace Dad got me from the quarter machine at Camponelli's Pizza.

My eyes trail away from the photograph but carefully avoid the hydrangeas as I turn up the creaky staircase. I reach the end of the hallway and ease open my door but then come up short.

My room should be dark, but it's not. Should be empty and silent, but it's not.

Wave after wave of this paralyzing shock crashes over me, but no matter how many times I blink, nothing changes.

The lamp beside the bed casts a shallow pool of golden light across the worn pink-and-blue quilt, the little dark-haired girl tucked into it, and the gap-toothed man sitting at her feet.

I'm looking at myself. I'm looking at Dad.

Eight

"DAD," I choke, but there's no sound. I try again, feel the vibrations in my throat, the movement of my tongue and lips, but still no sound.

"Tell me another one," the little girl—*me*—says from the bed.

Dad scratches the strawberry scruff on his chin. "Another one, huh, June-bug?"

"When Great-Great-Great-Great-Grampa Jonathan found our hill."

Dad nudges the younger me aside and swings his booted feet up onto the bed as he stretches out beside her. "So how's it start again, Junior?"

"Jonathan set out looking for a place to call home."

I take a shaky step forward, and neither of them looks at me.

"So he did," Dad says. He wraps an arm around the girl's skinny shoulders and kisses the crown of her head. My eyes shut for a long moment before I force myself to open them again, to keep watching. "And he looked all down the East Coast, but it was too hot and sticky, and the water was too salty, and the hills were too hilly. And when he planted cherry trees, their roots wriggled and writhed in the dirt, and their branches withered, and when the cherries came, they tasted like tears, and not the good kind."

"Was he sad?" she asks.

"Nah. Jacks don't get sad, and we get that from him."

"Was he scared?"

"Do *Jacks* get scared, June-bug?"

"Was he lonely?"

"Jacks like a lot of alone time," Dad says. "They also love an adventure, and Jonathan Alroy O'Donnell had plenty of both. He knew he'd find the right place, and that's why he never settled down anywhere else, no matter how many friends he made and adventures he had in a single place. You know, the night of Annie Oakley's debut at the Baughman and Butler Shooting Show, Jonathan bought her a soda and they spent the whole night wandering Cincinnati together. By the time the sun came up, they'd caught a band of bank robbers on the Ohio River, planted a dozen cherry trees, and gotten engaged. But Jonathan was looking for a home, and the cherries didn't take to the Ohio soil, so in the end, they parted ways, and he went south to Florida—too hot and sticky for the cherries, of course—then out west, and you know what he found?"

The pink floral drapes billow like wisps of hair as a warm breeze pushes through the open window, carrying quarter-sized specks of ethereal white: Window Whites.

I remember this moment. It's coming back to me, as it happens.

"He found sand." It's not a guess—it's the answer Dad taught me. Every part of every story was a line in a play we performed hundreds of times. I'd nearly forgotten about that.

"Sand," Dad repeats. "So much sand and sunlight. The cherries he grew there, they lacked that first-snow-of-the-year tingle a good Jack's Tart always has. But Jonathan took advantage of being in California, even if his cherries didn't. Jacks—you know Jonathan was the *first* Jack—are good at getting things un-lost. The gold rush was winding down, so on his way north to Washington, Jonathan followed the Siskiyou Trail. But one day, as he waded in the Columbia River, he dropped a cherry pit in the water and it jumped back out like a snake had bit it.

"He saw a glint there, and when he brushed aside the river muck, he found a solid brick of gold. Most people would've thought, *A brick of gold? Nothing more valuable than that.* But Jonathan wasn't most people. He knew you couldn't eat a brick of gold or bake it into your favorite pie. You couldn't bite into it and taste the whole world in its juice. So you know what he did?"

The girl sits up, her tangle of waves splaying against the headboard. "He traded it for more pits," she says.

Dad leans forward, grinning. "That's right, June-bug."

Tears prick my eyes, and the world slants in too many directions. I don't understand how this is happening. How I can see him so clearly. He's *here*, and of all the impossible things that happen on our land, something like this never has.

Dad, I say, still voiceless, and move toward him. His eyes stay locked on the sleepy eight-year-old in the ratty CHERRYFEST

T-shirt. I study the wrinkle in his forehead, the uneven tan from always riding with his left side half out the car window.

"So he went up the coast," Dad goes on. "And when he got to Washington, he liked it. Don't get me wrong—he did like it. But still, the ocean was too dark, and it rained too much, and it lacked that Special Thing, that *home* thing."

"So he came to Michigan." I mouth the words, but it's not my voice I hear. Or it's *mine*, but a slimmer, scraggly, younger version.

Dad's eyes crinkle and take on a gloss. I don't remember that—I don't remember him on the verge of tears maybe ever, so how can I see it now?

"He came across the North, and by then it was winter, and he passed through all kinds of snowstorms and blizzards and over lakes made entirely of ice."

"And was he scared then?"

"No way, Junior!" Dad replies. "He was having the time of his life. He loved the wildness of it. But he couldn't stand the landlocked-ness. Minnesota was better—tons of water there—but it wasn't a perfect fit. So he went on through Wisconsin and Illinois and over the lake into Michigan. It was spring when he finally reached the tiny town of Five Fingers, between the Five Fingers offshoot of Torch Lake and Lake Michigan. The water was a beautiful turquoise—so clear you could see your hand through it—and the rocks and cliffs were all red and gold, like a sunset. The forests were thick and thriving, full of pure sunlight and cool shadows and tiny, fluttering things. The women were strong as sequoias but lovely as the northern lights, which you could see on a clear night, a great blanket of green and purple and blue spread across the sky.

"Most dirt's just dirt, but in Five Fingers, the dirt *sang*. It *coursed*. It wanted to make life. It beat like it had a heart, and Jonathan, he knew this was home right off the bat. So he trekked through the woods until he came to a grassy hill, and he climbed it to choose where he would plant his first tree. But do you know what he found at the top of that hill?"

"A coyote."

"That's right." Dad nods. "And what else?"

"And a wolf."

"And?"

"A robin."

"Sleeping on the wolf's haunch," Dad finishes. "My great-great-great-grandfather knew right then that he'd stumbled into a thin place, a plot of land where, on a sunny day or a starlit night, you might get a glance at heaven. And he tore up a bit of earth and packed a cherry pit down nice and neat, and right there, he sat and watched the first tree grow before his eyes. By morning, the grass was covered in dew, and the boughs were heavy with plump cherries, and when he bit into the glossy skin, his eyes teared up. *Home*, he said, *it tastes like home*. And it was."

"I love that story," the little girl says.

I love that story.

"Someday I'm gonna write it down," Dad murmurs. "I'm gonna write down all my stories for you, June-bug, so you can know just where you came from." He rustles her hair and kisses her head again, and then my tears blur the scene.

You didn't *write them down*, I want to say. They're already lost, shadows flitting across my memory. *You're lost.*

And yet there he is, just out of reach. Real and impossible.

"Night, Junior." Dad stands to go. He ticks the lamp off and strides right past me, like I'm invisible, a ghost.

I chase him. "Dad," I beg. "Dad! Please."

He doesn't hear, and by the time I reach the hallway, it's dark, empty, as if he were never there.

Something tickles against my palm. I gasp and jump as the white tuft emerges from my lifeline, hovers for just a moment, then drifts toward the stairs.

I follow it, chase *him*—wherever he went.

He's dead, I think, *his trillions of cells sprinkled in Lake Michigan, and that little girl back there hasn't existed in ten years.* But still I'm running down the steps, searching for him, dodging the pile of shoes at the bottom, though it's unnecessary because, somehow, all those shoes have vanished.

I don't understand.

Why is this happening?

Why did I see him, and why is he gone again so soon?

I spin uselessly, tear through the dark kitchen. Dining room. Living room. The sunroom off the side of the house, its windows overlooking the hill and woods and stars. I find nothing. No one.

I barrel back up to my bedroom.

The lamp's off. The window's shut, the Whites gone. I'm alone.

But he *was* here.

At least I think he was.

Nine

"HAPPY Wednesday! Happy first day of senior year," Hannah sings down the hallway as she literally prances toward me. Her hair is slicked into an alarmingly neat fishtail braid that, combined with her gingham dress, makes her look like she should be running through a field of daisies, arms spread wide to catch the sun.

I swing my locker shut and kiss my fingers to greet hers. "You glorious sunburst of a person, did the birds dress you this morning?"

"Basically!"

It's been four days since I saw Dad in my bedroom, and, unable to bring myself to tell Mom what happened, I called Hannah immediately. After days of texting her feverishly during every break she took from her AP summer homework, it's a relief to finally be with her in person.

She slumps against the forest green lockers and jogs her violin case up her shoulder. "P.S. *One* of those little birdies passed along a rumor that Saul's planning on sticking around for a while."

"Oh?" My stomach clenches, and I forget what people usually do with their hands. "I thought you two weren't speaking after your messy split."

"Relax," she says. "I'm not going down *that* rabbit hole again."

Relax? Who, me? The girl leaning against her locker with her thumbs hooked into her belt loops like the hard-ass female cop in a CBS crime thriller? I am the definition of relaxed.

"Nate told me," she adds. "He thinks the four of us should 'totally chill again soon.'"

A pulse of heat drops low in my stomach. "Oof."

She laughs. "That's essentially the reaction I expected."

"I just . . . sort of think . . . Nate likes you."

Her face twists into a mask of not-quite-repulsion. "Nate?"

"Mhm."

"Nate Baars?"

"Yep."

"Nate, who walks like he's auditioning for the role of Cop Number Three?"

"The very same, Han." I rearrange my books in my arms, thinnest to thickest.

"Oof." Hannah tips her head back against the locker. "Maybe you're wrong."

"Maybe." I don't mention that Saul told me so. It'd be too hard to reference our private conversation on the Ferris wheel without broadcasting across my forehead: I HAVE A CRUSH ON

MY SWORN ENEMY SLASH THE (EX-?) BOY OF YOUR DREAMS. "Hey," I say, fumbling over a binder in my locker, "did you ever find out why Saul's back, anyway?"

Hannah scrunches up her mouth. "Nope. Just that he's here for the foreseeable future."

"I thought you would've done some expert digging by now."

"I know—a decade of Saulitis cured in one fateful night. Seeing him as the tragically beautiful stick-in-the-mud he really is freed me up to spend the last three days finishing my AP summer reading."

"Speaking of which, why haven't I seen you all day? Do they keep smart people in a separate wing now?"

Hannah's top lip curls. "Practically. If I have to sit next to Stephen Niequist in one more class, I'll freak. He's gunning for my salutatorian slot."

"Maybe you should flash him some boob, throw him off."

"Stephen Niequist is not into boob."

"Ah, see, I didn't know that, because they keep us simpletons in a separate pen."

"Oh please. You're in the simpleton pen by choice."

"Your misplaced confidence in me is charming, Han."

"And the fact that you won't even *apply* for the same schools as me is decidedly not."

"I'm not *going* to college," I remind her. I'm as incapable as I am uninterested. Instead I'm going to do what Dad and his dad and his dad's dad did: travel, see the world, rest up in Five Fingers, repeat.

"Anyway," Hannah says, "this doesn't matter in the scheme of things right now. How are you doing? Did any more of the"—she glances around furtively, then lowers her voice—"*you-know-what*s happen?"

I sink my teeth into my lip, fighting the drop in my chest. I know she's trying to help, but right now I almost regret telling her about what happened.

The weight of loss is so familiar to me by now that I've become a master at misdirecting myself: pinching my hand, biting my lip, grinding the heel of my shoe into the top of my other foot—any physical sensation to distract from the nonphysical pain.

I don't want to talk about this.

"No, no more hallucinations of my dead father," I murmur.

She squeezes my arm apologetically. She's sorry it happened in the first place. *I'm* sorry it hasn't happened again since.

"What class do you have next?" she asks, expertly steering me from the grief ledge.

"Creative writing."

"Hey, good for you, taking an elective instead of a study hall."

"I already have two study halls this semester. They wouldn't let me take any more."

Hannah laughs as the warning bell rings. "That's it, babe. Aim for the stars. I'll see you later."

"Probably not," I call after her. "Unless—wait, are you in my seventh-period *Would you like fries with that?*"

"Ha. Ha. Ha."

I straighten my books again and turn toward 204, the classroom listed on the schedule taped to my binder. Creative writing is always held in the same space: a cozy offshoot of the library's second floor with three walls and a ceiling comprising mostly windows. Originally, it was a greenhouse where some of the science classes would go for site-specific lessons, but most of the time it was basically treated as a vitamin D–rich alternative to the official teacher's lounge.

In Michigan, especially this far north, you take all the sunlight you can get, no matter the temperature outside. *If you wait for warmth to enjoy the outdoors*, Dad used to say, *the sun might die before you get there.*

It's almost funny, in a tragic way, that the fiery thing at the center of my universe did die and that I, a girl whose name is synonymous with summer, am expected to live without it.

A handful of kids are already seated in the blue Herman Miller scoop chairs lining the rectangular arrangement of tables. I take an open spot along the wall so I can look out the window at the pine trees beyond, though it will probably mean squinting into the sun most days. I recognize a few kids, most notably *the* Stephen Niequest, who plops down immediately to my left and opens a calculus textbook for some light reading until the bell rings and the final stragglers hurry in.

Everyone knows this class is pretty much a blow-off elective, taken by seniors like me who can't have a third study hall, but usually in classes like these, teachers still hand out detentions for tardiness—since, like, what else are you even getting graded on? Mrs. Strand is no exception, but, ironically, the moth-eaten woman isn't here yet.

Other kids have started to murmur about it when a girl at the head of the table formation rises from her seat and claps once.

"Hello, class." She rubs her manicured hands together, as if she's trying to start a fire. "I'm Ms. deGeest, and I'll be teaching creative writing this semester."

Everyone looks around at one another, and if I had to guess, it's because "Ms. deGeest" looks like sixteen-year-old Alicia Silverstone in *Clueless*.

"Are you kidding?" Drew Goodall calls from the back.

Ms. deGeest purses her lips and checks her student roster. "No, Andrew. Our satire unit's not for a few weeks. I'm here because Mrs. Strand retired, and I was thrilled to get the opportunity to work with all of you."

That elicits some chuckles, mostly from the group of boys surrounding Drew, who murmur variations of *Can't wait to work you either, baby*.

Her eyes blaze a trail across the corner the catcalls came from. She makes a swift gesture, like she's bisecting them with the edge of her hand. "You three. Office."

The boys exchange confounded looks. "Seriously?"

"Make sure to memorize some of your classmates' faces. You'll need to get today's assignment from someone later so that you'll be ready tomorrow." She doesn't seem mad, just calm, her tone deadpan. It has to be an act—the Tough Guy persona they teach any Dallas Cowboys cheerleader who decides to go into education.

Drew and his friends volley a few unsure looks back and forth as they pick up their books and mosey toward the door. "Close the door on your way out," Ms. deGeest says almost sweetly.

She has performed her first miracle: They obey. She faces the rest of us and claps once enthusiastically, and it's like the whole thing never happened.

"Narrative," she says. "All writing contains it. Even research papers have some semblance of story in them—conflict, resolution, specific evidence to build a thesis. A persuasive essay comes together through rhetoric, the tricks you use to *suggest* a narrative or outright portray one." She selects a marker from the shelf beneath the board and quickly scribbles, *For sale: baby shoes, never worn.* "Anyone recognize this quote?"

"Hemingway," Stephen says.

"Possibly," deGeest answers. "That's the legend, at least. Arthur C. Clarke, Ernest Hemingway, and John Robert Colombo were sitting around a table, eating lunch one day, when Hemingway bet them each a dollar that he could write a story in six words. When the money was on the table, he grabbed a napkin and wrote this line on it. Allegedly. But there had been a similar story in a 1910 edition of the *Spokane Press.* The week before there'd been an ad for a handmade baby bed and trousseau that had never been used. The *Spokane* piece homed in on the sadness of that statement, all the possibilities for why such an ad might exist.

"Today we're going to talk about story, and tonight you're going to write your own piece of flash fiction. Yours, however, will be one to five pages rather than six words."

A groan travels throughout the room. It's unanimous, an aural wave, until it reaches Stephen, who I suspect somehow already knew about the change in plans for this semester's creative writing class. His owl-like hazel eyes are fixed on the middle distance, and I can practically see the dozens of ideas skating over them.

I don't find myself disappointed about the homework either,

though unlike Stephen I have no slew of concepts barraging my beautiful near-salutatorian brain. I have exactly one idea, exactly one story I want to write down: Dad's.

That night, after dinner—and after the handful of minutes I spent staring into my room from the hallway, trying to summon my vision or hallucination or strangely vivid memory from last weekend—I sit at the kitchen table and start on my story.

Grayson and Shadow sprint circles around the downstairs, attacking each other with Nerf guns, and Mom and Toddy lie snuggled up on the couch, sipping wine and flirting in French.

French is Mom's first language, but Dad never learned it, and so I didn't either. I have all the touristy stuff down—*Où sont les toilettes? Je veux aller à la plage. Donnez-moi tout ce que vous avez*—but don't have a firm enough grasp on the language to have full conversations. Sometimes it makes me mad that Dad didn't learn, that they didn't teach me. Mostly when Grayson or Shadow is screaming, *À moi! T'as perdu!* (I win! You lose!) at the end of a wrestling match or particularly bloody round of video games.

Toddy, who's about as different from Dad as two friends could be, studied French in college and brushed up on it when he and Mom started dating. Sometimes they'll pass through the room and stop to muss the boys' hair, telling them to *rangez votre chambre* (clean your room). They'll share a quick back and forth beyond that, but it's lost on me.

It's not that I feel excluded, exactly. It's more like I thought that Mom's life with Dad and me was supposed to be the better one.

Like when we lost him, no one could possibly replace him or what he meant to us. And no one *could*, and Mom and Toddy both made sure I understood that.

But as I sit at the timeworn table beneath the pendant lamps Toddy installed, watching my half brothers, powered by sugar, surge through the house and hearing my parents laughing into each other's necks and speaking a language I don't understand, I can't help but feel like Mom's life wasn't supposed to be this good without Dad. Like things should be noticeably worse, and in a lot of ways, they're not. And it feels . . . *wrong*.

I know Dad would want Mom to be happy, for Toddy to take care of us. I've understood that since I was a kid, and their happy life hasn't made me hurt this way in a long a time. Reliving that memory four nights ago has left me feeling like I *just* lost him all over again. And *that* makes me feel like none of us should be happy right now.

All the good things in the world shouldn't make up for the best thing we had but lost.

But if I write down the things he told me, if I tell his stories and hold on to his memories, maybe it's not too late to capture some small part of Dad.

Mom glides in from the living room, carrying her and Toddy's empty wine glasses. She stops just in time for stocky Grayson to pound past her and into the hallway, followed by lanky Shadow, whose footsteps sound like snowfall by comparison—that's the way he got his nickname, actually, his impressive quietness. Poor Grayson's the only one of us without one, but then again, he got a pretty normal legal name, whereas I got a man's, and for some reason

Shadow got "Eustace." I think shortly after they filled out the birth certificate, Mom realized that "Eustace" sounds like Crayola code for "vomit," and he was such a quiet baby that he became Shadow.

"Whatcha working on, June?" Mom asks, leaning over me.

"Hoooomework," I say.

"Hoooomework," Toddy calls from the couch. "Those jerks gave you homework on the first day, Junie?"

"Yeah, will you sue?"

"Course we will, honey."

"Thanks."

"I think it's good you're being challenged," Mom says, setting the glasses in the blue-tiled sink Dad installed for her while he was between jobs. "It'll prepare you for medical school."

I snort, and she shoots me a disapproving glare. "Mom. What am I going to do at medical school? Like, is this homework going to prepare me to be the long-winded janitor there?"

She exhales and dodges the boys again to come sit at the table with me. "Baby, we can send you anywhere. You can do anything."

"Anywhere?" I gasp. "Anything?"

"Dental school," Toddy chimes in.

"Dentistry's a great business." Mom squeezes my hand in hers. I wonder if she and Ms. deGeest get their nails done at the same salon. "Toddy loves it, don't you?"

"Yep." He turns off the TV, stretches his arms over his head, and shuffles through the kitchen, stopping to kiss me on the head. "Night, Junior."

"No one loves dentistry," I mumble.

"They love the paycheck." He plants a kiss on Mom's cheek and ambles toward the stairs. "They love the hours, the vacation, and the fact that the worst news you have to deliver is that someone needs a root canal. What else is there to love?"

"What about gum cancer?" I ask. He waves me off.

Mom smiles at him like he's giving his first presidential address, then shoots me another semi-worried look and squeezes my hand again. "He's right, baby. Even if you didn't love college, who knows? Maybe you'd meet someone. Dentists really do have way better hours than other kinds of physicians—and less baggage too."

"Great, Mom. I'll keep that in mind. When I'm hitchhiking through Texas, I'll think fondly of the dentist I could have married had I gone to college."

She smiles, but it's a sad one. For a moment the veil of perfect contentedness slips from her face and I see her heartbreak all over again, just the way it looked back in the days right after Dad died, when I was binging on comfort cereal and Easy Mac and she was eating nothing at all.

"I had dreams, you know," she says softly, pushing her chair back to stand. She kisses me exactly where Toddy did. "I had them, and I waited too long to chase them."

She turns and sweeps toward the hall, clearing her throat. "Boys! Bedtime!"

They groan and whine, but Toddy claps his hands three times in this faux-authoritative manner at the bottom of the stairs, and they run past Mom and pound up the steps. He's always backing Mom up like this, the opposite of how Dad's smile and quiet refusal to be reined in for the night would draw her out onto the grass to stare up at the stars. Tonight, the discrepancy grates at me.

I love Toddy, but I'm not like him. I'm not a sensible dentist in the making. I'm like Dad—*hungry*, he would say. *So hungry you want to taste the sun and lap up the lake.*

I'd never thought of Mom as *hungry*, but as I watch my family retreat down the hall, I wonder what she meant. *I had dreams.*

To me, her story has always felt like Jonathan Alroy O'Donnell's: a part of some distant tapestry of fact turned legend. She moved to the states from her tiny hometown in France when she was sixteen to study ballet at Joffrey, and at eighteen she took a job with a professional company in Miami. There, she met Dad on one of his trips, when he walked into the bar where she waitressed part-time.

Jacks, according to lore, do *not* dance. And apart from the occasional waltz or twirl in the kitchen with Toddy, Mom doesn't either. I asked her once, when I was small, why she stopped. She just looked at me, smiled, and said, *With your daddy, life is the dance.*

Thinking about it now, I wonder if her dream was simply to dance, or if it was just to have the life she thought she'd signed up for, the one that was torn down the middle ten years ago. Either way, I feel sick for having thought she wasn't sad enough about Dad. She's in love, she's married, but her heart will always be a little bit broken, and there's nothing she can do about it.

Toddy intercepts Mom again on the bottom step at the end of the hall, and his voice drops into a whisper I strain to hear: ". . . know the Angert kid's back?"

She glances my way, and I feign concentration on my laptop.

I catch only one word from her mouth as they turn and climb the stairs together: *"Trouble."*

I quell the guilt burning up my stomach and focus on the

blinking cursor on my screen. I close my eyes and let my mind drift away from Saul. I try instead to remember the story of how Jonathan Alroy O'Donnell discovered our hill, our heavenly slice of thin space. Then I let it all pour out of me, gushing like it can't escape quickly enough.

When I look up from my work, it's one A.M. All is silent, all is still, apart from the chirp of crickets and the moths dancing around the pendant lamp, grazing my hair and shoulders. At some point, the sheen of pink appeared against the wall across from me.

Feathers flutters softly. She watches me.

Ten

MS. DEGEEST cuts a slow trail around the table formation as she passes back our first assignment. She's dressed in all black and gray: black shoes, gray skirt, black blouse, gray blazer, black earrings. She's more formal than most teachers, in both dress and attitude, probably another attempt to look old enough to work here.

At lunch yesterday, the first words out of Hannah's mouth were, "Tell me everything about creative writing, and don't leave anything out." Halfway through my rundown of what we'd read and written so far, she groaned and dropped her forehead against the table. "I can't believe Stephen Niequest got to take that class and I'm in AP U.S. history that period. God, I'd better get into it next semester."

"You realize it's not AP, right?" I pointed out.

"Doesn't matter. Colleges love well-roundedness."

"You literally told me the exact opposite of that last year."

"That was last year. Last year colleges wanted niche students, people with an intense focus on one itty-bitty thing. That's why I spent all freaking year volunteering with the music branch of the Arts Council. *Now* they want well-roundedness."

"Who tells you these things?" I asked. "Is this information dispersed telepathically to all you freaks? Do the thoughts just appear in your head with a little purple signature from Dawn at the Harvard admissions office?"

"Something like that," Hannah said, then went back to smacking her head on the table.

I didn't and don't care about well-roundedness, but something about writing down Dad's story two nights ago got to me. The work felt almost sacred, like one still, perfect instant of clarity and purpose—jumping from a cliff into the turquoise water of Torch Lake or the icy blue of Lake Michigan—that stretched across the many silent hours I spent hunched over the kitchen table.

Just like the memory or hallucination or *whatever* that spurred it, I haven't been able to stop thinking about the story that spilled out of me.

Ms. deGeest pauses in front of Stephen and me, first setting our stories facedown on the table.

"Great work on your first assignments," she says. "I was truly impressed. There's a lot of potential in this room, and it was evident you put a lot of thought into these flash fiction pieces. These grades, however, won't be counted toward your final grade. This is merely a marker for you, so you have an idea of what to expect from me as a teacher and what I expect from you in order to earn an A."

She's still rambling about work ethic and progress and the

importance of honest criticism when I catch Stephen positively beaming at the red and emphatically circled B+ on the front of his story. I slide my own story off the table.

My heart plummets into my stomach at the sight of the D+ scrawled over the entire first paragraph. I fight back tears and then feel so embarrassed that I have to fight back a *second* wave and basically spend the rest of class as an emotional pendulum swinging between humiliation and anger. As soon as the bell rings, I break for the door and hurry to my locker.

I've never been this upset by a grade. It's possible I've never been upset by any grade, *period*. I've known all along that I want to travel after graduation, then come back to Five Fingers, like all Jacks do, and a plan like that limits my college options to approximately zero.

But this isn't about college apps or career paths.

I loved that story. And either I butchered it or Ms. deGeest flat out hated it. Either way, it feels like I'm failing Dad—desecrating the only part of him I have left. That I'm not worthy of that memory, or hallucination, in which he held my hand in his and I felt his skin and breath and love.

"Hi," Hannah chirps, appearing beside me in a blur of blond.

"Hi." I don't look up from riffling through my locker for my backpack.

"What's wrong?"

"Bad grade."

Her eyebrows pucker together. "I'm so sorry, June." After a second, she shakes her head. "Wait, why do you care?"

"I don't wanna talk about it."

She lifts her hands, one of which is clutching the handle of her violin case. "Fine, totally understandable."

"Thanks."

She studies me. "You know what you need?"

"Bourbon."

"Girls' Night."

"Hallelujah."

"Yes?" she confirms.

"Very yes."

"Girls' Night it is."

Except it's not. At least not for long.

It's Girls' Night when we get to Hannah's neighborhood, a series of rustic lodges surrounded by a gorgeous mix of evergreen, and eat spaghetti with Mrs. Kuiper, who, rather than returning to "Miss Sowerbutts" kept her married name even after Hannah's dad left her for his pregnant mistress. It's Girls' Night when Han and I lie on our stomachs, flipping through the newest *Rookie* yearbook and laughing over flirting tips in her mom's old magazines ("Wear your underwear as a hair band!" "Be entirely naked!").

It's even Girls' Night on the drive to the movie theater and the blissfully ignorant walk from the parking lot to the lobby.

But that's where Girls' Night ends: in the popcorn-scented lobby of the Cineplex, with Nate Baars shouting, "Laaaaaaadies!" into his cupped hands and Saul standing next to him, looking a little horrified and a little amused.

At that point, Girls' Night crashes headlong into a four-way not-a-date in which no two people are in agreement over which couple they're not part of.

I look to Hannah accusatorily. Her face is pale, eyes wide as she waves back to Nate sheepishly.

"Are you serious, Hannah?" I demand.

Her eyes dart to mine, and she mumbles like a ventriloquist, "I swear I had no idea. Nate and I were texting, and—"

"Since when do you and Nate Baars *text*?"

"I told him we were going to the movies. He said, *See you there*, but I thought he was kidding!"

"Why?" I hiss. "*Why* would you think that was a joke?"

"I don't know—he used a winky face!" she whispers, teeth still gritted. "What do we do?"

"Leave?" Even as I say it, an itch of curiosity coils under my breastbone.

"Are you kidding?" she cries. "That's so awkward! They think we're meeting them here. Intentionally. We can't *leave*."

As I glance across the lobby toward Saul, that curiosity spirals up through me like a charmed snake. It's just a movie. Saul and I won't talk; we'll sit in silence and then part ways.

"You owe me," I say under my breath, then start across the planet-spangled carpet toward the boys.

"Add it to my tab," she says.

"*Finally*," Nate says when we reach them. He seems completely unconcerned about the forty-five seconds Hannah and I spent whisper-arguing on the far side of the lobby, and he folds over each of us in a hug. His arms are particularly linger-y with Hannah, but she must be in a good mood, because she doesn't shake him off. "Glad you girls could make it."

To our own Girls' Night? Same.

"Hi, Nate," I manage, which is a downright cheery greeting compared to Saul's single nod toward us. "Saul," I say in return. "My mortal enemy, good to see you in fine health. Frankly, I thought my voodoo doll would've been more effective."

He smiles, and I anticipate then physically *feel* the cusp of his gritty laugh rise then slip back down his throat, and a tiny and hopefully nonessential piece of my heart flakes off.

Nate laugh-barks. "You're so freakin' weird, O'Donnell. Love it."

I shoot Hannah a stare like a steak knife. "What can I say? I'm not like other girls. I've literally never eaten a salad in my life."

This time The Laugh surfaces, and my face heats. I can't look at Saul, so I look at Nate, who's nodding. "Really? Wild."

Hannah gifts him with an encouraging smile and saddles me with a pleading look.

Okay, technically speaking, Nate Baars is hot. He's an olive-skinned, espresso-haired stack of muscle who surfs in summer, snowboards in winter, and rock climbs year-round. But at this point, my brain replaces the sight of him with a giant, slobbering golden retriever.

"I want to be drunk," I accidentally say aloud to myself.

"Anyway," Hannah interrupts before this not-date can get any worse. "What are we seeing?"

Saul juts his chin toward the banner hanging over us. *"The Axe Murderer on Thirteenth Street."* He could not look any smugger that this is his first contribution to our conversation. I try to imagine that he has baby-soft hands and smells like Axe Body Spray and that his favorite food is mayonnaise, because otherwise he's so, so charming to me right now I want to die.

"Great," I say, heading to the counter. "Can't wait."

"Don't have to." Nate brandishes a strand of four red tickets. "You think we gentlemen would let you girls buy your own tickets?"

Saul stares at the floor, and I know he did not pay for a single one of those tickets.

"Great," Hannah says quietly, reverting to the timidity of the first hour and a half we spent with Saul at the carnival.

We file into the theater along the back row. Somehow Nate manages to corral Hannah between him and Saul, making the final seating arrangement Nate, Hannah, Saul, me. The lights dim and previews begin.

Saul leans over and whispers, "You didn't know you were meeting us here, did you?"

In the cool dark of the theater, his voice rushes over my skin like a creek full of cattails. "Long story. It involves a misinterpreted winky face."

"Oh, naturally." He straightens up, but a second later, he leans over again. "You wouldn't have come if you'd known?"

"I . . ." . . . have no idea what to say. "Don't know."

"Because I'm an Angert?"

I stifle a laugh, not wanting to draw attention to us. "No." *At least not entirely.* Part of me feels guiltier than ever for being here after seeing, or imagining, Dad; another part wonders if

81

this—disobeying him—is the way to trigger another moment like that again. I lift my backpack off the floor and sneak a swig from the flask.

"I drive you to drink," Saul whispers.

"Well, yeah, but that's not because you're an Angert."

"Is it because I chose this shitty movie?"

"You chose this?"

"I also wasn't thrilled about coming tonight." He lifts his feet up to rest on the back of the seat in front of us.

"Because I'm an O'Donnell?"

"Yes," he pans. I narrow my eyes, but he doesn't break into a smile for a full five seconds. "Because it's a little pathetic to drop out of school, move home, and start hanging out with your younger cousin's friends all the time—don't you think?"

"Sorry, I have no idea what you just said," I say. "I don't speak Baby Boomer."

"Hilarious, Junior."

"Hey."

His eyes snap to mine, and in the dark, they look almost black. "Huh?"

"I don't think it's pathetic," I whisper. "I mean, I have abnormally high self-esteem, so take this for what it's worth, but I don't think it's pathetic for you to hang out with us."

He's quiet for a second. "I never said *you*, by the way."

"What?"

"I didn't say it was pathetic to hang out with *you*."

I feel myself smiling like an idiot, but the slow burn of the whiskey takes the edge off my embarrassment. "Shh. I think the worst movie of all time is starting."

He trains his eyes on the screen. His Adam's apple shifts as he swallows. I do everything I can to make his words stop replaying in my mind. It's not enough.

I never said you, *by the way. I didn't say it was pathetic to hang out with* you.

Eleven

"WHAT'D you think?" Hannah asks Saul as we stream out of the theater. I try to hang back with Nate, but he keeps pace alongside them, so basically I'm just walking behind the group.

"It was probably in the top three worst movies I've ever seen," he answers. His eyes flash back to me, and he slows, as if to let me catch up.

I slow too, and he must notice, because he stops trying to lessen the gap between us and devotes his full attention to Hannah.

"God, it was *horrible*," she says. She sounds relieved to get that opinion off her chest. She eyes Nate accusatorially. "Why the hell did we go see that?"

Nate shrugs sheepishly. "Sorry."

"I chose it." Saul itches his collarbone, and I'm 60 percent sure he catches me zoned out on him, remembering plowing into him in the House of Mirrors. "My fault. I have famously bad taste in movies."

"I don't believe that," Hannah says. "When we were kids, you were always watching Hitchcock and Coppola and Stanley Kubrick. You were super into that stuff."

Saul's mouth opens a fraction of an inch, then closes. His ears turn pink, his chin and eyes dipping toward the floor. I'm *watching* him realize what's going on here, that the neighbor girl who barely spoke to him was silently spending her childhood gathering these details.

"Yeah, you're right. I was." Saul looks back up, all signs of embarrassment wiped clean from his face. "I was super into that stuff back then, but . . . I don't know, I'm kind of over art."

Nate laughs and slaps Saul's shoulder. "Totally, dude."

Hannah looks dumbstruck. Understandable, since the phrase *I'm kind of over art* is both striking *and* dumb. "Hey," Nate says, "we should all drive out to the falls tonight, take a night swim and rinse off the stink of that movie."

"That sounds awesome," Hannah recovers. "I'm in."

"I have to get home," Saul says, at the exact same time I say, "I can't."

Of course I've always been curious about the falls. They're a Five Fingers point of pride, famous for their preternaturally warm water. But I'm already breaking one of my parents' two rules, and in my house, going to the falls has always been treated as just as dangerous as walking through alleys alone in the dark or crossing a highway while wearing a blindfold.

"Bummer," Nate says. "Next time."

"No, you guys go on," Saul says, tipping his head toward Nate and Hannah.

"Hannah and I rode together," I point out.

"No problem," Saul says. "I can take you home. I'm staying with my dad at our old cabin. It's, like, two miles from your house. Nate can ride home with Hannah, right?"

"Hannah might not even want to go to the cliffs," I say. "Why don't you take her home and Nate can take me home?"

"In what universe does that make sense?" Nate laughs. "I didn't even bring a car. Saul drove, and Han drove you."

My mind scrambles for a way to rescue Hannah and finds nothing. I look toward her helplessly, but she's focused on Nate. "Sure," she says brightly. "I can take Nate home after the falls, and Saul can run June home. If that's okay?"

She meets my gaze, and the apples of her cheeks turn Jack's Tart pink.

Nate's face lights up. "Okay," he says. "Right on."

"Okay," Hannah repeats, face still reddening. I try to meet her eyes, to silently ask, *Is it really okay?* But she's actively avoiding my gaze and focused instead on Nate.

Oh my God. A slim but distinct new possibility blooms in my mind. Maybe Hannah really is over Saul.

Nate and I were texting, she'd said casually when we arrived. She'd been *texting* Nate Baars.

"Okay," Saul says, looking toward me for final approval. My whole body feels warm and fizzy, like my heart just started pumping ginger beer through my veins.

Or maybe I just *want* to believe Hannah's into Nate. Maybe she's being optimistic and kind because Hannah *is* optimistic and kind.

"What say you, Junior?" Nate says. "Okay or nay?"

"Okay," I murmur.

"Okay!" Nate guffaws one last time and hooks an arm around Hannah's neck. "We're off to have an adventure while you two downers go home and journal."

"Let me know you get home safe, Han?" I shout after them.

"Yeah." She nods. And then they're out the doors, and I'm sure I've made a mistake. I'm alone with Saul Angert.

"Ready?" Saul asks.

"You shouldn't have done that."

"What?"

"Forced Hannah into hanging out with Nate," I fume.

"I didn't force anyone to do anything. Seems like she wanted to go."

"How was she supposed to say no, Saul?"

"That didn't bother you when *you* were trying to force *me* to hang out with Hannah."

"What?"

"'You take Hannah, Saul,'" he imitates. "'Nate will drive me home in the car he doesn't have to the house he doesn't live by!'"

"It's not the same thing."

His body shifts as he lets out a huff of laughter. "Oh? How's that, Junior?"

"Nate likes Hannah. *You* told me that."

"You're going to make me say this, aren't you?"

"Say what?" I demand.

"I can't hang out alone with a teenage girl who's been harboring a childhood crush on me for a decade. Is she even eighteen?"

"Okay, this just got weird," I say, holding up my hands. "Do you have some kind of criminal record? I mean, should *I* be alone with you?"

He tips his head back and rubs the crease in his forehead. "It's different with you."

"That 'not like other girls' thing was a joke, Saul. I love a good salad."

"It's different because you're not into me."

"How would you know who's into you and who's not? It took you ten years to figure out Hannah was!"

"Fine, you *could* be into me," he says, meeting my eyes. "But my cousin's not trying to date you—you're not going to put me in a weird situation."

It's like the voice is coming from someone else. Like someone else has taken over my body and I'm just a ghost floating outside it. "Again, how would you know?"

"Because your best friend likes me."

"It was a childhood crush," I say, lowering my voice. "And she's over it. I believe her exact words were *tragically beautiful stick-in-the-mud.*"

His smile spreads slowly until his laugh crackles out like burning charcoal. "I still couldn't take her home when she and I were the only two people who drove."

Looking at him, I feel sort of like a burgeoning lightning storm staring down at the temptation of the Eiffel Tower, promising not to touch it. "Sorry," I say.

He lifts one eyebrow. "Sorry?"

For having a crush on you.

For trying to make you take Hannah home.

For starting a fight in a space-themed movie theater.

"For biting your collarbone."

His smile is faint. "Come on, Jack. Let's get you home."

That's the best idea anyone's had all night. The lobby might be empty now, but soon a more heavily trafficked movie than *Axe Murderer* is bound to let out, and I don't need to be standing here with Saul Angert for all of Five Fingers to see.

We walk out into the hot night, and some of the tension between us dissipates as we cross the lot to a dumpy black Saturn. Things feel almost normal, friendly. "This is your car?"

"That impressed, huh?" he says. "Maybe I *should* start hanging out with high school girls."

"Not impressed, Saul. Mystified. Perhaps no one's told you: You live in northern Michigan. It's unsafe to drive a tin can up here."

He climbs in, but when I pull on the passenger door's handle, it's locked. "Sorry," he says, his voice muffled by the glass. "I can't in good faith let such precious cargo ride in my tin can. Too dangerous."

"Too dangerous for *you*, Saul," I say. "Jacks are hardy stock."

"Got it." He unlocks the door, and I get in. "Angerts: small, weakling babies. O'Donnells: muscular, demigod Michiganders."

His grin glows in the half light, and I can't help but smile too as the silence stretches out.

During the two hours we spent watching body parts and blood spurt across the screen, the sun has slunk low on the horizon. Its nose barely juts between the trees, and the moon already hangs in the rapidly deepening blue, stars poking through like pinpricks in a sheet of colored paper. As we pull away, Saul manually cranks his window down, which I take as permission to do the same.

The air is stiffer than it's been all week—summer's last cry before fall crushes it—and as we slice through the night, I feel like we're being enveloped in a fleece blanket fresh from the dryer. We're quiet for a while, the hazy sound of the suburbs fading behind us and night a deep, yawning indigo unfurling ahead.

The air pulls my hair from behind my ears and whips it around, tickles me to the point that a laugh slips out, and when I glance at Saul, he's watching me, one corner of his mouth quirked. "I like having you around, Jack," he says over the snap of wind, and I grin like the maniac I'm quickly becoming.

"Why'd you come back?" I ask.

He looks my way again, takes a deep breath, slowly exhales. "My dad's sick."

"Oh," I say. "God, I'm sorry. Is it . . . ?" I trail off, thinking of Bekah.

"Cancer?" He shakes his head. "Alzheimer's. Runs in my family, but with him, it's happening fast, or—I don't know—maybe it's been happening for years. His agent just told me. If I waited any longer, I might've lost my last chance for him to recognize me."

"I'm sorry," I say weakly. It's not enough. That's what I learned from losing Dad: There are no right words. There's nothing another human being can say that makes it better or eases the pain. *Sorry* is a white flag, an *I can't help you.*

"Yeah." Saul swallows. His fingers tighten over the steering wheel. "We were never close. My sister was his pride. But."

"Still," I say.

"Still."

"I know another *sorry*'s nothing," I say. "I'd give you something better than that if I had it."

"I'd give it back," he says. "You know what they say about Angerts and O'Donnells. Your violent blow from the universe might be right around the corner, and then I'll have nothing to give you either."

"I think mine's already come for me," I murmur toward the glass, then turn to speak to him directly. "I thought you didn't believe in that."

I also thought *I did*, but would I really have gotten in the car with him if that were true? I glance at the windshield, almost expecting a tornado or out-of-control semi to come shrieking toward us, but we're alone on the road, slinking through a peace-fully swaying copse of trees.

"Old habits," Saul answers. "Or, I don't know, maybe it's being back here. It's like nothing ever changes."

"Some things do."

His mouth curls up, and his eyes flash between the road and me. "Some things do."

"You're making it hard to hate you," I tell him.

"All part of my evil plan."

"Did you hate leaving school?"

"Nah," he says. "That was the easiest part of all this."

"You know, I had a brief career as a writer."

"Oh yeah? How'd that go?"

"Quickly. Jacks are more doers than thinkers. I got a D on my first assignment and haven't touched the second."

Without a moment of pause, he says, "Do you want help?"

"Are you offering to take out a hit on my teacher?"

"Yes," he says. "And to tutor you."

"Oof. *Hi, Mom, here's my new tutor. He's the tattooed twenty-one-year-old dropout formally known as Saul, the youngest living member of Dad's least favorite family.*"

"Twenty," he says.

"What?"

"You said twenty-one. I'm twenty."

I swallow the knot of heat in my throat. "Twenty. Okay, yeah, I think she'll *totally* go for it."

Saul nods in time with the yellow lines shooting past our car. "Okay, remember how you were definitely *not* going to put me in a weird situation or turn me into a creep?"

"Fifteen minutes ago? Vaguely."

"What if we don't tell your mom who I am? How would she know I'm an Angert? I haven't been here in years, and hardly anyone knows I'm back. How would you and I have even met?"

"In a mirror maze, Saul! That's the first place she'll guess!"

He laughs: husky, warm. "Good point. Look, I'm not telling you to lie to your parents. But if you want help, I'll help you. Even if that includes lying to your parents."

"Your resolve against being put in a weird situation sure lasted long."

"I'd do anything for the written word, Jack."

"Really?" I lean over the middle console and rest my chin on my hand. "'Cause I'm kind of *over art*."

"Whoa, whoa, whoa!" He pushes my face away with his hand. "Low blow, Junior."

At the sound of my name, whole forests grow from saplings into moonlit redwoods beneath my collarbones. I can't wait for this feeling to stop, so I can be on Dad's side like I always have been.

But I also never want this feeling to stop.

"You wanna do something fun?" he asks.

I study his profile. "Such as?"

He flips on his blinker and follows the corkscrew road toward the street lined with million-dollar vacation homes overlooking turquoise water. "Break into one of the vacation homes' pools for a swim. I used to all the time in high school."

So did I, every summer including this last one. Sometimes with visiting boys I'd never see again. Or with the friends Hannah and I grew apart from since that last day of the summer before sophomore year, when we all (except Hannah) got tipsy on five-dollar champagne and swore we'd be friends forever. Or, most often, with *just* Hannah, whenever I itched so badly to do something risky that I pushed until she caved. We did it three weeks ago, on my birthday, floated beneath the moonlight in inflatable donuts, drinking Jones Soda and boxed pink wine Hannah's cousin got us.

"Don't you have somewhere to be?" I ask Saul.

"Yeah, tons of plans. I'm a busy guy."

"I just mean, you had your chance to go swimming at the falls and you passed. Or were you really so determined to land Nate that date?"

"Yeeeeah," he says. "Okay, so this is weird because I'm a grown-ass man and all—at least, kind of—but my parents always had a rule about the falls. They were freakishly strict about it. Basically convinced me I *would* die if I went. Again, old habits."

"No way." I don't realize my hand has snapped out to grab his arm until I see his eyes fixed on it. I retract it immediately.

"I know—not the parenting style you'd expect from the *New York Times* best-selling adventurer Eli Angert."

"No, I mean, my parents had—*have*—the same rule."

"Huh." Saul rubs his collarbone through his faded black T-shirt. He seems a little less put together than he did a week ago at the fair. I'm a fan. "A hint about why our families hate each other?"

"They never told you?" I say.

He laughs. "Oh, they've told me. It's because O'Donnells are arrogant, self-righteous assholes who thrive on my family's misfortune."

"Well, that's all true, but there's more to it. You don't know this?"

"June." He fixes me with a reproachful look. "Think about whatever story you're about to tell me, which no doubt makes my ancestors out to be fork-tailed demonoids, and ask yourself whether it explains why *my* family would hate *your* family back."

"It's about the cherries," I say confidently.

Saul snorts. "Isn't it always?"

"My great-great-whatever, Jonathan Alroy O'Donnell, came to Five Fingers looking for somewhere to grow cherries," I explain. "Your great-great-whatever owned the land Jonathan planted our first tree on. Ancestor Angert traded Ancestor O'Donnell the land for a basket of cherries. Jonathan wanted to build a farm nearer to the water, where the soil was sandier, so he talked Ancestor Angert into renting him *more* land. They shook on it, agreed on a fair yearly payment, swore on *the land itself*, and—what?" I interrupt myself to ask when Saul laughs.

"This is so rehearsed. You've clearly heard this story a million times."

"Anyway, as I was saying before I was brutally *Angerted*, they swore—"

"On the land itself."

"Right. Now fast-forward a couple of generations and *your* great-grandfather Jacob came to *my* great-grandfather Jack the First and demanded he pay him in full what the land was worth *then*. Like, fifty years later. Jacob told Jack he could either buy it or vacate it, but Jack had put every dime he'd made back into the farm, so he didn't have the money. Jacob kicked him off the land. He took everything Jack the First had, my family's entire legacy."

"Bullshit," Saul says immediately.

"What?"

"You want to know *my* family's version of that story?"

"The lie version?"

"Jonathan O'Donnell agreed to lease the land. There was a handshake and an oath *on the land itself*. Only, a couple of generations later, the O'Donnells hadn't paid in literally years. They'd send Jacob boxes of cherries instead of payments, and Jacob put up with it out of pity for a long time, until he stopped by the farm and realized Jack the First just kept buying more *stuff*. Equipment, tools, trees, employees. It was a huge operation, and Jack wasn't paying even pennies for it. Jacob gave Jack six months to come up with a down payment to buy the land. Five months into that, Jacob's son had a major breakdown. He needed full-time care. Medical bills piled up. Jacob needed the money, but Jack told Jacob he needed at least six more months. So Jacob evicted him. And rather than let the farm be sold, you know what Jack did? He burned the trees to the ground. The people who bought that land started all over, and for years the cherries tasted like ash."

I stare at him, hard, and he glances at me sidelong as he eases onto the break in front of one of the gated mansions. He holds my gaze, like we're playing eye chicken.

"You don't believe that, do you?" I say.

"No, June. That's the point. Eli can spin a story too. This is Five Fingers—*everyone* can. That was the tail end of the Great Depression. Times were tough for everyone. It doesn't justify being terrible to each other for three generations after that. Either something else happened or our families are assholes."

The idea that something else could have happened, something Dad *didn't* tell me, eats at my stomach like acid. I shake my head. "If your family destroyed *my* family, that would—"

"Even if they did," Saul says, "did *I* destroy your family, June? Did I ever hurt you?"

The longer we hold eye contact, the higher the pressure in the car rises, until the air feels so thick we're swimming in it.

I used to think what happened to Dad was somehow the Angerts' fault, or at least that they'd celebrated my loss.

But if that were true, then what about what happened to Bekah? Was that somehow *my* fault? Did Mom and Toddy revel in her death? The day I heard, I went home sick from school. I couldn't eat, sleep, do anything but lie in bed staring at the stars on my ceiling.

"Do you?" I ask. "Think I destroyed your family?"

His smile unspools like fishing line, nearly invisible yet luminescent all the same. "Every time you make fun of me, you cut me to my core. But no, June, I don't hold you personally responsible for anything bad that's happened to me or the people I love. In fact, if you're a fair representation of what a Jack O'Donnell is, I feel a little cheated."

Heat swarms my cheeks, and I'm grateful for the cover of dark. "If only you'd saved my life that day with the wasps. Could've saved you years."

"Nah, that wouldn't have worked out in my favor. You would've liked Bekah way more than me. I was the boring twin."

His easy smile fades, sending an ache through my center. "Well. I wish I'd had the chance to like her more than you."

"Me too." He stares at the steering wheel for a second. "Anyway. Now or never, June."

I balk. "What?"

He tips his head toward the glowing aquamarine pool visible behind the mansion beside us. "Up for a swim?"

The thrill in my chest fizzles at the memory of that day at the pool years ago, when I almost drowned and Saul dislocated his shoulder. Maybe it *was* just a freak accident. Maybe Saul's right about all of it, but I still feel guilty being here with him, especially without knowing for sure how Hannah would feel about it. "I probably shouldn't."

He holds my gaze for a beat. "Yeah, I probably shouldn't either."

I stifle a wave of disappointment. What did I expect, for him to beg me to go after I already said no?

"Some other time, maybe," he says. "If you want."

"Another time," I agree.

"Wow, that was easy."

"What can I say? I'm eas—not going to finish that sentence, because I didn't think it through."

Saul laughs more loudly, more openly than usual. I can almost see the dotted line that connects the quality of the sound to Nate for a second. It makes me appreciate Nate's bark more.

I smile involuntarily, and Saul smiles too, turning his eyes back to the road and drumming his fingers on the wheel as we pull away from the curb. In the moonlight, his tattooed arms make me think of ravine-riddled glaciers: icy white and etched in shadows of blue-black. "What are all your tattoos?" I ask when he catches me examining him.

"A whole lot of bad decisions, mostly." He shakes his head. "Next time I turn eighteen, I'm listening to everyone who tells me to wait awhile."

"They look pretty cool."

"Really?" His eyebrows pinch, and he inclines his forehead toward me as he lifts his forearm in front of his eyes, revealing the inked outline of a camera held between hands. It makes it look like he's taking a picture of me. "*This* is cool?"

"Wow, that's . . . a camera. Did it mean anything to you at the time?"

He smiles, nods, glances in his rearview mirror. "Yeah. It did."

I wait for him to go on, but he doesn't. We reach the mouth of my driveway, and he clicks the headlights off, ducking his head to look up at the farmhouse.

I try to see it how a stranger might. White, rickety. Lattice overgrown with ivy. The wild garden that Mom and Toddy rarely touch sprawling before the porch. A green-shingled roof, warped and sunfaded, and the first Jack's Tart tree leaning right, its branches like a gnarled umbrella. The plywood chicken coop off to the left and some of the Girls, as Dad called them, asleep in the grass beside it. Some beams partially chewed by termites, though never enough to warrant an exterminator—even the pests cooperate in thin places.

"It's beautiful," Saul says.

"Yeah," I agree.

"Can I walk you to your door?" His dark eyes meet mine, and I shake my head. He nods once. "Good night, June."

"Good night, Saul."

Twelve

THE following Tuesday I'm sitting on the blue metal table outside the cafeteria where I've eaten lunch every reasonably warm day for four years, glaring at the red *C- Needs more plot! More conflict!* burned into my latest creative writing assignment, when Stephen Niequist walks past on his way to the parking lot.

He jerks his chin toward the paper in my hands. "Ms. deGeest?"

"The one and only."

"She's a real ballbuster. She gave me a B," Stephen says. "On the one hand, it's like, if she's going to ruin my GPA, maybe I should drop. But on the other, I'm obsessed with getting that perfect grade from her."

I couldn't reach a perfect grade with a space shuttle. "Yeah."

Stephen messes with the strap of his messenger bag. "*Anyway,* you and Hannah are, like, best friends, right?"

"Yeah." I fold the story in half. "Why?"

"Is she dating Nate Baars?"

"Noooo."

"Good."

"Good? Why, are you interested?"

Stephen snorts. "Nate's one of my oldest friends. He's liked Hannah for years."

"And so she *shouldn't* date him?"

Stephen lifts his eyebrows. "Not if she doesn't get how real it is to him."

"What do I owe you for the advice, Stephen?"

He rolls his eyes. "You asking my fee, Junior? Don't drop creative writing. I heard we're going to start doing critique groups, and I do *not* want to get stuck reading any more *scoring the winning goal* personal narratives than absolutely necessary."

"Okay, done."

He sways on his feet, then sets off for the parking lot, leaving me to wallow. I shouldn't have made such an effort on the second assignment.

But when Saul dropped me off after the movie, one of Dad's stories *had* come to me—even without the help of another hallucination—and I'd needed to write it down: the story of the time Dad found the place the coywolves take the shoes. Whenever he told it, the purse of Mom's lips said she didn't believe him, but she couldn't see Feathers either.

I knew the story was true, that once, when he was small, my father ran outside and saw the farmhouse disappear before his eyes, leaving behind a towering pile of shoes surrounded by coywolves.

It was another story he'd never get to write down and another one I'd apparently butchered.

"Ready?" Hannah's voice drifts across the sunlit courtyard from the school's side doors. "What's that?"

"Another bad grade."

"In what?"

"Creative writing, forever and always."

"Girl, you know who can help you with that?"

"I already asked Toddy to buy me a better grade. Mom vetoed."

"Okay, second idea?" Hannah says. "Saul."

"I don't think so."

"Why not?" Hannah cries, looping her arm through mine and steering me toward the Subaru. "He's a prodigy! And Nate says he's doing, like, nothing with his time. No one knows why he's back."

"Huh," I say. Hannah's barely mentioned Nate since their trip to the falls. If something's going on between them, she's being tight-lipped about it. "I still don't think using my poor academics is the best way to design a third meet-cute for you and Saul," I say, watching her for a reaction.

She rolls her eyes. "Junie, you care about doing well in this class. *Let* yourself care. Let yourself succeed."

"I'll look into a tutor," I promise.

"Not *a* tutor. The *best* tutor. Nate says Saul's stuff is amazing."

"And we're trusting Nate's opinions on literature?"

Hannah buckles her seatbelt, cranking the windows down and radio up. "He's smarter than he seems. I think he's just shy, and it translates into . . . well, you know. Anyway, we actually had a good time last weekend."

"*How* good?" I ask. *Totally-over-Saul-and-into-Nate good?*

Looking over her shoulder, Hannah shrugs and backs out of the parking space. "Good," she says simply. "Which—segue—the weekend after next, camping at the dunes?"

"With Nate and Saul?"

"Yes."

"No."

"Think about it."

"Okay. No."

"Whyyyy?" Hannah says. "The weather will be perfect—chilly and cozy, probably foggy. Your fave. My fave. Everyone's fave."

"I find hanging out with Saul and Nate stressful."

"Seriously, I'm telling you, Nate's not that bad. Give him another chance."

"If you're so over Saul," I press, "why are you pushing this, Han?"

Blushing badly, she takes a deep breath. "Please know that I am deeply, thoroughly humiliated by what I'm about to admit to you."

"Hannah, what's going on?"

"Ooooooh my God," she groans, then, "ahhhhhhhhh," as if the car is plummeting over a cliff but she's on too much anesthesia to properly scream. "I might, maybe, possibly have a small—nay, *tiny*—crush, which is probably nothing, on Nate Baars."

"Oh my god!" I yelp. "Nate Baars. I knew it."

"You did *not*," Hannah cries, ocean-blue eyes flicking from the road to me.

"I wondered!"

"It's probably *nothing*," she insists, face rapidly reddening.

"Like, a total fluke. I'm ninety percent sure it was a full moon at the falls that night."

"Right." I erupt into laughter, and Hannah smacks my arm, fighting a smile herself.

"It's probably nothing," she repeats. "But going camping might be a good way to confirm it either way. At least consider it, June."

I consider telling her then, blurting out that I'm into Saul Angert, and if any part of her is still hung up on him, I can't be around him. But admitting it aloud seems like an uncrossable line: dangerous, traitorous.

The truth is, no matter how Hannah feels, I can't be around him, because he's Saul Angert.

"Junior?" Mom calls from the door. "Someone's here for you."

I heard the bell from the sunroom, where I'm writing, a process that can be described as staring at a blank page for fifteen minutes, typing a few choice swear words, backspacing, and repeating, while Feathers undulates in the corner.

I pass through the kitchen and living room, where the boys are annihilating zombies on the TV screen. It's seven thirty on a school night, and I have no idea who could be waiting at the door for me.

Halfway down the hall, I spot the boyish man, or mannish boy, on our porch, and my stomach flips.

"Hi." Saul stretches a hand out. He's wearing a long-sleeved button-down, but I think I can spot the outline of the camera tattoo through it. "I'm Mike, the tutor. Sorry I'm late."

I look, probably suspiciously, toward Mom, whose hand's still resting on the doorknob. "You didn't tell me you were expecting anyone, Junie."

"Sorry," I manage. "Totally forgot that was tonight."

"Huh." Mom doesn't seem totally convinced. Her turquoise eyes narrow on Saul, probably trying to place his familiar dark eyes, his lean build and sharp angles.

In a rush of panic, I step aside, blocking her view, to let him past. "Come in, Mike."

He regards the swarm of moths around the porch light uneasily, then ducks inside, hands wringing his backpack straps.

"You guys can work in the sunroom," Mom offers. "Down the hall and to the right, through the dining room, Mike. Junior will be right with you."

He nods and moves off, leaving Mom to appraise me. "You hired a tutor?"

I try to keep my face from broadcasting the truth. "I mean, yes, but the school funds it," I say. I have no idea if that's a thing schools do. "For seniors. For college prep."

Mom's smile practically explodes into a fireworks display. "College, huh?"

I roll my eyes. "Maybe." I turn down the hall. "Don't get your hopes up."

"My baby's going to college," Mom sings after me. Her pride makes my heart trill. And then freeze over. Because college is for Hannahs and Sauls and Toddys, not for Jacks, and she should know that.

"So, Mike." I step into the sunroom and close the door. Saul's already set up on the floral-padded wicker chaise, pulling books from his backpack. "How long have you been named Mike?"

He grins up at me. "Since my boring parents realized they gave birth to a boring baby who definitely would never be a part of an ongoing family feud that would bar him from tutoring a friend who happens to be both younger and a girl."

"You can trust your daughters with a Mike," I agree.

"Mikes have no sex drive," Saul says. "They don't even have genitalia. They're basically L.L. Bean mannequins."

"Ooh, sorry for your loss."

"It's okay. I'm Mike now, so I don't miss having a dick."

"That's good. But, hey—why are you here? I thought we agreed it wasn't a good idea for you to tutor me."

His smile falters, and he runs a hand over his mouth, clearing his throat. "Um. I was under the impression you'd changed your mind."

"Based on . . . ?"

"The *forwarded text* in which you asked Nate to schedule tutoring with me, which I'm realizing based on your facial expression wasn't from you."

I perch on the rattan chair, pulling my knees into my chest. "I'm guessing Hannah."

"You want me to leave?"

"No," I say, heart hammering. "I want you to help me."

"You have something I can read?"

"Do you want the D+ or the C-?"

"D+," Saul says.

I stand and slide the story off the garden table, handing it to him. I take a seat beside him and tuck my legs underneath me. "Now what?"

"Shh." His eyes roam back and forth across the first page. We sit in silence for probably twenty minutes, and the whole time, I'm as bored as I am embarrassed. I can't stop tapping on the back of the lounge until Saul reaches out and presses my hand flat on the cushion without interrupting his reading.

I expect him to take his hand away, but he doesn't, and I'm acutely aware of every spasm in my hand, the way my fingers involuntarily arch up between his as if to pull his fingers down through mine. His thumb starts moving gently back and forth on the back of my hand, which makes my whole body feel like I'm standing outside in a lightning storm. His fingers skim up mine and back down between them, and I don't totally remember how to breathe.

I watch him swallow. His hand leaves to turn the page and doesn't come back when he's finished, which is the worst kind of relief. Finally, his eyes drop off the last page, and he stacks the papers. I cover my face with my hands, and he grabs my wrists to pull them back down.

"Are you ready for the bad news?" he says.

"Fine," I groan.

"First, you didn't follow the assignment." He taps one of Ms. deGeest's notes: *FLASH fiction = SHORT.* "That probably lost you a letter grade, at least."

"Because I wrote *too much*?"

He nods. "That's not the biggest problem though."

"And what would the 'biggest problem' be?"

"This isn't a story."

"Okay. Have you considered becoming an ER doctor? Your bedside manner is killer."

"I have a *great* bedside manner," he says, and I pretend not to notice the innuendo. "If I were your teacher, I'd dance around it like these comments do, but I'm not your teacher. I'm your friend, and your writing—June, it's beautiful. It sounds like you, or like how you would sound if you had all the time in the world. You, but better. It's weird and good and—honestly, I'm relieved how good it is."

"Relieved."

"Yeah. I mean, I was a teaching assistant for a freshman writing class, and it was fine, because I wasn't friends with any of the students, but when friends and relatives ask me to read their stuff, it terrifies me. I've had relationships end because I didn't like someone's writing."

"That kind of makes you sound like an asshole, Mike."

"I know," he says. "It does. I am. It's not intentional. It's just, if I'm friends with—or drawn to—a person, and then I hate the thing they make, or think it's bad or bland or unoriginal, my interest just shuts down."

"You should stop explaining. You're making this sound worse."

He laughs, rubbing at his eyebrows. "June, you have a strong voice. Strong and singular. I wish I could write like that. All I do is imitate. Your language still has its own strangeness. If you can learn the rules but keep your idiosyncrasies, you'll be unstoppable. It's great. Except there's no *story* here."

"Stop saying that," I say. "There *is* a story. A man travels the entire country and finds a thin place to build his home on."

"Yeah, exactly," Saul says. "A man travels the country, making friends, tightrope walking across the Grand Canyon, picking the winning horse at the first Kentucky Derby, saving children from drowning in the street after a molasses-plant explosion, pulling babies from burning buildings—"

"That last part doesn't happen. When does that happen?"

"He wins his way across the nation," Saul continues, "and at the end he scores the jackpot of a homestead, and . . . nothing . . . happens. No conflict, no struggle, no sadness or pain of any kind. No opposition."

"I don't *want* to write something sad," I say.

"Junior, you're too smart to think this is the truth. You *know* life's not like this. Even when it's good, it's hard and terrible and you lose things you can't ever replace."

"Fine," I snap, "I know that. Why do I have to write that? Why can't I write the parts of life that *are* perfect?"

Saul sets my story on the couch between us: a moat, a wall, a ravine. "Okay, so the best story I ever wrote—the only one I really believe in—*was* about a perfect day. My parents and Bekah and I went on a picnic at the dunes. No one talked about Bekah being sick. Mom didn't look at her and start crying, Dad didn't *refuse* to look at her, period, and she ruthlessly mocked me after a bird shit on my head. We pretended she hadn't gone off chemo, that she wasn't sick. She fell asleep in the sun, and I watched her breathe. I saw my sister smile in her sleep."

"That's your happiest memory?"

"Not my happiest," he says. "The one I'll never let go of. If Bekah had never gotten sick, that day wouldn't exist. There'd be hundreds like it, and none of them would feel like that. I never would've appreciated a moment like that."

"So you're saying it was worth it."

"God, Junior, of course not," he says, looking hurt. "I'm saying that's the way it is. I'm saying a *narrative arc* should do more than capture an ordinary day, even if the main events take place on an ordinary day. Your story captures extraordinary adventures, but they're coming out bland because Jonathan Alroy O'Donnell never fails, never hurts. He doesn't have something to lose or want something he can't have."

We fall into silence, the chirp of crickets hanging in the air between us. Saul's teeth skate over his bottom lip, and his chin drops toward his chest. "There's a lot of stuff happening, but no tension. Does that make sense?"

"Take off your shoes," I say.

"What?"

I slide off the couch and start pulling at Saul's boots. "What are you doing?" He tries to move his feet out of my reach, but it's too late. I grab his boots and walk toward the back door of the sunroom, throwing it open. A few Whites who'd been batting against the door dodge the shoes as I toss them and then reconvene against the frame.

"What are you doing?" Saul asks again, scrambling off the couch.

"I'm throwing your shoes to the coywolves."

"*What—why?*"

Because I was thinking about kissing you, because I don't want you to leave, because talking about the things you can never have makes my heart ache for the things I've already lost and I'd rather stop thinking about it. "Because you insulted my story!" I squeal as I dodge his reach. "Because you're rude and elitist for a Mike."

He laughs, reaches for me again. "June."

"Better get your shoes before it's too late."

"Did I really hurt your feelings?" he asks, leaning against the doorframe. "I didn't mean to. I just think you can dig deeper. Your brain can't be entirely rainbows and candy."

"I see glinting eyes." I nod toward the flashes of white prowling at the forest's edge. "Better hurry if you like those boots."

"What?" he says. "I can't go out there *now*."

"They won't mess with you."

"Then you go get them."

"Fine," I sigh. "Back to Mike, I see. No fun at all."

"Wait, I'll—"

Right then—right as we both step through the door into the starlit backyard—I see the floating White get caught between us. I watch it sink into my arm or his or both. And when our feet touch the grass beyond the door, the night sky vanishes, a blindfold ripped off.

The yard isn't starlit anymore. We're facing the setting sun, golden light so intense that when we turn to each other we have to squint.

The biggest difference, aside from the change from night to day, is a four-foot-high pile of shoes in the middle of the yard. As we stand there, a coywolf picks across the grass, Saul's boots dangling from its jowls. It drops the shoes at the edge of the pile and turns aside, pausing to meet our eyes before trotting off.

Saul points at the shoes and says something. I can't hear him.

"*What the hell?*" he mouths, but makes no sound. He scans the sky like he's expecting to find a UFO hovering overhead. Instead, wispy cirrus clouds hang low across the yellowing expanse, and birds blot out bits of the sunlight as they sweep overhead to perch in the treetops. The gentle cluck of our hens draws my eyes to the coop.

Dad.

He's crouched low, holding one suntanned hand out toward a yellow beak. A little girl with dark braids stands beside him—*me again*. Like the other night.

Saul is still spinning beside me, searching for a way out of *whatever this is*. I take a few steps forward, heart burning from Dad's closeness, from his sweat-dirt-cut-grass smell and the particular hunch of his shoulders, which I'd nearly forgotten.

Saul notices then that we aren't alone. He jogs past me, trying to call for Dad's attention, waving his arms over his head.

Dad doesn't see or hear him; he doesn't see or hear me either.

"C'mere," Dad murmurs to the smaller version of myself. She moves closer, careful not to startle the hen bobbing toward Dad's outstretched hands. Dad swiftly catches the bird, subduing its flapping with sure fingers. He draws it in so she—*I*—can stroke its feathers. He lifts the now calm chicken to his ear, as though listening for the tick of a clock. "Wanna hear?" he asks.

Saul taps on Dad's shoulder fruitlessly then steps back,

bewildered, searching my face for answers. His eyes bounce from me to the little girl, examining the similarities in our bone structure and coloring. As his eyes lock back onto her, his mouth quivers open.

The girl crouches and presses her ear to the hen.

I remember this. How we listened to the bird's quick, viscid heartbeats.

The two heads stay bowed together, listening and counting. Three hundred and eight heartbeats in one minute. They hear three hundred and eight pulses, like a tiny mallet hitting a glob of paint. Three hundred and eight disseminations of blood and oxygen, of life. There's sweat on Dad's neck from working out in the yard and dirt on my knees and cheek from following along, pulling wild onions up and pretending to mix potions from them, biting into their sweet white heads only to spit them out across the grass.

It's warm, so warm, and they're huddled together, and I can't hear the three hundred heartbeats, but I remember their sound and the way I looked into Dad's eyes while I listened and how he just barely smiled and I knew he loved me.

"Do you hear it?" he hums. She nods, and he releases the chicken to strut toward a sunny patch. Dad lies on his side and presses his ear to the earth. She does the same, facing him. "You listenin', Bug?"

She nods. He smiles. The heartbeat of the world. That's what I'd been sure I heard that day. It made me feel small but safe too, like I was a tiny part of an unbreakable thing.

When you lose someone, you start to feel like there's an expiration date on your crying. All your friends and neighbors and teachers expect it for a couple of weeks. They'll ask you how you are, and as you're saying *Okay*, you'll begin to shake, and they'll fold their arms around you until it passes, maybe send you to the bathroom or the office. They expect that for maybe a month, any innocuous question might trigger a process in your brain: homework > you used to do homework at the kitchen table > Dad used to lean over you, chewing on chips as the crumbs fell onto your paper > Dad > Dad's dead.

It's not like anyone *says* you should get over it. But they think—and they're mostly right—that someday you won't think about it so much. Or maybe you will. But you'll only remember things you loved and appreciate that you had them, and the hurt will have burned off like morning mist does as the sun rises higher.

They don't expect that, in the middle of the night ten years later, you might find yourself lying in bed, staring at the stars that no longer glow on your ceiling, trying to remember how it felt when Dad threw you over his shoulder and carried you, squealing with laughter, around the house. Or how he'd hold on to your wrists and spin you so fast you flew out in a circle like those carousel swings. They don't know that, the more time passes, the more you forget, and the more you forget, the more it hurts—less often, sure, but worse. You want to dig your fingernails and teeth into the ghost that's slipping through your fingers.

I couldn't have known how much it would hurt to see him again, to remember his minutiae.

I watch Dad's and the little girl's mouths turn up in matching smiles, and I'm still a tiny thing and the world still feels unbreakable, but that no longer makes me feel safe. Because Dad is gone and the world doesn't notice; its heart keeps beating like he was never here.

Dad's eyes take on a watery sheen, as if he knows he's already gone, that this is only a memory and we're lost to each other. Almost like he misses me too. He sits up and runs a hand over the little girl's head. "Bug, why don't you go inside and get ready for dinner?"

She nods, because she loves him, because she would do anything he asked, then stands, a whopping three and a half feet tall, and runs across the grass to the house.

Dad stays where he is, staring at the woods. Saul nudges my arm, pointing out toward where Dad's looking. There, I see it: a dark, warbling shape. The sprite we never named, and by default, or maybe through fear, became Nameless. The cold, angry one whose touch made you feel alone, steeped in nightmare.

Who brought with it panic and death.

Dad gazes out at it until finally it vanishes. Then he stands and goes inside.

Thirteen

AS soon as Dad steps inside, all noise cuts out, and the rippling grass and bobbing branches pause. The world freezes as I chase after him, and Saul follows me. But when we cross into the sunroom, the light vanishes; the sound of owls and crickets cuts back in. A high moon and sparkling stars replace the sunset, blues and greens encroaching on the yellows and golds, an empty stretch of grass where the shoes were.

We freeze in the doorway, taking in the transformation. I look toward the point in the woods where the dark thing hovered. I remember now: The day after Dad showed me the chicken's heartbeat, we found that same hen torn up in the yard. I'd cried, and Dad had assured me the bird was in heaven now, flying better than it ever did on earth.

By that time next week, Dad was gone, and when I saw him in his casket, I'd thought of that bird. I'd tried to find comfort imagining my dad with big brown wings that let him soar over indigo water. Instead I kept seeing the visible muscle and ligaments pulled loose from the chicken's bones. Dad was supposed to be unbreakable, an essential piece of the universe, as important to our woods as the sun itself. So was the hen. So was I. We all were, but *especially* him.

"What was that?" Saul whispers. Now that we've emerged from . . . whatever that was, his voice is back. I shake my head. "I don't know. The past? A memory?" I press the heels of my hands against my eye sockets and try to shut the door to grief before it can flood me. "No," I hear myself say.

It sounds so futile. *No*, he can't be dead. *No*, I can't keep seeing him only to have him ripped away again. "I don't want him to be gone," I half-sob for the first time since I was eight, another fruitless sentence in a time when words are powerless.

Saul draws me into him, folding his arms around me. "I'm sorry," he says. "I don't understand how that happened, but I'm sorry it did."

I tighten my eyes against a wall of tears.

"I'm sorry all I have is *sorry*."

"I'm sorry about your shoes," I murmur.

He exhales a throaty laugh. "Forget the shoes."

"I think Dad saw the ghost watching him. I think . . ." My voice breaks off.

"What?" Saul presses gently.

"I think he knew. That he was going to . . . you know. That ghost is like an omen. Bad things follow it. What if he *knew*?"

"I don't know." Saul's eyes sweep over the lawn. "Maybe . . .

maybe he's trying to tell you something. You know, like, from . . . *beyond*?"

My chest constricts. When he died, I spent months watching for Dad's ghost. I lay awake praying, begging the house, the woods, the coywolves, whatever would listen to let him come back. I would've taken a blob of color, an amorphous rendering of him—anything.

But in ten years, no new feathery presence arrived. No secret messages or mysterious warmth wrapping around me like his arms. Just the pink sheen and the black one and the tufts of floating white, like always. I pull free from Saul. "I think it's the Window Whites—the tufts that look like dandelions? Like, somehow when you touch them, you . . . *see* things."

"You think . . . that could happen again?"

"It's not the first time."

"This is . . . *impossible*." He surveys the yard once more. I follow his gaze out across the lawn, toward a flutter of pure-black shadow receding behind a pine tree. Fear shoots through me, icy and jagged. My pulse speeds and my vision tunnels until the shadowy patch of woods is all I see. The shadow shifts as a deer picks its way out from behind the pine.

Just a deer. Nothing else. I repeat it until the wave of dizziness passes, until the darkness recedes to the corners of my eyes, but still I don't totally believe myself.

That thing, Nameless, was *watching* Dad.

I swallow a knot. "Saul, you should go."

"Are you kidding?" he says. "We have to try more. I mean, maybe the Whites *are* holding memories, but *whose* and why? That must've been your dad's, right? And you said they all hang out in the windows and doors—maybe they're trying to get inside."

"Saul," I begin.

"And if they *are*, then why? June, maybe there's something they, or *he*, want you to see."

My heart leaps against my ribs, and I glance toward the woods again. "You have no idea what you might see if that happens again," I tell him. I think of one day in particular, *the* day . . . and yet I already know I'm going to try to make whatever just happened, *seeing him*, happen again, regardless of that risk.

"Look, Junior," Saul says, "I know what it's like to lose someone. I promise I won't pity you or try to give you something more than *sorry* just so *I* don't feel useless. In fact, I promise to be useless—but let me be useless *with* you, while you figure this out."

"It's not a good idea."

"So you're not going to try to make it happen again? You're going to pretend we didn't just slip into the past or your family's memories or some alternate reality where you're still a kid and your *dad is alive*?"

"That's not what I mean, Saul," I say. "*This* isn't a good idea. I don't think we should be hanging out, period. I think you should go."

"I wasn't trying to . . ." He opens his mouth, closes it, nods. "Okay." He turns and stuffs his books into his canvas backpack, then pulls it on and looks from his shoeless feet to me. His eyes are so dark I feel like I'm falling into them. "You should rewrite that story. It could be really good."

He slips into the kitchen, sending me one last organ-melting look before turning to go. "Night, June."

When he's out of sight, I sit on the chaise, every cell in my body simultaneously buzzing and drained. Feathers resurfaces from the wall. "What?" I demand of her.

She's silent and, I think, sad.

"Do *you* think Dad's trying to tell me something?"

She sways cryptically.

"Yeah, I don't know either." I search the windows for Whites but find none.

I pull my notebook onto my lap and start to write. This time I tell the whole truth as I know it. The story about a girl named Jack and the magic house she lived in and the man she loved more than all the water in every lake.

How one day they listened to the heartbeat of a golden hen and the slow groaning of the earth. How when she went inside, he stared out at the darkness and began to cry.

How two weeks later, he was gone forever.

Or maybe not quite.

Fourteen

IN the middle of the night I wake myself up crying, tangled in my quilt, face wet, hair stuck to my cheeks. A cool rain blows through my window, speckling my bare legs.

I was dreaming about Dad, but the details flit away like a school of tiny silver fish, darting out of reach before I can grab hold of them.

I cross the floorboards to shut my window, and I find a White skating across the frame's chipped paint. It comes toward me as I extend my hand, bouncing against my palm. I close my hand around it, willing it to show me Dad again.

It slips between my fingers. I catch it once more, and it breaks apart, squeezing between my knuckles and reconvening as a single entity outside my grasp.

"No," I whisper. "You have to work."

The White ignores my plea. Feathers shifts sadly in the corner.

The moon stares down at me, and I'm still in my unlit bedroom, aching for impossible things.

Grief is an unfillable hole in your body. It should be weightless, but it's heavy. Should be cold, but it burns. Should, over time, close up, but instead it deepens. The pain of missing Dad these last ten years pales in comparison to the pain of having seen him again only to have him ripped away once more.

I spend the next few nights doing my homework in the sunroom, constantly checking the windows for Whites. There's an itch under my skin, a restlessness, especially whenever I see the shapeless pink sprite or the coywolves slinking through the grass, watching me as if I should be doing something I'm not. I see no sign of Nameless, but every motion in the corner of my eye makes me jump. Every innocuous shadow haunts me.

Nameless was watching Dad, and then he died. The thought is a constantly deepening pit in my stomach, but somehow that's not enough to drown out thoughts about Saul: Saul's smile glowing in the dark hall of the mirror maze, Saul's gravelly laugh in a dim movie theater, Saul in my house, sitting beside me.

I sleep terribly for the next two nights, and in the middle of the third, after hours of tossing and turning, I give up on sleep entirely and head downstairs. I'm hunched over a coffee mug in the sunroom, watching the fog roll across the yard, the pinks and oranges of sunrise peeking through, when I hear Mom croak, "Junior?"

She squints at me, then reties her powder blue robe and shuffles to the coffeepot. "What are you doing up so early, baby?"

"Homework."

"Oh."

In truth I'd been writing. Not a story, just words—thoughts, snatches of conversation. About Dad, about Hannah, Shadow and Grayson, Mom and Toddy. About Saul too. Since ignoring him for the past few days hasn't eased any of the pressure in my chest, I thought maybe pouring out my thoughts about him would.

I swing the notebook shut as Mom eases into the chair across from me. "You've been taking schoolwork pretty seriously lately."

"I guess."

"You like to write?"

"Mhm."

She takes a sip, then smooths the thick locks of hair that have escaped her ponytail. In the soft gray light, she looks young, less like a mother and more like . . . a girl who couldn't sleep.

"Do you miss Grandma and Grandpa?" I ask her.

"Grandma and Grandpa Girard?"

I nod. I've only met Mom's parents a handful of times, the first at Dad's funeral. For a while, Mom thought they might move here, but they ended up staying in France, in the same town Mom grew up in, running the same bakery where she'd learned to make buttercream macarons and apricot tarts.

"Sometimes," she says. "A lot of times. It's hard being far from the people you love. In a way, you never stop feeling like a child, even after you have your own."

"Really?"

She smiles at her mug. "When I'm sick, *all* I want is my *maman*."

"What would she do?"

"She'd take care of me."

"Doesn't Toddy take care of you? Didn't Dad?"

She hesitates. "Of course. But no one's perfect, Junior. There are times when someone hurts you, or falls short of what you expect, and you remember what you *used* to have. Only in memory it looks shinier than it was. You understand?"

"Sometimes it would be easier to be someone's daughter than someone's mother?"

"Something like that."

"What about dancing? Do you miss dancing?"

She smiles, delicate, wispy. "I think life is about learning to dance even when you're sitting still. You learn to dance when you cook and clean, when you bite into cherries, and when you lie in clean sheets. It's easy to believe that if you could do it all over, you'd do everything different."

"But would you?"

"No," she hums, standing. "Most of the time, when you regret something, you haven't seen what the thing you regret can lead you to, if you let it. Some of the worst things that have happened to me have led to some of the best."

I try to see how losing Dad could have possibly brought anything good into the world—for me or anyone else. Okay, so my brothers were a pretty direct result of losing him. Two lives for one, more than fair of the universe or whatever orchestrates it, but this morning it doesn't feel like enough. Nothing could.

I force a smile. "Thanks, Mom."

"I'm proud of you, June." She sweeps a trail of kisses across my forehead and slips away to get ready for her morning.

• • •

"That's all we have time for today."

Ms. deGeest slides a stack of papers off the table and starts her twice-weekly parade around Room 204, setting stories facedown as she goes. "For Monday, I want you all to try one of the poetic forms we discussed, and do so fearlessly. The forms are meant to spread your water droplet into an ocean." She pauses in front of Stephen and me and flashes a smile. "You'll be surprised by how much smarter the form is than you. Not that you aren't already brilliant, of course."

The class laughs politely; she's got even the Problem Students whipped by now.

She sets Stephen's assignment down on the table. "Aim high. Class dismissed." The bell rings, and she places my story in front of me. "Stay for a minute after class, Ms. O'Donnell?"

Stephen shoots me what can only be described as a grimace of apology as he shovels his books into his messenger bag and mock-salutes on his way out the door. Ms. DeGeest starts wiping the whiteboard down, and I nervously flip the story over, bracing for the worst grade yet.

There's no mark on it. Maybe I'm about to be forcibly transferred from the class?

"Ms. deGeest?"

"Would you close the door, please?" she asks without turning around.

That can't be good. And why do I care? Why does it matter if I have to transfer into seventh-period gym? I've never planned on going to college. I've *always* planned to follow in Dad's footsteps.

It's not that I want the perfect grade, but I realize then that I *do* want the perfect story. I want to feel that unfettered rush of writing again, *and* I want to learn how to get everything I *feel* onto the page. To make the stories sing like they did whenever Dad told them.

And just as I'm realizing I want that, I might be losing my shot to have it.

I close the door and perch on the edge of the table. Ms. deGeest swipes her hands together, wiping nonexistent chalk off them. "I'd like you to skip the poetry assignment."

"Oh. Okay."

"You have a knack for fiction. Or, rather, narrative nonfiction. Whatever you consider your first several assignments to be, that's what I'd like you to keep working on."

"You gave me a D."

"That grade was waived, you'll recall."

"Fine, you gave me a C."

"Junior, your work is too good to grade generously. An inflated mark and words of praise are not what you need. You have raw talent. Stop worrying about the grades the people around you are getting and push yourself. *You* are the competition here. I want everything you turn in to be like your last piece."

"You want me to write twenty stories about my dad seeing a death omen?"

Her mask of cool shudders. "I'm sorry for your loss, June," she says. "But yes, I see why it might feel like that's what I'm asking. I want you to write the things you have the most to say about *and* the things you're afraid of messing up."

"That's how I felt about the first two stories, and you hated those."

"I didn't hate them," she counters. "They just lacked conflict, motivation, a clear sense of purpose—the fundamentals we've been talking about in class. The most epic character in the world isn't much without something worth fighting for."

"There weren't goals in the last one. There wasn't any of that stuff."

She laughs. "The protagonist's *goal* was to protect his daughter from seeing Death. He succeeded initially but ultimately failed. Listen, you *need* to learn the rules so your technique doesn't hold you back, so don't mishear me—but sometimes there's so much heart in your words that the rules go out the window. You had me looking at that story as a *reader*, not a teacher. Your story made me pick up my phone and meet my parents for dinner."

"Your parents live in Five Fingers?"

"Born and raised," she admits. "You know what they say: Lake girls can't stay away." For an instant, it's like I'm looking at a friend, someone who loves this place like I do, who left it for college but came back. When I think of it as a place to write, to take classes like deGeest's, college sounds at least a little less boring. The thought of a path like this flutters in my chest, a new possibility I've never considered before.

I tap my story. "I don't know if I have more of that in me. But I'll try."

"Whatever you did last time, do that again."

"Right, so take more LSD."

The corner of her mouth twitches toward a smile. "That's not the kind of joke you should make to a teacher," she says, "for future reference."

I nod, hesitating in the doorway. "So, I know you said my work is too good to grade generously but . . ." I lift the papers.

She nods. "Let's say a B."

"B?"

She must think I'm disappointed, because she adds, "*Plus*."

Mom and Toddy are going to an Arts Council event downtown—Wine & Lines, which apparently no one else thought sounded like a cocaine reference—that Toddy's office sponsored, leaving me stuck watching the boys. But Hannah's so bogged down with homework that she's devoting her Friday night to AP calculus, so there's nothing else for me to do anyway. Other than hunt for Whites, of course.

In the days since Saul and I saw Dad in the yard, the need to see him—to smell, hear, *touch* him again—has spread through me like kudzu, but still none of the Whites I've caught have done anything but float away.

It's getting chillier as fall slogs closer to winter, so to get the boys outside before it becomes too frigid, I pretend Mom and Toddy banned video games for the night.

"They did *not*," Grayson calls me out as I stuff our designated picnic quilt into his arms and shove him toward the door.

"Did too."

Shadow looks skeptical but doesn't argue. He may be older, but he's much more reticent than Grayson, who shouts, "Nuh-uh! They don't care if we play video games!"

"Remember last winter, Gray?" I say.

"Yeah."

"Okay, so then you know that soon you're going to have whole months where you do nothing but play video games. You're going to cry from how cold it is when you walk to the bus stop. You'll barely go outside. If there's a house fire, you'll feel grateful."

"What are you talking about?" he growls, scrambling out of my grip.

"Enjoy the sunshine and fresh air, and in a while, I'll take you to get pizza and three kinds of candy."

Grayson looks toward Shadow, whose bony shoulders shrug. "Okay," Grayson answers for the both of them, and I push them out the door.

At first they make a game of gathering the shriveled cherries beneath the tree and planting them in a circle around it. When they tire of that, they move on to playing aliens, zombies, soldiers, superheroes, and any other comic book subject matter they can think of while I lie on my back in the sun, eyes occasionally searching the windows. Soon the boys are circling my quilt, sighing and complaining, "We're bored. When are we gonna go get pizza?"

Eventually, this devolves into Grayson kicking my legs and Shadow rolling on top of me while I pretend to be asleep. When that doesn't work, they resort to tickling me. "Fiiiine, you little monsters," I relent, rolling Shadow off me. "Go get Dad's car keys."

Grayson whoops and Shadow punches and kicks the air as they race to the house. "Lock the doors on your way out!"

When Mom and Toddy first got married, it was a balancing act, learning how to talk to and about him. There's what I've always called him: Toddy. There's how I think of him and Mom as a unit: Mom and Toddy. The way I talk about them: my parents. The way

I talk about just him: my stepdad or my dad, for the convenience of people I don't know at all; Todd, for adults; Toddy, for people who are like family. And of course there's how I refer to him when I'm talking to Grayson and Shadow: Dad.

It doesn't feel strange to me. At least no stranger than my own absurd smorgasbord of names.

I liked how Saul couldn't settle on one. I liked feeling like maybe he thought they all applied, in different situations.

The boys come streaming across the yard. "LOCK THE DOOR!" I yell again, and Shadow dashes back to check the knob, then flashes me a thumbs up.

We pile into Toddy's truck and pull down the driveway onto the country road. I usually beeline for the scenic route through the cutesy part of downtown, but for quick errands and junk food runs with the boys, I head straight for the derelict IGA grocery store and Camponelli's Pizza next door, which sells suspiciously old but not technically expired candy.

We pull into Camponelli's and hop out of the truck, and as we pass through the front door my eyes trail back to the car parked next to us. I'm milliseconds from figuring out where I recognize the junky sedan from when I walk straight into someone.

"Sorry," I say.

"Sorry," Saul says.

Both of us freeze, rattled. "Hi," he says.

The scratch of his voice makes my stomach flip. "Hi."

"Wow, hi," he says again, adjusting the pizza box under his arm.

"Who are you?" Grayson asks.

"He's Junior's teacher," Shadow offers, which makes Saul laugh uncomfortably. "Remember?"

"Tutor," I say.

"What's a tutor?" Grayson asks.

"He helps me with school."

"That's not fair," Grayson says. "That's cheating."

"Yeah," Saul says. "Come to think of it, it's *not* fair."

"Well, tutoring isn't cheating though," Shadow explains, I guess to all of us. "They don't do your homework for you or take your quizzes or anything. They're just older kids who are good at school, and they help you go over things you learn."

Grayson must already be bored with this topic, because instead of responding, he blurts out, "Does our mom know you have tattoos?"

"I . . . ?" Saul looks to me for help.

"She doesn't like tattoos," Grayson says. "She says it makes you look like you're trying too hard."

"Are you trying too hard, *Mike*?" I say.

"Mike, trying too hard?" he says. "Mikes don't try at *all*, Jack. Mikes pretty much just get individual pan-crust pizzas and go home to play video games in their fathers' basements."

"Is the pan crust good?" Grayson asks.

"No."

"Do you like video games?"

"Yes," Saul says.

"Do you want to come over and play video games with us?"

"Mom and Dad said no video games tonight," Shadow says softly.

"Nuh-uh, that was Junior."

"No video games," I say again, helplessly.

"I'll tell Mom Mike has tattoos," Grayson says.

"Go for it."

"Does Mike get a say?" Saul says. "Because Mike would rather your mom didn't think he was trying too hard."

Grayson scrunches his face. "Why are you talking like that?"

"Can we get ham and pineapple?" Shadow asks.

"Ew, no," Grayson says. "We're getting pepperoni with extra pepperoni."

"Junior, that's not fair. I want ham and pineapple."

"No, no, no, no, no," Grayson says while Shadow begs.

"Okay, who wants to go home and play video games?" I say to make them stop.

Grayson whoops. "With Mike!"

Saul glances at me sidelong, making my stomach flip. I shouldn't have Saul over.

"We can at least get *half* ham and pineapple, right, Junior?" Shadow says.

I'm going to have Saul over. "Fine. Let's get the pizza and go."

As the boys rush the counter, Saul says, "You sure, Jack?"

"Is that what you call me when you're mad at me?"

"It's what I call you when you're smirking."

I brush past him. "I don't smirk."

Fifteen

AT ten thirty, I force the boys into bed with the help of bribery (more candy, more pizza, another god-awful eighties horror movie to watch the next time Mike comes over) and drop onto the couch across from Saul, sending my mom what I hope is a casual *When will you be home?* text.

Another hour? She replies.

In case, though, Saul asks if he can borrow a sweatshirt to hide his tattoos.

"Why do you care if my mom thinks you're trying too hard?" I tease. "Are you trying to *woo* my mom, *Mike*?"

His elusive dimple flickers into view as he says seriously, "Do you think she'd have me?" I laugh and throw a couch pillow at him, which he knocks away. "Please, June. Just let me borrow a sweatshirt. It'll make me feel better."

"So I'm June when you want something."

"I guess so, June."

"Okay. I'll grab one."

"Hey," he says, stopping me. "Can I see your room?"

"Why?"

He shrugs. "I don't know. This is your parents' house, and I want to see the part that's yours."

"It's my great-great–et cetera–grandfather's house."

"I'm less curious which pop-star poster *he* had over his bed."

I laugh. "Yeah, you can see my room."

"I don't have to," he says.

"No, yeah, it's fine."

"No, yeah?"

"Follow me or don't, Mike." I move down the hall. He does follow, and for the first few seconds after stepping into my room we're immersed in darkness together, standing close enough that I can feel his cells bumping into some of mine. I turn the lamp on, and the light breaks through some of the tension, allowing me to breathe again. I break from Saul and disappear into the closet to look for a sweatshirt big enough to fit him.

I'm not much of an oversized-hoodie girl, and while Saul's thin, he's taller than me. The only legitimate option I have is a navy crew-neck sweatshirt that belonged to Dad, which I'm hesitant to lend out. I hug it to my chest, imagining I can smell Dad on it, imagining I even *remember* his smell. I tamp down thoughts about what he'd say if he knew an Angert would be wearing it. When I come back into my room, Saul's sitting on my bed, holding a picture frame. "Your dad," he says. "I recognize him from . . . the chickens."

I hold out the sweatshirt. "This was his too, so don't forget to give it back."

"I won't." He pulls it on. "So, Nate asked me to go camping tomorrow. I think your name was mentioned."

"Are you going?"

He studies me. "I told him I couldn't."

"Oh."

"Since you and I aren't hanging out and all."

I lean against the wall. "Right."

He looks out the star-washed window then back to me. After a few still, heavy seconds, he asks, "Is it because I'm older than you?"

My body begins to buzz. My stomach pulses, and an acorn of heat catches in my throat. It feels like, all along, we've been dancing closer and closer to this, to saying aloud the last thing an O'Donnell and an Angert should say to each other. I shake my head.

Saul's dark eyes stay intent on mine. "Because of Hannah?"

"No." The possibility that she wouldn't be *thrilled* about Saul and I hanging out still lingers, but sometimes I catch her texting Nate. If things really *could* go anywhere with Saul, I'd ask her flat out. But they can't, so why torture myself?

Saul studies me for a few more seconds. "Because you don't like me?"

There, the one thing I shouldn't say: *I like you*.

"June," he says.

I laugh from pure distress. Answering truthfully would be betraying Dad. But then again, what is this? I'm *flirting* with him. I've brought him into my house—*Dad's* house—lent him Dad's sweatshirt. I'm ignoring every warning my father gave me, every rule he had for me, for a boy I've only known a few weeks. I shake my head. "Saul, I can't."

Talk about this.

Do this.

Like you.

I ignore the voice that says, *It's too late. You can't walk away from this now.*

"Do you want me to leave?" he asks finally.

"Yes," I say. "No."

"June," he says.

I let out a frustrated sigh. "Yeah. You should go."

"Okay." He stands, and I cross to my dresser to grab the B+ short story, whose grade I filled in myself. I hand it to Saul, who smiles down at it.

"Keep it," I say. It feels like I'm offering him the memory of my father and the hens itself, a tiny token, a piece of a heart I'm strictly prohibited from sharing with him.

His eyes lock with mine for a long moment, and I think he's about to kiss me. Instead, he turns toward the hall, and I follow. We're halfway through the doorway when I see the White caught between our arms.

By then it's too late: The hall is gone. My *house* is gone. We're standing in an unfamiliar bathroom, and, with one look at Saul's face, I know where we are and who the girl lying on the mint-green tile is. She looks like him, though a bit younger—around seventeen, the age she died. Her skin is sheened with sweat, her dark hair shaved to the roots and cheeks sunken.

"Please stop," the girl whispers against the floor. "Make it stop."

Saul doesn't go toward her. He stares, jaw flexed.

There's a knock on the closed door. "Bekah?" a man's voice calls. "You okay in there?"

"Make it stop." Her eyes skirt toward the porcelain tub, inside which a pile of shoes sits. A shapeless darkness writhes over it.

Nameless.

Behind us, the door creaks open, and the ghost disappears as a gray-bearded man pushes into the room.

I don't see the Eli Angert of book jackets and news stories, the one who wears a tweed coat and sits in a leather chair framed by mahogany bookshelves, looking toward a window with an expression of almost brutal indifference.

This is a secret Eli hurrying into the bathroom, a private Eli kneeling on the floor beside the girl. This Eli wears half a pajama set—the pants—and a ratty undershirt stained with coffee. He cradles the back of his daughter's head with thick, blistered fingers. "Oh, kid," he whispers, voice quavering. "Oh, kid."

"I need it to stop," she murmurs.

"I know." He gently rubs her shoulder. "Let's get you into bed."

"No," she says more firmly, "I can't keep doing it, Dad."

"You're a fighter. You'll get through this."

"I don't wanna fight." Her voice swings high. Eli scoops her into his arms and stands. "I'm tired, Daddy."

He *shh*s her, kisses her cheek despite the flecks of vomit there.

"Dad?"

"Yeah, kid?"

"You'll forgive me if I stop?"

"Stop?"

"The chemo."

Eli Angert falters. He breaks. He stops before the bathroom door and breathes. His voice cracks though he says no words. His chest heaves.

Saul stares, body rigid like he can stop himself from cracking too.

"You'll beat it, baby." Eli carries her through the door, a White glistening in his wake.

Saul catches the fluff in his hand and studies it. As it sinks into his skin, I fold my fingers over his, nodding: *I'll go with you.*

We step forward and emerge into another moment.

We're halfway up a steep white dune overlooking Torch Lake, the turquoise water rocking over the happily shrieking bodies splashing through it. On the shore, a man and woman sit in folding chairs on a polka-dotted blanket, flanking two outstretched teenagers: the girl asleep with a wide-brimmed hat draped over her eyes, the boy watching her. A pile of shoes sits yards away, ignored by the beachgoers wandering past.

Saul takes a few steps down the hillside, the hot wind rippling through Dad's sweatshirt and mussing his hair. I touch his arm. *Is this it?* I ask without sound. *The day you won't let go of?*

He nods, then squints into the sunlight. Together we watch the waves hit, the gulls dive low for Dorito crumbs and dropped grapes. I know this must hurt him, but it seems like it makes him happy too.

Saul looks my way, shielding his eyes from the sun. I do the same, and he leans forward until our hands form an awning over us. *Hi*, he mouths.

Hi.

Want to go to the water?

Yes.

The sparkling lip of the lake is riddled with millions of floating memories. We climb down to the water's edge, and when our toes *should* meet the frigid fringe of the water, we instead step onto something solid and glassy.

We're on a frozen pond now, circled in velvety snow. The beach is nowhere in sight. A gangly boy and muscular girl in matching neon snowsuits skid wildly across the icy surface, and frosty shoes tower at the edge of the lake. The kids' shouts and giggles echo as they race across the frozen pond, sliding on their snow boots. The boy slips and cries out as he falls, landing on his back with his arms and legs splayed out.

"Saul!" the girl yelps and spins, gliding toward him. She drops onto her knees beside him, and he sits up, his hat askew to reveal a considerable amount of ear. I glance sideways at *my* Saul, adult Saul. His smile is tight but wide. His eyes glisten.

"You're okay." Bekah rolls her eyes exaggeratedly and hauls him up by his coat. "Stop being a baby."

"I'm not a baby!" Saul yells.

"You're five minutes younger than me. That makes you the baby! That makes you my *servant*."

The Saul beside me shifts to accommodate a laugh, but I can see the effort it's taking to hold himself together. The miniature

Angert twins are hurling snow at each other now, and while at first they seem genuinely annoyed, Bekah shrieks with laughter when a snowball spatters her face, and Saul breaks into an open-mouthed grin.

At the top of the tree-covered ridge beyond the pond, Eli Angert appears with a bundle of firewood perched on his shoulder. His cheeks are red and eyes tight against the brilliant winter sun. "Time to come home!" he calls.

The twins skate to the bank, passing through a cluster of Whites they don't seem to see. We follow their lead, but when we step from the frozen lake onto the snowy shore, the Whites rip us away again, and we find ourselves crashing through a solid wall of water.

Soaking wet and freezing cold, we emerge into a dark space, the thundering sound of falling water echoing around us.

Saul's hand grasps for mine in the dark, checking that I'm still here with him. Wherever *here* is.

It's as if each new threshold we cross—man-made or natural—tunnels us to whatever the White contains—like when the puffs cling to a doorframe or the lake's lip, the memories they hold become rooms on the other side, places you can simply step into. That must be why just holding one the other night didn't do anything—I needed to step *into* it, like Saul and I did when we passed from the icy shore to wherever we are now.

I wipe the water from my eyes as they adjust to the meager light. We're in a cave behind a waterfall—*Five Fingers Falls?* My eyes move past the dark, glimmering falls toward the interior of the cave, and I lurch backward when I realize we're not alone.

Behind a heap of soaked shoes, a boy and girl stand coiled

together with their foreheads resting against each other's, ignoring the Whites' lazy batting.

Saul squeezes my hand to get my attention. *Who are they?* he mouths. I shake my head.

They're not much older than us, both dressed in some kind of antique undergarments: the dark-haired boy in a pair of short shorts, the girl with strawberry blond curls and full cheeks in an ivory chemise that clings to her thighs.

The boy whispers something to her we can't hear over the roaring falls. His hands skim over her arms, and he lifts her chin to his.

Saul and I trade abashed looks when the couple moves on to some pretty serious groping, and he tilts his head toward the waterfalls. I nod, and he pulls me through the thundering water.

We stumble into my bedroom, immediately dry but still so cold we're shivering. "You didn't know them?" I stutter through the chill. Saul shakes his head. I can see pain in the torque of his face, the rigidity of his shoulders. "Are you okay?" I whisper.

"Were you?" he says. "After you saw your dad the first time, I mean."

"No." I shake my head. "But I wanted it to happen again. I wanted for it to never stop."

"Me too," he says, eyes low.

"I'm sorry, Saul." I want to pull him toward me, wrap my arms around him, make him feel that he's not alone. But I don't. "I'm useless, but I'm here."

He nods, his dark eyes lifting to meet mine. The corner of his mouth twitches with an attempt at a smile. "Thanks, Jack," he says quietly.

I step back and slump onto my bed, my own disappointment spreading through me like wildfire. I close my eyes against rising tears. "After last time," I say, "I thought maybe you were right, that my dad *was* trying to tell me something. But if that last memory was a total stranger's, then, what, they're random? I might never find a memory of him again?"

Saul lets out a long breath, and the bed sinks as he sits beside me. "Hey," he says, bumping my elbow with his. "Look, if the Whites were full of random memories, what are the odds you would've found a few of your dad's? Or we would've found some of Bekah's? Those odds are impossible, June. They're miracle odds. I can't promise this is a message from your dad, but this isn't random. It means something, for both of us."

I open my eyes again and look into his. They're dark and liquid, soft and warm. "This all started the night we met," I tell him. "I thought I saw the ghost that night—the dark one—and when I got home . . . it happened for the first time here. I saw my dad.

"When I was a kid, my dad told me only O'Donnells could see the ghosts—as far as I knew, *no one* else ever had. I thought it was our own private bad omen. But in that memory . . . in the bathroom, it seemed like . . . like Bekah saw it too."

Saul swallows and nods. "Yeah," he agrees. "It did."

"What does that mean?"

He shakes his head. "I don't know. But there's a lot about our families that a story about cherry trees can't account for."

An uncanny tingle crawls down my spine, and the silence stretches out between us.

I realize then that Saul still has my hand, and my eyes flash toward the door and then the alarm clock on my desk. Though it felt like we were only gone for a handful of minutes, the numbers flash *11:22.*

"You should go," I say. "My parents will be home soon."

"June, I can't pretend this didn't happen—whether Bekah and your dad are trying to tell us something or not, we have the chance to *see* them again."

"I know." I do. I understand how everything changed when we saw Saul's sister. This bit of magic doesn't only belong to me anymore, and I can't ask Saul to forget about it, about the possibility of seeing *her* again. "I know. But my parents will be home any minute, and if you're still here when they get here, *this*—you coming over—is going to get a *lot* harder."

He studies our linked hands, then nods and lets go. "Your story—I must've dropped it."

But there's no sign of it. The pages are gone, maybe gathering dust and pollen in a pile of lost shoes. "What's your e-mail address? I'll send it to you."

"Would you believe Saul Angert is a rare enough name that I have the unique fortune of owning Saul dot Angert at Gmail dot com?"

"Stop trying to impress me," I tease.

"Send me your story, Jack." He steps through the doorway, and I feel a half-formed surge of panic before I peek into the hall and confirm he didn't vanish into some other place or time. There are no Whites in sight as Saul heads toward the stairs. His phone rings, and he answers as he descends. "Takumi. What's up?"

As I listen to the gentle grit of his voice move down the stairs,

I think about life a few weeks ago, before Nameless reappeared, before the Whites tore open the old wound in my chest, before I met Saul.

Something major shifted when he came back. It's as if all along we've been on two paths bound for collision, O'Donnell and Angert, and now it's happened. We're inextricably tangled; even the Whites know it.

A few weeks ago, Saul had a different life too. Friends I don't know, professors who shaped him, maybe non-O'Donnell enemies, all tucked away in another place.

I want to know it all.

Two hours after Saul leaves, my phone buzzes on my bedside table with a new e-mail alert, and I realize I've been waiting for it.

I tap open the e-mail, Saul's reply to the story about my dad and the chickens.

I hope you're awake, I read. *I hope you don't fall asleep before I get to tell you that you're amazing. This is amazing, and also you.*

I stare at the words, intoxicating waves of warmth coursing through me as I debate how to reply.

Even if our collision was inevitable, even though it feels *good* to like Saul Angert, every step forward I take with him moves me a little further off my old path, the one that aligned with Dad's.

The mental gymnastics—justifying some things and drawing arbitrary lines before others, straddling loyalty to Dad and my interest in Saul—are exhausting.

I try for an innocuous reply: *Who's Takumi?*

Old roommate, Saul answers. *He's been trying to get ahold of me for weeks, but I hate the phone. Turns out he's getting married and moving to Indonesia to teach English.*

WOW! Congrats, Takumi! About time, I respond.

No kidding. He and Sarah have been together for, like, four months.

Oh . . . jeez. That's . . . four months, I write.

My thoughts exactly. Whatever, it's his funeral. Whoops, meant to say wedding.

Well, good for him. I can't believe I haven't been proposed to yet. Honestly, I'm offended.

This is awkward. I swear I was already going to ask this, but . . .

No, I will not be your date to Takumi and Sarah's wedding. I cannot support such a union.

Damn. Maybe next time one of my friends gets married, he'll know his fiancée's middle name and you'll feel differently.

After a long pause, I type, *How are you?*

Bad in some ways, good in one.

   Meaning?

Five minutes pass before my phone vibrates with his reply. One word:

June.

I fall asleep feeling bad in most ways, happy in one.

Sixteen

TUTORING? Saul's e-mail reads.

I snuggle deeper into the blankets, morning light washing across my face.

On a Saturday morning? I respond.

Okay, then what about Not Tutoring? he asks.

You mean White-hunting?

I watch dust twirl through the sunbeams, landing on the shaggy ferns and bulbous succulents Toddy helped me hang from the ceiling.

I want to see more.

Laughter, clinking pots, and the shrieks of a hyperactive

cartoon dog drift up from the kitchen. Toddy makes breakfast every chance he gets, partly to keep the boys from overdosing on Cap'n Crunch and partly because his and Mom's definition of a hot date has always been strolling hand in hand through an organic grocery store and coming home to make creamy *cassoulet* or flaky *gâteau Basque* with Jack's Tart cherries.

They'll cook for hours, feeding each other bites of cheese and sips of Bordeaux as they go, then sit down for a three-course meal. The food is always delicious, and the process is always—like now— *very* loud.

My sweet, sugar-addicted family is downstairs having their traditional lazy Saturday morning, and here I am plotting with Saul Angert to keep chasing memories of Dad and Bekah. Guilt gnaws at my stomach, and I burrow my face into a patch of sunlight. *Today won't work*, I tell Saul. *My whole family's home.*

Then I'll be Mike.

I should say no. For Dad but also because I *know* it's only a matter of time before my parents figure out who Saul really is.

But until then, I can't deny Saul the one thing we both want more than anything else: more time with the people we've lost.

Okay.

Fifteen minutes later I'm sweatered and blue-jeaned, rooting around for bagels in the pantry.

"Eat breakfast with us," Mom says, grabbing my hand.

"I have tutoring," I say. "He'll be here any minute."

"On a Saturday?" Mom says. "Okay, well, Mike can eat too. We're making omelets."

"I'm barely hungry. Bagel-hungry, not omelet-hungry."

The doorbell rings then, right as the boys start pummeling Toddy, who has a hot pan in his hand, with their new boxing gloves. Mom has to pull them off of him, shouting things like *Faites attention!* and *Péril!* One advantage of being significantly older than your siblings is that you can usually slip away unnoticed, which I do.

I open the door to Saul's smile. The air outside is cool and dry, chilly in the shade of the porch, but I'd guess warmer out in the sun.

"Hello, Jack."

I lower my voice so my parents can't hear me, if that's even possible over Grayson's shrieking. "Mr. Angert."

He shakes his head. "God, I hate that."

"Hey." I nod toward the cherry tree, where prickly green sprouts stick up from the grass in a circle.

"What?"

"Shadow and Grayson planted those."

"Huh. And they're coming up this late?"

"They planted them *yesterday*."

"Shit," Saul says. "You're rapidly turning me into a Five Fingers Truther."

"Good." I lead him past the kitchen, grateful Grayson doesn't notice his bud "Mike" walk by. We close ourselves in the sunroom along with the morning cold and plop down on the wicker couch. For a minute, we're caught in heavy silence, just staring at each other.

"So." Saul clears his throat. "Whites." The gravel in his voice rustles through me, and I want to touch him, or maybe tap my hand on the back of the couch until he sets his over it. He bumps my knee with his. "June, look."

A White skates across the sun-warmed glass, heading straight for the back door. It hovers there, expectant, and Saul and I exchange a look.

He holds his hand out, and I take it shakily. We stand, reaching for the White. It bumps against our interlaced fingers, rolls onto our hands, and settles.

"Ready?" Saul whispers.

Desperate.

Overwhelmed.

Terrified.

"Ready."

We take a breath and step outside.

Nothing changes.

At first, I think we've stepped into a memory of a day nearly identical to today, but then Saul's voice cuts through the morning quiet: "Where are the shoes?" He looks surprised to hear himself too. "I guess that answers my question."

"What do you mean?" I ask.

"In the memories, there's always a pile of shoes," he says. "But it didn't work, so of course there aren't any shoes."

The White is pushing up from our skin again, bobbing against our hands like it can't find a way in but also doesn't want to leave.

"I don't get it. What did we do wrong?" I say helplessly.

We step back into the sunroom, searching for some clue as to why it didn't work. My mind cycles through the other times we've stepped into memories. "The *shoes*," I say. "We were barefoot the other times."

Saul releases a gruff laugh, but he's already bent down to yank his shoes off.

"We should throw them in the yard."

"How many pairs of shoes do you think I own, Jack?"

"More than the rest of the boys in my graduating class combined."

He smirks and kicks my foot. I untie my boots and, with mild regret, toss them outside. No coywolves appear, but the White is still drifting, and Saul slides his rough fingers through mine again. This time, there's no *Ready?*

We catch the ball of fluff. It melts into our hands, and we take a step together, leaving the sunroom and the present behind.

It worked, I say silently.

Saul's grip tightens as we survey our surroundings. We're just inside the woods, and everything, even the pile of shoes behind us, is blanketed in a layer of frost. The sky is bright and cloudless, and in the distance, a boy and girl, all sharp elbows and big ears and black eyebrows, are trudging our way. Saul and Bekah can't be more than nine here, but they already look so *themselves*: he neat and elegant, she mud-smudged and tough.

I glance at *my* Saul and tug his ear teasingly. He rolls his eyes and bumps my shoulder with his, sending a rush of heat down into my stomach.

We look back toward the twins. Though he's taller than her, Saul's still struggling to keep up with his sister. "We're not *allowed*," he calls at her back.

Her laugh has a shade of his grit to it, but where his is level and low, hers is loud, unapologetic. "That's why it's fun! We're like spies."

As they pass us, we turn and follow them toward the edge of the woods, where white slivers of the farmhouse are visible between trees.

The boy stops walking a few feet from the lawn. "He'll be angry."

Bekah looks at him over her shoulder. "Just keep watch, okay?"

She takes off across the lawn, beelining toward the first Jack's Tart tree. She scrambles up it, if not *gracefully* then at least *powerfully*, and picks through the branches.

It's too early in the season, I think. Patches of snow still blanket the grass, and the end of winter nips in the air.

Bekah shakes a branch, and green pellets tumble down. Her brother takes a few steps closer and wraps his arm around a tree trunk as he watches her rearrange herself in the branches. She moves fearlessly, higher and higher, picking and rustling. Minutes pass.

Behind us, birds scatter noisily. We spin toward the commotion.

Eli is coming toward us in angry strides, and little Saul's eyes rim with white as he looks between his father and the cherry tree. He runs toward Eli, as if to hold him off. "It was just a game," he pants. Eli rips him out of the way and keeps moving.

Bekah's spotted her father from up in the tree. She slides down to the grass, watching him progress toward her. She barely bats an eye when he grabs her arm and drags her toward the woods. Both Sauls lurch out of Eli's stormy path, and the boy chases him. "It's not her fault!" he cries helplessly, pulling at his father's jacket.

"Completely disrespectful," Eli growls at Bekah. "If Jack O'Donnell had seen you, you have any idea what he might've done? He'd've had grounds to *shoot* you, kid."

Bekah writhes against him, huffing angrily. He tosses her over a fallen log and spanks her once. She grits her teeth and stares hard at the mud. Eli spanks her again, and Saul starts to cry. Eli spanks her a third time, and Saul runs at him, pulling at his father's arms. They scuffle for a second before Eli throws him off.

"*Please*," Saul says.

The ruddy heat leaves Eli's face. He straightens, studying Saul for a long beat. He wipes the sweat from his upper lip and jerks his head in the direction of their cabin. His eyes sweep over both twins. "Go home," he grunts. "Both of you."

The boy remains frozen, but Bekah slumps off the log and takes his hand, pulling him away. Eli sighs, resting his fingers on his hips, and watches them move off. He looks back and shakes his head at the cherry tree in the distance.

This must be Bekah's memory, because as she moves off, the natural rustle of the woods catch in a kind of loop. Like the woods are doing what she might have expected them to do in her absence: birds trilling in the same unsettling rhythms, her father sighing again and again.

We hurry away from the nightmarish scene and catch up with the twins. They walk in silence for a long while before Bekah says, "You shouldn't let him get to you."

The boy says nothing, and Bekah adds, "It doesn't *hurt*."

His voice is small: "He doesn't do it to hurt you. He does it to embarrass you."

"I'm not embarrassed," she says, matter-of-factly. She stops walking and dips her hand in her pocket, plucking from it two cherries, mostly pink though spotted with green. "You're a bad lookout," she says. "But an okay brother."

The boy grins, revealing a missing front tooth, and gingerly takes a cherry. "On three?" Bekah says. He matches her gaze and nods. The two of them count to three, then press the still-crunchy cherries into their mouths and bite down, jaws working awkwardly against the not-quite-ripeness. "What do you think?" she says around a mouthful, her face scrunched. "It's kinda sour."

Saul closes his eyes and chews slowly. "Not sour. *Bitter*."

Bekah lets out a bark of laughter and spits her cherry out. "Gross," she says. "Still worth it though. To say we did."

"The last taste," little Saul says. A crescent of smile passes over his face. He opens his eyes, and his grin cracks all the way open. "The last taste is like honey."

"The last taste should always be sweet," Bekah says solemnly. They start moving again, the crisp leaves crumbling loudly underfoot. Without looking over at him, she says, "Saul?"

"Yeah."

"You don't need to keep me safe. I'm older than you."

"Five minutes," he says. They've reached the end of the woods. They climb the cabin's stairs and go inside, leaving the world still and noiseless, as if without them it doesn't exist.

Whites wait along the edge of the forest, and Saul and I exchange another look. He nods, and we step through.

We're back outside the sunroom, but the grass is cropped, gleaming in the sunlight. A few wisps of cloud sail across the pale sky, and a breeze snakes through the treetops, sending dried-out blots of orange frittering from the branches of yellow birches and plasticky green ironwoods.

Two elegant coywolves pick across the yard, dropping our shoes at the edge of a pyramid of boots and sandals, then trot into the woods again.

A peal of laughter draws our attention to the sunroom as a little girl bursts from it: a blur of yellow dress and nearly black curls streaked rust-red by sun. She squeals with delight as her bare feet pound the grass. Saul looks from the little girl to me, comparing us.

"Watch out for nails and rocks, June-bug," a man's voice shouts. A second form careens through the sunroom doors, barreling down the hill in the opposite direction.

My stomach jerks within me.

No.

We can't be here.

My eyes judder to the hydrangea that curls wildly up the porch, blooms spread into orbs of blue.

No.

Some petals have fallen to the grass at the bush's base. I know exactly *when* we are.

The sunlight is harsh. The dirt has a sharp, acrid scent to it, like the dehydration of summer has boiled the earth down to its essential minerals. The lawn glimmers like sea glass, thirsty, almost translucent. The birdsong rings hollow.

Any moment but this.

"I'm gonna beat you, Daddy!" the girl shrieks as she runs, throwing a look of fiery delight over her shoulder at him.

I remember how it feels to be her right now. Happiness ballooning in her chest as Dad lopes after her, clumsy and powerful like some kind of circus bear, slowing himself to give her a lead.

The part of his lips. The gap between his front teeth. The crinkle in his sweat-streaked brow.

Blue hydrangeas bobbing in the wind. Petals falling—one, two, three, one, two, three—in a half dome around the roots.

We were playing a game. Racing to see who reached O'Dang! first.

I remember how, when I saw Dad's gap-toothed grin, those blue flowers, I thought I might burst from happiness. In the moment, I had him, all the way. I didn't know it was the last moment I would. The last time I would see his living smile ignite, his chest heave with breath, his eyes squinch against the sun.

DAD. I run. I chase him. *Dad, no!*

My child self has already disappeared into the forest, and Dad's headed in the opposite direction. I try to scream for them to come back. I try to scream for her to *follow* him.

If only I had followed him, everything *would be different.*

But that wasn't how we played the game.

We ran. Two entirely separate directions. Crashed through misty, sun-washed forest. Moving, moving, moving, sometimes in straight lines, sometimes right-left-right-left. But whenever Dad wanted to play, it worked: The woods let us both find our way to the gnarled tree that, at times, simply stopped existing. It was wide as a house, bits of bark peeling away to reveal a supple whiteness underneath.

Hemlock, Dad thought. Trunk so thick you could lie on the roots like hammocks. Streamers and ribbons were strung around it. Some had been there as long as I could remember; others appeared one day as if from thin air.

Dad was gone a lot, driving semitrucks cross-country, selling fancy knives from the trunk of his car, delivering soda to vending machines or packages to doorsteps—whatever work he could find that allowed him to travel. Mom said he got restless when he was home too long. Restless when he was gone too long too.

He'd be home for a few days or weeks or months in between jobs, and in those days we'd spend sunrise to twilight together, except for the occasional morning when he was out of the house by the time I woke up and still gone when I climbed in bed.

Whenever he was home, we played this game.

Whenever he was home, we raced barefoot to O'Dang.

As I sprint down the slick hillside after him, I remember what he used to say: *Can't get into heaven with your shoes on, June-bug. If we wanna break through the veil in this thin place, we gotta go the way we came into this world: barefoot.*

For eight years, racing Dad to O'Dang! was my favorite thing. For ten, the thought of it has made me sick.

I know Saul must be chasing me, but I don't look back. My heart thunders, and my feet hit hard and fast. I scream for Dad so hard it hurts, but I make no sound. He can't hear me.

And what if he could? How could I stop what's already happened? The only reason I'm here to relive this at all is because it already happened. How can I undo this blemish on my memory? My black hole. The grief at my core, sucking everything into it.

The feeling of getting to that tree, panting and sticky and happy-so-happy. And the fear that set in when the sun started fading and the air cooled and still Dad hadn't come.

I chase him into the woods. Tree branches whip and lash at my skin. They feel solid and scraggy against my arms, though I pass through them like a ghost.

He's too fast. His gait's too long. I see slashes of red fabric—his shirt—darting through the forest ahead of me.

Wild blue hydrangea curls through the woods. Blue petals twirl in the wind, their dry tang cloying in the air. Red and blue. Red and blue. Red and blue.

"JUNE-BUG?" Dad shouts.

I follow the voice. I thrash, I claw, I fight through the brush.

I burst into a clearing, golden light pouring over yellowing grass. Dad stands there, hands resting on his hips as he breathes hard.

Hydrangea petals spiral through the air. They catch in his hair. They'll still be there. They'll still be there when I find him.

Tears flood my eyes. My throat closes. I can't breathe. I can't breathe, but I'm still mouthing the word—*Dad*—as I move toward him.

Something shifts in the trees, and I freeze, a new shock of cold coursing through my veins. A darkness writhes into the clearing.

Nameless billows toward him. The branches come alive with cheeps and squeaks as birds and squirrels erupt into panic. The trees sway and tremor as every living thing retreats from the dark ghost. Every living thing except my father.

Dad, I beg.

He stares at the black thing, tears springing to his eyes. Like he knows. He knows what's coming.

Move, Dad! Move! I'm trying to scream. I try to pull at his hand. I can feel his skin, rough and warm, but he doesn't react. Doesn't budge. He's a statue, and I'm not even a breeze.

Tears roll down his cheeks—*how does he know what's coming?*

"Please." He's panting, can't catch his breath. The darkness closes in on him: hopelessness, fear, claustrophobia, suffocation. I feel it all, and still Dad breathes hard, too hard.

"You can have me, but leave June alone."

My stomach jolts at the sound of my name. The darkness touches him then. He lets out a grunt and sinks to his knees as the thing towers over him. Dad clutches at his arm. His face twists, and eyes flutter against pain. "She's not like us. She won't be. I promise you. Just leave her alone."

Dad, I sob.

The thing folds over him. He chokes—a tight, garbled sound. The sound he made as pain surged outward from his heart. *Acute myocardial infarction*, the doctors would later tell us. I memorized the words, repeated them to myself for weeks, trying to understand how something that sounded so mundane could have beaten my father, the biggest man on earth.

"Please." He shuts his eyes tight. They zigzag under his eyelids. *"Please show her."*

I fall onto my knees and wrap my arms around him, right

through the darkness and its cold. I try to drag him away. I try to shield him. I try to make myself solid for him. Audible. *Dad. Dad. Dad.* I say it a hundred times.

My voice is still lost, but I swear he feels my arms as he slumps forward and passes through them. His eyes search for something—for me?—but I don't think they see. "Junie," he chokes. "Jack."

I'm so sure he knows I'm there, that I'm holding him, but then, in a small voice, he says, "Dad? Are you there?"

HELP! I scream as hard as I can. *HELP. HELP. HELP.*

My throat feels raw, shredded, and still the only sound is the chatter of robins and gray jays, the distant caw of ring-billed gulls. The world insists it's a beautiful day, while I sit on my knees, holding my father, blue petals falling around us.

The light, his being, his Himness, fades from of his eyes. *DAD.* The torque of pain relaxes from his face.

I know. The second he's gone, I know. I feel the gap at the core of me, in the world, in the universe. I feel the place he should be, a tattered emptiness.

And just like that, everything freezes. The whole forest pauses.

And I know right then it's because this is where the memory ends. There's nothing left to it. The man who made it has *stopped*, ceased. Ended.

I push on his chest. I try to hold his head back and breathe into his mouth. I sob but make no sound. The birds are silent now; there is no such thing as sound here anymore. Even Nameless is frozen there, its coldness rendered neutral. There is no temperature, no feel to the air or smell or breeze.

Hands press against my shoulders and try to drag me away,

but I can't stand. I can't leave. I can barely see because I'm crying so hard, because the impossibly motionless sun is aflame, because what is there to see when your whole world dies in front of you?

Saul wraps himself around me. He lifts me. My head falls into his chest. Tears and snot dampen the long-sleeved shirt he wore to hide his tattoos from Mom back in another world.

I wanted to forget this feeling forever. The feeling of being ripped into two people: the you of before and the one you'll always be once you know what it is to lose something.

Saul carries me through the woods, jogging me up in his arms every few yards. When we get to the hill, he can't bear it any longer. He sets me on the grass and touches my teary cheeks. He mouths something and pulls my forehead against his throat, smoothing my hair. He pulls away, looks hard into my eyes, and squeezes my neck.

You're going to be okay, he silently promises. *It's over, June.*

I close my eyes against more tears, our hands twined together like old roots as we walk back to the sunroom. There's nothing else to do.

This moment is over. There's nothing left for us here.

Seventeen

I tell Saul I need to be alone. I beg him to leave. I tell him I never want to see him again. I tell him I need him to go, over and over, until he gives in. He slinks through the back door.

I sit in the sunroom until my face is placid, then tell Mom and Toddy I don't feel well and go upstairs.

They believe me—I don't look well.

I climb into bed and pray for sleep, for darkness to hide me. For time to stretch out while my eyes are closed so that when they next open, centuries will have passed and nothing will hurt like it does now.

Is this a sign? Punishment for spending time with Saul?

The words he said in the forest replay in my mind: *You can have me, but leave June alone.* Nameless wasn't just an omen. It *killed* Dad. Did it kill Bekah too?

Eventually, I fall into an agitated sleep.

"*No*," I wake myself a dozen times saying. "No, no. Please, no."
Don't let him be dead. Don't let that moment have happened. Wash it from my mind.

In the morning, I wake to a text from Hannah: *Need beach. Will die soon from calc overdose. Send help.*

I weakly push my covers away and sit up to glare at Feathers. She's been here all night, sorrowful and glistening, but her presence doesn't comfort me. It reminds me of the darkness wrapped around Dad in the woods. "It killed him," I whisper.

Feathers slumps, recedes into the wall.

My body's sore from crying. The precise moment the life left Dad's body is imprinted on my retinas in a way that feels permanent. I can't tell Mom what's happening; even if she'd believe me, I couldn't give her that burden. I need Hannah. And not the way our friendship has been lately, with gaps and secrets. I need her as my best friend. *Immediately*, I text her, then go to my dresser and sift through my drawers.

Fifteen minutes, she replies, then, *(read as: thirty)*.

I pull on a pair of jeans, a crop top, and a long crocheted sweater and grab my sun hat and purse from the hook on the wall. All the while, there's the feeling that I've forgotten something.

I remember this sensation, from when I was eight. For seconds, you forget. Like walking into a room and having no idea what you came for, your mind blanks. You know there's something you should be thinking about, because lately your only job has been to think about it.

But then—*ping*—it's back. You'll always remember.

I put on a pair of brown sandals then check for Whites before stepping into the hall. Part of me wants to look for a memory to overshadow last night's, some clue to understanding Dad's strange words. The majority hopes I never see a White again.

I tell Mom and Toddy where I'm going, give them both a kiss on the cheek, and step out onto the porch to wait. It's a balmy fifty degrees, and the sun's starting to haul itself over the trees—*ping.* Dad's dead.

The Subaru rumbles up the drive, and Hannah waves her arms dramatically from the driver's seat. "You're aliiiiive," I cry as I plop down beside her and offer my pre-kissed fingers.

Ping! Dad's not.

"I knoooow." She matches my hand's gesture, then reverses down the driveway and points the car toward Twin Gull Dunes. "How are you? I feel like I haven't seen you in forever."

"Or, like, Friday, when you gave me a ride home from school." My voice shakes, and she eyes me uncertainly.

"Not real, quality time," she says.

"No, definitely not." I clear the phlegmy rattle from my throat. "Is dropping out still on the table for you? Because I think we should consider that."

"Nah," she says. "The rumor mill suggests that creative writing class is draining Stephen Niequist's GPA, so I'm pretty much kicking his butt now. Anyway, what's going on, Junie? You look upset."

I chew on my bottom lip and shake my head. I don't know where to start: Saul, or the memories, or all the indescribable stuff in between. "Hannah."

Her eyes flicker to me. "Baby girl. What's wrong?"

Saul first. I don't understand how my heart can be moving so fast and fearfully while my stomach can feel so heavy and tight. "Can you pull over?"

"Sure." She swerves to the edge of the craggy asphalt.

I clear my throat again, bat my eyelashes dry.

"I need to tell you something because *not* telling you feels like lying."

"Okay," she says uneasily.

I blink back the sting in my eyes. "The reason I haven't wanted to go on those double dates isn't because I don't like Nate. And it's also not totally because of my family's problems with the Angerts."

Her hand flies to her chest. "Oh my god, did I do something?"

"No! No, Han." I swallow the tension bunching in my throat. "Okay, so that night at the carnival, when I met Saul, I guess . . . I was pretty into him."

Hannah laughs. "Of course you were! He's beautiful."

"Sure," I say. "But I don't just mean I noticed he was hot. You know he's not my type."

"He owns deodorant," she agrees.

"I was *really* into him, Hannah. Like into him enough that I didn't want to be around him because of my family, but also because I *knew* he was, like, your *forever crush*. And then you set up that tutoring session, and the more time I spent with him, the more I liked him. And I tried not to, because you're one of the most important people in my life, and I don't know how you feel, but I don't know how to turn this off."

Hannah drops her forehead onto the steering wheel and lets out a laugh.

"Hannah, I'm not joking."

"Nate and I made out!" she yelps, sitting up. Her entire face turns pink, making her blond hair look pearly in comparison. "Honestly, like, four separate times now. And I was going to tell you, but I was embarrassed, and I wanted to be sure how I felt."

"You made out. Four times. With Nate Baars."

"Don't say it like that!"

"Four times, like, for three minutes each?"

She gives me a reproachful look.

"Wow."

"I know."

"Wooow," I say. "So . . . not a full moon–induced fluke? You *like* Nate?"

She sighs. "I would go so far as to say I *really* like him."

I nod. "And . . . Saul?"

She snorts. "*You* were born to have chemistry with *dreamy* Saul Angert. *I* have been cursed to fall into Nate Baars's big, stupid mouth over and over again until I admit I don't even think it's that big! Or stupid!"

"You're seriously not upset with me?"

"Frankly, June, I'm annoyed you thought this would be a big deal. Am I so pathetic you thought I'd fall on my sword over you liking someone I've barely spoken to? I *had*—past tense—*had* a crush on Saul Angert like I had a crush on young James Dean, or Ryan Gosling. It's the kind of crush you share with the masses. If you called me and were like, *Hannah, young James Dean just brought a pizza to my door, do you think I should make out with him?* I would be like, *If you cut me, do I not bleed? What are you doing calling me at a time like this? Of course I want you to make out with him, and then I want you to call me and tell me everything.*"

I shake my head. "Second of all, Saul was in your MARRY column."

"My *what*?"

"In your closet."

She dissolves into laughter and covers her face with her hands. "Oh my God, June! Damon Salvatore and Gilbert Blythe were on that list! What do you think of me?"

Now I crumble into laughter too. For the first time in twenty-four hours, the knot in my stomach loosens.

Hannah reaches across the center console and threads her fingers through mine. "You cannot imagine how loved and special it makes me feel that you were worried about this," she says. "I mean, it also sort of makes me feel like a choad. But mostly it makes me *miss* you, June."

I kiss my fingers, and she kisses her; we press them together, promising to get through anything, to still be best friends on the other side. "Forever," I say.

"Always," she agrees. She restarts the car but doesn't pull back onto the road right away. "Is this what had you all upset?"

Ping!

"Um." My voice wrenches upward, and I close my eyes. "Well. I also saw my Dad die?"

"*What?*"

"The Whites showed me," I say. I close my eyes for a long moment, until I'm steady enough to say the rest. "It wasn't a heart attack—at least not *just* a heart attack. Nameless killed him."

"Oh my God. June," she says.

"It was terrible, Han." My voice shudders. "Dad was there, and then Nameless wrapped around him, and it was like suddenly he wasn't himself anymore. It was just his body, and I knew he was gone. I *felt* him leave."

"Oh, baby girl." Hannah folds me into her arms.

"They showed us some of Saul's sister's memories too," I murmur into her hair, and she sits back. "And some that belonged to strangers."

Her mouth quivers open, and her throat bobs. "Maybe the memories aren't at your house because they *happened* there but because of where your house is. On the thin place."

"Like they're coming back from . . . heaven?"

Hannah shrugs. "From somewhere. But there's no way you'd find your Dad's and Bekah's memories randomly, at least not more than once. *Something* must be bringing those memories to you specifically, right?"

When I finish telling her what I heard Dad say to Nameless, Hannah slumps in her seat, chewing on her lip. "June." She hesitates for a second. "If your dad *is* sending you these Whites, maybe . . ." She swallows hard, shaking her head. "Maybe it's a warning."

My stomach jerks within me. My vision splotches, and I dig my fingernails harder into my skin. *What if Nameless killed both Dad and Bekah? What if they're trying to warn us that Saul and I are next?* "Maybe," I whisper.

Hannah reaches across the car and pulls my hand into hers. "What do we do, June?"

I shake my head. I can think of only one thing, a thing I'm not sure I'm capable of doing again: going back into the Whites.

"I don't know yet," I answer.

"Well," Hannah says. "In the meantime, let's get our asses to the beach, lie in the sunlight, and smother you with love." She tries to smile. "You'll get through this, June. You shouldn't have to, but you will."

Eighteen

LIKE the first time I lost Dad, I'm surprised how quickly the white-hot pain fades into a gnawing ache. I've put ten years between me and that day, but today I feel eight again: mixed up, afraid of the world that once made me feel so loved, so safe.

The gaps of *forgetting* shorten until most of the time, a world without Dad is my new reality. Again.

All day at the beach, Hannah lets me talk things out. Tell stories about Dad that make me almost happy, slip back into crying, panic over the darkness that lurks in the woods, wander toward conversation about Saul and Nate and school.

I swear off the Whites then decide I *have* to keep investigating them a dozen times over.

Hannah's there with me as I settle into the rhythm of grief.

When I get home that night, I still haven't made a decision

about the Whites. I ignore the swarms in the windows and try to focus on my writing assignment.

I start, strike, and rewrite another one of Dad's stories, about the day he proposed to Mom. But thinking about the rich timbre of his laugh, the way he always leaned in when he told this story, the moments when he'd pause for dramatic effect—recalling each of these details makes me feel as if another nail is being driven through me, pinning me to the ground.

Like I'll never feel anything again except this invisible weight crushing my every inch.

Long after I've climbed into bed, my phone buzzes with an e-mail from Saul: *June.*

My blood turns to lava as I stare at it. I type a reply, *Saul,* but don't send it. Instead I stare until my phone light fades, then tap it back on and stare some more.

June.

Even if I'm not risking Hannah's friendship, the way I'm starting to feel about Saul *is* risking something. My whole life Dad told me to stay away from the Angerts, that *Bad Things happen when we cross paths.* It scares me how easy it's been to ignore all that since I met Saul.

But after what I saw yesterday, it's harder.

I close the message and think again of Dad's story, focus on it.

He'd been traveling a lot, and most recently he'd been in New Mexico when he saw smoke coming from a rounded summit to his north. He pulled his car over and left it on the scrubby side of the road as he wandered toward the stacks of soot, with nothing but the box of dried cherries he'd brought from home. He always took them when he traveled, partly because he could taste the sunlight on the lake in every bite and partly because, if he got a tickle in his throat or ache in his belly, he could swallow a few and wake up feeling good as new.

When he reached the bottom of the hill, everything was engulfed. The fire had raced quickly along the arms of dehydrated ponderosa pines to attack both cities at the base of the mountain. An overworked team of firefighters rushed around, trying to evacuate homes before the flames could stretch any farther, but there weren't enough of them. Dad set his box of cherries on a rock and dove in to help, ushering families to cars and buses. They worked tirelessly through the night, emptying the cities. Whenever they pulled a woman from a collapsed house, or dragged cats and dogs from flaming top floors, Dad returned to his box of cherries and gave a Jack's Tart to the injured, one bite miraculously healing their burns.

By morning they'd evacuated three hundred houses, and not a single person had died. Everyone was exhausted, ready to sleep when the bleary tangerine sun came up, but Dad had given out all his cherries and was tired in a different way, the kind that's run out of Home. So he got in his car and drove straight through the next day and night.

When he finally got there, he found Mom sitting at the kitchen table. Seeing her there made him homesick, even though he was back, like he realized right then how much time he'd lost with her and their farmhouse on the hill and had to catch up on all the *missing it* he'd forgotten to do while away.

Here's the thing about Dad, about all the Jacks: They're lake people, sponges. They have adventurous spirits but get restless when they're away from the water too long. Like Jonathan Alroy O'Donnell and his grandson Jack the First and great-grandson Jack II, Dad wanted to see the world, but he had to do it in spurts because he felt so wrong when he couldn't go stand at the edge of the lake and look out at the familiar way the sunlight bounced on its wriggling back. The cherries let him take the taste of home with him, but eventually, cherries got eaten and Jacks had to go home once again.

When Dad got back to Five Fingers and saw Mom at that table, the first thing he wanted to do was gather her in his arms and take her to the lake, so he could see his two loves side by side. It didn't matter that it was late January and the whole town was heaped in snow.

They climbed in his truck and drove to the falls, which had fully frozen over, turning the whole cave into a shimmering hall of ice. There, Dad got down on one knee and told Mom he would love her in warmth and cold, that she'd be as beautiful to him when she was old and cracking as she was when she was young and verdant; he would find something to love about her in every season of life, and he would always, always come home.

I loved the story as a kid. Dad told it to me all the time, and sometimes I asked Mom to too. She'd smile and say, "There are always at least two versions of everything, June. I've forgotten my own because I love your daddy's so much."

My daddy.

I start to cry.

Feathers wriggles at the foot of my bed, mourning or warning me or maybe simply being.

On Monday, the rest of the class turns in their poems to Ms. deGeest while I sit there empty-handed. When the bell rings and everyone files out of the room, I hang back, watching Ms. deGeest clean the board.

"I have a question," I say, and she turns around, swiping her hands together like she always does.

"All right. What's up, Junior?"

"I couldn't write it," I say. "I had an idea for a story, and I swear I tried, but I got stuck."

"You didn't turn anything in?"

"I was wondering if I could have an extension."

"I don't give extensions."

"Okay, well, will you at least read it when I *do* turn it in? I can take the zero—I don't care."

She's silent for a beat, her posture reminiscent of a hunting cat. "You shouldn't be okay with zeroes, Junior."

"Are you telling me to beg?"

"I'm telling you to do the work. I'll give you an extension this once, but here's what I'm going to do. I'm going to talk to the office and get your enrollment in this class re-designated as an independent study with me. You'll come here for both your study halls, so I know you're taking this seriously. And if you show up for the rest of the semester, I'm going to do two things: First, I'm going to write you an amazing recommendation letter that will at least partially explain your poor grades. Second, I'm going to talk to the principal about continuing your independent study into next semester. I'll use two of my planning periods each week to meet with you, and the other three you'll work silently in this room or the library. If you stop showing up, physically or mentally, I'll retract my recommendation, and I won't feel bad about it. Does that work for you?"

I stare, unsure what to say. *I'm not going to college? No letter of recommendation can make up for grades like mine? I want my study halls to be study halls?* Those are the things I would've said before this class, but that's not what comes out.

"That works."

She flashes a straight white smile. "Good. Close the door on your way out."

I'm distracted all night while I help Mom and Toddy cook dinner. While we're eating, Mom interrupts Grayson's dramatic retelling of a game they played at school to ask whether I'm feeling okay, and Toddy pushes back his chair to come feel my forehead.

"A little warm there, Junie," he says.

"I think I'll go lie down," I say.

"Do you feel sick?"

"A little." It's true. The thought of venturing back into memory nauseates me even as it pulls on me. What are the odds I'll see That Day again? Despite that risk, I need to see him. I need to understand what he knew about Nameless that Saul and I are missing.

Leave June alone. She's not like us. She won't be. I promise you. Leave her alone.

Shivers snake down my spine, and Mom reaches across the dinner table, worried, and touches my arm. "Take some ibuprofen, baby," she says. "It will help with the fever."

Upstairs, I slip my shoes off outside my bedroom, but there aren't any Whites in the doorway.

I scan the other doors at my disposal: Mom and Toddy's, Grayson and Shadow's, the bathroom—there, one lone White. I close the door to my bedroom so Mom and Toddy will think I'm sleeping if they check on me, then reach my hand out and let the White skate over me. It settles on my skin, and as it dissolves, I step into the bathroom.

The effect is immediate.

I'm downstairs in the dining room again, as though the hallways in my house got tangled and spit me out at the table. In this version of the dining room, it's late at night and the pink ghost ripples in the corner.

Dressed in pajamas and a long sweater, Mom sits at the table, her hand resting on the green corded phone she and Dad kept for posterity's sake well into my childhood. Her soft waves hang in a loose ponytail, and her eyes look puffy and wet. The wrinkles I'm used to seeing around her lips and eyes have vanished, and her cheeks are soft and round.

She stands and paces. Feathers follows her as she disappears around the corner into the sunroom. Everything stops, as it did in the forest—the crickets and cicadas falling silent, the whirring fan freezing. The drapes blowing inward from the moonlit windows pause. This memory is over.

A new White bobs against the doorframe Mom passed through.

I cup it, letting it take me through the doorway to another moment. I'm instantly back in the kitchen, seeing the exact same thing as before, only Mom's clothes are different and her hair hangs over her shoulders.

Again she stands and paces. Followed by Feathers, she turns and walks through the back door, pausing the memory. Again a single White waits for me.

I clasp it and follow.

I blink and find myself back at the entrance to the dining room.

The cycle repeats four more times, and every time I snap back into place beside the worn kitchen table, Mom looks more tired, her eyes a little pinker and puffier until finally she's sleeping with her head down against a place mat when there's a commotion down the hall.

Feathers recedes into the wall, and Mom lurches to her feet. She reaches for a knife from the block on the counter. Morning light spills through the front door as Dad comes down the hall. He stops, looks at Mom and the knife she's holding, then walks past and opens the refrigerator without a word.

"Where have you been, Jack?" she whispers.

"Went to New Mexico."

Mom sets down the knife and folds her arms around herself. "New Mexico?"

"I was thinking we could go see the ice caves this morning—what do you think, Le?"

Mom doesn't say anything at first. Dad smiles sort of sheepishly, and she says, "Okay."

"Get your coat." He grabs an apple from the fridge, swings it shut, and plants a kiss on Mom's forehead. She closes her eyes, the corners of her mouth tightening like metal twist ties. She pulls away and goes to the coat closet. I chase them through the front door, a White zipping to meet me there, to carry me away.

Across the threshold, I don't find myself in the yard. I'm in the cave again, and it's *exactly* how Dad described it: a wall of blue-green spears of ice stretching down to the snowy floor. The sun must be mostly up by now, because the whole place glitters as Dad circles it, running his hand along the icy wall. "Isn't it beautiful, Le?"

Mom stands with her hands in her coat pockets at the center of the cave. Dad glances at her. Shakily, she draws a folded piece of paper out and scrutinizes it. She holds it out to him.

Dad crosses to accept it. "What's this?"

"You know what it is, Jack."

"A plane ticket?" His voice sounds hollow. He storms away from her, then turns back. "Léa."

"You've been gone three weeks, Jack."

"I'm back."

"You didn't tell me where you were going or how long you'd be away." Her eyes cloud. "You left me there, alone, in your house, and I didn't know if you were coming back."

"I'm *back*," he repeats.

"How could you leave me there?"

"I don't know," he says. "I was confused."

"I miss my family," Mom says. "And now that your father's gone, there's no one here for me. When you're gone, I'm completely alone, and I can't keep doing that. I can't go through this again."

Dad starts to cry, hard. Harder than I would've thought possible, and Mom first looks stunned, then sad. She goes to him and draws his face up with her hands.

"I don't want to feel this way anymore," he says.

Mom's hands skim through his hair. "I know."

Dad drops forward onto his knees in the snow and buries his hands and face into Mom's stomach. "Marry me, Le."

She presses her fingers to her mouth, crying. "You know I can't."

Dad's eyes rove over her face. "I'll get help."

"Jack."

"I'll always come home," he promises. "I'll love you when I'm hot and when I'm cold. I'll love you as much as I do right now, forever, and I'll always, always come home."

"You know I can't say no," Mom cries into her hands. He stands, pulling her wrists down to cup her fingers between his.

"You can," he says. She twines her hands around his neck, nestling her face into the crook of his shoulder. "You don't have to believe me, but I'm going to get help. Whether you say yes or not. I don't want to live like this anymore. You can say no."

"Jack." Mom takes a deep breath. "I'm pregnant."

First his lips part. His eyes flick between her eyes and her mouth. A breathy laugh erupts from him. "You're pregnant?"

Mom nods, and Dad laughs again, which makes a smile stretch across Mom's teary face too. He grabs the sides of her face and kisses her. "You're pregnant."

"I'm pregnant."

And suddenly, they're happy. So happy they're laughing, so happy they're crying, but I can't breathe. Black splotches speckle my vision. Something heavy is pinned on my chest. The walls of ice are closing in.

This isn't how it happened. This isn't what I came from.

I wasn't the thing that made Mom stay. It was love, the thing that made me.

It was supposed to be love.

I stumble from the cave, collapsing against the frozen wall. I drag myself toward the shock of daylight. When I cross the threshold, I find myself back in the hallway outside my bathroom.

Laughter trickles up the stairs: Mom, Toddy, Grayson, Shadow. Happy, healthy, living.

I stagger into my bedroom, wheezing out hot tears. A shapeless dark writhes outside my window, watching me. "Why are you doing this to me?" I ask the house I once called magic. "Why are you haunting me?"

Nineteen

MS. DEGEEST looks up from the pages in her hand. She'd insisted on reading them immediately after class so we could discuss. My phone lights up with a message full of question marks from Hannah, who's waiting for me outside at our table.

Talking to deGeest, I type. *Be out ASAP but maybe wait inside just in case?* The temperature's hovering around forty degrees. We'll have snow by Halloween.

"You're going to be a phenomenal writer someday, Junior," Ms. deGeest says finally.

"Someday," I repeat.

"Don't get me wrong—it's good."

"Great. That seems worth not being able to look my mother in the eye."

"So this story is true?"

"Apparently. As of two nights ago, anyway." It had been

surprisingly easy to write, carried out of me in a rush of impotent anger I had nowhere else to exert.

She points a French-manicured finger at me. "You've nailed your problem. Sometimes, when we write about conflicts we're still in the middle of, we produce great emotion, strong feelings, but the technical aspects of the story fall to the wayside, because we don't understand the interconnectedness of all the elements of our own narrative yet."

"The interconnectedness?"

She opens the gray filing cabinet against the wall and pulls out one of those metal ball pendulums—a Newton's cradle, I think they're called. She sets it on the desk, lifts the metal ball on the right, and lets it drop, sending a shock wave through the three center balls that results in the far left ball swinging outward, then back in, where it sends the shock back again.

"I meant to use this for a lesson, but I totally forgot," she says. "Your work tends to create snapshots of powerful moments. But often it reads as a series of events. This happens, *and then* this, *and then* this, *and then* this. What we're looking for is: This happens, *therefore* this happens, *but then* this happens, *therefore* this happens.

"This scene you wrote works, but it might work better as part of a larger piece, once you're further off—when you can put things into perspective. I think you should consider working in the realm of fiction for a while. You can always come back to family history later."

"You don't know that," I say.

"Excuse me?"

"You don't *know* I can always come back. No one gets that guarantee. That's the whole point."

Ms. deGeest shakes her head. "The whole point of what?"

"That's why I have to piece this all together." I snatch the papers. "Because *usually*, when a person goes, the truth goes with him, and someday even the stories—the lies he told—are forgotten, and there's no way to recover them."

There's no way to recover *him*.

"Junior, wait!"

I'm already out the door.

"What's wrong?" Hannah asks as I brush past her.

"Everything," I choke. "It was all a lie, Hannah. He wasn't who I thought he was. I'm not who I've always thought I am."

Not the child of two adoring parents tragically ripped apart, but the child who made Mom stay when she should've left.

Not a house overlapping with heaven; an endless tunnel of bad memories.

Not a magic house, but a haunted one.

I'm a lie.

Hannah offers to take a night off from violin and studying to comfort me, but the look of trepidation on her face as she does is enough to make me decline. Instead, when she drops me off at home, I slip upstairs to "study," and spend the night staring at Feathers's lava-lamp burbling.

What's one white lie when Mom and Dad lied to me my whole

life? I feel so stupid for everything I used to believe. Who thinks it's *normal* for her dad to be gone for weeks at a time with no phone calls, no texts, no postcards? How naïve do you have to be to convince yourself your mom doesn't mind that kind of instability, that she's happy with it?

Leave June alone. She's not like us. Leave her alone.

I wrap myself in blankets, but I'm still cold and shuddering. What did he mean? What does any of this mean?

"Some help you are," I whisper to Feathers, and she withdraws.

Minutes pass. Hours pass. The sun goes down and the moon glides up. The stars twinkle and the crickets sing, voices thin, starting to die off in the cold. Still I stare at my dead-starred ceiling, unable to get warm.

After what the Whites showed me in the ice cave, everything's different. If Dad's stories weren't true, that changes everything. Who he was. Who *I* am. What his rules mean.

Maybe that's what the Whites wanted me to see, what they started telling me the night Saul came back.

I shove aside thoughts of Nameless and open Saul's last e-mail: *June.* When I read it, I can hear his voice, warm and rattling and close. I see slivers of his teeth glowing in the dark, moonlight across the slight dent in his nose as he drove me down the forested lane, snatches of his hands cupped around his eyes as he looked at me through the extraordinary light of the sun on the waves in Bekah's memory of the beach that day. His dimple shadowed purple, his mouth moving silently inches from mine: *Hi.*

It's nearly two in the morning when I send my reply: *Saul.*

He answers immediately. *June, at last.*

I attach my last story and send a blank e-mail back. Twenty minutes later, my phone buzzes again. *It happened again? You saw this?*

Yeah, I answer.

Are you okay?

No.

I'm useless, but I'm here.

My pulse quickens and blood warms. I'm running out of reasons and willpower to avoid him. *Tomorrow?* I say.

What about it? You'll have to be more specific.

I wonder if we're the first people since 2001 to have a real-time conversation via e-mail.

I like how permanent it feels, he says, then a minute later: *So you're not going to clarify about "tomorrow"?*

Nah.

Yes to tomorrow, he says. *What time?*

I have to go to high school during the day, because I'm in high school. So after that.

Can you pick me up from the nursing home after?

> *No, you're the only old person I'm not afraid of. You come to me.*

June.

> *Saul.*

You're incorrigible.

> *How does it make you feel to know I just had to look that word up?*

It takes so long for him to respond that I'm almost asleep when I feel the vibration beneath my hand. *Strangely charmed/appreciative that you need a tutor.*

Twenty

AT lunch the next day, feeble sunlight lances through the cafeteria windows, striping Hannah's face, and wind thunks angrily against the glass as she asks suddenly, "Are you going to try to make it happen again? See another memory?"

"I don't know," I admit. "I'm so overwhelmed by all of this." She nods understanding, and I ask, "Do you think it's possible what I saw in the cave wasn't real? Like, maybe some kind of ancient mold has been giving me and Saul shared hallucinations."

Hannah twirls her hair. "June, this is Five Fingers. Coywolves ignore sleeping chickens to score Old Navy dollar-bin flip-flops, and I've run through a feathery ghost, and once when we were playing hide-and-seek in the woods, I swear I saw my Grandma Ortiz climbing a tree. I mean, that woman moved at a nebbish shuffle the last five years of her life and there she was, hair ten shades darker and dressed in overalls, perched in a branch twenty-five feet off the ground. When I got to the tree? Gone.

"I'm sorry, babe, but the question isn't whether this is happening. It's *why*. You need to figure out what the memories are trying to tell you."

"That my life has been a lie?"

Hannah swishes her mouth back and forth. "Your life hasn't been a lie. I mean, my parents married for love and my dad *still* cheated and moved to Colorado and waited three months to so much as e-mail me. Your dad never would've done that. He never would've left you or your mom willingly."

"He did all the time."

"No," Hannah says sharply. "He always came back." She examines her tray. "Maybe that's what he wants you to know. That's a pretty good message from the afterlife, as far as messages from the afterlife go."

"I thought maybe it was about the Angerts," I say. "Like he, or *someone*, wanted me to forget about the feud."

Hannah nods thoughtfully. "You *did* say it started the night you met Saul."

She shakes her head once, and I can guess what she's thinking. That theory doesn't explain what I saw happen with my dad and Nameless.

She's not like us. Leave her alone. Please show her.

After school Hannah puts off her psych research to come over. We wander the house barefoot for an hour and a half, searching for Whites with no results.

"Your magic house doesn't like me as much as Saul," she groans. "I've never felt so betrayed."

"It's kind of a bitch. Don't feel bad."

"Why do you keep looking at the clock?" Hannah asks.

"I don't."

"Do too. What's the—" Hannah grins. "Ah."

"Just a tutoring session. I can reschedule."

"Stop," she says. "I have a violin lesson anyway."

"Oh, is *that* what you're calling Nate? And how is 'violin'?"

Her cheeks dimple. "Ridiculous. Still pestering me about camping at the dunes with you and his cousin."

"Wow."

"Acclimated to the idea yet?" she says. "Keep trying. Anyway, he asked me to be his girlfriend."

"Seriously?"

"First he asked me to prom. Then he remembered homecoming comes first, and he asked me to that, and then he got nervous and asked me out for real."

"What'd you say?"

"We'll see about prom, yes to homecoming, and let's talk about making it official *after* homecoming."

"Hannah!" I shake her elbow. "Nate Baars!"

"He's great. He's so different than he comes off. I think he gets nervous or something. He's actually kind of shy, and super sweet, and he just, like . . . *likes* people."

"Weird."

"I know, right? Anyway, I feel like he's kind of *rare*. I just don't know if I want a boyfriend this year. Seems like an unnecessary complication."

"Maybe."

"I don't want to get so swept up that I blink and it's time to leave, and I've hardly seen you. I already feel like I've done that with schoolwork, and those are weeks of weekends I'll never get back."

"You're not going to lose me, Hannah. Not to Nate, not to school, not to anything."

Not even to a curse, I silently vow.

"Same," she promises.

Mom comes in then, the boys whipping past her straight toward the fridge. "Hey, Hannah!" she sings, giving her a squeeze around the shoulders. "Haven't seen much of you lately. What are you girls up to tonight? Do you want to come to Shadow's basketball game with us?"

Shadow looks over his shoulder at us and blushes shyly at Hannah. He's had a crush on her since he was born. "Oh, man, I'd love to," Hannah says. "But I have a paper to write, and I think June has tutoring?"

"Hey, Mom, did you know Mike has tattoos but he's not trying too hard?" Grayson calls, popping open a can of Mountain Dew he definitely does not need.

"I did not, *mon chou*." Mom closes the fridge. "And though we would never get tattoos, it's none of our business that Mike did, right?"

Grayson runs toward the TV. "I'd get them. They're cool."

Mom shoots Hannah and me an *Oh, brother!* look. "Gray, there's no time for video games. We have to be back at school in an hour. Wash your hands and get ready for dinner." Grayson whines, and Mom turns back to us. "And, Junior, please stay in the living room or sunroom while Mike's here, okay? I'm not terribly comfortable having him here while Toddy and I are out."

"*Mom*," I say.

"Junior, please."

"I *will*."

As soon as she's out of earshot Hannah looks at me and says, "Or *don't*."

Saul shows up fifteen minutes before my family leaves for Shadow's game, and Mom and Toddy are *thrilled* to hear he wants to take me to the library. I get the feeling Toddy had planned to (attempt to) veto Mom's decision to let us have an unsupervised tutoring session and is relieved he doesn't have to play bad cop after all.

Saul's wearing long sleeves again, which I'm fairly sure I catch Mom trying to x-ray for signs of tattoos, but at least the cutting fall wind justifies his clothing choice this time. I, for my part, am doing my best to act politely indifferent to my tutor, instead of like my brain is filling with shooting stars at the sight of him. As horrible as our last day was together, I can still feel the ghost of his arms around me, his hands in my hair.

"What's at the library?" I ask.

"Books, June," he says, then curbs the flirtation in his voice by adding, "I reserved some stuff on craft I think you'll find helpful."

It doesn't matter that my parents and the boys are running late: Toddy fuddles in the kitchen "looking for a snack" until Saul and I are safely out the door. It's mostly dark out, and the grass crunches with a hint of frost as we make our way to the Saturn. Around the cherry tree, the sprouts Grayson and Shadow planted last week have grown to about a foot tall, stringy but vibrant.

"Books on craft," I say.

"Some," Saul replies. "Mostly books on thin places."

"And with your rigorous schedule you couldn't get them ahead of time?"

His ears turn the tiniest bit pink, and he scratches his jaw as we pull away. "You seem a little bit freaked out every time I come over," he says. "I mean, *not* by the magic stuff."

"I have been," I admit.

"Yeah."

I want to say, *I'm not anymore.* It's not quite true. In some ways, I'm more freaked out than ever. Seeing a more complete picture of my father may have freed up my opinions on the Angerts, my feelings for Saul, but it has also fundamentally changed who I've always believed I am.

I am a Jack, my father's daughter. All my life people have told me they see Dad in me, and now that means something different than it used to. My blood feels heavy in my veins.

I want to forget who I am.

I don't want to be a Jack. I want to be just June.

"We can go back to my house after we pick up the books," I say. "My parents will literally not do a thing."

"I want them to like me," Saul replies.

They won't, no matter what, I want to tell him, so we might as well break all the rules.

We park outside the library and run through the shrieking cold and skittering leaves to the door. Past the circulation desk, we find the shelves where they keep reserved books, trailing along the *A* surnames to *Angert*. Saul pulls out five books rubber-banded together and tagged with his name, and he passes me a couple before leading the way through the warmly lit stacks.

We turn down an aisle toward the study tables, and a blond girl in a houndstooth peacoat straightens from where she was crouched beside the bottom row and turns toward us. Saul stops short.

"Saul," Ms. deGeest says. "I wondered when I'd run into you."

"Allison," Saul says. "Hi. I didn't know you'd moved back."

"Yeah, a few months ago." She grabs his arm and gives a dazzling smile before her sharp blue eyes wander to me and try to blink either me or her confusion away. "Junior. Hi."

Her expression moves from puzzled to shocked understanding in four-tenths of a second. "You guys *know* each other." She looks pointedly at Saul. "Junior's in my creative writing class at the high school. She's a super bright kid."

"Oh," Saul says. "Cool. Yeah, June's talented."

Allison deGeest half-laughs, folds her arms across her chest, and shakes her head to toss her hair over her shoulder. "Yeah, *June's* great."

"Okay, we should get back to work," I say.

"Oh, are you tutoring her?"

For a second she seems to consider this a real possibility, but then Saul says, "Not tonight. Great to run into you, Allison. Have a good night."

"We should meet up." Her eyes dip toward me. "If you have time."

"Sure," Saul says. He steers me toward the study tables again. "So that's a high school friend of mine, Allison, who is a little bit terrifying and also your teacher now."

"I've never heard my own name sound so crude."

"Yeah, well, what can I say? I'm drawn to laid-back, un-snarky girls."

"Drawn to?"

A heavy smile tugs at his mouth. "Are you asking me something, June?"

"I wasn't going to."

"You can."

"Isn't she a little old for you?"

His laugh rattles in his throat. "She was the older sister of a friend. There was a brief . . . *thing*."

"Oh god. This is so . . . you and Allison deGeest?"

"June, come on. Local legend has it you once kissed Nate behind a slide."

"First of all, remembering that will never be any source of comfort to me. Second of all, is Nate responsible for your future? Does he give you grades, and if so, on what?"

Saul's forehead inclines toward me imploringly. *"June."*

"Can we leave now? I think the back of my head is two seconds from bursting into flames."

"It's not you," he says, blushing. "I mean, she's probably worried about you. I didn't have a great reputation back then. Also she thinks of me as her peer and you as her student."

"Ugh."

He gives one scratchy laugh. "Sorry. That was weird."

"Let's just go." We're silent for the length of the ride home. Saul keeps looking over at me, and I'm reminded of the night he drove me home from the theater. Maybe the reality of running into his former *whatever*, who also happens to be my teacher, has brought him back to where he was that night: feeling a little pathetic. Anxiety wrings my insides, and an ache of disappointment, embarrassment, and jealousy radiates low in my stomach.

Saul and the closest thing I have to a mentor.

Maybe this is the universe's last-ditch effort to separate two fatally star-crossed people before their collision destroys everything around them.

The image of the darkness closing in around Dad sizzles across my mind. *Leave her alone.*

No matter what the universe has to say about it, Saul and I can't walk away until we understand the Whites' message. *Their warning.*

When we get home, we spread the books along the coffee table. Some center around Celtic mythology, others the musings of Catholic priests on places where miracles happened. A couple of collections of essays investigate buildings and natural landmarks where the veil between heaven and earth is so flimsy the authors accidentally passed through and the world transformed before their eyes.

"We can start with reading and then try some Whites, or we can do the opposite," Saul says. "Preference?"

"Reading." I'm still sick over the last two memories I saw. Still so confused and frustrated with Dad that I can't imagine facing him, though his words loop endlessly in my mind. *She's not like us. Leave her alone. Please show her.*

We can't put off the past forever. Tonight, I want to pretend we can.

Saul and I each pick a book and sit on the couch, backs propped against opposite ends, knees bent up and facing each other in the middle. I start skimming *Thin Places: Transformed by the Edge of Heaven* only to fall immediately into a Saul/Ms. deGeest spiral. I don't notice I'm drumming my fingers against the back of the couch until Saul sets his hand on them. "That's fairly distracting," he whispers.

"Saul," I whisper.

"June."

"Did I end up making you feel like a creep?"

He laughs. "Why would I feel like a creep?"

"You want me to say it?"

He looks at me. It's Serious Saul, not Flirting Saul. "Kind of."

"Because you like me, and I'm a *super bright kid*."

He glances at the book propped against his knees. "I don't."

"Oh-kay."

"I don't feel like a creep," he clarifies. After a few lapsed seconds, he says, "Anything else?" I shake my head, and he goes back to reading. I turn my hand over, and Saul's fingers trace slowly up my palm, then fall into the gaps between my fingers. He looks up again, and after a moment, his body shifts with a tired laugh. "I can leave, if you want."

Neither of us moves, though, and the silence stretches indefinitely. My stomach feels like it's slowly filling with lava, warm and thick, piling toward my throat.

"Okay," Saul says finally, standing. "Okay." I follow him toward the door, but he stops by the sunroom and faces me. "I do like you." He rubs his jaw anxiously. "I don't know if I said that part."

The heat has fully flooded my stomach, my chest, my esophagus. It's found its way through my legs. Beyond the open windows, owls hoot, the wind bats the trees, and a sudden vacuum has seemingly opened, sucking the universe and its many obstacles between Saul Angert and me from the house.

"I meant to," he says. "But in case I didn't," he nods, "I do."

I mean to say, *I like you.*

I manage only: "Oh."

Saul laughs and scratches at the back of his head. He turns to leave, and I grab his hand, tugging him into the dark sunroom, out of sight from the front door. He stares at me, so still he must be holding his breath. Or waiting for lightning to strike us. I touch his waist.

He touches my elbows. "June?"

"Saul?"

He draws me closer, a sliver of smile beginning in the corner of his mouth. "I'm worried you don't realize this isn't the way out."

"It's not?"

"The other thing is"—he takes the sides of my neck gingerly in his hands—"I'm getting sort of mixed signals here, so I want to clarify: What should I be doing right now?"

I knot my fingers into his shirt and step into him. "I like you, Saul. If you're on a roll, you can keep talking, or you can stop and kiss me."

His laugh is warm and coarse. His mouth is warm and coarse.

Twenty-One

SAUL'S laugh is still grating through him when his mouth catches mine. It travels through my cheeks and my stomach, hips, and fingers.

His hands slide around my back, catching bare skin and conjuring goose bumps as he pulls me closer in increments of millimeters. It's possible I've spent my whole life flexing every muscle in my stomach and now, relaxing for the first time, I might liquefy.

His arms tighten as he steps me back to the wall and presses his mouth, unhurried and deliberate, against my throat. His palms climb down my hips and thighs, back up to my neck like they can't sit still, and I don't want them to.

We're both a little clumsy, and I keep laughing because he feels so good. His smile widens, and our teeth bump together, but neither of us cares. The warmth of his stomach melts into my skin, but he's still too far away. His hands skim my back, press into my legs, rise up; they circle my waist beneath my shirt and settle at the bottom of my ribs, fingers gliding along the grooves between them.

He kisses me again, for the span of four sharp heartbeats, and when he pulls away, his hair is *almost* messy. He lifts my wrist and kisses the inside of it. "Are you going to disappear again?"

"What do you mean?"

"Will it be days before I hear from you?"

"It depends what grade I get on my next story."

"June."

"No, Saul. It won't be days."

He folds his arms around my waist and draws my stomach into his. "Now all we have to do is figure out how to navigate a thin place and tell your parents."

"No problem. I'll write them a note: *Dear Mom and Toddy, My tutor and I made out in the sunroom. Here is a diagram indicating which wall and pieces of furniture you should consider burning. Best wishes.*"

His laugh turns into a pseudo-groan as he slides his hands down my legs. "Maybe we should start by telling them my real name."

"God, sometimes you can be such a *Mike*."

He rolls his thumb across my bottom lip thoughtfully, then sinks into me again, his teeth skating across my lip. At the front of the house, the door whines open, keys jangle, and a jumble of voices flood inside.

Saul and I run into the living room and toss ourselves onto opposite couches, swiping books off the coffee table as my family's parading in.

"Shadow won!" Grayson shouts, storming toward us. "Hey, Mike, do you want to play video games?"

Saul looks at me, smirking, and adjusts the book over his lap. "I think I need to get home. Can I play next time?"

"I did *not* win." Shadow tromps in. "I *scored*, but my team lost."

Scored, Saul mouths at me, and I badly hide a laugh within a cough. "Well, at least you did well, right, bud?"

"Next time's fine, Mike!" Grayson shouts over his shoulder as he turns the TV on.

Mom and Toddy filter in last, slowly appraising the situation. "Back from the library already, huh?" Toddy says.

"Too loud," I say without looking up.

"I hope that's okay." Saul looks over the back of the couch into the kitchen. His ears don't even flush pink. "I thought it might be less distracting here."

"Yeah," Mom says vaguely. "So, you guys had fun?"

"Mhm," I murmur into my hand, then turn the page. "Studying's a blast."

Saul stands and lifts his backpack. "Read as much as you're able, and let me know when you want to meet up again."

"Yep," I reply. "Thanks for your help."

Somehow, that's the thing that makes his ears color.

"Thank you, Mike," Mom says.

"Get home safe," Toddy allows.

"Good night," Saul says.

Five minutes after he leaves, I close my book, pick the stack up, and announce I'm going to bed. I haven't even started my writing assignment for tomorrow, but I decide to put it off until study hall and climb into bed. Five minutes after that, I get Saul's first e-mail.

Felt a little bit more like a creep once I was trying
to escape without accidentally teaching your little
brothers about boners. I hope you're not reading this
in the midst of giving a birds-and-the-bees talk.

No, I type out, *my mom thought it would be best if you gave that*
lecture yourself. P.S. What's a boner? Asking for a friend.

Are you hitting on me, June? And if so, can I have
your phone number?

Yes and yes.

I'm so happy I'm grinning into my pillow. I'm so happy the
feeling can't fit in my body.

And then, out of nowhere, it happens. Something pink glistens
in the corner of my room and—

Ping: My dad's dead.

Ping: He might be trying to tell me something from beyond
the grave.

Ping: I never really knew him.

Ping: There's a dark, writhing, nameless thing that watches my
house.

This is how grief works. It watches; it waits; it hollows you out,
again and again.

My classmates pour out of the creative writing room as the bell
rings, but I hang back. Stephen is packing his things with the

speed of a geriatric sloth, and I offer him five bucks to pick up the pace.

"Twenty if you keep your best friend from ruining my best friend's life," he retorts.

"Han's not going to ruin Nate's life. She likes him."

"She also likes Stanford. Which do you think she'll choose, Junior?"

"Stanford? Hannah's not looking at Stanford," I say. "That's in California." She's looking at schools in the area. Maybe not the *immediate* area, but within a bearable drive: University of Michigan, University of Chicago, Northwestern.

Stephen's eyebrows flick upward. "If you say so." He pulls his books into his chest and walks out, leaving me alone with the person I least want to talk to.

"Ms. deGeest," I stammer. "Can I talk to you for a second?"

She faces me and rests her fingers on the tabletop. "If it's about your writing or this class, of course."

"It's about my *future* in this class, and whether it exists." Not that it really matters, since I didn't end up turning anything in today.

She nods. "I'm an adult, Junior."

I stifle my laugh too late. "Okay."

She winces. "I meant, I'm a *professional*. My offer stands."

"Wait, really?"

"June." She shifts uncomfortably against the edge of the table. "June, your personal life isn't my business. I just want you to hear me say this: *You're talented*. And I know you and Saul Angert have similar interests, and you're both clever and capable, and you've been through similar situations, but your life's just beginning. You have every opportunity in the world ahead of you. People from this town have a habit of sticking around, but if any part of you wants to try college, you should pursue it. And Saul—he's not here to stay. Once he gets back on track, this town won't be enough for him. Don't give yourself a reason not to reach your potential. Especially not a reason that's temporary."

I swallow a knot. "Is that all?"

"That's all," she says. "I want you to consider what you want from life."

I walk, stunned, into the library, where Hannah and Nate are making out. I pass them without a word to let them wrap things up, but Hannah calls, "See you!" to Nate and jogs after me. "How was claaaaass?"

"Good. My teacher told me not to date Saul."

"Wait, what? Is there any context for this?"

"Oh," I say. "That's the best part. They had a *thing* in high school."

"No," Hannah gasps, latching on to my arm. "Junie, that's awful. So she was, like, trying to stake a claim?"

"I don't think so. She basically told me Saul shouldn't keep me from going to college, and she also implied I'm his quarter-life-crisis booty call. Apparently this town isn't enough for people like Saul." *Like you, Hannah*, I think, tears springing into my eyes. "Once they're on track, they'll get out of here and leave the rest of us behind."

"Hey." Hannah yanks me to a halt outside the front doors. It's freezing and semi-dark, all the school's windows either aglow with light or blue and glare-streaked by the street lamps. "Maybe you are Saul's quarter-life crisis, but so what? Maybe he's yours. Or maybe you two are the luckiest people in the world and you've already found your fireworks-in-the-sky, holding-hands-until-you-die Forever Person. Guess what? There are drawbacks either way.

"Maybe you break up and it sucks, but then you heal and move on and fall in love again. Or maybe this is it, the last person you'll ever have butterflies for, your last first kiss, but you get to grow up together, start your life together sooner. And you know what else? You don't have to be afraid to walk away either way, because *you*, Jack O'Donnell IV, are amazing and my best friend, and there's no expiration date on soul-love. And if you and I want to go away to college, dammit, we're going to go away to college, and it's *not* going to stand in our way of finding love or happiness, and it's definitely not going to amount to *leaving each other behind*. We need to chase our dreams, Junie, and I don't know about you, but in my best and brightest dreams, you're *always* there."

There are tears in Hannah's eyes, and she doesn't blink them away. And then I'm crying too, because it hits me, hard. The words crack as they pass through my lips: "You're gonna move to California, aren't you?"

Hannah wraps her arms around me, and we stand there in the parking lot, crying, holding on to each other. "You're my first great love," she tells me. "I won't lose you."

"I don't know how to be without you."

"You won't be. Not really. Never."

I want to believe that, but I can't. No one is forever.

Twenty-Two

I wake to a tickling on my face as Feathers floats over me toward the window, a tangled blob of warmth and sadness. The clock glows green: *4:44*.

She ripples there, beckoning me, and I stand to look across the yard. Dimly illuminated Whites thread through the cherry tree's branches and bounce against the window frame.

Feathers seems to nod, a gentle *Go on*.

"I don't want to," I tell her.

Her warbling seems to say, *I know*.

"I have to. Don't I?"

She bobs.

I slide the pane up, and three Whites alight on the veins near my wrist. They melt like snow, and Feathers drifts toward the hall.

I follow her downstairs and out the back door, the world

changing infinitesimally when I step through. It could almost still be tonight, except for Dad.

Alongside the ache to be cradled by him, I feel a brutal, helpless frustration I can't exert anywhere. He's younger than when I saw him in the ice cave, no older than twenty-five, the patchy scruff I'm accustomed to seeing on his jaw shaved clean and his hair swept neatly back.

He sits in a lawn chair beside an older man with the same wide mouth and square jaw, his body spotted with age and sun damage. The man is staggeringly tall, but something about the slump of his shoulders makes him look insubstantial.

My grandfather Jack II. I've seen pictures but never met him. He died months before my parents got engaged.

Dad didn't talk about him much, except to say he was a Jack, that he craved adventure but always came home, was quiet but brave. He probably meant *absent*, an abandoner.

Mom's reviews of Jack II were mixed. Sometimes when Dad talked about him, she'd stab her broccoli extra hard or go from casually wiping the counter to scrubbing a spot no one else could see. But other times she'd stare out the window over the kitchen sink and say, "We all do our best. God rest his soul."

I asked her once, when Dad wasn't around, whether she liked Jack II. "He loved your father" was all she'd said. "I believe that."

Now he sits in front of me, sallow, drawing a cigar to his square, O'Donnell mouth for a puff. "Winter's coming," Dad says. Jack II exhales.

They're silent awhile. "You gonna marry that girl or just let her live in my house forever?" Jack II says gruffly.

Dad studies him. "I love Léa."

Jack II coughs, never once looks at Dad. "Then you're as stupid as I thought. A girl like that won't be happy here."

Dad watches Jack II for a long minute, then stands and goes inside. My grandfather stares at the ground. He throws the half-smoked cigar down and stamps it out, then pushes to his feet, his hulking form still hunched, and looks into the kitchen through the back window. Inside, Dad pulls Mom into a waltz, the gold light splashing across her teeth, throwing rusty streaks through her hair. He spins her, dips her low.

When he pulls her close, he sings in her ear. There's no sign on his face of the conversation he just had.

I never saw them like this, never saw them dance.

My grandfather's eyes are glassy, his fists clenched. He looks over his shoulder at the woods. A darker-than-dark blemish billows there. "You're always there, aren't you?" Jack II whispers. "You'll never let me go, I know that. But what about my boy?"

The memory ends.

Twenty-Three

"YOU know what we should do?" Hannah says, sprawled out on my bed.

"Duct tape the boys' mouths shut," I guess. Downstairs, my parents are helping Grayson host a slumber party, and a half dozen voices keep sprinkling our conversation with screams of bloody murder.

When I messaged Saul this morning about what Jack II said to Nameless, he'd been eager to pass back through the thin places—*figure this out* and *maybe take a break to redecorate the sunroom*, he wrote—but a spontaneous Friday-night tutoring session would definitely raise a red flag for my parents, so Hannah and I decided to hang out instead.

"Duct tape, absolutely," she agrees. "*And* I think you and I should go to homecoming together."

"What about Nate?"

"We could go as a group, but you'd be my date. We'd get each other corsages and coordinate our dresses and mostly dance together. Halfway through we could get into a screaming fight, and you could throw punch in my face or whatever."

"Let's be real, Han. If one of us is going to get face-punched, it'll be me."

"True," she allows. "Isn't it weird how Stephen and Nate are like the boy versions of us?"

"What do you mean?"

"Think about it. Stephen is, like, this shy bookworm type, and Nate is, like, a little louder, smart but uninterested in school, pretty content with Five Fingers."

"Oh my God, *I'm* Nate in this scenario?"

"Hey!" Hannah throws a pillow at me. "That's my kind-of boyfriend you're talking about! And it's not like I'm thrilled to be Stephen—my *arch*nemesis."

"Oh, whatever. You guys love competing with each other."

"Anyway, if you were planning on taking Saul to homecoming, I get it."

"Only if Ms. deGeest is chaperoning. I want this dance to be as awkward as possible," I say. "No, I'm all yours for homecoming. Anyway, I'm pretty sure last year they made it a rule that your date's not allowed to be older than nineteen."

"Oh, that's *right*," Hannah says. "There's always that *one* girl with, like, a forty-five-year-old boyfriend she met at the Fry Shack."

"Barf. About the guys, not the Fry Shack. The Fry Shack is the best restaurant of all time."

"True." Hannah's phone chirps, and she smiles enormously as she checks it. "You know, I think my favorite parts of life are the things I didn't know I wanted."

Ping! Your father was a liar. Ping! Everything you thought you were and wanted to be was based on a person who didn't exist. Ping! You're just like him.

Hours later, Grayson and the boys settle down, and the house quiets. Hannah and I climb into bed and turn off the light, whispering a list of our favorite things back and forth: corn mazes and pumpkin carving; picnics on the frozen lake; walks through the rainy woods and tulip fairs and cherry festivals and lying in the sun; getting tipsy on coconut rum and Diet Coke; houseplants and sunny kitchens; blueberry salads and goat cheese and deep-fried pickles; falling in love; kissing and sometimes more; sunsets and fog and jumping into the deep crystalline teal of the lake; laughing until our stomachs hurt, until we cry, until we can't breathe; and the water itself, always the water.

Hannah's breathing falls into a peaceful rhythm, and I'm left alone to stare at the ceiling. My phone illuminates with a text, and I tip it up to read.

Has your magic house mentioned anything about giving you a doorway to me? Saul says.

House isn't that nice. Why do you only text me at two in the morning? Am I your quarter-life crisis?

Two A.M. is when I lose all my inhibitions and say

*yes to everything I want. I also just ate a shit-ton of
Taco Bell.*

Ah, I'm in good company then.

*It's also about twenty minutes after New York
Times best-selling novelist Eli Angert stops watching
the Game Show Network and goes to bed. And I
think I'm having less of a quarter-life crisis and
more of a "my dad keeps forgetting my mom left him
and my sister's gone" crisis, and if you're entangled
in that it's only because you're you and I'm me and I
want you.*

You know what I have, besides a magic house, Saul?

What? he asks.

*A magic forest that stretches from my door all the
way to yours.*

Are you asking me to meet you, June?

I steer my thoughts away from the last time I walked those
woods, searching for the ever-moving tree. I focus on the beautiful moments instead, the day Dad carried me through the rain and
stretched out my hand to catch a White in the branches.

But even that day is tinted differently now. Dad wasn't who I thought he was; knowing that rewrites every memory I have of him.

I'm asking you to try, I type. *Meet me at O'Dang! Don't wear shoes.*

Immediately.

I roll out of bed, stuff my feet into slippers, and creep downstairs to the coat hooks beside the door. I pull a scarf and coat on over my pajamas and step outside.

A coywolf hunches beyond the porch, eyes flashing, a sentry guarding a tear in the veil. I shed my slippers and set them on the bottom step.

Maybe I could toss them inside and it would work the same— but if I'm asking the land to take me to Saul, maybe I shouldn't be stingy.

The coywolf slinks forward, bows to take the slippers, and dashes off in a blur of silver and red. I hurry past the cherry tree and its circle of growing saplings to the woods beyond the yard, tearing my mind from blue hydrangeas and inky ghosts.

I step through the first row of eastern pines, and sunlight splashes over everything, the sounds of night breaking open for the song of morning.

It looks *exactly* how it did whenever Dad and I went to O'Dang!

Mist floats in clumps, and jays flit between branches, calling to one another. Ahead, I spot the coywolf trotting toward a shoe pile. She drops the slippers and disappears into the brush.

"Thanks," I say as her tail disappears. I'm surprised to hear my voice until I remember this isn't a memory trapped in a White. It's the same mysterious forest we used to explore. In this impossible thin place where the sun can shine in the middle of the night, I'm as solid as the birds and squirrels who watch me but don't scatter.

There's no path to follow, no right way to get where I'm going. Soon I turn a corner around a mossy boulder, and there it is: O'Dang!

Saul's staring up at the mammoth branches and the bits of ribbon and string and flags tied all over them. Sunlight pours through the leaves and dapples the sleepily dancing Whites, revealing billions of veins and wrinkles.

"Hi," I say.

Saul turns and smiles. "I can hear you."

"I can hear you."

He's dressed in the clothes he wore the night we met, minus shoes. He looks different, his details more pronounced, now that I know his face. He makes the leaves twirling in the breeze seem sparklier, the birds bouncing between dew-laden branches happier.

"You found me," he says.

"Jacks have an excellent sense of direction." *Ping! They're used to leaving.*

"Look what *I* found." Saul's fingers run over one of the thousands of carvings in the trunk, words etched into a living, breathing thing: O'DONNELL + ANGERT.

"Aw, we have a tree together?"

"Well, we share it with a bunch of other losers, but yeah, it would seem so."

"I don't understand. Does this mean another O'Donnell and another Angert came here? *Before* our families hated one another?"

"I'm a little annoyed," he says. "We were supposed to be the first to have a forbidden relationship." His eyes trail back to me, making my heart speed. "Why do you think we can hear each other right now?"

"It's not a memory," I say. "I think it's a place where the thin place is *even thinner*. Like it sort of exists in both places, sometimes."

Saul nods thoughtfully at the hundreds of Whites crawling over the branches. "Maybe they're coming back from the other side. Maybe all the magic—the coywolves, the Whites, the ghosts—all slip through here from . . . the *other* side."

I swallow a knot. "Hannah said that too. That maybe Dad's and Bekah's memories were coming back from the afterlife because of the thin place."

Saul brushes at the trunk. "One of my library books talked about a Scottish town with an old bridge. In the last fifty years, fifty dogs have leaped off it. People think it's a thin place."

"Because dog suicide screams *pathway to heaven*?"

"Well, *some* townspeople think it's haunted, like something bad happened there and the memory was preserved, and animals pick up on it. But the optimists think maybe the dogs are chasing something to the other side, to something people can't see."

"Dogs don't wear shoes," I point out.

Saul laughs. "I guess that could explain it. Maybe they wandered into some other place when they crossed the bridge, but their bodies were still physically with the owners? I don't know—most of the thin places I've read about are cathedrals Jesuit priests take pilgrimages to, or natural landmarks where artists experienced inspiration. Believe it or not, the books don't have much about dead relatives sending messages via memory-spheres."

"It *has* to be them though, right?" I say. "Trying to warn us about the dark ghost—" Something stirs in my periphery.

My lungs catch.

We're not alone. A barefoot girl stands in the distance, watching us.

Saul follows my gaze to her. She's dressed in a butter-yellow dress, her coppery hair tangled over her shoulders and crowned by a flutter of downy Whites.

It takes me a moment to place her as the girl from the cave.

Her stare worms into my chest as she lifts her hand.

"She sees us," Saul whispers.

"It's not a memory." I lift my voice: "Hello?"

The girl turns. She begins to hum as she wanders along a stripe of sunlight. "Wait a second!" Saul calls.

Her gaze snaps back to us *"Hurry,"* she says, grabbing either side of her skirt. She takes off running into the woods.

We sprint after her, through low-hanging branches and thorny brush. "Wait!" I scream.

"June!" Saul calls from behind me.

I lose her around a bend, then catch a flash of strawberry blond cresting a ridge ahead. "Who are you?" I shout, suddenly sure the memory we saw of her was neither random nor accidental.

We're almost out of the woods now—I can see the bare expanse, the steep hill slowing the girl. I burst through the edge of the woods and come up short.

A White must have jerked me away.

I'm in a dimly lit bar packed with bodies and lazy music. It's swelteringly hot, thatched fans spinning overhead and plastic ones plugged into every outlet around the narrow wooden-floored room. The breeze does nothing to prevent the sweat dripping down shoulders and foreheads and the necks of beer bottles. There's supple laughter, silky conversation.

From the bar, Dad watches the ebb and flow on the crowded dance floor. He looks younger than I've ever seen him, smooth-faced with hair that manages to be both short and messy. He absentmindedly spins his damp bottle, eyes following a woman with shoulders so tan they make her white halter top glow, and dark curls that stick with sweat to the edges of her round, lovely face.

Mom looks young and playful, gorgeously inelegant, blissfully sunlit, and little more than a teenager. The man she's dancing with whispers something in her ear that makes her throw her head back in laughter. Her reply gets lost in the music coming from the jukebox in the corner. As the song ends, they part ways, Mom shaking his hand and coming to lean across the bar beside Dad. His beer suddenly absorbs his attention.

Miami, I realize. *Where Mom used to live. Where she and Dad met. Is this when it happened?*

"You know," she says to him. "The staring would've been less unsettling if you'd spoken to me."

"That would've depended on what I said," Dad answers.

Mom turns to rest her elbow on the bar. "Would you have said something unsettling? You should know I'm friends with everyone in this bar. You would've been pulp."

Dad takes a swig, and a rivulet runs down his throat. "I wouldn't have said *anything*. That's the point."

Mom reaches out and catches the drop, eyeing it in the light. Somehow, it contains every color of the rainbow. Her eyes widen and narrow on it, as if she's seeing a miracle. She closes her forefinger against her thumb. "Why not?"

"You're too pretty," Dad offers. "You would break my heart."

"What a strange and backward view of women," Mom tsks. "There are plenty of beautiful women in here. You think they would break your heart too?"

"No."

Mom lifts an eyebrow. "Then what makes me different?"

"I see you," Dad says. "I see you, and somehow, from across the room, you convince me I know who you are. And if I'm wrong, you'll break my heart. And if I'm right, you'll break my heart too. A person shouldn't be so pretty it hurts to look at her."

Mom tips her head back and laughs again. "Jack, what are you doing back here?"

It's not the night they met. They already know each other.

Dad's gaze dips. "I was restless."

"I know you were," Mom says. "And I'd rather not get too attached to a man who has to up and leave because he misses a body of water, despite the ocean of it right outside that door—"

"Not that, Léa," he interrupts. "When I got home, I was restless for you."

She gives a derisive laugh and rubs at her sweat-dappled forehead. "I thought a dozen times about coming to find you," she says. "But I didn't. Because I know that's not how this works. You can't split your love between a woman and a lake. I don't want someone who can walk away like that, Jack."

Pain slices through my chest. *That's what you got.*

Dad takes Mom's hands in his. He kisses the backs of them one at a time. "Dance with me," he says.

"You don't dance."

"For you, I will."

She gives a closed-mouth smile, draws him onto the dance floor. A crackling Dean Martin song swells to life as Dad holds Mom close, rocks her side to side. "Did you know me when you saw me?" he asks.

She rests her mouth against his shoulder. "You know I did."

"And what did you know?"

"I knew you were full of shit."

Dad laughs, and Mom's smile spreads rapidly. This is how I want to remember her always—glowing beneath his eyes, not wilting. Not aching. Not staying because she had to, because of me.

"I was?" Dad says.

"You're a magic man who lives in a magic house and has magical adventures all around the country," Mom says. "Probably only half of what you say is true, but that's what I learned from talking to you."

"What did you know from looking at me?"

Mom glances at her sandaled feet as Dad twirls her. "Our whole lives," she says. "I saw it all, Jack. But I saw the best version of it, and that's not what we've got."

"No," he agrees. "We've got the broken one. We're all crooked and taped together. Especially me. Maybe if Jack the First hadn't done what he did, I could be better for you, Le. But I'm cursed. I'm destined to hurt you every time we collide, and we're *gonna* collide, because that's destined too."

If Jack the First hadn't done what he did? Cursed?

Mom steps clear of him. "Yeah, that's right, Jack. What you've got is a curse. It's not your fault you tore my heart up." She turns to walk away, and Dad catches her wrist but lets her go free when she tugs it. "I want what I saw when I looked at you. I don't want *this*. Get help, Jack."

She walks out the door, into the storm, and Dad stares after her. "I am," he says to himself. He sets a stack of bills on the bar and walks out into the pouring rain and heat-ridden wind.

Whites seethe in front of the door. There's no getting home now without passing through them.

Did the red-haired girl lead me here on purpose?

Stepping through the door, I'm returned to my yard. It's dusk, and a stringy teenager with a wide mouth and a gap between his teeth stands on the driveway wearing a bulky canvas pack.

Here, Dad's even younger than he was in the bar. He stands with his mother, my grandmother Charmaine, who wears her raven hair pinned back, its first gray streaks visible. In her plaid wool skirt and pearls, she looks like an aging Elizabeth Taylor, like Old Hollywood glamour hidden under rural dust and the callouses of hard work. She touches his shoulders lightly and draws him into a hug.

The front door opens, and Jack II ducks out, his hands in the pockets of his wool trousers, his button-down tucked and sandy hair cropped close. Standing on the porch behind his son and wife, my grandfather's height is more obvious than ever. The man I saw watch Mom and Dad dance in the kitchen light is hidden behind stern eyes and a flat, indifferent mouth.

"Jacky's going now," Charmaine tells him.

Jack II regards his wife and son.

"Bye, Dad," my father says.

Jack II nods curtly, sways on his feet, then goes inside. Charmaine rubs Dad's upper arm. She grabs his cheeks and pulls his head to eye level. "We love you, Jack."

"*You* do," Dad says.

"Your father's a haunted man," she answers. "But he loves you." Dad kisses the top of Charmaine's head, then takes off down the hill. As he goes, she shudders and eases herself onto the porch steps. Silently, she starts to cry. "I never asked for this," she whispers into her folded arms. "I've been a good person, haven't I?"

She sniffs hard, dabs her eyes with her skirt, and settles her face into a placid expression. Then she goes inside, and the memory freezes.

I want out, I say. *I'm tired of this.*

Whites surround the house in a circle; they block every door and window. They won't let me go, not until they've had their say.

I mount the porch stairs and accept the memories waiting at the front door.

I'm back in the woods. Ahead of me, massive Jack II has shed even more years. He walks alongside a freckly boy with a gap between his teeth, his jeans cuffed to show off red rubber boots. My grandfather's and father's chins are down, hands stuffed into pockets in an identical gesture.

The world is quiet, drenched in the last remains of a piercing sunset and the deep blue shadow in its wake. The dead fall leaves crunch under their shoes, life disintegrating into death. The air is cool, their noses dripping. Their cheeks are rosy with cold as they amble through the silence. Jack II reaches out and squeezes the back of the boy's—my father's—neck. He pats him on the back. The boy looks up at him, the last harsh spurt of sunlight glancing off his irises. His father smiles. He hangs his arm loose over his son's shoulders. The stiff leaves crunch. The sun glows. They keep walking.

Until they're so far off the memory fades.

I step back. I'm alone in my dark house. My phone vibrates, a message from Saul: *Did you see what I saw?*

That depends, I tell him. Did you see Love?

Twenty-Four

"A curse?" Hannah gasps. She brings the blush mug to her mouth and lets steam swirl up her nose. Her hair lies on her shoulders, glossy and untangled as though freshly flat-ironed rather than slept on.

"That's what Dad said," I confirm. "And my grandmother called my grandfather *a haunted man*. I think they were talking about Nameless. Mom didn't believe it, though. After she and Dad met, he went back to Michigan without telling her he was leaving, and she thought he used the curse as an excuse for hurting her."

Hannah lifts an eyebrow. "A fair assumption."

"Sure, but it *wasn't* an excuse—Saul saw a memory too, one from a couple of nights before my dad died. Bekah had *just* gotten her diagnosis, and that same day, the coywolves had killed one of our chickens. My dad found the dead bird and took it to the Angerts' cabin to show Eli. Dad said they *both* knew what the coywolves' behavior meant: that *the curse* was about to strike. According to

Saul, my dad was *really* freaked out—crying, begging. He was afraid I'd be next unless he and Eli 'made things right.'"

"What, like you were gonna catch Bekah's cancer?" Hannah gasps.

"You know what people say: When something bad happens to an Angert, the O'Donnells are next. I think Nameless does it—like somehow we're tied together, and if something happens to one of us, it attacks the other. I think Nameless is the curse."

"So what did your dad expect Eli to *do*?"

I shrug. "Saul said Eli was pissed—said even if he *could* help, he wouldn't. That if the curse was anyone's fault it was *ours*, and if something happened to *me*, it'd be fair."

"God. That's messed up." Hannah takes a careful slurp and hoists the blankets around herself again, forming a protective shell.

"I think the Whites *were* warning us about Nameless."

"Have you asked your mom about any of this?"

"She doesn't *believe* in it."

"But she knows what your dad thought."

"She's lied to me my whole life. I doubt she'll be any more forthcoming now."

"Why not? The jig is up." Hannah climbs out of bed and starts trading her pajama T-shirt and shorts for jeans, a top, and a thick sweater. "Even if the Whites are guiding you, it couldn't hurt to *ask* your mom about all this."

"I don't want more lies, Han. The memories have the truth."

"Okay, sure. You can walk into an imprint of the past, look around, smell the roses—but don't you think the truth is a little bigger than a play-by-play of events?"

"Meaning?"

"The Whites told you your dad left your mom for three weeks. They told you your mom was pregnant and considering leaving him—so *what*? Don't you care what your mom has to say? I mean, I get that it's your origin story, but it's your mom's *story* story. Doesn't she get a say in it?"

"I can't ask her, Hannah!"

"Why *not*?"

"I can barely look at her!"

Hannah falls silent. She reaches out and touches my hand. My face burns. "June."

"I trapped her," I say. "I trapped her here, and my whole life, all everyone's ever told me is how much like him I am, what a Jack I am to my core."

"She loved him," Hannah says.

My mind hearkens to Ms. deGeest's mini-speech: *I want you to consider what you want from life.* "All I used to want was to be like him. To live this big, untethered, rule-breaking life." I meet Hannah's eyes, tears flooding my own. "He wasn't having adventures, Hannah. He was running. He should've been here, trying to fix this, and instead he ran. He ran from *us*."

She pulls me into her arms, holding me tight around the neck, and kisses my head fiercely. "Know something great about your dad?"

"What?"

"He helped make you. And even if he was stupid enough to leave, he was smart enough to come back."

When you've been as lost as I have, as many times as I have, you get good at finding your way home, June-bug.

How is it possible to be so angry with someone you miss so much?

"Tell me about Dad," I say at the breakfast table.

Mom's eyes dart to Toddy, then to where the boys are watching cartoons in the living room. "What about him, baby?"

I shrug. "I don't know—why'd he travel so much?"

"For work."

"Always?"

Mom laughs. "What's going on?"

"I'm working on a story for creative writing," I lie. "There's a character who can't stay in one place for too long. He tells people it's because he's too curious, and it's true, but it's not the whole truth."

"Huh." Mom lifts an eyebrow.

"You know," Toddy says, "your dad saved my life once."

"Really?" A memory nudges the corner of my mind. Dad told me this story too. It got lost in a sea of similarly heroic and untrue tales, like Jack the First saving the kids in the Boston Molasses Explosion, or Jack II keeping Henry Ford and a couple of traveling entrepreneurs from turning Five Fingers into a live-in industrial compound by beating all three of them in an arm wrestling match—at once.

"We were fourteen," Toddy says. "We were down at the falls one day, jumping into the pool. Your dad, he wasn't allowed to be there—for good reason—but he was sitting down on the rocks, watching.

"It was my turn, and I stepped up, and for a second, I saw this piece of gold. I swear, a big gob of it, down in the water, and I took a step to get a better look, but the rocks were wet. I slipped. It wouldn't have been such a big deal, but it was getting dark. I leaned forward to catch myself, and my head hit the rock. Fell unconscious in an instant and tumbled right off the falls.

"Next thing I knew, he'd dragged me onto the shore. Started mouth-to-mouth until I woke up, coughing water. Your dad always insisted I said, *There! Knew I'd get you in the water, Jacky.*"

"Well, my dad had a bit of a lying problem, didn't he?" I say. I feel stunned, not by the story but by the glinting gold, the connection to the falls again. All these memories have to be connected, and somewhere within their web is the curse.

"No way, Jack." Toddy goes rigid. He's never called me Jack. It hurts in a way—that I'm not quite Toddy's, that I belong to the man who gave me his name. "Your dad wasn't a liar, and if anyone tells you that, you ignore them. He embellished, sure, but he never lied. He saw the truth of things." He looks at Mom and sets his hand on hers. "He looked at your mom and saw her beautiful heart even before her eyes, and I was there when he held you for the first time, and you know what he said?"

Mom's eyes sit low on the table. They lift heavily to mine.

"My life has been so small. And now it's finally big. Look at her. Look at my world." She stands from the table and turns away. "It was like he saw your whole life right then. He didn't miss a moment. He wouldn't have dared."

I think of Dad, of his own father watching him through a softly glowing window.

I think of Dad leaving home, of his mother kissing him good-bye. *Your father is a haunted man.*

I think of Dad as a boy, in a striped T-shirt and stiff Levis, looking up at his father in the forest, love in his sunlit eyes.

I wonder if, before he went, Dad remembered that moment. I wonder if he ever realized his father had been watching all along.

Twenty-Five

I'M getting ready for homecoming when Feathers's quivering reflection appears on the wall across from my window. She moves like a sheet dancing in the wind on a clothesline, carrying Whites toward my closet door.

They're here for me, as if I called them. As if they know I'm finally ready.

"Who was he?" I whisper. "Who was Dad?"

The Whites land along my arms and sink into my skin.

I step inside.

This time, it's different. I'm standing in the middle of a field, and on all sides of me, he's there. Dozens of places and times, dozens of my father living moments that have passed. Only when I focus in on one does it gain volume, the rest playing out as if muted.

In the first I latch on to, a gap-toothed little boy pounds down the porch steps and throws himself over a blue bike, pedaling down the hill after two other boys through failing sunlight. Their hoots and whoops echo through the trees as they career away from the porch, where hulking Jack II stands watching.

In another, night hangs over the farmhouse, and the boy, my father, walks up the gravel, dirt smudged on his cheeks and blood visible at the knee of his jeans. The porch light flicks on, and Charmaine hurries out. Jack II pushes past her and takes sharp hold of Dad's string-bean arm, shaking it. "Where have you been?"

"Sorry," the boy says.

"Sorry, *what*?" Jack II parrots.

"Sorry, sir," the boy says.

"You get into it with the Angert kid?"

The boy's eyes stay low. After a beat, he says, "No, sir."

"Don't lie to me."

The boy stumbles over another apology. Jack II claps his shoulder hard, somewhere between affection and anger. His voice mellows: "Get on inside."

In some memories, Dad's small and gawky, his auburn-haired head too big for his shoulders. In some, his hands are thrust into soapy water, scrubbing dishes at the sink beside Charmaine while Jack II sits on the sofa, staring at the ticking clock on the wall. Listening to the crackle of the radio. Distractedly tapping a cigarette against a crystal ashtray.

Dad, tiny and chubby, dressed in pinstriped overalls and carried through a gauntlet of sprinklers by a singing Charmaine. Being lifted to pluck cherries from the tree with plump baby fingers.

Lying in the grass, his feet kicking in rhythm with the heartbeat of the earth, as his mother smiles down, tickling his cheek with leaves, and his father watches from across the lawn.

Dad, awkward and gap-toothed with knobby knees, carrying pellet guns through the woods. Dad escaping the house on bike, a silent Jack II watching from the upstairs window. Dad staring in at his father through a downstairs one, taking aim with an imaginary weapon, one eye closed tight, then dropping his hands and staring through the glass to his parents moving around behind it.

"You hate me," he whispers to himself.

There are older Dads too in the carousel of moments. Dad replacing shingles on the roof. Building the garage, then the sunroom, where in later memories a silver-streaked Charmaine sits with books or knitting spread across her lap.

There's Dad in rain-swept bars dense with humidity. Dad dancing and sweating with Mom, pushing her hair behind her ear and whispering to her slick cheek, "I will always love you."

There's Dad how I remember him: scruffy and strong, wrinkled from laughter and sun. He sits on a green chintz couch across from a man in gold-rimmed glasses who asks, "What was your childhood like, Jack?"

Dad thinks for a long moment, then says, "My father was a haunted man."

"Did he hurt you?" the man with the gold glasses asks.

"No," Dad says. "He hardly touched me."

"No," Dad says in another memory much like this one. "He was a good man."

"No," he says in a third. "He did his best."

"No," he whispers to himself in the next memory over. He sits in the dark on the bed, Mom asleep behind him. "He couldn't stand to look at me."

I turn to another scene. The same green couch. The same bespectacled man asks Dad, "Are *you* a haunted man, Jack?"

Dad regards him. "I'm trying to change."

"And do you believe you can?"

"I'm cursed. We all are."

"We?"

"Jacks," he says. "My grandfather, my father, me."

"And you have a new baby at home," the therapist confirms. "Do you think she's cursed?"

"She's different," Dad says.

"How?"

"She's how things were before."

"Before?"

"The curse."

The man sets his notepad aside and leans his forearms on his knees. "And what exactly is this curse?"

Dad's eyes flicker up. "Darkness."

"Darkness?"

"Inside of us," Dad says. "It watches us. It tempts us."

"What does it tempt you to do?"

"To end it."

The man straightens, but his face stays placid. "To end your life?"

Dad regards him. "It's not what you think."

"Then tell me what it is."

"It shows us . . ." Dad's eyebrows pinch. "It shows us the things

231

that hurt us. Over and over again. And then it takes the thing we love most."

"I don't understand."

"It poisons us," he says. "And the people we love."

"And what do you think will happen if you end it?"

Dad's great shoulders shrug. "It will be satisfied. It will go away."

"What is this *it*, Jack?"

"It's Nameless."

"Jack, what do you think happens to Léa if you die? To your daughter?"

He drops his face into his cracked hands and starts to cry. "I don't want to leave. But the ghosts in that house—the ghosts won't leave me alone."

I don't know if I can take seeing any more. My heart feels cracked in half, but I have to keep going until I understand. Until I can *fix* this.

I turn toward a memory of a foggy morning on our hill, one of the earliest moments yet. My grandfather looks strong and limber. Dad is very small, one curl swooping down in the middle of his forehead. Together they carry tin buckets out to the hens. They stop at the coop, scattering the feed in the grass. Jack II's great form crouches as he reaches his hands out. A hen comes toward him, trusting and calm. He sweeps her up, lifts her to his ear, closing his eyes to better hear the *goop-goop-goop* of her heart.

The boy watches, and Jack II beckons his son forward, and the boy shuffles through the mud. He presses his ears to the speckled feathers, the tiny gasp that escapes his mouth making Jack II's smile grow.

"I used to think you could hear the whole world—even outer space—in the beat of a chicken's heart. That you could taste the sun itself in a cherry." Jack II sets the hen down and straightens. "It's strange how the smallest things and the biggest are so alike."

Dad gazes up at him. "Like you and me."

Jack II shakes his head, rustles his son's hair. "No. You're different. You won't turn out like me." Jack II seems to fade then, his eyes going vacant, his body becoming somehow less solid. He turns and goes inside.

I find my father young and old. In pain and ecstasy. Alone and with arms folded around Mom, holding me on his hip, whispering stories I'm too young to understand.

"When you were born, the sun cried," he whispers. "The lake danced. The dirt in Five Fingers sung, and all the coywolves stayed up past morning, hollering at the sky. The whole world rejoiced because *you* were finally in it."

In that moment, I find him.

The magic man who could talk roots into spreading.

The haunted man who ran from the people he loved.

My father, the sun, who warmed everything he touched. Who fought for us and for his place in the world.

The grass plot I'm standing on unfurls like a rug rolled out on top of the hundreds of scenes, vanishing them to make way for my own yard, my own hill encircled by magic forest.

My house is nowhere in sight. Nothing but sunlight and grass and pine needles.

Nothing with fingers or toes or eyes, apart from the three sleeping animals in the middle of the hill. A coyote curled up with a wolf, a yin and yang of red and gray fur, a robin resting on the wolf's snout. Their eyes are shut lightly as they nap beneath the cloudless sky.

In the distance, I see a flicker of color: a strawberry-haired girl watching me.

"Who are you?" My voice comes out. I'm no longer in the realm of memory but rather in the thin place.

She starts to walk away. When I try to follow, the threshold of the forest spits me back into my room from my closet.

Twenty-Six

WHEN I'm leaving that night for homecoming, I stop by the living room and stick Shadow and Grayson each with a kiss.

"Ew!" Grayson groans. "Stop!"

"You're a brat, and I love you," I tell him. "Shadow, you're not a brat, and I love you."

"You have germs," Grayson says. "Germs make people sick, and I don't want to be sick, because you can die if you're sick."

"I don't think most germs are as scary as you think," I tell him. "But I won't give you any more germs, if you don't want, even though I'm not sick."

It seems ridiculous to head out for a school dance in light of an *unbroken* curse on my lineage, but after everything I saw today, I feel fragile. I want this night with Hannah, and I don't want to let the curse steal it from me.

Nothing sounds better tonight than living my small life well.

I slip into the sunroom, where Mom's reading with her legs stretched over Toddy, who's watching a movie on his tablet.

"Hey." Mom looks up. Toddy takes out his earbuds. "You guys and Dad are and were the best parents in the universe."

They exchange a look. "You need some money for tonight, Junie?" Toddy asks. He's not joking. That's legitimately how spoiled we are: A compliment leads to an offer of cold, hard cash.

"No. I was just thinking about how lucky I am."

How I never would've described *any* of my parents as haunted. How all three of them have always looked at me, made me feel their love.

Mom closes her book. "We're lucky."

"So far you have been, yeah," I agree. "But when Grayson's old enough to go to homecoming, and he mentions how great you are, you might want to consider what he's going to buy with the cash you immediately offer him."

Mom chuckles, but Toddy's already somewhat small eyes narrow. "Oh shoot, Léa. You should've told me not all kids turn out like June before you roped me into two more."

Mom shrugs. "I was as naïve as you, and Shadow's angelic disposition certainly didn't help."

"Have fun, Junie," Toddy says.

"You staying at Hannah's?" Mom asks.

"Yep."

"Be safe, Junior."

"Love you."

I meet Hannah in the driveway, toss my bags in the back, and climb in. She offers me her kissed fingers. "Hey," she says gently.

I bypass our usual greeting and wrap her in a hug. "Thanks."

"For?"

"Being you."

"Anytime," she says. "Unless Adele has a sudden vacancy and I'm able to be *her*. Then I'm out of here."

I pull back. "You were right, Han. The memories aren't the whole story. But *hearing* about Dad from Mom and Toddy isn't the same as knowing him. And every time I step through a White, I get a chance to know him a little more. And it wrecks me to see him, and a lot of what I learn hurts, but I can't explain to you how little that matters. Because for the first time, I'm starting to really know him. To understand who he was, the good and bad. And I guess I'm just realizing that hurting someone doesn't mean you don't love them, and being mad at someone doesn't mean you stop loving them."

She studies me for a long beat, her mouth small. "It's different," she says quietly. "I know what you're saying, but it's different with your dad than mine."

"I know," I agree. "And it's not up to me whether you should forgive your dad, or if he can be trusted to come back into your life, but if you ever want to try, I just want you to know I'll be there. I'll hold your hand when you call, go with you to Colorado, whatever. Anything. Or if you want to fly out there and toilet paper his house, I'll do that too."

Hannah leans across the console to pull me into another hug. "Don't you ever leave me, June O'Donnell," she whispers into my hair.

"Never," I say fiercely.

"We have to break that curse."

"We will," I try to promise.

Despite the fact that Hannah and I are allegedly each other's dates, Nate and Stephen meet us at Hannah's in a hunter green sedan, our chariot to the dance.

"Giiirls!" Nate calls from the driver's side window, through which he's squeezed the top half of his body.

"Don't you feel like you should be throwing eggs at him?" I ask Hannah.

She gives me a reproachful purse of her lips and smooths her vintage baby blue minidress. "June, be nice."

The car stops, and Nate hops out to open the door for us, making a big show of bowing and offering his hand. "He thinks *I'm* weird," I mumble.

"Hey, Hannah. Hey, Junior," Stephen says from the passenger seat, giving us a tight smile in the imperfectly angled rearview mirror.

"Hey, Stephen," I offer. Hannah says nothing, her primal sense of academic competition taking over her body. Stephen seems simultaneously amused and annoyed.

Fifteen minutes later we park and follow the droves of students into the school to the gym. There's a vague Under the Sea theme, which mostly means we're all wearing various shades of blue, though some of the girls Hannah and I used to hang out with are in coconut bras and grass skirts, arguing fervently with Principal Michaelson, who's literally holding out a handful of Five Fingers High School Bears T-shirts and begging them to put them on.

I half-expect Hannah to ditch me and Stephen for Nate, but instead she grabs my hand and leads me down the bleacher stairs to the refreshments table on the floor of the gym.

We fill our cups with punch and shuffle to a dark recess to spike it with Dad's flask—though it seems someone's already beaten us to the *punch*, ha-ha-ha. Soon Hannah and I are on the basketball court, underneath the flare of strobe lights and tangle of blue streamers and metallic fish cutouts, dancing wildly with a crowd of kids who act like we never grew apart, screaming, "*Han! June!*" over the sound and pushing through bodies to give us sweaty hugs, cranberry juice and something sharper on their breath.

It's not our usual scene, but we're both determined to commit to the concept of homecoming like we never have before. Eventually we manage to reconnect with Stephen and Nate in the sea of bodies, and soon Hannah and her non-boyfriend are making out in the middle of the dance floor, where they're safe from the flashlights the chaperones keep shining into the crowd as they circle, hunting for contraband and breaking up the more ferociously grinding dance partners.

"Want water?" Stephen shouts.

I look back to let Hannah know where we're going, but decide not to interrupt. I take Stephen's hand to keep from getting separated on our way out. We fill new cups at the Rubbermaid jug and sit on the bottom bleacher. I chug my water, then flip my head upside down to pull my hair into a sweaty knot.

"I like your jumpsuit," Stephen says, leaning back. "Comfy yet sophisticated."

"Thanks." I touch the dark blue halter straps. "So you like my jumpsuit, but you still hate my best friend?"

Stephen rolls his eyes. "I've already told you I like Hannah."

"Then why do you seem sulky?"

He laughs. "I had a date—first time in all four years I had a date for a school dance. Then Hannah decides she doesn't want to go with Nate after all, so he talks me into canceling with Thomas so we could go stag together one last time, and somehow I didn't think that would end with the two of them cannibalizing each other on the dance floor while I hang out with someone who's—no offense—not even really my friend."

"No offense taken," I say. "It does suck. Senior year's just weird, you know?"

"How so?"

"I don't know—your defenses are down, you're more open to new people and things, and that means you might start falling in love with something or someone new, and you kinda feel like you have to devote as much time as you can to it until it's too late, but you're also trying to cram all your time with the stuff you already love and don't want to leave."

Stephen studies me for a long moment. "I wish I were more like you, like 'lake people.' There's nothing here I don't want to leave."

"Seriously?"

He shrugs. "I don't get along great with my parents. I hate winter. My sister's already at school in Ohio, and Nate's my only *close* friend. I spend most of my time studying, and we're so far away from the rest of the world that there's *still* hardly anyone out of the closet at our school. I can date, like, two people publicly and another six who won't be seen in public with me because they haven't told their friends or family yet. Aside from that, I'm not particularly into camping, kayaking, rock climbing, or getting drunk and eating fried food, so there's not a whole lot for me to do when I'm *not* drowning in schoolwork."

"I do not understand how you're best friends with Nate Baars."

Stephen shrugs and gulps more water. "Nate talks a lot, but he's also a good listener. And he cares about hearing what his friends care about. I'll miss him a lot, but not enough to stay."

"Hm." I think of what deGeest said about Saul, how eventually he'll move on from here and that I should too. Before her class, I'd never even thought about college. I'd never thought about leaving Five Fingers for more than a couple of months, and when I imagined those trips, it wasn't libraries and science labs I saw.

All those days I spent sitting at the edge of the driveway, waiting for Dad to come back, I told myself the same kind of epic stories Dad told about his time away. I gave myself shiny reasons why the man I loved more than anything in the world would leave me.

And when he was gone, I told myself I'd be like him. That I'd be cunning and fearless and wild, and I would never be far from him.

No matter how mad I am at him, I don't know how to handle wanting something different from what he had. I don't want to hurt the people I love like he hurt me and Mom, but I don't want to lose any more of him than I already have.

Maybe the thing Jacks *really* have in common, apart from the curse, is that we're all trying to correct the mistakes of our fathers.

But how did we get this way, cursed and Angert-hating?

"Look, I don't want to ditch you," Stephen says, "but I kind of want to salvage my last chance to take a real date to homecoming."

I glance around. "Is your date here? It's, like, eleven—the dance is almost over."

Stephen shakes his head. "No, but he only lives a couple of blocks from here, and rumor has it you can dance anywhere. Can you tell Nate I had to go?"

"Sure."

"Can you convince him I'm not mad at him?"

"No, because I think you are."

Stephen stands. "Think maybe you're projecting? Have a good night, Junior."

As he climbs the stairs to the school's lobby, I fish my phone out of my chiffon pocket and search for a new message that's not there. The music fades out, the lights brighten, and Hannah and Nate come staggering toward me, yelping about how badly their feet hurt. At the far end of the gym, I notice a woman in a svelte black dress, her white-blond hair slicked into a bun with one stray wave framing her face. All done-up, Ms. deGeest looks more like an adult. A super beautiful one. I fight a twinge of jealousy and embarrassment about our last conversation. Her eyes fix on me, and I look away.

"Where's Stephen?" Nate asks.

"He had to go. He's not mad at you."

"Huh." Nate nods. "Okay. Well, you know what we need?"

Hannah looks up from under the curve of his arm draped over her shoulders. "What?"

"A fourth person to camp out with. Any ideas, Junior?" He

practically winks, and Hannah grabs my phone off my lap and starts typing.

"Hey, Han," I say. "Maybe if you taught me how to type, I could send my own texts."

"This is faster!" Hannah chimes. "Let's go!"

On our way out, I glance back at Ms. deGeest. I swear she's still watching us. I shove my phone back into my pocket.

In the parking lot, Hannah's smile glows as bright as the moon, and Nate is nearly charming. In the car, he keeps grabbing Hannah's hand across the console, grinning almost madly.

We swing by Nate's house first and go through the gate to the basement door. We change into the sweats we brought, then pack Nate's tents, sleeping bags, a lantern, and a couple of flashlights in the trunk while Hannah calls her mom to tell her we got back to my house okay. Her mom believes her, because when has Hannah ever lied before? We're throwing the last few bags in the trunk when Saul pulls up and gets out of his car, looking too clean, too good.

"Hey, man," Nate calls.

Saul nods and drops his backpack into the trunk but keeps a sweatshirt folded in his arms. "Hannah, June."

"Glad you could make it," Hannah says.

"Me too," Saul answers.

Nate claps and rubs his hands together. "All right, let's get going. Nature waits for no man." He looks to Hannah. "No matter how beautiful."

She rolls her eyes. Saul glances at me, smirking, and the four of us pile into the car and head out. "So where exactly are we going?" I ask.

"Back to where it all began—where this beautiful woman fell in love with me."

"I don't think we can camp in the Fry Shack, Nate."

He eyes me earnestly in the rearview mirror. "Not the Fry Shack, Junior—the *falls*."

He doesn't notice the expression on my face or the way my body goes rigid; I guess it's hard to see on the outside that all my organs just set off simultaneous alarm bells. But Saul knows, and Hannah definitely knows, this is the one of *two* rules I've ever had to follow.

"Did you know about this?" I ask Saul. He shakes his head uneasily.

"Please don't be mad, Junie," Hannah says. "No one's going to make you get in the water if you don't want to."

"Hannah," I snap.

"*June*," Hannah pleads. "This is a town tradition we literally might never have another chance to take part in. I swear nothing's going to happen to you. We'll all be right here with you. You're going to be so glad you did it. Remember the last rule you didn't want to break? Total B.S."

This feels different. What does it mean that both Saul and I are forbidden from the falls?

His gaze is as warm and tangible as if his hands were on me. "If you want, we can drop them off," he says softly. "Then I'll take you home."

"Sure," Nate agrees from the front. Hannah crosses her arms and slumps aggressively in her seat. He reaches over and tugs her elbow.

"Fine," she sighs. "If you really don't want to go."

"What do you want to do?" I ask Saul.

The dark and silence between us are heavy and warm. Finally, the corner of his mouth twists up. "That last rule *was* total B.S."

I feel my smile mirroring his. His hand finds mine on the seat between us, his fingers rough and careful. "True," I agree.

And what about the memories I've seen there? The stories I've heard secondhand? Dad hadn't been allowed there either, but he'd gone. Everyone I know has been to the falls—camping there is *the* senior tradition. I don't want to miss out on that because of a rule Dad himself didn't follow.

I meet Hannah's eyes in the rearview mirror once more.

"I'll go."

"Yes!" Hannah gasps.

"*Yeah* you will, Junior," Nate says. "You're no wimp."

Saul's smile glows in the dark. I want to touch his teeth. Maybe climb inside his mouth.

Something Dad said floats into my mind. *It shows us the things that hurt us. Over and over again. And then it takes the thing we love most.*

Tomorrow, I think. *Tomorrow I'll keep working on the curse.*

Twenty-Seven

WE park on the side of the dirt road that runs up to a few formerly beautiful houses that now have shattered windows and lawns covered in old baby toys and broken appliances. This really might be our last chance to do what thousands of Five Fingers kids have done before us—Toddy's always saying it's only a matter of time until these houses are bulldozed to make room for condos. Then there will be some kind of gate blocking all the cars that park here in summer.

We pull our stuff from the trunk and climb the bank beyond the road, into the forest. It's two miles to the water, and following the single-track path with flashlights that catch creatures' eyes and mysterious shapes within hollowed nooks has me on edge. I'm beginning to suspect the hike will never end when finally we find ourselves on a cliff overlooking the falls and the deep pool below them.

One by one we come to stand at the ledge, turn our flashlights off, and stare into the water. There are some things that leave even Nate Baars speechless.

The surface looks dark, an oily blue, and in it millions of stars twinkle—the whole sky duplicated in one still basin, the churning strip where the falls hit seeming to suck up and pump out more constellations all the time.

No one says the word *beautiful*.

It doesn't feel right to give something so marvelous, so dizzyingly wild, a compliment. That'd be claiming that *we* have the right to look at this water and decide whether it's beautiful. And looking at the pool is the opposite of that: It's feeling very small, both incidental and fortuitous, like maybe the star-matted water would look at us and say, *I think they're pretty*, and the moon and the cave and the falls would nod: *You always did have good taste. How could you not? You're the center of the universe.*

Nate whips his shirt off, kicks his shoes to the side, and drops his pants and boxers, letting out a whoop as he flings his bare body into the water. When he crashes back up to the surface, we watch the warbling starlight to find him. "Warm," he calls. "Good."

Beside me, Hannah starts scrambling out of her clothes, hesitating when she gets to her underwear. Determinedly, she looks away and takes those off too. Her squeal and her bare butt arc up toward the sky then down. The water shouts when she hits it, and her laughter bounces back as she resurfaces. Saul and I smile tentatively at each other from a couple of yards apart.

"Hi," he says.

"Hi."

"Do you want to get in the water?"

"Yes," I admit.

"Are you going to?"

"Are you?"

"It depends on your answer."

"I shouldn't," I say. He nods to himself, then flicks the fluorescent lantern on and fumbles over some pieces of the tent. He holds up a post and scratches his head. "Clearly an outdoorsman."

"You love to mock me."

"You're an easy target." I spread out the bright blue tarp, staking down its corners.

He crouches beside me. "Hey, we okay?"

It's still hard to be close to him and think about anything but his mouth, but somehow my conversation with Ms. deGeest keeps intruding. I pull the posts out of his hand and snap them together. "Yeah?"

I finish with the tent frame, and he brings me the cover to slide over it. We work in silence, and when we finish, we set up the other tent too, Hannah's and Nate's voices and laughter rising up to us, then finally falling suspiciously quiet. "Hey, how long did you and Ms.—Allison—deGeest, like, date?"

Saul laughs. "I wouldn't call it dating. I would say we had about three *encounters*." I toss the sleeping bags inside the tents. "Why? Is that what's been bothering you?"

"No," I say. "So what did you mean when you said you're *over art*?"

My tone sounds more mocking than I mean it to. Saul stares at me for a couple of seconds before he walks away and sits at the edge of the cliff. I follow and sit beside him, leaving some space between us. Hannah and Nate are nowhere in sight, meaning they're probably in the same cave where Saul and I first saw the strawberry-haired girl and dark-haired boy.

"Saul," I begin after a moment. "I spend a lot of time thinking about you. A ridiculous amount, if you consider all the more pressing things I have to think about right now."

He smiles, murmurs quietly, "Feeling's mutual, Jack."

"And I love hanging out with you."

"Life-threatening curse notwithstanding," he says, "it's the best."

"But there's a lot you don't talk about. Like what's happening with your dad, or school—whether you plan to go back, and what happens then." My chest aches, and I focus on the starlit water below. "If I'm just a distraction from everything terrible you're going through, I get it, but—"

"June." He catches my hand and draws me toward him. I let him pull me across his lap and sink into him when he wraps his arms tight around me. He buries his face into the side of my neck, his breath drawing chills there. "Please don't think that," he whispers.

I fold my hands into his shirt, and he pulls back to look into my eyes, his own serious and intent under pitched eyebrows. He smooths the hair back from my face. I feel too teary and sensitive to say anything. I just nod.

"I want to know you, June," he says. "Not just who you are now, or who you were in a handful of memories, but all of you. And if you want to know me like that, I want that too."

"I do," I manage.

He's quiet for a long moment as he thinks. Finally he nods to himself. "Okay," he says quietly. "Did you know Bekah was a youth archery champion?"

I shake my head.

"She was tough," he says. "And brilliant. I mean, she could tell you the name of any tree in this forest. She and my dad used to take these trips. Do things Mom and I had no interest in. She went through a partial remission when she was fourteen, and they took a dogsled trip in Montana."

"Wow. Intense."

He nods. "I *always* wanted to be a writer. I was never interested in the hunting and fishing stuff like she and my dad were. Writing seemed like a good way to connect with him, I guess, so I started writing stories, and then when Bekah got sick, it was practically all I did, and then she died, and I went away to school."

He glances at me then back to the falls. "I'd be fine for a couple of weeks. Stretches where it wouldn't seem so bad. And then something would happen—or nothing would—and I'd *really* remember she was gone. And I'd plummet and write and plummet some more. I wanted to move on, to stop being sad, but I wasn't ready. So I crammed my schedule, stayed on campus to take classes over my first two summers, applied for a residency for this past one. I didn't expect to get in, and when I did, I felt terrible."

"You didn't want to go?"

"I didn't deserve to," he says. "I was—*am*—twenty years old, and all I do is imitate other writers. I mean, you know how some people are excellent at standardized testing and some people—no matter how smart—just bomb?"

"I'm aware of the second group," I say. "I refuse to believe in the first."

He forces a smile. "Yeah, well, I'm part of the first. I'm not any smarter than anyone else. I work hard and pay attention and I *copy*. I either got into the York residency because of who my dad is or because I studied until I could write like someone else. I burned out fast. A week in, I stopped writing altogether. I'd sold this book of essays—a lot of stuff about growing up in Five Fingers, about Bekah—but it turned out my editor wanted more of *an intimate look* at Eli Angert, and I couldn't do it. I couldn't make myself write a word about him. When Bekah died—I don't know. Writing was the only thing I could focus on. When I wasn't doing it, every minute was terrible, and all I could do was wait for enough time to pass that I could go back to sleep.

"When I wrote, things sort of came into focus for a while, and I could find pieces of my sister; I knew what I wanted to say, and I could pass the time saying it. When I found out about my dad's Alzheimer's, it was completely different. Even before Bekah died, things were complicated with Dad, and I think I'd always kind of written for him?" He says it like a question, like he's asking himself. "To prove I was like him. And then knowing that soon he'd be gone, it just felt like a pointless exercise."

I take Saul's hand, and his other tightens around my waist. "I didn't want to go to that residency. But I was scared to come back to Five Fingers. I didn't want to see what was happening to him. Or remember everything that happened here. And at the same time, ever since I saw those memories of Bekah, the past is all I think about. Except you."

I stare up at him until his molten eyes dip to me. "All *I* ever wanted was to be like my dad," I tell him. "I didn't *want* to forget. But now, with everything I've seen in the Whites—I don't know. Everything was different than I thought it was. *He* was different." I glance at Saul, moonlight slanting across his face. "When I'm with you, I remember there's such a thing as a present, and a future. It feels almost okay that he wasn't who I thought he was. Because now there are all these other things I never considered being or having, and I want them. And I feel like it's okay to want them."

Saul cups my face in his hands, his thumbs drawing circles on my jaw. He kisses me softly, and I thread my hands through his hair. He eases me back toward the cool earth, and I draw him with me. His rough hands slide to my waist beneath my shirt; his touch is light and potent. It wakes up my skin, drips heat into me. He kisses me again, his jaw gently grating mine, and the lines in his back tighten and soften in rhythm with our breaths.

His mouth slides down my neck, the side of his face settling over my heartbeat. "I hear you," he whispers, kissing my collarbone. "I can hear all of you, rushing around in there. A million Jacks and Juniors and Junes, a city of them."

I pull him back to me and lift myself against him. His knee slides between mine, and his stomach presses into me as he lowers himself, his warm mouth nestling into my throat. He moves down the length of me, kisses the center of my chest and stomach, my hips. My skin buzzes everywhere he touches and pulses where he doesn't.

"Go in the water with me," I say.

He grins. "Now?"

"Now. While we're not afraid." There are things I want to say and do that are scarier than the pool lit up with galaxies, and it makes me feel reckless and unstoppable. I want to be in the water, where our boundaries will lose their firmness. I want to do something I never would have done two months ago, and I want to do it with Saul Angert. "Let's go in," I whisper as his face lifts toward mine.

"Are you sure?"

I touch his nose, cheeks, jaw, cataloguing him. This is a moment I'll want to relive. "You were scared to come back. I was scared to leave. The last thing we're scared of is down in that water, and we can swim through it, and if we make it, we're done being scared."

He lets out a particularly gravelly laugh. "That's it? We go in the water and then we're fearless, June?"

"That's it. Nothing can stop us." *Not even curses.*

"Okay, Jack. Let's be fearless." He stands and pulls me up. He peels his sweatshirt and shirt off, and it's hilarious how exaggeratedly I am *not watching*.

Saul notices my sudden shyness and turns, leaving me to undress in semiprivate. "Do you want me to jump first?"

I look out over the ledge.

"Hello? We're coming down now," I shout. When I hear no answer, I say, "Let's jump together." Saul turns around slowly, and we both try to Not Look at each other too much or too long, but it turns out those things don't exist. I like having him look at me as much as I like looking at him—his luminous skin and gleaming hair and narrow smile. The real obstacle is the freezing cold air.

"You're beautiful, June O'Donnell," he says.

"Is that a surprise?"

He shakes his head once. "It shouldn't be, and it is."

"For me too." It *is* a surprise to see him and realize he's just a person, a handsome boy with all the same parts and pieces and lines I know to expect, and somehow everything is different too, because it's him. He holds out a hand, and I twist my fingers into his, step into him so close I feel the warmth of his body though only our hands are touching.

Together we step to the edge of the world and throw ourselves into the outstretched arms of the glittering sky.

We fall as one, and the world is nothing but strands of light and dark zooming past us. Air that's cold-hot-cold again, and Saul's hand, always Saul's hand. We hit the blanket of warmth—*yes*, the water is, like everyone says, *impossibly warm*—and it folds around us, dragging us down.

Even after eighteen years of stories about the warmth of the falls, I'm still so surprised, my eyes snap open beneath the surface.

That's how I find out that the stars in the water weren't just a reflection.

At first they look like jellyfish: fragile spheres of glowing purples and blues, swimming down-down-down toward the sandy floor we can't see. Many are pebble-small, others the size of snow globes. I catch one of the delicate orbs, and it turns foggy white, as if I'm holding a tiny cloud. Saul jerks his chin toward the surface, and we kick back up, the cloud-thing still in my hand.

We break through the water, gasping for breath. The air is as frigid as ever, and our teeth immediately start chattering.

I rub the water from my eyes and find that something's changed.

Night is gone. The pool is cloaked in the gray that comes when the sun has begun to lift enough to pierce the trees and bring color to the earth. Everything's a richer, darker version of itself, and fog coils around our shoulders and speckles our faces.

"It happened," Saul whispers, because when the rest of the world is this quiet, it feels like you *have* to whisper. "We're not where we were." He points to where our tents and lantern should be. There's nothing but fog rolling over a patch of blue-green brush.

"Hannah? Nate?" I hiss, treading water. He's right—they're gone. Or *we* are.

"What does it mean?" Saul murmurs. "We're not in a memory—is this a thin place too?" He slicks his hair back and swims closer to examine the orb in my fingers. Crooked in my palm, it looks different than in the water: soft, feathery.

"A Window White," I breathe. "I've only ever seen them by my house before." The White skirts off my hand and drops into the water with an almost inaudible *plop!*

"The one place we're not allowed to go," Saul says, "and yet multiple memories have brought us here. *And* there are Whites here. June, this place has something to do with us."

In the gray morning, the water appears opaque, the sparks of colorful light dulled to look like rocks catching enough sun to glitter. I think of Toddy's story, how he thought he saw gold in the water.

"I don't get it," I say. "Why aren't we allowed to come here? My dad broke the rule, and he was fine. And if the rule was made because the thin places are dangerous, wouldn't they have kept us out of the woods?"

"Maybe—" Saul stops. A quiet rustling rises from the brush. Branches quiver and jump. The rustle grows. Louder, nearer.

"Hannah?" I whisper. Cold fear trickles down my spine. The water near the shore begins to bubble and froth. "Nate?"

All at once, a school of fish breaks the surface, mouths gaping, eyes wide and strange. Their silver bodies seize, churning the water. Two flop up onto the bank, bodies beating the mud as the fish choke over oxygen. Agitated cheeps and chirps swell through the trees. The hiss and slither of snakes undulate through the brush.

There's one beat of silence, and then the whole forest erupts. Squirrels and birds flee from the branches, clearing out from the ledge Saul and I jumped from. White-tailed deer bolt along the shore, eyes wild. A colony of bats shrieks into the sky, and two collide, gnashing at each other as they tumble toward the earth, wings twisted in sickly angles. A snake at the edge of the cliff jerks to a stop, its sinuous upper body lifting before it strikes toward its own tail, jaw yawning as it begins to devour itself.

Saul grabs for my arm in the water and yanks me toward him, face blanching.

Up on the ledge, half-hidden in the trees, a dark and terrible silhouette billows forward. Cold stabs my heart like a shot of adrenaline. The forest seems to close in, darken, seethe as Nameless moves closer. The fish are still writhing, suffocating. A stampede of tiny wings and paws reverberates out from the shadowy ghost.

"*Go!*" Saul pushes me toward the falls.

We swim. As fast as we can. Stroke toward the waterfall. He throws himself over the slick ledge and hauls me up through the falls to the cave.

Inside we stand, panting, staring through the rushing stream. My heart thrums louder than the water's angry roar, and Saul's choppy breaths jolt through my arm. We stay frozen for minutes, waiting.

"It must be gone," Saul says. I'm not sure he believes it.

Whites are drifting through the waterfall now, convening like tiny magnets until their combined mass is too thick to see through.

"June-bug?" The familiar voice echoes from behind me.

Everything in my body shoots up toward my throat, then plummets. I spin, searching the empty cave. I can hear my rapid breathing—we're not in a memory—but my father's disembodied voice reverberates against the stone again: *"Jack IV?"*

Shivers crawl along my skin. My eyes zigzag, finding nothing but wet rock and Whites.

"Hello?" I manage.

"June?" Saul's eyes look almost black against his drained face. "Who are you talking to?"

"Found you, June-bug!" Dad says. *"I found you."*

"Dad?" I stammer

Saul spins away from me, his shoulders suddenly rigid, then looks back. "You hear him, don't you?"

"He's here." *Somehow.*

"No, June." Saul's voice is strained and low. "It's the Whites, I think. It's a trick."

"He's *here*." Desperation swells in me. His voice is everywhere now, rebounding endlessly against the walls. *June, June, June*, it swirls around me. "Dad, can you hear me?" I scream over the chorus.

"June, it's not them," Saul rasps. "I hear her too, but it's not them."

That's when I see it: Nameless, twitching against the cave wall. It comes forward, the Whites gliding along with it, and the voices rise in number and volume until they reach the waterfall. Saul jerks me back against the wall.

"*June*," Dad's voice says, fearful now as it's sucked through the waterfall. "*June-bug.*"

The sound cuts out as the Whites pass though the falls, and I run after them. I can't explain it, but the thought is there pulsing in my mind:

He's here. He's really in there this time.

You're going to lose him again. You can't lose him again.

Saul's shouting something I can't make out. I leap through the falls and hit the water, drop-drop-drop, billions of bubbles erupting, buffeting the glowing orbs away from me. There are *so* many, but I'm somehow convinced I'm looking right at the one that held Dad's voice—not a memory, but *Dad*, my brain repeats.

I dive after it, deeper and deeper, and I keep going even when my lungs start to stutter, and still my hands can't clasp the ball of light slipping away from me.

I'm out of breath.

Out of air.

I've gone too deep. There's no way back out. Panic sets in. My lungs spasm.

Ahead of me a waterlogged voice calls out: *June.*

The eerie blue glow stops its descent, then timidly moves back toward me. I can't explain it, but if I can get my hand around the

White, somehow the dark spots popping across my vision won't matter. The nameless thing at the bottom of the pool and the water seeping into my lungs won't matter.

Nothing matters but the voice.

My fingers graze the sphere.

I see his smile: gap-toothed, bright.

Twenty-Eight

I'M coughing. So hard it hurts.

No, throwing up.

"Oh God, Junie," I hear Hannah sob.

"She's fine," Nate says. "She's fine, Han."

"What happened? Where the *hell* did you guys go?"

The voices swim through darkness, emitting little meaning until my eyes focus on the faces hovering over me.

"Hi," Saul says softly, helping me sit up. Nate passes him a blanket, which Saul and Hannah wrap around my shoulders. I'm still naked. I'd forgotten I was in the first place. It hadn't mattered. Nothing had but the voice. There's a hollow pang in the pit of my stomach.

"Why did you let her get in the water?" Hannah demands of Saul tearfully.

"Han, come on—we were in too," Nate tries.

"You knew she didn't want to! You knew she wasn't supposed to!" Hannah's anger bows and snaps. She's crying again. "God, Junie. I should've listened to you." She folds her arms around me and cries into my wet hair.

Saul's eyes are intent on me, trying to understand what he must see on my face: fear and loss and *hope* wrapped into one.

He was down there.

"I'm okay."

He was down there.

We're on a lower ledge of rock, farther out from the falls. The water still glitters with the reflection of the stars, but the Whites are gone. The urge to throw myself back in and tear down to the bottom is powerful.

Saul catches my gaze. "We shouldn't have gone in."

What he means is: *You shouldn't do it again. Whatever you heard, it wasn't there.*

He's wrong.

I should've seen it sooner. If the Whites are slipping through cracks from the other side, there's a way for us to slip through too. All the way.

It's in that water. He's in that water.

"What happened, June?" Hannah asks.

"I dove too deep," I say. "I couldn't get back up."

She gnaws on her bottom lip. "We should get you to a hospital."

I scoot back from her, from all of them. "I'm fine."

"You're not fine," Saul says. "You nearly drowned."

"Let's at least get you home," Nate says. "Your lungs could have water in them—sleeping out in the cold is a bad idea."

I need to go back down.

Saul touches my jaw. "June?"

The spell of the water fades when I meet his eyes. I jam my mouth shut, force a nod. "Okay."

By the time we tear down the tents, hike back to the car, and start driving, heat blasting, to my house, the first rays of sun are poking through the forest lining the road. Faint pinks and yellows brush past, catching the leaning, ivy-smothered telephone poles and the flapping wings of newly awakened birds.

In my mind I still hear the spastic scream of bats, see the snake swallowing its own tail. I close my eyes until the image vanishes. *Nameless isn't here. Saul and I are safe.*

But for how long?

We slog partway up the driveway, and Nate parks to let me out. I'm banking on my parents still being asleep and more specifically on not having to tell them that I went to the falls with Saul Angert. That I saw the embodiment of Dad's curse. That, by disobeying their rule, I nearly drowned. And despite that, that I don't regret it.

Dad is there.

I strap my duffle bag, garment bag, and purse around my shoulders and shuffle up the hill. For the first time since we brought them home, I'm eager to submerse myself in the books about thin places. I need to understand how to get through. Could it be as simple as diving to the bottom?

I know we need to break the curse, but it falls to the back of my mind as other possibilities pile on top of it.

Like the possibility that I can see Dad again, not in a memory but in a place where he can look at me, talk to me, hold me.

As I approach the house, several coywolves vanish into the woods. Toddy's truck is gone; he must be having an early gym day. I unlock the door and ease it open, trying for silence and ending up with one shrill squeak of the hinges.

At the end of the hall, Mom sits at the kitchen table in her robe. She looks so eerily like those versions of herself from the past that I wonder if, even with my shoes on, I've stepped into a memory. Then she looks at me, her face tear-streaked and furious.

"Where have you been, Junior?"

"Hannah's?"

She stands and folds her arms over her chest. "And where has Hannah been? Because her mother certainly hasn't seen her."

"Mom," I groan. "We went camping. I'm sorry I didn't—"

"I had a call from your teacher." Mom holds up a hand, and her eyes flutter closed like she can't look at me while speaking these words.

"What are you talking about?"

"Ms. deGeest," Mom says. "She was concerned about where you might be headed after the dance. And with whom."

"Mom." My stomach drops, hard and fast. "Whatever she told you, I'm sure it's only loosely connected to the truth."

Mom's hands fall to her sides, and her voice drops to a whisper. "Go upstairs, Jack. I can't look at you right now."

"Mom."

"You lied to me. You had Toddy and me terrified out of our minds for half the night, calling everyone we could think of. I've never seen him so mad. You'll be lucky if he hasn't already started a war with Eli Angert."

"Toddy?" The combination of him and Eli in the same thought racks me with hot anger. "This has nothing to *do* with Toddy. This is about *Dad's* rule, and if *he* were here, he'd listen to m—"

"You father is gone, June!" Mom's scream hits me like a slap. She gathers herself in the silence. "Toddy and I are your parents, and we don't want you anywhere near that boy. He's trouble—"

"You can't honestly believe that! Saul's—"

"Enough, Junior," Mom interrupts. The tremor in her composure tells me she doesn't want to hear Saul's name. "Go upstairs, *now*."

Twenty-Nine

THE storm outside shakes leaves from the branches. Whites linger outside my window, as if waiting for the rain to let up before they drift back to wherever they go when they're not here.

The other side.

The place at the bottom of the falls.

My body's one ball of frenetic energy, legs bobbing and hands tapping. More than ever, I feel restless. Like I'm all dried out and I *need* the water.

Hours after our fight, Mom knocks on my door and lets herself in. She sits beside me on the bed, but I keep my eyes fixed on the rainy windowpane. She swings her legs up beside mine so we're facing each other. "I'm sure you're upset." After a long silence, she continues, "I don't expect you to understand, but the bad blood between our families runs back a long ways."

"Why?" I ask her. "Because Jack the First lost a farm you and I have never even been on?"

"It doesn't matter why, Junior," she insists. "It doesn't matter whether *you* think it's a good enough reason. Your father did, and Todd and I do too. I'm telling you to stay away from the Angerts."

"I'm eighteen."

"Fine," Mom says. "I'm *asking* you to stay away from them. And if you're going to live under our roof, you'll abide by that rule."

"It's as much my house as it is yours. Dad left it to both of us. He said it should always be owned by a Jack."

Mom recoils, hurt. I know it was cruel, but it's hard to care. "Do you think he would want you to own his grandfather's house when you can't follow his two rules for you?" she says.

"You can't let Dad's rules go because you feel guilty," I snap. "You *never* took them seriously. But now he's gone and you're sticking to them even though, if he were here, I'd get him to give them up."

Mom laughs, but the sound is empty. "Your father believed he could trace everything bad that ever happened to this family back to the Angerts. That wasn't something you or I could've changed. You need to let this go, Junior. I don't expect you to understand. I just wanted to say I'm sorry it has to be this way."

"You could try being honest with me sometime instead."

Mom sets a hand on my leg. "You could have too. But you didn't. And that's all I need to know about the effect this boy is having on you."

She grabs my phone and my laptop from my desk, then leaves my room. "Three days," she says from the hallway. "Then we'll talk about you getting your phone back."

"I kind of need my computer for homework."

"And you can use it. Down in the kitchen, where I can see you."

I want to scream, but I don't argue. Mom's never grounded me to the house before, let alone taken away my connection to the outside world.

There's a cruel lack of Whites, but I try doorways for a while anyway before flopping onto my bed with one of the thin-place books.

Like Saul described, the essays in the book are mostly meditations on the serenity of beautiful places. But there is one excerpt, attributed to a writer named Sheridan Llewelyn, that I find myself rereading.

The Celts called these spaces "thin places," places both visible and hidden, where the veil between this world and the next is lifted, and the light spills through. Space carved out to form the shape of God: holy ground.

The light spills through: the memories, the voices from the past.

The veil between this world and the next: the doorways that take me somewhere they shouldn't, the misty sunlit woods that sometimes open up to me, and the pool beneath the falls. I want to think it means what I so deeply believed while under the water, that there's a way to step through the veil and truly see Dad again.

Thunder rumbles the house, and the ivy outside my windows shivers, dispelling a few hidden Whites.

I set the book in the middle of the bed as a translucent pink blob appears in the corner. "Hi."

Feathers wobbles, her warmth palpable despite the chill sneaking through the old bones of the house.

"Are you trying to take me somewhere? Do you know how to get to him?"

She sails forward through my windowpane. I shove it open and let a White land on my hand. But every time I try to carry it to my closet, the wispy sphere blows back toward the window where Feathers billows. Beckoning me.

I slide the window all the way up. Beneath it there's a thin ledge, and under that, a platform of rickety lattice entwined in shaggy greens extends over the porch.

I swing one leg over the windowsill, setting the bare ball of my foot on the weathered wood. I give it more weight until it fully supports me. A White lands on my arm as I swing my other leg over.

Immediately, I'm down in the yard, lightning crackling to illuminate a pile of drenched shoes. A slim man with a cleft chin emerges from the woods, bent against the wind. Even with his dark hair and tailored clothes whipping in the storm, he looks *neat*. The angle of his cheekbones and the heat in his eyes announce him as an Angert. Something gray and mangled hangs in his hand, and he mutters to himself as he stalks to the porch and pounds the door.

A heart-shaped face framed in dark curls peeks out. My grandmother Charmaine. With a soft murmur, she sends the gap-toothed child pulling at her hip back into the house. She and the Angert man begin to argue in hushed mutters, then he tosses the mangled thing onto the porch. Charmaine bends to examine the lump: a dead rabbit.

She slips inside, and a minute later Jack II stoops his head to step out.

When Dad used to claim his father had been six foot seven, Mom would give him that *You're exaggerating* look. But the way Jack II carries himself now makes his height more pronounced than in other memories, those in which he seemed to hide within himself, eyes vacant and so quiet he was nearly invisible.

His sandy head towers over the thin man. His wide mouth presses into a thin line as his eyes dip to the fleshy thing at his feet. "What are you doing here, Zeke?"

"You know what." Zeke's voice is a raspy growl. "I found that on my doorstep. Coywolves are agitated."

Jack II nudges the rabbit with his foot.

Zeke runs a hand over his mouth hastily. "Call it off, Jack."

That vacant look passes over Jack II's face. He reminds me of a cellar door, rusted shut and covered in weeds. "Call what off?"

"The curse, dammit. This isn't our fight, Jack."

Jack II's face darkens, and he crosses his burly arms. "It's not?"

"You know as well as I do, it wasn't Abe's fault what happened. They were kids. As long as we keep this fight going, *this*"—he nudges the rabbit with his boot—"is gonna keep happening."

Jack II's stare is empty. It's the face of a black hole, and I recognize it as if looking into a mirror: the grief sucking the world into itself.

Right then, I know my grandfather lost something. I see it in the twist of his mouth, the tension in his right temple, the hollows behind his eyes.

What did the curse take from you?

Zeke twists his hands together. "He lost his mind with grief, Jack. Forty years passed, and he still couldn't sleep through the night. Not to mention how it all ended. Wasn't that enough retribution?"

"And what do you expect me to do?" Jack II demands. "You think I'm a sorcerer? I can wave my hand and bring Abe back, make his mind the way it was before? Sounds like your brother finally paid for his sins. I hope he's *still* paying, wherever his soul went."

"It wasn't his fault!" Zeke hisses. "They'd never have even gone to that wretched place if they hadn't been hiding from your father. So don't you go acting all high and mighty, Jack O'Donnell. Don't you *dare* pretend this started with Abe. Until we *both* make it right, it's not going to stop—not for you, not for me. Your father brought evil into this place, and it's not only Abe who was punished. It'll be all of us in the end. Your family and mine."

Jack II steps forward, forcing Zeke to stumble back. "Do you ever relive it?" he whispers, deadly calm.

Zeke's dark eyes widen. "I relive all sorts of things."

"But not that night," Jack II says. "No, you weren't there, Zeke. You were at home, asleep in your bed. And they don't come for you, do they? Maybe other Moments, but not that one."

"You're wrong." He shakes his head. "I see it too."

"Then you know I wouldn't help you if I could. The only curse I see on this land is you, Zeke. You and your damned family. Now get off my property before I make you." The fire fades from his eyes, leaving Jack II empty and trapped within himself.

He turns and goes inside, brushing aside the little boy waiting in the foyer and closing the door.

Zeke Angert stalks toward the woods, his gait lithe and graceful, like his grandson's. I take off after him, but the memory releases me when I cross into the woods. I'm still in the forest, but Zeke is gone, and my heavy breaths are audible. Dusky sunlight drapes over the foliage, puffs of mist visible in the stripes of gold breaking through the ancient branches.

I'm not in a memory, but I'm not just in the woods either. I'm in the overlap.

The answers were all there, cut into a million pieces that need to be placed together.

Jack the First *brought evil into this place.*

As long as we keep this fight going, this *is gonna keep happening.*

We were right: The Whites were warning us about the curse. But what's more, *all* the Jacks and Angerts that came before us knew about it too. They knew Nameless wandered the woods, disturbing the thin place. They knew the curse robbed us of the things we loved, and maybe—*maybe*—they even knew how to break it.

A fire blazes in my chest. Someone *must* be sending these moments to us.

He's down there. On the other side of the veil.

Thirty

IF Dad knew, Eli knows.

I sprint toward Saul's house. My lungs burn; my feet hammer the earth. I pass O'Dang!, eyes flashing across the names carved into the bark: O'DONNELL + ANGERT.

The mystery of our families is taking shape, but it won't be complete until Saul and I are together.

The forest thins, and the reddish cabin resolves ahead, but as soon as I hit the clearing around it, I'm ripped away again.

Why? I scream voicelessly. At the Whites. At Feathers. At Dad. At whoever's leading me. *I thought this was what you wanted!*

I'm back at the farmhouse, in the flat dark of night, electric light casting an imperfect circle on the front porch. Mom and Dad sit in patio chairs, wrapped in blankets, their hands loosely knotted. An owl hoots, moths flutter, but my parents are silent.

"Don't you think it's time to put an end to this silly fight?" Mom says quietly.

"You don't know anything about it, Le."

She shoots him a sidelong glance. "You never used to want to be like your father."

"He was a haunted man." Dad scratches at his pant leg. "Want to or not, I'm like him. It's his blood under my skin."

Mom lets out a long sigh. "You know, at some point you have to decide whether it's more important for you to be a Jack or to be happy."

She stands and goes inside, leaving him on the porch. He leans over his knees and eyes the sky. "What do you think, Issa?" he murmurs.

Issa?

"You think I should let it go? You ready to get out of here for good?"

He pushes on his legs to stand and walks inside.

A thousand Whites converge in front of the door, and I burst through them, my skin alive and hot as, all at once, memories hit me in sharp fragments, overwhelming my senses with kaleidoscopic color. I force myself to stay upright as the competing memories focus into something comprehensible.

I'm alone in a dark maze of mirrors. Some of the mirrors reflect me, as I am right now, but others show me as a toddler, as a preteen with braces, as an eight-year-old with a bloody knee. I stop in front of a mirror that shows my father.

He stares blankly out at me, doesn't react when I touch

the glass in front of him. Other mirrors show Mom and Toddy, Shadow, Grayson, Jack II and Charmaine, Jack the First and his tiny flaxen-haired wife, Annie. In some, my Grandma and Grandpa Girard stare out, and others show people I don't recognize, women with Mom's nose and shoulders, men with her chin. People who are pieces of her, like she's a piece of me.

Off to one side, I see the strawberry-blonde from the cave. She blinks slowly, then steps sideways from her mirror, disappearing in the gap between that one and the next.

I turn, searching for her, and face a whole new set of mirrors. Front and center, as if he's the immediate reflection of myself, I see Saul. Spreading out behind him, I see Sauls with missing front teeth, with sunburns and bowl cuts. I see a man in a tweed coat with a face as brutal as winter, Saul's father, Eli. Lean and elegant Zeke, and another Angert patriarch I don't recognize, with the same angular jaw and captivating eyes. I see Bekah, her crooked smile and thick eyebrows, and a curvy brunette with deep-set eyes—her and Saul's mother, Rachel.

And then I see the boy.

The dark-haired boy who held the red-haired girl in the cave.

He presses his hands to the glass, his nose flattening against it. He begins to scream. His fingernails claw at the surface of the mirror. He thrashes against it.

I hit the glass too, trying to free him. His eyes are wild and fearful. Whites are alighting all over the mirror, and he's still screaming. *I'm trying*, I say.

I throw myself at the glass, and it shatters in every direction, leaving me tumbling onto the hill where my house should be.

There's no one here. Just a wolf and coyote and robin asleep in a yin and yang formation, and a springy green cherry sprout dancing in the breeze.

Now the scenes unfold around me, another carousel of moments.

I focus first on one that shows Jack II, middle-aged and hunched. He sits in a high-backed chair in a room lined with lilac wallpaper speckled by vines and plump golden fruit—the room Mom now shares with Toddy.

The man lying in the bed beside Jack II has a sickly yellow tint to his skin, and his breaths rattle in his lungs. Where Jack II is shadowy and insubstantial, this man is all intensity and sharp lines, despite the trembling of his puffy fingers against the quilt.

I recognize Jack the First from his one and a half eyebrows. According to Dad, my great-grandfather lost the other half over in France during World War I, when he threw himself between a friend and a grenade. Shrapnel had lodged itself in Jack the First's left knee, which never worked quite right after that, and in his left eyebrow, which had never fully grown back.

He'd been beloved in Five Fingers before that; afterward, he was a hero.

A clock ticks on the wall, and dust floats through spears of sunlight.

"You can leave," Jack the First coughs. "Don't need nobody watchin' me die."

Jack II rocks forward over his knees. "I'm not leaving, Pop."

The clock ticks onward; the dust drifts.

Jack the First clears his throat. "Why not?" His glassy eyes roll toward the corner as an inky darkness materializes there, twisting hatefully. "You find anything dead in the yard?"

Jack II's chin lifts. "No, Pop."

"Don't lie to me, boy," my great-grandfather spits. "You think I don't know? It's been watching me ever since that little shit finally drowned. It wants revenge, son."

Jack II winces and sits back, putting space between him and his father. His eyes have that vacant look again, as if his soul has walked off for a coffee break.

"I don't care, son," Jack the First says. "Don't give a damn how this spirit tortures me. I don't have any regrets, except that I didn't kill him myself."

Jack II's eyes lift. "You did."

"What's that?"

Jack II shakes his head.

"Speak up," his father demands. "You got something to say then talk like the fucking man I raised."

"You *did* kill him."

Jack the First tries to scoff, but his throat's too weak to let anything but a cough through. "You pity that piece of shit? After what he did to us?"

Jack II studies the floor. "You don't have any regrets? Not one?" His eyes glimmer, light reflecting against their abyssal surface.

His father regards him, mouth juddering open like a fish gasping for water and finding only air. He jams it shut. If the first Jack had any regrets, they're trapped within him for good. "Get me a drink, would you, son?"

Jack II tips his head toward a porcelain bowl resting beside the bed. "How about some cherries, Pop?"

"Scotch," his father replies. "Neat."

Jack II hesitates, as if considering pointing out that a man inches from death, skin jaundiced and hands shaking, shouldn't shoot liquor. He shakes his head and unfolds his great height from the chair, crossing toward the door.

Jack the First's eyes shut, and he groans. "I'm coming, honey," he whispers. "Not long now."

Jack II pauses in the doorway. I see something then, a kind of *caving in*, as if everything on the outside of him is collapsing inward, creating his black hole. He tries to say something. His wide mouth presses tight. He walks into the hall.

Jack the First opens his eyes as Nameless approaches him. "Do your damnedest," he growls at the ghost. "Show me anything you want. I'll be with her soon, and you'll still be trapped here."

The thing folds over him. Jack's eyes close, and a smile curves up his lips. The anger leaves his body, the tension abandoning hundreds of muscles at once, finally permitting them a moment of peace. The memory freezes as the sounds of others push forward.

I turn toward the memories circling me. A long-legged, sandy-haired child who must be Jack II barrels through the front door and scampers down the hillside. He pumps his arms, gasps for breath, bare feet pounding the wet grass. Jack the First stumbles out the front door, the bottle in his hand knocking the doorframe and his left leg swinging stiffly. "Come back, you little coward!"

Jack II keeps running, eyes blinking against sweat. "Take me away," he hisses, breath frosty as he sprints for the woods. "Take me away. Take me away."

He hits the edge of the woods and vanishes, the memory stilling.

I turn to the next and see Jack the First's wife, Annie, holding her only son atop her knees. She kisses his forehead, smooths his sweat-streaked hair. She murmurs, "He doesn't mean any of it, my love."

"He does," little Jack II says. "He hates me."

Annie presses her lips to her child's head again and stares at the wall of the bedroom where Grayson and Shadow's bunk beds now sit.

"Was it my fault?" Jack II looks at her. A smile blossoms then withers on her painted lips. She pulls a green-jeweled pin from her yellow hair and closes his hand around it.

"You are blameless, my love." Her eyes become distant. If Jack II grew up to be a collapsed heart, a black hole, his mother was a meteor hurtling through space: beautiful but burning out, screaming but kept silent by the vacuum. "Go to sleep, angel." She maneuvers her son from her arms into his narrow bed, then pulls the blankets to his chin and kisses him once. She hesitates, kisses him again more slowly.

He seems to know this means something—that tonight, she kissed him *again*. Annie hurries, crying, from the room. She glances backward one last time before she cups her hand over her mouth and escapes.

The memory stops, and I dread the one that comes next even as I turn to it.

Here Jack II sits on the same bed in the dark, his lanky legs dangling over the side as he stares at the pulsing pink patina. His fingers roll the hairpin back and forth. "She's gone," he tells Feathers. "She's gone and you're gone and all that's left is him, and he hates me." His fingers lift the pin and press it to his head where Annie kissed him goodbye.

Feathers encircles him, fluttering, warming. "You promised," he whispers. "You said we'd get out."

I want it to stop. I need it to stop, so I run. I run straight through another memory: Jack the First bending beneath the shade of the first Jack's Tart, putting his heart to Annie's stomach, hands gently clasping her waist. "I hear it," he says, voice soft and warm as sunlight through his smile. "The heartbeat of the whole world, and it's in my wife's belly."

"Little Jack," Annie says, touching the side of her husband's face.

I keep running.

What happened to destroy this?

What took the man I see now and made him into the one I watched die?

And what's it going to do to me and Saul?

Two families.

Two ghosts—one warm and sad, one cold and hungry.

Two tears in our world—one at an impossible tree and one in a starlit pool.

One curse, tying the puzzle together, and infinite memories holding the answer to what created the hungry darkness, the brutal cycle that will eventually swallow Saul or me.

I run to the end of the yard, right into the ice cave again, right through the bar where Dad stared at Mom in the middle of a monsoon, down a dune past a family napping on the sand, and into the water, and there—

I'm on the cliff overlooking the waterfall, sunlight-sprinkled mist hanging heavily over everything.

Whites *plop* against the surface, sinking under it.

"*June-bug?*" one says. "*Junie?*"

"*Dad.*"

I need him. To tell me how to make the flood of memories stop, how to rewrite a history of grief and break the curse before Saul and I lose any more of the things we love most.

I need *Dad* and all the things he never told me, and I need his arms.

I step to the ledge and study the delicate light beneath the water.

I take a deep breath and prepare to jump.

"NO!"

I spin back and see her: the girl from the cave, the woods, the hall of mirrors. "You'll drown," she hisses, her eyes wild. "You mustn't let him do this to you!"

"Let *who*?" I step toward her. "Who are you?"

"Come away from the water, Jack."

The Whites pull at my back, tell me not to walk away. The girl scans the misty forest, her pale arms hanging at her sides. "When are you going to stop this?" she screams.

"Who are you talking to?"

She faces me again. "Someone who has forgotten what it's like to have a name."

"Nameless?"

Her airy voice shakes. "The water doesn't lie. But it doesn't tell the whole truth either. If you want to break the curse, you must *both* go in. You and Saul together."

"But you said I'd drown," I stammer.

"Yes." She smiles sadly, then steps behind a thick eastern white pine. I curve around the tree's feathery branches, but she's gone. The mist has lifted, the sparkling sunlight replaced by thunderclouds and rain. I'm soaking wet, as though I've been standing out in the downpour for hours.

Standing there, in front of me, is Saul.

Thirty-One

HE rushes toward me and catches me in his arms. "I've been trying to get ahold of you all day," he says. "I thought you'd—I was scared you'd gone back to the water."

"The red-haired girl," I manage, still searching for her.

"From the cave?"

"She came to me—she said I'd drown. I don't know what they did, Saul, but our great-grandparents caused all of this—everything bad that's happened to us and our families, all of it."

His brow furrows. "June, what happened?"

My mind buzzes. I try to think back to the beginning. "Allison deGeest called my mom. My parents know I was with you. They know you're . . . you."

He nods. "Your stepdad was at my house when I got home."

"Seriously? What happened?"

He looks up the tree, rubbing his jaw. "He tried to hit me."

"Oh God."

"I almost felt like I should let him."

"Saul," I say sharply.

"I can't blame him."

"Look, I love Toddy, but he needs to drop the pee-on-everything-you-think-you-own outlook. This has nothing to do with him. I made my own decision, and besides, we have more pressing issues than he or my mom realize. Something bad happened here, and if we're going to fix it, we need to go in the water."

"June, you *just* said that girl appeared and told you you would *drown*."

I swallow a knot that scrapes like it's made of thorns. "She also said that we both had to go in to break the curse. I saw more memories, Saul. The dark ghost didn't just kill my dad; it killed Jack the First too. And your grandfather Zeke—he came to see my grandfather, like my dad went to see yours. Zeke had a dead rabbit—he *knew*, Saul. Our grandfathers knew about Nameless and the curse, and I think—Saul, if we don't fix this, I think we're next."

Saul trains his eyes on me. "How does going into the water fix it, June? What if that was Nameless trying to drown you? What if he's using your dad's and Bekah's voices to—"

"The girl *told* me, Saul."

"And who is she? How do we know she's not part of the curse? That she's not *helping* Nameless kill us?"

I massage the space between my eyebrows. I'd been sure I'd be able to convince Saul to go into the water with me. Not only because we need to break the curse, but because I *know* he must want to see Bekah again as badly as I want to see Dad, and we can *get to them.*

"We can't rush this, June," he says. "If we're going back there, we have to know for sure. We have to let the memories take us to the beginning."

"I don't care about the memories. I want to go through the veil, to where the memories come from, and *see him again.*"

He takes the back of my head in his hand and draws me into his rain-soaked chest. "The past is what it is, June. Can't the present be enough for you? Your mom and Todd and your brothers and Hannah. Me."

I close my eyes and breathe him in. *He's safe,* I tell myself. *We're safe. Focus on that.* "I don't understand how it can be enough for *you.*" I open my eyes again and watch the rain slide down his face. "How did you close up *your* black hole? How can *you* move on?"

The corner of his mouth inches up, and he cups my face. "Because I have to. The sun keeps rising, and the seasons keep changing, and there are still people here I don't want to lose."

Focus on that. There are still people here I don't want to lose.

"We need to find out about Abe Angert," I say.

"Abe?"

"You grandfather Zeke told Jack II he thought the curse was Jack the First's fault. But Jack II said it was Abe's—is that your great-grandfather?"

Saul shakes his head. "Abe was Zeke's brother, my great-uncle—I don't know much about him."

"We need to talk to someone who does."

Saul grimaces as he anticipates where I'm heading.

"Saul, every O' Donnell and Angert who came before us knew about the curse. We need to talk to your father."

He folds my fingers into his. "I never know what to expect when I get home. He may not remember the curse, or Abe. He may not even remember me." He looks poised to go on, but instead he rests his mouth against my forehead.

"I'll be there with you," I tell him. "If Eli doesn't remember you, I'll still be there."

His eyes move back and forth across my face, reading me. He nods and turns, leading the way through the woods.

Thirty-Two

THUNDER crackles, shivering the foundation of the Angert cabin.

It's never had quite the mythos of our farmhouse, but people *do* talk about it, guess what kinds of oddities hang on the walls or sit on dusty bookshelves. Because for all intents and purposes, this log cabin *was* the beginning of Five Fingers.

Before Jonathan Alroy O'Donnell arrived, the Angerts had already built their cabin and opened the sawmill that put Five Fingers on the map. For a long time, they'd owned most of Main Street, but they'd been selling it off for generations now. When Eli hit it big with his first novel, he sold the rest—everything except the Cape Cod–style house they bought on the water and that rickety cabin in the woods.

When Rachel and Eli split up, they sold the Cape Cod too. The original Angert cabin is all they have now, just like the farmhouse and the lone Jack's Tart tree are all *we* have.

Saul steps inside and runs a hand through his hair, shaking out the rain. I follow him past a staggeringly disorganized office piled with books and maps and old cassette tapes into a conjoined kitchen and living space, whose rear wall of windows reveals long swaths of storm gray and lush forest.

"Wait here." Saul turns to a brown leather couch draped in a set of red bedsheets, a dull plaid blanket, and some pillows. "I'll check the bedroom."

As he treads down the hall, I realize how tiny the house is. It's the kind of place you might rent for a long weekend with one or two friends, and judging by the bedding on the sofa, there's no spare bedroom for Saul. I imagine him and Bekah camped out on the couches, telling ghost stories and watching the windows for the glint of coywolf eyes.

There's sadness in this house—a fireplace overflowing with soot, counters littered with orange pill bottles, and the kind of quiet that feels less like peace and more like absence—but the warmth isn't gone entirely. A crayon drawing is still stuck to the fridge door, four stick people swimming under the lake, and notches in the back door record changes in Saul's and Bekah's heights. As miserable as they were when Bekah was suffering, I bet there still was softness and love in these walls. Moments, at least seconds, to feel bone-breaking crushes of happiness at being here together.

Beneath the coffee table, my feet bump a hidden cardboard box, eliciting a metallic rattle. I drag it forward and move aside the crumpled newspaper to find a stack of picture frames. I slide one out and stare into the black-and-white image: the gleaming eyes of a toothy girl whose dark freckles sprinkle her cheeks like constellations. Pollen and leaves cling to the sweat streaks in her messy bangs.

She can't be much older than fifteen, but she's got the crow's-feet and fine wrinkles of someone mid-laugh.

It's absolutely beautiful.

I set it down and keep riffling. Many are portraits; some were taken at wide angles; all are of kids: siblings, parents with their children. They're uniformly tender, saturated in the many shades of gray and black, eyes shining and endless, freckles and wrinkles holy.

They all have the same candidness of real living moments captured.

My chest twinges when I reach the last photograph. A girl lies in a hospital bed, tubes in her nose, dark hair a mess on the pillow. She's lifting herself up and pointing across the room, an open-mouthed smile ablaze across her face. Her unruly eyebrows are lifted in surprise.

You can't see what she's pointing at, but it doesn't matter. She is the sun. She is what matters, not whatever brought her that overflowing happiness.

Her eyes and hair are dark, her skin fair and jaw sharply angled. She looks like her brother, only three years younger, permanently seventeen.

"He's sleeping." Saul's voice is low as he returns to the living room. I set the frame down. The sound and the sight of him, here in this place, breaks my heart. Not the way that losing Dad did, a constant, ever-deepening spiral into all the things I hadn't realized I'd lost right away. No, this is a sharp break, a flood crashing through a dam, because Saul has—and his father and mother and Bekah have—hurt more than any person should.

He sits beside me, taking the photograph in his hands. A crease burrows between his eyebrows. I touch the camera inked onto his skin. "Is this what the tattoo was about?"

His eyes barely reach mine before turning back to the photograph.

"They're beautiful," I say. "They're alive."

He raises an eyebrow. "Yeah. Can't do anything that's not ironic, I guess."

"What do you mean?"

His fingers splay on the glass, touching Bekah's teeth. "All these people, they're all dead."

"*What?*"

"I mean, not *all*. But someone from every picture. So if there's only one person, then, you know. I started this . . . um, not technically a business, because it was free . . . but this thing in college where I'd take pictures for families who had kids or partners with terminal illnesses."

I look at the open-mouthed girl again, expecting to see the haze of death, some kind of emptiness printed over her. She's obviously ill—medical equipment visible all around her—but she's still full of life, this indescribable *twinkle* I can't imagine ever being stamped out.

Dad had that too. Maybe some people die gradually, move away from their bodies over time, but others—people who shine—go in an instant. You can see their souls in their eyes until the last possible second, feel the gap in the world the second they're lost.

"They're incredible, Saul."

He sets the frame down. "You know, back when I used to pray, all I ever asked was to be able to tell stories. So I could be like my father." He juts his chin toward the box. "Telling stories never came naturally to me, but I was good at capturing moments. When I was a kid we had my photos hanging all over this place. When I left, I'd mail prints home for him—didn't tell him about the whole *sick kids* thing, just sent them along. I never expected that when I got home they'd all be in a box. Even the ones that used to be hanging. I guess that's the thing about moments. They always pass."

I thread my fingers through his. "You know what my least favorite thing is?"

"What's that, Jack?"

"When people find out you've lost someone and they get uncomfortable and embarrassed and pitying and weird."

"It's the worst."

"But not because I hate being pitied. I *do*, but it's more than that. When people pity you, it's like they honestly don't realize the exact same thing's coming for them. And then *I* feel embarrassed and uncomfortable and have to pity *them*, because, like, do you not realize it's always someone's turn? You haven't noticed *everyone* gets a few blows that seem so big you can't survive them? And then here is this person looking at you and dramatically murmuring, *I'm sorry for your loss.* And you have to look at them and hope your eyes aren't saying, *Don't be too sorry. You're next.* You have to spend all this energy making your face say, *Yes, it's horrible, and extremely*

*rare. I can't believe I was the person who lost my father. You certainly
won't lose anyone. You'll die first, out of everyone you love, on the eve
of your hundredth birthday."*

"June." Saul says it so gingerly my eyes well with tears. He pulls
me against his side and rests his chin on my head.

We both know that pain comes for us all.

It's almost a relief. Because if all of us are going to someday lose
the people we love most, or be lost by them, then what is there to
do but live? But that doesn't seem like a good enough answer. The
answers to the hard questions *never* seem good enough.

"I'm sorry," I say. "I don't want to cry about someone who
wasn't mine to lose. I feel like I'm co-opting your grief."

His hands stop tracing idle circles on my back. "I think once
you've felt grief, it's hard not to catch someone else's. Especially
when the person grieving is someone you love."

The word, *love*, swells painfully in my chest. "Or maybe when
you've felt grief, it's hard not to love someone else who has too."

Saul eases my shoulders back to look me in the eye. "No," he
says. No declarations or arguments or speeches. Just *no*, and it's all I
want, all there's room for in this tiny house of ghosts.

"I'm so sure we can get to them," I tell him. "Like they're right
there, on the other side, trying to help us."

"I know it feels like that. But our parents told us to stay away
from the water for a reason, June. Nameless was *there*."

"I don't think I *can* stay away."

His fingers graze my spine and stop against my neck, where he
knots them through my hair. "I know you think my dad can tell us
what *really* happened between our families. But, June, some days he

doesn't know what shoelaces are. Sometimes he doesn't remember how to ask. If he can't help us, promise me you won't go back to the falls until we're *sure* that's what we need to do."

My chest cinches. *I can't wait that long.* "He'll remember."

"Just in case." Saul goes to the mahogany liquor cabinet on the wall and pulls a notepad and pen from the bottom drawer.

"Still hiding your diary?"

"You know what I like about you?" he says.

"My bite."

"Precisely. Being mocked by you mere moments after holding you in my arms restores my faith in humanity." He sets the notepad on the ottoman. "If you *must* know, my dad uses this to take notes on different scotches. I figured we could write down—" He drops off.

"What?"

"Um." He stares down.

I pull the notebook from his hands and look at the shaky handwriting there: *Your son is Saul. Your daughter is Bekah. Bekah is dead.* I flip through the pages and find more notes: *This is your house. You live here alone.*

The name *Rachel* alone on one page; on the next, *Rachel is gone.*

Eggs go in the refrigerator.

Your laundry room is in the cellar.

Your agent's name is Miriam.

Saul pulls the notebook out of my hand, avoiding my gaze as he flips to an empty page.

"Saul."

He shakes his head. "I can't, June," he says, voice phlegmy. "I can't talk about it."

"Okay."

He scribbles names in opposite corners along the page's bottom end. He writes Bekah's beside his and Shadow's and Grayson's beside mine. "Saul, what are you—"

"Making a family tree." He starts four generations back, drawing a thin line marrying *Jacob Angert* to *Abigail Marshall Winston.* "This is when both our families say the feud started, and even if they're lying about the farm being the cause of it, Zeke blamed the curse on Jack the First, so it's a safe bet we only need to look this far back."

Beneath Jacob and Abigail, Saul lists their sons, *Ezekiel "Zeke" Angert* and *Abraham "Abe" Angert.* He connects Zeke to his wife, *Elisa Avila,* and beneath them he places their son, *Eli.* Finally, Saul links his father to *Rachel Stolarz,* then connects them to *Saul* and *Bekah* below. He slides the notebook my way. "Your turn, Jack."

As I start filling out my half, I realize how little I know about anyone but the Jacks. Like the Angerts, the O'Donnells are an antiquately patriarchal line. I scribble *Jack I* and *Annie* at the top, and below that I write *Jack II* and his wife, *Charmaine,* who produce a line to *Jack III.* I connect Dad to Mom, *Léa Girard.*

As I scan it, I catalogue all the evidence of the curse: Jack the First seeing Nameless on his deathbed; Jack II splitting his time between watching the dark ghost in the woods and the son he could barely look at through the window; Jack III clutching his chest in a forest clearing as the ghost throttled him and stole my whole world. "That's all I've got."

Saul analyzes the web of names, rubbing the wrinkle between his eyebrows. I'm distracted by his hands. Despite our current situation, his arm grazing mine still makes me feel a little like my organs might liquefy.

For a few seconds, the curse becomes less urgent to me than Saul's rain-dampened skin. Or the scratch of his fingers against his jaw's shadow. His eyes slope down my legs then return to the words on the page, and my stomach swelters. He glances my way again, and a slow smile quirks the corner of his mouth. "Why are you grinning?"

"I'm not."

"Yeah, June, you are. We're looking at our cursed family trees, and you're grinning."

I shrug, and he jogs my knee in his hand. I set my hand over his, and his smile widens until he lets out a heavy breath and refocuses on the notebook, leaving me to burn up by myself. I'm about to suggest we take a brief and steamy recess from the History of Grief when a low voice rattles behind us.

"What is she doing here?" Eli asks from the doorway, his mouth twisted downward. He feebly grips the doorjamb, shaking his gray head. "Can you see her, son?" he chokes out as he takes one stumbling step back, half-supported by the wall. All the heat in me turns icy then, because I see it so clearly in his face: Eli Angert is afraid of me. "Can you see the ghost?"

Saul rises and approaches his father. "Dad, this is my friend Junior. She's not a ghost. You're confused."

Eli stumbles, shaking his head frantically, eyes flashing between us in a frenzied corkscrew. "I didn't do anything," he cries at me, voice crackling. "Don't take my baby!" he screams. "Don't take my Bekah!"

I shake my head, speechless. I'm trembling as badly as he is. His eyes are clear, homed in on me. He doesn't look confused; he looks like he sees something dark and brutal.

"Dad," Saul tries again, inching nearer to him.

Eli scrambles for the door. "Leave us alone, Maolissa. You can't have her—leave us alone!"

He bolts into the thunderstorm, and Saul takes off after him, leaving me to chase them both.

When I reach the forest, sunlit mist replaces the rain.

Ahead, Saul's gaining on his father. Eli stops shambling from tree to tree and slumps against a trunk, his fingers digging into the bark. Saul gets an arm around him, but Eli's hysterical now, waving his arms against Saul's grip.

When he sees me, his knees sink onto a broken tree limb. His fingers curl into Saul's leg. "There," he cries, "you see her too. The dead O'Donnell girl. Issa."

Saul registers shock, and I look down at myself, half-expecting to see my clothes covered in blood or some visible evil circling me. But Eli and Saul are staring past me.

I turn and balk.

Within Feathers's rose-tinted aura, crisscrossed by Whites, stands a girl.

Not blood-smattered or grisly, but timid and barefoot. Impossibly still, like a tear in the world pulling everything toward her. Her strawberry waves hang on her shoulders, and her white shift clings to her, damp.

The dead O'Donnell girl, Issa? Issa, who Dad spoke to the night Mom asked him to end the feud?

Is Feathers *Issa O'Donnell*?

She beckons me from the edge of the woods, noiseless in her prompting. I look over my shoulder at Saul, who's still bodily supporting Eli. If Feathers is a dead O'Donnell, then we're on the cusp of understanding what happened to destroy our families.

On the cusp of breaking the curse.

Of diving through the water and seeing him again.

Saul gives one curt shake of his head. "June, no. I don't think—"

I step past the tree line, through the feathery softness. I've hardly caught the first desperate note of Saul's shout when a tremendous warmth sinks into me and I'm tugged into a new world.

Thirty-Three

I'M standing beside O'Dang!

Feathers—Issa—is gone.

I circle the sprawling roots, disrupting sleeping Whites that rise and twirl as I pass. Each time I curve around the trunk, I cross a new threshold and find different people there, eyes that don't see me, ears that don't hear me.

Children tightrope walk along roots. Preteens play chicken on low branches, slapping one another's hands and screeching with laughter when one finally topples off. Couples kiss in dirt pressed with pine needles, against the trunk, in crooks between branches. Dozens of people. Hundreds of bare feet.

They carve names and hearts, symbols and dates into the flaky bark. Flags are strung up, torn down. Mardi Gras beads tossed over limbs, bird feeders hung from the most inviting branches.

I walk past Dad and me.

I'm in the floral shorts that were my favorite at the time and the too-big yellow dinosaur shirt I often slept in. Dad won it for me in a milk-can toss. I'd wanted the stuffed tiger, but he'd talked me into the shirt: *You can only have the toy in the house,* he reasoned. *You can wear that shirt for years, anywhere you go, June-bug.*

That was Dad, all about mobility, being able to walk away when he wanted and come back when he needed. I wriggle my toes into the mud and watch them together until eventually they turn away.

A new White hovers at my sternum.

I observe its fragility, the way light bends and refracts through it nonsensically. I clasp it and keep circling the trunk.

I've come to her moment.

The red-haired girl, Issa, stands, facing the tree, beside the dark-haired boy she kissed in the cave. She holds a pocketknife to the bark, and he grips a nail between two knuckles, both etching lines into the tree.

"I'm writing yours." Her voice shimmers. I don't know how else to describe it. It's not purely a matter of sound; it's the way he reacts to it, his eyes squinting and mouth curling, ears pink. It's the way her words hit him and reverberate through his grin, the fullness that sparks and palpitates between them.

"I'll write yours," he says, and his voice shimmers into her too.

I feel Feathers—*Issa's ghost*—hovering behind me, watching.

A whistle cuts through the air. They both stop carving. "He's calling you," the boy says.

She folds the pocketknife and presses it into his palm. He slides his hand around her neck and kisses her slowly. "Tomorrow," she says.

"Tomorrow," he promises.

"I love you, Abe."

Abe.

"Always," Abe says. He leans against the tree and watches her retreat. Over his shoulder, their unfinished carvings are visible: O'D ANG.

Here—where wolves and coyotes lie together and robins sleep on the haunches of wild dogs, where cherries taste like sunlight and chickens run free—here, it was possible for an O'Donnell and an Angert to fall in love. So what happened to it all?

Why hadn't I heard Issa's name before?

Why does no one talk about her, though her ghost still wanders our house?

Issa's ghost leads me to the forest's edge, where another bobbing White waits for me. I cradle it, breathing deeply, and step through.

The blazing light of a setting sun skirts across the waves I'm facing. Peals of laughter rise amid the crash of water on sand. Down the shore, made into shadow by the intense last light of day, a man with pants rolled to the knee chases a little girl with long red curls in and out of the water. She squeals as she dodges him, her curls bouncing across her back.

Behind them, a petite woman with pinned-up hair walks barefoot across the wet sand, hand outstretched to a chubby toddler. The wind ruffles his Peter Pan collar and poufy shorts, dances through her yellow curls and blue dress.

The light slices around the four of them, shaping their silhouettes. Hunched like an amateur wrestler and swinging his stiff left leg, the man shuffles after the delightedly shrieking girl. "Oh no you don't!" he growls, bending to splash her. She shrieks and splashes him back, and he sweeps her into his arms, pretending to gobble her belly as she flails with laughter.

"Don't eat me, Papa!"

He swings her onto his hip and jogs her there, her hair glinting down her back like a blaze of fire. "I won't eat you, Issa," he says. "What kind of a man would eat his own heart?"

She grins, her face partially hidden under deep blue shadow. Beneath his one and a half eyebrows, the first Jack's eyes sparkle in the light. He cradles her head and kisses her above her temple.

Annie lifts a fussy Jack II into her arms and steps into the water beside her husband. They watch the half dome of sun melt into the waves; they squint against the wind. For a moment, my family— the first Jack, Annie, Issa, and Jack II—are happy.

I take a step into the water behind them, wanting to become a part of this memory. Instead I find myself back on the hill.

A pinkness, the aura of a red-haired girl, dances on the porch, and my chest aches with the memory of the one ghost who's *not* inside that house.

For the people who are left, I go inside.

Thirty-Four

"STRAIGHT to school and straight home," Mom says sharply, pressing my phone into my hand. "*Only* for emergency calls."

"You're seriously going to make me stay home on Halloween?" I say.

"Oh, you're not staying home," she says. "You're coming to Shadow's basketball game."

"Mom, come on."

"We've been over this."

We "went over it" for two hours last night when I walked in, rain-soaked, through the front door, which, thanks to the Whites, Mom and Toddy hadn't seen me walk out of in the first place.

"I have half a mind to keep your phone even during the day," she says, "and if I see you've been sending texts or using data, I *will* keep it tomorrow."

Hannah leans on the horn outside.

"I'm going to *fail* creative writing without his help. I'm not going to get a letter of recommendation."

A fifth honk from Hannah's car.

"I'll call your teacher and get a referral for a tutoring service," Mom says. It's both a genuine offer and a threat. Another *end of story, final answer, no Saul Angert for you while you live with me.*

Is this really as simple as a fight over the land, over money? Why would Mom care about that?

Since I got back last night, Feathers has been hovering against my Whiteless wall. "At least tell me Saul and Eli are okay," I begged of her, but no matter how much I hissed and threw paper wads at her, she took me nowhere, gave me no new answers, and I spent the night willing Saul to be safe, praying nothing happened to him or Eli.

Hannah honks again, and I throw Mom one last glance. "I can't make you tell me what happened between our families," I say, "but I'm going to find out either way."

Her mouth tightens. "For your sake, I hope you don't."

"But we *always* spend Halloween together." Hannah stabs her pasta salad with her fork and waves it toward the fake spider webs strewn over the cafeteria doors. "I'll beg. Parents love me."

"One of the benefits of being a real-life Disney princess, Han, which, after our attempted campout, you're officially not. You're a brazen hussy like me now. How's it feel?"

"You know, it felt pretty good," she says, "until Léa called my mom."

"I can't believe *you* didn't get grounded. I think my mom

would care less if I'd talked you into stealing a car than she does that *you* talked *me* into spending half a night at the falls with an Angert."

Hannah sets her fork down and studies me.

I'd told her this morning about what happened in the woods last night—who Feathers was, that Issa and Abe were in love, that Saul and I would have to go in the water to break the curse, and what I heard at the falls last weekend—and the crease of worry between her brows hasn't let up since.

I look down at the pathetic tacos on my tray, a mess of low-grade beef and wilting iceberg lettuce. There's some serious cognitive dissonance going on with the summery food they're serving us and the actual snowflakes falling outside.

"How did it feel?" Hannah asks quietly. "Hearing his voice."

Like nothing else mattered. Like he was really there.

I stand and swipe the rest of my food into the trash can. "It hurt so much I thought I would die."

On my way to study hall, I stop by the office to pick up a drop/add slip on my way to the library, where I slide into the last computer in the row along the rear wall. I can see a sliver of Ms. deGeest through the open door to her classroom.

A storm of anger and shame rages in my stomach.

I'm furious with her for telling my parents about Saul, but I'm also furious with myself for spending the last four years obsessed with following in Dad's footsteps. Now any other future I might want hinges *entirely* on my ability to write myself out of the hole of a straight-C student.

And I can't do it. Can't face deGeest. Can't write. Can't figure out who I want to be or where I want to go. All I can think about right now is breaking this curse before it hurts someone else.

I start an e-mail to Saul, telling him about the tree with O'D ANG carved into it and the moment on the beach with Jack the First, Annie, Jack II, and Issa—*she was his daughter, I think*. I write about Feathers guiding me through it all and my fight with Mom. I ask if Eli's okay, whether he said anything after I disappeared after Feathers, then I hit SEND and wait.

I open a word document—*one last try*—but I have no story, just broken pieces of one.

I lay my spinning head on the desk. The computer pings, and I sit upright to find an e-mail waiting for me.

Jack, I'm so happy you're okay. A few seconds later another comes in: *Sorry, I wanted to say that before I finished reading the e-mail. Back now.* New York Times *best-selling author Eli Angert is fine, but I couldn't get anything out of him. Pretty much right after you ran off, he forgot he'd ever seen you. Have I mentioned how happy I am you're okay? It's almost enough to make knowing I can't see you all right. Just kidding, I'm more selfish than that.*

Meet me tonight, I type.

He doesn't respond for four minutes, each of which takes approximately one hour to pass. When his message comes in, it reads: *Juuuune.*

Sauuuuuuul, I reply.

I didn't think I'd ever get to kiss you.

*I'll give you six dollars and kiss you again if you
meet me tonight.*

Your family's really upset, June.

I stare at the words, chest burning, hands aching, eyes stinging.
The next message that comes in reads: *Promise me you'll stay away
from the water, June.*
    Being apart sucks, I say.
    It does, he says. *Promise me, June.*

*I can't wait any longer. I can't spend every night
waiting for something terrible to happen to my
family, or to you. We have to end this tonight.*

Another six minutes pass. *Where and when?*

Thirty-Five

"JUNIOR, could you stay after class?"

It's infuriating that Ms. deGeest can even look at me, embarrassing that *I* can't look at *her*.

After the rest of the class files out, I count thirty seconds of pindrop silence before Ms. deGeest crosses her arms and leans against the table. Her lipstick is miraculously crisp for this late in the day. Every detail of her seems curated, like her four years' advantage over me gave her the time to determine the precise message she wanted her hair, makeup, wardrobe, and posture to communicate.

"You didn't turn in an assignment," she says.

"I haven't written anything."

"Any particular reason?"

"My life took a particularly weird turn this week."

Her eyes flicker sideways, betraying an instant of discomfort before she pulls her Grown-Up Teacher mask on. "I understand why you're upset."

Now I do meet her eyes. "You're *from* here," I say. "You must know about the bad blood between my family and Saul's. You might've stepped into my business out of some misguided desire to protect me, but you have no idea what—"

"I'm sorry." She straightens the papers on her desk. When she looks up her cheeks are pink. "Okay? I'm new at this, and I crossed a line. I messed up, and you don't need to forgive me, and you certainly don't have to like me, but this thing you do? Writing? It's not a hobby, not a phase. *You* are a *storyteller*. You have a chance to shape your world. You have talent and opportunities and something to say, and you're choosing to blow it because you think this town defines you. I've watched your effort in this class dwindle—you haven't turned in *anything* since I ran into you that night—and if I overstepped, it was only because I thought you were getting involved in a situation that wasn't good for you, and if I were your mother, I'd want—"

I can't contain a jab of laughter. "My mother? To be my mother, you'd have to have gotten pregnant when you were four years old."

She lifts her hands. "The point is, don't let my mistake be an excuse to give up on this class, and don't let Saul be an excuse to stay here. Believe me, June, I know what it's like, how hard it is to leave, to let yourself be different. And I know Saul. What the world stands to lose if he walks away from writing. Look, your grammar's a mess, your vocabulary's slim, and you could line the Great Wall with your adverbs, but you *have* something to offer. That's a *gift*.

And if you master the tools that go along with it, well . . . the world will be better for it. It's okay to be angry with me—and it's okay to take breaks from writing, and fine, college isn't for everyone. But if you take this seriously, you need to fight for your future. Do *something*."

"I *am* doing something," I say, frustration mounting. "I'm just not *writing* because sometimes *writing* isn't worth anything. Sometimes your actual *life* takes over and you don't have time to stare at a computer for four hours."

"I understand." Her voice dims to a hum. "I do. But you shouldn't feel guilty about taking time to nurture a part of yourself that matters. And aside from that, you *need* to turn in your homework. I can't possibly communicate how ridiculous it would be for you to fail this class because you didn't take an hour to pull together *something* to turn in."

I take the slip of paper from my pocket and set it in front of her. She lifts it between two polished fingernails. "This is a drop slip."

"Yeah."

"We're weeks from the end of the semester."

"A month."

"It's too late for this."

"The office gave it to me," I counter. "They'll do anything to get a few more seniors though graduation."

"And you think you won't graduate without dropping my class?"

I nod.

"Because you plan to fail?"

"Are you going to sign it?"

She tears it in half and places the halves in front of me. "It's too late."

"Okay." It doesn't change anything. I'm not going to do the work, because writing down the past is meaningless. I hate so much of my family's past, who I am because of it. I want to undo it, not preserve it as record. All that matters is undoing it.

"I can't do the work for you," she says. "You can't save anyone, no matter how hard you try. I want good things for you, but that doesn't matter if you don't want them for yourself."

Her stare has at *least* as much steel in it as I imagine mine does. "I don't need saving. I just don't have anything to write."

"I'm not asking you to make something perfect. I'm asking you to put the work in."

"I'm not like you, okay? I'm stuck here. This town *is* me."

"Fine." But I can tell it's not fine. She's upset and disappointed, and right now it's easy to see she's not much older than me. While she may have *learned* you can't save anyone, she hasn't stopped trying or feeling bad when she can't.

A strange feeling tangles in my chest.

I want her to be right about me.

"I'll try," I say over my shoulder.

It feels like a lie. I guess I'm still nothing if not a Jack.

Thirty-Six

"I can't believe her." Hannah takes another slurp of her Diet Coke. We're sitting in the bleachers of the Five Fingers Elementary gymnasium, watching Shadow's basketball game. "Doesn't she realize she's your *teacher*, not your mother?"

"Shh." I tip my head toward Grayson, the only buffer between us and Mom and Toddy. Thankfully, Mom made an exception to the No Fun, No Friends rule and let me bring Hannah along. When Toddy found out, he was huffy. They'd almost certainly made a pact not to cave on my punishment, and Mom's already broken it. Out on the basketball court, tennis shoes squeal over the floor and high-pitched shouts echo as the boys call for one another to pass the ball to them. It seems like *everyone* on the court is saying, *Here! Here!* I half-expect Grayson to join in from the way he's bouncing on his butt.

Hannah drops her voice into a whisper. "I'm serious, Junie. You could probably get her fired for that. It's freaking *creepy* how she keeps getting into your business."

I feel a barb of defensiveness, like when someone else joins in when you're complaining about your siblings. "Yeah, well, it's not like she's the only problem. There are billions of things keeping us apart."

Hannah's lips turn down in an exaggerated frown. "It's a *week* without a phone, not a prison sentence. I'm sure he's at home moping and pining, like *you've* been doing all day. It's a bump in the road, Junie."

"A cursed bump."

Hannah shakes her head, bangs swinging over her blue eyes. "You're not going to try and do it alone, though, right? Issa *told* you not to go without him."

"No. We're going to try to meet up tonight."

Her gaze flashes toward my mom, and she whispers, "Maybe you should slip Léa some Ambien."

"Frankly, I think she could muscle through on sheer willpower."

"I want candyyyy!" Grayson announces then, kicking the shoulder blade of the woman sitting in front of us. She turns around with a glare, and Mom flashes an apologetic smile.

Toddy leans forward. "The game's almost over, Gray."

"I'm soooo hungry," he groans. "And I'm about to pee my pants!"

The buzzer sounds then, signaling a Five Fingers loss. As we make our way out to the snowy lot, Grayson skips along dramatically clutching his crotch and squealing in faux misery and true delight at the way the people crane their necks to watch him.

When we get home, everyone else slips inside, but Mom catches me on the porch. "Could you give us a minute?" she asks Hannah.

When the door is shut behind her, I say, "What, don't want an audience while you attach a house-arrest tracker to my ankle?"

Mom gestures toward one of the garden chairs, and I plop down as she eases herself into the other. It's freezing out, and our teeth are fighting a chatter. "You know I hate this, June. I would much rather trust you."

"Then do."

She sets her hand on top of mine. "I didn't want to tell you this, but Todd thinks you should know." After a long beat of silence, she gives her head one firm shake. "Abraham Angert was a murderer."

I stare at her, uncomprehending. "What?"

"He killed your grandfather's sister, your great-aunt. Issa. It happened when Jack II was very young, but it affected him profoundly. Your father grew up hearing about it—older people in town were still talking about it. Jack II was a sad, sad man. Losing his sister destroyed his family."

My mind grasps at the words, but they don't make any sense. Abe *couldn't* have killed the girl he loved. And even if he did, that wouldn't be an excuse for banning me from Saul.

"She was only seventeen," Mom continues. "Abe *said* he had no recollection of doing it, and by the time of the trial, his counsel had persuaded him to plead insanity."

"What do you mean he *said* he had no recollection?"

"Issa's father, Jack the First, never believed it. So her brother, Jack II, didn't quite believe it either, and your father *really* didn't believe it. They thought the Angerts were . . . dangerous."

My scoff isn't enough to show how completely ludicrous that sounds. "Dangerous. And that's what *you* think?"

"I don't know, Jack." Her face twists at the sound of my name. She frees her hand and sinks into her chair. The snowfall has picked up. The lawn is almost entirely coated with white, Shadow and Grayson's cherry sprouts bowing under the weight, and the treetops glint silver. "I think there was more to it than any of them ever let on. And I loved your daddy, but he was *not* the most forthcoming person—he wanted the world to be rosy and bright for us all the time, even at the expense of the truth."

"I know."

Mom narrows her eyes as if trying to see through my skin. Finally, she gives up, and they soften. "I don't know why he thought what he did, but he was afraid of them, June. And there wasn't much else he was scared of.

"I can't protect you forever." Her voice quivers as she stands, a cloud of ice crystals hovering in the air from her breath. "I'm going to while I can." She looks back, resting her hand on the weather-rusted doorknob. "I can't lose you too."

I know what we're risking if we go to the water. But I also know what we're risking if we don't.

"You won't, Mom," I whisper.

Thirty-Seven

INSIDE, Hannah's already got her homework arranged on the kitchen table. The boys are on the couch, watching old episodes of *Adventure Time*, flat out shrieking with laughter, and Toddy's setting up Happy Lamps, his yearly effort to sprinkle the house with imitation sunlight as we slog toward winter, which likely won't let up until April or May.

He emerges from the basement carrying the clock he bought me last year, the kind with a light that clicks on an hour before your wake-up time, intensifying gradually until it theoretically wakes you up with the misconception you're going to see the sun that day.

Against my wishes, my coldness toward him thaws.

Mom comes and sets my phone down beside me, tapping the tabletop with her manicured fingernails. "I still don't want you communicating with him," she says.

Toddy halts his dig through the hall closet, standing still in a hopelessly obvious attempt to listen in. I nod, and that's that. Toddy huffs and heads upstairs. Mom follows him, and I stare at my phone, debating whether it's safe to text Saul.

Han looks up from the calculus problem she's been scowling at and whispers, "You can use my phone to text him if you want."

I glance toward the stairs and shake my head. "We're meeting tonight anyway." I dig my folders out of my backpack, and Hannah shrugs and returns to her work. I last two minutes before I cave and start a message to Saul. I rephrase it eleven times but still find no delicate way to tell him what Mom told me. I settle on: *My mom said Abe killed Issa.*

I let out the breath I'm holding and pick up the photocopied notes I harangued Stephen for, my last attempt not to fail Ms. deGeest.

The top page is a sort of timeline printed in uneven shades of gray, covered in streaks of highlighter and Stephen's chicken-scratch notes. "STORY ARC," it says at the top.

My phone buzzes. I check the stairs again for Mom or Toddy before opening Saul's reply.

Eli won't tell me anything about Abe. He shuts down whenever I ask. I don't know what happened, but I can't imagine the guy we saw making out with Issa in the cave hurting her. There's more to this.

Agreed, I respond. *Mom finally left me alone. I'll see if I can track down some Whites before tonight.*

My phone buzzes almost immediately. *Please don't do that. What if they take you to the water again?*

I sigh. I keep making promises I can't keep. That I'll stay away from Saul, that I won't go to the water without him, that I'll do my creative writing homework despite the utter chaos inside my brain. *What will you give me if I wait?*

Apple fritters by the dozen. I'm at Egrets with NYT-blah-blah-blah Eli Angert right now.

Egrets, the storefront downtown that sells pastries and cider from Egret Orchard, is a Five Fingers autumn staple. It's only open a few months a year, during which everyone eschews their usual cafés in favor of apple everything. *See you at two then.*

I turn again to the STORY ARC timeline and try to focus.

The main horizontal path curves across the page like a speed bump, vertical lines labeled "TURNING POINT" dividing it into sections.

Stephen's labeled the first section of the timeline: "ORDINARY WORLD."

Before I met Saul, my mind fills in the blank.

"TURNING POINT 1: NEW OPPORTUNITY."

"NEW SITUATION."

"TURNING POINT 2: INTRODUCTION OF MAIN GOAL."

"PROGRESS TOWARD GOALS/TESTS, ALLIES, ENEMIES."

Feathers/Issa—ally? Nameless—enemy? Ms. deGeest—mentor?
Enemy? Ally?

"TURNING POINT 3: POINT OF NO RETURN." It's the halfway point on the line, with two more big turning points marked afterward.

Point of no return: *the cliffs over the swimming hole.*

I can feel Saul's knuckles grate against mine. I remember the fall breeze rustling over our naked skin, drawing goose bumps on our arms and legs. His eyes on me, his breath, half the stars strewn across the sky and half warbling in the oily water.

There is no returning from what I heard in the cave or what I found in the water. And there's no returning to how things were before I knew Saul Angert.

I drag my laptop to me and start to type. I begin by describing the way Saul fumbled over the tent and how it made my insides turn into bumblebees. I write about the way he kissed me, breathed against me. How the water drew us into it with the false promise that anything that happened within it would be sacred, unknowable, secret, and safe. I write it all.

I could be embarrassed at the thought of Ms. deGeest reading this, but I'm not sure she ever will. I'm writing this for myself.

So I can remember.

So if someday the curse squeezes my heart so hard the blood stops pumping, I can disappear from this world knowing that night won't be lost. The truth won't be lost.

I, Jack O'Donnell IV, love an Angert.

"More coffee?" Han swipes our mugs up and carries them into

the kitchen. I look up, feeling like I've just emerged from the warm water beneath the falls.

The boys have changed into pajamas and moved on from cartoons to a boxing video game.

Shadow keeps saying, "Gray! You don't have to move side to side! Your character does that automatically!"

Grayson keeps kicking and half-elbowing Shadow as he waves the wireless controllers around in a frenzy.

Hannah glides back with our refilled mugs. "So I chose my AP psych paper topic: the fallacy of memory. Thought the research could help with your little . . ."

"Curse?" I finish.

"I was going to say *problem*." She drops into her seat. "Anyway, it turns out memories are rarely totally accurate, and the more we're asked about them, and the *way* we're asked about them . . . well, it changes them."

"Example?"

"Um, this guy showed a video of a car accident to two groups of people. To one group, he asked questions about what happened when the cars were *smashed into*. He asked the other what happened when the cars were *hit*. A week later, the *smashed* group remembered seeing shattered glass in the video. Which there wasn't."

"Huh." I think about all the memories I've seen so far, the way that, though I'm not *really* there, I can still *feel* them.

"You know how sometimes you remember something specific from your childhood, and your parents can confirm it happened, but when you picture it, it's less like a memory and more like you're watching it happen to someone else, like a video?

Memory is mostly about making connections. We have snippets of real information, bits of imagination and emotions, and we combine them to tell ourselves stories. That could explain *how* you experience the memories. Sure. They could belong to your dad, but maybe you don't see them through his eyes because *he* didn't really either. His brain created a full to-scale replica of the moments you're visiting."

"Weird."

"If you think *that's* weird, you should hear about this rat experiment these scientists did."

"'Rat experiment' is basically my middle name."

"They found out they could pass phobias down through generations of rats."

"Everything about that grosses me out."

Hannah laughs, but her eyes widen at the prospect of talking science. "It's called genetic memory. It's present in animals at birth, leftover information gathered by previous generations. Like, rats learn to be afraid of cats, and cats learn to be afraid of dogs. Not every new rat or cat has to have firsthand experience with the enemy to learn that fear, you know? Some are born with it."

"Maybe that's how O'Donnells are with the falls and with Angerts. Maybe it's genetic memory."

"That's not the same thing," I point out. "I was freaked out by the falls *because* my parents were *constantly* telling me to stay away from them."

"True," Hannah says. "Bad example. Anyway, what are *you* working on? Seems like you're over your writer's block?"

"In this exact moment, yes."

"Well, you know what they say: Rome was built in one exact moment."

"What's writer's block?" Grayson hollers over his shoulder.

Hannah whispers, "How can one tiny organism make that much noise while simultaneously catching every word we say?"

"He's got to be some kind of reincarnated god," I answer, then shout, "It's when you can't write."

"I get that," Grayson says.

"Oh? What are you writing?"

"Homework stuff." He sends one of his controllers flying into the wall.

"Hey, bud, use the wrist straps with those things, okay?"

He chases it and picks it up, but it's too late: Shadow's character has knocked Grayson's out. "Is Mike going to come over and help you with your homework?" Grayson asks.

Shadow glances back at us. "Yeah, tell Mike to come over. Grayson's too easy to beat."

"Mike?" Hannah asks.

I'm distracted by a lone White sifting down the hall toward the stairs.

"June?"

"Mike does Junior's homework," Grayson answers Hannah.

"He's her *tutor*," Shadow corrects him.

The White twirls up the banister. I know I told Saul I wouldn't, but it's here for me—sent to me, like I'm now sure all the memories have been.

My heart begins to race. "Be right back," I tell Hannah and jog upstairs. The White clings to my closet door.

Why can't I let this go?

Because *he's* sending them.

The White dances like a dandelion in a summer breeze. I reach a shaking hand out and hungrily accept its warmth into my skin.

I can't resist. I step through the doorway.

I'm still inside my closet, but I'm facing out into my bedroom now. Shouts are coming from downstairs: screams—a man and woman—and the shatter of porcelain.

A teenage Issa hurries into the room, pulling little Jack II in after her. She closes the door, shutting out some of the noise, but Jack II is still crying. She shoots him a forced yet fierce smile, then hurries to the bed and starts ripping the blankets off it.

Jack rubs his eyes and takes a tentative step. "What are you doing?"

She flings the smile over her shoulder, golden-red curls falling into her face. "I'm building a safe house."

"A safe house?"

"Take the pillows and follow me, Jack." She carries the bundle of bedding into the closet, passing right through me. She begins tying the corners of the sheets to the shelves along the wall, stringing up a fort.

Jack II's chin snaps over his shoulder at the sound of another shout. "Jackie," Issa says, taking his shoulders.

He stares at her with saucerlike eyes. "What's a safe house?" he whispers.

She studies him, the expression on her heart-shaped face as serious as that on his round one. "A safe house is a doorway to a magical place."

"Like the thin place."

"Yes, like the thin place. When we go inside, we won't be here anymore. We'll be somewhere no one can find us. A secret place for you and me alone. How's that sound?"

Jack nods solemnly, and Issa squeezes his shoulder, then ducks into the blanket fort. He follows, a look of wonder spreading as he inspects the light spilling through the blankets. "We'll be safe," he says.

"We will."

"Why is he so angry?" Jack asks.

A sadness flickers over Issa's face. "I think because he is afraid."

"Afraid of what?"

"Of losing what he loves."

Jack's mouth forms a perfect circle of concern. "The cherries?"

Issa folds her legs underneath herself and pats the pillow beside her. Little Jack curls up there, letting his sister smooth his hair. "He's very lonely, Jack," she says. "He's watching the world as he's always known it change into a place he doesn't fit. He resents those who know how to change with it and those who pity him. I think he even resents those who love him." She squeezes his shoulders. "You and I won't ever be alone like that. Someday you'll be grown up, and when you are, we'll escape together."

"Where will we go?" Jack asks.

"Anywhere you want. With anyone we want."

"I don't want him to hate me," Jack whispers.

She discreetly brushes tears from her eyes and kisses the crown of his head. "Have I ever told you about the night you were born?"

He shakes his head, and her lips press into a smile. "Papa was in Maryland. Everyone wanted Jack's Tart, and people had money to spend back then, so he'd gone to sell seeds to a farmer down there. He hadn't wanted to go, but you weren't due for another two weeks, and Mama told him there was a better chance of every fish in Lake Michigan turning silver than your being born in the next two days.

"But you had other ideas, and sure enough, when Papa reached the hotel that night, there was a message waiting for him: You were on your way. He was so happy, he picked the clerk up and spun him around, gave him all the cherry seeds he'd brought to sell. Then he hopped right back in the car without so much as a glass of milk for dinner and headed for home. But as he drove, he saw, out of the corner of his eye, a star falling over Backbone Mountain.

"And then another, and another, until the sky was alight with a meteor shower. Papa knew then you had arrived. He started crying so hard he couldn't see—from happiness that you were here and sadness because he'd missed your grand arrival. He couldn't return home with nothing to give his new son, so he pulled over and climbed to the top of Backbone, and at its peak, with his bare hands, he caught a falling star."

I've heard this story, though in my father's version, Jack the First had chased the star on horseback and caught it on a dare from Jacob Angert. I wonder, then, if I'm witnessing the story's first telling. If it was less an exaggeration and more an outright fabrication that Issa created to soothe Jack II in this moment. Something that affected him profoundly enough that he'd pass it along to his own son, who would pass it to me, all its details chopped up and rearranged.

"And though the star badly burned," Issa continues, "he ran to his car and drove all the way home through the night with it, ignoring the heat on his palm. When he reached Five Fingers, he threw the star into the lake, and just like that, every fish turned bright, shimmering gold. Papa caught one with his hand and carried it to the hospital, where he found me and you and Mama waiting for him. *Hi, Jack*, he said to you, *I'm your father, and this is how much I love you. Enough to climb a mountain. Enough to catch a star. Enough to carry it home as it burns. Someday you'll know what it's like. Someday you'll love something so much it turns every brown fish gold.*"

Jack's lungs have fallen into a steady rhythm, his eyes pressing shut.

"I love you, Jack," Issa whispers. "Even if he's forgotten how to, I won't. I love you, and I'll never let you go."

When he finally drifts into sleep, the memory freezes.

You promised, I remember Jack II crying on the bed to the pink ghost. *You promised we'd get out.*

He knew Feathers was his sister. She was supposed to take him away, somewhere safe. She *was* his somewhere safe. I know what that's like to watch that disintegrate. To lose the one thing you never thought you could.

But how? How did he lose her?

Did Abe really kill her?

Dread creeps through me, mingling with the ache of grief.

I slip back into the bedroom—mine, in the present. The sound of Shadow's and Grayson's laughter, of Hannah's playful teasing drift up to me. I'm home.

I set my alarm for two A.M. and get in bed. I must drift off, because

I jerk awake sometime later, choking, convinced my lungs are filled with the water from the falls.

The cold burn in my chest fizzles, but there's no way I'm getting back to sleep, so I creep downstairs. Mom's sitting up at the table, tearfully scribbling in a notebook. Fresh worry needles me. I want to go to her—comfort her—but I can't jeopardize my impending escape.

I sneak back upstairs to wait. My nerves spark when a text from Saul comes in. I'm suddenly afraid he'll call off our plans, feel too guilty or worried to meet me in the woods. I tap it open.

Hey. An ambiguous bait-message. An implied *We need to talk.*

I figure if I don't respond, he won't be able to cancel. There's no way Saul Angert will leave me to wander the woods alone.

Another message comes in. *That was my impression of a loser who doesn't know how to say what he's thinking.*

Convincing, I can't resist replying.

It's all about commitment. If I'd texted you any sooner, with more than one word, it might not have been so convincing.

Great, I say, then add, *Are you trying to cancel?*

No.

Then why are you texting me an hour before we're supposed to meet?

Why do you think?

So it's my job to answer the question for you.

I don't want to wait an hour, he says.

That eager to dive into memories, huh?

Sure. *That's it.*

Flirting with me on the very brink of discovering what caused a century-old family curse.

I'm shameless. Shameful? Both?

I think you mean "hot."

Get over here, Jack.

I'm trying, I tell him.

Not hard enough, apparently.

Is that a euphemism?

Hitting on me on the very brink of breaking a century-old family curse, huh, June?

I go into my closet for a coat and a pair of boots, then sit on my bed and pull them on. A faint illumination comes from the window. The Whites are back, silently grazing one another as they shift within the pane.

This time when I sneak downstairs, Mom's on the couch snoring peacefully, a pilled carmine throw tossed over her. Guilt coils around my stomach.

You're doing this for her too, I tell myself. *For everyone you love.*

The windows are frosted and dark, but I can make out a doe picking its way through the snowy lawn, two fawns ambling after, stopping to sniff and munch. At one point they freeze and stare at me, their ocher eyes blinking at me through the glass.

I remember a morning like this one. Dad nudged me awake and led me downstairs to show me how, through one window, you could see coywolves hiding in the trees and, through the other, a deer lying in the snow as though it were a bed of hay.

"Is it true that in another forest, the coyotes or the wolves would kill her?" I whispered.

Dad nodded solemnly and twisted the knob on the back door, nodding permission for me to step outside. Our toes purpled in the below-zero temperature, and our breath was visible as we watched the creatures. "Anywhere else the deer would run too," Dad whispered. "But this is sacred ground."

"Marta Griggs didn't believe me," I told him. "Even though her family believes there used to be a magic garden and a snake slithered into it and spread evil. She says that's why people kill one another and why they get sick too."

Dad's face tensed. "You know, June-bug, evil's something you can decide to do every day, and it gets easier every time. But the more good you bring into the world, maybe the more the rest of the world would look like this. Like paradise."

I ease the back door open, and the wind cuts through me. I close it before the bite can wake Mom, and I step onto the porch, heart trilling in my chest because we're so close to figuring everything out *and* because I'm going to see Saul again. Finally.

As I set off across the yard, a snowshoe hare darts past me, followed by two more, their feet pricking holes in the crunchy snow. I watch the point where they vanish into the dark folds of the trees, amazed by how much ground something so small can cover in so little time. I pick up my pace, jumping in surprise as a deer gallops jerkily past, dashing into the forest exactly where they did, its white tail fading into the night.

An outburst of flapping wings erupts behind me, and the feeling of free fall hits me all at once, the sensation of my stomach flying into my mouth, the ground dropping out from under me.

I know before the stampede of living things hits—the porcupines and opossums, starlings and house sparrows, weasels and woodchucks all scuttling furiously past me, all shrilling and wild-eyed. Before I've turned to face the chicken coop, I know what I'll find.

The blackness thrashes in front of it, stretched out in every direction, twice its usual size, and everything caught within its grasp screams and seizes. Instead of huddling around the heater in the coop, the chickens flap through the grass, pecking and flailing; field mice move drunkenly among them, falling onto their backs and twisting in agony.

A hen—neck twisted, blood and feathers spread—lies strewn across the shining white.

"Saul." My teeth chatter, lips shiver. I turn and run, whipping my phone from my coat. I dial as fast as I can, counting the seconds as the line rings. Once.

Twice.

Three times.

Six.

Seven.

"Hi, you've reached Saul. Sorry I can't take your call. Leave—"

"No," I say aloud. I call again.

One ring. Two. Three. Five. Seven. *"Hi, you've reached—"*

I turn back to the writhing darkness, to the nameless thing following me, hating me. "You can't have him."

It vanishes.

I take off running.

Thirty-Eight

IT'S not too late, I tell myself.

I'll get to Eli's cabin soon, and Saul will be fine, I tell myself. *I'll be fine.*

I keep running, my heart raging against my rib cage.

A twig snaps within the forest—the footfall of a coywolf, or gravity taking its toll on a dead branch, probably. But I *feel* something watching me.

Another snap. A rustle. I spin.

A dark shape dives into the shadows.

I lunge after it, throw myself through the brush, feet pounding the snow, calves burning, lungs heaving, heart *aching* because *where is Saul and why isn't he answering his phone?*

A half dozen coywolves scatter from the brush as I pick up my pace. I run until everything is a blue-green blur. The trees thin ahead, moonlight breaking through.

I stumble into the clearing around the cabin. A rabbit lies dead in front of the steps, and the front door hangs open, the wind pounding it against the side of the house. Dead leaves skitter across the floor, the crispy noise like a lifeless version of Saul's laugh.

I bound up onto the porch and move into the dark hallway. "Saul?"

The house is a mess: an antique console table flipped on its side, a ceramic vase shattered, its dried-out contents spilling across the wood grain. A green lamp knocked over on a fifties walnut table, its age-yellowed shade askew and the lightbulb flickering from the loosened connection.

"Saul?" My voice crackles as if interrupted by static.

Soft whimpers rise from behind the couch. I pick up a broken slab of ceramic from the ground as I advance. "Hello?"

I sidle around the edge of the coffee table until I can see the gap between the couch and the loveseat. On the floor, a man in rumpled pajamas rocks against the wall, tears still rolling down his wrinkled cheeks.

"Eli." I hurry to his side.

His vacant eyes drift to me, blinking against the stuttering lamplight. The wintry bite I'm used to finding in his face is nowhere to be seen, but neither is the man who cradled his daughter on a bathroom floor.

"Who are you?" He sounds young, lost.

"I'm Ja—Junior," I decide on. "Saul's friend."

"Saul." Eli looks at his hands. They're clutching a triangular slice of ceramic, like mine, but his are smeared with blood. His arms are sliced in purposeless sweeps of dark red. I bite down on the words—*Oh God*—rising in my chest.

I pry the makeshift weapon from his fingers. "Eli. Where's Saul? What happened?"

"Saul." Something passes over his eyes, as if his mind just slid into place behind his pupils. A gurgle gets trapped in his throat. "Saul's my son." He covers his trembling mouth with one hand. *"Bekah's gone."*

"Eli."

His eyes snap toward mine, teeth chattering. "She came."

Shivers spring up over my legs as the wind's howl whips through the open front door. "Bekah?"

"No. Maolissa." The open door claps against the side of the house. Eli's eyes pinch shut, and he releases a half-formed grunt, the tears starting to fall anew as he slumps toward the wall.

"Eli, *what happened*?"

"Maolissa came. She tried to take him from me. I told him not to go," Eli gasps between tears. "He wasn't going to. But then *he* came."

I touch his shoulders. "Who, Eli?"

His eyes rove around the room, his face contorting. "Abe."

That familiar chill passes through me. "Abe is . . . the other ghost. Abe is Nameless?"

Eli sniffs. "I told Saul he wouldn't hurt us. Abe only hurts *them*." *Them.*

"I tried to tell him, but he ran, and Abe left too. It was just me and her then." Eli sinks into himself, wrapping his arms around his own shoulders. "She showed me," he sobs. "I don't want to remember. I don't want to see it. Please don't make me see my baby like that. I didn't do anything. *It wasn't my fault. It wasn't . . ."*

He curls up on the floor. I touch his shoulder, but he hardly seems to notice. "Eli, who are *they*?" I say, needing confirmation. "Who does Abe hurt?"

All at once, his crying stops. His dark eyes relax. He blinks up at me. "You must be one of Bekah's friends. She's out back."

I swallow the lump pressing into the top of my throat, brace myself against the hollow weight crushing my chest. He's lost. He can't answer, but I don't need him to.

"They're good kids," Eli whispers. "Good."

I hold back tears and take his hand. "They love you."

Eli's eyebrows sink. His face is open, childlike. "Who, now?"

I straighten, lifting the lamp upright as I do. I leave him huddled on the floor, like the chickens clustered in the coop, like the coywolves gathered in the woods. Like everything on this land we share that seems to know:

Death is coming.

Thirty-Nine

"SAUL." The wind swallows my voice as I emerge from the ramshackle cabin.

Saul would've gone to my house when he saw Nameless—*Abe*—like I went to his. And what would he find?

A dead chicken and me missing. He'd think the worst, like I had about him.

I check my phone—no missed calls—and dial again. No luck.

Issa quivers in front of a furry pine, the moonlight stripping her bubbly reflection of color.

"Help me," I beg her.

The pain in my chest is deep and violent, lodged in the endless vacuum of grief inside me. As badly as I want to see Dad, I don't want to die. I don't want to lose Mom or Toddy or the boys or Hannah or Saul. I need him to live. I need *both* of us to live.

Shadows splotch Issa's non-body: Whites from the woods drift through her.

"No more memories. Take me to *Saul*!" I shout through the wailing wind. "Before it's too late."

Issa sways. I remove my boots and cross the stiff snow barefoot. When I step through Whites, I appear on top of the waterfall, current gushing around my ankles like angry salmon.

Two bare, moonlit bodies stand ahead of me at the edge of the waterfall. Even though Saul and I jumped from the cliffs to the right, I can't help but think for a second that it's *us* I see.

"Ready?" Abe Angert asks the red-haired girl beside him. A smile parts her full lips, dimpling her cheeks. She looks as if her happiness is on the verge of spilling into laughter. As happy as she was that day on the beach with her family.

Abe studies her, momentarily forgetting the breeze, the water, their nakedness. He reaches out, and she does too. They look at their entwined fingers with breathless wonder, as if watching the earth's foundations being laid.

As if they can see the bones shaping their hands, the tendons stretched there, the joints attached and ligaments tied, the veins threaded through and muscle wrapped. As if they can see the pulse of her heart racing from her chest down to her palm, thrumming against his lifeline until his heartbeat and hers are in sync.

Until the two of them are in sync.

Abe and Issa: one thing, one intangible thing that cycles between two bodies.

"I love you," he tells her quietly.

Her eyes flutter shut as she smiles. "You aren't allowed to love me."

"No," he says. "It's you who isn't allowed to love *me*. I have no such rule. What did your father call me—a snake in the grass?"

Her smile fades. "It's not you, Abe." She opens her teary eyes. "He hasn't always been so angry. The world doesn't have money for cherries anymore. He gives them away by the dozens just to keep them from rotting on the ground, and I think . . . I think he needs someone to blame, because otherwise it's just him. *Him* who failed us, who lets us be hungry. He can't look at us. He's angry all the time. He tries to find other work, but there's none here. And your father, he's been so generous, but . . . my father resents feeling indebted. I see it in his face, Abe: He believes he's losing the world, and that makes him angry with anyone who's managing to hold on. But once he *knows* you . . ."

"Issa." Abe touches her cheek, running his thumb up to the corner of her lashes. "Your father sees his land as the Garden of Eden and me as the snake trying to tempt you away."

"Then he's as foolish as the devil was," Issa says. "This may be as close to Eden as any place, but no man, not even Jack O'Donnell, can be God."

Abe's smile is so similar to Saul's that my heart speeds. "Yes," Abe replies, fighting to appear solemn, "God is much too lovely to be a man. She's far more likely to look like you."

Issa erupts with laughter. "You are shameless."

"Is that what you love most about me?"

"It is," she says. "Though it may also be one reason I'm forbidden from loving you. Or do you so easily forget the other girls you've carried on with all through town?"

A flush starts at his ears. He tucks his nose against the side of Issa's face. "Yes," he whispers. "Easily, immediately, wholly."

"That doesn't flatter me, Abe."

"Then what does?" He steps back. "How I dream of you, Is? The sketchbooks devoted to your neck and shoulders and hands? How when I bite into a cherry, it's not the sun I taste but you? How, for me, the whole world isn't made up of lakes and trees but of your millions of shades?"

"Obsession," she says. "Infatuation. And when you follow the only work left in the state to another city, what then?"

"How long have I loved you, Issa?"

She arches one eyebrow. "Always, to hear you tell it."

"Always," he says. "Before you would even look my way."

"I looked your way," she teases. "It was only that you hadn't yet grown into your ears, so looking did little."

"Maolissa O'Donnell," he says, "I have loved you since you were six years old and I found you at the disappearing tree. I loved you when you, at twelve, turned up your nose and said, 'Abe, I'm going to travel the world, probably marry a prince, so you need to understand the nature of this friendship.'"

Issa keens with laughter, and Abe winds his arms around her waist. "Tell me, Issa. Is that still your plan?"

Her smile falls, leaving tenderness and vulnerability exposed. "Sometimes," she whispers, "I think you are the snake."

"*Issa.*"

"Don't draw me away from them only to leave me," she says. "You say these things—you make me feel as though, if you stop loving me, I'll die."

"You won't," he murmurs. He shakes his head once. "I won't."

"Promise me."

He takes her hands in his. He kisses one, then the other. "I promise you. I promise the stars. I promise the lake and falls, coywolves and robins. I promise earth and heaven: I will love you long after the last human has taken his last breath. When the stars burn out and the oceans freeze over and the whole world is ash and dust and ice, our names will still be carved into the tree of life, side by side, and I'll still be loving you."

Issa's voice trembles. "Maybe in the water we'll be reborn. When we come up, you will be only you, and I will be only me. On the other side, nothing will keep us apart."

"Nothing *will* keep us apart," he answers solemnly.

Her smile is the kind that hides something. I think of the memory of that day on the beach, when Jack the First chased her through breaking waves and her laughter spilled out like gemstones. Her love for her father is as essential to her being as her love for Abe, or either's love for her. I think of the coyote and the wolf then, and instead of marveling at Dad's description of them lying together, it's the robin that awes me.

The delicate thing with soft feathers and hollow bones that lies between two wild and unpredictable beasts, untouched by both. Fearless, trusting.

Issa looks at Abe one last time. "Ready," she whispers.

They take a running leap off the ledge, and squeals fling out of them as they drop to the water. I rush forward and watch Abe Angert and Issa O'Donnell hit the pool below. They splash; they plunge; they sink, bubbles jostling to the surface in their wake. Everything falls silent for three breaths, and then Abe tops the water, gasping, his smile vivid. He treads water, turning in slow circles.

"Issa?" The walls around the pool catch his voice and mute it. "Is!"

No answer. He glances right-left-right, dives down again. He's gone for a long moment, too long. He resurfaces alone.

"ISSA?" The water sloshes as he twists. "IS? ISSA!"

He dives under, emerges again, hoarsely shouting her name. The cliffs absorb his voice. The water mocks him with its quiet. Still no red-gold hair or slim shoulders. No gemstone voice responding to his call.

I stumble from the ledge. Stagger, trip. Stomach bile rises in my throat, and vertigo rocks me off balance.

My head cracks against something hard, stars popping in my vision, a wall of hot whites and reds.

The colors fade; the shadows hanging over me resolve into foliage. I'm back in the forest. *I just saw someone die.*

I saw someone die.

I saw—

Saul. I'd forgotten about Saul. About the dead hen and the ghosts.

I lurch to my feet and run for my house, calling out for him in case he's still in the woods. My bare feet are numb as they trample the snow, and I try to shake the Whites from my hair and clothes. There's no time for this.

But when I reach my yard, lush grass catches my feet where there should be frost.

A warm breeze wriggles through my coat. A pile of shoes sits to the right of the porch, and the moon hangs high.

At the bottom of the hill, I see movement: a hunched blur.

"HELP!" Abe's now familiar voice is cracking, muffled by distance. "HELP!"

Lights flick on in the windows.

"HELP!" Abe screams again. He struggles to keep his legs under him, to keep hold of the limp thing in his arms.

The front door flings open. Jack the First careens out, bad leg buckling with each step. Abe lets himself fall now, now that there's someone to witness what's happened. The porch light barely spills across the girl's face.

"What happened?" Jack the First rasps. "What happened?"

He's a record stuck on a note, skipping, scarred. He touches the sides of Issa's face. He drags her out of Abe's arms and across his own lap, keening with horrible bearlike sounds. "What did you do?" he screams, voice threadbare, at Abe.

A long-legged little boy with sandy hair breaks from the front door and runs across the shadowy yard. Annie chases Jack II, her nightgown fluttering, and catches his shoulders. A strangled noise dies in her throat as she sees, then understands. She shakes her head and sinks, pulling Jack II to her. His round face is scrunched. He shakes his mother off and runs for the woods, runs right past me, runs like he can never stop. Like if he looks back, he'll die, and if he keeps moving, it won't hurt so bad.

"What did you do?" Jack the First shrieks again.

"The falls," Abe musters. He shakes his head. "I thought that if she could have the cherries—"

"The cherries?" Jack rasps, returning to himself.

"—if she had a healing cherry," Abe chokes.

Jack's on his feet, standing over the crumpled boy. He bears down on him, and Abe makes little more than a grunt when Jack kicks him in the ribs. He doesn't scream when Jack hauls him up by the neck or hits him across the face. He collapses onto his stomach, tries to scramble away, but Jack drags him back and stomps on his shoulder.

Abe goes limp though not unconscious. There's blood under his nose, and in this light it looks more like syrup or chocolate. It blooms across a cheek, an elbow, a gaping mouth on a pale boy.

A scream tears through me, making no sound. Stars dance behind my eyes, and the ground sways. I crumple and grip the grass between my fingers, wanting to stop this thing that's already happened.

Feathers flickers at the far edge of the woods, weeping as only a thing without eyes can. Kneeling without knees.

Abe doesn't see her. Does he see anything anymore? He stares at the sky, unblinking, mouth twisted as Jack hits him, sickly thud after sickly thud. Crunch after snap. Snap after thwack. There's blood, so much blood, and I can't tell where it comes from—Jack's split-open knuckles or Abe's cheek.

Whether it's Jack's thumb that's broken or Abe's eye socket.

Jack splattered in Abe's blood or Abe splattered in Jack's.

Jack's heart torn in two or Abe's drowned in the water.

A snake rustles in the grass beside me, slithering toward the woods. I wish I could close my eyes and shut out the sounds of flesh hitting flesh, lungs heaving.

The wolf at the coyote's throat.

The robin dead in the water.

Eventually Jack's throws come slower, his breathing heavier. He slumps sideways off Abe, onto the ground.

Annie sways in the breeze, her hair lifted off her neck.

Abe just stares, as though his mind has become untethered from his body.

There's blood in the grass, none of it hers, and she's still dancing, weeping at the edge of the woods.

Jack the First crawls to Issa, presses his forehead into her shoulder. He knots his fingers into the grass beside her.

The snake is gone. It's over. This place is broken, and now I understand.

Forty

I enter the house and am ejected into the present, a new sense of terror cleaving to me.

It's not just me and Saul at risk tonight.

Issa's hovering form follows me upstairs to the boys' room. I listen for their breathing, search the dark corners and shadows for the ghost we've always called Nameless.

When I'm sure Shadow and Grayson are safe, I stand outside the master bedroom and listen to Toddy's snores, then slip back downstairs, where Mom turns over on the couch, sighing in her sleep.

They're safe. It does little to ease the spastic clip of my heart. *What about Saul?*

I leave the house, feet still bare and approaching frostbite, I'm sure, but I need to be able to follow wherever Issa leads.

Wherever Saul is.

Issa takes me back into the woods. They're misty and sunlit, as though night were nothing but a dream, and in this golden haze she becomes solid: pale with strawberry hair and dimpled cheeks. She smiles sadly—the way she smiled when Abe said nothing would keep them apart—and leads me, calling for Saul as I go, through the forest.

We pass the billions of fluttering Whites, the mass of vines and branches circling O'Dang! like women holding hands around a maypole, and Issa keeps moving.

"Where is he?" I ask.

She says nothing.

Ahead, the trees thin. My heart thunders. I know where Issa's taking me—I can already hear it.

We crest the cliff overlooking the falls. Beneath the glassy surface, delicate spheres float like lazy jellyfish, membranes in otherworldly shades of blue, purple, and white.

Warmth wafts off the water, carrying a whispered word: "*June.*"

I try to shut out the sound of my father's voice. I dig my feet into the earth to keep myself from leaping in pursuit of him. "Where's Saul?" I demand of Issa, who has shifted into a fluctuating pink aura again.

She wavers at the lip of the cliff, as if peering into the water, and every pump of my heart carries ice through my veins.

"*June-bug.*"

"*Junie.*"

"*Junior.*"

Dad's voice becomes insistent, harder to block out.

"You said I would drown if I went in alone," I snap. "Why did you bring me here?"

Issa billows, all her movement pointing to the water. The ice in my veins stops, reverses, plunges into my heart. "Did Saul go in the water?"

She dips. It's as close to a nod as I can imagine a thing like her doing. I eye the sleek surface, and the voices escalate into a feverish pitch: "*June, June, June.*"

The Whites sound sinister now: hungry. Less like Dad and more like Nameless. *Abe.*

I step to the edge, sending rocks scrabbling down the cliff side.

"If Saul went down before we got here . . ." He would've been under for a full minute by now—and that's only if he went *right* before we got here. "Why would he *do* that? He knows how dangerous it is."

My mind spins, trying to piece the night together. I think back to the dead hen in my yard and the rabbit outside Eli's cabin. Issa had gone there, Abe too, and Eli had told Saul what the memories had revealed in pieces to me: that Nameless hurts O'Donnells.

He would've come to check on me, only to find a hen dead in the snow and me already gone. Whether because he assumed I'd gone there or because he knew we were out of time—

Saul went in the water.

"*June. June. June. JUNE. JUNIOR.*" The voices mix with the hiss of creatures scuttling through the branches, slinking along the forest floor. The voices begin to *shout* over the burbling of the water as fish rise, flailing.

An inky shadow rolls across the falls.

He's here. Maybe he planned all of this exactly as it's happening. Maybe he knew sending Saul in would send me in after.

Maybe Abe's here to drown me.

But it doesn't matter. The voices are so loud they feel as if they're coming from within my head, and the forest buzzes in anguish at the cold ghost's presence. From this close, I feel the shapeless thing's turmoil worm into me, stoke me into a frenzy.

"Saul," I say, grounding myself.

Stay focused. For Saul.

I jump.

The warm water seems to reach up to snatch me, drag me down. Hundreds of waterlogged Whites scream and moan in my father's voice. I don't fight the pull.

I dive.

Deeper, deeper, deeper, until I have to kick hard to keep moving through the barrage of Whites. I ignore the push on my lungs, the water slipping up my nostrils, the panic saying *up-up-up*.

Closer to the bottom, the Whites are packed more densely. Their light dazzles so brightly I can see nothing else. I kick harder.

Closer. So close I can touch the wall of white. I can taste it.

I push myself into it. It envelops me, light everywhere. Nothing but light.

It recedes from the center of my vision, radiating toward the outsides.

I'm immersed in a memory, the whole scene washed out by the brilliant luminescence hanging over everything. I'm downstairs in my house.

Dad sits in a high-backed chair at the console table in the dining room. He's hunched, his oversized hand gripping a pen, scribbling on a sheet of loose-leaf paper.

In the kitchen, Mom is boiling noodles. I can smell marinara, tangy and sweet and loaded with garlic. Steam spirals up from the pot, finely sheening her cheek with humidity. She sweeps her forearm up to her hairline to catch the sweat accumulating there.

"Junior?" she says. The burning whiteness seems to drape over her voice, distilling it into the pure sound of her. "Come help Mama."

The eight-year-old girl drawing at the dining room table stands but hesitates there, between her parents—her mother at the stove a few yards to her left, her father at the desk on her right. She ignores her mother and goes to her father.

I remember.

She tries to climb on his back. He wriggles her off, leaving her to squeal and giggle and try harder. "Not now, June-Bug," he says.

"Jackie, please," Mom says. "Get the silverware, baby."

She keeps climbing on him. He stops what he's doing and pulls her off. Holding her by the elbows, he leans back to study her, smiling softly. After a few seconds of silence, he kisses the wiggling girl's forehead. "You go help Mom, Bug."

She huffs and turns away. Dad folds the letter he'd been working on.

I remember. This happened the night we found the dead hen.

He writes something on the outside of the note, then walks toward the door. "Be right back," he tells me and Mom.

I strain my eyes to see the word on the folded letter: *Junior*.

White light bursts across my vision, and I feel the water all around me again. I kick one last time, but somehow I've been turned around. I'm kicking *up* not down, and that one kick sends me over the surface.

Forty-One

THE white is hot against my eyes. I blink it back, treading water. Slowly, color filters into the edges of my vision.

The forest is gone. So is the waterfall.

I'm in an ocean, or maybe a Great Lake, some vast gray body beneath a mist-filled sky. In the distance, I spy a white shore. A girl with red-gold hair sits at the edge of the tide. *Issa.*

"Hello?" I call, checking whether I'm in a memory. My voice is audible but barely; a blanket of hot wind roars over it.

The water is as dense with Whites as the pool under the falls. Billions of them filling up this massive space. They all seem to be swimming away from the shore where Issa sits, across the softly rollicking waves where I emerged. In several places throughout the watery expanse, the Whites stop swimming *out* and dive *down*, forming little cyclones of fluff.

To gaps in the veil, I think, *like the woods and the falls.*

I stroke through them, grazing dozens at a time, and even though I'm not crossing thresholds, their contents flash bright across my mind.

A red sled whipping down a hill, the sweet tastelessness of a snowflake on my tongue, the crackle of a gas fireplace, and piles of snow melting on boot toes in a tray inside a green door.

A hammer in my hand, yellow floral curtains, the earthy smell of sweat, and a buttery laugh.

Popsicles staining mouths Tang-orange, slivers in my feet, fights with a mother who isn't mine, a glass shattering in the sink, drawing blood from the skin between my thumb and forefinger.

Downy fur soft against my face.

The memories course through me, and it's everything I can do to keep treading water. Sometimes, though, the memories feel so real I forget and start to slip beneath.

A tug of the tide pulls me back to reality, and I kick to the surface and keep swimming.

Until my arms ache. My legs ache. My shoulders burn and lungs feel like someone's taken sandpaper to every inch of them, and still I'm far from the shore.

Issa sits, watching serenely.

"SAUL?" The wind swallows my voice. I don't know whether I'm calling out for him or asking Issa if he's here. I can't let myself think about what could've happened to him.

I swim until it's all I can do to keep my nose above water. And then I can't even do that.

I kick my legs, windmill my arms, but I'm no longer above the surface, and every muscle in my body throbs with exhaustion. I open my eyes and watch armies of Whites swim past.

I see full cities beneath me—sunken homes and skyscrapers, bicycles and cobblestone and awnings, Whites cloistering around the waterlogged windows. Overlapping places, maybe, or maybe places that haven't existed for a long time.

My lungs stutter until they're on fire. *It won't end here, Abe,* I think with all my might and keep swimming. *I'm fixing it.*

I ignore the voice that says it's already over. I repeat in my mind: *Saul will be okay, you will be okay, everything will be okay,* even as my muscles stop responding to my commands and my lungs twitch and cold dread tangles around me.

Now other memories crash over me—not from the Whites but from my own mind: Mom's hands in my hair, Toddy's chin resting on her head, Grayson and Shadow wrestling me in the yard, Hannah pulling me close in the school parking lot as snow falls on our hair, Saul looking into my eyes and saying, "I can hear all of you, rushing around in there. A million Jacks and Juniors and Junes, a city of them," bees awake beneath my skin, buzzing eagerly toward him.

I DON'T WANT TO DIE.

I think it like a scream, like a battle cry. Even if it means seeing Dad, I don't want to die. There, I admit it and fight a losing fight against the water, thrash, scream with my body as I can't with my mouth, and *fight.*

I WANT TO LIVE. I WANT TO LIVE. I WANT TO LIVE.

My toes graze something solid.

Sand. The valley beneath me starts sloping upward to meet the shore in the distance. I kick, and soon my feet hit ground. My knees hit ground. I'm crawling up the shore.

And then there's air.

Shocking, hot, abundantly dry.

My face is above water. I collapse onto my stomach, greedily gulping oxygen. I'm shaking, unable to stand. I curl into the fetal position, too tired to acknowledge the girl sitting behind me, and dig my hands into the sand.

It's not sand at all. It's cool on my hands but doesn't melt. Warm on the soles of my feet but doesn't burn. I let a fistful sift through my fingers. It floats to the earth like trillions of Whites crushed to bits. The ground is made of crumbled memories.

Every spare inch of me has been dusted chalky white, as if I've rolled in a vat of flour. I wipe at it, but it doesn't even smear.

Craning my neck, I look at the sky. Out over the water it's a gray-blue, but past Issa, the sandy shore extends into a desert plain, and billowing mist forms a high wall in the distance, blocking the horizon from sight. The Whites are coming from the haze, carried by the wind. I'm closer than ever to wherever they come from.

In a way this place is familiar. I imagine this is what you see when you open your eyes after a plane crash or car accident, in that moment *before* you register the truth of wreckage, blood, and rocks. This is a place you see as you're falling asleep, and you think it must've come from your brain, but you have no clue where you got the idea.

I've crossed through the veil.

Hot wind batters me, loud but strangely calming. I struggle out of my coat and stand, forming a visor with my hands to shield my eyes from the light and the whip of my hair.

"He's not dead."

Issa's voice startles me. She's standing now, water lapping at her feet. She dusts the white stuff off her skin; it doesn't cling to her as it does to me.

"Saul?"

She tips her head toward the wall of mist. "Walk with me."

My muscles groan in protest, but I fall into step beside her, her copper curls lashing her creamy face and pink lips like streaks of sunlight. "What is this place?"

Her shoulders barely hitch in a shrug. "It doesn't need a name, does it?"

"Everywhere else has one."

"Then call it the place that isn't everywhere else. Or perhaps the *other* place."

"Is it an afterlife?"

Issa laughs, a sound not dissimilar to the wind in its crisp, vital quality. She sets her hand against a twisted tree that grows out of the sand, casting slight shade. "It's just a place," she says. "Like any other. This world is outside your world. If your world is the womb, this is the person it belongs to. It carries you everywhere, but you don't see it until you're born."

"You mean *until you die*." My voice shakes. "I drowned, didn't I?"

"You don't have to die to get here," Issa says. "Most do, but your world has cracks in its walls. Sometimes things get in, sometimes they get out. It takes a great amount of luck or coincidence for a person to squeeze through."

"And which brought *me* here?" I say.

"I did. And *you* did."

I shake my head. "I don't understand."

"I hoped you would choose to come here as you did," she says. "Alive rather than dead."

"I didn't make a choice. I came to find Saul."

"Yes." Her lips lift a blaze of smile. She keeps walking, guiding me through the Whites and wind. The gray overhead never changes. I see no sun or moon or stars, only the white underfoot, the shifting mass of water molecules ahead, and the Whites blowing past us. Sometimes I hear seagulls, distant and blithe.

"Can we go back?" I ask her. "Home, I mean."

"Perhaps." She doesn't go on.

"What about the curse—is it broken now?"

"Our house sits in a special place," Issa says. "Things were meant to be better there. Quiet, peaceful, *good*. Grief tore through it. You understand that, don't you?"

"I saw what happened at the falls, what your father did when Abe brought you to him."

She squints into the wind. "Grief isn't a curse, June. Pain affects us all, even those of us who live a little closer to paradise than the rest. But my father's grief turned into poison. It ate through his heart and changed our family: his son, his son's son, you. And Abe's shame destroyed him. Shame, many say, was the first curse."

"Abe isn't cursed," I argue. "He *is* the curse. He killed my father *and* your father. He even killed Bekah."

"What you saw between Abe and my father," she says, "was one haunted man trying to find solace in revenge against another. What you saw happen to your father was the nameless thing that used to be Abe lashing out when he saw what was happening to Bekah. He never hurt her. When you saw him linger near her, when she was ill, you witnessed a haunted ghost remembering what it is to weep."

"You're saying he was *justified*?"

"He *has* been our family's curse—exerting his pain, exacting his idea of justice—but this didn't start with him. And he's not the only one to blame, just as our family isn't the only one cursed. What my father did to Abe broke something in him, June. Abe lived with it until the day he ended his life. His curse—*Saul's* curse—is different from ours but every bit as real. Shame steals from them. It eats at their vast, vivid minds until they become small and shadowy, trapped alone in a dark, wordless place."

"What about Bekah? The cancer?"

"That wasn't the curse. That was life, all its brightness and its dark. But the way the Angerts forget—that, I think, is a little of both: life *and* the curse. Life has made them want to forget, conditioned their bodies for it. The curse takes every tendril of memory, pulse of life, every touch and whisper and golden moment from them while Abe watches and, in his pain, strikes out. The only way to end this is to release the past. To be the one who lets go first, with no guarantee the other will follow."

"Then why did you bring me here?" I demand. "Why did you show me all that? If we need to let the past go, then why haven't *you* moved on?"

She smiles wordlessly.

It seems like we've been walking for hours. There are no signifiers for time or distance, and my body never gets more tired than it already was—absolutely wrecked with fatigue. My mind feels empty as when morning draws you from a dreamless sleep, but my throat feels swollen and dry.

It's hard to hold on to the truth here, even harder to remember the outside world. I try to picture my father, my mother, but their faces are blurry. I picture Saul's eyes. I hold on to them as we walk.

"Saul?" I manage to ask her.

She smiles and walks onward. I have to believe she's taking me to him.

I keep moving, moving, moving. At some point I must have fallen without noticing. I'm on my stomach, dragging myself forward. Issa walks evenly alongside me.

Coywolves pass us, their keen eyes watching me, belly-down and crawling. Ahead, blurs of color in the roaring wall of mist become squiggly silhouettes. Wind sprays water against my face, and I open my mouth to swallow it, but it's not enough. Even without the sun, my skin feels raw and scorched.

My mind slithers toward the moisture, its tongue lolling, praying for a drink, but my limbs won't listen, and the mist remains out of reach.

At its edge, small white tufts whiz like snowflakes.

I focus on Issa's ankles and keep moving.

My skin begins to burn, as if the dust on it is poison. I scratch at it, tear into it with my fingernails trying to get it off me, more desperate with every passing second of white-hot pain.

"June," Issa says.

"My skin," I rasp, "it hurts." I slash and scrape at my arms and legs, tears pouring down my face, but still the coat of Whites won't smudge. "It won't come off." The pain hits me in waves, sending grotesque images through my mind: a pool of blood overflowing my cupped hands, spreading up my arms, covering my body.

I scream and rub at my arms, seeing nothing but red now where white was. Red all over, blood covering me, and I know—somehow I know—it's Abe's.

I'm bathed in it. The memories of that night on the hill flap against me like a thousand angry bats.

"I didn't do it," I gasp as I try to writhe away, but I can't escape the memory. It's everywhere; the blood is everywhere.

Issa crouches and gingerly frees my hands from my hair. "What's happening?" I sob.

"You were supposed to have cherries that tasted like sunlight, a house full of love, and a peaceful forest," she says. "But instead, this is what was passed down to you, and I'm sorry for that, June, but you can't get it off yourself."

I see it all: I've inherited the man who swept his daughter from the water, laughing, and who held her empty body, weeping in dew-slicked grass.

The little boy who watched it happen, the man he became, who learned to turn invisible, who saw ghosts and feared love because he knew what it was to lose.

My legacy is the little boy who grew up haunted, who thought his father couldn't see him. Who left me and my mother whenever the house became too crowded with ghosts of his childhood. The man who abandoned me again and again and didn't know how to stay, no matter how badly he wanted to.

My birthright was Issa's death, Abe's assault, Jack the First's refusal to forgive.

Two ghosts: vengeance and grace.

The blood on my hands may not be real, but I was born with it all the same.

My inheritance is grief and sunlight, and the ability to choose which to hold on to.

"How?" I sob, the pain of my own skin becoming unbearable. "How do I make it stop?"

"I'm taking you to the one who can," Issa says.

Forty-Two

ISSA helps me to my feet. The burning still sears through me, but her arm is strong under mine as she guides me onward.

We're closer to the mist now, and the blurs of color take on the shapes of people. Peals of laughter, snippets of conversation, slip through the wind.

"When you come here, you're meant to wash time off. To let your past settle." Issa kicks one foot through the not-sand underfoot. "Your Moments are meant to rest. But our two families live in a place riddled with cracks, and instead of crumbling when I washed, my Moments were drawn back through the holes by someone who hungered for them. I was free to move on, but I stayed. For Abe.

"When he arrived, he wasn't ready to let go. He didn't wash himself, so the pull on his Moments drew him back through the veil too. For four generations, our families' inability to let go has brought Moments back. The hate between our families has anchored Abe, has allowed us to stay."

"They weren't being sent to us," I whisper. "Saul and I were bringing them?"

"In a way, the memories *belong* to you—they're pieces of what made you—so when you longed for the things you'd lost, the Moments came, as they had for your father and for his. All of you were born already holding on to the pain of the past and hating Angerts, because my father had."

Genetic memory. Memory passed through DNA. I shake my head. "But I never hated the Angerts. Not really."

"Not all coyotes dislike wolves," Issa says. "In another life, perhaps your lack of hate might have been enough to let our family's darkest memories rest. But you and Saul were each looking for the person you'd lost. And there were fragments of those people—shared DNA—in the Moments that came to you, and within Abe and me."

"I thought . . . I *hoped* my dad was sending them."

Issa's cerulean eyes flick across my face. "Whenever I could, when cracks and thin places in your world and this one aligned, I came through. I didn't bring the Moments, but I guided you to those I thought you needed. Abe—the thing that used to be Abe—he guided your father and grandfather to the Moments that hurt most."

"It *all* hurt, Issa." Tears squeeze from my eyes from the effort of holding in the screams of pain. I focus on the meager relief the mist brings my sizzling skin. "The happy memories hurt just as bad, maybe worse."

She studies me. "I know. But that kind of pain teaches you something different, June."

Finally, we're within the mist, each drop cooling the burning of my skin and clearing my mind. It snags on something Issa said. "You said Abe guided my dad and grandfather to the Moments that hurt most. What about me?"

"Abe's watched you grow up, June." Her lips pull into a straight line, the wind lashing strands of hair across her face. "Of the three Jacks I've tried to guide, you're the first who was ready to listen. It was harder, I think, for Abe to hate you. Otherwise he would've come for you when Eli lost Bekah. You were too innocent then, even to the thing he'd become. But tonight, I could see it in him. He was going to hurt you."

How could he take the thing I loved most but hesitate to hurt *me*? Didn't he know he'd already torn out my heart? That he'd hurt me worse than any physical pain could? A coywolf trots past, and I clear my throat of its teary thickness. "And whose side are the coywolves on?"

Issa almost laughs. "Did you know there's a fungus that drives everything it infests to spread itself? The fungus infects hosts with a desire to destroy. Evolution—nature—did that."

I shake my head. "I don't understand."

"The coywolves are the antithesis of nature. They have no capacity for revenge, no instinct to kill. They're driven by *wholeness*, the impulse to heal. They try to draw everything here, to be washed clean. They steal your shoes so you can leave your world— you must be barefoot and wide-eyed, just as you entered it.

"The coywolves weren't trying to show you memories; they

361

were trying to bring you here. Thresholds are more than randomly chosen divisions between rooms. They're places where change—transformation—happens, and whenever you slipped through one, barefoot, to a thinner piece of the veil, you saw the memories as we're able to in this place."

"And O'Dang!? That's here too?"

"There's only one of that tree," she confirms. "Where you live, you might wander through a thousand different cracks to find it. The same with the water you came through—it overlaps with the pool beneath the falls and a hundred others. Our families' darkest Moments are drawn to that water, *because I died there.*"

We've reached another shore. Fog hangs thick in the air above us, but ahead, the water is a healthy teal, waves topped by half domes of refracted light, and the clear sky gleams cornflower blue.

All around us, people emerge from the mist. Some, like me, are led by dustless people, but most are alone, covered to varying degrees in White-dust.

"We're meant to be washed clean, June," Issa says. "To let our burdens fall away and moments come apart like dandelions. It happened long ago, to the wolves and coyotes and birds who stumbled through, before any human tread on that grassy hill—and it's still happening."

She nods toward an old woman shuffling into the glittering froth of the tide. "Most people, when they come here, are finally free, but what they don't realize is that they could've been all along if they'd just let go."

Issa faces the wall of mist, where a shape emerges, its details filling out as a stooped man in a tartan hat limps forward, damp eyes rising and falling to take in the sight. He begins to cry as his gaze locks onto something behind us: the woman bathing in the water. Her layer of white has started to rinse off, and when she sees him, a laugh breaks free from her throat. She runs for him, falling in the water, and he catches her, gripping her tightly.

"When I first arrived, I waited here for the boy I loved," Issa says. "And when he came, I saw him, shrouded in mist but so very, clearly, excellently him."

She squints across the light-dappled water, and I can recall the feel of her sadness, the feathery warmth.

"He waded toward me, but he didn't let time wash off. The stars hadn't yet burned out. The planet wasn't cold. And I was waiting. Even then, he couldn't let go. He turned away—slipped back through, though he no longer had a body to wear there." She swipes a gold-streaked curl from her eyes. "I know what you must think, but he isn't lost, Jack. There's still hope. For you and Saul *and* for him."

I search the freckles on her nose, the glints in her eyes. "How can you say that? He's tortured us for decades, Issa."

"You must be tired from carrying all that Past around," she replies. "It must be exhausting to live for four Jacks."

"I'd rather do that than let go and lose him."

"Letting go is not forgetting. It's opening your eyes to the good that grew from the bad, the life that blooms from decay."

"My dad was supposed to be here," I whisper." He was supposed to always be here. I *needed* him, and Abe took him from me."

Issa lets a Moment alight on her hand. She sets it in mine and curls my fingers around it. I see a pure, bright memory: sun in my eyes, dirt underneath my fingernails, teeth sinking into a cherry, spraying tart juice on my chin.

She scoops another few and drops them over my fist. They hit my closed fingers, then bounce away. "June, Moments are like cherries. They're meant to be relished, shared—not hoarded. You can clutch one terrible Moment or experience all the rest. Your life is slipping past in brilliant little bits, and I know it feels as though you're holding on to *him*, as though opening your hand is letting him slip away."

Now she opens my hand, and the Moment in it floats to the ground. "But when Moments pass and crumble, they become seeds. They grow into new trees. And I promise you, he'll be in every new leaf. He will *never* be far from you.

"But if you *don't* let go of all that Abe did, you'll be haunted like the rest of them. You will miss the chance to live the life you want because you've accepted the one that's been passed down to you."

I swallow the knot in my throat. "Is he gone, Issa?"

Her mouth quivers. "When your father came here, he came in through the front door, no regrets. He shed his skin and stepped through a free man. He bathed in the water, and he wasn't sad about the way things were anymore. He was ready to move on."

I'm trying to parse out her meaning when an abrupt smile splits her face and she illuminates with happiness, bright and salient. I follow her gaze over my shoulder.

A lean boy with dark hair approaches through the mist, his angles sharpening into focus as the fog between us thins. "Saul."

My heart flares with relief so concentrated it overwhelms me with tears. He can't see me yet, but I know it's him. With every bone and muscle and ligament, I *know* him.

I look back to Issa, but she's turned away, wading into the water, her dress floating out around her. She turns toward me again, shielding her eyes against the light. "It's a miracle," she calls, grinning.

"What is?"

"That with your hand shut so tightly, he managed to slip in. That with his hands gripped like they were, he saw the shimmering possibility of a future when he met you."

Her smile widens, but tears still prick her eyes. "Wash yourselves, June," she calls. "Your curse will be broken. Abe won't be able to follow you back. If that's not enough to free him, there's nothing else I can do. It's his decision now. I'm moving on."

I run down the beach toward her. "And if I don't? Go back? If I want to stay and find *him*?"

Issa looks out across the water, where a series of islands has become visible, some drifting toward the shore and others away. "You swim," she says.

"What's there?"

Issa laughs, and while it should be eerie, it's shiny and gorgeous. "I don't know yet. Either way, don't delay your decision—there are people waiting for you, Jack O'Donnell."

I watch her shrink, feeling the wind at my back and an unbearable cleaving in my heart. Feathers, the sprite, my sweet pink ghost, is gone.

"June?"

And then I turn. I see him. And for a moment, the happiness, the light, the *deeply good* outweighs all the bad.

Everything in me swells, threatens to pop like an overblown balloon.

Saul's face is sunburned and muddy. Hair sandblasted, skin bleached by Whites. Through the crashing waves and seagulls, he says my name.

I run to him, and he crushes me to his chest. His lips are cracked and bloody as he kisses me, but I don't care. I don't care that I'm covered in blood. I forget the scalding of my skin.

I take his mist-speckled face between my hands, and he knots his fingers into my hair and laughs, gravelly, warm, *him*.

"You're alive," he says, and I nod, and laugh, and cry. His hands stroke through my hair. "Jack O'Donnell IV, we're alive."

I cling to him, damp wind cycling around us. Safe, steady, whole.

"I went to the falls," he says in a rush. "I saw Nameless and Feathers. There was a dead rabbit, and I thought the worst, June. I went to your house, but you were *gone*. I didn't know what else to do."

"Issa," I say. "Issa and Abe. That's who the ghosts are. She brought me here."

He presses his face into my neck, and a cracking sound climbs his throat. "I thought you were already gone. I told myself if I jumped, I could find you." He pulls me into him, blocking me from the wind.

"I'm here." I spread my fingers over his heart, feeling its beat. "I'm not gone." I repeat it again, a promise.

Saul straightens, and his eyes register the blood on me. "June, what happened?" He tries to wipe it off, but it doesn't smear.

"It's a stain," I tell him. "Look." I point to the bruises on his arms. I gently lift his shirt and find more blue-black welts rising from his ribs. "Did you see what happened to Abe on the hill?"

Understanding crosses Saul's face as his fingers skim the bruises. "You think these are from what Jack did to him? Takes *chip on your shoulder* to a whole new level."

"Chip in your bloodstream," I say. "Blood in my DNA."

"Are we dead, June?"

"We won't feel this close to dying when we're dead."

Saul laughs. "True. I've never been so thirsty."

We start to walk, and the pain needling my skin hits anew with each step we take out of the mist. The sparkling water and blue sky come into view. Up and down the shore, blemishes of color become visible, all moving, like us, toward the water.

"Where are we?" Saul asks.

"The world outside ours?" I say helplessly.

One of the islands has drifted closer, a small one smack-dab in the water, on which a white farmhouse basks in the light, ivy sprawling through its lattice, flowers and a cherry tree leaning in its yard. Another island floats in tandem with it, vacant apart from a massive tree with gnarled roots.

"Your house," Saul says. "And O'Dang!"

I nod. "You think that's the way home?"

"Is that the way back?" Saul shouts to a barefoot woman in an olive dress. She and several other newcomers are wading into the water, splashing their wind-beaten faces. She looks up, droplets sliding off her face, then follows Saul's gaze to the farmhouse.

"Not for me," she shouts back. "The others said the islands come when it's your turn."

"Turn?" Saul asks.

She shrugs and lowers herself into the water. As she does, something strange and lovely happens. White puffs wash off her—off everyone who's wading in. Like snakeskin being shed, snow from a window, dust bunnies blown free from a book cover.

"This is where they come from," Saul says.

The woman's grinning as she slurps from her cupped hands.

"Is the water drinkable?" I call.

She laughs and slicks her wet hair back. "It's water!"

We push our faces into the crash of the tide and gulp.

We lie in it, roll through it. The snow-sand starts to wash from our hair and clothes, settling to the bottom without a fight. The Whites shed from me, but the blood doesn't rinse off no matter how I scrub.

Saul takes my hands in his and runs his fingers through the blood, drawing wet streaks through it. He scoops water in one hand and pours it over my forearm, and the blood runs off in minuscule red rivers, though the water doesn't seem to muddy. Pour by pour, the blood disappears, rinsing off beneath his cupped hands until it's gone.

Saul kisses my clean fingers, one by one.

I touch the bruises on his cheek, those on his arms. I massage the water into them, watching the dark purple fade from beneath his tattoos until the bruises become nothing. I pull his shirt over his head and wash his sides, his ribs.

I rinse his shoulders, his spine. I watch the welts vanish, and when they're gone, I kiss his forehead, his cheeks, his mouth.

We fall under the water and sink and twist, are buoyed back up, water and Moments sliding off us like avalanches. Our Whites drift off. They crumble, one by one, and sink.

We lie back on the White-sand, smiling and breathing deep. I can't explain the feeling in my body. At first, we're both laughing breathlessly, and when the giddiness settles, I feel heavy, so calm I could melt into the beach, become a part of it like all our Moments. Saul's fingers twist through mine, and he looks over to me, a million droplets glistening on him like marbles.

"I knew who you were in the mirror maze," he says. Somehow, here, we're *below* the wall of wind, *above* the crash of water, in a quiet slice of space. "I knew who you were, and I was so happy you didn't seem to recognize me. I wanted to stay there as long as I could, to spend as much time as possible before you found out."

I try to remember why. I remember what happened but not why it mattered so much, why I believed anything was keeping me and Saul apart. I think of what Issa said to Abe on top of the waterfall: that he would leave and forget her. "What if I want to travel?" I ask Saul.

"Then you'll travel, Jack."

"What if I want to go to college?"

"You'll live in a dorm and join the literary magazine," he says. "Go to readings and sneak out with your friends the night before

National Poetry Day to cover the campus with poems; drink Jell-O shots and shave your head in a frat-house bathroom and quit shaving your armpits and live in a new city and learn how to make sushi and whatever else you want. I can wait."

I close my eyes and grin at the sun—or the *not-the-sun.* "What if our curse makes all the stars burn out and we're left in the dark?"

Saul touches my bottom lip, and I open my eyes. The crescents of refracted light in the water droplets on his face make him glitter like the ocean. "We aren't cursed anymore, June."

"How do you know?"

"Because I'm happy," he whispers. "I saw all there was to see, all the worst parts, and I'm still furiously happy."

He's right—our blood and bruises are gone, like Issa said—but what about Abe? What happens to him now? I curl myself against Saul, pressing my face into his wet shirt. "Maybe everyone's cursed."

"Not us," he murmurs in my hair.

"What makes us so special, Saul?"

"We're in love."

"Are we?" I whisper.

He gingerly takes the sides of my face in his hands. "June O'Donnell, I like that you know you can't fix the thing that hurts in me. And that you understand it gets better but you never stop missing people. I like that you *know* no human being will ever make it okay that you lost another one. And that you're smart and funny and willing to go on horrible double non-dates for your friend and that you want to write things that are happy, and of course I like your butt and eyes and teeth and hair and the way your fingernails are always badly painted and that when you laugh, you have no chin.

"And I don't know what exactly makes it love, but when I saw you in the House of Mirrors, it was like I already knew exactly who you were. And I should've been wrong—that would've made more sense—but I wasn't, and I love you. I'll always love you. And someday maybe we'll have a bad breakup or grow apart and—curse or not—all the stars will burn out and the planet will have another ice age, but I'll go on loving you because I see you, June O'Donnell, and I can't unsee you."

He lowers his mouth to mine, and we kiss how we drank the water. Our teeth collide like they did that night in the sunroom, from too much smiling.

When we pull apart, his eyes flick down my face and out toward the twin islands docking near the shore: O'Dang! and my house.

All along I'd been so sure Dad was trying to tell me something, and even now that Saul and I are here together, legs outstretched in sparkling waves and invisible sun blanketing us, I still feel a deep ache. "One will take us home," I murmur.

"And the other?"

I meet Saul's dark eyes. "To *them*."

"Is that for you?" the woman in the olive dress calls, tipping her head toward the farmhouse on the island. "You might want to wade out there while you can, if it is. Looks like it's starting to drift back out." She returns to wringing her hair out, knotting it into a braid.

She's right. The island is floating away, a new one visible on the horizon.

Saul and I stand. "Which do we take?" he asks.

"I don't know yet."

We wade into the water, and when we're in to our waists, we let our fingers fall apart. The sun on our backs and arms, we climb onto the floating island and look up at my house. "Saul?"

"June?"

Maybe for some people, falling in love is an explosion, fireworks against a black sky and tremors rumbling through the earth. One blazing moment. For me, it's been happening for months, as quietly as a seed sprouting. Love sneaked through me, spreading roots around my heart, until, in the blink of an eye, the green of it broke the dirt: hidden one moment, there the next.

"I like your hair and arms and laugh. And the pictures you take and that you came home even though you were scared and that you apologize and expect apologies. I like that you don't get embarrassed often but when you do, your ears turn pink, and I like your jaw and stomach and how you think about the worst things that have happened in a way that doesn't *justify* them but finds the tiny specks of good circling them, and I love you. I love you, Saul Angert."

His smile is slow and faint. "I know, Jack."

"Cocky," I tease.

"Confident."

Forty-Three

WE fold our fingers together and step toward my porch. It's nearly silent, apart from the gulls overhead. Butterflies spiral around the ivy-wrapped lattice, and birds chirp in the bushes.

Something crawls on the nape of my neck. I turn, and across the water, I see a shape moving out of the haze toward the shore where we bathed.

"June?" Saul touches my elbow, then follows my gaze.

Abe's blue-gray button-up ripples in the wind. The worn fabric of his pants lashes his legs, and his dark hair ruffles.

I expect to feel hate, anger, fear—but I only feel sadness. His dark eyes, the sharp angles of his face—they're so familiar, shadows of a person I love. How did the boy on the waterfall, the one who'd loved Issa since they were six, turn into the darkness that haunted us? Was it in that moment he found her? When the light left his eyes as Jack the First attacked him?

Or did it happen over years of missing her, being hated by the family *she* loved? In the end, he's nothing but a mess of color: the white of memory dust, the red of the blood on his hands, the purple of the bruises the world inflicted on him.

"Our curse is broken," I say. "He can't follow us back. Whether he moves on is his decision."

We watch him and he watches us for an extended moment.

He steps into the water, his pants clinging and rocking with the tide. I try to see the darkness in him or feel the cold that rushed into me whenever he was near, but here he's nothing but a human being. A mass of guts and cells and all the Moments that hurt him.

Behind him, a little girl emerges from the mist. A woman down the beach lets out a yelp, and the girl turns toward her, a smile breaking across her face. They run for each other, the girl's yellow braid bouncing behind her. Their bare feet slap the not-sand, making a sound like the heartbeat of the earth.

The woman's knees hit the ground as the girl collides with her, their arms wrapping tightly around each other, faces burying themselves in curves and muscle and fabric.

That.

That was the moment I had wanted. A reunion.

Saul's hand tightens, silent acquiescence: *me too.*

Still watching us, Abe lowers himself to his knees. Whites spit out from him like soap bubbles beneath a showerhead. He plucks one off, brings it to the surface, and meets my eyes again.

He shakes his head, opens his mouth, then closes it again. Silently he releases the White.

It doesn't sink. It's pulled along by the breeze straight toward me. The dead bit of memory, the outermost layer of moments, pulled away to leave behind only the supple truth.

Abe stands, his liquid eyes shifting away from us to search the horizon. He doesn't find what he's looking for there, and the light draws a vein down the silvery slope of his cheek.

His mouth forms words: *"I'm sorry, Issa."*

He doesn't wash any more of his time away. He turns toward the mist and returns the way he came.

"What does this mean?" Saul whispers. "I thought the curse was broken."

"For us, it is," I answer.

"But if he's not moving on, he'll keep torturing us."

I shake my head. "He can't come back."

"Then why stay here?"

I stare into the mist and its white noise. "I don't think he was ready to face her."

Because he blamed himself for her death. Because of the way he tore through her family and broke all his promises. Issa said shame was the first curse, and when you've held on to shame that long, it must be nearly impossible to let go. *Nearly.*

Maybe not now, but someday he'll let the girl who loved him look at him again. And when he does, she'll be waiting.

Saul nods at the White floating toward me. "What do you think is in that?"

I wrap my arms around his neck and bury my face in his chest. I can't look at it, or the house, or O'Dang! "I don't know."

He lowers his forehead to mine. "What do you want to do, June?"

"I want to know Dad's okay. I want a promise that I'll see him again. I want that love back, Saul."

Saul tips my face up. "The kind of love your dad had for you, that's not the kind of thing that can die. Look at Issa. This whole thing—she had us play out their lives so we could understand this fight and stop it. After everything Abe did, she brought us here for *him*. *That* kind of love—the kind that doesn't stipulate or caveat— doesn't die. That's what you had with your father. That's what I had with Bekah. That's what we have, June, and they're *here, right now*."

"You want to stay?" A sharp pain passes through me. I never would have believed I'd feel this way, but since I dove into that water, *I'm* different. *I WANT TO LIVE* burns like an ember in my chest.

For Saul, for Mom and Toddy, Shadow, Grayson, Hannah. And for myself.

Saul shakes his head. "June, the past three years have felt like one never-ending night. And then, a few months ago, I was running through a hall of mirrors, and I collided with you, and I remembered it was just an optical illusion. Your teeth hit me in the shoulder, and I saw morning in you. And if the world can surprise me with something as bright as June O'Donnell's teeth in my shoulder once, it can do it again."

His thumb runs over my jaw, and his eyes tighten at the corners. "I love my sister, and until I die, I'll never stop missing her. But I want to be good to the people I haven't lost yet. I want to live, with you."

He brushes tears from my eyes.

"Those are some transcendent bicuspids I've got," I whisper.

He grins. "If you'd hit me with your molars, I would've seen the face of God right then."

"I bet we could catch a boat to that attraction from here."

"For sale: face of God; price: future."

"For sale: baby shoes; misread eBay description; thought they were adult shoes."

Saul's laugh is all husk and warmth. He pulls me sideways so he can kiss the top of my head. "Even if you can't see morning in me, I hope you can see it somewhere."

My heart fills with homesickness—for all three of my parents. I look up at the house in front of us. I can imagine Mom sitting at the table, wearing her two wedding bands, staring down at the smooth wooden surface she's washed clean a million times.

"June." Saul tips his head toward Abe's fluttering White as it finally reaches us. "Do you want to see it?"

I flatten my palm, and the White dances over it. Though it touches my skin, it doesn't reveal its secrets. I think of that day in the woods. *Please*, Dad said as the darkness folded over him. *Please show her.*

I tighten my fingers around the pulsing Moment, but the memory doesn't play out for me. This island must be more a part of our own world than this one, where merely brushing the White is enough to send its contents dancing through you. I need a threshold.

I look up at the only door within reach: the door to my own house.

"I think he left it for me," I say. "My dad."

Saul studies me.

377

"Thank you for not stating the obvious."

He laughs. "What, in this impossible place, could possibly be obvious, June?"

"That I'm holding a message from my dad in my hands, and the only apparent way to see it is to go through that door, probably back to Five Fingers. Away from him."

"I thought 'the obvious' was that you already had dozens of messages from him: about how much he loved you and what he wanted for you. The obvious is that whether you had that White or not, your dad would want you to go back to your life and live it well."

"I want to say goodbye first."

"It's not goodbye." Saul threads his hand through mine. We circle the far side of the island and stand with our toes in the water. There are islands coming closer, others moving out, and there, at the edge of sight, the thin line of the horizon: dark greens and browns, the hazy half image of mountains spearing the sky. Saul sweeps my hair behind my shoulders, and the wind carries it out behind me. I lock my fingers into his, and we stare.

"Are you there?" I whisper.

There's silence, but it's Dad's. Bekah's. The specific silence that can come only from their mouths. I know. I have to believe.

"I love you," I say.

"I love you," Saul says, and I know he's not talking to me, just like I wasn't talking to him.

I cup my hands around my mouth and scream, as loud as I can, as big and long as I can so it will be a promise with gravity and truth. "SEE YOU."

Saul laughs beside me and lifts his T-shirt to wipe his eyes. He cups his hands around his mouth and screams: "SEE YOU."

We stand for one more beat of silence, and then we turn back toward the house.

We climb the steps to the porch, and I stop Saul by the arm. "I think . . . I think I need to see this alone."

"You're sure? This is what you want?"

I nod, and Saul pulls me into one last hug, then kisses my forehead. "See you on the other side, Jack."

I gather all of myself, and it's not that much. All the Jacks that clung to me, all the ghosts, are gone, and I'm just me.

Light.

Breezy.

Free.

Jack IV.

I go through the door.

Instead of stepping into my house, I find myself in the side yard, behind a dark, writhing shape. Abe's ghost is watching through the window as my father sits at the console table in the kitchen, scribbling a note. Every so often, Dad stops and looks up through the pane of glass, straight at Abe.

I watch the eight-year-old version of me climbing on Dad and see him frown and disentangle her from him. "I'll be right back," his muffled voice comes. He disappears down the hall.

I follow Abe's fluctuating form to the front of the house, where Dad is bounding down the porch steps into the night. He's holding a note, labeled JUNIOR, clipped to a leather-bound book. I follow him into the woods.

Suddenly, the night blinks away, replaced by golden light and soft fog. I trudge through the strange quiet, listening to my father's breaths, counting the beats of his heart, all the way to O'Dang!

When we reach it, Dad climbs, one arm over the other, to the first level of branches, to a hollow made by an animal. He pulls the book and note from his jacket and glances toward Abe—*at me*—then at the book. He tucks it in the hole.

He left something for me. He left a note *for me, something I've never seen before.*

I go toward the tree as if to climb it, but he's already climbing down.

I chase his long strides back to the yard, to the sudden night and porch-light glow, the overgrown ivy and shaggy grass, the cicada chirp and twinkle of stars and glint of coywolf eyeshade.

Dad stops beneath the Jack's Tart tree, eyes lifted to the moon. He looks over his shoulder at Abe—*at me*—and gives a closed-mouth grin, full tears rolling down his cheeks.

Dad, I say, though of course I have no voice. He faces the house again.

This is the last time I'll see him, at least for a long time. I'm shaking like a leaf despite the warmth as I cut a circle to stand in front of him.

His eyes flash up to my bedroom window, then drop again. They look right at me, or through me. "June-Bug," his voice squeezes out as a throaty whisper.

Dad. My heart races so fast I vibrate with it.

He holds his arms out to his sides, like he's hugging the house, the night, the world. His eyes neither shift nor focus. They stare, wide open, lashes thick with tears. I reach out and touch his hand, feel its warmth and solidness. "Look," he whispers.

I follow his eyes to the stars. Once, when we lay gazing up at the night, he told me the stars we saw were only the tiniest fraction of the stars that burned above us.

I'm looking.

His eyes move vaguely back and forth. "I don't know if you'll find this, Bug." His voice is small. "I hope that if you find *any* of them, if you figure out how the Whites work, this is the one you find. I think I'm running out of time." His breath catches in his chest, and he wipes his eyes with the heel of his hand. "I wanted to be a better man than my father, but I made so many mistakes. Someday you'll know that. I hope you know the good parts too. I hope you know I loved you."

He waves his free arm up in a slow arc across the sky. "You look for me there, baby," he says. "I'll look up. We'll see the same stars."

I remember something else he told me about stars: that their light traveled so far we might see some shining that had already burned out. They might reach us after their lives had ended. The light was real and warm, though it came from something that, elsewhere, no longer existed.

What if there are no stars in that other place, Dad? I ask, starting to cry.

He opens his arms again—this time as if to hug me, and I walk into them. I feel his heartbeat against my chest, warm and real though it comes from someone who, here, no longer exists. *I love you so much,* I say.

"I love you so much," he says.

Don't ever let go of me.

"I'll never let go of you, June," he says. "The first time I held you, I saw it all. I didn't miss any of it. I hope you find this. I hope you know. Go live, baby. The world's waiting."

Dad.

Abe's torn-free memory shivers, breaks. Darkness spills in through it like water through holes in a ship. The woods break. The coywolves come apart like dandelions. The stars wink out. Dad's heart keeps beating. Dad's arms stay warm. "See you, June-bug," he says.

See you.

Forty-Four

I crash through. There isn't a doorway to go by. Instead the memory crumbles around me. I don't have the presence of mind to hold my arms up over my head.

I simply sob. I feel my tired legs collapsing and then solid arms around me. "You're okay," he says again and again.

"He loved me," I cry.

"He loves you."

"I miss him."

Saul holds me. We lean together on the front porch, and it's not the front porch of the *other* place. It's the true front porch. Of the here, the now. The one with a frosty cherry tree ringed with sweet saplings.

The hill Jonathan Alroy O'Donnell came to. The hill Jack the First stood on. The hill Jack II rode his bike across and where Jack III showed me the stars. Our home. A thin place.

Where life goes on and the stars keep shining and the person who loved me most has moved on but his heart has somehow stayed behind.

"We're home."

Saul nods.

I touch the doorknob. It's unlocked. I start to shake again, but this time with happiness, relief. Because of what I've come home to.

All the things of the present I'd forgotten to treasure: a mother with dreams and long, elegant fingers that dance in all they do, a stepfather who fixes broken toilets and cleans teeth and protects me like his own, brothers with boundless energy and chalkboard-fingernail voices and sometimes sweetness just for me.

And Saul, a boy who loved me when history said he couldn't.

"I'm home," I cry. "Mom! Toddy! Shadow! Grayson!"

The stair lights flick on.

"I'm home."

"*Baby*," Mom's voice says.

I am so happy, so relieved. For the first time, I feel big.

We've been gone three days, they tell us.

They thought the worst.

The police were looking, Hannah was panicking, Eli was found wandering in the street, his home torn up.

Tonight, they agree to ask no questions. ("But we *will* talk about this tomorrow.")

Tomorrow, the answers will matter again, but they'll still be impossible things.

Hannah gets here in twenty minutes, and we're crying on the

floor in the living room. Grayson and Shadow are shy, unsure how to be around the sister they thought had left them and broke their parents' hearts.

Only I will ever know how seriously I considered doing just that. How could I willingly do that to them?

The answer, deep down, is that I couldn't have. There's too much in this world, under the slowly dying stars, that I love.

For Saul, I know what hurts worst is Eli.

"We'll see him tomorrow," Mom promises. She's the one who got him into the assisted living facility after Saul disappeared, when the police found him in the median of the highway, disgruntled and murmuring with bloody hands.

"It should've been me," Saul says.

"You're here now," Mom says. "There's still time."

"Maybe," Saul says. "Or maybe he won't know me."

Mom hesitates. "He talks about you. He has your pictures on the walls."

And in this way, I know we *did* break a curse when we washed each other clean. Because my mother, an O'Donnell, or the former wife of one, at least, visited *New York Times* best-selling author Eli Angert these past three days. An O'Donnell paid his bills and made sure he had books to read and pictures on the wall. An O'Donnell took an Angert a box of dried cherries, and an Angert accepted them.

He had taken them between his teeth, and tears had flooded his eyes. *They taste like home,* he'd said.

"The ghosts are gone now," I tell Mom quietly.

She smiles knowingly. Or maybe skeptically. It's hard to

say—it's the same smile she gave when Dad told stories from his trips or talked about the magic tree in the forest.

"I know Dad wasn't perfect," I say. "I know . . . he used to leave."

Mom laughs. "Of course he wasn't perfect. But he was ours. And we were his."

"Was that enough?"

Her eyes sweep over my face. "When it came down to it, yes. That was enough."

For the first time since this started, I'm sure my father wasn't a liar. A liar would've changed his memories. A liar would've projected that shiny version of his proposal to Mom, the version he always told, not kept the truth close to his heart, guarded in a little sphere of white. "It was enough."

We eat even though we're not hungry yet.

"So you don't get sick," Toddy says gently, tousling my hair. "It's good to keep a little something in your stomach."

He wanted to take us to the hospital but settled for scheduling doctors' appointments in the morning. We eat everything they put in front of us: two bowls of bland tomato soup, one half-frozen piece of turtle cheesecake, a peanut butter sandwich apiece, slabs of reheated macaroni casserole. I let them wrap blankets around me. I let Mom comb through the tangles in my hair. Every gesture is an *I love you*, and I collect them, my way to say, *It is so good to be loved by you*. I drink every cup of water they bring, and when Mom surreptitiously pours each of us a tiny taste of whiskey, I let its warmth settle in my stomach, thinking fondly of the worst movie of all time.

"How's Nate?" I ask Hannah, and she laughs in surprise.

"He's going to be good. He's going to be really good when he gets my message that you're both okay."

"I'm sorry," I say again.

She wraps an arm around me and clears her throat. "I knew you'd never leave me, Junie."

I kiss my forefinger and middle. She kisses hers. "Never. Not in the important ways." But the sting is still there in my chest, and I pull away, fighting tears. "I think I need to step outside for a second."

Everyone tenses, Mom and Toddy especially, but they nod and let me go. This time, I won't pass into a memory. Our families' Moments are gone, but there's still something unnerving about passing through this doorway, knowing how it conspired with memory and magic to show me so much. I sit down on the porch and breathe in the pine. I can almost see the outline of Dad standing in the yard. I look up at the stars, and I see him there too.

I feel his stories burbling up in my chest, and I know that tomorrow I'll begin to write them down for Ms. deGeest, and this time I'll tell the truth.

The door clicks open, and Saul lowers himself to sit beside me. After a minute I say, "The night we met, I didn't see you coming either."

He smiles. "I would try to make out with you right now, but I don't know if in the last three days your mom and Todd had a chance to teach Shadow and Grayson about the birds and the bees, and I'm too tired to explain it."

I laugh despite myself. It's easier than I would've guessed. "Tomorrow then."

"Tomorrow," he agrees.

"And the next day. And the day after that. In every room and every Five Fingers establishment."

"A Makeout Tour," he says. "Maybe we can do a signing."

"And what about after that?"

His dark eyes are serious despite the trace of smile in the corner of his mouth. "I don't know, Jack. College? Grad school? Indonesia with Takumi and Sarah? The world is your oyster."

"And you?"

"I'll be here with Eli," he says. "For now, at least. And after now, I'll still be close, if you still want me."

"Nowhere the stars can't reach you?"

"If I have anything to say about it, I'll be well within celestial-light range."

"Good," I say.

"Good."

We sit for hours, the door opening every once in a while as, one by one, the others join us on the porch until we're a row of seven. From one end, Toddy passes a box of dried Jack's Tart. I cradle one between my teeth.

"Look." Mom points across the yard toward the first streak of yellow. "Morning's coming."

I bite down and taste it all, the heartbeat of the world.

Forty-Five

The Complete History of Jack O'donnell

I find it in the woods, in the crook in O'Dang!, right where he left it.

June,

If you find this, it means you see them too: the ghosts, the memories, all of it. It means they tortured you like they tortured me, with pieces of our story.

Baby, I'm sorry, for everything. I'm sorry I gave him fodder to hurt you. I'm sorry I messed up enough that when you saw the truth, it was always going to hurt. I never wanted you to stop looking at me like I was the sun, but now you know how things really happened. At least, as well as a series of moments can tell it.

I always meant to write the truth down, June, and here it is. This book has all you need to know about me. The things that mattered. The important things.

I love you, June, always. Always.

I lean into the crook of the branch and tuck the note into my pocket. I take a deep breath and push a cherry between my teeth, sunlight and warmth and dirt rushing over my tongue, a million glimmers of Jack, both sweet and bitter. I open the book, THE COMPLETE HISTORY OF JACK O'DONNELL III.

This is all you need to know about me. Not every moment, not the things I saw or the places I went. You need to know where my heart was.

That the most important thing I ever did with my life was love you, and my favorite sound was your snorting laugh. I don't have time to tell you any more bullshit stories, and I wouldn't tell you even if I did.

Here, so close to the end, all that means so little.

When I was a kid, I dreamed about exploring pyramids and riding on elephants' backs. I wanted to sail across the world and climb Mount Everest and look down over everything. I thought that was the life I'd lead and that the moments of mine that were closest to that would be the ones that made me.

The truth is, I stopped dreaming about those things, June, the day you were born.

Here is what I'll take with me from this world: a thousand moments spent watching you sleep, tracing the freckles over your mom's eyebrow as she Windexed a mirror, rubbing her wrists when the cold made them sore, combing your hair when it got tangled, a deep hurt in my belly from the way it hurt you.

I am very small, and I don't find myself wishing I were any bigger.

All I want, with my one tiny moment, is to love you.

If you remember anything about me, remember the truest thing: I will love you after all the stars have burned out, after the sun has died and ice has covered the earth, after the last human has taken her last breath.

I'm happy, so happy to be a tiny fleck of a thing alongside you. We may just be moments, June, but to love a handful of people very well, that's a good life.

I was just a blip, a spark, the blink of God's eyes. Because of you, it was more than enough. It was everything.

I was just a moment, and you gave me a million Junes.

I was just a moment, and you made me forever.

Thanks

FIRST, I need to thank my incredible parents (and grandparents) and promise my mother (and grandmother) she *will* get a book dedication, just as soon as I write the right book. I am so lucky to have spent my life with two loving parents in my corner, and I wouldn't trade you for anything or anyone.

Thanks to my brothers and sisters, for always coming through for me and for each other. If I ever move to a deserted island, I hope you'll come too. (This includes you, Megan and Noosha.)

Thank you to Brittany Cavallaro, Parker "Charker" Peevyhouse, Anna Breslaw, Jeff Zentner, Janet McNally, Katie Kennedy, Lindsay Eagar, and anyone else I am traitorously forgetting who offered early (and late) reads on this book. I am so, so lucky to have friends with brains and hearts as brilliant and beautiful as yours.

Thanks also to Kerry Kletter, Jack Sjogren, Hallie Bateman, Matthew Baker, Shannon Parker, Roshani Chokshi, Kathryn Purdie, Erin Summerill, Julie Eshbaugh, Margot Harrison, Ashley Blake, Dahlia Adler, Katherine Locke, Sara Taylor Woods, Tristina Wright, Meg Leder, Adriana Mather, Riley Redgate, Jeff Giles, Tehlor Kinney, Cam Montgomery, Eric Smith, ALL the Sweet 16s, and everyone else who makes my writing and reading world so much brighter on a daily basis.

To my Hope College family, you are the best. Always.

To all my book blogger, bookstagram, and bookseller friends:

You've made this whole process so much less daunting and more fun. Thank you, thank you, thank you.

To my agent, Lana: You have been my rock this past year. Thanks for all that you do to keep me going and to make everything I write 300 percent better.

To my editors, Liz and Marissa: Liz, I am floored by your generosity and kindness. I, and this book, owe you so much. Neither would be the same without all your hard work and passion. Marissa, thank you for stepping up and kicking you-know-what in the eleventh hour. You are a master slicer and dicer (of words), and your support has meant so much to me.

Anthony Elder and Corina Lupp: I don't think *anyone* deserves a cover as a beautiful as the one you've given me, but I'll gladly accept it.

Kim Ryan and Jennifer Dee, thank you for being such wonderful advocates for *A Million Junes*. You are empresses. Thanks you, Kate Frentzel, for fixing my many randomly capitalized phrases and so much more.

To Ben Schrank, and everyone else at Razorbill and Penguin Young Readers Group, thank you for all that you've done for me and for this book. I'm so grateful to have landed among you.

Thanks also to Hermione Granger, without whom probably none of us would be alive.

And finally, thank you to Joey: Every moment that I'm loved by you is an incomprehensible gift. You've already given me a million Junes.